THE
COLLECTED TALES
OF
WALTER DE LA MARE

THE
COLLECTED TALES
OF
Walter de la Mare

Chosen, and with an Introduction, by

EDWARD WAGENKNECHT

ALFRED A KNOPF

NEW YORK

1950

THIS IS A BORZOI BOOK,
PUBLISHED BY ALFRED A. KNOPF, INC.

32728   FIRST EDITION OF THIS COLLECTION

TO

Robert, David, & Walter Wagenknecht:

these Three:

with the blessing of the Tale-Teller

SEPTEMBER I, 1949

INTRODUCTION

I

IT IS A proud and a perilous privilege to "introduce"—though not that they need introduction!—the stories of Walter de la Mare. In behalf of such a writer the critic must at once enter very high claims. But unless he is a very young critic, he will long since have learned that to do just that for any subject of one's enthusiasm is often to render him the worst possible service. For there is an ugly something in human nature that impels us somehow to use every means at our disposal to drag our heroes down to our own level: else why the hospitable reception invariably accorded to every bit of scandal, believable or unbelievable, about famous men and women? "Whatever people on the other side of the question may advance," said Keats, "they cannot deny that they are always surprised at hearing of a good action, and never of a bad one." Witness, here, the considerable number of supposedly reputable writers who are currently accepting serious allegations against the private character of Charles Dickens, in spite of the fact that nothing really resembling evidence has ever been brought forward to substantiate them. I cherish, too, the wryly delightful story of the young American scholar engaged in research upon a distinguished New England writer of unimpeached—and unimpeachable—reputation who, one day, came out from the manuscript room rubbing his hands because he had at last encountered a letter in which the poet had expressed an undecorous enthusiasm for a woman whom he had encountered abroad. "Frau Boudour" was what it looked like in a handwriting that had not been particularly designed for the comfort of scandalmongers to come; he must have been hurt and grieved when a better pair of eyes discovered that what the great man was being enthusiastic about was merely the poetry of the Troubadours. And whatever the difficulties of my position, my worst possible course would be to attempt to take

vii

refuge in modesty. I shall not, therefore, attempt to confine myself to describing how much *I* enjoy Mr. de la Mare's work or what it "means to me." To reward such pusillanimity I could only expect—and should richly deserve—to hear a voice coming back at me from the gallery with "But who are *you*?"

My concern in this place is, of course, with only one segment of a singularly multiform output singularly unified in its inspiration. Mr. de la Mare appears between these covers only as a teller of tales. He is also, as everybody knows, a poet and a novelist. To my way of thinking—and I am not alone in my opinion—his *Memoirs of a Midget* is the most distinguished novel that has come out of England in our time. Nor can I think of any competent judge who would deny that as a poet of the dream-world and the supernatural, de la Mare stands with Coleridge, Poe, and their all too few peers in any literature, while as a poet of childhood (which is a very different thing from a man who makes verses either for or about children), he has no peer at all.

In addition to all this, de la Mare has a considerable number of what are for him "minor" books, any one of which would suffice to earn a reputation for a less important writer. In *Love; Come Hither;* and *Behold, This Dreamer!* he lifted that last refuge of the literary hack, anthology-making, to a plane where only something like genius can handle it, for these books are each an incomparable piece of mosaic work, quite as expressive of de la Mare's personality as his "creative" work itself. In *Stories from the Bible* he produced the only modern paraphrase I know that does not travesty its original. If he could only be persuaded to apply the same method to the Gospels—and it is only, I think, an excessive sense of reverence that has hitherto restrained him—I am fully persuaded that he could produce the best literary life of Christ that has ever been written. He has, too, an altogether delightful way of giving us, every now and then, a completely unclassifiable book that he alone could have written. What can you say of *Early One Morning in the Spring* except that it is an encyclopædic compilation of child lore? what of *Desert Islands and Robinson Crusoe* beyond its being a lecture with elaborate annotations? what of *Ding Dong Bell* save that it is a collection of enchanting epitaphs in a prose-fiction setting? And yet how utterly all these words fail to convey the flavor of what is, in each instance, a unique book!

Often, of course, the ostensible subject is hardly more than a point of departure. In the de la Mare cosmos, every mundane object becomes, sooner or later, a point of departure. In 1948 an impressive number of important British writers collaborated to produce for Faber & Faber an already excessively scarce volume known as *Tribute to Walter de la Mare on His Seventy-fifth Birthday*. In his contribution to this symposium, that perspicacious student of fiction, Lord David Cecil, points out that de la Mare is a writer "concerned with some of the profoundest and most critical issues that confront the human soul," "occupied with nothing less than the ultimate significance of experience." One might indeed say of him what Maunders says of Anthony in the story "Lispet, Lispett and Vaine": that there is "more in him than in most of us [that] had come from elsewhere." His characters, too, even when there is nothing supernatural about them, live in worlds from which they can be "called back"—at times!

These things must, I fear, be grasped at the outset if de la Mare's work is to be read with understanding. I cannot honestly acquit him at every point of the charge of obscurity, which has often been made against him. I believe, for example, that certain points in ."The Connoisseur"—in some ways the most wonderful story he has written—are extremely obscure. It is, by the way, both odd and interesting in this connection that though de la Mare's later poems are certainly far more "intellectual" than the early ones, and in their harmonies far more complex, there has not been here, as there was with his celebrated relative, Robert Browning, an increase in obscurity through the years; on the contrary, I think de la Mare the poet more successful in communicating his meanings now than he used to be. On the whole, he is certainly no more "difficult" than any other modern writer who is not avowedly aiming at "mass circulation" and who has consequently been reduced to the necessity of writing so that the illiterate may both run and read. Mary Garden once told me that she did not care for Italian music because Italians "sing all over the place." On that score de la Mare's withers are unwrung. He sometimes *seems* obscure because we go to him with our minds set on yarning when all that he wishes to do is to create a mood. It would be almost as unreasonable to go to "The Vats" for a "story" as it would be to approach what is sometimes called "absolute music" for the same end. But it may as well be said frankly that much of what has been called de la Mare's obscurity is due merely to the fact that such a writer as he cannot be apprehended by the use of the analytical mind alone. Yet, alas! in this dreadful hour of the world's history the analytical mind is unhappily all that many readers have to work with. As St. Paul once sadly remarked, the preaching of the Cross of Christ is foolishness to them that perish.

The implied comparison is, in a sense, misleading, for de la Mare can hardly be said to conceive salvation in Pauline terms. Yet the note of austerity is common to both writers. Where, for example, is the New Testament more absolutist in its claims than "The Connoisseur"?

Every great writer, like every great teacher, makes certain assumptions about life. Joseph Conrad, for example, earnestly opposed (in the ordinary sense) didacticism in fiction; yet, says Conrad, "every subject in the region of intellect and emotion must have a morality of its own if it is treated at all sincerely; and even the most artful writer will give himself (and his morality) away in about every third sentence." If the reader cannot understand the assumptions made, or cannot grant them even as the frame of reference for a work of art, then—there is no help for it—the writer's world is closed to him. De la Mare, too, has his assumptions, and, gentlest of men though he is, there are "hard sayings" among them.

"Realism," for example, "in the accepted sense," is only, as he sees it, "a kind of scientific reporting." "What is called realism is usually a record of life at a low pitch and ebb viewed in the sunless light of day. . . ." Nature itself "resembles a veil over some further reality of which the imagination in its visionary moments seems to achieve a more direct evidence." There are the senses, of course. But the senses "can tell us only what they are capable of being sensible *of*." And this is quite inadequate, for "what we see and hear is only the smallest fraction of what is." Even when you have found a material explanation for a given set of phenomena, "it doesn't follow . . . that they didn't mean something else too."

Some of these quotations are from de la Mare's stories; some of them are from Mr. de la Mare speaking *in propria persona*. None of them, I think, misrepresent him; for, as I have already suggested, his is a notably varied yet remarkably single voice. And it should not be difficult, I think, to guess along what lines a writer who makes such assumptions would be likely to proceed.

If he is a serious writer, he must, necessarily, first of all seek to pierce "the veil," to "achieve a more direct evidence" of the things that matter than the senses can give. And, be it carefully noted at the outset, there is no element of "escapism" in this. "How," asked the wise London *Times* reviewer of *The Connoisseur,* "How can you be said to be fleeing the real, or the actual, when you are merely opening your eyes to what the simplest fragment of it, in your view, involves?" De la Mare has never fled through the veil to the comforting delights of a Never-Never Land; there are dreadful terrors in Tishnar—greater terrors indeed than any he could have encountered had he been content to remain earth-bound. But the essential point is that had Walter de la Mare stopped where, say, Mr. Maugham stops, that would have been, for him, the real "escapism"; for on that basis he must have left out not merely *a* segment of human experience but what seems to him *the* most important segment of all.

Now, obviously, the man who would pierce the veil must approach it at some point where it promises to be pierceable. Where do these points of entry lie? They are somewhat differently located, no doubt, for different writers. But there can be no question of where they lie for de la Mare. He finds his points of entry through dreams; through childhood ("Children . . . live in a world peculiarly their own." "They are not bound in by their groping senses. Facts to them are the liveliest of chameleons. Between their dream and their reality looms no impassable abyss"); through adventures, "psychic" or what-you-will, on the frontiers of consciousness; and, as has already been indicated, through the use of the artistic imagination ("An imaginative experience is not only as real but far realer than an unimaginative one"; for it is "in our individual imagination" that "the essential truth for each one of us lies").

And with this we have come, I think, very close to the themes and motives of the de la Mare fantasy; close enough, at any rate, to be clear in our own minds that none have been idly or arbitrarily chosen. To take a specific example, de la Mare has not written about children rather than about businessmen because he "likes" children better. He may, to be sure, "like" children better than businessmen. But his "liking" or not "liking" is a quite irrelevant consideration. He has been driven to the use of certain symbols, certain materials, because only through them can he express an apprehension of life which, in the last analysis, he did not choose, but which was chosen for him.

The adumbration of these matters is, however, in his case, less simple than it sounds. It is true, as Lord David Cecil says, that he is concerned with the human soul almost altogether, yet he is not, in the usual sense of the term, a religious writer; true that he has given more attention to childhood than almost any other writer of his rank, yet he is hardly ever sentimental about his children; true that he is fascinated by the twilight side of life, but he is almost unique among writers of whom that can be said in that there is no slightest suggestion of unhealthiness about him.

It is very interesting in this connection to study the use that he has made of madness in his poems and stories. For many centuries madness has opened wickets through the veil. Now, de la Mare understands the use of madness for this purpose as well as Shakespeare did or the makers of popular balladry; yet he himself has lived through a great Age of Unreason without ever falling victim to that worship of unreason—and its accompanying violence —by which so many gifted writers of the period have been ensnared. He understands, I believe, what Wordsworth means by his denunciation of the "meddling intellect," comprehends, for their suggestive value at least, the older poet's tributes to the ass and the idiot boy, but he does not therefore emulate the painter who tells his pupils that they "must not think but do"! It would be difficult, for example, to prove that Miss Duveen in the story owes her lovely qualities to the *fact* that she is mad. And her final, unglimpsed condition was, clearly, horrible enough.

As for the children, they are not precisely little angels in "The Trumpet," "The Almond Tree," "An Ideal Craftsman"—one might easily continue the roll. The boy of "In the Forest" refuses to go for the doctor when his little sister lies dying. Philip Pim, of "The Orgy"—who never did turn out very well—learned early how to simulate the sound of croup and bring his mother quickly to his side! Even Miss Duveen's friend has something of the hardness of childhood about him, and though the Nicholas of "The Bowl" is more attractive, it is clear that he lives in a world of his own, equally impenetrable to the understanding of the stupid adults round about, whether they slander him or gush over him. But if children are not angels, they are always human beings. Even the most sinister among them, the Craftsman, is humanly childish at the end; he is not a monster, even though his unhealthy imagination has once nerved him to the performance of a monstrous deed.

Nearly every critic who has written about de la Mare has compared him with Blake; in *The Three Royal Monkeys* he has even, like Blake, created his own mythology. But there is also a fairly general recognition of the fact that he has not explored the "further reality" quite in the Blakian manner, has not (this is to say) torn himself clear of the here and now. Occasionally, to be sure, he has nearly achieved this. There are tales like "The Creatures" and "The Vats" in which we travel off to a mysterious realm of otherness which seems to cling only by sufferance to the naked shingles of the world. But though such stories are less anomalous in the de la Mare canon than, say, "The Great Good Place" is for Henry James, it still remains true that the more characteristic form of the de la Mare supernatural story—"All Hallows," "Seaton's Aunt," and even, in its own way, "The Riddle"—deals rather with supernatural beauty or terror in the act of invading this mundane sphere in which we live. There is something in the nature of the problems he poses as artist, something also, I think, in his own temperament and in the mood of the age in which he lives, that causes de la Mare to prefer to concern himself with these glimpses of reality that come to us here rather than actually to attempt to portray the Ultimate Beatitude.

This is no doubt a limitation, but it is a limitation without which the de la Mare charm as we know it could not exist, for the roots of that charm sink quite as deep into this world as in the other; and what we think of as de la Mare's sanity is due quite as much to his refusal to sacrifice this world as it is to any other consideration. He has always been a practical man, with a practical man's ability to make terms with life—a husband, a father, a businessman. Did he not earn his living for many years as a statistician in the office of the Anglo-American Oil Company and write his first novel, *Henry Brocken,* upon Anglo-American scrap paper? (He still has two copies of the manuscript in this form.) One can hardly imagine him, for all his interest in the occult, being swept off his feet by the phenomena of the seance-room. In the novel *The Return* and in "The Imagination's Pride"—

> Be not too wildly amorous of the far,
> Nor lure thy fantasy to its utmost scope—

he may be said to have conveyed a solemn warning from the man who came whither he went that human beings can do worse things than take each world as it comes.

There are stories in this collection in which his mastery of the "real" is abundantly demonstrated: "Cape Race," "Physic," "The Nap," "The Almond Tree" with its complicated sexual tangle, and "Missing," which Forrest Reid called the most appalling murder story ever written, though the word "murder" is never mentioned in it. Run through the tales some time with no other idea in mind save to notice the minor characters that are made to live, if only for a moment, and to glow with colors that are brighter than life. To mention no others, there are the sailor in "Cape Race"; Mrs. Sullivan in "The Trumpet" ("When I was a young girl I nearly brooded all the blood out of my body thinking of things like that . . ."); the vergers of "All Hallows" and "Strangers and Pilgrims"; the barmaid of "The Three Friends" and the waitress who inquires about the bus ("It's a 'Ighteen") in "Missing"; the secretary in "The Orgy"; the fat woman who has killed Jacobs in "An Ideal Craftsman"; and the people in the little butcher's shop at the close of "Seaton's Aunt." They all have the Dickensian vividness, though we see them only in flashes, which recalls de la Mare's suggestive observation about his own inward eye: "It can see its object with the utmost clearness; but it cannot, I think, except for a moment or two, remain fixed and watch it." He has

watched it, notably I think in the *Midget*. But the remark is a
tantalizing one nevertheless, and it suggests one possible explanation of why he has devoted so much of his time to the short story
and the short poem.

That Mr. de la Mare has a never-failing delight in the varied
phenomena of earth and sky no reader of his poems can need to
be told. But the tales attest the same passion. Nor is it only lovely
things that enthrall him—the sight of the stars in "All Hallows"
or the beauty of the sleeping child in the verger's house: "He had
flung back his bedclothes—as if innocence in this world needed
no covering or defence—and lay at ease, the dews of sleep on lip,
cheek, and forehead." Look at the zest in the picture of the
middle-class kitchen of "The Nap" or the concrete realities of the
city street at the beginning of "The Connoisseur." De la Mare
has, indeed, the same kind of visualizing imagination that he has
attributed to the narrator of "Missing," to whom Mr. Bleet's simple "we—I—suffer from want of a plentiful supply of water"
called up "a picture of a gaunt yellow-brick building perched
amid sloping fields parched lint-white with a tropical drought, its
garden little more than a display of vegetable anatomies." There
is pleasure in such conjuring even when the pictures are ugly.
What an impressive "property," in the theatrical sense, is Mr.
Bleet's obscenely melting "ice"; with what gusto did the Ideal
Craftsman first perceive, when his eyes fell upon Jacob's dead
body in the cabinet, that the hitherto feared and detested creature
was actually a *little* man. But de la Mare knows too the comfort
that can be derived from the very unspirituality of material objects. The tortured woman in "Physic," half of her consciousness
busy with her children's illness, the rest with her husband's newly
discovered defection, finds everything in her familiar bedroom
"doing its utmost to reassure her": "*things* stay where they are
put" in this world, "do not hide, play false, forsake and abandon
us," even if human beings do. This whole side of de la Mare's
genius is a ballast to his more dazzling faëry unsubstantiality, and
though it is less than half the truth about him, it has its own importance.

It has, for one thing, enabled him to become a writer of fiction,
rather than, say, an anatomist like Burton or a brooding rhapso-

dist like Sir Thomas Browne, both of whom, in some of his moods, he resembles. For the artist, unlike the philosopher, must, in the nature of the case, concern himself with concretions, can, indeed, illustrate the universal only as it manifests itself in the particular. As an artist, Dante presents Paradise in terms of a series of images, but because he was also a theologian—or the disciple of a theologian—he annuls each image, as soon as he has employed it, with another image: this is *not* Paradise, he seems to be saying; this is merely what Paradise is *like!* So the other side of de la Mare's delight in physical realities manifests itself in his use of symbolism, symbols of that which satisfies the human spirit, that which *is*, "emblems of an ineffable peace." Once, indeed—in "Lispet, Lispett and Vaine"—he goes so far as to suggest, very much in the Hawthorne manner, that it is only as symbols that objects can have value at all. De la Mare's symbols may be chosen from nature, like the Vats or the Tree—the garden in "The Creatures" cries " 'Hospital' to the wanderers of the universe"—or they may be works of man, like the cathedral of "All Hallows": "There are buildings . . . that have a singular influence on the imagination." The Bowl is almost a talisman, an object of magic, curiously tied up with the intuitive insight of childhood.

The most daring of all de la Mare's symbols is the manure-pile in "The Wharf," which becomes the means of saving a woman's reason. Not even Henry James ever set himself a more difficult problem than that story, nor brought it off more triumphantly. But "The Wharf" is, even for de la Mare, a somewhat special case. The essential point about all these symbols is the importance of remembering that they *are* symbols and of maintaining one's detachment. To love a human being as the child of God is to achieve deliverance from the shell of self, but to make him an end in himself is idolatry. This is precisely the kind of thing which, on another level, the Connoisseur in the story cannot achieve: therefore beauty itself is for him damnation, and he sinks to a lower level of life than the serpent on the rocks, who died for love.

How "modern," then, is de la Mare? (When "The Wharf" was reprinted in my anthology, *The Fireside Book of Romance*, one unconscious humorist among the reviewers conferred a brittle immortality upon himself by referring to its author as "the ultra-modern, realistic de la Mare"!) It was once said of the Hardy whom de la Mare so greatly admires that though no contemporary writer was sharper in his break with tradition, none other would have been more at home upon the earth a thousand years ago. Different as he is from Hardy, de la Mare has at least this much in common with him, that his work, like the older writer's, is full of curious remnants of animism and folk-belief that live on in the heart of the people and in the hearts of children. But modern as he is in his technique—which is always indirect and implicational—one feels always that his sense of values is more firmly grounded and widely nurtured than could be that of one whose roots go down into the soil of this age alone. The social setting, to be sure, is dominantly late-Victorian, but this has little to do with the fact, sometimes made a source of reproach against him, that de la Mare's ethic is based upon what are now often spoken of as "the old-fashioned virtues." The point is rather that he belongs to the type of artist whose creativity operates largely upon the basis of his experiences and emotions in childhood and whose creative range is conditioned by the associations of his early years. Willa Cather was, in recent American literature, another outstanding example of these things, though Willa Cather was much less inventive and far-reaching technically than de la Mare.

But there is a yet more important question concerning de la Mare's "values." Graham Greene, writing in the same *Tribute* to which I have already referred, declared that de la Mare had never accepted—or even speculated upon—"the Christian answer" to the problems with which his art is preoccupied. "Christianity when it is figured in these stories is like a dead religion of which we see only the enormous stone memorials." He is not, I think, alone in this feeling, though I know no other writer who has made the observation quite so sharply. When I mentioned the point to Mr. de la Mare, he replied, most interestingly, as follows:

As far as my small consciousness permits (and it is difficult to realize in the least the narrowness of its range), I feel that the Christian and

Catholic idea of Man and the Universe is the richest, profoundest, most "imaginative" and creative, beautiful and reasonable conception of any I have any knowledge of (and there once more come in the inevitable restrictions). Therefore, as it seems to me, it is, quite apart from anything else, the most *likely* to be true. It is certainly true that the best in our fellow creatures and in fellow objects is what is most essentially true about them. Only three days ago, I was having the liveliest talk with a friend on the subject of good and evil. My feeling was that as with "absolute cold" and the prodigious range in regard, say, to stellar temperatures, so with these. There is a limit to evil but no limit to good, or, as one might put it, cold is the absence of heat, and evil the absence of goodness. Whether this could be argued on to the end, I cannot say. . . .

I am by no means sure that these considerations would cause Mr. Greene to wish to alter his statement. From the standpoint of the dogmatic (as it were, "classical") Christian theology to which he adheres, he might well still find his position defensible. But it seems to me equally indisputable that, in a larger sense, Mr. de la Mare's statement is a statement of faith. It is true, as I have already suggested, that his mysticism itself makes life more perilous than life could otherwise be. How much more dreadful than the atomic bomb is the spiritual attack in "All Hallows"! how terrible the vampire-triumph of "Seaton's Aunt"! Yet "he" of "The Creatures" sees "that other gate . . . for ever ajar into God knows what of peace and mystery," and if this statement is not in harmony with the impression made by the author's work as a whole, then I have interpreted it altogether amiss. That courageous story "The Wharf" faces the ultimate question of whether it be possible that Satan occupies the throne of the universe, and calmly and deliberately rejects it as the fantasy of a diseased mind. In the radiant Gulliver episode of *Henry Brocken* one of Swift's Yahoos is made to lay down his life for his friend. In his own person, de la Mare has made it clear that he prefers in art an implicit, not an explicit, statement of the "poet's faith." We must not ask a writer to "answer each of our riddles in turn; 'tidy things up.' He shares our doubts and problems; exults in them, and at the same time proves that life in spite of all its duplicity and deceits and horrors, is full of strangenesses, wonder, mystery, grace and power: is 'good.'" "Illuminated by the imagination, our life—whatever its defeats and despairs—is a never-ending, unforeseen strangeness and adventure and mystery. This is the fountain of our faith and of our hope." We live in a world in which the ultimate cost is often asked of goodness, in which those who undertake impossible journeys may well be asked to leave their bones in the sun. But that in itself is no indictment either of the value of the journey or of its goal, any more than the life of Christ was robbed of its meaning by the fact that it ended upon the Cross. When the Connoisseur asks St. Dusman whether the journey has a goal, the saint replies: "Surely! Were you uncertain even of that?"

II

Something like that, inadequate as it is, represents, I think, what *needs* to be said. There is much more that *could* be said, that in a way inevitably *will* be said. But these things each reader may quite as well say for himself. Memorable art requires two things: that the writer shall have something to say that is worth saying, and that he shall be able to communicate it in a form of sufficient beauty so that men shall not be willing to let it die. Under the first aspect, one may sum up, as I have tried to sum up here; but in so far as the second is concerned, the only possible proof of the pudding must be the eating. And from that eating —one of the best bills-of-fare (to hark back to Fielding) that any restaurateur has provided in our time, I have already kept the paying guests far too long away.

Among the individual stories each reader may best find his own favorites, for we contrary mortals always tend to love best the things we have discovered for ourselves rather than those which others have presented to us—pre-digested, pre-arranged, or pre-appreciated, as the case may be. No author has ever succeeded perfectly in expressing just what was in his mind, and no reader has ever succeeded perfectly in understanding what the author had expressed. Our own experience is the tiny golden key with which we must unlock the treasures that have been stored up in books. It is generally inadequate, but we continue to make use of it for the simple reason that there is no other key anywhere that we can use at all. And because no two of us have had exactly the same experience of life, exactly the same story never exists for any two persons. Sir Herbert Tree used to be fond of saying that every man has the god he deserves. In reading, too, we find, inevitably, the things that were destined for us.

I have already mentioned some of my favorites among these tales; of others I have said little or nothing. I have said little of "The Riddle," for example, perhaps because I have said so much of it elsewhere.[1] Yet "The Riddle" seems to me already as clearly one of the inescapable things as "Jack and the Beanstalk," *The Merchant of Venice*, "Rip Van Winkle," or the Story of Joseph. Men *have* lived on this planet without knowing these stories— how strange that seems! For that matter, there was an idiot of a woman on one of the quiz programs the other day who had never heard of "Rip Van Winkle."

Not only do we use our own past experiences in interpreting art as it comes to us, but fresh associations cluster round the reading itself and blend in our memories with the thing that is read. Such experiences I covet for the readers of this book, and such I expect; for this is a book which if it is read at all will be read again and again. Myself I am fortunate enough to remember the Saturday night in the early 1920's when the celebrated author of *Memoirs of a Midget* came to the University of Chicago to lecture in Mandel Hall. Edith Rickert did not go to hear him because she didn't want to miss Frederick Stock's Mozart at Orchestra Hall, which is interesting because it shows what a strange mistake even a very great and wise human being can make! A very different sort of memory is that of the night when, at another university on the Pacific Coast, I gave a public reading of "Seaton's Aunt," and a student of mine who had the bad judgment greatly to admire me brought his own aunt—a visitor in town—to hear

---

[1] See my article: "Walter de la Mare's 'The Riddle,' A Note on the Teaching of Literature with Allegorical Tendencies," *College English*, November, 1949. I have discussed de la Mare's long fictions in my *Cavalcade of the English Novel* (New York: Henry Holt & Co.; 1943).

the reading. Encountering me only in my Miss Seaton aspect, she at once gave me a place in her imagination as a kind of second Boris Karloff, and it was as such that she would inquire concerning me, to my great delight, whenever she would see the nephew who had so unaccountably blown me up. I remember, too, that *The Riddle and Other Stories* was one of the books that my wife and I took along on our honeymoon. But it is clear that I am now merely maundering, and since this is not my autobiography, I hasten to step out of the way. . . .

There remains, however, in common honesty, the necessary admission that I have, inevitably, restricted your understanding of Mr. de la Mare, and your capacity for appreciation, by the fact that it is my choice of his tales to which you are here limited. This volume is "collected" in the sense that there is no other single volume which contains so much, but it is by no means complete. In the six volumes into which de la Mare's stories have hitherto been gathered, there are sixty-three titles in all. From two of these collections—*Broomsticks* (1925) and *The Lord Fish* (1933)—I have, because they were addressed primarily to children, taken nothing for these pages. The twenty-four stories printed here have been chosen from the other four volumes: *The Riddle and Other Stories* (1923); *The Connoisseur and Other Stories* (1926); *On the Edge* (1930); and *The Wind Blows Over* (1936). I should add that the story called "The Connoisseur" appears here not in the abbreviated form in which it was printed in the volume of similar title, but complete, as it appeared in *Two Tales,* published in a limited edition in London, by "The Bookman's Journal" Office in 1925, and in this country, serially, in the *Yale Review.* The order in which the stories appear is only roughly chronological; in general the early stories are in the first half of the book. But chronology has yielded, on occasion, to other considerations.

EDWARD WAGENKNECHT

Boston University
August 27, 1949

CONTENTS

THE
COLLECTED TALES
OF
WALTER DE LA MARE

Walter de la Mare

THE RIDDLE

So THESE seven children, Ann, and Matilda, James, William and
Henry, Harriet and Dorothea, came to live with their grandmother. The house in which their grandmother had lived since
her childhood was built in the time of the Georges. It was not a
pretty house, but roomy, substantial, and square; and an elm tree
outstretched its branches almost to the windows.

When the children were come out of the cab (five sitting inside
and two beside the driver), they were shown into their grandmother's presence. They stood in a little black group before the
old lady, seated in her bow-window. And she asked them each
their names, and repeated each name in her kind, quavering
voice. Then to one she gave a work-box, to William a jack-knife,
to Dorothea a painted ball; to each a present according to age.
And she kissed all her grandchildren to the youngest.

"My dears," she said, "I wish to see all of you bright and gay
in my house. I am an old woman, so that I cannot romp with
you; but Ann must look to you, and Mrs. Fenn too. And every
morning and every evening you must all come in to see your
granny; and bring me smiling faces, that call back to my mind
my own son Harry. But all the rest of the day, when school is
done, you shall do just as you please, my dears. And there is only
one thing, just one, I would have you remember. In the large
spare bedroom that looks out on the slate roof there stands in the

corner an old oak chest; ay, older than I, my dears, a great deal older; older than my grandmother. Play anywhere else in the house, but not there." She spoke kindly to them all, smiling at them; but she was very aged, and her eyes seemed to see nothing of this world.

And the seven children, though at first they were gloomy and strange, soon began to be happy and at home in the great house. There was much to interest and to amuse them there; all was new to them. Twice every day, morning and evening, they came in to see their grandmother, who every day seemed more feeble; and she spoke pleasantly to them of her mother, and her childhood, but never forgetting to visit her store of sugar-plums. And so the weeks passed by.

It was evening twilight when Henry went upstairs from the nursery by himself to look at the oak chest. He pressed his fingers into the carved fruit and flowers, and spoke to the dark-smiling heads at the corners; and then, with a glance over his shoulder, he opened the lid and looked in. But the chest concealed no treasure, neither gold nor baubles, nor was there anything to alarm the eye. The chest was empty, except that it was lined with silk of old-rose, seeming darker in the dusk, and smelling sweet of pot-pourri. And while Henry was looking in, he heard the softened laughter and the clinking of the cups downstairs in the nursery; and out at the window he saw the day darkening. These things brought strangely to his memory his mother, who in her glimmering white dress used to read to him in the dusk; and he climbed into the chest; and the lid closed gently down over him.

When the other six children were tired with their playing, they filed into their grandmother's room as usual for her good-night and her sugar-plums. She looked out between the candles at them as if she were unsure of something in her thoughts. The next day Ann told her grandmother that Henry was not anywhere to be found.

"Dearie me, child. Then he must be gone away for a time," said the old lady. She paused. "But remember all of you, do not meddle with the oak chest."

But Matilda could not forget her brother Henry, finding no

pleasure in playing without him. So she would loiter in the house thinking where he might be. And she carried her wood doll in her bare arms, singing under her breath all she could make up about him. And when in a bright morning she peeped in on the chest, so sweet-scented and secret it seemed that she took her doll with her into it— just as Henry himself had done.

So Ann, and James, and William, Harriet and Dorothea were left at home to play together. "Some day maybe they will come back to you, my dears," said their grandmother, "or maybe you will go to them. Heed my warning as best you may."

Now Harriet and William were friends together, pretending to be sweethearts; while James and Dorothea liked wild games of hunting, and fishing, and battles.

On a silent afternoon in October Harriet and William were talking softly together, looking out over the slate roof at the green fields, and they heard the squeak and frisking of a mouse behind them in the room. They went together and searched for the small, dark hole from whence it had come out. But finding no hole, they began to finger the carving of the chest, and to give names to the dark-smiling heads, just as Henry had done. "I know! let's pretend you are Sleeping Beauty, Harriet," said William, "and I'll be the Prince that squeezes through the thorns and comes in." Harriet looked gently and strangely at her brother; but she got into the box and lay down, pretending to be fast asleep; and on tiptoe William leaned over, and seeing how big was the chest he stepped in to kiss the Sleeping Beauty and to wake her from her quiet sleep. Slowly the carved lid turned on its noiseless hinges. And only the clatter of James and Dorothea came in sometimes to recall Ann from her book.

But their old grandmother was very feeble, and her sight dim, and her hearing extremely difficult.

Snow was falling through the still air upon the roof; and Dorothea was a fish in the oak chest, and James stood over the hole in the ice, brandishing a walking-stick for a harpoon, pretending to be an Esquimau. Dorothea's face was red, and her wild eyes sparkled through her tousled hair. And James had a crooked scratch upon his cheek. "You must struggle, Dorothea, and then I shall swim back and drag you out. Be quick now!"

He shouted with laughter as he was drawn into the open chest. And the lid closed softly and gently down as before.

Ann, left to herself, was too old to care overmuch for sugar-plums, but she would go solitary to bid her grandmother good-night; and the old lady looked wistfully at her over her spectacles. "Well, my dear," she said with trembling head; and she squeezed Ann's fingers between her own knuckled finger and thumb. "What lonely old people we are, to be sure!" Ann kissed her grandmother's soft, loose cheek. She left the old lady sitting in her easy chair, her hands upon her knees, and her head turned sidelong towards her.

When Ann was gone to bed she used to sit reading her book by candlelight. She drew up her knees under the sheets, resting her book upon them. Her story was about fairies and gnomes, and the gently-flowing moonlight of the narrative seemed to illumine the white pages, and she could hear in fancy fairy voices, so silent was the great many-roomed house, and so mel-lifluent were the words of the story. Presently she put out her candle, and, with a confused babel of voices close to her ear, and faint swift pictures before her eyes, she fell asleep.

And in the dead of night she arose out of bed in dream, and with eyes wide open yet seeing nothing of reality, moved silently through the vacant house. Past the room where her grandmother was snoring in brief, heavy slumber, she stepped light and surely, and down the wide staircase. And Vega the far-shining stood over against the window above the slate roof. Ann walked in the strange room as if she were being guided by the hand towards the oak chest. There, just as if she was dream-ing it, was her bed, she laid herself down in the old rose silk, in the fragrant place. But it was so dark in the room that the movement of the lid was indistinguishable.

Through the long day, the grandmother sat in her bow-window. Her lips were pursed, and she looked with dim, inquisitive scrutiny upon the street where people passed to and fro, and vehicles rolled by. At evening she climbed the stair and stood in the doorway of the large spare bedroom. The ascent had shortened her breath. Her magnifying spectacles rested upon her nose. Leaning her hand on the doorpost she peered in towards the glimmering square of window in the quiet gloom. But she could not see far, because her sight was dim and the light of day feeble. Nor could she detect the faint fragrance, as of autumnal leaves. But in her mind was a tangled skein of memories—laughter and tears, and little children now old-fashioned, and the advent of friends, and long farewells. And gossiping fitfully, inarticulately, with herself, the old lady went down again to her window-seat.

The Riddle and Other Stories (1923)

THE ALMOND TREE

MY OLD friend, "the Count" as we used to call him, made very strange acquaintances at times. Let but a man have plausibility, a point of view, a crotchet, an enthusiasm, he would find in him an eager and exhilarating listener. And though he was often deceived and disappointed in his finds, the Count had a heart proof against lasting disillusionment. I confess, however, that these planetary cronies of his were rather disconcerting at times. And I own that meeting him one afternoon in the busy High Street, with a companion on his arm even more than usually voluble and odd—I own I crossed the road to avoid meeting the pair.

But the Count's eyes had been too sharp for me. He twitted me unmercifully with my snobbishness. "I am afraid we must have appeared to avoid you to-day," he said; and received my protestations with contemptuous indifference.

But the next afternoon we took a walk together over the heath; and perhaps the sunshine, something in the first freshness of the May weather, reminded him of bygone days.

"You remember that rather out-of-the-world friend of mine yesterday that so shocked your spruce proprieties, Richard? Well, I'll tell you a story."

As closely as I can recall this story of the Count's childhood I have here related it. I wish, though, I had my old friend's gift for such things; then, perhaps, his story might retain something of the charm in the reading which he gave to it in the telling. Perhaps that charm lies wholly in the memory of his voice, his companionship, his friendship. To revive these, what task would be a burden? . . .

"The house of my first remembrance, the house that to my last hour on earth will seem home to me, stood in a small green hollow on the verge of a wide heath. Its five upper windows faced far eastwards towards the weathercocked tower of a village which rambled down the steep inclination of a hill. And, walking in its green old garden—ah, Richard, the crocuses, the wallflowers, the violets!—you could see in the evening the standing fields of corn, and the dark furrows where the evening star was stationed; and a little to the south, upon a crest, a rambling wood of fir trees and bracken.

"The house, the garden, the deep quiet orchard, all had been a wedding gift to my mother from a great-aunt, a very old lady in a kind of turban, whose shrewd eyes used to watch me out of her picture sitting in my high cane chair at meal-times—with not a little keenness, sometimes, I fancied, with a faint derision. Here passed by, to the singing of the lark, and the lamentation of autumn wind and rain, the first long nine of all these heaped-up inextricable years. Even now, my heart leaps up with longing to see again with those untutored eyes the lofty clouds of evening; to hear again as then I heard it the two small notes of the yellow-hammer piping from his green spray. I remember every room of the old house, the steep stairs, the cool apple-scented pantry; I remember the cobbles by the scullery, the well, my old dead raven, the bleak and whistling elms; but best of all I remember the unmeasured splendour of the heath, with its gorse, and its deep canopy of sunny air, the haven of every wild bird of the morning.

"Martha Rodd was a mere prim snippet of a maid then, pale

and grave, with large contemplative, Puritan eyes. Mrs. Ryder, in her stiff blue martial print and twisted gold brooch, was cook. And besides these, there was only old Thomas the gardner (as out-of-doors, and as distantly seen a creature as a dryad); my mother; and that busy-minded little boy, agog in wits and stomach and spirit—myself. For my father seemed but a familiar guest in the house, a guest ever eagerly desired and welcome, but none too eager to remain. He was a dark man with grey eyes and a long chin; a face unusually impassive, unusually mobile. Just as his capricious mood suggested, our little household was dejected or wildly gay. I never shall forget the spirit of delight he could conjure up at a whim, when my mother would go singing up and down stairs, and in her tiny parlour; and Martha in perfect content would prattle endlessly on to the cook, basting the twirling sirloin, while I watched in the firelight. And the long summer evenings too, when my father would find a secret, a magic, a mystery in everything; and we would sit together in the orchard while he told me tales, with the small green apples overhead, and beyond contorted branches, the first golden twilight of the moon.

"It's an old picture now, Richard, but true to the time.

"My father's will, his word, his caprice, his frown, these were the tables of the law in that small household. To my mother he was the very meaning of her life. Only that little boy was in some wise independent, busy, inquisitive, docile, sedate; though urged to a bitterness of secret rebellion at times. In his childhood he experienced such hours of distress as the years do not in mercy bring again to a heart that may analyse as well as remember. Yet there also sank to rest the fountain of life's happiness. In among the gorse bushes were the green mansions of the fairies; along the furrows before his adventurous eyes stumbled crooked gnomes, hopped bewitched robins. Ariel trebled in the sunbeams and glanced from the dewdrops; and he heard the echo of distant and magic waters in the falling of the rain.

"But my father was never long at peace in the house. Nothing satisfied him; he must needs be at an extreme. And if he was compelled to conceal his discontent, there was something so bitter and imperious in his silence, so scornful a sarcasm in his speech, that we could scarcely bear it. And the knowledge of the influence he had over us served only at such times to sharpen his contempt.

"I remember one summer's evening we had been gathering strawberries. I carried a little wicker basket, and went rummaging under the aromatic leaves, calling ever and again my mother to see the 'tremenjous' berry I had found. Martha was busy beside me, vexed that her two hands could not serve her master quick enough. And in a wild race with my mother my father helped us pick. At every ripest one he took her in his arms to force it between her lips; and of all those pecked by the birds he made a rhymed offering to Pan. And when the sun had descended behind the hill, and the clamour of the rooks had begun to wane in the elm-tops, he took my mother on his arm, and we trooped all together up the long straggling path, and across the grass, carrying our spoil of fruit into the cool dusky corridor. As we passed into the gloaming I saw my mother stoop impulsively and kiss his arm. He brushed off her hand impatiently, and went into his study. I heard the door shut. A moment afterwards he called for candles. And, looking on those two other faces in the twilight, I knew with the intuition of childhood that he was suddenly sick to death of us all; and I knew that my mother shared my intuition. She sat down, and I beside her, in her little parlour, and took up her sewing. But her face had lost again all its girlishness as she bent her head over the white linen.

"I think she was happier when my father was away; for then, free from anxiety to be for ever pleasing his variable moods, she could entertain herself with hopes and preparations for his return. There was a little green summer-house, or arbour, in the garden, where she would sit alone, while the swallows coursed in the evening air. Sometimes, too, she would take me for a long walk, listening distantly to my chatter, only, I think, that she might entertain the pleasure of supposing that my father might have returned home unforeseen, and be even now waiting to greet us. But these fancies would forsake her. She would speak harshly and coldly to me, and scold Martha for her owlishness, and find nothing but vanity and mockery in all that but a little while since had been her daydream.

"I think she rarely knew where my father stayed in his long absences from home. He would remain with us for a week, and neglect us for a month. She was too proud, and when he was himself, too happy and hopeful to question him, and he seemed to delight in keeping his affairs secret from her. Indeed, he sometimes appeared to pretend a mystery where none was, and to endeavour in all things to make his character and conduct appear quixotic and inexplicable.

"So time went on. Yet, it seemed, as each month passed by, the house was not so merry and happy as before; something was fading and vanishing that would not return; estrangement had pierced a little deeper. I think care at last put out of my mother's mind even the semblance of her former gaiety. She sealed up her heart lest love should break forth anew into the bleakness.

"On Guy Fawkes' Day Martha told me at bed-time that a new household had moved into the village on the other side of the heath. After that my father stayed away from us but seldom.

"At first my mother showed her pleasure in a thousand ways, with dainties of her own fancy and cooking, with ribbons in her dark hair, with new songs (though she had but a small thin voice). She read to please him; and tired my legs out in useless errands in his service. And a word of praise sufficed her for many hours of difficulty. But by-and-by, when evening after evening was spent by my father away from home, she began to be uneasy and depressed; and though she made no complaint, her anxious face, the incessant interrogation of her eyes vexed and irritated him beyond measure.

"'Where does my father go after dinner?' I asked Martha one night, when my mother was in my bedroom, folding my clothes.

"'How dare you ask such a question?' said my mother, 'and how dare you talk to the child about your master's comings and goings?'

"'But where does he?' I repeated to Martha, when my mother was gone out of the room.

" 'Ssh now, Master Nicholas,' she answered, 'didn't you hear
what your mamma said? She's vexed, poor lady, at master's
never spending a whole day at home, but nothing but them
cards, cards, cards, every night at Mr. Grey's. Why, often it's
twelve and one in the morning when I've heard his foot on
the gravel beneath the window. But there, I'll be bound, she
doesn't *mean* to speak unkindly. It's a terrible scourge is jealousy,
Master Nicholas; and not generous or manly to give it cause.
Mrs. Ryder was kept a widow all along of jealousy, and but a
week before her wedding with her second.'

" 'But why is mother jealous of my father playing cards?'

"Martha slipped my nightgown over my head. 'Ssh, Master
Nicholas, little boys mustn't ask so many questions. And I hope
when you are grown up to be a man, my dear, you will be a
comfort to your mother. She needs it, poor soul, and sakes
alive, just now of all times!' I looked inquisitively into Martha's
face; but she screened my eyes with her hand; and instead of
further questions, I said my prayers to her.

"A few days after this I was sitting with my mother in her
parlour, holding her grey worsted for her to wind, when my
father entered the room and bade me put on my hat and muffler.
'He is going to pay a call with me,' he explained curtly. As I
went out of the room, I heard my mother's question, 'To your
friends at the Grange, I suppose?'

" 'You may suppose whatever you please,' he answered. I
heard my mother rise to leave the room, but he called her back
and the door was shut. . . .

"The room in which the card-players sat was very low-ceiled.
A piano stood near the window, a rosewood table with a fine
dark crimson work-basket upon it by the fireside, and some little
distance away, a green card-table with candles burning. Mr.
Grey was a slim, elegant man, with a high, narrow forehead and
long fingers. Major Aubrey was a short, red-faced, rather taciturn
man. There was also a younger man with fair hair. They
seemed to be on the best of terms together; and I helped to
pack the cards and to pile the silver coins, sipping a glass of
sherry with Mr. Grey. My father said little, paying me no attention, but playing gravely with a very slight frown.

"After some little while the door opened, and a lady appeared. This was Mr. Grey's sister, Jane, I learned. She seated herself at her work-table, and drew me to her side.

" 'Well, so this is Nicholas!' she said. 'Or is it Nick?'

" 'Nicholas,' I said.

" 'Of course,' she said, smiling, 'and I like that too, much the best. How very kind of you to come to see me! It was to keep *me* company, you know, because I am very stupid at games, but I love talking. Do you?'

"I looked into her eyes, and knew we were friends. She smiled again, with open lips, and touched my mouth with her thimble. 'Now, let me see, business first, and—me afterwards. You see I have three different kinds of cake, because, I thought, I cannot in the least tell which kind he'll like best. Could I now? Come, you shall choose.'

"She rose and opened the long door of a narrow cupboard, looking towards the card-players as she stooped. I remember the cakes to this day; little oval shortbreads stamped with a beehive, custards and mince-pies; and a great glass jar of goodies which I carried in both arms round the little square table. I took a mince-pie, and sat down on a footstool near by Miss Grey, and she talked to me while she worked with slender hands at her lace embroidery. I told her how old I was; about my great-aunt and her three cats. I told her my dreams, and that I was very fond of Yorkshire pudding, 'from under the meat, you know.' And I told her I thought my father the handsomest man I had ever seen.

" 'What, handsomer than Mr. Spencer?' she said laughing, looking along her needle.

"I answered that I did not very much like clergymen.

" 'And why?' she said gravely.

" 'Because they do not talk like real,' I said.

"She laughed very gaily. 'Do men ever?' she said.

"And her voice was so quiet and so musical, her neck so graceful, I thought her a very beautiful lady, admiring especially her dark eyes when she smiled brightly and yet half sadly at me; I promised, moreover, that if she would meet me on the heath, I would show her the rabbit warren and the 'Miller's Pool.'

" 'Well, Jane, and what do you think of my son?' said my father when we were about to leave.

"She bent over me and squeezed a lucky fourpenny piece into my hand. 'I love fourpence, pretty little fourpence, I love fourpence better than my life,' she whispered into my ear. 'But that's a secret,' she added, glancing up over her shoulder. She kissed lightly the top of my head. I was looking at my father while she was caressing me, and I fancied a faint sneer passed over his face. But when we had come out of the village on to the heath, in the bare keen night, as we walked along the path together between the gorse bushes, now on turf, and now on stony ground, never before had he seemed so wonderful a companion. He told me little stories; he began a hundred, and finished none; yet with the stars above us, they seemed a string of beads all of bright colours. We stood still in the vast darkness, while he whistled that strangest of all old songs—'the Song the Sirens sang.' He pilfered my wits and talked like my double. But when—how much too quickly, I thought with sinking heart—we were come to the house-gates, he suddenly fell silent, turned an instant, and stared far away over the windy heath.

" 'How weary, stale, flat—' he began, and broke off between uneasy laughter and a sigh. 'Listen to me, Nicholas,' he said, lifting my face to the starlight, 'you must grow up a man—a Man, you understand; no vapourings, no posings, no caprices; and above all, no sham. No sham. It's your one and only chance in this unfaltering Scheme.' He scanned my face long and closely. 'You have your mother's eyes,' he said musingly. 'And that,' he added under his breath, '*that's* no joke.' He pushed open the squealing gate, and we went in.

"My mother was sitting in a low chair before a dying and cheerless fire.

" 'Well, Nick,' she said very suavely, 'and how have you enjoyed your evening?'

"I stared at her without answer. 'Did you play cards with the gentlemen; or did you turn over the music?'

" 'I talked to Miss Grey,' I said.

" 'Really,' said my mother, raising her eyebrows, 'and who

then is Miss Grey?' My father was smiling at us with sparkling eyes.

" 'Mr. Grey's sister,' I answered in a low voice.

" 'Not his wife, then?' said my mother, glancing furtively at the fire. I looked towards my father in doubt, but could lift my eyes no higher than his knees.

" 'You little fool!' he said to my mother with a laugh, 'what a sharpshooter! Never mind, Sir Nick; there, run off to bed, my man.'

"My mother caught me roughly by the sleeve as I was passing her chair. 'Aren't you going to kiss me good-night, then,' she said furiously, her narrow underlip quivering, 'you too!' I kissed her cheek. 'That's right, my dear,' she said scornfully, 'that's how little fishes kiss.' She rose and drew back her skirts. 'I refuse to stay in the room,' she said haughtily, and with a sob she hurried out.

"My father continued to smile, but only a smile it seemed gravity had forgotten to smooth away. He stood very still, so still that I grew afraid he must certainly hear me thinking. Then with a kind of sigh he sat down at my mother's writing-table, and scribbled a few words with his pencil on a slip of paper.

" 'There, Nicholas, just tap at your mother's door with that. Good-night, old fellow'; he took my hand and smiled down into my eyes with a kind of generous dark appeal that called me straight to his side. I hastened conceitedly upstairs, and delivered my message. My mother was crying when she opened the door.

" 'Well?' she said in a low, trembling voice.

"But presently afterwards, while I was still lingering in the dark corridor, I heard her run down quickly, and in a while my father and mother came upstairs together, arm in arm, and by her light talk and laughter you might suppose she had no knowledge of care or trouble at all.

"Never afterwards did I see so much gaiety and youthfulness in my mother's face as when she sat next morning with us at breakfast. The honeycomb, the small bronze chrysanthemums, her yellow gown seemed dainty as a miniature. With every word her eyes would glance covertly at my father; her smile, as it were, hesitating between her lashes. She was so light and girlish and so versatile I should scarcely have recognized the weary and sallow face of the night before. My father seemed to find as much pleasure, or relief, in her good spirits as I did; and to delight in exercising his ingenuity to quicken her humour.

"It was but a transient morning of sunshine, however, and as the brief and sombre day waned, its gloom pervaded the house. In the evening my father left us to our solitude as usual. And that night was very misty over the heath, with a small, warm rain falling.

"So it happened that I began to be left more and more to my own devices, and grew so inured at last to my own narrow company and small thoughts and cares, that I began to look on my mother's unhappiness almost with indifference, and learned to criticize almost before I had learned to pity. And so I do not think I enjoyed Christmas very much the less, although my father was away from home and all our little festivities were dispirited. I had plenty of good things to eat, and presents, and a picture-book from Martha. I had a new rocking-horse—how changeless and impassive its mottled battered face looks out at me across the years! It was brisk, clear weather, and on St. Stephen's Day I went to see if there was any ice yet on the Miller's Pool.

"I was stooping down at the extreme edge of the pool, snapping the brittle splinters of the ice with my finger, when I heard a voice calling me in the still air. It was Jane Grey, walking on the heath with my father, who had called me, having seen me from a distance stooping beside the water.

" 'So you see I have kept my promise,' she said, taking my hand.

" 'But you promised to come by yourself,' I said.

" 'Well, so I will then,' she answered, nodding her head. 'Good-bye,' she added, turning to my father. 'It's three's none, you see. Nicholas shall take me home to tea, and you can call for him in the evening, if you will; that is, if you are coming.'

" 'Are you asking me to come?' he said moodily, 'do you care whether I come or not?'

"She lifted her face and spoke gravely. 'You are my friend,' she said, 'of course I care whether you are with me or not.' He scrutinized her through half-closed lids. His face was haggard, gloomy with *ennui*. 'How you harp on the word, you punctilious Jane. Do you suppose I am still in my teens? Twenty years ago, now— It amuses me to hear you women talk. It's little you ever really feel.'

" 'I don't think I am quite without feeling,' she replied, 'you are a little difficult, you know.'

" 'Difficult,' he echoed in derision. He checked himself and shrugged his shoulders. 'You see, Jane, it's all on the surface; I boast of my indifference. It's the one rag of philosophy age denies no one. It is so easy to be heroic—debonair, iron-grey, fluent, dramatic—you know its captivation, perhaps? But after all, life's comedy, when one stops smiling, is only the tepidest farce. Or the gilt wears off and the pinchbeck tragedy shows through. And so, as I say, we talk on, being past feeling. One by one our hopes come home to roost, our delusions find themselves out, and the mystery proves to be nothing but sleight-of hand. It's age, my dear Jane—age; it turns one to stone. With you young people life's a dream; ask Nicholas here!' He shrugged his shoulders, adding under his breath, 'But one wakes on a devilish hard pallet.'

" 'Of course,' said Jane slowly, 'you are only talking cleverly, and then it does not matter whether it's true or not, I suppose. I can't say. I don't think you mean it, and so it comes to nothing. I can't and won't believe you feel so little—I can't.' She continued to smile, yet, I fancied, with the brightness of tears in her eyes. 'It's all mockery and make-believe; we are not the miserable slaves of time you try to fancy. There must be some way to win through.' She turned away, then added slowly, 'You ask me to be fearless, sincere, to speak my heart; I wonder, do you?'

"My father did not look at her, appeared not to have seen the hand she had half held out to him, and as swiftly withdrawn. 'The truth is, Jane,' he said slowly, 'I am past sincerity now. And as for *heart* it is a quite discredited organ at forty. Life, thought, selfishness, egotism, call it what you will; they have all done their worst with me; and I really haven't the sentiment to pretend that they haven't. And when bright youth and sentiment are gone; why, go too, dear lady! Existence proves nothing but brazen inanity afterwards. But there's always that turning left to the dullest and dustiest road—oblivion.' He remained silent a moment. Silence deep and strange lay all around us. The air was still, the wintry sky unutterably calm. And again that low dispassionate voice continued: 'It's only when right seems too easy a thing, too trivial, and not worth the doing; and wrong a foolish thing—too dull. . . . There, take care of her, Nicholas; take care of her, "snips and snails," you know. *Au revoir,* 'pon my word, I almost wish it was good-bye.'

"Jane Grey regarded him attentively. 'So then do I,' she replied in a low voice, 'for I shall never understand you; perhaps I should hate to understand you.'

"My father turned with an affected laugh, and left us.

"Miss Grey and I walked slowly along beside the frosty bulrushes until we came to the wood. The bracken and heather were faded. The earth was dark and rich with autumnal rains. Fircones lay on the moss beneath the dark green branches. It was all now utterly silent in the wintry afternoon. Far away rose tardily, and alighted, the hoarse rooks upon the ploughed earth; high in the pale sky passed a few on ragged wing.

" 'What does my father mean by wishing it was good-bye?' I said.

"But my companion did not answer me in words. She clasped my hand; she seemed very slim and gracious walking by my side on the hardened ground. My mother was small now and awkward beside her in my imagination. I questioned her about the ice, about the red sky, and if there was any mistletoe in the woods. Sometimes she, in turn, asked me questions too, and when I answered them we would look at each other and smile, and it seemed it was with her as it was with me—of the pure gladness I found in her company. In the middle of our walk to the Thorns she bent down in the cold twilight, and putting her hands on my shoulders, 'My dear, dear Nicholas,' she said, 'you must be a good son to your mother—brave and kind; will you?'

" 'He hardly ever speaks to mother now,' I answered instinctively.

"She pressed her lips to my cheek, and her cheek was cold against mine, and she clasped her arms about me. 'Kiss me,' she said. 'We must do our best, mustn't we?' she pleaded, still holding me. I looked mournfully into the gathering darkness, 'That's easy when you're grown up,' I said. She laughed and kissed me again, and then we took hands and ran till we were out of breath, towards the distant lights of the Thorns. . . .

"I had been some time in bed, lying awake in the warmth, when my mother came softly through the darkness into my room. She sat down at the bedside, breathing hurriedly. 'Where have you been all the evening?' she said.

" 'Miss Grey asked me to stay to tea,' I answered.

" 'Did I give you permission to go to tea with Miss Grey?'

"I made no answer.

" 'If you go to that house again, I shall beat you. You hear me, Nicholas? Alone, or with your father, if you go there again, without my permission, I shall beat you. You have not been whipped for a long time, have you?' I could not see her face, but her head was bent towards me in the dark, as she sat—almost crouched— on my bedside.

"I made no answer. But when my mother had gone, without kissing me, I cried noiselessly on into my pillow. Something had suddenly flown out of memory, never to sing again. Life had become a little colder and stranger. I had always been my own chief company; now another sentimental barrier had arisen between the world and me, past its heedlessness, past my understanding to break down.

"Hardly a week passed now without some bitter quarrel. I seemed ever to be stealing out of sound of angry voices; ever fearful of being made the butt of my father's serene taunts, of my mother's passions and desperate remorse. He disdained to defend himself against her, never reasoned with her; he merely shrugged his shoulders, denied her charges, ignored her anger; coldly endeavouring only to show his indifference, to conceal by every means in his power his own inward weariness and vexation. I saw this, of course, only vaguely, yet with all a

child's certainty of insight, though I rarely knew the cause of
my misery; and I continued to love them both in my selfish
fashion, not a whit the less.

"At last, on St. Valentine's Day, things came to a worse pass
than before. It had always been my father's custom to hang my
mother a valentine on the handle of her little parlour door, a
string of pearls, a fan, a book of poetry, whatever it might be.
She came down early this morning, and sat in the window-seat,
looking out at the falling snow. She said nothing at breakfast,
only feigned to eat, lifting her eyes at intervals to glance at my
father with a strange intensity, as if of hatred, tapping her foot
on the floor. He took no notice of her, sat quiet and moody with
his own thoughts. I think he had not really forgotten the day,
for I found long afterwards in his old bureau a bracelet purchased but a week before with her name written on a scrap of
paper, inside the case. Yet it seemed to be the absence of this little
gift that had driven my mother beyond reason.

"Towards evening, tired of the house, tired of being alone, I
went out and played awhile listlessly in the snow. At nightfall
I went in; and in the dark heard angry voices. My father came
out of the dining-room and looked at me in silence, standing in
the gloom of the wintry dusk. My mother followed him. I can see
her now, leaning in the doorway, white with rage, her eyes
ringed and darkened with continuous trouble, her hand trembling.

"'It shall learn to hate you,' she cried in a low, dull voice.
'I will teach it every moment to hate and despise you as I—
Oh, *I* hate and despise you.'

"My father looked at her calmly and profoundly before replying. He took up a cloth hat and brushed it with his hand.
'Very well then, you have chosen,' he said coldly. 'It has always
lain with you. You have exaggerated, you have raved, and now
you have said what can never be recalled or forgotten. Here's
Nicholas. Pray do not imagine, however, that I am defending
myself. I have nothing to defend. I think of no one but myself—
no one. Endeavour to understand me, no one. Perhaps, indeed,
you yourself—no more than—. But words again—the dull old
round!' He made a peculiar gesture with his hand. 'Well, life is

. . . ach! I have done. So be it.' He stood looking out of the door. 'You see, it's snowing,' he said, as if to himself.

"All the long night before and all day long, snow had been falling continuously. The air was wintry and cold. I could discern nothing beyond the porch but a gloomy accumulation of cloud in the twilight air, now darkened with the labyrinthine motion of the snow. My father glanced back for an instant into the house, and, as I fancy, regarded me with a kind of strange, close earnestness. But he went out and his footsteps were instantly silenced.

"My mother peered at me in terrible perplexity, her eyes wide with terror and remorse. 'What? What?' she said. I stared at her stupidly. Three snowflakes swiftly and airily floated together into the dim hall from the gloom without. She clasped her hand over her mouth. Overburdened her fingers seemed to be, so slender were they, with her many rings.

" 'Nicholas, Nicholas, tell me; what was I saying? What was I saying?' She stumbled hastily to the door. 'Arthur, Arthur,' she cried from the porch, 'it's St. Valentine's Day, that was all I meant; come back, come back!' But perhaps my father was already out of hearing; I do not think he made any reply.

"My mother came in doubtfully, resting her hand on the wall. And she walked very slowly and laboriously upstairs. While I was standing at the foot of the staircase, looking out across the hall into the evening, Martha climbed primly up from the kitchen with her lighted taper, shut-to the door and lit the hall lamp. Already the good smell of the feast cooking floated up from the kitchen, and gladdened my spirits. 'Will he come back?' Martha said, looking very scared in the light of her taper. 'It's such a fall of snow, already it's a hand's breadth on the window-sill. Oh, Master Nicholas, it's a hard world for us women.' She followed my mother upstairs, carrying light to all the gloomy upper rooms.

"I sat down in the window-seat of the dining-room, and read in my picture-book as well as I could by the flame-light. By-and-by, Martha returned to lay the table.

"As far back as brief memory carried me, it had been our custom to make a Valentine's feast on the Saint's day. This was my father's mother's birthday also. When she was alive I well remember her visiting us with her companion, Miss Schreiner, who talked in such good-humoured English to me. This same anniversary had last year brought about a tender reconciliation between my father and mother, after a quarrel that meant how little then. And I remember on this day to have seen the first fast-sealed buds upon the almond tree. We would have a great spangled cake in the middle of the table, with marzipan and comfits, just as at Christmastide. And when Mrs. Merry lived in the village her little fair daughters used to come in a big carriage to spend the evening with us and to share my Valentine's feast.

"But all this was changed now. My wits were sharper, but I was none the less only the duller for that; my hopes and dreams had a little fallen and faded. I looked idly at my picture-book, vaguely conscious that its colours pleased me less than once upon a time; that I was rather tired of seeing them, and they just as tired of seeing me. And yet I had nothing else to do, so I must go on with a hard face, turning listlessly the pictured pages.

"About seven o'clock my mother sent for me. I found her sitting in her bedroom. Candles were burning before the looking-glass. She was already dressed in her handsome black silk gown, and wearing her pearl necklace. She began to brush my hair, curling its longer ends with her fingers, which she moistened in the pink bowl that was one of the first things I had set eyes on in this world. She put me on a clean blouse and my buckle shoes, talking to me the while, almost as if she were telling me a story. Then she looked at herself long and earnestly in the glass; throwing up her chin with a smile, as was a habit of hers in talk. I wandered about the room, fingering the little toilet-boxes and knick-knacks on the table. By mischance I upset one of these, a scent-bottle that held rose-water. The water ran out and filled the warm air with its fragrance. 'You foolish, clumsy boy!' said my mother, and slapped my hand. More out of vexation and tiredness than because of the pain, I began to cry. And then, with infinite tenderness, she leaned her head on my shoulder. 'Mother can't think very well just now,' she said; and cried so bitterly in silence that I was only too ready to extricate myself and run away when her hold on me relaxed.

"I climbed slowly upstairs to Martha's bedroom, and kneeling on a cane chair looked out of the window. The flakes had ceased to fall now, although the snowy heath was encompassed in mist; above the snow the clouds had parted, drifting from beneath the stars, and these in their constellations were trembling very brightly, and here and there burned one of them in solitude larger and wilder in its shining than the rest. But though I did not tire of looking out of the window, my knees began to ache; and the little room was very cold and still so near the roof. So I went down to the dining-room, with all its seven candlesticks kindled, seeming to my unaccustomed eyes a very splendid blaze out of the dark. My mother was kneeling on the rug by the fireside. She looked very small, even dwarfish, I thought. She was gazing into the flames; one shoe curved beneath the hem of her gown, her chin resting on her hand.

"I surveyed the table with its jellies and sweetmeats and glasses and fruit, and began to be very hungry, so savoury was the smell of the turkey roasting downstairs. Martha knocked at the door when the clock had struck eight.

" 'Dinner is ready, ma'am.'

"My mother glanced fleetingly at the clock. 'Just a little, only a very little while longer, tell Mrs. Ryder; your master will be home in a minute.' She rose and placed the claret in the hearth at some distance from the fire.

" 'Is it nicer warm, mother?' I said. She looked at me with startled eyes and nodded. 'Did you hear anything, Nicholas? Run to the door and listen; was that a sound of footsteps?'

"I opened the outer door and peered into the darkness; but it seemed the world ended here with the warmth and the light: beyond could extend only winter and silence, a region that, familiar though it was to me, seemed now to terrify me like an enormous sea.

" 'It's stopped snowing,' I said, 'but there isn't anybody there; nobody at all, mother.'

"The hours passed heavily from quarter on to quarter. The turkey, I grieved to hear, was to be taken out of the oven, and put away to cool in the pantry. I was bidden help myself to what I pleased of the trembling jellies, and delicious pink blancmange.

Already midnight would be the next hour to be chimed. I felt sick, yet was still hungry and very tired. The candles began to burn low. 'Leave me a little light here, then,' my mother said at last to Martha, 'and go to bed. Perhaps your master has missed his way home in the snow.' But Mrs. Ryder had followed Martha into the room.

" 'You must pardon my interference, ma'am, but it isn't right, it isn't really right of you to sit up longer. Master will not come back, maybe, before morning. And I shouldn't be doing my bounden duty, ma'am, except I spoke my mind. Just now too, of all times.'

" 'Thank you very much, Mrs. Ryder,' my mother answered simply, 'but I would prefer not to go to bed yet. It's very lonely on the heath at night. But I shall not want anything else, thank you.'

" 'Well, ma'am, I've had my say, and done my conscience's bidding. And I have brought you up this tumbler of mulled wine; else you'll be sinking away or something with the fatigue.'

"My mother took the wine, sipped of it with a wan smile at Mrs. Ryder over the brim; and Mrs. Ryder retired with Martha. I don't think they had noticed me sitting close in the shadow on my stool beside the table. But all through that long night, I fancy, these good souls took it in turn to creep down stealthily and look in on us; and in the small hours of the morning, when the fire had fallen low, they must have wrapped us both warm in shawls. They left me then, I think, to be my mother's company. Indeed, I remember we spoke in the darkness, and she took my hand.

"My mother and I shared the steaming wine together when they were gone; our shadows looming faintly huge upon the ceiling. We said very little, but I looked softly into her grey childish eyes, and we kissed one another kneeling there together before the fire. And afterwards, I jigged softly round the table, pilfering whatever sweet or savoury mouthful took my fancy. But by-and-by in the silent house—a silence broken only by the fluttering of the flames, and the odd far-away stir of the frost, drowsiness vanquished me; I sat down by the fireside, leaning my head on a chair. And sitting thus, vaguely eyeing firelight and wavering shadow, I began to nod, and very soon dream stalked in, mingling with reality.

"It was early morning when I awoke, dazed and cold and miserable in my uncomfortable resting-place. The rare odour of frost was on the air. The ashes of the fire lay iron-grey upon the cold hearth. An intensely clear white ray of light leaned up through a cranny of the shutters to the cornice of the ceiling. I got up with difficulty. My mother was still asleep, breathing heavily, and as I stooped, regarding her curiously, I could almost watch her transient dreams fleeting over her face; and now she smiled faintly; and now she raised her eyebrows as if in some playful and happy talk with my father; then again utterly still darkness would descend on brow and lid and lip.

"I touched her sleeve, suddenly conscious of my loneliness in the large house. Her face clouded instantly; she sighed profoundly: 'What?' she said, 'nothing—nothing?' She stretched out her hand towards me; the lids drew back from eyes still blind from sleep. But gradually time regained its influence over her. She moistened her lips and turned to me, and suddenly, in a gush of agony, remembrance of the night returned to her. She hid her face in her hands, rocking her body gently to and fro; then rose and smoothed back her hair at the looking-glass. I was surprised to see no trace of tears on her cheeks. Her lips moved, as if unconsciously a heart worn out with grief addressed that pale reflection of her sorrow in the glass. I took hold of the hand that hung down listlessly on her silk skirt, and fondled it, kissing punctiliously each loose ring in turn.

"But I do not think she heeded my kisses. So I returned to the table on which was still set out the mockery of our Valentine feast, strangely disenchanted in the chill dusk of daybreak. I put a handful of wine biscuits and a broken piece of cake in my pocket; for a determination had taken me to go out on to the heath. My heart beat thick and fast in imagination of the solitary snow and of myself wandering in loneliness across its untrampled surface. A project also was forming in my mind of walking over to the Thorns; for somehow I knew my mother would not scold or punish me that day. Perhaps, I thought, my father would be there. And I would tell Miss Grey all about my adventure of the night spent down in the dining-room. So moving very stealth-ily, and betraying no eagerness, lest I should be forbidden to go, I stole at length unperceived from the room, and leaving the great hall door ajar, ran out joyously into the wintry morning.

"Already dawn was clear and high in the sky, already the first breezes were moving in the mists; and breathed chill, as if it were the lingering darkness itself on my cheeks. The air was cold, yet with a fresh faint sweetness. The snow lay crisp across its perfect surface, mounded softly over the gorse bushes, though here and there a spray of parched blossom yet protruded from its cowl. Flaky particles of ice floated invisible in the air. I called out with pleasure to see the little ponds where the snow had been blown away from the black ice. I saw on the bushes too the webs of spiders stretched from thorn to thorn, and festooned with crys-tals of hoar-frost. I turned and counted as far as I could my foot-steps leading back to the house, which lay roofed in gloomy pallor, dim and obscured in the darkened west.

"A waning moon that had risen late in the night shone, it seemed, very near to the earth. But every moment light swept in-vincibly in, pouring its crystal like a river; and darkness sullenly withdrew into the north. And when at last the sun appeared, glit-tering along the rosy snow, I turned in an ecstasy and with my finger pointed him out, as if the house I had left behind me might view him with my own delight. Indeed, I saw its windows trans-muted, and heard afar a thrush pealing in the bare branches of a pear tree; and a robin startled me, so suddenly shrill and sweet he broke into song from a snowy tuft of gorse.

"I was now come to the beginning of a gradual incline, from the summit of which I should presently descry in the distance the avenue of lindens that led towards the village from the margin of the heath. As I went on my way, munching my biscuits, looking gaily about me, I brooded deliciously on the breakfast which Miss Grey would doubtless sit me down to; and almost forgot the oc-casion of my errand, and the troubled house I had left behind me. At length I climbed to the top of the smooth ridge and looked down. At a little distance from me grew a crimson hawthorn tree that often in past Aprils I had used for a green tent from the showers; but now it was closely hooded, darkening with its faint shadow the long expanse of unshadowed whiteness. Not very far from this bush I perceived a figure lying stretched along the snow and knew instinctively that this was my father lying here.

"The sight did not then surprise or dismay me. It seemed but the lucid sequel to that long heavy night-watch, to all the troubles and perplexities of the past. I felt no sorrow, but stood beside the body, regarding it only with deep wonder and a kind of earnest curiosity, yet perhaps with a remote pity too, that he could not see me in the beautiful morning. His grey hand lay arched in the snow, his darkened face, on which showed a smear of dried blood, was turned away a little as if out of the oblique sunshine. I understood that he was dead, was already loosely speculating in what changes it would make; how I should spend my time; what would happen in the house now that he was gone, his influence, his authority, his discord. I remembered too that I was alone, was master of this immense secret, that I must go home sedately, as if it were a Sunday, and in a low voice tell my mother, concealing any exultation I might feel in the office. I imagined the questions that would be asked me, and was considering the proper answers to make to them, when my morbid dreams were suddenly broken in on by Martha Rodd. She stood in my footsteps, looking down on me from the ridge from which I had but just now descended. She hastened towards me, stooping a little as if she carried a burden, her mouth ajar, her forehead wrinkled beneath its wispy light brown hair.

"'Look, Martha, look,' I cried, 'I found him in the snow; he's dead.' And suddenly a bond seemed to snap in my heart. The beauty and solitude of the morning, the perfert whiteness of the snow—it was all an uncouth mockery against me—a subtle and quiet treachery. The tears gushed into my eyes and in my fear and affliction I clung to the poor girl, sobbing bitterly, protesting my grief, hiding my eyes in terror from that still, inscrutable shape. She smoothed my hair with her hand again and again, her eyes fixed; and then at last, venturing cautiously nearer, she stooped over my father. 'O Master Nicholas,' she said, 'his poor dark hair! What will we do now? What will your poor mamma do now, and him gone?' She hid her face in her hands, and our tears gushed out anew.

"But my grief was speedily forgotten. The novelty of being left entirely alone, my own master; to go where I would; to do as I pleased; the experience of being pitied most when I least needed it, and then—when misery and solitariness came over me like a cloud—of being utterly ignored, turned my thoughts gradually away. My father's body was brought home and laid in my mother's little parlour that looked out on to the garden and the snowy orchard. The house was darkened. I took a secret pleasure in peeping in on the sunless rooms, and stealing from door to door through corridors screened from the daylight. My mother was ill; and for some inexplicable reason I connected her illness with the bevy of gentlemen dressed in black who came one morning to the house and walked away together over the heath. Finally Mrs. Marshall drove up one afternoon from Islington, and by the bundles she had brought with her and her grained box with the iron handles I knew that she was come, as once before in my experience, to stay.

"I was playing on the morrow in the hall with my leaden soldiers when there came into my mind vaguely the voices of Mrs. Ryder and of Mrs. Marshall gossiping together on their tedious way upstairs from the kitchen.

" 'No, Mrs. Marshall, nothing,' I heard Mrs. Ryder saying, 'not one word, not one word. And now the poor dear lady left quite alone, and only the doctor to gainsay that fatherless mite from facing the idle inquisitive questions of all them strangers. It's neither for me nor you, Mrs. Marshall, to speak out just what comes into our heads here and now. The ways of the Almighty are past understanding—but a kinder at *heart* never trod this earth.'

" 'Ah,' said Mrs. Marshall.

" 'I knew to my sorrow,' continued Mrs. Ryder, 'there was words in the house; but there, wheresoever you be there's that. Human beings ain't angels, married or single, and in every—'

" 'Wasn't there talk of some—?' insinuated Mrs. Marshall discreetly.

" 'Talk, Mrs. Marshall,' said Mrs. Ryder, coming to a standstill, 'I scorn the word! A pinch of truth in a hogshead of falsehood. I don't gainsay it even. I just shut my ears—there—with the dead.'

Mrs. Marshall had opened her mouth to reply when I was discovered, crouched as small as possible at the foot of the stairs.

"'Well, here's pitchers!' said Mrs. Marshall pleasantly. 'And this is the poor fatherless manikin, I suppose. It's hard on the innocent, Mrs. Ryder, and him grown such a sturdy child too, as I said from the first. Well, now, and don't you remember me, little man, don't you remember Mrs. Marshall? He ought to, now!'

"'He's a very good boy in general,' said Mrs. Ryder, 'and I'm sure I hope and pray he'll grow up to be a comfort to his poor widowed mother, if so be—' They glanced earnestly at one another, and Mrs. Marshall stooped with a sigh of effort and drew a big leather purse from a big loose pocket under her skirt, and selected a bright ha'penny from among its silver and copper.

"'I make no doubt he will, poor mite,' she said cheerfully; I took the ha'penny in silence and the two women passed slowly upstairs.

"In the afternoon, in order to be beyond call of Martha, I went out on to the heath with a shovel, intent on building a great tomb in the snow. Yet more snow had fallen during the night; it now lay so deep as to cover my socks above my shoes. I laboured very busily, shovelling, beating, moulding, stamping. So intent was I that I did not see Miss Grey until she was close beside me. I looked up from the snow and was surprised to find the sun already set and the low mists of evening approaching. Miss Grey was veiled and dressed in furs to the throat. She drew her ungloved hand from her muff.

"'Nicholas,' she said in a low voice.

"I stood for some reason confused and ashamed without answering her. She sat down on my shapeless mound of snow, and took me by the hand. Then she drew up her veil, and I saw her face pale and darkened, and her dark eyes gravely looking into mine.

"'My poor, poor Nicholas,' she said, and continued to gaze at me with her warm hand clasping mine. 'What can I say? What can I do? Isn't it very, very lonely out here in the snow?'

"'I didn't feel lonely much,' I answered, 'I was making a—I was playing at building.'

"'And I am sitting on your beautiful snow-house, then?' she said, smiling sadly, her hand trembling upon mine.

"'It isn't a house,' I answered, turning away.

"She pressed my hand on the furs at her throat.

"'Poor cold, blue hands,' she said. 'Do you like playing alone?'

"'I like you being here,' I answered. 'I wish you would come always, or at least sometimes.'

"She drew me close to her, smiling, and bent and kissed my head.

"'There,' she said, 'I am here now.'

"'Mother's ill,' I said.

"She drew back and looked out over the heath towards the house.

"'They have put my father in the little parlour, in his coffin; of course, you know he's dead, and Mrs. Marshall's come; she gave me a ha'penny this morning. Dr. Graham gave me a whole crown, though.' I took it out of my breeches pocket and showed it her.

"'That's very, very nice,' she said. 'What lots of nice things you can buy with it! And, look, I am going to give you a little keep-sake too, between just you and me.'

"It was a small silver box that she drew out of her muff, and embossed in the silver of the lid was a crucifix. 'I thought, per-haps, I should see you to-day, you know,' she continued softly. 'Now, who's given you this?' she said, putting the box into my hand.

"'You,' I answered softly.

"'And who am I?'

"'Miss Grey,' I said.

"'Your friend, Jane Grey,' she repeated, as if she were fond of her own name. 'Say it now—always my friend, Jane Grey.'

"I repeated it after her.

"'And now,' she continued, 'tell me which room is—is the little parlour. Is it that small window at the corner under the ivy?'

"I shook my head.

"'Which?' she said in a whisper, after a long pause.

"I twisted my shovel in the snow. 'Would you like to see my

father?' I said. 'I am sure, you know, Martha would not mind; and mother's in bed.' She started, and looked with quiet, dark eyes into my face. 'Where?' she said, without stirring.

" 'It's at the back, a little window that comes out—if you were to come this evening, I would be playing in the hall; I always play in the hall, after tea, if I can; and now, always. Nobody would see you at all, you know.'

"She sighed. 'Oh, what are you saying?' she said, and stood up, drawing down her veil.

" 'But would you like to?' I repeated. She stooped suddenly, pressing her veiled face to mine. 'I'll come, I'll come,' she said, her face utterly changed so close to my eyes. 'We can both still—still be loyal to him, can't we, Nicholas?'

"She walked away quickly, towards the pool and the little darkened wood. I looked after her and knew that she would be waiting there alone till evening. I looked at my silver box with great satisfaction, and after opening it, put it into my pocket with my crown piece and my ha'penny, and continued my building for a while.

"But now zest for it was gone; and I began to feel cold, the frost closing in keenly as darkness gathered. So I went home.

"My silence and suspicious avoidance of scrutiny and question passed unnoticed. Indeed, I ate my tea in solitude, except that now and again one or other of the women would come bustling in on some brief errand. A peculiar suppressed stir was in the house. I wondered what could be the cause of it; and felt a little timid and anxious of my project being discovered.

"None the less I was playing in the evening, as I had promised, close to the door, alert to catch the faintest sign of the coming of my visitor.

" 'Run down in the kitchen, dearie,' said Martha. Her cheeks were flushed. She was carrying a big can of steaming water. 'You must keep very, *very* quiet this evening and go to bed like a good boy, and perhaps to-morrow morning I'll tell you a great, great secret.' She kissed me with hasty rapture. I was not especially inquisitive of her secret just then, and eagerly promised to be quite quiet if I might continue to play where I was.

" 'Well, very, *very* quiet then, and you mustn't let Mrs. Marshall,' she began, but hurried hastily away in answer to a peremptory summons from upstairs.

"Almost as soon as she was gone I heard a light rap on the door. It seemed that Jane Grey brought in with her the cold and freshness of the woods. I led the way on tiptoe down the narrow corridor and into the small, silent room. The candles burned pure and steadfastly in their brightness. The air was still and languid with the perfume of flowers. Overhead passed light, heedful footsteps; but they seemed not a disturbing sound, only a rumour beyond the bounds of silence.

" 'I am very sorry,' I said, 'but they have nailed it down. Martha says the men came this afternoon.'

"Miss Grey took a little bunch of snowdrops from her bosom, and hid them in among the clustered wreaths of flowers; and she knelt down on the floor, with a little silver cross which she sometimes wore pressed tight to her lips. I felt ill at ease to see her praying, and wished I could go back to my soldiers. But while I watched her, seeing in marvellous brilliancy everything in the little room, and remembering dimly the snow lying beneath the stars in the darkness of the garden, I listened also to the quiet footsteps passing to and fro in the room above. Suddenly, the silence was broken by a small, continuous, angry crying.

"Miss Grey looked up. Her eyes were very clear and wonderful in the candlelight.

" 'What was that?' she said faintly, listening.

"I stared at her. The cry welled up anew, piteously, as if of a small remote helpless indignation.

" 'Why it sounds just like—a little baby,' I said.

"She crossed herself hastily and arose. 'Nicholas!' she said in a strange, quiet, bewildered voice—yet her face was most curiously bright. She looked at me lovingly and yet so strangely I wished I had not let her come in.

"She went out as she had entered. I did not so much as peep into the darkness after her, but busy with a hundred thoughts returned to my play.

"Long past my usual bed-time, as I sat sipping a mug of hot

milk before the glowing cinders of the kitchen fire, Martha told me her secret. . . .

"So my impossible companion in the High Street yesterday was own and only brother to your crazy old friend, Richard," said the Count. "His only brother," he added, in a muse.

The Riddle and Other Stories (1923)

IN THE FOREST

WHILE my father was away at the war, I marked off each day with my knife on a piece of wood. He had started when it was scarcely light beneath the trees. I was very sleepy so early in the morning while he ate his breakfast, and as I watched him on the other side of the lighted candle drinking his steaming tea in his saucer, my eyes kept rolling back of themselves because I was so tired. And everything in the room was plain one moment and the next all blurred and wavering. The baby was asleep in the cradle. The wind was still roaring in the tops of the trees, but the candle burned clear, because the wind did not come down into the house.

When my father opened the door I saw that the grass was strewn with green leaves, and falling leaves were in the air, and the wind overhead sounded like water, though the tree trunks hardly swayed even, down here. But it was not raining when he started, only the leaves were wet with rain and the bark of the trees was darkened with wet. I asked him to bring me back a long rifle. He kept rubbing his hands over his face and blinking his eyes and listening to the wind as if he heard the guns. Two or three times he came back to say good-bye to my mother. And even when at last he didn't come back he kept turning his face, looking over his shoulder at us. There was no sun shining yet that morning, but the bright light of the sky gleamed on the wet leaves. I asked mother if father was glad to be going to the war. But she was crying over the baby, so I went out into the forest till dinner.

My mother was more cheerful at dinner, and we had some hot soup. After dinner I chopped up some wood in the shed. It made me very hot and excited chopping up the wood. It was getting dark when I came back, carrying the logs. It seemed that the wind grew more angry in the twilight, and although it still roared like the mill-water in the village, yet it whistled too, and the leaves kept dropping, heavy with rain. And now it was not clear, but cold and misty round the hut. I went in with the logs.

Mother was sitting in the wooden chair with the baby in her arms. She looked as if she were pretending. I went close and stared at her, and found that she was fast asleep. The baby was asleep too, but it scarcely seemed to be really breathing—it was like a moth fluttering on a pin; its face was quite pale and still in its sleep, but its cheeks were very red. I thought I would make a fire again without asking mother's leave, so as to be more cheerful; besides, I could feel the cold air oozing through the crannies of the timbers, and it was getting so dark I could see only the white things in the room. The rushing sound of the wind never ceased at all.

As soon as the flames began to spring up, and the sparks to crack out of the wood, my mother woke up. She looked at me with a curious face; but soon she remembered that she had been asleep, and she enjoyed the warmth of the fire.

On the next day I woke up where I had fallen asleep by the hearth, and it was a very quiet morning. I looked out of the window, and saw the sun shining yellow between the branches; and many of the boughs were now all but bare. But the fallen leaves lay thick on the ground as far as I could see, and some of them were still quite large and green. I was glad my father was gone away, because now I could do just as I pleased. I did not want the trouble of lighting the fire, so I went out into the forest, and down to visit the snares. There was a young hare caught by the leg in one, and the leaves were all round him. His eyes were bleeding, and not very bright. I killed him with a crack on the neck as I had seen father kill the hares, and carried him back by his hind legs. The leaves made an incessant rustling as I walked through them. I could see the blue sky above the trees; it was very pale, like a ribbon. I stood still a minute, carrying the hare, and listening to find if I could hear the guns. But I heard only a bird singing and a rushing sound, as if a snake were going away under the leaves. Sometimes I came to branches blown down to the ground, and even now, here and there, a leaf would fall slowly through the air, twirling, to be with all the rest. I enjoyed my broth for dinner very much, and the hare lasted for three days, with some turnips.

I asked mother how long father would be away. She said she could not tell. And I wondered how they would carry back his body if he was killed in the war.

I stayed out in the forest nearly all that day because the baby kept on crying. It was dark, and the window was lit up when I came home, and still the baby was fretting. Its eyes were gone dull, and it would not go to sleep in the night, though mother kept walking up and down, crooning and mumbling to it, and rocking it in her arms. She said it was very ill, and she held it pressed close to her. I asked her if it was going to die, but she only walked a little faster, and, as I was very sleepy, we did not talk much that night. The baby was still crying when I woke up, but not so loud. It was bleating small and shrill; like a young lamb, I told mother. I felt very refreshed after my sleep, and very hungry. I lit the fire and boiled the kettle, and put the plates on the table, and the loaf.

After breakfast I told mother I was going down to the old pool to fish, and that I would bring her some fish for dinner. But she looked at me and called me to her.

"The baby is dreadfully ill," she said, "and we must go without the fish. Feel its poor thin hot hands. That's the fever. Do you love it? Then take it in your arms."

But I shook my head. It looked very ugly because its face was all puckered up, and it just wailed and wailed like a gnat in the air.

"I think I would *like* to go fishing, mother," I said, "and I promise you shall have the biggest I catch."

But she kept on persisting that the baby was too ill to wait, that it was very queer, and that I must go for the doctor in the village. It wasn't so very far, she said, and I could fish to-morrow.

"But it *is* far," I told her; "and it doesn't look so very bad; and it might be windy and cold to-morrow. It's only crying," I said. And I ran out before she could catch me.

But I did not catch any fish. I suppose they would not bite because I had been wicked. So I tied up my lines and came home about three in the afternoon. As I stood at the door waiting before going in, I heard a sound far away, and then, in a while, again, through the forest. And I knew it was the guns and cannons on the other side of the forest. The baby was not crying now, when I went in. But my mother did not turn her head to speak to me. She was kneeling beside its old rocking-cradle, some of her hair hanging down on her shoulders.

"I'll go for the doctor now, mother; but the guns are firing; you can hear them now if you come and listen at the door."

But when I told her about the guns, she began to cry out loud, and hid her face in the coverlet on the cradle. I watched her a little while, and I could hear the cannons going off quite plainly now; only far away, like a drum when you put your hand on it.

I got very hot standing still, so I put my tackle on the hook and sat down by the hearth.

"Shall I go for the doctor now, mother? It'll be dark before I get back."

Mother turned on me very wild. "Oh, you coward, you coward," she said. "Dark—it's dark enough for me!"

She startled me very much by saying this and I felt very uncomfortable. I went nearer and looked. The baby's face was white, and its eyelids were like white wax. Its lips were the colour of its hands, almost blue.

"Is it dead, mother?" I asked. But she did not answer me, only shook her shoulders. I walked away and looked out of the door.

First I felt hot and then my back shivered. And I began to cry too, because I had not gone in the morning for the doctor. I did not dry my eyes because the tears ran quite hot down my cheeks, and I could hear them dripping off my chin upon my jacket. I liked to have the door open, although it was cold and grey in the afternoon.

My mother came to the doorway and drew me close to her as if she were sorry, with her hand clutching my head. I could not cry any more now, but stood still; and even then the guns and cannons went on firing. And sometimes birds silently flew between the trees away from the sound. I wondered if father was fighting near the cannons.

The next day it was so cold again my mother made me a jacket out of an old coat of father's. It was just hemmed up, and I wore it instead of my other jacket when I went out. She had drawn the coverlet over the baby's face, so that it now lay in a kind of little house in its cradle. I thought I would please mother, so found the place and read out of the Bible about Herod; but the candle burned very sooty and smoky, so that I could not read very well, and left out the long words.

The next morning mother told me to go down to the village and tell the sexton that the baby was dead so that it could be buried in the churchyard.

I started out with my switch, about ten o'clock. It was a warm day; so I was wearing my old jacket again, and the air smelled of the leaves, which were withered and yellow and brown. I went on, whistling; but it was more than five miles to the village. The robins were singing on the twigs, and I saw some crows flying in the sky. It was so quiet in the forest, that the cannons seemed to shake the air with their sound.

And while I was walking along, not very fast, and looking out for wild berries, I heard a noise in the distance of men running, and then the sound of a rifle quite near, and a scream like a rabbit, but much more loud and awful. I hid behind a tree, and when the forest was quiet again, I ran home as quickly as I could. But I did not like to tell mother that I had been frightened of the soldiers, because she had called me a coward already. So I said instead that the sexton was nowhere to be found in the village, that he must have gone to the war himself, and that no one would come for fear of the soldiers.

She looked me full in the face with her eyes. She looked so earnestly and so hard at me that I could not help moving my shoulder a little. And at that she turned away, and I felt very wretched because I knew that she had seen it was a lie. But I did not say anything.

All the while I sat there my eyes would not keep from looking at the cradle. I was very hungry. But since mother was putting on her shawl I knew that she was going out presently. Then, I thought, when she is gone, I will eat as much as ever I can. There were some bones in the cupboard well worth picking, I knew. When mother had put on her shawl and her bonnet, she lifted the baby out of the cradle.

"I must carry it to the churchyard myself," she said, but more to herself than to me. There were no tears in her eyes; they were dark all round.

"Won't you kiss your little brother, Robbie?" It was wrapped up in her wedding shawl, which she had sometimes shown me of an evening, out of the chest. I began to cry when I kissed its forehead. It was as cold as a stone, as a piece of dough, and looked very heavy, yet thin, and its face was quite still now.

"Take care of the house, Rob," she said. "Don't go out; and bolt the door after me."

I watched her hasten off along the narrow path between the trees. There was a light like crimson in the forest, and I knew that the sun would soon be setting. It was silly of her not to have gone earlier. It was very quiet now; and I was afraid it would soon be dark.

Soon she was out of sight, and only the trees seemed to come a little nearer and stand still. I left the door open, went into the room and put the candlestick on the table. I kicked the log till it began to flame. Then I went to the cupboard and took out the loaf and the bones, and a few puckered old apples. I ate from the dish, sitting by the hearth, looking out of the door. When I had finished I fell asleep for a little while.

By-and-by I opened my eyes. It was darker, and I saw some animal looking in at the door. I jumped up, and the animal ran away. Then I shut and barred the door and put some more wood on the fire until it was blazing high up the chimney. But I did not like to look over my shoulder towards the square window; it was so dark and silent and watchful out there. I could not hear the cannons now, either because they weren't sounding or because the flames made a loud bubbling noise as they ran up and waved. I did not dare to let them fall quiet, to only the red embers, so I kept putting wood on the fire as fast as it burned away.

Mother did not come back, and it seemed I was sitting in front of the warm hearth in a dream that would never come to an end. All was still and motionless, and there was no ordinary sound at all that I could hear in the forest, and even the cannons were more muffled now and further away. I could not cry, though I felt very angry at being left alone, and I was afraid. Besides, I didn't know what I would say to mother when she came back—about the food. Yet I longed for her too, and got a pain with it, and felt that I loved her, and was very sorry for my wickedness.

I fell asleep unawares. When I woke it was broad daylight. I felt very glad and relieved to see the light, even though mother had not come back. It seemed to me that some noise had awakened me. Presently there came a groan at the doorway. Kneeling down and peeping through a crevice between the planks, I saw my father lying there on the doorstep. I took down the bar and opened the door. He was lying on his stomach; his clothes were filthy and torn, and at the back of his shoulder was a small hole pushed in in the cloth. There was dark, thick blood on the withered leaves. I tried to see his face, but couldn't very well. It was all muddy, bleared and white, and he groaned and swore when I touched him. But he didn't know who I was, and some of what he said didn't seem to me to have any sense.

He asked for some water, but I could not turn him over so that he could drink it. And it was all spilt. I told him about the baby dying, but he didn't show that he could hear anything; and just as I finished I heard mother coming back from the churchyard. So I ran out and told her that it was father.

The Wind Blows Over (1936)

THE TALISMAN

In the little town of Weissehäuser there are—or at any rate there used to be—three bridges, two cold and beautiful spires, innumerable gables, and at least one old curiosity shop. Of these charming things I confess I liked the shop best. It was my own discovery—made during the first evening walk I took through the wind-swept starlit streets. I was young, had never before been out of England, knew little German. Nevertheless the queer old dealer in "antiques," Adolph Gessen, whose shop it was, not only tolerated my idling there at every opportunity, but, I verily believe, had taken a fancy to me; and I became his constant visitor.

It was an obscure and poky shop as seen from its stone-silled many-paned window, but it ran far back into the twilight of green trees, and it was packed from end to end with his fantastic merchandise. In a gloomy recess no bigger than a cupboard, Gessen used to sit all day beneath a lamp, mending clocks and watches. From here, in a tarnished tilted mirror framed with Cupids, he could scan his customers, of whom the jangling bell above his door had already given him warning. He was an angular, lean old man, his absurd skull on scraggy neck bulging from fleecy fluffs of silvery hair behind it. But his profile was aquiline, his expression keen and whimsical, and he had the biggest hands that can ever have been capable of doing such deft and delicate work.

What trade he enjoyed I cannot surmise. Nor can I recall ever having missed any article on which I had cast a covetous glance. It seemed as likely as not indeed that the clock which I usually found him nodding and glaring over he had himself many times put together and taken to pieces again! He knew, perhaps, a little more English than I German. And so we managed to converse very happily together, since neither of us had words enough ever to become wearisome. For though we talked little we told much. His eyes beneath his thick eyebrows could reveal a whole world of human experience, and its effects; his hands scarcely less. Perhaps, too, it was the common secret bond between us that lightened all difficulties. For the poor old fellow loved, and loved in vain. And so then did I—with my hopeless, sorrowful, youthful passion for Pauline Dussenaine.

In those few sad rapturous days I used to loaf off on long solitary walks. My father had his own concerns and found little pleasure in so raw a companionship as mine. Thus I got to know well all that I cared about in the town, in the valleys, beside the rivers. Moonlight I knew, and the melancholy beauty of the rain. But rarely a day passed without at least one visit brief or prolonged to my friend Gessen.

There I would sit and talk, or pry, or watch him over his little wheels. Sometimes he would frown and nod and whisper—or sigh of his ancient *affaire*. And I, too, would make my mournful confidences. Occasionally, out of my scanty pocket-money, and prompted, I suppose, by English instincts, I bought some trifling thing—"to pay my way." But it angered him inwardly, for he guessed my motive, and immensely overcharged me, I fancy, for what I would not accept as a gift. "Frents," he would say, "vat then?"

He used to eat his vegetable dinner in a sort of cobwebby cupboard, pushing back his tools and gewgaws to make room for his plate when it was brought in, hot in its napkin, by the little white-haired child from the baker's with the serious blue-eyed smile. He ate with a spoon, in extraordinary haste, with immense gusto, and it was not until after this very audible display, one afternoon, that I first perceived the sound of ticking in his latest acquisition—a dark and battered old rosewood bureau.

It was one of those rare pieces of furniture which are of no conspicuous grace or beauty and on which one either turns a cold indifferent eye or—well, falls in love with at first sight. Having then a tendency that way, *I* fell in love with it. I could not discover where it had come from, although Gessen was spluttering guttural explanations between the aftermaths of his dinner. Nodding and pointing, I asked him if he had explored it yet. He had; and busied his great hands and dangling eyebrows in describing its inward charms. But it was this faint, all but imperceptible ticking that had arrested *my* quickened ear. When he was silent I listened. And at last I managed to make him understand, and he listened too, his old fallen lantern-jawed cheek pressed tight against the wood. He disembowelled the beautiful chest once more; but in vain; the ticking continued.

A "death-watch," I thought to myself; for my old friend Miss Barlow and I had listened together to *that* ticking but just before I had sailed from England. But whether he understood me, agreed with me, or not, Gessen made no sign. Like a doctor engrossed with his first wealthy patient, he again stooped bonily over his prize, and again laid his hairy ear against the smooth dark wood. He then took his smallest hammer and tapped very gently, very heedfully all over the precious thing, that was certainly not less black than any coffin ever made. And then I knew it could not be the death-watch beetle, for that abstruse morsel of life desists from telling tales the moment it detects even the vestige of an answer.

The ticking went steadily on, a little louder if anything now that the drawers were removed, and the bureau was reduced to a shell. I had to leave Gessen, tapping, scratching, ruminating, in order to dine with my father. But I sat and sipped without appetite, gazing dreamily out on the gold and blue and beauty, that faraway yet ever-present pulsation—that summons—in my head, like the sound of the heart of a child, and only a very little more rapid. My father raised his eyebrows at me once or twice; scrutinized his elegant fingers; offered me, very politely, more. But that evening I was in a sour humour, I remember. Had he not that very morning presented roses to Pauline, and caught my jealous eyes fixed on them both? If, indeed, I laugh now to think I could then be jealous of my own father, what must my jealousy have been of Arthur, a second cousin of hers, a dandy neatly moustached, and, I acknowledge, no fool; always laughing, boasting, and at ease,

and who is now the father of Pauline's four charming children,
Pauline II, Harry, Antoinette, and John!

I hastened out, leaving my father faintly smiling over his wal-
nuts, and there before me, as if rapt but an instant before clean
out of paradise, stood Pauline herself, in her beloved blue dress. I
bowed distantly. She smiled.

"I hope," I muttered with a ridiculous attempt at irony, "that
the flowers are as fresh as ever."

Her brows gathered into a tiny frown of perplexity. Then she
remembered. "Oh those," she said. "I was immensely flattered.
But if . . ."

But I much preferred to nurse my gnawing little grievance than
to ponder her smiling "if." I cast her a tragic glance of upbraiding
and entreaty, coldly and loftily bowed again to her gentle sparkling eyes, and passed on.

There was a solitary candle burning in a rusty old candelabrum
when I once more entered the little shop. Gessen was sitting in a
chair beside the open window, gazing vacantly out into the green
evening solitude of his garden. Silence lay as deep in it as the
waters of a well. He did not stir when I entered. He seemed to
be lost in thought. But I was accustomed to his moods, knew of
whom he was thinking, and my whole attention had at once
centred on the curious object which lay on the top of the old black
bureau. In shape it was a delicate oval and seemed to be of a very
pale gold. Beneath its thick crystal glass, and above a markless
face there moved a single slender hand, telling no hours, no minutes, no seconds even; only Time. Despite that faint ticking, I
could not detect the least "check" in its stealthy yet rapid movement. One slender hand only—and a motto, in minute German
characters, beyond my wits to decipher, engraved around its
margin.

Why, I know not—I hesitated to pick it up. It was so quiet in
the centuries-old shop. Bells were ringing across Weissehäuser's
waters. And here, among these fantastic relics of Man—Man the
curious, the engrossed, the eager, the infatuated, the transitory—
ticked on this hourless, beautiful timepiece; sat the gaunt old love-
sick dealer, whose treasure trove it was, lost in reverie. I caught a

glimpse of my own face in a grimy mirror as I turned at last from examining it—and saw, as it seemed, another reflection, a phantom face, Pauline's. *"She* never told her love"—but then Viola *could* have done so, and in the loveliest verse, let only the moment come and the loved one, together; whereas I myself, in those greenhorn days, really needed some kind of sorcery to enable me to utter a fraction of what mine meant to me. But Gessen had turned with a sigh in his chair, sneezed, and looked up at me. Then he rose—still sighing—and came and stood beside me.

"It is strange—it is very strange, this," he said, touching my sleeve. "Take it, my goot boy, and tell me dreams. It is a wonder. It goes here!" He laid his enormous hand upon his heart. "And this"—he pointed with his long black fingernail to the motto on the dial—"this too is a—a . . ." He opened wide his pale-blue innocent eyes, shut them, frowned, opened them again, and shook his head; and I understood that *this* was a mystery.

He gave me a little wash-leather bag to keep the watch in, and a steel chain to secure it. And I slipped it into a pocket inside my waistcoat, not far from some dead gentians, and buttoned it over twice. Gessen stood watching me from over his spectacles. It seemed he had something further to say. He opened his mouth more than once, but at length, shaking his head, said nothing, sighed loudly, blew out the candle, letting the moonlight steal in across the dry and dusty floor, and, muting its dangling bell for me, opened the door.

I pined to buy the watch, even to borrow money from my father, to pay for it; but I knew, had realized instantly at one look into the old man's face, that it was not for sale—never would be for sale. It was a thing Fate sends, and Fate alone; and Fate was the one other revered mistress of my forlorn old friend.

I went out into the town. I knew not why then, but never had night shone with such exalted beauty as this. The moon hung low in the sky above the hueless snows of the mountains. The stars: it seemed that the faint multitudes which confuse the eye and imagination were scarcely visible—with so much splendour burned the constellations. There was an air across the darkened town cold as hill-water and clear as valleys seen in dream. And as I mounted the narrow cobbled street which led over a bridge to our inn, I saw with a kind of wild and sweet assurance Pauline standing there looking down into the water.

Forgotten every grievance then—every poisonous fang of that cur named Jealousy! I called to her. She started and turned; and we looked into each other's faces in the dim heavenly light.

"Why, Harry," she said, "what's the matter? You've fallen in love!"

"No," I said, "not fallen—mounted!"

"Dear me!" she said, opening her eyes a little. "But really, now, tell me! Tell me! What is it? *Who* is it? When?"

"Ah," I said. "I will. But now come a little down. It is so much —it would take eternity; and all life is only an instant, Pauline. Listen! The waters mean only that. They roar, they come from the hills, and go down to the sea, as we, poor wandering ghosts, go too. We *are* ghosts, you know, you and I. How could you else be so beautiful and—and mock me so?"

I listened, amazed, to this harangue—I who hitherto never had a syllable to say, who even at a simple "Good morning" flushed and stammered. And yet I could not be silent. All my fishlike dumbness had vanished. My thoughts were sparkling in my mind like bubbles in wine.

"Come, at once," I said, touching her hand. "The moon will soon be down. It is late."

She drew back, smiling. "You mad boy," she said. "I am waiting for someone. *I* am early. He will be here at any moment."

"Let him, then, wait for Thee!" I mocked.

"But who said 'him'?" she cried, laughing.

"Ssh! now," I said, "we will soon be back, and *he* could not grow much colder; creep down behind me; we'll see the moon make rainbows."

Half silly with delight, scarcely able to breathe, I led the way down the steep, slippery old stone steps; and with a kind of incredulous amusement and astonishment Pauline was following me. I drew her back, her heart beating, into the shadow of the arch. Above the unpausing clamour of the water we had caught faintly a footstep, and her own name called softly. I pressed her hand in mine—it seemed, indeed, that such slender fingers must be unreal, unreal the pale smiling face so close to mine in the shadow of the cold arch echoing with the Lorelei.

"But, Harry, you know, how dare you do this? Where are you taking me, you mad, ridiculous boy?"

"Ah, you call me a boy," I said, "but still you had to come—you had to come, Pauline. Even now, if fifty Arthurs called you, you still would stay here. This way; the shadows lengthen as the moon sinks lower, and a little further down where that moth is fluttering, is the path that leads to the rainbows. And then—*then,* Pauline, I'll tell you how much I love you."

"Oh!" she cried softly; "but then *I* mustn't listen—not even to you."

"*He* hasn't told you," I called triumphantly above the clamour. She smiled gravely. "No, my friend, but he's going to."

"Why, yes," I said, "and I will teach you what to say in answer."

The path fell ever nearer and nearer to the snowy swirl and tumult of the river. Above our heads the trees hung motionless festoons beneath their silvered boughs. There seemed to be voices calling, birds, music, laughter, and enchantment. And on, on, like some restless conscience, I felt, as if against my heart, the unhastening beat of Gessen's curious timepiece.

We walked hand in hand. And as I gazed at the pale profile of that beloved and beautiful face, it was transfigured even in my young ardent eyes; like that of one entranced, a face seen in a dream. The dark beauty of the night was in her eyes. Frowning, smiling, wistful, meditative, she listened to my unconscionable babble. We sat under a tree whose heights touched heaven and shut out half the stars. And, looking on the changing moon-bows of the fall, I told her my dreams. My heart was full. It seemed I was entrusting into her hands all that my childhood had so long been hoarding. No deed too noble could there be, no glory too remote, no bravery too forlorn, but that I would choose for her service! Here was my very self revealed. Here was the meaning of life—the goal of its strange journey! She heard me out—unable to do otherwise.

"No, no, you mustn't!" she kept repeating, searching half in wonder, half in amusement and mockery my poor haggard, beatified countenance! She promised she would think of me, even that she would dream of me. To love me, *that* she could not promise. "Oh, but I love someone else!" she kept repeating, almost as if in doubt of her own words, and still with my fingers clasping hers. "But what, dear friend, *makes* you? You look so— well, I suppose one may say it—so beautiful, Harry. Your eyes! What have you been doing? Are you bewitched?"

"No," I said, with happy sadness; "it is only that I love you."

"Love me!" she frowned. "But then, *can* you, and you only a boy?"

"I am eighteen," I said truthfully.

"Well, can one *then*?" she answered gently. "I am twenty-four, but oh, centuries and centuries older than you, dear friend!"

"Please not, 'dear friend,'" I said. "If you knew how I—oh! Pauline, there's nothing here, nothing that can ever be hoped for, dreamed of, which I could not give you, *have* given you. The water—listen! How it cries above its music. The stillness, the shadows—all, all they mean: dearest Pauline, I love, because you only are they, and they are you."

"Yes, yes," she said, "I do, indeed, believe you. But then, when you come to know how many things there are in this world that won't—can never match. . . . But there, forgive me. I am not so true, not so good as you are. How sad you have made me! I *will* think of you. I do—often. I *like* you, oh, very, very much; who could help it? But . . . but now, tell me," she leaned forward, looking into my face, "where have you *been*? What has made you —suddenly—so—different?"

I told her of my day's adventure; never dreamed of keeping it secret. It never occurred to me then that there was any mystery in this wild hour of freedom from a tortured and stupid timidity. I never suspected *what* had been my mentor, the source of all my madness. If indeed it had!

She listened eagerly, and I took out my curious treasure and in a beam of moonlight laid it in her hand. We stooped together over its oval face, its one pale delicate finger following the unrecorded hours. And there, beneath the tree, the moonlight glinting on the crystal, she read out the German inscription in a slow faltering voice, and put it into English for me:

> For him who bears me I of Love and Death tell out Eternity:
> While Life tells only Moments.

The face she now turned to me had become grave and absent. Some sudden resolve seemed to have arrested and darkened her eyes. Her breast rose like a dove's to a sigh, yet no sigh came. "What does it mean? Who said *that*? Do you believe it?" she said. "It's wildly romantic—sentimental!"

"I don't know what it means." Weariness and revulsion had come over me. I shivered. My good angel had left me. I felt how much was gone from me, lost, betrayed—my secret self. Could anyone have ever imagined it worth even a pinch of dust—the hoard of one of Gessen's cobwebs?

But she seemed to be completely indifferent to what was passing in my mind, merely pelted me with questions about Gessen, about the shop, the bureau, the "charming curio." Did I believe in it? And might she wear it—for only one night, one day? Just to *see*?

"To see what?" I asked dully.

"Oh, to *see*. Do let me, dear, dear friend! I do think of you. Who knows?—why love *might* come. One day only—I will give it back to-morrow, here—here in this very moonlight. Fancy, all your kindness, and I not a single word in reply!"

She stooped her head at the foot of the narrow steps, and kissed my hand! I drew back awkwardly, on fire, loving her so much in my heart that—yet again!—all words seemed blasphemous, and the fool's voice I had been listening to, as if in a dream, insane.

She ran up in front of me, and waved me good-night. . . .

From over Weissehäuser the moon had long descended. Its cataracts roared faintly. A few of its upper windows still showed lights behind their blinds—one by one they went out. As had mine! All dark—but empty. What had been said—had it not now been irrevocably lost and wasted? I might still love; but could I ever love so truly? The nightingale having sung, falls silent. How different are the two silences—before the song and after!

I went to bed; slept soundly, without dream; and woke unhappy.

All that morning I haunted Pauline's doorstep, not daring to inquire, nor daring to return to Gessen again without his treasure. At last, a little after two, I saw her descending the hill from the pine woods; and Arthur was her companion. I turned back, burning tears pricking my eyes; remorse, anger, vanity, envy, despair, and faithful love battling for mastery in my irrational foolish heart.

She left him and ran to me, her face a little anxious, her every movement one of rapture.

"There!" she said, putting the watch into my hand. "My promise. It is a mystery. What does it mean?—what *does* it mean? Don't tell Arthur. Not a word—oh, no. And congratulate me, Harry. You will? You do? And forgive. You have never been angry with me, not for a single moment. And you see I cannot *help* being happy, can I now?"

I took the watch, staring vaguely into her eyes. Gloom and resentment seemed to vanish as if by enchantment. Why! after all, I was alive, I could still live on. There never was such sunshine as this upon her hair; never such shadows in unfathomable wells of water as these within her eyes.

"Forgive you!" I cried. "Oh, may you be always happy! I love you. I shall never never forget you. Good-bye, Pauline."

I turned from her and hastened away. My thoughts were so many, and they raced so fast through my mind that I hardly seemed to think at all. Beauty was left—the beauty of remembrance; and could there be despair where there had never been hope? It is difficult to recall the mazy meanderings of one's youth. Still, one must at least attempt to be just—even to a past self— for who knows what future self may not some day be upon us! I loved her foolishly, guilelessly; but it was my love that was my riches; her peace—*that* was its hope. Yes, I verily believe that that bemused and obsessed young man was as insufferably unselfish as all that!

Gessen met me at his shop door. I poured out in broken jargon all my doings into that long, bristling ear. We seemed to be lifelong friends, old comrades. He understood me. It was, after all,

but his own heart's confusion made articulate. He patted my
shoulder; he purred; he glared; asking no questions. And when
I had finished, as best I could, tears were running down his
cheeks. He stooped, and putting his hands tenderly on my shoulders, kissed my cheek.

It was childish, fatuous, infamously un-English. At the back of
my mind I realized, even while my heart seemed to have swollen
too big for my body, that he was a sentimental old fool, who
might much better be preparing for his winding-sheet than doting
on a dark, taciturn, sensual woman who—as I guessed—had never
perhaps looked twice at him, unless in the hope of extorting something really worth her while. But he and I now shared a sovereign
secret. He had not been a magician in vain—the craftsman who
had set these wheels revolving, and who had graved his cryptic
wisdom on the dial!

"Ah, it was prave, prave," the old man kept repeating. "You
vlowed out, my goot boy. Luff, luff, luff! Haf courage! It vill be
vell. It vill be very vell."

He stretched out his great hands, head on one side, and beamed
on me through his tears. But his was the delusion now. His own
vaporous, futile sentiment prompted him. Hope like a pyramid
blossom had sprung up in his heart. Here was his fate at last. I
left him as twilight gathered, sitting in the gloom of his narrow
shop, the watch in his hand, his face like some old children's book
of Märchen.

Yet somehow, I knew not why, all that evening I continued to
think of him, as well as of Pauline—of his love, and of hers, and
of mine. Was there ever such a trio! Would his be as disastrous
too, his hour of many hours? Would it be better to hold his
peace? make no mad venture? Better the plateau than the abyss.
What would *his* to-morrow be—rejected?

I ran out late, and through deserted streets. No need to knock
—his door stood unlatched. A candle burned beneath his wooden
mirror, with its vacantly smiling shadowy Cupids. He sat in his
workaday chair, in his beautiful best clothes, polished, starched,
and shaven. His astonished face was grey, and smiling in its stillness; his mouth queerly ajar. His body was slightly bent, his head
stooping, his eyes looking down. And pale beneath the candles,

in his great seamed open palm, lay the beautiful and mysterious
object that seemed in some fantastic fashion to have been the
cause of our common undoing. And though my poor old friend's
heart in *that* mortal body would never stir again, I could still
hear—thin, ecstatic, unhastening, through, above, and beneath the
babble of the pendulums around us—the infinite small summons
of its tick.

But when in panic haste I had run off to the baker's—and in
spite of the gleam above the fanlight, showing that he was busy at
his job, I knocked for ten solid minutes on his too too solid door
before he appeared—and then returned with him; there sat Gessen precisely as I had left him, but his open hand was empty; the
watch was gone.

The Wind Blows Over (1936)

MISS DUVEEN

I SELDOM had the company of children in my grandmother's house
beside the river Wandle. The house was old and ugly. But its
river was lovely and youthful though it had flowed for ever, it
seemed, between its green banks of osier and alder. So it was no
great misfortune perhaps that I heard more talking of its waters
than of any human tongue. For my grandmother found no particular pleasure in my company. How should she? My father and
mother had married (and died) against her will, and there was
nothing in me of those charms which, in fiction at any rate,
swiftly soften a superannuated heart.

Nor did I pine for her company either. I kept out of it as much as possible.

It so happened that she was accustomed to sit with her back to the window of the room which she usually occupied, her grey old indifferent face looking inwards. Whenever necessary, I would steal close up under it, and if I could see there her large faded amethyst velvet cap I knew I was safe from interruption. Sometimes I would take a slice or two of currant bread or (if I could get it) a jam tart or a cheese cake, and eat it under a twisted old damson tree or beside the running water. And if I conversed with anybody, it would be with myself or with my small victims of the chase.

Not that I was an exceptionally cruel boy; though if I had lived on for many years in this primitive and companionless fashion, I should surely have become an idiot. As a matter of fact, I was unaware even that I was ridiculously old-fashioned—manners, clothes, notions, everything. My grandmother never troubled to tell me so, nor did she care. And the servants were a race apart. So I was left pretty much to my own devices. What wonder, then, if I at first accepted with genuine avidity the acquaintanceship of our remarkable neighbour, Miss Duveen?

It had been, indeed, quite an advent in our uneventful routine when that somewhat dubious household moved into Willowlea, a brown brick edifice, even uglier than our own, which had been long vacant, and whose sloping garden confronted ours across the Wandle. My grandmother, on her part, at once discovered that any kind of intimacy with its inmates was not much to be desired. While I, on mine, was compelled to resign myself to the loss of the Willowlea garden as a kind of No Man's Land or Tom Tiddler's ground.

I got to know Miss Duveen by sight long before we actually became friends. I used frequently to watch her wandering in her long garden. And even then I noticed how odd were her methods of gardening. She would dig up a root or carry off a potted plant from one to another overgrown bed with an almost animal-like resolution; and a few minutes afterwards I would see her restoring it to the place from which it had come. Now and again she would stand perfectly still, like a scarecrow, as if she had completely forgotten what she was at.

Miss Coppin, too, I descried sometimes. But I never more than glanced at her, for fear that even at that distance the too fixed attention of my eyes might bring hers to bear upon me. She was a smallish woman, inclined to be fat, and with a peculiar waddling gait. She invariably appeared to be angry with Miss Duveen, and would talk to her as one might talk to a post. I did not know, indeed, until one day Miss Duveen waved her handkerchief in my direction that I had been observed from Willowlea at all. Once or twice after that, I fancied, she called me; at least her lips moved; but I could not distinguish what she said. And I was naturally a little backward in making new friends. Still I grew accustomed to looking out for her and remember distinctly how first we met.

It was raining, the raindrops falling softly into the unrippled water, making their great circles, and tapping on the motionless leaves above my head where I sat in shelter on the bank. But the sun was shining whitely from behind a thin fleece of cloud, when Miss Duveen suddenly peeped in at me out of the greenery, the thin silver light upon her face, and eyed me sitting there, for all the world as if she were a blackbird and I a snail. I scrambled up hastily with the intention of retreating into my own domain, but the peculiar grimace she made at me fixed me where I was.

"Ah," she said, with a little masculine laugh, "so this is the young gentleman, the bold, gallant young gentleman. And what might be his name?"

I replied rather distantly that my name was Arthur.

"Arthur, to be sure!" she repeated with extraordinary geniality, and again, "Arthur," as if in the strictest confidence.

"I know you, Arthur, very well indeed. I have looked, I have watched; and now, please God, we need never be estranged." And she tapped her brow and breast, making the Sign of the Cross with her lean, bluish forefinger.

"What is a little brawling brook," she went on, "to friends like you and me?" She gathered up her tiny countenance once more into an incredible grimace of friendliness; and I smiled as ami-

cably as I could in return. There was a pause in this one-sided
conversation. She seemed to be listening, and her lips moved,
though I caught no sound. In my uneasiness I was just about to
turn stealthily away, when she poked forward again.

"Yes, yes, I know you quite intimately, Arthur. We have met
here." She tapped her rounded forehead. "You might not suppose
it, too; but I have eyes like a lynx. It is no exaggeration, I assure
you—I assure everybody. And now what friends we will be! At
times," she stepped out of her hiding-place and stood in curious
dignity beside the water, her hands folded in front of her on her
black pleated silk apron—"at times, dear child, I long for company
—earthly company." She glanced furtively about her. "But I
must restrain my longings; and you will, of course, understand
that I do not complain. *He* knows best. And my dear cousin,
Miss Coppin—she too knows best. She does not consider too
much companionship expedient for me." She glanced in some
perplexity into the smoothly swirling water.

"I, you know," she said suddenly, raising her little piercing eyes
to mine, "I am Miss Duveen, that's not, they say, quite the thing
here." She tapped her small forehead again beneath its two sleek
curves of greying hair, and made a long narrow mouth at me.
"Though, of course," she added, "we do not tell *her* so. No!"

And I, too, nodded my head in instinctive and absorbed imita-
tion. Miss Duveen laughed gaily. "He understands, he understands!" she cried, as if to many listeners. "Oh, what a joy it is in
this world, Arthur, to be understood. Now tell me," she continued
with immense nicety, "tell me, how's your dear mamma?"

I shook my head.

"Ah," she cried, "I see, I see; Arthur has no mamma. We will
not refer to it. No father, either?"

I shook my head again and, standing perfectly still, stared at
my new acquaintance with vacuous curiosity. She gazed at me
with equal concentration, as if she were endeavouring to keep
the very thought of my presence in her mind.

"It is sad to have no father," she continued rapidly, half closing
her eyes; "no head, no guide, no stay, no stronghold; but we have,
Oh yes, we have another father, dear child, another father—
eh? . . . Where . . . Where?"

She very softly raised her finger. "On high," she whispered, with extraordinary intensity.

"But just now," she added cheerfully, hugging her mittened hands together, "we are not talking of Him; we are talking of ourselves, just you and me, *So* cosy; so *secret!* And it's a grandmother? I thought so, I thought so, a grandmother! Oh yes, I can peep between the curtains, though they do lock the door. A grandmother—I thought so; that very droll old lady! *Such* fine clothes! Such a presence, oh yes! A grandmother." She poked out her chin and laughed confidentially.

"And the long, bony creature, all rub and double"—she jogged briskly with her elbows, "who's that?"

"Mrs. Pridgett," I said.

"There, there," she whispered breathlessly, gazing widely about her. "Think of that! *He* knows; *He* understands. How firm, how manly, how undaunted! . . . *One* t?"

I shook my head dubiously.

"Why should he?" she cried scornfully. "But between ourselves, Arthur, that is a thing we *must* learn, and never mind the headache. We cannot, of course, know everything. Even Miss Coppin does not know everything—" she leaned forward with intense earnestness—"though I don't tell her so. We must try to learn all we can; and at once. One thing, dear child, you may be astonished to hear, I learned only yesterday, and that is how exceedingly *sad* life is."

She leaned her chin upon her narrow bosom, pursing her lips. "And yet you know they say very little about it. . . . They don't *mention* it. Every moment, every hour, every day, every year— one, two, three, four, five, seven, ten," she paused, frowned, "and so on. Sadder and sadder. Why? why? It's strange, but oh, so true. You really can have no notion, child, how very sad I am myself at times. In the evening, when they all gather together, in their white raiment, up and up and up, I sit on the garden seat, on Miss Coppin's garden seat, and precisely in the middle (you'll be kind enough to remember that?) and my *thoughts* make me sad." She narrowed her eyes and shoulders. "Yes and frightened, my child! Why must I be so guarded? One angel— the greatest *fool* could see the wisdom of that. But billions!—with their fixed eyes shining, so very boldly, on me. I never prayed for so many, dear friend. And we pray for a good many odd things, you and I, I'll be bound. But, there, you see, poor Miss Duveen's on her theology again—scamper, scamper, scamper. In the congregations of the wicked we must be cautious! . . . Mrs. Partridge and grandmamma, so nice, *so* nice; but even that, too, a *little* sad, eh?" She leaned her head questioningly, like a starving bird in the snow.

I smiled, not knowing what else she expected of me; and her face became instantly grave and set.

"He's right; perfectly right. We must speak evil of *no* one. *No* one. We must shut our mouths. We—" She stopped suddenly and, taking a step, leaned over the water towards me, with eyebrows raised high above her tiny face. "S—sh!" she whispered, laying a long forefinger on her lips. "Eavesdroppers!" She smoothed her skirts, straightened her cap, and left me; only a moment after to poke out her head at me again from between the leafy bushes. "An assignation, no!" she said firmly, then gathered her poor, cheerful, forlorn, crooked, lovable face into a most wonderful contraction at me, that assuredly meant—"But, *yes!*"

Indeed it was an assignation, the first of how many, and how few. Sometimes Miss Duveen would sit beside me, apparently so lost in thought that I was clean forgotten. And yet I half fancied it was often nothing but feigning. Once she stared me blankly out of countenance when I ventured to take the initiative and to call out "Good morning" to her across the water. On this occasion she completed my consternation with a sudden, angry grimace—contempt, jealousy, outrage.

But often we met like old friends and talked. It was a novel but not always welcome diversion for me in the long shady garden that was my privy universe. Where our alders met, mingling their branches across the flowing water, and the kingfisher might be seen—there was our usual tryst. But, occasionally, at her invitation, I would venture across the stepping-stones into her demesne; and occasionally, but very seldom indeed, she would venture into mine. How plainly I see her, tiptoeing from stone to stone, in an extraordinary concentration of mind—her mulberry petticoats, her white stockings, her loose spring-side boots. And when at last she stood beside me, her mittened hand on her breast, she would laugh on in a kind of paroxysm until the tears stood in her eyes, and she grew faint with breathlessness.

"In all danger," she told me once, "I hold my breath and shut my eyes. And if I could tell you of every danger, I think, perhaps, you would understand—dear Miss Coppin. . . ." I did not, and yet, perhaps, very vaguely I did see the connection in this rambling statement.

Like most children, I liked best to hear Miss Duveen talk about her own childhood. I contrived somehow to discover that if we sat near flowers or under boughs in blossom, her talk would generally steal around to that. Then she would chatter on and on: of the white sunny rambling house, somewhere, nowhere—it saddened and confused her if I asked where—in which she had spent her first happy years; where her father used to ride on a black horse; and her mother to walk with her in the garden in a crino-lined gown and a locket with the painted miniature of a "divine" nobleman inside it. How very far away these pictures seemed!

It was as if she herself had shrunken back into this distant past, and was babbling on like a child again, already a little isolated by her tiny infirmity.

"That was before—" she would begin to explain precisely, and then a crisscross many-wrinkled frown would net her rounded forehead, and cloud her eyes. Time might baffle her, but then, time often baffled me too. Any talk about her mother usually reminded her of an elder sister, Caroline. "My sister, Caroline," she would repeat as if by rote, "you may not be aware, Arthur, was afterwards Mrs. Bute. *So* charming, *so* exquisite, *so* accomplished. And Colonel Bute—an officer and a gentleman, I grant. And yet . . . But no! My dear sister was *not* happy. And so it was no doubt a blessing in disguise that by an unfortunate accident she was found *drowned*. In a lake, you will understand, not a mere shallow noisy brook. This is one of my private sorrows, which, of course, your grandmamma would be horrified to hear —horrified; and which, of course, Partridge has not the privilege of birth even to be informed of—*our* secret, dear child—with all her beautiful hair, and her elegant feet, and her eyes no more ajar than this; but blue, blue as the forget-me-not. When the time comes, Miss Coppin will close my own eyes, I hope and trust. Death, dear, dear child, I know they *say* is only sleeping. Yet I hope and trust *that*. To be sleeping wide awake; oh no!" She abruptly turned her small untidy head away.

"But didn't they shut *hers?*" I inquired.

Miss Duveen ignored the question. "I am not uttering one word of blame," she went on rapidly; "I am perfectly aware that such things confuse me. Miss Coppin tells me not to think. She tells me that I can have no opinions worth the mention. She says, 'Shut up your mouth.' I must keep silence then. All that I am merely trying to express to you, Arthur, knowing you will regard it as sacred between us—all I am expressing is that my dear sister, Caroline, was a gifted and beautiful creature with not a shadow or vestige or tinge or taint of confusion in her mind. *Nothing.* And yet, when they dragged her out of the water and laid her there on the bank, looking—" She stooped herself double in a sudden dreadful fit of gasping, and I feared for an instant she was about to die.

"No, no, no," she cried, rocking herself to and fro, "you shall *not* paint such a picture in his young, innocent mind. You *shall* not."

I sat on my stone, watching her, feeling excessively uncomfortable. "But what *did* she look like, Miss Duveen?" I pressed forward to ask at last.

"No, no, no," she cried again. "Cast him out, cast him out. *Retro Sathanas!* We must not even *ask* to understand. My father and my dear mother, I do not doubt, have spoken for Caroline. Even I, if I must be called on, will strive to collect my thoughts. And that is precisely where a friend, you, Arthur, would be so precious; to know that you too, in your innocence, will be helping me to collect my thoughts on that day, to save our dear Caroline from Everlasting Anger. That, that! Oh dear: oh dear!" She turned on me a face I should scarcely have recognized, lifted herself trembling to her feet, and hurried away.

Sometimes it was not Miss Duveen that was a child again, but I that had grown up. "Had now you been your handsome father —and I see him, oh, so plainly, dear child—had you been your father, then I must, of course, have kept to the house . . . I must have; it is a rule of conduct, and everything depends on them. Where would Society be *else*?" she cried, with an unanswerable blaze of intelligence. "I find, too, dear Arthur, that they increase —the rules increase. I try to remember them. My dear cousin, Miss Coppin, knows them all. But I—I think sometimes one's *memory* is a little treacherous. And then it must vex people."

She gazed penetratingly at me for an answer that did not come. Mute as a fish though I might be, I suppose it was something of a comfort to her to talk to me.

And to suppose that is *my* one small crumb of comfort when I reflect on the kind of friendship I managed to bestow.

I actually met Miss Coppin once; but we did not speak. I had, in fact, gone to tea with Miss Duveen. The project had been discussed as "quite, quite impossible, dear child," for weeks. "You must never mention it again." As a matter of fact I had never mentioned it at all. But one day—possibly when their charge had been less difficult and exacting, one day Miss Coppin and her gaunt maidservant and companion really did go out together, leaving Miss Duveen alone in Willowlea. It was the crowning opportunity of our friendship. The moment I espied her issuing from the house, I guessed her errand. She came hastening down to the waterside, attired in clothes of a colour and fashion I had never seen her wearing before, her dark eyes shining in her head, her hands trembling with excitement.

It was a still, warm afternoon, with Sweet Williams and linden and stocks scenting the air, when, with some little trepidation, I must confess, I followed her in formal dignity up the unfamiliar path towards the house. I know not which of our hearts beat the quicker, whose eyes cast the most furtive glances about us. My friend's cheeks were brightest mauve. She wore a large silver locket on a ribbon; and I followed her up the faded green stairs, beneath the dark pictures, to her small, stuffy bedroom under the roof. We humans, they say, are enveloped in a kind of aura; to which the vast majority of us are certainly entirely insensitive. Nevertheless, there was an air, an atmosphere as of the smell of pears in this small attic room—well, every bird, I suppose, haunts with its presence its customary cage.

"This," she said, acknowledging the bed, the looking-glass, the deal washstand, "this, dear child, you will pardon; in fact, you will not see. How could we sit, friends as we are, in the congregation of strangers?"

I hardly know why, but that favourite word of Miss Duveen's, "congregation," brought up before me with extreme aversion all the hostile hardness and suspicion concentrated in Miss Coppin and Ann. I stared at the queer tea things in a vain effort not to be aware of the rest of Miss Duveen's private belongings.

Somehow or other she had managed to procure for me a bun— a saffron bun. There was a dish of a grey pudding and a plate of raspberries that I could not help suspecting (and, I am ashamed to say, with aggrieved astonishment), she must have herself gathered that morning from my grandmother's canes. We did not talk very much. Her heart gave her pain. And her face showed how hot and absorbed and dismayed she was over her foolhardy entertainment. But I sipped my milk and water, sitting on a black bandbox, and she on an old cane chair. And we were almost formal and distant to one another, with little smiles and curtseys over our cups, and polished agreement about the weather.

"And you'll strive not to be sick, dear child," she implored me suddenly, while I was nibbling my way slowly through the bun. But it was not until rumours of the tremendous fact of Miss Coppin's early and unforeseen return had been borne in on us that Miss Duveen lost all presence of mind. She burst into tears; seized and kissed repeatedly my sticky hands; implored me to be discreet; implored me to be gone; implored me to retain her in my affections, "as you love your poor dear mother, Arthur," and I left her on her knees, her locket pressed to her bosom.

Miss Coppin was, I think, unusually astonished to see a small strange boy walk softly past her bedroom door, within which she sat, with purple face, her hat-strings dangling, taking off her boots. Ann, I am thankful to say, I did not encounter. But when I was safely out in the garden in the afternoon sunshine, the boldness and the romance of this sally completely deserted me. I ran like a hare down the alien path, leapt from stone to stone across the river; nor paused in my flight until I was safe in my

own bedroom, and had—how odd is childhood!—washed my face
and entirely changed my clothes.

My grandmother, when I appeared at her tea-table, glanced at
me now and again rather profoundly and inquisitively, but the
actual question hovering in her mind remained unuttered.

It was many days before we met again, my friend and I. She
had, I gathered from many mysterious nods and shrugs, been
more or less confined to her bedroom ever since our escapade, and
looked dulled and anxious; her small face was even a little more
vacant in repose than usual. Even this meeting, too, was full of
alarms; for in the midst of our talk, by mere chance or caprice,
my grandmother took a walk in the garden that afternoon, and
discovered us under our damson tree. She bowed in her dignified,
aged way. And Miss Duveen, with cheeks and forehead the colour
of her petticoat, elaborately curtseyed.

"Beautiful, very beautiful weather," said my grandmother.

"It is, indeed," said my friend, fixedly.

"I trust you are keeping pretty well?"

"As far, ma'am, as God and a little weakness of the heart permit," said Miss Duveen. "He knows all," she added, firmly.

My grandmother stood silent a moment.

"Indeed he does," she replied politely.

"And that's the difficulty," ventured Miss Duveen, in her odd,
furtive, friendly fashion.

My grandmother opened her eyes, smiled pleasantly, paused,
glanced remotely at me, and with another exchange of courtesies,
Miss Duveen and I were left alone once more. But it was a grave
and saddened friend I now sat beside.

"You see, Arthur, all bad things, we know, are best for us.
Motives included. That comforts me. But my heart is sadly
fluttered. Not that I fear or would shun society; but perhaps your
grandmother . . . I never had the power to treat my fellow creatures as if they were stocks and stones. And the effort not to
notice it distresses me. A little hartshorn might relieve the *palpitation,* of course; but Miss Coppin keeps all keys. It is this shouting
that makes civility such a task."

"This shouting"—very faintly then I caught her meaning, but

I was in no mood to sympathize. My grandmother's one round-eyed expressionless glance at me had been singularly disconcerting. And it was only apprehension of her questions that kept me from beating a retreat. So we sat on, Miss Duveen and I, in the shade, the day drawing towards evening, and presently we walked down to the waterside, and under the colours of sunset I flung in my crumbs to the minnows, as she talked ceaselessly on.

"And yet," she concluded, after how involved a monologue, "and yet, Arthur, I feel it is for your forgiveness I should be pleading. So much to do; such an arch of beautiful things might have been my gift to you. It is here," she said, touching her forehead. "I do not think, perhaps, that all I might say would be for your good. I must be silent and discreet about much. I must not provoke"—she lifted her mittened finger, and raised her eyes— "Them," she said gravely. "I am tempted, terrified, persecuted. Whispering, wrangling, shouting: the flesh is a grievous burden, Arthur; I long for peace. Only to flee away and be at rest! But," she nodded, and glanced over her shoulder, "about much—great trials, sad entanglements, about much the Others say, I must keep silence. It would only alarm your innocence. And that I will never, *never* do. Your father, a noble, gallant gentleman of the world, would have understood my difficulties. But he is dead. . . . Whatever that may mean. I have repeated it so often when Miss Coppin thought that I was not—dead, dead, dead, dead—but I don't think that even now I grasp the meaning of the word. Of you, dear child, I will never say it. You have been life itself to me."

How generously, how tenderly she smiled on me from her perplexed, sorrowful eyes.

"You have all the world before you, all the world. How splendid it is to be a Man. For my part I have sometimes thought, though they do not of course intend to injure me, yet I fancy, sometimes, they have grudged me *my* part in it a little. Though God forbid but Heaven's best."

She raised that peering, dark, remote gaze to my face, and her head was trembling again. "They are saying now to one another —'*Where is she? where is she? It's nearly dark, m'm, where is she?*' Oh, Arthur, but there shall be no night *there*. We must believe it, we must—in spite, dear friend, of a weak horror of glare. My cousin, Miss Coppin, does not approve of my wishes. Gas, gas, gas, all over the house, and when it is not singing, it roars. You would suppose I might be trusted with but just my own one bracket. But no—Ann, I think—indeed I fear, sometimes, has no—" She started violently and shook her tiny head. "When I am gone," she continued disjointedly, "you will be prudent, cautious, dear child? Consult only your heart about me. Older you must be . . . yes, certainly, he must be older," she repeated vaguely. "Everything goes on and on—and round!" She seemed astonished, as if at a sudden radiance cast on an old and protracted perplexity.

"About your soul, dear child," she said to me once, touching my hand, "I have never spoken. Perhaps it was one of my first duties to keep on speaking to you about your soul. I mention it now in case they should rebuke me when I make my appearance there. It is a burden; and I have so many burdens, as well as pain. And at times I cannot think very far. I *see* the thought; but it won't alter. It comes back, just like a sheep—'*Ba-aa-ah,*' like that!" She burst out laughing, twisting her head to look at me the while. "Miss Coppin, of course, has no difficulty; gentlemen have no difficulty. And this shall be the occasion of another of our little confidences. We are discreet?" She bent her head and scanned my face. "Here," she tapped her bosom, "I bear his image. My only dear one's. And if you would kindly turn your head, dear child, perhaps I could pull him out."

It was the miniature of a young, languid, fastidious-looking officer which she showed me—threaded on dingy tape, in its tarnished locket.

"Miss Coppin, in great generosity, has left me this," she said, polishing the glass on her knee, "though I am forbidden to wear it. For you see, Arthur, it is a duty not to brood on the past, and even, perhaps, indelicate. Some day, it may be, you, too, will love a gentle girl. I beseech you, keep your heart pure and true. This one could not. Not a single word of blame escapes me. I own to my Maker, *never* to anyone else, it has not eased my little difficulty. But it is not for us to judge. Whose office is that, eh?" And again, that lean small forefinger, beneath an indescribable grimace, pointed gently, deliberately, from her lap upward. "Pray, pray," she added, very violently, "pray, till the blood streams down your face! Pray, but rebuke not. They all whisper about it. Among themselves," she added, peering out beneath and between the interlacing branches. "But I simulate inattention. I simulate . . ." The very phrase seemed to have hopelessly confused her. Again, as so often now, that glassy fear came into her eyes; her foot tapped on the gravel.

"Arthur," she cried suddenly, taking my hand tightly in her lap, "you have been my refuge in a time of trouble. You will never know it, child. My refuge, and my peace. We shall seldom meet now. All are opposed. They repeat it in their looks. The autumn will divide us; and then, winter; but, I think, no spring. It is so, Arthur, there is a stir; and then they will hunt me out." Her eyes gleamed again, far and small and black in the dusky pallor of her face.

It was indeed already autumn; the air golden and still. The leaves were beginning to fall. The late fruits were well-nigh over. Robins and tits seemed our only birds now. Rain came in floods. The Wandle took sound and volume, sweeping deep above our stepping-stones. Very seldom after this I even so much as saw our neighbour. I chanced on her one still afternoon, standing fixedly by the brawling stream, in a rusty-looking old-fashioned cloak, her scanty hair pushed high up on her forehead.

She stared at me for a moment or two, and then, with a scared look over her shoulder, threw me a little letter, shaped like a cock-hat, and weighted with a pebble stone, across the stream. She whispered earnestly and rapidly at me over the water. But I could not catch a single word she said, and failed to decipher her close spidery handwriting. No doubt I was too shy, or to ashamed, or in a vague fashion too loyal, to show it to my grandmother. It is not now a flattering keepsake. I called out loudly I must go in; and still see her gazing after me, with a puzzled, mournful expression on the face peering out of the cloak.

Even after that we sometimes waved to one another across the water, but never if by hiding myself I could evade her in time. The distance seemed to confuse her, and quite silenced me. I began to see we were ridiculous friends, especially as she came now in ever dingier and absurder clothes. She even looked hungry, and not quite clean, as well as ill; and she talked more to her phantoms than to me when once we met.

The first ice was in the garden. The trees stood bare beneath a pale blue sunny sky, and I was standing at the window, looking out at the hoar-frost, when my grandmother told me that it was unlikely that I should ever see our neighbour again.

I stood where I was, without turning round, staring out of the window at the motionless ghostly trees, and the few birds in forlorn unease.

"Is she dead, then?" I inquired.

"I am told," was the reply, "that her friends have been compelled to have her put away. No doubt, it was the proper course. It should have been done earlier. But it is not our affair, you are to understand. And, poor creature, perhaps death would have been a happier, a more merciful release. She was sadly afflicted."

I said nothing, and continued to stare out of the window.

But I know now that the news, in spite of a vague sorrow, greatly relieved me. I should be at ease in the garden again, came the thought—no longer fear to look ridiculous, and grow hot when our neighbour was mentioned, or be saddled with her company beside the stream.

The Riddle and Other Stories (1923)

THE BOWL

I<small>T WAS</small> one autumn evening—in the month of October, I think, for I can just remember that the thin gold and tawny beech leaves were still floating down in the garden in the hazy sunshine, and that already a fire burned in the grate to cheer the colder twilights, when first my very young eyes fell in wonder upon Mrs. Orchardson's silver bowl. Perhaps it had always been there, and always as conspicuous. But it was now, I am sure, that I first noticed it. It stood on the sideboard beside a cut-glass decanter reflecting the ruddy colour of its wine in the smooth cheeks of its two laughing Cupids. It had handles, two pendant rings as plain in workmanship as the buckle on a child's shoe. I stood and stared up at it, as young eyes will at any such magical object. There was a sort of secret jollity in the very look of it—an air to blow bubbles in, cool as an orchard, or as the half-hidden valleys of a summer cloud.

I was astonished at it, entranced by it; longed to touch and handle it, and even felt, I verily believe, a kind of covetousness and an envy of the friend whose bowl it was. And if I had been a jackdaw of equal proportions to myself, I should certainly have carried it off to hide in the chimney or hole in the wall, wherever my nest might be. As it was, I at least carried off a very vivid remembrance of it in my mind—which, fortunately, in a world hedged about with a superfluity of *Dont's,* is not a felony.

Anyhow, when one dark rainy morning the sharp need came for *something* of this kind, it was I who thought of the bowl, which, after all, could contain almost as much Jordan water as could the freestone font in St. Barnabas's, and was twenty times more beautiful.

All through the night, while I had been placidly asleep, I learned at my lonely breakfast, my friend Mrs. Orchardson's little baby had been simply burning like a coal at death's door. It was a most interesting and enthralling piece of news. And I'm not so sure that I did not speculate how it was that in my long nocturnal journeyings in the wilds of dreamland, I had not heard its wailing cries as it, too, a much smaller spirit, ran along into the shadowy valley. For after all, abstractions like death are for a child little more than a vague and menacing something in a dream.

Mrs. Orchardson's baby had, of course, been sickening for some little time past. I had been angry and jealous more than once because it had been the cause of my seeing very little of her, and of my being entertained a good deal less than I thought proper on so short a visit. I could remember well enough its little blue-eyed puckered face and slatey-blue eyes, with an expression in them too, almost as dull as slate. Indeed, one morning, not long before —an unusually hot morning for October—she and I and it had sat on a rug in the garden together under the elms. A few withered wild flowers still showed in the grass, I remember, with nothing but their swollen seed vessels left of their summer.

And I had noticed, too, how peculiar a shiningness had come into Mrs. Orchardson's grey eyes when she talked to her baby. Yet anxiety kept her forehead frowning even while she was smiling, as she stared down into its small ugly wizened face. I didn't think it was in the least a pretty baby, and was vexed at its persisting in being ill.

These last few days, indeed, I had been left almost entirely to myself, with nobody to say a word to, except Esther, the parlour-maid—a sandy-coloured woman with a thick down on her face—and now and then to Mrs. Orchardson's cook, who had a way of speaking to me as if I were a kind of clockwork image incapable of even hearing her words. "And how is the poor little infant this morning?" I asked her once, mimicking the old doctor. She looked at me as if I were a snake in the grass—as no doubt I was.

But to come back to the silver bowl again. I had finished my bread and milk, had for the third time shooed away the cat from getting on to the table, and now sat staring through the long rainy window with my spoon in my mouth, when the door opened, and Mrs. Orchardson put her face in at it. It was grey, almost like wet chalk, and her eyes were so sharp and far-off-looking that she seemed scarcely to be aware of me at all. She was certainly looking at me, and yet as if through me, and with almost as horrified an expression as if she could see the very bones in my body. And then, suddenly she came in, almost fell down on her knees beside my chair, clasped me round, and hid her face in my lap. "Oh, Nick, Nick, you poor lonely thing," she said, sobbing, "she is worse, much, much worse. She is dying."

"Oh, dear!" I said in a mournful voice, "oh, dear!"

"So you will just try," she went on hurriedly, as if she were saying something that at any moment might be forgotten, "you will just try to be quiet and happy, by yourself. It won't be long; not very long." She paused, and I sat on as still as the loaf of bread on the table. She did not seem even to be breathing. But in a minute or two she lifted her wet face from my pinafore, and was looking entirely different from herself. I should hardly have recognized her—and yet she was quite calm, though her cheeks were almost like clay and her eyes as if they had fallen a little back into her head. "And now, you see," she added, as if not to me at all, "Mr. Cairns is coming to christen her, to make her God's little child. As you are, Nick."

"Isn't it going to be taken to church, then?" I said in a sepulchral voice.

"No," she answered, listening, but not to me.

"But why?" I said in disappointment. She put her hands to my cheeks, cupping my chin in them, and simply looking at me.

"But," I said wriggling away, "there's no font here: there *must* be a font like as at church." I frowned, looking at her a little scornfully out of the corner of my eye. "It won't be much good, if you don't. At least that's what Esther says."

She only shook her head, still gazing at me, and listening. "*I* know!" I said, "will that big silver bowl on the sideboard do for a font, Mrs. Orchardson? It's a very big bowl."

She smiled at me brightly.

"Why, of course, you strange creature, that will do beautifully. . . . And now—" She got up, and stood looking for a moment

out of the window, as if she had forgotten my presence altogether. "In all this loveliness!" she almost whispered, though all
that she could see was just an ordinary wet morning. . . .

Dr. Sharp would not return again for an hour, so there were
only Mrs. Orchardson and Esther and Mr. Cairns in the bedroom besides myself and the baby. The cook, I heard, wouldn't
come, because she was afraid of being upset. That seemed silly
to me. When I went into the room, a little square table already
stood between the fire and the window, and it was covered with
a linen napkin with a fringe. On this were burning two tall
white candles in silver sticks; and in the midst was the bowl
with a little water in it which by tiptoeing I could just manage
to see. I stared between surprise and dismay at Mr. Cairns when
he came in in his surplice. He seemed to be a person absolutely
different from the two Mr. Cairns I knew already—the one a
smiling, but rather silly-smiling elderly man in his old clerical
clothes in the Vicarage garden; the other, of course, looking
almost artificial, as he stood intoning the service in church.

Having blown out the candles, and placed them on the
dressing-table, he signed to us to stand up, myself being between
Mrs. Orchardson and Esther, and the baby lying still and
scarlet and open-eyed and without a single sound in Mrs.
Orchardson's arms. Once I remember, as he leaned over towards
her, Mr. Cairns's surplice brushed my cheek with its peculiar
dry perfume of cambric. And when he dipped his fingers into
the bowl I saw the water-butterflies jig on the ceiling.

He did not seem to have noticed that I was there, though for
a moment or two his glasses blazed on me like lanterns when
he fronted the window. He took the little baby in his great hands.
It had begun to cry then. But its crying was more like a very, very
old woman's than a natural baby's, and the fingers it spread out
in the air an instant were like white match-sticks, they were so
thin and shrunken. I smiled at it and made a grimace to please it,
but it looked at me like purple glass, as if it was not there to see
me or to be amused.

When the service was done, Mr. Cairns stooped down and
kissed the baby and he looked a very old man indeed; and yet
when he stood up again and had taken off his stole and surplice,

he was exactly the same as when I had seen him reading in his garden.

"My dear, dear lady, you must not grieve overmuch," he said to Mrs. Orchardson, at the door of the bedroom, "He knows His lambs, all His lambs. And He is merciful."

He leant his chin, and smiled towards me with a curious wrinkle on his face. His brown eyes reminded me of berries. They were full of kindness even though the look in them was not very attentive. I whispered to Esther, asking if I might be allowed to carry the silver bowl downstairs again. And all she gave me was a sharp shake of the head and a greenish look, because I don't think she liked to say no while Mr. Cairns was in hearing. He must have heard what I said, because he put his fingers on my hair and smiled at me again, so that I had to go downstairs in front of him, and I think he must have told Mrs. Orchardson meanwhile what to do with the bowl and the water.

In the hall he talked for a minute or two in secret with Esther. "In that case send the little boy to me, then," I heard him say. "Mrs. Cairns will be at home. Poor tiny lamb! To think it must have suffered like you and me!" Esther shut her fair-lashed eyes a moment as if to show it would be a mercy if the baby did die, and then opened them again very stern and mournfully when she saw me watching her.

Yet in my heart of hearts I was perfectly sure that Mrs. Orchardson's little baby would *not* die. I cannot tell whence this assurance came. It may have been the fruit of a child's natural intuition; or even of his exquisite eyesight—experienced, as it would seem, to see through, and not only on the surface. But for one thing, I had all along felt a firm belief in the inherent virtue of the bowl, and was contemptuous of Esther for shutting her eyes like that. It seemed impossible that the clear shallow water in its shadowy deeps should not wash all taint of sickness away. Besides, I had thought of it.

This, I think, was the reason why I flatly refused to accept Mr. Cairns's invitation to go to the rectory, when Esther told me to do so. I knew perfectly well she wouldn't be able to make me go against my will while the baby was so ill. At last she gave a furious empty toss with my grey wool scarf that she was carrying in her hand, and looked at me as if no tongue could express her hatred.

"And don't you feel *no* pity for that poor suffering mite upstairs, you obstinate boy?" she asked me in a low compressed voice. I merely stared at her without answering, and she had to turn her eyes away.

"He don't even know the meaning of the word!" she said, and shut the door of the dining-room after her as if she hoped its wood would stick for ever after to the lintel. But I did not mind her temper. Presently she came in again, looking even angrier and whiter than before.

"Is this the time for building and Noah's-arking," she almost shouted in my ear as I sat on the hearth-rug; "is *this* the time?—when that poor little innocent is rattling its very life out over your head?"

I looked no further up at her than at the tray in her hand. "You little imp!"

"I suppose when it gets well, it will have to be christened all over again, *properly,* won't it?" I inquired. I knew she was staring at me, and hating me for not caring what she said.

"Where,"—she gasped almost losing herself in her rage, "where you pick up such evil heathenish notions from, I can't think. Not from *this* house. There's not a speck of sin left in the whole of that infant's body now; not a speck. And if you had gone to that kind Mr. Cairns as he arst, he would have *told* you so."

"I didn't want to go, and Mrs. Orchardson wouldn't have tried to make me." The blood seemed to rise up in my body and I could hear my own voice growing more insolent and trumpeting every moment. "What's more, Miss Esther, I don't believe a bit in your old holy water. It isn't *going* to die, and even if you hope it will, it won't. And you're treading on one of my animals."

At that she deliberately kicked down the fort I was building with her foot.

"You are a little devil incarnate; that's what you are," she screamed at me, if one can scream without raising one's voice. "A little devil. You ought never to have been allowed in a Christian house. It's Tophet and the roaring flames that you're bound for, my young man. You've *murdered* that poor mite. You mark my words!"

I was so much enraged at this that I hit at a little bulge in her boot with one of my bricks.

"You're a beast," I bawled at her in a voice no louder than her own. "You're a filthy beast. And I don't mind where I go, so long as *you* aren't there. Not a—not a *dam'*."

Her face was so close to mine in its hatred that I saw her eyes change, and her lips stiffen, as if she was afraid. "You wait, Master Nicholas; you wait! For that vile horrid word! You wait! The master shall hear of that."

I laughed at her sneeringly. "I dare you to say it to him. He wouldn't care; he thinks you're a stupid hairy woman. And *I* think you're *hateful*." She lifted her hand and shut her eyes. "Oh, my God," she said, "I can't stand it," and all but ran out of the room.

When she was gone—with the inside of my stomach feeling as if it were on fire—I climbed the stairs to my bedroom, and, boots and all, flung myself down on the white quilt of the bed.

Nothing happened. The house remained in silence. A flying shower rattled on the window-pane, and then the sun returned and shone grey and golden on the raindrops. And I hated everything I looked at. I thought how I would kill Esther; and how I would kick her body when she was dead.

But gradually the furnace within me began to die down, my "thoughts" wandered away, and my eyelids were drooping into a drowse when I heard a muffled sound of footsteps to and fro, to and fro, ascending from the bedroom immediately beneath me, and I remembered the baby. And suddenly a dark shivering horror turned me to ice, and there, as I lay, I prayed to be forgiven for having been myself, and implored God to let me take its sufferings or to die instead of it. So I lay; flat on my stomach, and prayed.

The afternoon had now grown a little darker in the room, and in a while after this, I must have emptily fallen asleep. For the next thing I remember is finding a cold arm round me in the dregs of the dusk and lips close to my face softly whispering and murmuring, their soft warm breath on my cheek.

"Guess, Nick! Guess!" said that soft, thrilling voice, when I stirred a little nearer. "Guess!"

I put back my head, and by staring close could just see the light from the window reflected in Mrs. Orchardson's eyes. A curious phosphorescence was there too; even her skin seemed very faintly to shine.

"Why," I said, "she's much better."

At which those eyes gazed through the narrow air between us as incredulously as if at an angel. "You knew it; you *knew* it? You precious holy thing! And all this while you have been brooding up here by yourself. What can I say? How can I tell you? Oh, Nick, I shall die of happiness."

She squeezed herself closer to me in the vacant space on the bed, clasping me round—her shoulders shaking with what just for a minute I thought was laughing.

"I never *can* say how, Mrs. Orchardson," I managed to murmur after a long pause. "But I was quite sure, you know. I don't think grown-up people understand."

"And I don't, either," she said with a little hysterical laugh. "Indeed, indeed I don't. But there—" she raised her face, sat up, put her hands to her hair, and smiled down on me. I too scrambled up; and could see her plainly now as if by a thin mist-like light from her own body. "Bless me, Nick, I have made your hair all wet with crying. God bless you, my dear. It was all you; all you."

She sat in silence a moment, but not as if she was thinking. Then suddenly she breathed, and lifted her head. "And now I must go, and we mustn't make the teeniest tiniest little crick of a sound. She is asleep. Follow me down—just two shadows. And don't, Nick, *don't* let me vanish away."

"Will everything," I asked her when we were safely downstairs; "will everything be just as ordinarily again now, Mrs. Orchardson?"

"You have missed me, you dear thing?" she asked, glancing over her shoulder, in the glaring light that now stretched down on us. She was kneeling at the sideboard.

"Esther never says a word, except to make me hate her," I replied. "So, of course, most what she says about me is true. So I think now that the baby's quite better, Mrs. Orchardson, I had better go home again. Even Mr. Cairns wouldn't let me carry the bowl downstairs. And if it hadn't been for that . . . "

The blue of her eyes shone across at me like bits of the sky seen through a window. They opened wider and wider. "But, Nick, my *dear!*" she cried at last, clear and small as a bird. "I hadn't a notion that you had been unhappy. Indeed, indeed I hadn't. Blind selfish creature that I am. He is shaking, poor darling. He is absolutely worn out!"

And at that I could refrain my self-righteousness and self-commiseration no longer. I ran over to her, bowed myself double beside her on the floor, and sobbed "as if my heart would break."

The Riddle and Other Stories (1923)

THE TREE

ENCASED in his dingy first-class railway carriage, the prosperous Fruit Merchant sat alone. From the collar of his thick frieze greatcoat stuck out a triangular nose. On either side of it a small, bleak, black eye gazed absently at one of the buttons on the empty blue-upholstered seat opposite to him. His breath spread a fading vapour in the air. He sat bolt upright, congealed in body, heated in mind, his unseeing eye fixed on that cloth button, that stud.

There was nothing else to look at, for his six narrow glass windows were whitely sheeted with hoar-frost. Only his thoughts were his company, while the coach, the superannuated coach, bumped dully on over the metals. And his thoughts were neither a satisfaction nor a pleasure. His square hard head under his square hard hat was nothing but a pot seething with vexation, scorn, and discontent.

What had invited him out so far, in weather so dismal, on a line so feebly patronized? Anger all but sparkled in his mind as he considered the intention of his journey, and what was likely to be the end and outcome of it. Twelve solid yet fleeting years divided him from his last encounter with his half-brother —twelve *cent. per cent.* years—shipload on shipload of exotic oranges and lemons, pineapples, figs, and blushing pomegranates. At this very moment three more or less seaworthy ocean tramps were steaming across the watery channels of the world laden with cargoes of which he was the principal consignee. He stretched out his legs, crossed his feet. He was a substantial man. There was nothing fantastic about *him*.

To put on airs when you couldn't afford them; to meet a friendly offer with rank ingratitude; to quarrel with the only relative on earth who had kept you out of the workhouse—he had sworn never to set foot in the place again. Yet—here he was: and nothing but a fool for his pains. Having washed his hands of the whole silly business, he should have kept them washed. Instead of which he thrust them deeper into his capacious pockets and wondered to heaven when his journey was to come to an end.

No, it was with no charitable, no friendly, no sentimental motive that he was being glided joltingly on. A half-brother— and particularly if he owes you a hundred pounds and more— need not be even fractionally a being one smiles to think of for the sake of auld lang syne. There was nothing in common between the two of them, except a father now twenty-five years in his grave and a loan that would never be repaid.

That was one galling feature of the situation. There was another. In plain print and in his own respectable morning newspaper the Fruit Merchant had chanced but a week or two ago on the preposterous fact that a mere woodcut of a mere "Bird and Flower," initialled P. P., had fetched at Christie's ninety-seven guineas. Ninety-seven guineas: sixty-eight crates of excellent Denia oranges at thirty shillings a crate. What the devil! His small eyes seemed to congest and yet at the same time to protrude from their sockets.

"P. P."!—perfect pest; paltry poser; plaguey parasite. And yet —hardly a parasite. You couldn't with a term like that dish a half-brother who hadn't sent you a single word of greeting for twelve solid fleeting prosperous years. Even if he did owe you a hundred pounds. Even if he hadn't the faintest wish to remind you of the fact. Not that the Fruit Merchant *wanted* his hundred pounds. He wasn't a debt-collector. He wasn't even vindictive. It was the principle of the thing.

For if half an hour's silly scratching over a little lump of wood could fetch you £101 17s., about twenty-nine and a half minutes would bring in a round hundred. And there were more birds and more flowers in that infernal tree than Noah could have found room for in his Ark. The tree!—the very thought of it swept a pulsating cloud of rage over the Fruit Merchant's eyes. Cool, quiet insolence—he could have forgiven that, and could almost have forgotten it. But the faintest recollection of the tree, and of the talk under it, never failed to infuriate him. It infuriated him now almost beyond endurance, simply because he knew, in the secrecy of his thoughts, that *this* was the decoy which was dragging him on these fifty-three interminable miles on a freezing hideous country afternoon.

The tree: never in all his life had he met with such an exhibition of sheer, stark, midsummer madness. And yet with every inch of his journey the recollection grew on him. He couldn't get it out of his head. Curiosity, resentment, vindictiveness, a cold creeping cunning—a score of conflicting emotions zigzagged to and fro in his mind. He glared through them at the walls of his cage. But worst outrage of all was the creeping realization—and his body stiffened at the thought—that he was even now, and perhaps even a little more than ever, afraid of the tree. When you finally deal with a relative and a bloodsucker who has been a pest to you all your life, the one thing you do not look for is an interference of that kind.

He could not deny it, the tree had impressed him. Ever since that first swimming stare at it, the moment he thought of his brother, of the country, even of his boyhood—there it was. It had impressed him so much that the upholstered button had now completely disappeared, and he seemed to be actually in the presence of it again. He saw it as vividly as if its image hung there before his very eyes in the slightly self-warmed air of his solitary compartment. The experience filled him with so sudden a flood of aversion and resentment that the voice of the guard chaunting the name of his destination reached him only just in time to set him frantically pulling down his frozen window and ejecting himself out of the train.

One hasty glance around him showed that he was the sole traveller to alight on the frosted timbers of the obscure little station. A faint rosiness in the west foretold the decline of the still wintry day. The firs that flanked the dreary passenger-shed of the platform stood burdened already with the blackness of coming night.

He was elderly, he was obese, his heart was none too sound, at least as compared with his head. Yet if he intended to catch the last train home, he had scarcely a couple of hours in which to reach his half-brother's wretched little house, to congratulate him on his guineas, to refuse to accept repayment of his loan, to sneer at his tree, and to return to the station.

A bark at a weedy young porter in mittens, with mouth ajar over his long teeth, sent him ambling off for a conveyance. The Fruit Merchant stood under the shed in his frieze coat and square hard hat and watched the train glide out of the station. The screech of its engine, horning up into the windless air, had exactly expressed his own peculiar sentiments.

There was not a living being in sight whereon to breathe a curse. Only himself, a self he had been vaguely cursing throughout his tedious journey. The frozen landscape lay white in the dying day. The sun hung like the yolk of an egg above the still horizon. Some menace in the very look of this sullen object hinted that P. P. might long since have crossed the bourne from which no belated draft on any earthly bank had ever been known to transpire.

The thought diverted into ruggeder channels the current of the talk which he had intended to engage in with his half-brother. In other words, he would give the silly fool a bit of his mind. The fact was, their last quarrel—if anything so one-sided could be called a quarrel—had tinctured the Fruit Merchant's outlook on the world a good deal more densely than he would until now have confessed. A frown settled above the sullen eyes.

No living creature, no sound stirred the air. The fair country lay cold as if in a swoon. Like a shallow inverted saucer a be-calmed sky curved itself over the unbroken quiet of the fields. His broad cleft chin thrust into his muffler, his hands into his capacious pockets, the stranger to these parts stood waiting, just stood there, with his small black eyes staring desolately out of his clothes. Why, you might just as well be marooned in a foreign land, or on a stage—sinister, cold, vacant, and not a single soul in the audience. At the sound of wheels and hoofs he coughed as if in uncontrollable indignation; and turned smartly on his heels. . . .

With a gesture of disdain the Fruit Merchant sourly thrust a shilling into the weedy porter's immense knuckled hand and mounted into the cab. At his onset the whole square fusty interior leaned towards him like an extinguisher over the stub of a candle. The vehicle disgraced the universe. Even the man on the box resembled some little cautious and obscure animal that had been dug up out of the earth. When given his direction his face had fallen into an indescribable expression beneath its whiskers: an expression, it appeared, which was its nearest approach to a smile.

"And don't spare your—horse," had barked his fare, slamming the rickety door behind him.

A railway carriage even of the most antique description, when its glass is opaque with rime, is a little less like a prison cell than a four-wheeled cab. For which reason, perhaps, as the vehicle ground on beneath the misty leafless elms, the frigid air was allowed to beat softly in from the open window upon its oc-cupant's slightly impurpled face.

And still on and on, now here, now there, memory retrieved for the sombre shape within it every incident of his last ex-perience on this self-same road. It had been summertime—June. He had been twelve years younger, a good gross of years less prosperous, and not perhaps quite so easily fanned into a peculiar helpless state of rage.

Indeed, his actual meeting with his half-brother at the little white garden-gate had been almost friendly. So friendly that it would hardly have been supposed they were in any way unpleasingly related to one another, or that the least responsibility of each to each could have caused any kind of festering recrimination. Not that P. P. was even then the kind of person one hastens to introduce to one's friends. You not only never knew how he would look or what he would say. You weren't even certain what he might do. A rolling stone that merely fails to gather moss is a harmless object by comparison with one that appears to gather momentum. And even the most trifling suggestion, not so much of eccentricity as of an alien and crooked gleam in the eye, is apt to make the most respectable company a little uneasy.

Not that the two half-brothers had ever discussed together their aims and intentions and ideas about life; their desires or motives or hopes, or aversions or apprehensions or prejudices. The Fruit Merchant had his fair share of most of these human incentives, but he also had principles, and one of them was to keep his mouth shut.

They had met, had shaken hands, had exchanged remarks on the weather. Then P. P., in his frayed jacket and slippers, with his meagre expressionless face, had aimlessly led off his visitor into the garden, had aimlessly dropped a few distant remarks about their common past; and then, surrounded as they were by the scenery, scents, and noises of summer, had pushed his knotted hands into his trousers pockets, and fallen silent; his grey, vacant eyes fixed on the tree. The Fruit Merchant had tried in vain to break the silence, to shrug his way out of it. He also could only stand and stare up and up—at the tree.

Solitary, unchallenged, exotic in its station all but at the foot of the broken-hedged, straggling garden, it rose to heaven, a prodigious spreading ascendant cone, with its long, dark, green, pointed leaves. It stood, from first springing branch to apex, a motionless and somnolent fountain of flowers.

If his half-brother had taken the Fruit Merchant into a dingy little greenhouse and had shown him an ailing plant that with care, water, and guano had been raised from some far-fetched seed—well, that might have been something to boast about. He himself was in the trade. He knew a Jaffa orange from a mandarin. The stuff has to *grow,* of course; and he was broad-minded enough to approve of rural enterprise. Giant Mangolds and Prize Pumpkins—they did no harm. They encouraged the human vegetable. But the . . .

At last he had come to his senses and had peered fretfully about him. The garden was a waste, the hedges untrimmed, a rank lusty growth of weeds flaunted their flowers at the sun. And this tree—it must have been flourishing here for centuries past, a positive eyesore to any practical gardener. P. P. couldn't even put a name to it. Yet by the fixed idiotic dreamy look on his face you might have supposed it was a gift from heaven; that, having waved his hands about like those coloured humbugs with the mango, the thing had sprung up by sheer magic out of the ground.

Not that the Fruit Merchant had denied that it was unique. He had never seen, nor would he ever want to see, its double. The sun had beaten down upon his head; a low, enormous drone filled the air; the reflected light dazed his eyes. A momentary faintness had stolen over him as he had turned once more and glanced again into his half-brother's long bony face—the absent eyes, the prominent cheek, the greying hair dappled with sunlight.

"How do you *know* it's unique?" he had asked. "It may be as common as blackberries in other parts of the country—or abroad. One of the officers on the *Catamaran* was telling me . . ."

"I don't know," his half-brother had interrupted him, "but I have been looking at trees all my life. This resembles all, reminds me of none. Besides, I'm not going abroad—at least for the present."

What had he meant by that? The Fruit Merchant hadn't inquired; had merely stood there in the flowers and grasses, blinking up once more into the spreading branches, almost involuntarily shaking his head at the pungent sweetness that hung dense and sickly in the air. And the old familiar symptoms

began to stir in him, as he now sat jolting on in his cab—
symptoms which his intimates would have described in one
word: fuming.

He was not denying it, not he—the tree had been remarkable
as trees go. For one thing, it bore two distinct kinds and shapes
of blossom. The one circular and full and milky in a dark cup-
like calyx, with clusters of scarlet-tipped pistils; the other a pale
yellow oval, three-petalled, with a central splash of orange. He
had surreptitiously squeezed a couple of the fallen flowers into
his pocket-book, had taken them out at his office in the Borough
the next morning to show them to the partner he had afterwards
advantageously bought out of the business, only to find them
black, slimy, and unrecognizable, and to be laughed at for his
pains.

"What's the use of the thing?" he had next inquired of his
half-brother in a gross voice. "Is it edible?" At which, with the
faint smile on his face that had infuriated the Fruit Merchant
even as a boy, the other had merely shrugged his shoulders.

"Why not try it on the pigs?"

"I don't keep pigs."

Keep pigs, indeed; there wasn't the faintest symptom that he
would ever be able to keep himself!

"Well, aren't there any birds in these parts?" It had been a
singularly false move.

"It has brought its own," had been his half-brother's muttered
retort.

There was no denying it—at least so far as the Fruit Merchant's
small ornithological knowledge went. At that very moment
birds of a peculiarly vivid green sheeniness were hovering and
dipping between the deep blue of the sky and the mountainous
blossoming. Little birds, with unusually long and attenuated bills,
playing, fluttering, lisping, courting, and apparently sucking the
heady nectar from the snowy and ivory cups, while poised like
animate gems on the wing. He had again opened his mouth, but
his half-brother had laid a lean tingling hand on his sleeve.
"Listen!" he said.

Half-stifled, jetting, delirious bursts of song twinkled, belled,
rose, eddied, overflowed from the tented depths of the tree, like

the yells and laughter of a playground of children suddenly released for an unexpected half-holiday. Listen, indeed! The noise
of the creatures was still echoing in his ears as he sat there bulkily
swaying, his eyes fixed on the pallid, gliding hedgerow from his
fusty cab.

P. P. had not positively claimed that every single chorister in
the chorus was an exotic visitant. He had gone further. He had
gently bent down a low-lying fan of leaves and bloom, and not
content with exhibiting one by one living specimens of a little
spotted blue iridescent beetle, a horned kind of cockchafer, and a
dappled black-and-yellow-mottled ladybird—all of them following their lives in these surroundings; he had also waved a lean
hand in the direction of a couple of gaudy butterflies intertwining
in flight down the slope of the garden, had pointed out little
clumps of saffron and sky-blue flowers, and a rank, ungainly
weed with a cluster of black helmet-shaped florets at its tips,
asserting that they were as rare—as unprecedented—in those
parts as the tree itself.

"You don't mean to say because the thing's brought its own
vermin that it's any the better for that? Lord, we can do that
in the fruit trade."

"It's brought me," said the other, mooning meanwhile in the
opposite direction.

"And where do you raise your pertatoes and artichokes and
scarlet runners? It looks to me like a dam' waste of soil."

The wandering greenish-grey eyes had rested for a moment
on the puffy contemptuous face a few inches beneath them without the faintest symptom of intelligence. Empty eyes, yet with a
hint of danger in them, like a bright green pool of water in a
derelict quarry. "You shall have a basket of the fruit; if you'll
risk it. It never really ripens—queer-looking seeds."

"You eat it yourself, then?"

The eyes slid away, the narrow shoulders had lifted a little.
"I take things as they come." It was precisely how he had afterwards taken the cheque.

Seated there, on either side of the deal table, in the bare, un-
carpeted, uncurtained living-room of the cottage over a luncheon

of bread and dry cheese and onions, with the reflected light of
the tree on his half-brother's face, the talk between the two of
them had gradually degenerated into an altercation.

At length the Fruit Merchant, with some little relief, had
completely lost his temper. A half-empty jam-pot buzzing with
bees was no more appetizing an object because the insects were
not of the usual variety. He had literally been stung into repeating a few semi-fraternal truths.

To submit to being half-starved simply because nobody with
money to waste would so much as look at your bits of drawings;
to sit there dreamily grinning at a tree in your back-garden,
twenty times more useless because there wasn't its like for miles
around, even *if* there wasn't; to be content to hang like a bloodsucker on the generosity of a relative half-blood and half-water—
well, he had given P. P. a bit of his mind.

The Fruit Merchant instinctively drew a cold fat hand down
his face as a more and more precise recollection of the subsequent
scene recurred to him. Mere silence can be insulting, and there
was one thing about his half-brother—worse than all the rest
of his peculiarities put together—that had never failed to reduce
him to a feverish helplessness: his eyes. They didn't see you
even when they were fixed on you across a couple of feet of deal
board. They saw something else; and with no vestige of common
courtesy.

And those hands—you could swear at a glance that they had
never done a single honest day's work in their owner's lifetime.
Every sight of them had made it easier for the Fruit Merchant
to work himself up into a blind refreshing rage. The cottage
had fairly shaken to his abuse. The raw onions had danced under
his fist on the table. And twining in and out between his roarings
and shoutings had meandered on that other low, groping, dispassionate voice—his brother's.

He had found his own place; and there he intended to remain.
Rather than sit on a stool in a counting-house writing invoices
for crates of oranges and pineapples he would hang himself from
the topmost branches of the tree. You had your own life to lead,
and it didn't matter if you died of it. He was not making any

claims. There was nothing the same in this world for any two individuals. And the more different everything was, the more closely you should cling to the difference.

Oh, yes, he had gone on, it was mere chance, or whatever you liked to call it, that had brought him here; a mere chance that the tree had not even been charged for in the rent. There it was, and it would last him his lifetime; and, when that was over, he wouldn't complain. He had wagged his skimpy beard, a pencil between his fingers. No, he wouldn't complain if they just dug a hole in the garden and shovelled his body in under the grass within reach of the rootlets. What's your body?—"They'll buy me all right when I'm safely dead. Try it—it's a fair speculation."

"Try what?" The Fruit Merchant's countenance had suddenly set like a gargoyle in cast-iron.

His half-brother had nodded towards a dingy portfolio that stood leaning against a half-empty bookcase. And at that his guest had laid about him with a will. "So that's the kind of profit you are hoping to make out of your blighted old bee-bush? That's your profit? *That's* your fine airs—your miserable scribblings and scragglings."

He had once more slammed down his fat fist on the table and delivered his ultimatum. "See here, I give you a hundred pounds, here and now. There's no claim on me, not a shred. We don't even share the same mother, even if we share the same dad. You talk this abject rubbish to me. You have never earned a decent penny in your life. You never will. You are a fool and a loafer. Go to the Parish; and go for good. I'm sick of it, d'ye hear?— sick of it. You sit there, whiffling that I haven't eyes in my head, that I don't know black from white, that you'd rather hang your miserable carcass in your wretched old tree than take a respectable job. Well, hang it there—it won't break the branches if this is the only kind of meal you can give a visitor! I'm done with you. I wash my hands of you. Do you hear?"

He had—inaccurately—pantomimed the operation, sweeping over the jam-pot as he did so, and now drew in his breath—a cold breath, too; as, with eyes fixed on the ever-lightening hedgerows beyond his oblong window, he remembered the renewed red-hot stab of pain that had transfixed the ball of his thumb.

It recalled him instantaneously to his surroundings. Scrambling up from his seat he ejected his head out of the cab into the open. "Whoa, there! Whoa, I say: I'm getting out."

The horse was dragged up on to its haunches, the cab came to a standstill, and, to the roaring suspirations of the animal, the Fruit Merchant alighted on the tinkling ice of a frozen wayside puddle of water. He turned himself about. Time and the night had not tarried during his journey. The east was a blaze of moonlight. The moon glared in the grey heavens like a circular flat little window of glass.

"Wait here—" the Fruit Merchant bade his cabman in the desolation. "You've pretty near shaken the head off my body."

The cabman ducked his own small head in reply, and saluted his fare with a jerk of his whip. "You won't be long," he sang out between his whiskers.

"What did he mean by that?" was the Fruit Merchant's querulous question to himself as he mounted the few remaining yards of by-lane towards the crest of the slope. He was tired and elderly and cold. A pathetic look, one almost of sadness, came into his face. He pushed up his muffler and coughed. There replied the faintest echo from the low copse that bordered the lane. Grass, crystalled with hoar-frost, muffled his footsteps. What had he meant by that? repeated self to self, but not as if expectant of an answer.

When well out of sight of the cabman and his vehicle beneath the slope of the hill, the Fruit Merchant paused and lifted his eyes. League beyond league beneath him, as if to the confines of the world, the countryside spread on—frost-beclad meadow, wood and winding lane. And one sole house in sight, a small, tumbledown, lightless, huddling cottage, its ragged thatch and walls chequered black with shadow and dazzling white with wash of moonshine. And there—lifting itself into the empty skies, its twigs and branches sweeping the stars, stood, as if in wait for him, the single naked gigantic tree.

The Fruit Merchant gazed across at it, like an obese minute Belial on the ramparts of Eden. He had been fooled, then; tricked. He might have guessed the fatuity of his enterprise. He *had* guessed it. The house was empty; the bird had flown. Why for a single instant had he dreamed otherwise? Simply because all these years he had been deceived into believing there was a kind of honesty in the fellow. Just that something quixotic, stupid, stubborn, dense, dull, demented which—nothing but lies, then.

That bee in his bonnet, that snake in his grass: nothing but lies. There was no principle by which you could judge a man like that; and yet—well, after all, he was like anybody else. Give him a taste of the sweets of success, and his boosted solitude, his contempt for the mere decencies of life, his pretended disgust at men more capable and square-headed than himself had vanished into thin air. There were fools in the world, he had now discovered, who would pay ninety-seven guineas for a second- or third-hand scrabble of a drawing. "Right you are; hand over the dibs, and I am off!"

A scornful yet lugubrious smile stole over the Fruit Merchant's purplish features. He would be honest about it; he positively enjoyed acknowledging when a rival had bested him over a bargain. He would even agree that he had always nursed his own little superstitions. And now all that fine silly talk—sheer fudge. He had been himself childish fool enough to be impressed by it; yes, and to have been even a little frightened by—a tree.

He eyed it there—that gaunt, prodigious weed; and then, with one furtive glance over his round shoulder towards the crest of the slope behind which lay his way of escape from this wintry landscape and from every memory of the buffoon who had cheated him, he slowly descended the hill, pushed open the broken gate, and entered the icy untended garden.

Once more he came to a standstill in his frieze coat, and from under the brim of his hard hat stared up into the huge frigid branches. There is a supple lift and ease in the twigs of a tree asleep in winter. Green living buds are everywhere huddling close in their drowsy defences. Even the Fruit Merchant could distinguish between the dreaming and the dead, or, at any rate, between the unripe and the rotten.

And as he looked, two thoughts scurried like rats out of the wainscot of his mind. An unprecedented foreboding descended

on him. These lean shrunken twigs, these massive vegetable bones
—the tree was dead. And up there—he shifted rapidly to and fro
in order to secure an uninterrupted view of a kind of huddling
shape up aloft there, an object that appeared to be stooping crazily
forward as if on a similar quest in respect to himself.

But, no. He took a deep breath. The muffled knocking against
the wall of his head ceased. He need not have alarmed himself:
an optical illusion. Nothing.

The tree *was* dead. That was clear—a gaunt, black, sapless
nightmare. But the ungainly clump and shape, hoisted midway
among its boughs was not a huddling human body. It was only
yet another kind of derelict parasite—withered mistletoe. And
that gentle spellican-like rattling high overhead was but the fingering of a faint breeze in the moonlight; clacking twig against
twig.

Maybe it would have simplified matters if— But no need to
dwell on that. One corpse at a time was enough for any man on a
night like this and in a country as cheerless as the plains of Go-
morrah. A phrase or two out of his familiar bills of lading recurred to the Fruit Merchant's mind—"the act of God." There
was something so horrific in the contorted set of the branches outthrust in ungainly menace above his head that he was reminded
of no less a depravity than the devil himself. Thank the Lord, his
half-brother had *not* remembered to send him a parcel of the
fruit.

If ever poison showed in a plant, it haunted every knot and
knuckle of this tree. Judgment had overtaken it—the act of God.
That's what came of boasting. That's what came of idling a useless life away in a daydream at other people's expense. And now
the cunning bird was flown. The insult of his half-brother's triumph stabbed the Fruit Merchant like a sword.

A sudden giddiness, the roar as of water, caused in part no
doubt by the posture of his head, again swept over him, reverberated in his ears. He thrust a cautious hand into the breast of
his coat and lowered his eyes. They came to a stay on the rugged
moonlit bole. And there, with a renewed intensity of gaze, they
once more fixed themselves.

The natural living bark of the tree had been of a russet grey,

resembling that of the beech. Apart from a peculiar shimmering-
ness due to the frost that crystalled it over, and as the skin of a
dead thing, that bark now suggested the silveriness of leprosy. So
far, so good. But midway up the unbranched bole, at the height of
five to six feet from the ground, appeared a wide peculiar cicatrice.
The iridescent greyness here abruptly ended. Above it stretched
a clear blank ring of darker colour, knobbed over, in and out,
with tiny sparkling clusters of fungi.

The Fruit Merchant stole in a pace or two. No feat of the inhuman this. Cleanly and precisely the thick rind of the tree must
some time since have been cut and pared away in a wide equal
ring; a ring too far from the ground to have been the work of
pigs or goats, too smooth and sharp-edged to have been caused by
the gnawings of cattle. It was perfectly plain; the sap-protecting
skin of the thing had been deliberately cut and hacked away. The
tree had been murdered. High in the moonlit heavens it gloated
there: a victim.

Not until then did the Fruit Merchant stealthily turn and once
more survey his half-brother's house. The slow and almost furtive
movement of his head and shoulders suggested that the action was
involuntary. From this garden side the aspect of the hovel was
even more abject and disconsolate. Its one ivy-clustered chimney-
stack was smokeless. The moonbeams rained softly and merci-
lessly on the flint walls, the boarded windows, the rat-and-bird-
ravaged thatch.

Only a spectre could be content with such a dwelling, and a
guilt-stricken wretch at that. Yet without any doubt in the world
the house was still inhabited. For even now a slender amber beam
of light leaned out at an obtuse angle from some crevice in the
shuttering wood into the vast bath of moonshine.

For a moment the Fruit Merchant hesitated. He could leave the
garden and regain his cab without nearing the house. He could
yet once more "wash his hands." Certainly, after sight of the
maniac's treacherous work on his unique God-given tree he hadn't
the faintest vestige of a desire to confront his half-brother. Quite
the reverse. He would far rather fling a second hundred pounds
after the first than be once more contaminated by his company.
There was something vile in his surroundings.

In shadows black as pitch, like these, any inconceivably evil creature might lie in covert. If the tree alive could decoy an alien fauna to its succulent nectar, the tree dead might well invite even less pleasing ministrations. Come what come would, he was prepared. It might startle him; but he was dead-cold already; and when your whole mind is filled with disgust and disquiet there is no room for physical fear. You merely want to shake yourself free —edge out and be off.

Nevertheless, the human intruder in this inhuman wilderness was already, and with infinite caution, making his way towards the house. On a pitch-black night he might have hesitated. Hadn't venomous serpents the habit of stealing for their winter slumber into the crannies and hollows of fallen wood? Might not even the lightest northern zephyr bring down upon his head another vast baulk of timber from the withered labyrinth above? But so bright was the earth's lanthorn, so still the starry sky, that he could hear and even see the seeds from the humbler winter weeds scattering out from their yawning pods, as, with exquisite care, he brushed on through the tangling growths around him.

And having at length closely approached the walls, standing actually within a jutting shadow, he paused yet again and took a deep breath into his body before, gently lifting himself, he set his eye to the crevice from which poured out that slender shaft of light.

So artificially brilliant was the room within—by comparison with the full moonlight of the Fruit Merchant's natural world without—that for an instant or two he saw nothing. But he persevered, and after a while his round protruding eye found itself master of at least half the space on the other side of the shutters. Stilled through and through, his fingers clutching the frosted sill, he stood there half suspended on his toes, and as if hypnotized.

For scarcely more than a yard distant from his own there stooped a face—his half-brother's: a face to haunt you to your dying day. It was surmounted by a kind of nightcap, and was almost unrecognizable. The unfolding of the hours of twelve solitary years had played havoc with the once-familiar features. The projecting brows above the angular cheekbones resembled polished stone. The ears stood out like the vans of a bat on either

side above the corded neck. The thin unkempt beard on the narrow jaw brushed the long gnarled hand that was moving with an
infinite tedious care on the bare table beneath it.

Motionlessly the hanging paraffin lamp poured its radiance
upon this engrossed cadaverous visage, revealing every line and
bone, hollow and wrinkle.

Nevertheless its possessor, this old man, shrunken and hideous
in his frame of abject poverty, his arms drawn close up to his
fallen body, worked sedulously on and on. And behind and
around him showed the fruit of his labours. Pinned to the scaling
walls, propped on the ramshackle shelf above his fireless hearth-
stone, and even against the stale remnant of a loaf of bread on the
cracked blue dish beside him, was a litter of pictures. And everywhere, lovely and marvellous in all its guises—the tree. The tree
in May's showering loveliness, in summer's quiet wonder, in
autumn's decline, in naked slumbering wintry grace. The colours
glowed from the fine old rough paper like lamps and gems.

There were drawings of birds too, birds of dazzling plumage,
of flowers and butterflies, their crimson and emerald, rose and
saffron seemingly shimmering and astir; their every mealy and
feathery and pollened boss and petal and plume on fire with
hoarded life and beauty. And there a viper with its sinuous molten scales; and there a face and a shape looking out of its nothingness such as would awake even a dreamer in a dream.

Only three sounds in that night-quiet, and these scarcely discernible, stirred in the watcher's ear: the faint shrill sing-song of
the flame of the lamp, the harsh wheezy breath of the artist, and
a faint scuttling as of rats or mice. This austere and dying creature
must have come in at last from the world of nature and mankind
a long time ago. The arm that had given the tree its quietus had
now not the strength to lift an axe. Yet the ungainly fingers toiled
assiduously on.

The Fruit Merchant, spying in on the old half-starved being
that sat there, burning swiftly away among his insane gewgaws,
as nearly broke out crying as laughing. He was frightened and
elated; mute and bursting with words. The act of God! Rather
than even remotely resemble that old scarecrow in his second
childhood pushing that tiny-bladed knife across the surface of a

flat of wood, he would— An empty and desolate look stole into
the gazing eye.

Not that he professed to understand. He knew nothing. His
head was completely empty. The last shred of rage and vindictiveness had vanished away. He was glad he had come, for now he
was going back. What little of the present and future remained
would soon be the past. He, too, was ageing. *His* life also was
coming to an end. He stared on—oh, yes. And not even a nephew
to inherit his snug fat little fortune. Worldly goods, shipload on
shipload—well, since he could not take them away with him, he
would leave them behind. He would bequeath them to charity, to
the W.F.M.P.A. perhaps; and he would make a note of the hundred pounds.

Not in malice; only to leave things business-like and in order;
to do your duty by a greedy and ungrateful world even though
you were soon to be washing your hands of that, too. All waste,
nothing but waste. But he thanked the Lord he had kept his sanity, that he was respected; that he wasn't in the artificial-fruit
trade—the stuff your grandmother belled under glass. He thanked
the Lord he wasn't foul to look at; foul probably to smell; and a
poison even to think about.

Yet still he peeped on—this old Tom, though at no Lady Go-
diva. "They" would buy right enough—there was no doubt of
that. Christie's would some day be humming with the things. He
didn't deny the old lunatic that. He knew a bird when he saw it—
even on paper. Ninety-seven guineas: at that rate there was more
money swimming about in this pestilent hovel than ever even he
himself could lay his practised hands on.

And there were fools in plenty—rich, dabbling, affected, silly
fools—dillytanties, you called 'em—who would never know that
their lying, preposterous P. P. had destroyed the very life of the
tree that had given its all for him. And why? And why? The
Fruit Merchant was almost tempted to burn down the miserable
cabin over his half-brother's head. Who could tell? . . . A gust
of wind stirred in the bedraggled thatch, feebly whined in the
keyhole.

And at that moment, as if an angry and helpless thought could
make itself audible even above the hungry racketing of mice and

the melancholic whistling of a paraffin lamp—at that moment the corpse-like countenance, almost within finger-touch on the other side of the table, slowly raised itself from the labour of its regard, and appeared to be searching through the shutter's cranny as if into the Fruit Merchant's brain. The glance swept through him like an avalanche. No, no. But one instantaneous confrontation, and he had pushed himself back from the impious walls as softly as an immense sack of hay.

These were not eyes—in that abominable countenance. Speck-pupilled, greenish-grey, unfocused, under their protuberant mat of eyebrow, they remained still as a salt and stagnant sea. And in their uplifted depths, stretching out into endless distances, the Fruit Merchant had seen regions of a country whence neither for love nor money he could ever harvest one fruit, one pip, one cankered bud. And blossoming there beside a glassy stream in the mid-distance of far-mountained sward—a tree. . . .

In after-years an old, fat, vulgar, and bronchitic figure, muffled up in a pathetic shawl, would sometimes be seen seated in a place of honour, its hard square hat upon its thick bald skull, within positive reach of the jovial auctioneer's ivory hammer. To purchase every "P. P." that came into the market was a dream beyond even a multi-millionaire's avarice. But small beetles or grubs or single feathers drawn "from the life" were within scope of the Fruit Merchant's purse. The eye that showed not the faintest vestige of reflected glory from the orange of the orange, the gamboge of the lemon, or the russet bronze of the pomegranate—in their crated myriads—would fitfully light up awhile as one by one, and with reiterated grunts of satisfaction, he afterwards in the secrecy of his home consigned these indifferent and "early" works of art to the flames.

But since his medical man has warned him that any manifestation of passion would almost unquestionably prove his ultimate manifestation of anything, he steadily avoided thinking of the tree. Yet there it remained, unexorcizable, ineradicable, in his fading imagination.

Indeed, he finally expired in the small hours one black winter's morning, and as peacefully as a child, having dreamed that he was looking through a crevice into what could not be hell, but might be limbo or purgatory, the place of departed spirits. For there sat his half-brother, quite, quite still. And all around him, to be seen, haunted gay and painted birds and crystal flowers and damasked butterflies; and, as it were, sylphs and salamanders, shapes of an unearthly beauty. And all of them strangely, preternaturally still, as if in a peepshow, as if stuffed.

The Riddle and Other Stories (1923)

AN IDEAL CRAFTSMAN

Away into secrecy frisked a pampered mouse. A scuffling of bedclothes, the squeak of a dry castor followed, and then suddenly the boy sat up and set to piecing together reality with scraps of terrifying but half-forgotten dreams.

It was his ears had summoned him, they were still ringing with an obscure message, a faint *Qui vive?* But as he sat blinking and listening in the empty dark he could not satisfy himself what sound it was that had actually awakened him. Was it only a dying howl from out of one of his usual nightmares, or had some actual noise or cry sounded up from the vacancy of the house beneath? It was this uncertainty—as if his brain were a piece of mechanism wound up by sleep—that set working a vivid panorama of memories in the little theatre of his mind—cloaked men huddled together in some dark corner of the night, scoundrels plotting in the wind, the pause between rifle-click and the loose fall, finally to culminate in the adventure of glorious memory—raiding Jacobs.

He groped under his pillow for the treasures he had concealed there before blowing out his candle—a box of matches, a crumbling slice of piecrust, and a dingy volume of the *Newgate Calendar*. The last usually lay behind the draughty chimney of his fireplace, because Jacobs had the habits of a ferret and nothing was safe from his nosings. He struck a match soundlessly on the edge of his mattress. Its flare lit up his lank-haired head, his sharp face and dazzled eyes. Then the flame drooped, went out. But he had had time to find the broad glossy belt he had cut out of a strip of mottled American cloth and the old sheathed poniard which he had months ago abstracted from his father's study. He buckled on the belt round his body in the dark over his nightshirt and dangled the rusty blood- (or water-) stained poniard coldly on his hip. He pulled on his stockings, tilted an old yachting cap over his eyes, and was fully equipped.

In this feverish haste he had had little time to ponder strategy. But now he sat down again on the edge of his bed, and though he was pretending to think, his brows wrinkled in a frown, he was actually listening. Even the stairs had ceased to creak. And the star that from a wraith of cloud glittered coldly in the night-sky beyond the rift between his curtains made no sound. He drew open his door, inch by inch, still intent, then stepped out on to the landing.

The first danger to be encountered on the staircase below was his father's bedroom. Its door gaped half-open, but was it empty? It was here on this very spot, he remembered with a qualm, that Jacobs had once leapt out on him. He saw in memory that agile shape stepping hastily and oddly in the dusk, furious at sight of the eavesdropper. And in an instant the tiny blue bead of gas on the landing had expanded into a white fan-shaped glare. Not so to-night. With a gasp and an oblique glance at the dusky bed and the spectral pendent clothes within, he slid by in safety on his stockinged feet, and so past yet another door—but this one tight shut, with its flower-painted panels—the door of his mother's gay little sitting-room, his real mother's, not the powdery eyebrowed stepmother who a few hours before had set out with his father, on pleasure bent.

A few paces beyond he trod even more cautiously, for here was a loose board. At the last loop of the staircase Jacobs's customary humming should issue up out of the gloom beneath—the faint tune which he rasped on and on and on, faint and shrill between his teeth, superciliously, ironically, in greasy good-humour or sly facetiousness—he would hum it in his coffin perhaps. But no, not a sound. The raider hesitated. What next? Where now? He listened in vain.

And then, he suddenly remembered that this was "silver" night. And doubtless—cook and housemaid long since snoring in their attic—a white glittering array of forks and spoons, soup ladles, and candlesticks were at this very moment spread out in be-daubed splendour before the aproned tyrant. For Jacobs was not only queer in his habits and nocturnal by nature but a glutton for work. But if it was silver night, why this prodigious hush? No clang of fork ringing against its neighbour; not a single rattle of whitening brush on metal reached his ears.

Slim as a ferret himself, he hung over the loop in the staircase as he might have hung over the Valley of Death; but still all was strangely quiet. And so, with a pang of disappointment, and at the same moment with a crow of relief, the boy came to the con-clusion that Jacobs was out. And not for the first time either. He must have had a visitor—the woman in the black bonnet, with the silver locket dangling on her front, perhaps. As likely as not they had gone off gallivanting together, and would reappear about eleven o'clock, Jacobs either swearing and quarrelsome or amiably garrulous.

But the boy was no fool. In spite of this sinister hush in the house—as if its walls were draped with the very darkness of night —Jacobs *might* perhaps be busy over his silver. Shammy, how-ever hard you rub with it, makes little sound. And if he were, then too much confidence would mean not only a sudden pursuit, a heart-daunting scuttle up the stairs, and Jacobs with his cane cutting at his legs from behind, but the failure of his raid alto-gether. Nothing then but a bit of stale piecrust for his midnight feast. So he trod on velvet down the stairs, his damp palm shun-ning the banister (*that* squeak would wake an army!), his lips dry and his tongue rolling in luxury of anticipation. And soon he was in the hall, with all the empty rooms of the house above his head, and minified in his own imagination to a mere atom of whiteness in the dusk, a mouse within smell of the cat. His rusty poniard clutched tight between his fingers, his stomach full of fear and his heart noisy as a cockcrow, he pushed on.

The staircase ran widely and shallowly into the hall; there was more light here, a thin faint glow of gas-light, turned low. He could distinguish the dark shapes of the heavy furniture, as he stalked on through this luminous twilight. But the back passage to the kitchen quarters was hidden from elegant visitors by a muffled door with a spring, which Jacobs, when it suited him, kept propped wide open. This passage, if followed to the end, turned abruptly at right angles; and at the inner angle near the fusty entry to the cellars he paused to breathe and then to listen again. Once round the corner, along the passage in front of him the kitchen door would come into view, ajar or wide open, on the right; and the larder itself a few paces further on, and exactly opposite the raider. But before reaching it, the boot cupboard, sour den of long-legged spiders and worse abominations, must be passed, and the window with the panes of coloured glass, looking out on a monstrous red, yellow, or blue garden of trees and stars.

The boy's lean dark face had in his progress become paler and leaner. His legs were now the skinny playthings of autumnal draughts, and at this moment a sound *had* actually reached his ears—the sound as of a lion panting over a meal. A sort of persistent half-choked snuffling. This was odd. This was surprising. Even when, with sleeves turned up and sharp elbows bared, Jacobs was engrossed in any job, he never breathed like that. In general, indeed, he scarcely seemed to be breathing at all; when, for example, he stooped down close handing a dish of cabbage or blancmange at the Sunday dinner table of a taciturn father. *This* breathing was husky and unequal, almost like a snore through nostrils and mouth. Jacobs must be drunk, then; and that would mean either a sort of morose good-humour, or a sullen, drowsy malice, as dangerous as it was sly. The adventure was losing its edge. Even the hunger for romance in the boy's Scots-French blood died down within him at recollection of the dull, dull-lidded eyes of Jacobs half drunk.

There came a sudden *crkkk* and the squeak as of a boot. The boy bit hard on his lip. Yet another slow sliding step forward; the kitchen door *was* ajar. A spear of yellow light warned the intruder. But light—spear or no spear—was as vitalizing as a sip of wine. Red-capped, pock-marked faces, all sorts and conditions of criminals, buccaneers, and highwaymen, gore and glory, flocked back again into the boy's fancy. An icy delicious shiver ran down his spine, for now Jacobs, tied with a tape round the middle, in his green baize apron, must be sitting at not much more than arm's length from the door. Or if not, who?

Inch by inch, courage restored, he slid on soundlessly, his stockinged foot first pushing forward into the light, then the white edge of his nightshirt. He pressed skin-close to the further side of the passage, and was actually half past the door ajar, when through a narrow chink he glanced into the kitchen, and so— suddenly found himself squinting full into the eyes of the fat woman in the black bonnet. Crouching a little, stiff and motionless, her eyes bolting out of her face, she stood there full in the light of the gas jet over her head, the faded brown hair that showed beneath her bonnet wreathing it as if with a nimbus. The boy stood frozen.

Not for an instant did he imagine he could be invisible to such a stare as that, to eyes which, though they were small and dark, showed as round and shining as the silver locket that rose and fell jerkily upon her chest. His mouth opened—mute as a fish; every sinew in his body stiffened in readiness for flight. But the woman never so much as stirred. Every fibre and muscle in *her* body was at stretch to aid her ears. It looked as if she might be able to hear even his thoughts moving. So would a she-wolf stand at gaze under a white moon, with those unstirring eyes; famished and gaunt. And yet, what in the world was there for *her* to be afraid of? If anybody else was there she would have spoken. She was alone, then? His fingers suddenly relaxed, the scabbard of his poniard rattled against the wall behind him, and there slipped off his tongue the most unlikely question that would ever else have come into his mind. "I say; where's Jacobs?"

The lids over the little black eyes fluttered and the woman's lips opened in a squawk. Her two rough red hands were suddenly clapped on either side of her mouth. For a moment he thought she was going to scream again, and was thankful when only a shuddering sob followed. "Oh, sir, how you did startle me. Mr.

Jacobs, sir, why just as you was coming—he's gone, sir; he's gone."

The boy pushed open the door and stood on the threshold. He had supposed it impossible that so stout a woman could speak in so small a voice. Sheer curiosity had banished all alarm. Besides, if Jacobs was out, there was no immediate danger. He looked about him, conscious that he was being closely watched from between those square red fingers, and that the forehead above them was deeply wrinkled, almost as if the woman were helpless with laughter.

"Why, lor," she was muttering as if to herself, "it's only the little boy. My! I thought he was his pa, I did; God bless him. He's come down for a drink of water. That's what he wants. And all in his pretty nightgown too."

Tears were now gushing down her round cheeks and gurgling in her voice. She walked in angles to a chair and sat there rocking her body to and fro and smiling at him—an odd contorted smile of blandishment and stupidity sicklied over with fear. He blushed, and stared back at her as hot and angry as when in days gone by bent-up wrinkled old ladies used to stop his nurse in the street to ask questions about him, and had even openly kissed him.

This end to his adventure, which seemed to be leading him into difficulties he had never dreamed of, was a bitter disappointment. A drink of water! He resented the presence of this fat woman in the kitchen. He resented even more his own embarrassment. He wriggled under his nightshirt, and was profoundly relieved when those flabby florid cheeks suddenly faded to a mottled mauve, the rocking ceased, and two heavy eyelids slowly descended upon the small black terrified eyes. Even if she *were* going to faint, she would at any rate have to stop staring.

But his troubles were only begun; ugly grunts were proceeding from that open mouth, and the woman's head was twitching oddly. Still, he had had experiences of this kind before. He knew what was to be done, and a scientific callousness gave his remedy zest. On the kitchen table besides some empty bottles of beer and a decanter stood a tumbler half full of water. This he liberally sprinkled on the woman's face and trickled a few drops, not without waste, between her teeth. Grunts expostulated, and the silver locket almost danced. She was coming to. Success stimulated him to fresh efforts; he snatched a scrap of brown paper from among the spoons and climbing up on to a chair lit it at the gas, and thrust it under her nose. It was enough. Such a smother would have stupefied an apiary.

But though the cure was now complete, and worthy of being proudly recorded, one pretty keepsake had been degraded for ever —the memory of his mother, lying on a sofa, and two blue eyes like dawn shining up amid the dewdrops sprinkling her fair cheeks. This fat stranger's petticoat was of coarse red dingy flannel. She was clammy and stupid and ridiculous. Nevertheless, the absurd fear of him or whatever it might be that had brought her to this pass seemed for the moment to be clean forgotten. For when her dazed eyes rolled down from under their lids again and looked out at him, precisely the same expression had come into her face as he had seen on it when he had watched her smiling mawkishly at Jacobs himself.

"Are you better now?" he asked coldly, flourishing the smouldering paper.

The woman smiled again, and nodded.

"I'm afraid I may have burnt you. But there's no other way, you see, though the smell's pretty beastly." The woman went on vacantly smiling. Not that this stupid wrinkling up of her mouth and cheeks seemed to mean anything. She might have been made of wax. Further parleying, he decided, would be wasted.

"You needn't mention it to Jacobs, you know," he began. "*I* shan't say anything. You see, I just happened to notice you through the door. I think I'll be going back now. Jacobs is a bit of a . . ." Nothing very conciliatory could come after that "bit." At all events he decided to keep back the word that had so nearly slipped out. The silver locket began to jolt again, and clumsy fingers fumbled at it. The smile was beginning to crystallize into the familiar wrinkled stare.

"You *look* better, *much* better," said the boy uneasily, edging towards the door. "I remember once my mother . . ." But his tongue refused for shame to say what he remembered. Also he found it difficult to turn his back on the woman, though when at last he reached the door he whipped round quickly.

"Little boy," called the woman in a fulsome voice, "come back! I say!—little *boy!*"

He frowned. Her eyes were now searching his face intently and suspiciously. She had begun to think again. And at sight of their hostility his own underlip drooped into a sullen obstinacy. He didn't mind *her.* If she decided to sneak to Jacobs, that was her look-out: meanwhile he could easily manage her alone.

"What?" he said.

"I was took ill, wasn't I? The heat's something awful. *Phh!* But there isn't any need to stare, little boy. I shan't eat you." Cunning peeped out of the unctuous face, and he merely waited for the trap. "Not me; and what a pretty belt he's got on," she continued, rolling her dingy handkerchief into a ball; "and ain't he got a nice new dagger!"

But even such flatteries as these produced no response. The dagger wasn't new, and the belt was not meant to be pretty. "I must be going now, thank you," he repeated. "Besides, I suppose he'll be back in a minute?"

Her hands stayed motionless, her head had suddenly jerked a little sideways like a thrush's intent on the stirrings of a worm.

"Going," she repeated; "why, of course, he must be going, poor lamb: he'll get his death of cold. And wasn't he *good* to me; *good* to me he was. And that clever! You'd have thought he was a doctor!"

Her glance meanwhile was roving in confusion into every corner of the room as though she were looking for something, and was afraid of what she might find. He could hardly keep his own from following them. "That kind and gentle he was! Just like a doctor he was!" And again a menacing silence swallowed up her words. The boy's face reflected a distrust deepening into hostility. Was the whole thing a cheat then? Was Jacobs as usual playing the sneak? Would he suddenly leap out on him? In any case he knew he was only being cajoled, if not ridiculed.

"There, now!" she suddenly broke out, "if he isn't *thinking* again. That's what he's doing. He's thinking about what I was saying to meself when that funny dream came over me. That's what he's doing. And why not, I should like to know. Eh?" She shot him a searching, ogling glance.

"I didn't notice," he answered. "Your *eyes* looked rather queer, with the whites gone up, and your skin twitched just as if the water burnt it. But *I* didn't mind."

"How long was you there, then? Tell me that?" Her nails were now gripped uncomfortably sharp on his arm. "You stand there frowning and sulking, my young soldier. And by what rights, may I ask? Just you tell me how long you was there!" Her face had grown hard and dangerous, but he shut his mouth tight and returned sullenly stare for stare. "So help me," she half whispered, releasing him, "now I've been and frightened him again. That's it. He thinks I'm angry with him. Lord love you, my precious, I didn't mean anything like that. Not me. P'raps you just came down for a bit of fun, eh?"

She fixed her eyes on the dagger, and shuddered. "What was I saying? Ah, yes. How long—*how long* was—you—there?" She stamped her foot. "That's right, saucer-eyes, stare, stare! Didn't I *say* I'm old and ugly! Ain't *he* said it too? Oh, oh, oh! What shall I do, what shall I do?" She hid her face in her hands and her tears gushed out anew.

The boy stood stiffly at her side. This unexpected capitulation unnerved him, and his heart began to heave menacingly.

"I'm sorry; but I must go now," he repeated, trying with as little obvious aversion as possible to drag his hand from her hot wet cheek. "And I don't see what good crying will do." As if by magic the snuffling ceased.

"Good! Who said, what good? It's *me* who must be going, my young man, and don't you make any mistake about *that!*" She shook out her skirts, and searched in vain for the bonnet on her head. He nearly laughed out, so absurd was the attempt—for the bunched-up old thing was dangling by its strings behind her back. But this retrieved, she drew it on, pushing under it wisps of her iron-grey hair. Then she opened a fat leather purse, stuffed with keys and dirty crumpled papers.

"Now what have I got here?" she began wheedlingly, as she pushed about with her finger and took out a sixpence. "What have I got here? Why, a silver sixpence. And who's that for? Why, for any nice little boy what won't spy and pry. That's what that's for." She stooped nearly double, holding it out to him with bolting eyes in her purpled face. "What? He won't take it? Shakes his head? Too proud to take it. Oh, very well, very well."

She opened her purse again and with shaking fingers pushed the sixpence back. She was not crying now, but her face had gone a deathly grey, and a blank, dreadful misery had crept into it. This woman was a very strange woman. He had never met any-one who behaved in such a queer way. He watched her as she went waddling off out of the kitchen and over the stone floor into the darkness beyond. Her footsteps ceased to sound. She was gone, then? And she must have left the garden door open behind her; the wind was bellying in his nightshirt and icy under his arms. Here was the cat come in, too, rolling in its sodden fur on the oilcloth at his feet. "Puss, Puss," he said. Where had *he* been to get in such a state? The boy stood dismayed and discomfited, while the cat rubbed its body and its purring jaws against his stockinged legs.

A stark unstirring silence had spread into the kitchen, though the gas was faintly singing—high and from very far away. And, as if to attract his attention, a wisp of hair was patting his fore-head under his ridiculous cap-brim. The silence entangled his thoughts in a medley of absurd misgivings productive only of chicken-skin and perplexity. Something had gone wrong—the house was changed; and he didn't know how or why. He glanced up at the clock, which thereupon at once began to tick. His eyes dodged from side to side of the familiar kitchen and then it was as if a stealthy warning finger had been laid upon his thoughts, and chaos became unity.

His roving glance had fallen on the cupboard door. For there in the crack at the bottom of it, shut in and moving softly in the wind, showed a corner of green baize. Jacobs was there, then; bunched up there, then: smiling to himself and waiting and lis-tening in there, then? The boy stood appalled, his bright black eyes fixed on this flapping scrap of green baize apron. The whole thing *was* a trap! And yet, as he tried hard to keep his wits, he had known instantly there was something wrong—something he couldn't understand. That was just like one of Jacobs's jokes!— jokes that usually had so violent and humourless an ending. And yet . . . Suddenly the hinges of the outer door had whinnied; he jerked round his head in alarm. It was the woman again. She had come back. Bead-bright raindrops glittered on the black of her jacket, on her bonnet, in her hair. That rigid awful stare of horror had come back into her face. He could move neither hand nor foot; could only stare at her.

"Eh, eh, now!" she was choking out at him. "So you've *seen* now, my fine young gentleman, have you? That's what you've done. Then what do *I* say; *me!* Keep a civil tongue in your head, that's what *I* say. And tell me this—" The face thrust so close down to his had grown enormous and unspeakably dreadful. Her hot breath enveloped him. "Where's the gate? Where's the gate, I say? I got lost there among them bushes. I can't get out. D'ye see? I've lost the gate. It's dark. It's come on raining. Where's the *gate?*"

Tiny beads of blood stood on her skin—she must have stumbled into the holly hedge at the foot of the garden by the cucumber frames. She smelt not only of her old clothes but of the night and the rain. And still he made no answer. He had been driven back by that awful and congealed look on her face—beyond fear. He was merely waiting—to find *his* way: this mystery, this horror.

"Eh, now"; she had turned away, her heavy head crooked down over one shoulder, and was speaking this time to herself: "quiet and silly, that's what *he* is. Nothing much anybody could get out of *him*. But see you here!" She had twisted round. "It's no good you playing the young innocent with me. You've seen and you know. That's what you've done. And you just tell me this. How *could* I have done it? how *should* I have done it? That's what I'm asking. Just you tell me that. Haven't I come of honest people? And didn't he promise me and promise me? And nothing but lies. And then, 'You ain't the first,' he says. And me as I am! 'You ain't the first,' he says. Ay, and meant it. 'What, what!' I says. And then he hit me—here, with his clenched-up fist, *here*. 'I shan't leave you,' I said, 'and you can't make me.' And all I wanted was just to keep body and soul together. 'And you can't make me,' that's what I said. 'That's all,' I said. And then he laughed. 'You ain't the first,' he says, laughing. And me as I am! . . . Oh, my God, he *won't* understand. Listen, little boy. I didn't know what I was doing; everything went black and I couldn't

see. And I put out my hands—to push him off, and my fingers
went stiff and a smudge of red came over my eyes, and next thing
he fell down like a bundle, and wouldn't speak, wouldn't speak.
Mind you, I say *this,* if I hadn't drunk the beer, if I hadn't drunk
the beer, if I hadn't—done—that . . ." She faltered, her face went
blank as she swayed.

Her listener was struggling hard to understand. These broken
words told him little that was clear and definite, and yet were
brimming over with sinister incomprehensible meanings. He
frowned at the contorted, dark-red moving face and loose lips.
One fact and one fact alone was plain. He had nothing to fear
from Jacobs. Jacobs was not going to pounce out on him. Simply
because Jacobs was gone. Then why . . . ? He twisted about,
and kneeling down on the floor by the cupboard beside the cooling kitchen range—with scarcely a glint of drowsy red now in its
ashy coals—he struggled with the metal tongue that held back the
door. Usually loose, it now turned stiffly and hurt his fingers.
Then suddenly it gave way.

And the boy's first quick thought was: Why, he's quite a little
man! And the next was one of supreme relief that all this wild
meaningless talk was now over. He leaned forward and peered
into the puckered-up clay-coloured face, with its blackened lips
and leaden-lidded eyes. The chin was dinted in with the claw
pin in the cravat. A gallipot stood near—a trap for crickets—
touching one limp hand, still smeared with pink plate powder.
The door-tongue was stiff, the boy supposed, because the corner
of the baize apron had got stuck to the varnish of the frame.
You'd have hardly thought, though, there'd be room in the cupboard. But the important thing, the illuminating, inspiring, and
yet startlingly familiar thing was the gallipot!

It had touched a spring, it had released a shutter in his mind
and set his thoughts winging back to a sooty, draughty chimney
where only a few minutes ago—minutes as vast and dark and
empty as the sea—he had hidden a book with a wedge of piecrust
on top of it. In that book he had read of just such a gallipot as this
—but not as a trap for crickets—a gallipot with a handful of spade
guineas in it, which had belonged to an old man who had been
brutally strangled in the small hours by his two nephews. They

had never been caught either; nobody had even suspected them. They had planned a means of escape—so vile and fantastic that even to watch them at it had made his skin deliciously creep upon him and his hair stir on his head. But it had succeeded, it had *worked*. To the dead old man's four-poster bed they had strung up the body of their victim, and until one of them, on his death-bed, had made confession, the old man's bones had lain beneath the tramplings of the cross-roads. For everybody, even his own relatives, believed that he had hanged himself. This evilly romantic picture had flamed up with an ominous glow in the boy's imagination as he stood there contemplating his quiet enemy. The woman had become utterly unimportant. She was standing by the table, twisting, now up, now down, her dark-green bonnet-strings.

"How did you do it?" said the boy, looking up and leaning back with a shuddering sigh upon his heels. "How on earth? Did he struggle? He couldn't have struggled *much,* I suppose. He's so small. He *looks* so small."

The questions were unanswered and were unrepeated. He was merely drinking the scene in. That mole upon the bluish close-shaven cheek was certainly grown blacker than it had been in life, more conspicuous.

"But you aren't of course going to leave him like this?" he broke out sharply. "You can't, you know; you simply can't." But the woman was paying him no attention. "Don't you *see?* They'd find it out in no time," he added petulantly.

Yet even in the midst of this callous analysis, the woman's childlike attitude attracted his sympathy. At sight of the mute, huddled contents of the cupboard, she seemed to have forgotten the danger she was in. A vacant immeasurable mournfulness quietened her face. She was crying. "I'm sorry, but it's no good crying," he went on, still kneeling on the cold oilcloth. *"That* won't be of any help; and I'd be awfully pleased to help you all I *can*. As a matter of fact I didn't much care for old Jacobs myself. But then, he's dead now. He *is* dead?"

The woman smothered his momentary fear with an eye-shot of horror. "Well, if he is, I can't see why you shouldn't say so." She remained motionless. "Oh, dear," he muttered impatiently, "don't you under*stand*? We *must* do *something*." A heavy frown had settled under the streak of dark hair on his forehead. "You wouldn't stand the ghost of a chance as it is. They'd catch you easy."

The woman nodded. "I don't care; I hope they will. I don't care *what* happens now—because I can't think."

"That's all rot," said the boy stoutly. "You've got to."

The woman was irritating and paradoxical in this mood, and more than ever like a senseless wax model, which, with diabolical tremors, moves its glazed eyes and turns a glossy head. He peered again into the cupboard. Only once before had he seen Jacobs asleep—stretched out on a sofa in the dining-room one sultry afternoon in the streaming sunshine—gaping, sonorous. Then he had gone out as he had come in, on tiptoe. Now he stooped a little closer towards the cupboard, examining what was in it, stretching out even an experimental finger towards the small pallid hand.

He compared the woman's face and this other face, and found a fancy strangely contradictory of the facts. Jacobs was really and truly the man of blood; Jacobs was just the kind of person you'd expect to be a murderer. Not this woman, so fat and stupid. Nobody would be surprised to find *her* body in any cupboard. But Jacobs, small and ferrety, softly rasping his tune between his teeth, on and on! And now Jacobs was dead. So that's what *that* was like. He jerked his head aside, and his eyes became fixed once more on the gallipot. *That* was the real and eloquent thing. His mind had completed its circuit. He stood up convinced.

"It's no good going on like this," he explained lucidly, almost cheerfully. "This would be the very first place they would look into. I should look in here myself. But don't you see, you needn't be caught at all if you do what I tell you. It's something I read in a book of mine."

The woman lifted a mechanical head and looked at him; and as if for the first time. She saw—a meagre boy with linnet legs and narrow shoulders, a lean clean-cut face of a rather bilious brown, and straight dark brown hair beneath a yachting cap; a boy in black stockings, a nightshirt, and a shiny belt; his dark eyes, narrowed and intent, set steep in his head. This boy frightened her. She pushed on her bonnet and loosened her dress about her throat.

Manifestly she was preparing to go. He spoke more decisively. "You don't *see*. That's all," he said. "Really, on my word of honour, it would be all right. I'm not just saying so. A baby could do it."

The woman knelt down beside him in a posture not unlike the inmate's of the cupboard, and solemnly stared into his face. "Tell me, tell me quick, you silly lamb. *What* did you say? A *baby* could do it?"

"Why, yes," said the boy, outwardly cool, but inwardly ardent, "it's as easy as A B C. You get a rope and make a noose, and you put it over his head and round his neck, you know, just as if he were going to be hanged. And then you hang him up on a nail or something. He mustn't touch the ground, of course. You throttled him, didn't you? You see there's no blood. They'll say he hanged himself, don't you see? They'd find old Jacobs strung up in the kitchen here and they'll say he's hanged himself. Don't you *see*?" he repeated.

"Oh, I couldn't do it," she whimpered, "not for worlds. I couldn't. I'd sooner stay here beside him till they come." She began to sob in a stupid vacant fashion, and then suddenly hiccuped.

"You could, I tell you. A baby could do it. You're afraid. That's what it is! I'm going to, I tell you, whether you like it or not." He stamped his stockinged foot. "Mind you, I'm not doing it for myself. It's nothing to do with me. You aren't taking the least trouble to understand." He looked at her as if he couldn't believe any human being could by any possibility be so dense. "It's just stupid," he added over his shoulder, as he sallied out to the boot cupboard to fetch a rope.

Once more the tide of consciousness flowed in the woman's stolid, flattened brain. Two or three words of this young hero had at last fallen on good ground. And with consciousness, fear had come back. She came waddling after the boy. The vagrant crawling inmates of the cupboard had been swept carelessly from the corner, and now he was trailing a rope behind him as he went on into the larder for brandy. His match died down meanwhile, scorching his fingers, and he stayed on in the dark, the woman close behind him, rummaging gingerly among the bottles and dishes. And soon his fingertips touched the sharp-cut stopper. He returned triumphant, flipping from them the custard they had encountered in their search. The woman followed close behind him, stumbling ever and again upon his trailing rope, and thereby adding to her fears and docility. She was coming alive again. Brandy set her tongue gabbling faster. It gave the boy the strength and zeal of a stage villain.

He skipped hither and thither, now on to, now off the kitchen chair he had pushed nearer; then—having swept back the array of pink-smeared silver candlesticks and snuffers that were in his way, he scrambled up on to the table, and presently, after a few lasso-like flings of it, he had run the rope and made it fast over one of a few large hooks that curved down from the ceiling, hooks once used, as Jacobs had told him, to hang up hams on. His mouth was set, his face intent; his soldier grandfather's lower lip drawn in under the upper. The more active he was, the more completely he became master of the ceremonies, the woman only an insignificant accomplice, as stupid as she was irresponsible. Even while she helped him drag out the body from the cupboard on to the flat arena of oilcloth, she continued to cry and snivel, as if *that* would be of any help. But a keen impassive will compelled her obedience. She followed the boy's every nod.

And presently she almost forgot the horror of the task, and found a partial oblivion in the intensity of it, though the boy was displeased by her maunderings. They were merely a doleful refrain to his troublesome grisly work. But he uttered no open reproof—not even when she buried her face in the baize apron and embraced the knees of the dead man. Only once she made any complaint against the limp heedless hung-up creature. "If only," she assured her young accomplice, "if only he hadn't gone and *said* as how I wasn't the first. I ask you! As if I didn't know it." But to this he paid no attention.

And now, at last, he drew back to view his handiwork. This he did with an inscrutable face, a face flattered at his own extraordinary ingenuity, a young face, almost angelic in its rapt gaslit look and yet one, maybe, of unsophisticated infamy. The dwarfish body seemed to be dangling naturally enough from its hook in the ceiling, its heels just free of the chair. And it did to some extent resemble the half-sinister, half-jocular cut that adorned his *Calendar*. Yet somehow he wasn't perfectly satisfied. Somehow the consummation was as yet incomplete. Some one thing was wanting, some blemish spoiled the effect and robbed it of unity. What? He stood hunting for it without success.

He followed the woman into the passage. She walked unsteadily, swaying bulkily to and fro, now and again violently colliding with the wall. "Oh, it was crule, crule," she was muttering.

After her stalked the boy, deep in thought. When she stopped, he stopped; when once more she set forward, as patiently he too set forward with her. Which of them was led, and which leader, it would be difficult to say. This dogged search after the one thing wanting continued to perplex and evade him. He decided that it was no good trying. It must be looked to when the woman was gone; when he was alone.

"I think you had better go now," he said. "He'll be coming home soon—my father, I mean, and . . . It's just ten to twelve by Jacobs's clock." The words conjured up in his mind a vision of his handsome dressed-up stepmother, standing there in the kitchen doorway half-hysterical before her swaying manservant. It faintly, and even a little sadly, tickled his fancy.

He opened the front door. It was still raining, and the smell of the damp earth and ivy leaves came washing into the house. The woman squatted down on the doorstep. "Where shall I go?" she said. "Where shall I go? What's the use? There ain't *no*where." The boy scowled at the dripping trees. The house was surrounded by night—empty and silent but for the smothering soft small whisper of the rain, and the flat *drip, drip* of the drops from the porch.

"What's the use? There ain't *no*where," again wailed his poor bedraggled confederate. He scrutinized her scornfully from under his tilted yachting cap. "Wait a minute," he said. He raced at full speed up the three dark flights of stairs to his bedroom. The book, the mouse-nibbled piecrust were tossed on to the hearth-rug and a florin was dug out of the gritty soot. Down he came again pell-mell.

Like a cat venturing into a busy street, the woman now stood peering out from the last of the three shallow crescent-shaped stone steps under the porch. "I've brought you this," he said superciliously.

"Thank you, sir," said the woman.

She paused yet again, looking at him, in an attitude now familiar to the boy—the fingers of her knuckled left hand, with its thick brassy wedding-ring, pressed closely against mouth and cheek. He wondered for a moment what she was thinking about, and he was still wondering when she stepped finally off out into the rain.

A shrill shout followed her. "I say! mind that ditch there in the road!" But the only result of this was to bring the woman back again; she knelt and clasped him tightly to her bosom.

"I don't know why or anything. Oh, my lamb, my lamb, I didn't mean to do it and now I haven't got anywhere to go." She bent low and hid her weeping face on his shoulder. "Oh, oh, I miss him so. The Lord God keep you safe! You've been very kind to me. But. . . ."

She released him, and waddled out once more under the flat-spread branches of the cedar tree, while the boy rubbed the smarting tears from his neck. He shut the door indignantly. This tame reaction was mawkish and silly. Then he paused, uncertain what to do next. And suddenly memory rendered up the one thing wanting—the master-touch.

Why, of course, of course! Jacobs must have kicked a chair down. You couldn't hang yourself like that without a drop. It was impossible. The boy's valour, after all, was only a little shaken by the embrace. Into the kitchen he walked victorious. The gas was still singing, as it had sung all the evening, shedding its dismal flaring light on wall and clock and blind and ceiling and wide array of glossy crockery. The puckered clay-coloured face looked stupidly at him with bolting, dull, dull-lidded eyes. What was now to be done must be done quickly. He ducked sharply and upset the chair—a little too sharply, for a light spring-side boot had tapped him on the cheek. He leapt back, hot and panting. The effect was masterly. It was a triumph. He stared, with clenched fists, and whispered over his shoulder to a now absent accomplice. He was alone! Only Jacobs was there—with that drowsy slit of eye—tremulously dangling. And as if, even for him, as if even for *his* clear bold young spirit this last repulsive spectacle were suddenly too much, the martial spirit of his ancestors within him wilted, surrendered, vanished, leaving behind it nothing but a small boy in his nightshirt—the timid half-stifled raider of Jacobs's pantry. The whisper in the dark outside of the uncertain wind, the soft bubbling whistle of the gas, the thousand and one minute dumb things around him in the familiar kitchen —nothing had changed. Yet *now* every object had become suddenly stark, menacing, and hostile. Panic seized him. He ran out to the front door and bawled into the dark after the woman.

No answer came. The rain was falling softly on the sodden turf; and here, beneath the porch, in large ponderous drops. The widespread palms of the cedar tree under the clouded midnight lay prone and motionless. The whole world was gone out—black. Nothing, nothing; he was alone.

He ran back again into the house—as if he had been awakened out of a dream—leaving the door agape behind him, and whimpering "Mother!" Then louder—louder. And all the blind things of the house took wooden voices. So up and down this white-shirted raider ran, his clumsy poniard clapping against sudden corners, his tongue calling in vain, and at last—as he went scuttling upstairs at sound of cab-horse and wheels upon the sodden gravel—falling dumb for very terror of its own noise.

On the Edge (1931)

SEATON'S AUNT

I HAD heard rumours of Seaton's aunt long before I actually encountered her. Seaton, in the hush of confidence, or at any little
show of toleration on our part, would remark, "My aunt," or
"My old aunt, you know," as if his relative might be a kind of
cement to an *entente cordiale.*

He had an unusual quantity of pocket-money; or, at any rate,
it was bestowed on him in unusually large amounts; and he spent
it freely, though none of us would have described him as an "awfully generous chap." "Hullo, Seaton," we would say, "the old
Begum?" At the beginning of term, too, he used to bring back
surprising and exotic dainties in a box with a trick padlock that
accompanied him from his first appearance at Gummidge's in a
billycock hat to the rather abrupt conclusion of his schooldays.

From a boy's point of view he looked distastefully foreign,
with his yellow skin, and slow chocolate-coloured eyes, and lean
weak figure. Merely for his looks he was treated by most of us
true-blue Englishmen with condescension, hostility, or contempt.
We used to call him "Pongo," but without any much better excuse for the nickname than his skin. He was, that is, in one sense
of the term what he assuredly was not in the other sense, a sport.

Seaton and I, as I may say, were never in any sense intimate at
school; our orbits only intersected in class. I kept deliberately
aloof from him. I felt vaguely he was a sneak, and remained quite
unmollified by advances on his side, which, in a boy's barbarous
fashion, unless it suited me to be magnanimous, I haughtily ignored.

We were both of us quick-footed, and at Prisoner's Base used occasionally to hide together. And so I best remember Seaton—his narrow watchful face in the dusk of a summer evening; his peculiar crouch, and his inarticulate whisperings and mumblings. Otherwise he played all games slackly and limply; used to stand and feed at his locker with a crony or two until his "tuck" gave out; or waste his money on some outlandish fancy or other. He bought, for instance, a silver bangle, which he wore above his left elbow, until some of the fellows showed their masterly contempt of the practice by dropping it nearly red-hot down his neck.

It needed, therefore, a rather peculiar taste, a rather rare kind of schoolboy courage and indifference to criticism, to be much associated with him. And I had neither the taste nor, perhaps, the courage. None the less, he did make advances, and on one memorable occasion went to the length of bestowing on me a whole pot of some outlandish mulberry-coloured jelly that had been duplicated in his term's supplies. In the exuberance of my gratitude I promised to spend the next half-term holiday with him at his aunt's house.

I had clean forgotten my promise when, two or three days before the holiday, he came up and triumphantly reminded me of it.

"Well, to tell you the honest truth, Seaton, old chap—" I began graciously: but he cut me short.

"My aunt expects you," he said; "she is very glad you are coming. She's sure to be quite decent to *you*, Withers."

I looked at him in sheer astonishment; the emphasis was so uncalled for. It seemed to suggest an aunt not hitherto hinted at, and a friendly feeling on Seaton's side that was far more disconcerting than welcome.

We reached his home partly by train, partly by a lift in an empty farm-cart, and partly by walking. It was a whole-day holiday, and we were to sleep the night; he lent me extraordinary night-gear, I remember. The village street was unusually wide, and was fed from a green by two converging roads, with an inn, and a high green sign at the corner. About a hundred yards down the street was a chemist's shop—a Mr. Tanner's. We descended the two steps into his dusky and odorous interior to buy,

I remember, some rat poison. A little beyond the chemist's was the forge. You then walked along a very narrow path, under a fairly high wall, nodding here and there with weeds and tufts of grass, and so came to the iron garden-gates, and saw the high flat house behind its huge sycamore. A coach-house stood on the left of the house, and on the right a gate led into a kind of rambling orchard. The lawn lay away over to the left again, and at the bottom (for the whole garden sloped gently to a sluggish and rushy pond-like stream) was a meadow.

We arrived at noon, and entered the gates out of the hot dust beneath the glitter of the dark-curtained windows. Seaton led me at once through the little garden-gate to show me his tadpole pond, swarming with what (being myself not in the least interested in low life) I considered the most horrible creatures—of all shapes, consistencies, and sizes, but with whom Seaton seemed to be on the most intimate of terms. I can see his absorbed face now as he sat on his heels and fished the slimy things out in his sallow palms. Wearying at last of these pets, we loitered about awhile in an aimless fashion. Seaton seemed to be listening, or at any rate waiting, for something to happen or for someone to come. But nothing did happen and no one came.

That was just like Seaton. Anyhow, the first view I got of his aunt was when, at the summons of a distant gong, we turned from the garden, very hungry and thirsty, to go in to luncheon. We were approaching the house when Seaton suddenly came to a standstill. Indeed, I have always had the impression that he plucked at my sleeve. Something, at least, seemed to catch me back, as it were, as he cried, "Look out, there she is!"

She was standing at an upper window which opened wide on a hinge, and at first sight she looked an excessively tall and overwhelming figure. This, however, was mainly because the window reached all but to the floor of her bedroom. She was in reality rather an under-sized woman, in spite of her long face and big head. She must have stood, I think, unusually still, with eyes fixed on us, though this impression may be due to Seaton's sudden warning and to my consciousness of the cautious and subdued air that had fallen on him at sight of her. I know that without the least reason in the world I felt a kind of guiltiness, as if I had been "caught." There was a silvery star pattern sprinkled on her black silk dress, and even from the ground I could see the immense coils of her hair and the rings on her left hand, which was held fingering the small jet buttons of her bodice. She watched our united advance without stirring, until, imperceptibly, her eyes raised and lost themselves in the distance, so that it was out of an assumed reverie that she appeared suddenly to awaken to our presence beneath her when we drew close to the house.

"So this is your friend, Mr. Smithers, I suppose?" she said, bobbing to me.

"Withers, aunt," said Seaton.

"It's much the same," she said, with eyes fixed on me. "Come in, Mr. Withers, and bring him along with you."

She continued to gaze at me—at least, I think she did so. I know that the fixity of her scrutiny and her ironical "Mr." made me feel peculiarly uncomfortable. None the less she was extremely kind and attentive to me, though, no doubt, her kindness and attention showed up more vividly against her complete neglect of Seaton. Only one remark that I have any recollection of she made to him: "When I look on my nephew, Mr. Smithers, I realize that dust we are, and dust shall become. You are hot, dirty, and incorrigible, Arthur."

She sat at the head of the table, Seaton at the foot, and I, before a wide waste of damask tablecloth, between them. It was an old and rather close dining-room, with windows thrown wide to the green garden and a wonderful cascade of fading roses. Miss Seaton's great chair faced this window, so that its rose-reflected light shone full on her yellowish face, and on just such chocolate eyes as my schoolfellow's, except that hers were more than half-covered by unusually long and heavy lids.

There she sat, steadily eating, with those sluggish eyes fixed for the most part on my face; above them stood the deep-lined fork between her eyebrows; and above that the wide expanse of a remarkable brow beneath its strange steep bank of hair. The lunch was copious, and consisted, I remember, of all such dishes as are generally considered too rich and too good for the school-boy digestion—lobster mayonnaise, cold game sausages, an immense veal and ham pie farced with eggs, truffles, and numberless delicious flavours; besides kickshaws, creams, and sweetmeats. We even had wine, a half-glass of old darkish sherry each.

Miss Seaton enjoyed and indulged an enormous appetite. Her example and a natural schoolboy voracity soon overcame my nervousness of her, even to the extent of allowing me to enjoy to the best of my bent so rare a spread. Seaton was singularly modest; the greater part of his meal consisted of almonds and raisins, which he nibbled surreptitiously and as if he found difficulty in swallowing them.

I don't mean that Miss Seaton "conversed" with me. She merely scattered trenchant remarks and now and then twinkled a baited question over my head. But her face was like a dense and involved accompaniment to her talk. She presently dropped the "Mr.," to my intense relief, and called me now Withers, or Wither, now Smithers, and even once towards the close of the meal distinctly Johnson, though how on earth my name suggested it, or whose face mine had reanimated in memory, I cannot conceive.

"And is Arthur a good boy at school, Mr. Wither?" was one of her many questions. "Does he please his masters? Is he first in his class? What does the Reverend Dr. Gummidge think of him, eh?"

I knew she was jeering at him, but her face was adamant against the least flicker of sarcasm or facetiousness. I gazed fixedly at a blushing crescent of lobster.

"I think you're eighth, aren't you, Seaton?"

Seaton moved his small pupils towards his aunt. But she continued to gaze with a kind of concentrated detachment at me.

"Arthur will never make a brilliant scholar, I fear," she said, lifting a dexterously-burdened fork to her wide mouth. . . .

After luncheon she preceded me up to my bedroom. It was a jolly little bedroom, with a brass fender and rugs and a polished floor, on which it was possible, I afterwards found, to play "snowshoes." Over the washstand was a little black-framed water-colour drawing, depicting a large eye with an extremely fishlike intensity in the spark of light on the dark pupil; and in "illuminated" lettering beneath was printed very minutely, "Thou God Seest ME," followed by a long looped monogram, "S.S." in the corner. The other pictures were all of the sea: brigs on blue water;

a schooner overtopping chalk cliffs; a rocky island of prodigious steepness, with two tiny sailors dragging a monstrous boat up a shelf of beach.

"This is the room, Withers, my brother William died in when a boy. Admire the view!"

I looked out of the window across the tree-tops. It was a day hot with sunshine over the green fields, and the cattle were standing swishing their tails in the shallow water. But the view at the moment was only exaggeratedly vivid because I was horribly dreading that she would presently inquire after my luggage, and I had not brought even a toothbrush. I need have had no fear. Hers was not that highly-civilized type of mind that is stuffed with sharp, material details. Nor could her ample presence be described as in the least motherly.

"I would never consent to question a schoolfellow behind my nephew's back," she said, standing in the middle of the room, "but tell me, Smithers, why is Arthur so unpopular? You, I understand, are his only close friend." She stood in a dazzle of sun, and out of it her eyes regarded me with such leaden penetration beneath their thick lids that I doubt if my face concealed the least thought from her. "But there, there," she added very suavely, stooping her head a little, "don't trouble to answer me. I never extort an answer. Boys are queer fish. Brains might perhaps have suggested his washing his hands before luncheon; but —not my choice, Smithers. God forbid! And now, perhaps, you would like to go into the garden again. I cannot actually see from here, but I should not be surprised if Arthur is now skulking behind that hedge."

He was. I saw his head come out and take a rapid glance at the windows.

"Join him, Mr. Smithers; we shall meet again, I hope, at the tea-table. The afternoon I spend in retirement."

Whether or not, Seaton and I had not been long engaged with the aid of two green switches in riding round and round a lumbering old grey horse we found in the meadow, before a rather bunched-up figure appeared, walking along the field-path on the other side of the water, with a magenta parasol studiously lowered in our direction throughout her slow progress, as if that were

the magnetic needle and we the fixed Pole. Seaton at once lost all
nerve in his riding. At the next lurch of the old mare's heels he
toppled over into the grass, and I slid off the sleek broad back to
join him where he stood, rubbing his shoulder and sourly watching the rather pompous figure till it was out of sight.

"Was that your aunt, Seaton?" I inquired; but not till then.
He nodded.

"Why didn't she take any notice of us, then?"

"She never does."

"Why not?"

"Oh, she knows all right, without; that's the dam' awful part
of it." Seaton was about the only fellow at Gummidge's who ever
had the ostentation to use bad language. He had suffered for it
too. But it wasn't, I think, bravado. I believe he really felt certain
things more intensely than most of the other fellows, and they
were generally things that fortunate and average people do not
feel at all—the peculiar quality, for instance, of the British schoolboy's imagination.

"I tell you, Withers," he went on moodily, slinking across the
meadow with his hands covered up in his pockets, "she sees
everything. And what she doesn't see she knows without."

"But how?" I said, not because I was much interested, but because the afternoon was so hot and tiresome and purposeless, and
it seemed more of a bore to remain silent. Seaton turned gloomily
and spoke in a very low voice.

"Don't appear to be talking of her, if you wouldn't mind. It's—
because she's in league with the devil." He nodded his head and
stooped to pick up a round flat pebble. "I tell you," he said, still
stooping, "you fellows don't realize what it is. I know I'm a bit
close and all that. But so would you be if you had that old hag
listening to every thought you think."

I looked at him, then turned and surveyed one by one the
windows of the house.

"Where's your *pater*?" I said awkwardly.

"Dead, ages and ages ago, and my mother too. She's not my
aunt by rights."

"What is she, then?"

"I mean she's not my mother's sister, because my grandmother married twice; and she's one of the first lot. I don't know what you call her, but anyhow she's not my real aunt."

"She gives you plenty of pocket-money."

Seaton looked steadfastly at me out of his flat eyes. "She can't give me what's mine. When I come of age half of the whole lot will be mine; and what's more"—he turned his back on the house —"I'll make her hand over every blessed shilling of it."

I put my hands in my pockets and stared at Seaton; "Is it much?"

He nodded.

"Who told you?" He got suddenly very angry; a darkish red came into his cheeks, his eyes glistened, but he made no answer, and we loitered listlessly about the garden until it was time for tea. . . .

Seaton's aunt was wearing an extraordinary kind of lace jacket when we sidled sheepishly into the drawing-room together. She greeted me with a heavy and protracted smile, and bade me bring a chair close to the little table.

"I hope Arthur has made you feel at home," she said as she handed me my cup in her crooked hand. "He don't talk much to me; but then I'm an old woman. You must come again, Wither, and draw him out of his shell. You old snail!" She wagged her head at Seaton, who sat munching cake and watching her intently.

"And we must correspond, perhaps." She nearly shut her eyes at me. "You must write and tell me everything behind the creature's back." I confess I found her rather disquieting company. The evening drew on. Lamps were brought in by a man with a nondescript face and very quiet footsteps. Seaton was told to bring out the chess-men. And we played a game, she and I, with her big chin thrust over the board at every move as she gloated over the pieces and occasionally croaked "Check!"—after which she would sit back inscrutably staring at me. But the game was never finished. She simply hemmed me defencelessly in with a cloud of men that held me impotent, and yet one and all refused to administer to my poor flustered old king a merciful *coup de grâce*.

"There," she said, as the clock struck ten—"a drawn game, Withers. We are very evenly matched. A very creditable defence,

Withers. You know your room. There's supper on a tray in the dining-room. Don't let the creature over-eat himself. The gong will sound three-quarters of an hour *before* a punctual breakfast." She held out her cheek to Seaton, and he kissed it with obvious perfunctoriness. With me she shook hands.

"An excellent game," she said cordially, "but my memory is poor, and"—she swept the pieces helter-skelter into the box—"the result will never be known." She raised her great head far back. "Eh?"

It was a kind of challenge, and I could only murmur: "Oh, I was absolutely in a hole, you know!" when she burst out laughing and waved us both out of the room.

Seaton and I stood and ate our supper, with one candlestick to light us, in a corner of the dining-room. "Well, and how would you like it?" he said very softly, after cautiously poking his head round the doorway.

"Like what?"

"Being spied on—every blessed thing you do and think?"

"I shouldn't like it at all," I said, "if she does."

"And yet you let her smash you up at chess!"

"I didn't let her!" I said, indignantly.

"Well, you funked it, then."

"And I didn't funk it either," I said; "she's so jolly clever with her knights." Seaton stared fixedly at the candle. "You wait, that's all," he said slowly. And we went upstairs to bed.

I had not been long in bed, I think, when I was cautiously awakened by a touch on my shoulder. And there was Seaton's face in the candlelight—and his eyes looking into mine.

"What's up?" I said, rising quickly to my elbow.

"Don't scurry," he whispered, "or she'll hear. I'm sorry for waking you, but I didn't think you'd be asleep so soon."

"Why, what's the time, then?" Seaton wore, what was then rather unusual, a night-suit, and he hauled his big silver watch out of the pocket in his jacket.

"It's a quarter to twelve. I never get to sleep before twelve—not here."

"What do you do, then?"

"Oh, I read and listen."

"Listen?"

Seaton stared into his candle-flame as if he were listening even then. "You can't guess what it is. All you read in ghost stories, that's all rot. You can't see much, Withers, but you know all the same."

"Know what?"

"Why, that they're there."

"Who's there?" I asked fretfully, glancing at the door.

"Why, in the house. It swarms with 'em. Just you stand still and listen outside my bedroom door in the middle of the night. I have, dozens of times; they're all over the place."

"Look here, Seaton," I said, "you asked me to come here, and I didn't mind chucking up a leave just to oblige you and because I'd promised; but don't get talking a lot of rot, that's all, or you'll know the difference when we get back."

"Don't fret," he said coldly, turning away. "I shan't be at school long. And what's more, you're here now, and there isn't anybody else to talk to. I'll chance the other."

"Look here, Seaton," I said, "you may think you're going to scare me with a lot of stuff about voices and all that. But I'll just thank you to clear out; and you may please yourself about pottering about all night."

He made no answer; he was standing by the dressing-table looking across his candle into the looking-glass; he turned and stared slowly round the walls.

"Even this room's nothing more than a coffin. I suppose she told you—'It's all exactly the same as when my brother William died'—trust her for that! And good luck to him, say I. Look at that." He raised his candle close to the little water-colour I have mentioned. "There's hundreds of eyes like that in this house; and even if God does see you, He takes precious good care you don't see Him. And it's just the same with them. I tell you what, Withers, I'm getting sick of all this. I shan't stand it much longer."

The house was silent within and without, and even in the yellowish radiance of the candle a faint silver showed through the open window on my blind. I slipped off the bedclothes, wide awake, and sat irresolute on the bedside.

"I know you're only guying me," I said angrily, "but why is the house full of—what you say? Why do you hear—what you *do* hear? Tell me that, you silly fool!"

Seaton sat down on a chair and rested his candlestick on his knee. He blinked at me calmly. "She brings them," he said, with lifted eyebrows.

"Who? Your aunt?"

He nodded.

"How?"

"I told you," he answered pettishly. "She's in league. You don't know. She as good as killed my mother; I know that. But it's not only her by a long chalk. She just sucks you dry. I know. And that's what she'll do for me; because I'm like her—like my mother, I mean. She simply hates to see me alive. I wouldn't be like that old she-wolf for a million pounds. And so"—he broke off, with a comprehensive wave of his candlestick—"they're always here. Ah, my boy, wait till she's dead! She'll hear something then, I can tell you. It's all very well now, but wait till then! I wouldn't be in her shoes when she has to clear out—for something. Don't you go and believe I care for ghosts, or whatever you like to call them. We're all in the same box. We're all under her thumb."

He was looking almost nonchalantly at the ceiling at the moment, when I saw his face change, saw his eyes suddenly drop like shot birds and fix themselves on the cranny of the door he had just left ajar. Even from where I sat I could see his colour change; he went greenish. He crouched without stirring, simply fixed. And I, scarcely daring to breathe, sat with creeping skin, simply watching him. His hands relaxed, and he gave a kind of sigh.

"Was that one?" I whispered, with a timid show of jauntiness. He looked round, opened his mouth, and nodded. "What?" I said. He jerked his thumb with meaningful eyes, and I knew that he meant that his aunt had been there listening at our door cranny.

"Look here, Seaton," I said once more, wriggling to my feet. "You may think I'm a jolly noodle; just as you please. But your aunt has been civil to me and all that, and I don't believe a word you say about her, that's all, and never did. Every fellow's a bit off his pluck at night, and you may think it a fine sport to try your rubbish on me. I heard your aunt come upstairs before I fell asleep. And I'll bet you a level tanner she's in bed now. What's more, you can keep your blessed ghosts to yourself. It's a guilty conscience, I should think."

Seaton looked at me curiously, without answering for a moment. "I'm not a liar, Withers; but I'm not going to quarrel either. You're the only chap I care a button for; or, at any rate, you're the only chap that's ever come here; and it's something to tell a fellow what you feel. I don't care a fig for fifty thousand ghosts, although I swear on my solemn oath that I know they're here. But she"—he turned deliberately—"you laid a tanner she's in bed, Withers; well, I know different. She's never in bed much of the night, and I'll prove it, too, just to show you I'm not such a nolly as you think I am. Come on!"

"Come on where?"

"Why, to see."

I hesitated. He opened a large cupboard and took out a small dark dressing-gown and a kind of shawl-jacket. He threw the jacket on the bed and put on the gown. His dusky face was colourless, and I could see by the way he fumbled at the sleeves he was shivering. But it was no good showing the white feather now. So I threw the tasselled shawl over my shoulders and, leaving our candle brightly burning on the chair, we went out together and stood in the corridor.

"Now then, listen!" Seaton whispered.

We stood leaning over the staircase. It was like leaning over a well, so still and chill the air was all around us. But presently, as I suppose happens in most old houses, began to echo and answer in my ears a medley of infinite small stirrings and whisperings. Now out of the distance an old timber would relax its fibres, or a scurry die away behind the perishing wainscot. But amid and behind such sounds as these I seemed to begin to be conscious, as it were, of the lightest of footfalls, sounds as faint as the vanishing remembrance of voices in a dream. Seaton was all in obscurity except his face; out of that his eyes gleamed darkly, watching me.

"You'd hear, too, in time, my fine soldier," he muttered. "Come on!"

He descended the stairs, slipping his lean fingers lightly along the balusters. He turned to the right at the loop, and I followed him barefooted along a thickly-carpeted corridor. At the end stood a door ajar. And from here we very stealthily and in complete blackness ascended five narrow stairs. Seaton, with immense caution, slowly pushed open a door, and we stood together looking into a great pool of duskiness, out of which, lit by the feeble clearness of a night-light, rose a vast bed. A heap of clothes lay on the floor; beside them two slippers dozed, with noses each to each, two yards apart. Somewhere a little clock ticked huskily. There was a rather close smell of lavender and Eau de Cologne, mingled with the fragrance of ancient sachets, soap, and drugs. Yet it was a scent even more peculiarly commingled than that.

And the bed! I stared warily in; it was mounded gigantically, and it was empty.

Seaton turned a vague pale face, all shadows: "What did I say?" he muttered. "Who's—who's the fool now, I say? How are we going to get back without meeting her, I say? Answer me that! Oh, I wish to goodness you hadn't come here, Withers."

He stood visibly shivering in his skimpy gown, and could hardly speak for his teeth chattering. And very distinctly, in the hush that followed his whisper, I heard approaching a faint unhurried voluminous rustle. Seaton clutched my arm, dragged me to the right across the room to a large cupboard, and drew the door close to on us. And, presently, as with bursting lungs I peeped out into the long, low, curtained bedroom, waddled in that wonderful great head and body. I can see her now, all patched and lined with shadow, her tied-up hair (she must have had enormous quantities of it for so old a woman), her heavy lids above those flat, slow, vigilant eyes. She just passed across my ken in the vague dusk; but the bed was out of sight.

We waited on and on, listening to the clock's muffled ticking. Not the ghost of a sound rose up from the great bed. Either she lay archly listening or slept a sleep serener than an infant's.

And when, it seemed, we had been hours in hiding and were cramped, chilled, and half-suffocated, we crept out on all fours, with terror knocking at our ribs, and so down the five narrow stairs and back to the little candlelit blue-and-gold bedroom.

Once there, Seaton gave in. He sat livid on a chair with closed eyes.

"Here," I said, shaking his arm, "I'm going to bed; I've had enough of this foolery; I'm going to bed." His lips quivered, but he made no answer. I poured out some water into my basin and, with that cold pictured azure eye fixed on us, bespattered Seaton's sallow face and forehead and dabbled his hair. He presently sighed and opened fishlike eyes.

"Come on!" I said. "Don't get shamming, there's a good chap. Get on my back, if you like, and I'll carry you into your bedroom."

He waved me away and stood up. So, with my candle in one hand, I took him under the arm and walked him along according to his direction down the corridor. His was a much dingier room than mine, and littered with boxes, paper, cages, and clothes. I huddled him into bed and turned to go. And suddenly, I can hardly explain it now, a kind of cold and deadly terror swept over me. I almost ran out of the room, with eyes fixed rigidly in front of me, blew out my candle, and buried my head under the bedclothes.

When I awoke, roused not by a gong, but by a long-continued tapping at my door, sunlight was raying in on cornice and bedpost, and birds were singing in the garden. I got up, ashamed of the night's folly, dressed quickly, and went downstairs. The breakfast-room was sweet with flowers and fruit and honey. Seaton's aunt was standing in the garden beside the open French window, feeding a great flutter of birds. I watched her for a moment, unseen. Her face was set in a deep reverie beneath the shadow of a big loose sun-hat. It was deeply lined, crooked, and, in a way I can't describe, fixedly vacant and strange. I coughed, and she turned at once with a prodigious smile to inquire how I had slept. And in that mysterious way by which we learn each other's secret thoughts without a sentence spoken I knew that she had followed every word and movement of the night before, and was triumphing over my affected innocence and ridiculing my friendly and too easy advances.

We returned to school, Seaton and I, lavishly laden, and by rail all the way. I made no reference to the obscure talk we had had, and resolutely refused to meet his eyes or to take up the hints he let fall. I was relieved—and yet I was sorry—to be going back, and strode on as fast as I could from the station, with Seaton almost trotting at my heels. But he insisted on buying more fruit and sweets—my share of which I accepted with a very bad grace. It was uncomfortably like a bribe; and, after all, I had no quarrel with his rum old aunt, and hadn't really believed half the stuff he had told me.

I saw as little of him as I could after that. He never referred to our visit or resumed his confidences, though in class I would sometimes catch his eye fixed on mine, full of a mute understanding, which I easily affected not to understand. He left Gummidge's, as I have said, rather abruptly, though I never heard of anything to his discredit. And I did not see him or have any news of him again till by chance we met one summer afternoon in the Strand.

He was dressed rather oddly in a coat too large for him and a bright silky tie. But we instantly recognized one another under the awning of a cheap jeweller's shop. He immediately attached himself to me and dragged me off, not too cheerfully, to lunch with him at an Italian restaurant near by. He chattered about our old school, which he remembered only with dislike and disgust; told me cold-bloodedly of the disastrous fate of one or two of the old fellows who had been among his chief tormentors; insisted on an expensive wine and the whole gamut of the foreign menu; and finally informed me, with a good deal of niggling, that he had come up to town to buy an engagement-ring.

And of course: "How is your aunt?" I inquired at last.

He seemed to have been awaiting the question. It fell like a stone into a deep pool, so many expressions flitted across his long un-English face.

"She's aged a good deal," he said softly, and broke off.

"She's been very decent," he continued presently after, and paused again. "In a way." He eyed me fleetingly. "I dare say you heard that—she—that is, that we—had lost a good deal of money."

"No," I said.

"Oh, yes!" said Seaton, and paused again.

And somehow, poor fellow, I knew in the clink and clatter of glass and voices that he had lied to me; that he did not possess, and never had possessed, a penny beyond what his aunt had squandered on his too ample allowance of pocket-money.

"And the ghosts?" I inquired quizzically.

He grew instantly solemn, and, though it may have been my fancy, slightly yellowed. But "You are making game of me, Withers," was all he said.

He asked for my address, and I rather reluctantly gave him my card.

"Look here, Withers," he said, as we stood together in the sunlight on the kerb, saying good-bye, "here I am, and—and it's all very well. I'm not perhaps as fanciful as I was. But you are practically the only friend I have on earth—except Alice. . . . And there—to make a clean breast of it, I'm not sure that my aunt cares much about my getting married. She doesn't say so, of course. You know her well enough for that." He looked sidelong at the rattling gaudy traffic.

"What I was going to say is this: Would you mind coming down? You needn't stay the night unless you please, though, of course, you know you would be awfully welcome. But I should like you to meet my—to meet Alice; and then, perhaps, you might tell me your honest opinion of—of the other too."

I vaguely demurred. He pressed me. And we parted with a half promise that I would come. He waved his ball-topped cane at me and ran off in his long jacket after a 'bus.

A letter arrived soon after, in his small weak handwriting, giving me full particulars regarding route and trains. And without the least curiosity, even perhaps with some little annoyance that chance should have thrown us together again, I accepted his invitation and arrived one hazy midday at his out-of-the-way station to find him sitting on a low seat under a clump of double hollyhocks, awaiting me.

His face looked absent and singularly listless; but he seemed, none the less, pleased to see me.

We walked up the village street, past the little dingy apothecary's and the empty forge, and, as on my first visit, skirted the house together, and, instead of entering by the front door, made our way down the green path into the garden at the back. A pale haze of cloud muffled the sun; the garden lay in a grey shimmer—its old trees, its snapdragoned, faintly glittering walls. But now there was an air of slovenliness where before all had been neat and methodical. In a patch of shallowly-dug soil stood a worn-down spade leaning against a tree. There was an old broken wheelbarrow. The roses had run to leaf and brier; the fruit trees were unpruned. The goddess of neglect brooded in secret.

"You ain't much of a gardener, Seaton," I said, with a sigh of ease.

"I think, do you know, I like it best like this," said Seaton. "We haven't any man now, of course. Can't afford it." He stood staring at his little dark square of freshly-turned earth. "And it always seems to me," he went on ruminatingly, "that, after all, we are nothing better than interlopers on the earth, disfiguring and staining wherever we go. I know it's shocking blasphemy to say so, but then it's different here, you see. We are further away."

"To tell you the truth, Seaton, I *don't* quite see," I said; "but it isn't a new philosophy, is it? Anyhow, it's a precious beastly one."

"It's only what I think," he replied, with all his odd old stubborn meekness.

We wandered on together, talking little, and still with that expression of uneasy vigilance on Seaton's face. He pulled out his watch as we stood gazing idly over the green meadows and the dark motionless bulrushes.

"I think, perhaps, it's nearly time for lunch," he said. "Would you like to come in?"

We turned and walked slowly towards the house, across

whose windows I confess my own eyes, too, went restlessly wandering in search of its rather disconcerting inmate. There was a pathetic look of draggledness, of want of means and care, rust and overgrowth and faded paint. Seaton's aunt, a little to my relief, did not share our meal. Seaton carved the cold meat, and dispatched a heaped-up plate by an elderly servant for his aunt's private consumption. We talked little and in half-suppressed tones, and sipped a bottle of Madeira which Seaton had rather heedfully fetched out of the great mahogany sideboard.

I played him a dull and effortless game of chess, yawning between the moves he himself made almost at haphazard, and with attention elsewhere engaged. About five o'clock came the sound of a distant ring, and Seaton jumped up, overturning the board, and so ending a game that else might have fatuously continued to this day. He effusively excused himself, and after some little while returned with a slim, dark, rather sallow girl of about nineteen, in a white gown and hat, to whom I was presented with some little nervousness as his "dear old friend and schoolfellow."

We talked on in the pale afternoon light, still, as it seemed to me, and even in spite of a real effort to be clear and gay, in a half-suppressed, lack-lustre fashion. We all seemed, if it were not my fancy, to be expectant, to be rather anxiously awaiting an arrival, the appearance of someone who all but filled our collective consciousness. Seaton talked least of all, and in a restless interjectory way, as he continually fidgeted from chair to chair. At last he proposed a stroll in the garden before the sun should have quite gone down.

Alice walked between us. Her hair and eyes were conspicuously dark against the whiteness of her gown. She carried herself not ungracefully, and yet without the least movement of her arms and body, and answered us both without turning her head. There was a curious provocative reserve in that impassive and rather long face, a half-unconscious strength of character.

And yet somehow I knew—I believe we all knew—that this walk, this discussion of their future plans, was a futility. I had nothing to base such a cynicism on, except only a vague sense of oppression, the foreboding remembrance of the inert invincible power in the background, to whom optimistic plans and love-making and youth are as chaff and thistledown. We came back, silent, in the last light. Seaton's aunt was there—under an old brass lamp. Her hair was as barbarously massed and curled as ever. Her eyelids, I think, hung even a little heavier in age over their slow-moving inscrutable pupils. We filed in softly out of the evening, and I made my bow.

"In this short interval, Mr. Withers," she remarked amiably, "you have put off youth, put on the man. Dear me, how sad it is to see the young days vanishing! Sit down. My nephew tells me you met by chance—or act of Providence, shall we call it?—and in my beloved Strand! You, I understand, are to be best man—yes, best man, or am I divulging secrets?" She surveyed Arthur and Alice with overwhelming graciousness. They sat apart on two low chairs and smiled in return.

"And Arthur—how do you think Arthur is looking?"

"I think he looks very much in need of a change," I said deliberately.

"A change! Indeed?" She all but shut her eyes at me and with an exaggerated sentimentality shook her head. "My dear Mr. Withers! Are we not all in need of a change in this fleeting, fleeting world?" She mused over the remark like a connoisseur. "And you," she continued, turning abruptly to Alice, "I hope you pointed out to Mr. Withers all my pretty bits?"

"We walked round the garden," said Alice, looking out of the window. "It's a very beautiful evening."

"Is it?" said the old lady, starting up violently. "Then on this very beautiful evening we will go in to supper. Mr. Withers, your arm; Arthur, bring your bride."

I can scarcely describe with what curious ruminations I led the way into the faded, heavy-aired dining-room, with this indefinable old creature leaning weightily on my arm—the large flat bracelet on the yellow-laced wrist. She fumed a little, breathed rather heavily, as if with an effort of mind rather than of body; for she had grown much stouter and yet little more proportionate. And to talk into that great white face, so close to mine, was a queer experience in the dim light of the corridor, and even in the twinkling crystal of the candles. She was naïve—appallingly naïve; she was sudden and superficial; she was even arch; and all these in the brief, rather puffy passage from one room to the other, with these two tongue-tied children bringing up the rear. The meal was tremendous. I have never seen such a monstrous salad. But the dishes were greasy and over-spiced, and were indifferently cooked. One thing only was quite unchanged—my hostess's appetite was as Gargantuan as ever. The old solid candelabra that lighted us stood before her high-backed chair. Seaton sat a little removed, with his plate almost in darkness.

And throughout this prodigious meal his aunt talked, mainly to me, mainly at Seaton, with an occasional satirical courtesy to Alice and muttered explosions of directions to the servant. She had aged, and yet, if it be not nonsense to say so, seemed no older. I suppose to the Pyramids a decade is but as the rustling down of a handful of dust. And she reminded me of some such unshakable prehistoricism. She certainly was an amazing talker —racy, extravagant, with a delivery that was perfectly overwhelming. As for Seaton—her flashes of silence were for him. On her enormous volubility would suddenly fall a hush: acid sarcasm would be left implied; and she would sit softly moving her great head, with eyes fixed full in a dreamy smile; but with her whole attention, one could see, slowly, joyously absorbing his mute discomfiture.

She confided in us her views on a theme vaguely occupying at the moment, I suppose, all our minds. "We have barbarous institutions, and so must put up, I suppose, with a never-ending procession of fools—of fools *ad infinitum*. Marriage, Mr. Withers, was instituted in the privacy of a garden; *sub rosa,* as it were. Civilization flaunts it in the glare of day. The dull marry the poor; the rich the effete; and so our New Jerusalem is peopled with naturals, plain and coloured, at either end. I detest folly; I detest still more (if I must be frank, dear Arthur) mere cleverness. Mankind has simply become a tailless host of uninstinctive animals. We should never have taken to Evolution, Mr. Withers. 'Natural Selection!'—little gods and fishes!—the

deaf for the dumb. We should have used our brains—intellectual
pride, the ecclesiastics call it. And by brains I mean—what do
I mean, Alice?—I mean, my dear child," and she laid two
gross fingers on Alice's narrow sleeve, "I mean courage. Consider
it, Arthur. I read that the scientific world is once more beginning
to be afraid of spiritual agencies. Spiritual agencies that tap, and
actually float, bless their hearts! I think just one more of those
mulberries—thank you.

"They talk about 'blind Love,'" she ran inconsequently on as
she helped herself, with eyes roving on the dish, "but why blind?
I think, do you know, from weeping over its rickets. After all,
it is we plain women that triumph, Mr. Withers, beyond the
mockery of time. Alice, now! Fleeting, fleeting is youth, my
child. What's that you were confiding to your plate, Arthur?
Satirical boy. He laughs at his old aunt: nay, but thou didst
laugh. He detests all sentiment. He whispers the most acid
asides. Come, my love, we will leave these cynics; we will go
and commiserate with each other on our sex. The choice of two
evils, Mr. Smithers!" I opened the door, and she swept out as if
borne on a torrent of unintelligible indignation; and Arthur and
I were left in the clear four-flamed light alone.

For a while we sat in silence. He shook his head at my
cigarette-case, and I lit a cigarette. Presently he fidgeted in his
chair and poked his head forward into the light. He paused to
rise and shut again the shut door.

"How long will you be?" he said, standing by the table.

I laughed.

"Oh, it's not that!" he said, in some confusion. "Of course, I
like to be with her. But it's not that. The truth is, Withers, I
don't care about leaving her too long with my aunt."

I hesitated. He looked at me questioningly.

"Look here, Seaton," I said, "you know well enough that I
don't want to interfere in your affairs, or to offer advice where
it is not wanted. But don't you think perhaps you may not
treat your aunt quite in the right way? As one gets old, you
know, a little give and take. I have an old godmother, or something. She talks, too. . . . A little allowance: it does no harm.
But hang it all, I'm no talker."

He sat down with his hands in his pockets and still with his eyes fixed almost incredulously on mine. "How?" he said.

"Well, my dear fellow, if I'm any judge—mind, I don't say that I am—but I can't help thinking she thinks you don't care for her; and perhaps takes your silence for—for bad temper. She has been very decent to you, hasn't she?"

" 'Decent'? My God!" said Seaton.

I smoked on in silence; but he continued to look at me with that peculiar concentration I remembered of old.

"I don't think, perhaps, Withers," he began presently, "I don't think you quite understand. Perhaps you are not quite our kind. You always did, just like the other fellows, guy me at school. You laughed at me that night you came to stay here—about the voices and all that. But I don't mind being laughed at— because I know."

"Know what?" It was the same old system of dull question and evasive answer.

"I mean I know that what we see and hear is only the smallest fraction of what is. I know she lives quite out of this. She *talks* to you; but it's all make-believe. It's all a 'parlour game.' She's not really with you; only pitting her outside wits against yours and enjoying the fooling. She's living on inside, on what you're rotten without. That's what it is—a cannibal feast. She's a spider. It doesn't much matter what you call it. It means the same kind of thing. I tell you, Withers, she hates me; and you can scarcely dream what that hatred means. I used to think I had an inkling of the reason. It's oceans deeper than that. It just lies behind: herself against myself. Why, after all, how much do we really understand of anything? We don't even know our own histories, and not a tenth, not a tenth of the reasons. What has life been to me?—nothing but a trap. And when one is set free, it only begins again. I thought you might understand; but you are on a different level: that's all."

"What on earth are you talking about?" I said contemptuously, in spite of myself.

"I mean what I say," he said gutturally. "All this outside's only make-believe—but there! what's the good of talking? So far as this is concerned I'm as good as done. You wait."

Seaton blew out three of the candles and, leaving the vacant room in semi-darkness, we groped our way along the corridor to the drawing-room. There a full moon stood shining in at the long garden windows. Alice sat stooping at the door, with her hands clasped, looking out, alone.

"Where is she?" Seaton asked in a low tone.

Alice looked up; their eyes met in a kind of instantaneous understanding, and the door immediately afterwards opened behind us.

"*Such* a moon!" said a voice that, once heard, remained unforgettably on the ear. "A night for lovers, Mr. Withers, if ever there was one. Get a shawl, my dear Arthur, and take Alice for a little promenade. I dare say we old cronies will manage to keep awake. Hasten, hasten, Romeo! My poor, poor Alice, how laggard a lover!"

Seaton returned with a shawl. They drifted out into the moonlight. My companion gazed after them till they were out of hearing, turned to me gravely, and suddenly twisted her white face into such a convulsion of contemptuous amusement that I could only stare blankly in reply.

"Dear innocent children!" she said, with inimitable unctuousness. "Well, well, Mr. Withers, we poor seasoned old creatures must move with the times. Do you sing?"

I scouted the idea.

"Then you must listen to my playing. Chess"—she clasped her forehead with both cramped hands—"chess is now completely beyond my poor wits."

She sat down at the piano and ran her fingers in a flourish over the keys. "What shall it be? How shall we capture them, those passionate hearts? That first fine careless rapture? Poetry itself." She gazed softly into the garden a moment, and presently, with a shake of her body, began to play the opening bars of Beethoven's "Moonlight" Sonata. The piano was old and woolly. She played without music. The lamplight was rather dim. The moonbeams from the window lay across the keys. Her head was in shadow. And whether it was simply due to her personality or to some really occult skill in her playing I cannot say: I only know that she gravely and deliberately set herself to satirize the

beautiful music. It brooded on the air, disillusioned, charged
with mockery and bitterness. I stood at the window; far down
the path I could see the white figure glimmering in that pool
of colourless light. A few faint stars shone, and still that
amazing woman behind me dragged out of the unwilling keys
her wonderful grotesquerie of youth and love and beauty. It
came to an end. I knew the player was watching me. "Please,
please, go on!" I murmured, without turning. "Please go on
playing, Miss Seaton."

No answer was returned to my rather fluttering sarcasm, but
I knew in some indefinite way that I was being acutely scrutinized, when suddenly there followed a procession of quiet,
plaintive chords which broke at last softly into the hymn, *A
Few More Years Shall Roll.*

I confess it held me spellbound. There is a wistful, strained,
plangent pathos in the tune; but beneath those masterly old hands
it cried softly and bitterly the solitude and desperate estrangement of the world. Arthur and his lady-love vanished from my
thoughts. No one could put into a rather hackneyed old hymn-
tune such an appeal who had never known the meaning of the
words. Their meaning, anyhow, isn't commonplace.

I turned very cautiously and glanced at the musician. She was
leaning forward a little over the keys, so that at the approach
of my cautious glance she had but to turn her face into the
thin flood of moonlight for every feature to become distinctly
visible. And so, with the tune abruptly terminated, we steadfastly regarded one another, and she broke into a chuckle of
laughter.

"Not quite so seasoned as I supposed, Mr. Withers. I see you
are a real lover of music. To me it is too painful. It evokes too
much thought. . . ."

I could scarcely see her little glittering eyes under their penthouse lids.

"And now," she broke off crisply, "tell me, as a man of the
world, what do you think of my new niece?"

I was not a man of the world, nor was I much flattered in my
stiff and dullish way of looking at things by being called one;
and I could answer her without the least hesitation.

"I don't think, Miss Seaton, I'm much of a judge of character. She's very charming."

"A brunette?"

"I think I prefer dark women."

"And why? Consider, Mr. Withers; dark hair, dark eyes, dark cloud, dark night, dark vision, dark death, dark grave, dark DARK!"

Perhaps the climax would have rather thrilled Seaton, but I was too thick-skinned. "I don't know much about all that," I answered rather pompously. "Broad daylight's difficult enough for most of us."

"Ah," she said, with a sly inward burst of satirical laughter.

"And I suppose," I went on, perhaps a little nettled, "it isn't the actual darkness one admires, it's the contrast of the skin, and the colour of the eyes, and—and their shining. Just as," I went blundering on, too late to turn back, "just as you only see the stars in the dark. It would be a long day without any evening. As for death and the grave, I don't suppose we shall much notice that." Arthur and his sweetheart were slowly returning along the dewy path. "I believe in making the best of things."

"How very interesting!" came the smooth answer. "I see you are a philosopher, Mr. Withers. H'm! 'As for death and the grave, I don't suppose we shall much notice that.' Very interesting. . . . And I'm sure," she added in a particularly suave voice, "I profoundly hope so." She rose slowly from her stool. "You will take pity on me again, I hope. You and I would get on famously—kindred spirits—elective affinities. And, of course, now that my nephew's going to leave me, now that his affections are centred on another, I shall be a very lonely old woman. . . . Shall I not, Arthur?"

Seaton blinked stupidly. "I didn't hear what you said, aunt."

"I was telling our old friend, Arthur, that when you are gone I shall be a very lonely old woman."

"Oh, I don't think so," he said in a strange voice.

"He means, Mr. Withers, he means, my dear child," she said, sweeping her eyes over Alice, "he means that I shall have memory for company—heavenly memory—the ghosts of other days. Sentimental boy! And did you enjoy our music, Alice? Did I really stir that youthful heart? . . . Oh, oh, oh," continued the horrible old creature, "you billers and cooers, I have been listening to such flatteries, such confessions! Beware, beware, Arthur, there's many a slip." She rolled her little eyes at me, she shrugged her shoulders at Alice, and gazed an instant stonily into her nephew's face.

I held out my hand. "Good-night, good-night!" she cried. "He that fights and runs away. Ah, good-night, Mr. Withers; come again soon!" She thrust out her cheek at Alice, and we all three filed slowly out of the room.

Black shadow darkened the porch and half the spreading sycamore. We walked without speaking up the dusty village street. Here and there a crimson window glowed. At the fork of the high-road I said good-bye. But I had taken hardly more than a dozen paces when a sudden impulse seized me.

"Seaton!" I called.

He turned in the moonlight.

"You have my address; if by any chance, you know, you should care to spend a week or two in town between this and the—the Day, we should be delighted to see you."

"Thank you, Withers, thank you," he said in a low voice.

"I dare say"—I waved my stick gallantly to Alice—"I dare say you will be doing some shopping; we could all meet," I added, laughing.

"Thank you, thank you, Withers—immensely," he repeated. And so we parted.

But they were out of the jog-trot of my prosaic life. And being of a stolid and incurious nature, I left Seaton and his marriage, and even his aunt, to themselves in my memory, and scarcely gave a thought to them until one day I was walking up the Strand again, and passed the flashing gloaming of the covered-in jeweller's shop where I had accidentally encountered my old schoolfellow in the summer. It was one of those still close autumnal days after a rainy night. I cannot say why, but a vivid recollection returned to my mind of our meeting and of how suppressed Seaton had seemed, and of how vainly he had endeavoured to appear assured and eager. He must be married

by now, and had doubtless returned from his honeymoon. And I
had clean forgotten my manners, had sent not a word of con-
gratulation, nor—as I might very well have done, and as I knew
he would have been immensely pleased at my doing—the ghost
of a wedding present.

On the other hand, I pleaded with myself, I had had no invitation. I paused at the corner of Trafalgar Square, and at the
bidding of one of those caprices that seize occasionally on even
an unimaginative mind, I suddenly ran after a green 'bus that
was passing, and found myself bound on a visit I had not in the
least foreseen.

The colours of autumn were over the village when I arrived.
A beautiful late afternoon sunlight bathed thatch and meadow.
But it was close and hot. A child, two dogs, a very old woman
with a heavy basket I encountered. One or two incurious tradesmen looked idly up as I passed by. It was all so rural and so still,
my whimiscal impulse had so much flagged, that for a while I
hesitated to venture under the shadow of the sycamore tree to
inquire after the happy pair. I deliberately passed by the faint-
blue gates and continued my walk under the high green and
tufted wall. Hollyhocks had attained their topmost bud and
seeded in the little cottage gardens beyond; the Michaelmas
daisies were in flower; a sweet warm aromatic smell of fading
leaves was in the air. Beyond the cottages lay a field where cattle
were grazing, and beyond that I came to a little churchyard.
Then the road wound on, pathless and houseless, among gorse
and bracken. I turned impatiently and walked quickly back to
the house and rang the bell.

The rather colourless elderly woman who answered my inquiry
informed me that Miss Seaton was at home, as if only taciturnity
forbade her adding, "But she doesn't want to see *you*."

"Might I, do you think, have Mr. Arthur's address?" I said.

She looked at me with quiet astonishment, as if waiting for an
explanation. Not the faintest of smiles came into her thin face.

"I will tell Miss Seaton," she said after a pause. "Please walk
in."

She showed me into the dingy undusted drawing-room, filled
with evening sunshine and with the green-dyed light that

penetrated the leaves overhanging the long French windows. I sat down and waited on and on, occasionally aware of a creaking footfall overhead. At last the door opened a little, and the great face I had once known peered round at me. For it was enormously changed; mainly, I think, because the old eyes had rather suddenly failed, and so a kind of stillness and darkness lay over its calm and wrinkled pallor.

"Who is it?" she asked.

I explained myself and told her the occasion of my visit.

She came in and shut the door carefully after her and, though the fumbling was scarcely perceptible, groped her way to a chair. She had on an old dressing-gown, like a cassock, of a patterned cinnamon colour.

"What is it you want?" she said, seating herself and lifting her blank face to mine.

"Might I just have Arthur's address?" I said deferentially. "I am so sorry to have disturbed you."

"H'm. You have come to see my nephew?"

"Not necessarily to see him, only to hear how he is, and, of course, Mrs. Seaton, too. I am afraid my silence must have appeared . . ."

"He hasn't noticed your silence," croaked the old voice out of the great mask; "besides, there isn't any Mrs. Seaton."

"Ah, then," I answered, after a momentary pause, "I have not seemed so black as I painted myself! And how is Miss Outram?"

"She's gone into Yorkshire," answered Seaton's aunt.

"And Arthur too?"

She did not reply, but simply sat blinking at me with lifted chin, as if listening, but certainly not for what I might have to say. I began to feel rather at a loss.

"You were no close friend of my nephew's, Mr. Smithers?" she said presently.

"No," I answered, welcoming the cue, "and yet, do you know, Miss Seaton, he is one of the very few of my old schoolfellows I have come across in the last few years, and I suppose as one gets older one begins to value old associations . . ." My voice seemed to trail off into a vacuum. "I thought Miss Outram," I hastily began again, "a particularly charming girl. I hope they are both quite well."

Still the old face solemnly blinked at me in silence.

"You must find it very lonely, Miss Seaton, with Arthur away?"

"I was never lonely in my life," she said sourly. "I don't look to flesh and blood for my company. When you've got to be my age, Mr. Smithers (which God forbid), you'll find life a very different affair from what you seem to think it is now. You won't seek company then, I'll be bound. It's thrust on you." Her face edged round into the clear green light, and her eyes groped, as it were, over my vacant, disconcerted face. "I dare say, now," she said, composing her mouth, "I dare say my nephew told you a good many tarradiddles in his time. Oh, yes, a good many, eh? He was always a liar. What, now, did he say of me? Tell me, now." She leant forward as far as she could, trembling, with an ingratiating smile.

"I think he is rather superstitious," I said coldly, "but, honestly, I have a very poor memory, Miss Seaton."

"Why?" she said. "*I* haven't."

"The engagement hasn't been broken off, I hope."

"Well, between you and me," she said, shrinking up and with an immensely confidential grimace, "it has."

"I'm sure I'm very sorry to hear it. And where is Arthur?"

"Eh?"

"Where is Arthur?"

We faced each other mutely among the dead old bygone furniture. Past all my scrutiny was that large, flat, grey, cryptic countenance. And then, suddenly, our eyes for the first time really met. In some indescribable way out of that thick-lidded obscurity a far small something stooped and looked out at me for a mere instant of time that seemed of almost intolerable protraction. Involuntarily I blinked and shook my head. She muttered something with great rapidity, but quite inarticulately; rose and hobbled to the door. I thought I heard, mingled in broken mutterings, something about tea.

"Please, please, don't trouble," I began, but could say no more, for the door was already shut between us. I stood and looked out on the long-neglected garden. I could just see the bright green-ness of Seaton's old tadpole pond. I wandered about the room. Dusk began to gather, the last birds in that dense shadowiness of trees had ceased to sing. And not a sound was to be heard in the house. I waited on and on, vainly speculating. I even attempted to ring the bell; but the wire was broken, and only jangled loosely at my efforts.

I hesitated, unwilling to call or to venture out, and yet more unwilling to linger on, waiting for a tea that promised to be an exceedingly comfortless supper. And as darkness drew down, a feeling of the utmost unease and disquietude came over me. All my talks with Seaton returned on me with a suddenly enriched meaning. I recalled again his face as we had stood hanging over the staircase, listening in the small hours to the inexplicable stirrings of the night. There were no candles in the room; every minute the autumnal darkness deepened. I cautiously opened the door and listened, and with some little dismay withdrew, for I was uncertain of my way out. I even tried the garden, but was confronted under a veritable thicket of foliage by a padlocked gate. It would be a little too ignominious to be caught scaling a friend's garden fence!

Cautiously returning into the still and musty drawing-room, I took out my watch, and gave the incredible old woman ten minutes in which to reappear. And when that tedious ten minutes had ticked by I could scarcely distinguish its hands. I determined to wait no longer, drew open the door, and, trusting to my sense of direction, groped my way through the corridor that I vaguely remembered led to the front of the house.

I mounted three or four stairs and, lifting a heavy curtain, found myself facing the starry fanlight of the porch. From here I glanced into the gloom of the dining-room. My fingers were on the latch of the outer door when I heard a faint stirring in the darkness above the hall. I looked up and became conscious of, rather than saw, the huddled old figure looking down on me.

There was an immense hushed pause. Then, "Arthur, Arthur," whispered an inexpressibly peevish, rasping voice, "is that you? Is that you, Arthur?"

I can scarcely say why, but the question horribly startled me. No conceivable answer occurred to me. With head craned back, hand clenched on my umbrella, I continued to stare up into the gloom, in this fatuous confrontation.

"Oh, oh," the voice croaked. "It is you, is it? *That* disgusting man! . . . Go away out. Go away out."

Hesitating no longer, I caught open the door and, slamming it behind me, ran out into the garden, under the gigantic old sycamore, and so out at the open gate.

I found myself half up the village street before I stopped running. The local butcher was sitting in his shop reading a piece of newspaper by the light of a small oil-lamp. I crossed the road and inquired the way to the station. And after he had with minute and needless care directed me, I asked casually if Mr. Arthur Seaton still lived with his aunt at the big house just beyond the village. He poked his head in at the little parlour door.

"Here's a gentleman inquiring after young Mr. Seaton, Millie," he said. "He's dead, ain't he?"

"Why, yes, bless you," replied a cheerful voice from within. "Dead and buried these three months or more—young Mr. Seaton. And just before he was to be married, don't you remember, Bob?"

I saw a fair young woman's face peer over the muslin of the little door at me.

"Thank you," I replied, "then I go straight on?"

"That's it, sir; past the pond, bear up the hill a bit to the left, and then there's the station lights before your eyes."

We looked intelligently into each other's faces in the beam of the smoky lamp. But not one of the many questions in my mind could I put into words.

And again I paused irresolutely a few paces further on. It was not, I fancy, merely a foolish apprehension of what the raw-boned butcher might "think" that prevented my going back to see if I could find Seaton's grave in the benighted churchyard. There was precious little use in pottering about in the muddy dark merely to discover where he was buried. And yet I felt a little uneasy. My rather horrible thought was that, so far as I was concerned—one of his extremely few friends—he had never been much better than "buried" in my mind.

The Riddle and Other Stories (1923)

LISPET, LISPETT AND VAINE

MAUNDERS's little clear morning town was busy with dogs and tradesmen and carriages. It wore an almost childlike vivacity and brightness, as if overnight it had been swept and garnished for entranceable visitors from over the sea. And there—in the blowy sunshine, like some grotesque Staffordshire figure on a garret chimney-piece—there, at the street corner, sat so ludicrous an old man that one might almost have described him as mediæval.

A peak cap, of a slightly marine appearance, was drawn down over his eyes. Beneath it, wisps of grey hair and a thin beard helplessly shook in the wind; and before him stood a kind of gaping wallet, of cracked American cloth, held yawningly open by its scissor-legs.

From this receptacle, ever and again, he extracted a strand of his dyed bast, or dubiously rummaged in its depths for his scissors. Whereupon he would gingerly draw the strand between his lips —a movement that positively set one's teeth on edge—and at the same moment he would cast a bleared, long, casual glance first down the street to his right—High Street; and then up the street to his left—Mortimer Street; as the bast drew him round.

I had watched him awhile from under the canvas window-blind of Lister Owlett's, the curio shop, in which my friend Maunders was chaffering with a dark sardonic-looking man over a piece of Sheffield plate, and, at last, with that peculiar mixture of shame, compassion, amusement, and horror which such ineffectual (though possibly not unhappy) beings produce on one, I had crossed the road and had purchased an absurd little doll bast marketing basket. Oddly, too, *after* I had actually selected my specimen, and had even paid its price, the queer remote old creature had insisted on my taking a rather more ornate example of his wares. . . .

"You know, Maunders," I said, when we were a hundred yards or so beyond the old gentleman's pitch, "this thing isn't at all badly made. The pattern is rather pretty, and there's a kind of useless finish to it. There's still something to be said for the amateur. Anyhow, Bettie will like it."

Maunders turned his long, large, palish face and looked at me with his extraordinary eyes. For the ninety-ninth time at least I noticed that their faint blue and his necktie's azure called each to each, as deep calls to deep.

"Amateur!" he echoed blandly, though a peculiar fixity of attention had gathered into his gaze; "why, that old gentleman is the last of—of the Lispets." He turned his head away—a queer-shaped, heavy head—and added: "Quite the last."

"Lispets, Maunders; what are they?"

"My dear K., believe me," said Maunders almost mincingly, "not everything is a jest. You must now have trodden the streets of this small town at least a dozen times. The Works—what remains of them—are not seven miles off. And yet, here you are, pleasantly fluting that you have lived a life of such obscurity as never to have heard of Lispet, Lispett and Vaine's. It's an affectation. I can scarcely forgive you. Nor will Henrietta."

He was—as usual—gently thrusting out before him his handsome malacca cane in a manner which frequently persuaded approaching pedestrians that he was blind. And he repeated *sotto voce,* and as if out of an ocean of reflection, " 'Lispet, Lispett and Vaine; Mercers to Their Majesties . . .' I wish I could remember exactly how the old title went. In latter times, I mean."

"Who were 'Their Majesties,' then?"

" 'Their Majesties'?" said Maunders. "Oh, mere kings and queens. In the firm's heyday they were, of course, the crowned heads of practically the whole barbaric globe. But what is history—mummified fact; desiccated life; the irretrievable. You are merely one of the crowd who care not tuppence for such things. The present generation—with its Stores and Emporiums and Trusts and 'Combines'—is blind to the merest inkling of what the phrase 'Merchant Prince' implies. We are not even conscious of irony in little Tommy Tucker's *Nation of Shopkeepers*. Other times, better manners. The only 'entirely honest merchant' of late years—so far as I have definitely heard—is bones in Shirley graveyard. Still, the Lispet tradition was not one of mere honesty."

"What, then?" said I.

"Well, in the first place," replied Maunders, sliding me a remote ruminative glance, "it rambles back almost to prehistoric times. You may hunt down the aboriginals of the firm for yourself, if you feel so inclined. They appear to have been Phœnicians. Tyre, maybe, but I gather non-Semitic. Some remote B.C. glasswork in the Egyptian galleries of the British Museum bears their 'mark'—two inverted V's with a kind of P between. There are others—a cone 'supported by' two doves; a running hound, a crescent moon, and a hand—just a slim, ungrasping hand. Such marks have been discovered, they say, woven into mummy linen, into Syrian embroidery, Damascus silks, and tapestry from the Persian Gulf.

"The priestesses of Astaroth, according to Bateson, danced in gauze of L. L. & V.'s handiwork. They exploited the true bombyx ages before Ptolemy; their gold thread gleamed on the Ark of the Covenant; and it was fabric of their weaving in which the Queen of Sheba marvelled before Solomon. The shoes of his apes, sewn-in with seed pearls and splinters of amethyst were— But what's the good of chattering on like this? I'm not," groaned Maunders with a muffled yawn, "I'm not a perambulating encyclopædia. Some old pantaloon of a German, long before Bateson, burrowed in true German fashion into the firm's past. You may go to bed with his book, if you like—this very night. And then, of course, there are one or two of their old ledgers and curios in the local Museum. But I'm not an antiquarian. My only point is that the past even of a soapboiler is none the worse for being the distant past. What's more, they knew in those days that objects are only of value when representative of subjects. Has it never occurred to you (no, I suppose not) that the Wisest's apes, ivory, and peacocks were symbolical? The apes representing, of course—"

"*Of course,*" I interrupted hurriedly. "But what I'm after, Maunders, is something faintly resembling matter-of-fact. These

Lispet people—what is *really* their history? Subsequent, I mean, to the Apocrypha on which you have already drawn. Honestly, that pathetic old guy with the pouch of bast at the corner rather interested me."

" 'Drawn on!' he says," drawled Maunders. "When I have not even distantly referred to Joseph's Coat, or that she-devil Jezebel's headdress, or to the Grand Khan, or to the Princess Assinimova, or to the tanned Barbary kid cuirass of steel and emeralds in which Saladin met his end. A firm that, apart from clients celebrated in Holy Writ, once happily wrote off bad debts incurred with such customers as Semiramis, Sappho, Paris, and the Arch— or, as we amused moderns suppose, the exceedingly arch—Druids, might well boast—though it didn't—not only of its repute but also of its catholicity.

"No, no"; he mooned slowly about him. "Your precious old 'matter-of-fact'! As if you were a clerk in unholy orders, as if you bought your boots in Scotland Yard, as if you were a huckster of hardware. By all means you shall have the facts. But for heaven's sake—for heaven's sake, precocious K., be careful with them. A friend of mine (an earnest man) was once given a fact, and it exploded—in his bathroom."

Dangling the last-of-the-Lispet's little basket on my forefinger, I awaited the facts.

"The point is," Maunders murmured on, "what of the slightest interest to you can there be to say of a firm that is now dust, and that followed a tradition which in these days would within six months clap its partners in Bedlam or the Bankruptcy Court? You must confess that that kind of sweet reasonableness, hardly less than the modern variety, is as last death to any decent humanity. At long last, maybe. And how divine a decay! Anyhow, there they were—and there, too, are the ruins of them, edging the smooth sloping crest of Adderley Hill, on the other side of the town. Henrietta shall take you there to-morrow, if you're a polite guest. She loves to expatiate on that kind of rubble—the Failures.

"Still, try to imagine it, my dear K., in its green and early days. A long range of low buildings, part half-timbered Tudor, with a few wombed-in bits of thirteenth- and fourteenth-century work, and a fringe of excellent eighteenth-century—weathered and lovely moulded brick. In its prime it must have been a ravishing sight, with its hanging sign of faded blue and gold, its walls and thatch, and shingles, cobbled alleys and water-conduits, worn and mellow with the peace of a thousand thousand sunsets, the mosses and rain-stains and frost-flowerings of centuries of autumns and winters—just England's history, moral and actual, in antique stone and gable and mullion.

"That's as it may be. I have no wish to exaggerate. There is no particular virtue in mere age—except to the imagination. Still, your mere 'facts' are something I suppose. The fact that they were spinning silk—here in England—before the Conqueror came over. The fact that they were world-renowned glovers long before Elizabeth's time. The fact that their Egyptian cotton must have been abob on the Mediterranean when Lancashire, please God, was a verdant solitude, and *your* forefathers, my poor dear, were gadding about in woad.

"They had their foreign agents, of course, netting in handiwork from all over the globe, on which they themselves set the final seal. I won't labour the point. All I suggest is that you should ask a Bond Street dealer to supply you with a Persian rug of L. L. & V. workmanship. But avoid the First of April for the enterprise. And yet, do you know, there was really nothing at the root of them but—well, a kind of instinct: to keep themselves clean. Animals share it. That, and the pride with which a single virtue darkens and suffocates a man if he isn't for ever toiling to keep its growth under. The one secret of their stability, of their being, and, in times past, of their success, was simply this—that nothing they should, would, or could ever conceivably offer for sale need disturb for a breath of a sob or the weight of a dewdrop the ashes of their sleeping forefathers in Adderley Churchyard. The like of which their forefathers had done by *their* forefathers.

"Why, if the ancient Hebrew Jews bequeath the very droop of their noses, why shouldn't an old English 'House' bequeath its tradition? They believed—not Athanasian fashion but in their insides, so to speak—they believed in that perfect quality and consummate workmanship which, naturally, only exorbitant prices can assure. Exorbitant prices, mind you, not profits. They valued their fair fame. Only what was good enough for a Lispet could hope to satisfy a partner who spelt his name with two t's, and only what satisfied a Lispett left unashamed the conscience of a Vaine.

"In plain Anglo-Saxon, the whole thing in decent practical moderation was merely the positive forecast of a Utopian dream. If ever you pass that way, rest for a moment at the mouth of the Well at the World's End. And drink, pretty creature. Perhaps you will discover a cone supported by two doves scrawled on the bottom of its bronze bucket."

"Perhaps," I echoed, as cheerfully as possible.

"At an extreme, of course, this tradition became the very devil. I don't say they made any claim to be gentry, or that they refused any kind of exalted alliance if nicely and unostentatiously proffered. There's an old tale of one of their apprentices who went sightseeing in the fourteenth century. Among other little romantic adventures, he hunted the Unicorn, got a siren with child, fought a demon in Babylon, and bartered tiaras with the reigning Pope in Avignon—very much at that precise moment at a loose end.

"Still a tale's only a tale, though none the worse for that. You want naked facts—a most indecorous variety; and one of them is that during the nearer centuries the three families riotously intermarried, making the green one red, as the poet says. They were self-sufficient—like Leonardo. Except, of course, that they were artists only in the sense that they designed and distributed objects of flawless craftsmanship; while he was a consummate craftsman only by degree of his supreme art. And that was—or was not—between himself and the infinite, so to speak."

"I love your 'so-to-speaks,' Maunders."

"It's very nice of you," said Maunders. "But what I really want to say is that gradually the 'standing' of the firm lost everything in the nature of the precarious. Then, enter Beelzebub. Their only conceivable corruption could come from within, in one of two forms, putrefaction or petrifaction. Well, you shall see. In their earlier annals they can never so much as have tasted temptation to sink to trade devices. Progress, on the other hand, was practically denied to them. Their monopoly was the only one to be had for the asking—their integrity.

"I am not joking. Their wares were as innocent of guile and as beautiful as the lilies of the field. All they needed for mere prosperity was the *status quo*. Does Nature? The high and mighty sought them out for precisely the same reason as a young man with imagination pursues that will-o'-the-wisp called Beauty. Have you ever noticed how different a respect one has for an *advertised* article and for an article whose virtues have been sweetly absorbed into one's soul?

"Compare, for instance, a cottage loaf with *foie gras;* or the Mr. Anon of the Scottish Ballads with Sappho; or Lord Loveaduck's 'brilliance' with Gamma in Leo. Lispet, Lispett and Vaine would have as gladly catalogued their goods as have asked for references. Advertise! Why, a lady might as well advertise her great-grandmother's wig. They were merchants of the one true tradition. Their profits were fees. Their arrogance was beyond the imagination of a Tamburlaine, and their—what shall we call them?—their *principles* were as perennial as the secret springs of the Oceans. It was on similar principles that Satan sold the fruit to Mother Eve."

"I see," said I. "If one *can,* Maunders—through a haze of contradictions."

"You cannot see," said Maunders. "But that is simply because your modern mind is vitiated by the conviction that you just *pay* a tradesman to sell you a decent article, that you can with money buy quality. You can't. L. L. & V. merely graciously *bestowed* on their customers the excellence of their wares, of their 'goods' in the true old meaning of the term—a peculiar something in the style and finish which only the assurance of their history and their intentions—their ideals, if you like—made possible.

"Good heavens, man, isn't there a kind of divination between one's very soul and a thing decently made—whether it's a granite Rameses or a Chelsea porringer? The mere look of a scarf or a snippet of damask or of lawn or of velvet, a stomacher or a glove of L. L. & V. make is like seeing for the first time a bush of blowing hawthorn or a nymph in a dell of woodruff, when, say, you are nine. Or, for the last, when you are nine-and-ninety."

"My dear Maunders," I smiled benignly. "What on earth are you talking about? I have always supposed that speech was intended to disclose one's meaning. Nymphs!"

"Well," replied Maunders, imperturbably shoving his "Sheffield" candlestick at last into his slate-covered greatcoat pocket; "I merely mean that there is a kind of goodness in good work. It confers a sort of everlasting youth. Think of the really swagger old boys we call the masters. What do you actually get out of them? The power to be momentarily immortal, that's all. But that's beside the point. What I wanted to tell you about—and you are a poor receptacle—is, of course, the firm's inevitable degradation. I have kept you pining too long. First they petrified, and then the stone began to rot away. The process must of course have been very gradual. It was Anthony Lispett who at the same time finished it off, and who yet—at least according to *my* notion of the thing, though Henrietta does not agree—and who yet redeemed the complete contraption.

"He must have come into the firm when he was a comparative youngster, say nineteen, towards the end of the eighteenth century. Needless to say, not a single one of the partners, not at least to my knowledge, ever went to a university or any fallalery of that kind. They held aloof from alien ideals. Their 'culture' was in their history and in their blood; and not a Methuselah's life-time could exhaust even a fraction of that. They had no ambitions; did not mix; kept to themselves. Their ladies made their own county society—sparrowhawk-nosed, sloping-shouldered, high-boned, fair-haired beauties for the most part. It was an honour to know them; to be known by them; a privilege—and one arrogantly reserved—to be among their 'customers.' They were Lispet, Lispett and Vaine.

"Well, this Anthony seems to have been something of an exotic leaven. From the beginning, he was two thirds himself, *plus,* if you like, three thirds a Lispett. There is a portrait of him in his youth—an efflorescent Georgian dandy, whiskers, *hauteur,* eyebrows all complete; a kind of antique Beau Brummel. No doubt the old boys squinted askew at him out of their spectacles, no doubt they nodded at each other about him over their port. No doubt their good ladies pursed their mouths at him over their teacups.

"But they could no more resist the insidious growth of the creature than Jack's mother could have held down the sprouting beanstalk. He was clearly the fruit of breeding-in, and of a kind of passive vaingloriousness, as you will see when Henrietta exhibits the Family Tree.

"Old John Vaine Lispet Lispett had married his first cousin Jemima Lispett, and Anthony, it seems, was their only child. There is a story that old John himself in his youth had—well, gossip is merely gossip, and gossamer's merely gossamer, however prolific it may be. And, whether or not, there is no doubt that Anthony in his boyhood had made an attempt to run away. They picked him up seven miles from the coast—half-starved and practically shoeless. He must have been off to Tyre or Damascus, or something of that kind. One knows how one's worm may turn.

"Poor child—just that one whiff of freedom, and he was back once more, gluing his nose, beating his fledgling plumes, against an upper window of the house on the hill. The whole thing, top to bottom, was a kind of slavery, of course. The firm had its own Factory Laws.

"No 'hand,' for example was allowed to wear, at least within sight of those windows, any fabric not of the firm's weaving. No hand ever came into direct contact with one of the partners. There was a kind of hereditary overseer—a family of the name of Watts. Every hand, again, was strictly forbidden to starve. If he or she misbecame himself or herself, instant dismissal followed; and a generous pension.

"So drastic was the relation between the valley-village and the hill that for upwards of two hundred and fifty years, only one hand *had* so misbecome herself. She had smiled a little smile one spring morning out of her little bottle-glass casement above her loom at the middle-aged Vaine; and she drew her pension for six months! They say she drowned herself in the Marshes. It is as if you went and hanged yourself for having too short a nose."

"I cannot see the analogy," said I.

"No," said Maunders, "but your Maker would—the Jehovah that blessed the race of the vulture that sold me this old replica of a candlestick. Can't you understand that her smile was a natural thing (just out of herself), and that he was a kind of sacrosanct old Pharaoh? The discipline was abominable according to our sentimental modern notions. But then, the perquisites were pretty generous.

"The long and the short of it was that every single one of the firm's employees was happy. They were happy in the only sense one *can* be truly happy—in service. Corruptions have swarmed in now, but in the old days the village in the valley must have been as beautiful as a picture of this green old world hung up in the forecourt of paradise.

"It had houses contemporary with every wing of the Works on the hill-top. Its wages were for the most part the only decent wages one can accept. They were in *kind*. What, I ask you, in the sight of heaven is the fittest payment to John Keats for a sonnet— a Thousand Guineas or a plume of your little Elizabeth's golden fuzz?

"I don't want to sentimentalize. J. K. had to live, I suppose (though why, we may be at loggerheads to explain). But what is porridge without cream, and what is cream if you loathe the cow? I ask you, my dear K., is not a living wage simply one that will keep the *kind* of life it represents fully alive?

"Give them the credit, then. L. L. & V. kept their hands positively blossoming with life. I don't mean they theorized. Marx is merely the boiled-up sentiment of a civilization gone wrong. They weren't philanthropists. Nor am I, please heaven. The quality of the L. L. & V. merchandise ensured quality in their hands. Where we walk now—this macadamized road—was once a wood of birches and bluebells. Can you even imagine its former phantom denizens to have been knock-kneed or under-hung?"

"Perhaps not," said I, "but are you intending to imply that the 'phantom denizens,' as you call them, manufacture the bluebells?"

Maunders made an indescribably guttural noise in his throat.

"What I am saying," he replied, "is that the village was as lovely a thing to see and live and laugh and love and dream in as were the bodies of the human beings that occupied it. *Their* stock, too, had climbed from grace to grace. They enjoyed a recognizable type of beauty. The girls were as fair-skinned as a plucking of apricots, with hair of a spidery fine silkenness, and eyes worthy of their veiling. Just Nature's mimicry, I suppose; like an Amazonian butterfly, or the praying mantis or—or the stick caterpillar.

"I can see them—and so could you, if you had the eyes—I can see them dancing in the first of early moonlight, or bathing in what, prior to the human spawning of tin cans and old boots, was a stream crystal as Pharpar. I can see them sallying out and returning on their chattering to-and-fro in the morning dews and the greying twilight. No set hours; only a day as long or as short as love of its task could make it. What indeed is breeding, my dear K., but the showing forth of a perfectly apt and peculiar excellency? Just fitness for its job. Puma, pelican, Patagonian papalja, pretty Poll."

"What is a papalja, Maunders?" I inquired.

"I don't know," said Maunders. "But imagine them—with whatever effort is necessary—ascending and descending that hillside through their Fruit Walk! It is about the nearest approach to any earthly vision I can achieve of Jacob's ladder. Give even your abominable old London a predominent L. L. & V.—well, *then,* but not till then, you may invite me to the Mansion House for its annual November 9th. But there, I'm not an iconoclast."

"I wish, Maunders," said I, "you would at your leisure re-read *Unto This Last;* and that you would first make the ghost of an attempt to tell a decent story. What was the Fruit Walk?"

The Town's puddley, petrol-perfumed, outlying streets were still busy with pedestrians—nurses and perambulators, children in woollen gaiters, and young ladies with red hair. It was, therefore, almost as difficult to keep abreast with Maunders as it was to follow his obscure meanderings.

"Oh, the Fruit Walk," he muttered, staring vacantly through a dairyman's window at an earthenware green-and-grey pelican with a fish in its bill. "The Fruit Walk was merely the cherries and quinces and crab-apples and damsons that had been planted in rosy, snowy, interlacing, discontinuous quincunx fashion; half circling and straggling over and down the green mounting and mounded hill to the very edge of the quarry. Not a miserable avenue, of course, but a kind of to-and-fro circuitous chace between village and Works. Once, your eyes might actually have seen that divine chimneyed cluster, tranquil as an image in water, on the dark emerald hill-top in the dying, gaudy sunset. And, shelving

down, that walk in bloom! One might almost assume that
L. L. & V. weather habitually haunted the scene. Things do react
on one another, you know; and Nature wears fourteenth-century
sleeves."

"Oh, for pity's sake, Maunders, let's get back to Anthony. What
about Anthony?"

Maunders, softly striding along like an elephant in his flat
square-toed shoes, appeared to be pondering.

"Well," he began slowly, "the 'what-about' of Anthony covers
a rather wide field. I fancy, do you know, there was a tinge of
Traherne in his composition. The beau was only the chrysalis
stage. Of course it was Blake's era. I fancy Anthony sowed pretty
early his wild oats. There are many varieties, and his were mainly
of the mind.

"He was not, I venture to add, to make things *quite* clear to
you, either a marrying or an un-marrying man. And, of course,
like all instinctive creatures with a never-waning fountain of life
in them, he shed. Some of us shed feathers, some fur, some innocence, some principles, and all shed skin—the seven year's spring-
cleaning, you know, that leaves the house in the flooding May-day
sunlight a little bit dingier than it was before.

"Well, Anthony seems to have shed what one mistakes for arti-
ficialities. He shed his ringlets, his foppish clothes, his pretences
of languor, his dreamy superiority. He shed his tacit acceptance
of the firm's renown, and so discovered his own imagination.
Only in the 'tip-toppers' do intellect and imagination lie down together, as will the lion and the lamb.

"Then, of course, he seems gradually or suddenly to have shed
the L. L. & V. pride and arrogance. He must have begun to think.
All these centuries, please remember, the firm had been gradually
realizing why, actually *why,* their stuff was super-excellent in the
eyes of humanity. And that—oh, I don't know; but to realize that,
perhaps, is to discount its merits elsewhere. Anthony, on the other
hand, had come to realize, in his own queer vague fashion, that
one's only salvation is to set such eyes squinting. And yet, not of
set and deliberate purpose. He was not a wit. Art, my dear, dear
K., whatever you may like to say, *is* useless; unless one has the
gumption to dissociate use from materialism."

"I was not aware," said I, "that I had said anything. You mean, I suppose, that a man has only to realize that his work is excellent for it to begin to lose its virtue. Like beauty, Maunders, and the rouge-pot and powder-puff? Still, I prefer Anthony to trade ethics. What did the rest of them do?"

"What I was about to tell you," replied Maunders mildly, "is that Anthony had bats in his belfry. Not the vampire variety; just *extra*-terrestrial bats. He was 'queer.' Perhaps more in him than in most of us had come from elsewhere. And the older he grew, the more the hook-winged creatures multiplied. No doubt the firm would have edged him out if it had been practicable. No doubt the young hedge-sparrows would edge out the squab-cuckoo, if that were manageable. But it was not. Anthony was double-dyed, a Lispett with two t's, and it would have been *lèse majesté,* domestic high-treason to acknowledge to the world at large that he was even eccentric.

"Well, there he was, a smallish man, with short-growing hair, a little like Thothmes II, to judge from his portrait—a man of extraordinary gifts in his craft, of an exquisite sensibility to quality and design, but seldom, I imagine, at the Board Meetings. Often, it seems, he used to ramble off into the country. He appears to have especially hated a sort of Frenchiness that had crept into the firms' wares. But much worse than mooning about to soak in Englishness again, he would ramble off into the country of his *mind,* and there you need to have a faint notion of where you are before you can safely go any further. It's difficult, of course, to know exactly what his broodings were. But the story goes that he would complete his nocturnal pilgrimages by climbing up before daybreak into one of the fruit trees on the hill, a magnificent mulberry—to see the sun, I suppose; to 'look down' as far as possible on the Works; to be up among the morning birds, like the old man in the limerick."

"An odd bat, that," I interposed.

"There he would squat," continued Maunders imperturbably, "poor old creature, peering out of the leaves, the rose of dawn on his face, as when it lightened Blake's. And presently, the angels up from the valley would pass by, singing and laughing, to their work. A pretty sight it must have been, with their young faces and pure colours and nimble practised gestures. For, mind you, it was still a happiness to be one of the hands in the firm—as compared, at any rate, with being a grimy paw elsewhere. Only at long last would *they* become aware of the glowing gloom in the heads. Not merely were the brains of the firm tending in one direction and the members remaining more or less static in another, but things outside were beginning to change. The god of machinery was soon to spout smoke and steam from his dismal nostrils, and man to learn the bright little lesson that not only necessities, but even luxuries, can be the cheaper if they are manufactured a gross at a time."

"Yes," said I; "there he would squat; and then?"

"Then," breathed Maunders, "one morning, one shafted scarlet morning, it seems he saw—well, I cannot say what exactly he did see. No hand anyhow, but a light-embodied dream. A being lovelier than any goddess for whom even an L. L. & V. in the service of the Sorceress of Sidon could have been moved from bowels of superstitious horror to design sandals. A shape, a fleetingness, a visitant—poor old Bat-in-the-Belfry—evoked by a moment's aspiration and delight out of his own sublime wool-gatherings. And so this ageing creature, this extra-Lispetted old daydreamer, fell in love—with a non-entity."

"My dear Maunders; pause," I said. "In mere self-respect! How could such an occurrence as that have been recorded in the firm's annals? No; no."

"Weren't there letters?" sighed Maunders, turning suddenly on me, malacca cane in air. "Wasn't there a crack-brained diary? Haven't you a vestige of old-fashioned and discredited gumption? Wait till I have finished, and let your sweet-smelling facts have a show. Ask Henrietta. I say," he repeated stubbornly, "that between the dawn and the daytime, down out of his broad foliage, the hill-side in indescribable bloom, this old meandering Query, this half-demented old Jack-o'-Dreams saw a Vision, and his heart went the same way as long since had gone his head. Haven't I told you he was what the dear old evolutionists, blind to the inexhaustible graces of creation, esteem a *sport*?

"The Family Tree had blossomed out of season, for the last time, jetting its dwindling virtue into this final, queer, anomalous bloom; rich with nectarous bane. It had returned upon itself. 'Tis the last rose of summer that sighs of the spring. 'Ah, yes, but did the vision see *him*?'—you are sneering to yourself.

"And to that I reply: I don't know. Do they ever? Or is it that only certain long-suffering eyes can afford them the hospitality of becoming visible? Anyhow, *I* see her. And in a fashion that is not only the bliss but the very deuce of solitude. Ignore its bidding, K., and we are damned. Oh yes, I know. The inward eye is all very well. I know it. But to share that experience with these outward groping orbs, I'd—well, I'd gladly go bankrupt. Ask Henrietta."

"What happened then?"

"This happened. The wool-gathering wits flocked back and golden-fleeced him. One might almost say he became equally astute and extravagant. As a matter of fact, of course, only willing and selfless service can bring every human faculty to bear." Maunders sighed. "He sent a cheque for a thousand guineas or so to a Dutch bulb-farm, and planted the hill-walk with tulips, April-blue scyllas and *Narcissi poetici. Narcissi poetici!* He tapped an earthbound spring and set up fauns and dryads, amoretti and what not, spouting subterranean water. He built a shrine of alabaster—with an empty niche.

"It appeared to be mere scatter-brained fooling. Still, it was in a sense in the L. L. & V. tradition, and his partners appear to have let him have a free hand. Don't forget their even then almost illimitable resources. They'd far far rather—even the strict-whiskered Vaine of the period, who in unhappier circumstances might have sat for the typical alderman—they'd infinitely rather he exhibited his peculiarities within their sphere, so to speak, than bring them to mockery before the world at large."

"I see."

"They hadn't till then perhaps baldly recognized the world at large, except as a hot-bed of prehistoric or sycophantic customers. And they never—not for an instant—even surmised his depredations would prove active from *within*. None the less, like some secret serpent, spawn of the forgotten fabulous, he was in fact gnawing at the very vitals of the tradition. Let me put it bluntly, in terms which even you, my dear K., will appreciate. Anthony

Lispett had 'gone balmy' on his Vision. She—and therefore he—was 'beside *himself.*'

"I do not suggest that he mixed her up with his superannuating old *corpus vile;* nothing vulgar to talk of, and tragic to think of, in that sort. He merely lived on from that daybreak dream to dream with but one desire in his poor cracked old cranium—to serve her idea. Aren't we, all of us, myth-makers? Grins not the Lion at the Unicorn? Does not the soapboiler bedizen our streets with Art—and 'atmosphere'? Anthony's myth was from elsewhere—neither from his stomach, his pocket, his reputation, his utilitarian morals, nor his brains. That was all. And as he served her, I suppose, he found himself cherubically treading yet more secretly and inwardly her hesperidean meads."

I glanced at Maunders in some dismay. "How?"

"Well," said he, "it is not easy to divine how exactly Anthony began his malpractices. But clearly, since he was perpetually haunted by this illusion of a divine, unearthly stranger, a sort of Athene haunting his hill, his one desire could not but be to set the Works working for *her.* He could bide his time. He could be quiet and gradual. Anyhow, we know the event, though we can't say precisely how it evolved.

"One may assume, I suppose, that he would steal to and fro among the nocturnal looms and presses and vats and dyeing-rooms, and, ten times more richly gifted by his insane inspiration than he was even by nature, that he just doctored right and left. He would experiment night after night with the firm's materials in the raw. Worse, he rationed himself in his tree-gazing; and climbed to his leafy perch only during certain conjunctions of the planets. Mere circumstances seem to have waited on him, as did the sun on Joshua.

"But the Lispet and the Vaine of this time were nothing but hidebound old bachelors—intent only on saving the face of convention. The last Double-T died the day after the site of the shrine was decided on. There was no young blood in the firm. And with an almost diabolical ingenuity Anthony seems to have executed only the orders of such clients as wanted the firm's very finest and rarest handiwork. Even those, of course, who coveted or could afford only the commoner materials were already beginning to dwindle in numbers.

"The other customers he kept waiting, or insulted with questions, or supplied with more delicate and exquisite fabrics than they required.

"The story goes that a certain Empress renowned for her domestic virtues commanded a trousseau for yet another royal niece or what not. A day or two before the young woman's nuptials, and weeks late, arrived silks and tissues and filigrees spun out of some kind of South American and Borneo spider silk, such as only a nymph could wear. My dear K., it nearly hatched a European War. That particular court was little but a menagerie of satyrs.

"Countesses and suchlike soliciting 'fives' and 'fours' in gloves, and 'ones' in stockings, might still faintly hope to be accommodated; and even then their coveted wares were a tight fit. For a while the firm seems to have survived on the proceeds from merchandise intended for grown-ups which your cosmopolitan Crœsuses snapped up for their children. At second hand, of course, since few of them could extort a 'reference' to the firm for love or even for money.

"Henrietta has a few bits of embroideries and silk of the time. Perhaps she will show them to you. Even a human craft can reflect a divine disaster. And the linens!—of a quality that would derange the ghost of an Egyptian embalmer.

"Even worse, Anthony seems to have indulged an extraordinary sense of propriety. He would lavish L. L. & V. urbanities on some sylph of an actress who had no more morals in the usual acceptation of the term than a humming-bird, and flatly returned fabulous cheques (with the order) to old protégés of the firm merely convicted of fortune-making, or of organized 'philanthropy,' or of 'bettering the conditions' of their fellow creatures. He seems to have hated the virtuous for their own sake alone.

"In short, he grew madder and madder, and the custom, the good-will, even the reputation of the firm melted like butter in the sun. The last Lispet followed the last Double-T—expired of apoplexy in the counting-house, and was sat on by the coroner.

The reigning Vaine turned religious and was buried in a sarcoph-
agus of Portland stone under the foundations of the Unitarian
Chapel which he himself had laid in the hope perhaps to lay the
L. L. & V. devil at the same time.

"The hands dwindled, died out, dropped away, or even emi-
grated to the paws. Only a few with some little competence and
an impulsive fund of gratitude and courtesy worked on for a
master of whom because they loved him, they asked the paltriest
wages. The Fruit Walk mutinied into a thicket; the fountains
choked themselves with sighing and greened with moss; the tulips found a quieter nirvana in mere leaf. And Anthony made at
last no pretence even of patronizing the final perishing flower of
the firm's old clientele.

"He trafficked in a kind of ludicrous dolls' merchandise—utterly beautiful little infinitesimals in fabrics worth a hundred
times their weight in rubies. So ridiculous a scandal had the
'business' at last become that when its few scoffing creditors for
old sake's sake sold it up, not a single bid was made for the property. It is in ruins now. Consult Ezekiel. Or Henrietta.

"I have no wish to sentimentalize; I am not a cynic or a philosopher. Yet I slide my eyes back to that narrow hilled-in strip of
sea-coast whence once rose walled Tyre and Sidon, Arvard and
Jebail, and—well, I merely remind myself that the Rosetta Stone
is but a hornbook of the day before yesterday's children of men.
Things *do* as a matter of fact seem to rot of their own virtue—inverted, so to speak. It's not likely to occur again. I mean, not for
some time. The Town was almost apologetic. Democracy rarely
runs to extremes—unless one may so describe the guillotine. But
I am no politician. Enough of that. Even transatlantic visitors are
now rare."

Maunders and I were standing together by this time under the
laurels and bay trees, not of his own planting, beside his garden
railings; he with his bulging, pale-blue eyes—and his sham candlestick branching out of his pocket; and I—well, irritated beyond
endurance.

"Good heavens, Maunders," I exclaimed, "the stuff you talk!
But one would not mind that so much if you could spin a decent

yarn. You haven't even told me what became of the Belfry. Was he *nothing* but bats at last?"

"Old Anthony?" he murmured softly. "Why, there is nothing in that. He lived on—for years—in the Works. You could see his burning candle from the valley, even on nights of full moon. And, of course, some gay imbecile set the story about that the whole lovely abandoned derelict place was haunted. Twangling strings and vanishing faces, and a musing shape at a remoter window, her eyes reflecting a scene which only an imagination absolutely denuded of common sense could hope or desire to share with her. After all, one does ignore the ghost until it is well out of the body. Ask Henrietta."

"But, Maunders," I called after him.

Too late: his shapeless slouching slate-grey body with its indescribable hat and malacca cane had vanished among the "evergreens," and the only answer I received was the dwindling rumour of my own expostulatory voice among their leaves— "Maunders . . ."

Strange to say, it was in this moment of helplessness that I discovered that my little bast basket was gone. When? How? For an instant I hesitated—in pure cowardice. It was a quarter past one, and Mrs. Maunders, a charming and active hostess, if a little of a martinet, disapproved of unpunctual guests. But only for an instant. The thought of Bettie's fair glad little face decided me; and I set out to retrace my footsteps in search of the lost plaything. Alas, in vain.

The Riddle and Other Stories (1923)

THE THREE FRIENDS

THE STREET was narrow; yet, looking up, the two old friends, bent on their accustomed visit, could discern—beyond a yellow light that had suddenly shone out into the hushed gloom from an attic window—the vast, accumulated thunder-clouds that towered into the darkening zenith.

"That's just it," continued Mr. Eaves, more emphatically, yet more confidentially, "it isn't my health, Sully. I'm not so much afraid of my health. It's—it's my . . ." He took off his hat and drew his hand over his tall, narrow head, but pushed on no further towards the completion of his sentence.

Mr. Sully eyed him stonily. "Don't worry, then," he said. "Why worry? There's worry enough in the world, old sport, without dreaming about it."

"I know," said Mr. Eaves; "but then, you see, Sully—" They had paused at the familiar swing-door, and now confronted one another in the opaque, sultry silence. And as Mr. Sully stood for an instant in close contact with his old crony in the accentuated darkness of the mock-marble porch, it was just as if a scared rabbit had scurried out of Mr. Eaves's long white face.

"Look here," Mr. Sully exclaimed with sudden frivolity, "we'll ask Miss Lacey"; and was followed by his feebly protesting companion into the bar.

The long black stuffed bench and oblong mahogany table, darkened here and there by little circular pools of beer, stood close against the wall, and Mr. Sully began to divulge his friend's confidences even before Miss Lacey could bring them their glasses. A commissionaire sat in the further bar, nodding over an old newspaper; and Mr. Eaves kept his eyes fixed on his oblong lurching head, while he listened, fascinated and repelled, to his friend's facetiousness.

"Now, supposing, Miss Lacey, my dear," began Mr. Sully shrewdly, half-closing his eyes as if to gloss over his finesse, "supposing a young man, a nice, curly-headed young man—just about our old friend's age here"—Miss Lacey, with a kind of arch and sympathetic good-nature, leaned a large, dark head to glance at Mr. Eaves—"supposing a nice young gentleman—just as it might be our old friend himself here—came, like an innocent, to entrust to your blessed bosom a secret—a sacred secret: what would you do?"

"Lor' bless me, Mr. Sully, sir, is that all you was coming to! A secret? Why, keep it, to be sure; and not the first time neether." Miss Lacey advanced to the bar, black, precise and cheerful, with the two small, thick glasses in her hand.

"Good," said Mr. Sully, with an almost professional abandon. "Good. *So* far. But step number two; supposing, my dear, you couldn't for the life and love of you *help* him in his little difficulty —dependent on his secret, let's say—what then?"

"Why, I'd keep it all the more," cried Miss Lacey brightly.

"A woman's answer, Eaves; and none the worse for that," said Mr. Sully. "But on the other hand, supposing you were a practical"—he paused with the little water-jug hovering an inch or two above his friend's glass—"supposing you were a practical, unromantic old blackguard like me—why, you'd go and tell it to the first lovely blooming creature that came along." He eyed her steadily yet jocosely. "And that's why I'm going to tell it to you, my dear!"

"How you do tease, to be sure!" said Miss Lacey. "He's a real tease, isn't he, Mr. Eaves?"

Mr. Sully's eyes suddenly sobered with overwhelming completeness. He pointed coldly with his stick. "He's been dreaming of hell," he said.

Mr. Eaves, on his part, withdrew large, weak, colourless eyes from the uneasy head of the commissionaire, and turned them on Miss Lacey. She glanced at him swiftly, then stooped, and took up a piece of sewing she had laid down on her wooden chair, in the little out-of-the-way bar.

"I don't approve of such subjecs," she said, "treated frivolous."

"Gracious goodness, Eaves," said Mr. Sully, "she says 'frivolous.' Hell—'frivolous'!"

"Why," said Miss Lacey lucidly, "I'm not so green as I look."

"Well, you couldn't look younger, if being young's to be green," said Mr. Sully; "and as sure, my dear, as that was a flash of lightning, it—it's the real thing."

When the faint but cumulative rumble of thunder that followed had subsided, Miss Lacey seemed to have withdrawn her attention. Mr. Sully edged slowly round on his feet and faced his friend. "You old skeleton at the feast! You've alarmed the poor child," he said.

Miss Lacey spoke without raising her eyes, bent closely on her needle. "Not me," she said; "but I don't hold with such ideas."

"Tell her yourself," said Mr. Sully to his friend; "tell her yourself: they never *will* believe *me.*"

Mr. Eaves shook his head.

"Why not?" said Mr. Sully.

"God bless me," said Mr. Eaves, with sudden heat, "I'm old enough to be her father."

Miss Lacey looked up over her sewing. "You'd scarcely believe *me,*" she said mysteriously; "but there was a young gentleman down Charles Street, where I used to be, that had dreams—well, there, shocking! Nobody but me had the patience to listen to him. But you can't give all your attention to one customer, can you? He," she cast a curious glance into the shadows brooding over the commissionaire—"he got up out of his bed one night, just as you or me might—he was living in private apartments, too—struck a match, so they said, and cut his throat. Awful. From ear to ear!" Her thimbled finger made a demure half-circuit of the large pearls of her necklace.

Mr. Sully gazed roundly. "Did he, though? But there, you see," and he leant in great confidence over the counter, "Mr. Eaves here doesn't shave!"

Mr. Eaves smiled vaguely, half-lifting his stick, as if in coquettish acknowledgment of his friend's jest.

"No, no, old friend," he said, "not that, not that, I hope."

"Gracious goodness," said Mr. Sully cordially, "he mustn't take it to heart like that. A dream's a dream."

"Why, of course it is," said Miss Lacey. "You ought to take more care of yourself, sir; didn't he, Mr. Sully?"

Mr. Eaves gazed dispassionately, and yet with some little dignity, in the isolation of attention he had evoked. He turned slowly towards the bar, and stooped a little—confidentially. "Not once, not twice," he said ruminatingly, "but every blessed night. Every blessed night."

Miss Lacey eyed him with searching friendliness.

"Tell her," said Mr. Sully, walking slowly and circumspectly to the door, and peeping out through the cranny into the darkened street.

Mr. Eaves put his empty glass deliberately upon the counter, drew his hand slowly across his lips, and shook his head. "It's nothing to tell, when you come to that. And . . ." he nodded a questioning head towards the solitary occupant of the other bar.

"Oh, fast; bless you," said Miss Lacey. "As reg'lar as clockwork —you'd hardly believe it."

"He'll break his neck, some day," remarked Mr. Sully tersely, "with that jerking."

"You see, my dear," continued Mr. Eaves trustfully, "I don't mind my old friend, Mr. Sully, making a good deal of fun at my expense. He always has: eh, Sully? But he doesn't *see*. You don't *see*, Sully. There the thing is; and truth all over it. Facts are facts —in *my* belief."

"But fire and brimstone, and suchlike; oh no!" said Miss Lacey with a dainty little shudder. "I can't credit it, reelly; oh no! And poor innocent infants, too! You may think of me what you like, but nothing'll make me believe *that*."

Mr. Sully looked over his shoulder at Mr. Eaves. "Oh, that," said his old friend, "was only Mr. Sully's fun. He says it's hell. I didn't. My dream was only—*after;* the state after death, as they call it."

"I see," said Miss Lacey, lucidly, summoning all her intelligence into her face.

Mr. Eaves leaned forward, and all but whispered the curious tidings into her ear. "It's—it's just the same," he said.

"The same?" echoed Miss Lacey. "What?"

"The same," repeated the old man, drawing back, and looking out of his long, grey, meaningless face at the little plump, bright, satiny woman.

"Hell?" breathed Miss Lacey.

"The state after death," called Mr. Sully, still peering into the gloom—and stepped back rather hurriedly in the intense pale lilac illumination of a sudden flickering blaze of lightning.

Thunder now clanged directly overhead, and still Mr. Eaves gazed softly yet earnestly into nothingness, as if in deep thought.

"Whatever you like to call it," he began again, steadily pushing his way, "that's how I take it. I sit with my wife, just the same; cap and 'front' and all, just the same; gas burning, decanter on the table, books in the case, marble clock on the mantelpiece, just the same. Or perhaps I'm walking in the street, just the same; carts and shops and dogs, all just the same. Or perhaps I'm here, same as I might be now; with Sully there, and you there, and him there," he nodded towards the commissionaire. "All just the same. For ever, and ever, and ever." He raised his empty glass to his lips, and glanced almost apologetically towards his old friend. "For ever, and ever," he said, and put it down again.

"He means," said Mr. Sully, "no change: like one of those blessed things on the movies; over and over again, click, click, click, click, click; you know. I tell him it's his sentence, my dear."

"But if it's the same," Miss Lacey interposed, with a little docile frown of confusion, "what's different?"

"Mark me, Eaves, my boy," cried Mr. Sully softly at the door; "it's the ladies for brains, after all. That's what they call a poser. 'What's different,' eh?"

Mr. Eaves pondered in a profound internal silence in the bar. And beyond the windows, the rain streamed steadily in a long-drawn gush of coolness and peace. "What's different?" repeated Mr. Sully, rocking infinitesimally on his heels.

"Why," said Mr. Eaves, "it seems as if there I can't change; can't. If you were to ask me how I know—why, I couldn't say. It's a dream. But that's what's the difference. There's nothing to come. *Now*: why! I might change in a score of ways; just take them as they come. I might fall ill; or Mrs. Eaves might; I might come into some money; marry again. God bless me, I might *die!* But there, that's all over; endless; no escape; nothing. I can't even die. I'm just meself, Miss Lacey; Sully, old friend. Just meself, for ever, and ever. Nothing but me looking on at it all, if you take me—just what I've made of it. It's my"—his large pale eyes roved aimlessly—"it's just what Mr. Sully says, I suppose; it's my sentence. Eh, Sully? wasn't that it? My sentence?" He smiled courageously.

"Sentence, oh no! Sentence? You!" cried Miss Lacey incredulously. "How could you, Mr. Sully? Sentence! What ever for, sir?"

Mr. Eaves again glanced vaguely at the sleeper, and then at his friend's round substantial shoulders, rigidly turned on him. He fixed his eyes on the clock.

"You've never done no harm, Mr. Eaves!" cried Miss Lacey, almost as if in entreaty.

"You see," said the old gentleman, glancing over his shoulder, "it isn't what you do: so I seem to take it." Mr. Sully half turned from the door, as if to listen. "It's what you are," said Mr. Eaves, as if to himself.

"Why, according to that," said Miss Lacey, in generous indignation, "who's safe?"

A day of close and tepid weather followed the storm. But it was on the evening of the next day after that—an evening of limpid sunshine and peace, the sparrows chirping shrilly in the narrow lights and shadows of the lane, that Mr. Sully came in to see Miss Lacey.

She was alone: and singing a little quiet tune to herself as she went about her business. He shook his head when she held up two glasses; and raised just one forefinger.

"He's dead," he said.

"Oh, no!" cried Miss Lacey.

"This morning . . . in his sleep." He gazed at her with an unusual—with a curiously fishlike concentration.

"Poor, poor gentleman," said Miss Lacey. "He *was* a gentleman, too; and no mistake. Never a hard word for nobody; man, woman, or child. Always the same. But it's shocking. Well, well. But how dreadfully sudden, Mr. Sully, sir!"

"Well, I don't know," said Mr. Sully, almost irritably. "And if so, where's the change?" His round shoulders seemed with slight effort almost to shrug themselves.

"Goodness gracious," Miss Lacey cried, "you don't mean—you don't mean to think—you don't say it's true? What he was telling us, Mr. Sully?"

"I'm not so sure," her visitor replied vaguely, almost stubbornly. "Where else, after all, knowing all that, why, where else *could* he go?"

"Mr. Eaves, Mr. Sully? Him? oh, no!"

Mr. Sully, in the intense clear quiet of the bar, continued to stare at her in a manner something like that of an over-glutted vulture. He nodded.

Miss Lacey's kind brown eyes suddenly darkened as if with a gust of storm. "But, then, what about us?" she asked piteously, and yet with the tenderest generosity.

"Well," said Mr. Sully, opening the door, and looking out into the sunny evening air, "if you ask me, that's merely a question of time."

The Riddle and Other Stories (1923)

WILLOWS

THE 2.17 p.m. this lovely, sleepy, precocious afternoon left only one passenger behind it on the wooden platform of the minute country station of Ashenham. Its volumes of vapour went ballooning up under the immense blue dome of the heavens; its nearly empty compartments rolled by; it was gone. And lo, Ronnie Forbes. With a shortsighted but observant glance at his rural whereabouts he stuffed his French novel into his pocket, gave up his ticket, passed through the booking-office, and looked round for a cab. Here, however, the only signs of life were an empty farm-wagon, a gaudy red and yellow reaping machine, and a bevy of sparrows engaged in a dust-bath.

He turned back, and with that bland air of assurance which sets its possessor at ease in any company, he inquired of the porter if he knew of a house called Willows. The porter was so old and so old-fashioned that he touched his hat when he replied. He knew Willows well. Mrs. Cotton's house. And he gave Ronnie copious and reiterated directions how to get there. It lay about two and a half miles distant. You turned to the left at the signpost after passing the "Green Man," took the third turning on the right—a little before you reached the old windmill—and went straight on until you came to a little old stone bridge over a stream. And there you were. Why, yes, there *was* a fly, and it *could* be fetched from the village—and that was a mile or so in the other direction. But it was an easy walk if you liked walking; "And you can't miss it, sir," he repeated again and again. It was as though here was an ardent pilgrim, and there, Mecca. Ronnie didn't quite see himself descending on his prey in lonely grandeur in the village cab, and he had plenty of time. He waived the suggestion, and at once set out.

No rain seemed to have refreshed the white dusty road for months past; indeed, on a chalky soil even a plenteous fall of dew vanishes into thin air when once the morning sun is up. But the meadows beyond the leafy hedgerow on the one side were as gay as a picture, and the dark acres of ploughland on the other were already sheened over with the first blades of sprouting corn. Sophisticated and urban creature though he looked amid this rural scene, Ronnie went on his way rejoicing.

Nor did his footsteps flag until he had passed the rather tumble-down "Green Man" and the incredibly old traditional broadside gaffer in gaiters who sat with his beard and his blue-and-white mug on a bench under its motionless sign. Still, it was warm work, and as soon as a gateway showed, Ronnie came to a standstill and took off his hat. He leant both arms on the gate and looked over and in. The pasture in front of him rose in a smooth wide curve of the embosoming earth against the pure blue of the sky, and there in the tender sunshine stood browsing sedate old mother ewes, while others, no less stolidly maternal of aspect, sat motionless in the lush young grass. How human, and how stupid, they looked, thought Ronnie: and how engaging!

And round about these sober dames was a host of long-legged lambs, their small inquisitive faces all turned in his direction, with sudden tremors of dangling flat woolly tails, and zigzag leapings and skippings aside in full butt of their mothers' dugs. What adorable country! And the woods over there, a faint purple with their bare twigs, though a few were now full in their virgin young leaf! Larks, too—it was impossible to say how many. It was as though each one of them had its own spiral pitch in the blue, and had only to range that airy and invisible tower to keep its walls for ever echoing with song.

Ronnie took a deep breath: it was little short of absurd—the combination of such a day and such an errand! None the less he had made pretty certain of fine weather before setting out. For he hadn't the faintest notion what kind of house and what kind of people were awaiting him. They might be perfectly awful, quite too impossible. Imagine that and a shivering leaden day together! On the other hand, the house might prove to be empty. Imagine *that,* and rain pelting down upon its abandoned porch! However, the porter had settled the question: "Mrs. Cotton's house"—his very words. She was still there, then. But had the inquiring emphasis he had put on the name suggested something the least bit formidable? Ronnie shuddered. He did so dislike raw, unpleasant, intractable people.

What a silly expedition! It all came of this touching greed on the other side of the Atlantic for the academic; this thesis craze. But data at second hand, was that really quite proper? Ronnie was still dubious. Surely any young zealot bent on a thesis should conduct his own investigations, should himself play sexton to his dead and buried subject, and with his own privy paw dig it up again. It was the least one would expect of him.

Yet here was this young American friend of his—and with the

most endearing enthusiasm in the world—calmly devolving this little obligation on himself. Ronnie had agreed, of course, that James Cotton's poems were worth excavation, and that could hardly be said of most of his contemporaries. Brief life was here *their* portion. And though a few of them were still alive their works were almost as dead as mutton. Not so James Cotton: precisely the reverse in fact. His achievement had been rivalled only by his promise—a promise, however, which could scarcely be said to have been kept, since after the publication of that first "slender" volume—to use the reviewers' unanimous epithet—it had dwindled away into a mere pamphlet, the contents of which had been luminous enough in sparks, but in general so obscure as to be almost disconcerting.

What these later poems "promised"—and four whole years separated the two books—well, Ronnie couldn't for the life of him imagine. It was veiled in an Egyptian darkness. Not that he knew even the little of James Cotton there was to know by *heart*. By no means. He felt a little conscience-stricken at thought of it—just in case in an hour or two he might be in for a catechism on the subject.

The truth was, of course, that in American seats of learning nowadays there are not nearly enough themes-for-theses to go round. You can hardly see literature for the *littérateurs*. For that very reason it was a stroke of pure luck for his young friend to have chanced on James Cotton. Except for an article—"an appreciation"—published about nine years before in one of the heavier Reviews, James was still practically virgin soil. And what an owlish and incredible performance that had been.

Take, for example, the lovely country in which Ronnie was now disporting himself. There hadn't been a single word in the article from start to finish to suggest what delightfully Blake-like surroundings the young poet had enjoyed in his childhood. The little shallow stream that was now tinkling at Ronnie's side over its sunny stones beneath a screen of vast-boughed elms with their clanking chaffinches; that hill over there, almost gaudy from crown to base with budded larch—it was all so rich, so gentle, and so deliciously English.

And then, after the barest mention of Ashenham, to have

asserted that the poet had gone and died in foreign parts! Byron and Shelley were exiles, of course, and so was Landor. Keats had gone to die in Rome. Cyril Charlton in his paper had been eloquence itself about all *that*. But Trinidad! Ronnie, all alone as he was, all but burst out laughing at the sound of the syllables in his mind. A charming asphaltic island, no doubt, but if you were pulling the long and sentimental bow why not have said Tobago —which has at least a pleasing suggestion of tapioca. But Trinidad! Those dreadful d's—like the slabs of a sarcophagus.

And his enthusiastic young American friend in every single letter on the subject had been so emphatic about Trinidad. He had even coquetted with the prospect of embarking for Port of Spain to look up the poet's inscription on his tombstone. How deliciously naïve. But Ronnie knew better. Wherever else *his* James Cotton may have deceased—he waggled his cane in the air to emphasize the point—he hadn't closed his eyes for the last time on *that* island. And, among other little duties, Ronnie was now well on his way to prove it.

He smiled to himself and, as there was plenty of time if he was to arrive at a polite hour, he came to a standstill again, and stooping his slightly tubby figure over the warm lichenous stones of the little old bridge, gazed into the amber running water beneath. Minnows—he watched them disporting themselves in their watery sun-dappled shallows, and almost subsided into a daydream. The simple little fishes had reminded Ronnie that he had once been young himself, and was now, well, getting middle-aged. Whither had fled their visionary gleam? In those far years they wouldn't have reminded him of whitebait! Yet Ronnie, too, in his salad days had published a sheaf of essays.

Yes. But what ages ago they seemed, and how raw a Ronnie then! One can't really *live* in two worlds at once. Yet even the most dilettantish of interests in some other than the prosperous one he was now occupying was, perhaps, better than none. A faint splendour lightened his mission. Whatever else he might have been, James Cotton's venture into poetry had been the real thing. And now Ronnie was on his way to inquire exactly how and when and where and why, and so on. A literary Sherlock Holmes.

With a look that might almost be described as grumpy he abandoned the minnows and went on. And now the stream had left him, *fa lero lero loo.* It had sallied off under a low-vaulted arch, danced over with reflected sunbeams, and a high stone wall flanking the lane had taken its place; an old wall too, with a rain-worn stone coping and with clumps of matted ivy and valerian bunching over it here and there.

"A little cottage girl" in a pinafore and with lank strands of yellow hair was approaching. When Ronnie asked for "Willows" she put her finger into her mouth and, gazing at him out of forget-me-not blue eyes, pointed mutely to a gateway not thirty yards distant. She might have come straight out of "We are Seven." Ronnie smiled at her as cherubically as he could manage, and yet, though he could not have said why, out of a mist of misgivings.

"Don't for Jehoshaphat's sake *write* to these Cotton people," his young American friend had implored him. "Even that Charlton guy seems to have been a little dubious about his reception. And no wonder! He is deadly effusive under that mincing style; but after *that,* if they had any warning they might stave you off for good. As I say, it's ten to one there will be nobody to remember J. C. now, but please be a dear and make sure. It would be no end of a scoop if I could get really fresh new-laid first-hand stuff about him—all his little ways and wiles, a few private letters *par excellence,* and photographs, of course. He seems to have been a hermit even in his twenties, and who knows what queer fish may not have shared his pond. But for heaven's sake don't *write* to them; just press the button and say you've come. *You*'ll know best, of course; and this is sheer hippopotamus talk."

This, of course, as Ronnie had decided at the time, was all very nice and exuberant and pleasant and characteristic. But now, as—after surveying the one faint word "Willows" on the old green paint—he pushed the gate open, and turned in on the weedy path, he couldn't help noticing that he felt a little self-conscious, even *gauche.* The very grass, the bead-bright moss on the pebbles, hinted at seclusion. Even the blackbirds seemed to be surprised to see a visitor. The rustic lettering of that "Willows," the serenity and unnoticeableness of it all—Ronnie all but then and there experienced a change of heart.

Even if one does publish a book of poems when one is scarcely out of one's teens—*i.e.,* even if one does scatter one's pearls before a public that much prefers wash—it doesn't in itself exactly justify any more fastidious inquirer from the country of the Gadarenes in pushing his nose in years after one has died and been buried in Trinidad merely to pick up tasty bits of gossip for a thesis! Good heavens, what deeds are done in thy name, O Muses!

The path wound round. The persistent shallow stream rippled into view again, and over there, across a verdant meadow, not yet in the buttercup stage, stood bushed in beauty—not a few crazy old pollard relics of willows, but a full-boughed bountiful grove of them. And a little to eastward of them, in the haze of the afternoon sun, lay a smallish, low-roofed, quite ordinary-looking, quiet and glinting country house. Not very old, but on the other hand, not very new.

Some poets have opened their eyes for the first time on the amenities of Camberwell; some, on those of Chicago. Weeds may flourish, with an effort, in a gravel path. But little James Cotton had been fortunate indeed in the place where he was born, even though there appeared to be no surplus income just now to keep it up. No actual neglect, but obviously no under-gardener. Did thick creepers make a house damp or did they keep the bricks dry? It was one of the two, but Ronnie couldn't remember which. And anyhow, the *Pyrus japonica,* with its shallow-cupped wine-red flowers, and the bushy-bloomed laurestinus did not seem to mind.

Ronnie took it all in, though his eyes remained discreetly downcast, just in case he was being observed from the windows. Better no appearance of boldness. And so, cane in hand, light overcoat over arm, he stepped at last into the embowered porch, and gave a vigorous tug at the twisted iron bell-pull. Its distant tinkling dwindled away, and except, as he fancied, for the sound of a firm but hasty footstep that had immediately followed it, only the shrillings of the skylarks overhead now broke the quiet.

Ronnie was no Miss Brontë. He was not one of those shy (and sometimes even elderly) creatures that ring and run away. He was entirely unalarmed at strangers. Nevertheless, as he stood waiting there, he was hoping solely for the best—that nobody was at home. Why not? He had enjoyed his country walk. Here was the house. Let sleeping poets lie. He would have done his duty, and theses might go to the devil.

A moment after, at sight of a stiff, high-capped, ageing, and obviously unfriendly maidservant, he changed his mind. The least symptom of opposition not only decoyed him on, but increased his natural suavity. He inquired if this was "Willows," and on being assured by an abrupt nod that it was, he asked if it were still occupied by a lady of the name of Cotton, and *that* being so, might he perhaps be favoured with a few minutes of her valuable time.

"Mrs. Cotton is not well enough to see visitors," was the stony retort. And the grey eyes that continued to regard him after the narrow lips had shut again, hinted that for the word "visitor" he might, if he chose, substitute such a synonym, say, as hawker or tax-collector. But Ronnie was easily able not to feel a little piqued. He smiled, and remarked, "I am Mr. Ronald Forbes," and at the same time drew out of his pocket-book, and presented this dragon with—a visiting-card. "I wouldn't detain Mrs. Cotton for more than a few moments," he assured her, sagaciously raising his voice a little. "It is merely to ask her kindness in a matter in which we are both deeply interested. And for this reason I hoped she would forgive me anything in the nature of an intrusion."

The maid took the card between finger and thumb. She appeared to be still hesitating whether to keep it as a trophy or to return it, when a voice out of the beyond, and apparently from the landing of the shallow staircase nearly opposite the door, decided the question.

"Show this gentleman into the drawing-room, please, Fanny. I will be with him in a few moments."

Having proffered his hat to his enemy, who far from accepting it did not even waste a glance on its beautiful lining, Ronnie laid it with his light overcoat on a small mahogany bench that stood beneath an engraving of one of Raphael's masterpieces. And he stood up his cane beside it. He glanced at the barometer which hung on the "flock" crimson-papered wall on the other side, and an instant afterwards found himself in a room, his first impression of which suggested that he had been shown into a hothouse by mistake.

It was not only a study in all shades of green, but even more verdant in effect than anything which spring had managed to regale him with on his way from the station. Ronnie had a lively eye for colour. It roved from the moss-green carpet to the curtains of green French flowered brocade, to the sage-green wall-paper, and so, one by one, on to the Victorian "easy" chairs, upholstered in a colour which in cooler circumstances would have suggested the cucumber.

But this verdure was not all artifice. In a recess near the shut small-paned window on his left stood a wooden erection of shelves, upon which pots of flowers in full bloom were banked in the utmost profusion. With the result that the room—much longer than it was wide, its French windows at the further end being also tight shut, though the afternoon sun swept steadily through them in a motionless cascade—the room smelt like some delicious fruit-pie. Freesia, perhaps.

Ronnie stood there in his elegant West End clothes, right in the middle of it, as if he were an egg-cup under the crust of the low-moulded ceiling, while portraits in oils of what he assumed to be deceased Cottons surveyed him from every wall. He was warm after his walk in this precocious spring weather, and though his reception had been a little chilly his present haven was very much the reverse. And as he glanced from portrait to portrait he was conscious of an almost irrestible impulse to giggle, and at the same time more disquietingly aware than ever that his dossier, so to speak, was rather on the nebulous side. Ronnie had read the poems, but not lately. He could appreciate verse with extreme rapidity; but now that the crisis was at hand, actual remembrance of salient specimens, and even of the precise quality of the collections, had suddenly eluded him.

Perhaps this was in part because the low firm voice he had heard on the staircase had continued to sound on in his ear. He was still vaguely engaged in an attempt to recover his *amour propre,* of which he had an ample supply, when the door by which he had entered opened, and he found himself, smile for smile, confronting a lady of substantial proportions, whom he judged to be somewhat on the other side of sixty. Her elaborately dressed hair closely fitted her square practical head. There were still traces of auburn in its grey. And out of the wide flattish face beneath, with its small square formidable nose, green-grey eyes motionlessly examined him.

With a curt but not unfriendly nod of her head this lady referred him to a low flounced arm-chair, which splayed its short Victorian legs full in the light of the French windows, while she seated herself in a less comfortable one immediately opposite him.

Ronnie cleared his throat, but paused.

"I understand you wished to see *me*," she said. "Am I right in supposing that I owe the pleasure of your visit to an interest in the writings of my son, Mr. James Cotton?"

Ronnie's neatly proportioned hand wandered to his necktie, and he opened his mouth to reply.

"I see," Mrs. Cotton continued pleasantly—"I see I have guessed right. Please tell me then exactly what I can do for you."

If only, thought Ronnie, the good old lady would look the other way for a moment, he might hope to make a much better show. On the contrary she sat stoically upright in her chair, her shoulders squared above her fortified bosom, her knees close together over her square-toed shoes, her whole frame encased in a primrose-coloured afternoon gown—its only adornments a cameo brooch on a small black bow, a thin gold chain about her neck, and a cluster of sapphires on her wedding-ring finger— while she steadily continued to hold his eyes.

"It is very kind indeed of you," began Ronnie. "I was afraid that a visit like this from a complete stranger, and without any warning or introduction, could not but seem in the nature of an intrusion. To be quite candid, Mrs. Cotton, I was afraid that if I wrote to you first, asking for the privilege of such an opportunity, I might be—well, misunderstood."

"That," was the reply, "would all depend on what you actually said in your letter."

"Yes," retorted Ronnie warmly. "But then you know what letters are. Besides, as a matter of fact I have come, not on my own behalf—though, in a sense, that very much too, for I am, of course, *deeply* interested—but on behalf of a friend of mine, a young American, now at the University of Ohio. He is most anxious to—"

But Mrs. Cotton had suavely interrupted him. "Almost exactly nine years have gone by, Mr. Forbes, since I have heard of any one being interested enough in my son's writings to come all the way from London, as I see you have—let alone America—to tell me so. I receive letters now and then, but very few. But although, as I say, nine years have gone by, that particular occasion is still quite fresh in my mind. Your friend may not perhaps have seen an article which appeared about that time in the *Modern Literature Review*?"

"That was the very reason—" began Ronnie, but Mrs. Cotton had once more intervened, almost as if she were anxious to save him even from the most candid of white lies.

"It is a relief to me that you *have* seen the—the article. I wonder if you would be very much surprised, Mr. Forbes, or whether perhaps you will think me ungracious, if I say that I didn't entirely approve of it. What are *your* feelings?"

The light-coloured eyes under the square brows never swerved by a hair's breadth, while Ronnie at last managed to get in his reply.

"You mean, of course," he said, "Cyril Charlton? Well, quite candidly, Mrs. Cotton, and I can say it without the faintest vestige of disloyalty, for I haven't the pleasure of knowing Mr. Charlton, I thought his paper was amateurish and superficial. He is a critic of sorts, of course; and I have no doubt he—meant well. But, how shall I say it?—the whole thing was so fumbling and uncertain. He didn't seem to—"

"In some respects," Mrs. Cotton interjected, rounding her eye at him as inquiringly as might a robin perched on a sexton's shovel, "in some respects hardly '*uncertain*,' surely?"

"Oh, you mean in the facts," said Ronnie.

"I mean in the facts," said Mrs. Cotton. "I am not suggesting that Mr. Charlton was anything but perfectly polite and, if one may say so, plausible, though I use the word in no damaging sense, of course. He knew my son's poems, I won't say by heart, but certainly by rote. He sat where you sit now and quoted them

to me. Stanza after stanza, as if they had just been dug up out
of the grave, as I understand Mr. Rossetti's were. As if I had never
read a line of them myself. He was, he assured me, profoundly
interested in literature, 'profoundly.' He was astonished, seemed
genuinely astonished, at the thought that so few lovers of poetry
—his own words—had even so much as heard of my son's books.
A fair, rather silly-looking young man; with a cheek like a girl's.
I couldn't have conceived such fluency possible. He talked and
talked. That, of course, was exceedingly nice of him and, so far
as it went, reassuring. But, believe me, Mr. Forbes, he almost took
my breath away. I said to myself, here is a young man whose zeal
has outrun his good sense, and *therefore*, of course, I gave him all
the help I could. Such overflowing, such disarming enthusiasm—
what harm could there be in that?"

Ronnie tried hard to prevent his face from showing the smallest
change of expression while he hastily masticated this question.
In these domestic surroundings, ordinary enough in some respects
but startlingly novel in others, it was so difficult to be certain what
degree of irony this rather formidable lady intended. And at
whose expense? Ten years ago: yet still the very accents of that
flaxen ass of a Charlton seemed to be haunting these green recesses! Ronnie became so horribly tongue-tied at last that he
felt a blush mounting up into his cheek—as he sat mutely on,
seeking inspiration and finding none in the view from the French
windows.

The lawn beyond had been recently mown. Its daffodils stood
as motionless in their clusters as if they had been drugged by
the sunshine. In a looping flash of blue a tomtit alighted for an
instant on the dangling coconut shell in the verandah, glanced in
from its reptilian blunt little head at Ronnie, and with a flutter
of wing posted off again. And still he could think of nothing
to say.

Meanwhile, it seemed, Mrs. Cotton, by no means expecting an
answer, had been steadily engaged in taking him in. Her slightly
mannish and astringent voice again broke the silence.

"We have used the word 'facts,' Mr. Forbes," she suavely invited him. "Tell me what—in that absurd account of my son's
early years—amused you most?"

"Quite frankly?" Ronnie, suddenly refreshed, turned quickly about and met her eyes. "Well, quite frankly, Mrs. Cotton, that he had died in Trinidad. I felt morally certain that *that* was, well," he shrugged his shoulders, "fiddlededee." . . .

The rather frog-like ageing face had not faltered at this intimate reference, and Ronnie at once pressed on.

"Trinidad, first. And next, the fantastic little account of how while he was still only an infant in arms he used to dance in his nurse's lap at the window during a thunderstorm and clap his hands at the lightning. It wasn't so much the thing in itself, but simply Charlton's namby-pamby way of putting it. It simply wasn't true, and had been cribbed of course from Coleridge. Or was it Walter Scott? Oh, a host of things."

What resembled a merry but not very resonant peal of laughter had greeted this burst of scepticism.

"I see," cried Mrs. Cotton, still laughing, "but *why* did you conclude—Trinidad?"

Ronnie had begun to breathe a little more freely again.

"Why, don't you see, things surely, even apart from words, are true—right, I mean—only in their appropriate setting. The thunderstorm at the nursery window (even though he didn't say lattice or casement), manifestly wasn't. It wasn't in the *picture,* or rather—to put it exactly opposite to that—it was just what a writer like Cyril Charlton would be bound to say, when once he had started on that kind of thing. He led himself on. Just roses, roses all the way; and nothing to show that he knew one variety from another. He *meant* well, oh yes. But there is simply no bottom to the abyss of mere blague into which such a sentimentalist can sink. Oh, I think you can rely on me in that. As a matter of fact"—it was a bold move Ronnie felt in the circumstances, but he risked it—"it was chiefly *because* of—of all this that I ventured to inflict myself upon you to-day. Trinidad! It was to say the least of it so idiotically inartistic. I almost burst out laughing at thought of it on my way from the station. And what adorable country!"

But Mrs. Cotton ignored the enticing compliment.

"And yet, Mr. Forbes," she was saying, and much more thoughtfully than the truism seemed to warrant, "Trinidad or no

Trinidad, I suppose we all have to die somewhere. Nor did I
realize there was anything 'inartistic' in his saying that. To me it
was merely untrue. It *may* have been my mentioning that my
husband was at *Trinity* led him astray; but even at that—well,
it was so completely out of the blue. Even, too, if Trinidad *had*
been the—the scene of my son's death, what then?"

But for the life of him, Ronnie couldn't blurt out the question
that had at once offered itself. He merely went on listening.

And for a moment Mrs. Cotton watched him doing so. "But
since," she pressed on, "you have used that particular word—
'inartistic,' I mean—do please enlighten me. What kind of people
really enjoy Mr. Charlton's kind of writing? It was more or less
new to *me* at the time; but I have noticed since then that though
his performance was a little sillier than most, it was quite in the
new fashion. Nowadays one has only to write a book, it seems, to
make even one's kitchen cat an animal worth adorning a newspaper with. And not merely literary men but quite young actresses, apart from soaps and cigarettes and cosmetics and that sort
of thing, are invited, almost as a matter of course apparently, by
editors of newspapers who must be quite intelligent men, to air
their views on marriage, or the soul, or a future life—on *that* sort
of thing. Quite as a matter of course. Do you think it much
helps?"

Ronnie gallantly met her eye. "Whom?" he said.

"Ah, who? I was thinking myself of what is called the 'man
in the street' and the woman under his roof. But then, I suppose,
there have always been a few talkative sillies in the world who
completely underestimate the common sense of people in general.
Or is it getting old, Mr. Forbes, that makes the sillies of one's
latter days seem a little sillier than usual? My own small view is
that life may be tragic and sorrowful enough in the long run—
and for the young actresses, too, poor things; they've much to
lose: but that it isn't—well, just Trinidad and thunderstorms.
There may be things, I mean, better left unsaid."

Ronnie stirred in his chair. He hadn't intended this little turn
to the talk. "Exactly," he agreed. "Still you wouldn't suggest even
Cyril Charlton meant to be as bad as all that?"

"Be fair to me, Mr. Forbes. Haven't I already confessed that I thought him an almost entirely harmless-looking young man? 'Meant to be,' indeed! I doubt if he was conscious of so much as brushing the down off a butterfly's wing. Yet, would you believe it, my brother Major Winslow, at that time in India, was inclined, though not for my son's sake only, to take more drastic steps. It was only with the greatest difficulty that I persuaded him not to consult his lawyer."

Yet again a curiously muffled and not quite unjangled peal of little bells sounded between the walls. Mrs. Cotton had laughed. And at sound of it a remote, fiery, defiant gleam had flamed up and vanished in Ronnie's brown eyes.

"If I may venture to say so," he said stoutly, "I think that course would have been as ill-advised as it would have been ineffective."

Mrs. Cotton graciously beamed at him. "I am delighted to hear you say so," she assured him. "Those were, I believe, almost the precise words I used in my reply to Major Winslow. Idle nonsense of that sort, however shallow and however false, is *not* libellous. And—whether or not *after* actual consultation with his lawyer, I cannot say—he came round in the end to our way of looking at it. Poor Mr. Charlton! I can see him in the witnessbox! But I referred to Major Winslow merely as an example of what I suppose would be called the Philistine view of Mr. Charlton's form of entertainment. My brother's and mine. What is more, I am entrusting these little confidences to your ear alone, simply because even if we neither of us have any particular friendliness for this young man, we don't bear him any ill-will. So far as I am concerned, he can be left to stew in his own juice." Mrs. Cotton nearly doubled her substantial shape in two as she leaned forward in her chair to insist on this vulgarism.

"You see," she hurried on, "I am taking it for granted that *you* are really interested in my son's work, and would be far more severe on some of Mr. Charlton's shortcomings—the artistic ones, for instance—even than I should be myself: his own mother, I mean. But tell me, has this young American friend of whom you speak any intention of *publishing* his thesis? If so, I hope I may be allowed to see it. Or is it to be a little private venture undertaken solely with the intention of keeping to the poems and of putting Mr. Charlton *right*?"

For a moment or two Ronnie pondered both these questions. They seemed to be equally crucial and dangerous. Ponder, alas, when he could hardly hear himself think, so loud were his inward execrations of the young friend in question. *Solely* with the intention of putting that silly, precious, sentimental ass of a C. C. right!—he could picture the young post-graduate's exultant grin at such an opportunity, even to the glinting gold of his exquisite "dentures." He gave a sharp impatient tug at his hardly less exquisite Bond Street trousering, and briskly crossed his legs.

"Publication *was* his intention," he replied, "and not merely to do as you suggest." But he wished the accents in which he had uttered this confession had not sounded as if he were a company promoter apologizing for a balance sheet.

"In other words, Mr. Forbes, I am to understand, then, that your visit to me to-day is not solely with a view to the success of this young man's university studies? You, too, have come to see me—not, of course, on your own behalf, but in kindness to your friend—in order to glean what you can of my son's personal and private affairs?"

The challenge was unmistakable. It rang out like a trumpet, and Ronnie could neither smile now nor reply. He moistened his lips. Though of late years more and more easily bored, he was still interested in human nature. The poet's mother had proved to be of a type he seldom encountered even on the outskirts of his ordinary orbit. He dearly enjoyed, too, a battle of wits. But this was hardly "wits," and he was as yet uncertain exactly where he himself was likely to remain—on which side of the fence, that is. All he could blurt out at last sounded much less pacifying than he intended to make it.

"You will forgive me," he said, "if I don't entirely agree with you. I mean on the principle of the thing. Surely, Mrs. Cotton, the publication of a book implies that the author of it is to that degree sharing himself with the world at large. Poetry in particular. He puts into print what he wouldn't confide in secret even to his closest friend. It is a confessional wide as the heavens!

Within certain limits, then, isn't the world at large justified in being interested not merely in him as a writer but as a human being? I agree that this can go too far, that it usually does, in fact. Mere prying curiosity is odious. And there's no need to be vulgar. But how can one separate entirely a man from his work, and especially if the *one* one *is,* as it were, explanatory of the other? Besides"—he took the fence that offered itself in one sprightly bound—"one doesn't have to be a Paul Pry to be grateful, say, for William Shakespeare's second-best bed."

Mrs. Cotton smoothed down her unmodishly long skirts over her lap. She, too, paused with stooping head, as if listening, or as if her thoughts had wandered. Then once again she openly faced him.

"In a moment or two I shall be ready and perfectly willing, Mr. Forbes," she answered him, "to answer *any* question you like to ask me. I won't say that I agree either in principle or in detail with what you have said. And—though I can only guess how dreadfully ignorant it must sound—I know nothing whatever about William Shakespeare's second-best bed. Weren't beds very expensive in those days? I seem to have read that somewhere. But all this apart, I should like to consider you, if I may, not only as a confidant, but as a friend. That being so, first, I propose to make a little private confession. Please listen to me as patiently as you can."

All Ronnie's native gallantry had mounted into his head at this appeal. For the first time for years he was the victim of an enlarged heart. He composed himself to listen.

"You must realize in the first place that I know very little *about* books and nothing whatever about poetry. I am not even a great reader; indeed if I were, that would be quite another question. Poetry is not in me, it is not in *my* family. As a child I detested it, the very word. I was therefore made to learn as much of it as a stupid governess could make me. I see myself at this moment, with tear-grimed cheeks and nose flattened to my nursery window, looking out on a world of rain and wind, and some thumbed, dog's-eared, horrid little book of poetry clutched in my grubby paw, containing not only poems, mind, definitely intended to do me good, but such famous pieces as 'Piping down the valleys wild,' and 'The Assyrian came down.' That kind of thing. Well, I hated them *all* with an almost physical hatred. Which merely means, I suppose, that even as a child I was of a practical and matter-of-fact turn of mind. But that, I believe, is true of many young children. As we are, so we remain; at least in deficiency of mind: it is a dreadful consideration, Mr. Forbes. Whether interest in poetry and in works of the imagination would ever have been mine in happier circumstances I cannot say. I can only confess that it never has. My husband was precisely the opposite, and my son, spared, in his childhood at least, the thorns and thistles which the little donkey that I used to be discovered in what I was fed on, took after him.

"I have heard of mothers, Mr. Forbes, who have been jealous of the love and intimacy between a child and its father. That's beyond my understanding. But when my husband died, I was for many years my son's only real company. You can be delicate in spirit as well as in body—a delicacy, I mean, that is none the less the very reverse of weakness. So you see, as time went on, he was practically compelled to confide in *me*. Apart from the craving to express oneself—though that, too, is not in me—little though you may be supposing it just now!—there is the craving to share what comes of it, afterwards. I can understand that. And though I could listen with all my heart and soul, to *share* I could only pretend. My son soon realized this, though I hid it from him as much as I could.

"Yet I tried—believe me, Mr. Forbes, I honestly tried—to educate, to force myself into his way of thinking. You'd be vastly amused to hear how much poetry I have read solely with that end in view, and almost always with complete unsuccess."

A sudden unbosoming smile swept over her face, like a burst of sunshine over corn-shocks at harvest-tide. "If I go on like this," she broke off, "you will be suspecting that I think it is *my* confessions you are after!"

Ronnie greeted this sally as amply as he knew how, inwardly speculating the while how it came about that with so easy and bountiful a field to glean Cyril Charlton had carried off so mingy a sheaf. Why, even a raw reporter . . . ! But Mrs. Cotton was hastening on.

"Egotist or not," she was saying, "I toiled on at my task, and at least became a little more capable of realizing the force and the strain of my son's secret idolatry. There was only one thing in the world for him—poetry. At first I believe he hadn't the faintest desire or intention to share this craving with any other human being except his father. Afterwards, I happened to be there, and—there wasn't anybody else. And though I had fallen far short of any true appreciation, I had become aware of two things: first, that there *is* such a thing as poetry, and next, that I had a pretty shrewd notion of what poetry *isn't*.

"Poetry, Mr. Forbes, as I have tried to understand it,"—she waved her hand towards the window—"is all *there,* just waiting for us. But it won't necessarily show itself at call or even at need. *Un paysage est un état de l'âme*; and so of poetry. One must— am I right?—have the mind, the sense, the spirit within—to invoke it. *That* I realize. It is a way of looking at things, a way of feeling about them, almost of being them—a way of *living.* And it is, I suppose—you will let me go groping on—as inseparable, if you *have* that particular sense and insight—as inseparable, I say, from the world at large and everything in it as its scent is from a flower. And no *more* inseparable either, for just as you can extract its scent from a flower and shut it up in a bottle, so you can extract the poetry from the life around and within you and put it into words and them into a book. *Is* that so? Am I even in the right direction?" She stooped towards her silent visitor as if her very life might depend upon his answer— an answer that none the less failed to come. "Well, I am being dreadfully clumsy, dreadfully commonplace. But I believe all that as surely, though maybe as gropingly, as a blind man believes that there is such a thing as light.

"Yet the thing itself is hidden from me, shut out from me. Try as I may, I cannot grasp or share it. On the one side my son, almost coldly conscious, I might say, of these volcanic feelings, pursuing this strange mystery, this mirage, eating his heart out, never satisfied, ready to sacrifice anything, everything, for its sake; and on the other, myself—stuttering and pretending, but so far as heart and soul are concerned, absolutely as dumb and insensitive as a fish.

"In spite of this, he was always generosity itself to me, though I knew that if the worst ever came to the worst even a mother would have to be sacrificed on that altar. But at last, as you know, his poems were published. Published."

The rather flat yet mobile face had cleared at the word as if, for the moment at least, these riddles and perplexities were over, as if she had steered clear of the reefs. "You will be amused to hear that I myself arranged all that: the printing, the paper, the binding—*his* final choice, of course. I saw the publisher, a Mr. Crown, in London, again and again, and settled *everything* —expenses, advertising, commission, everything. He, too, in spite of his dingy little office and a *very* extraordinary secretary, seemed to be a most enthusiastic admirer of poetry, though, as I have since discovered—and here Mr. Charlton could give me surprisingly little information—I was treated on severely business-like principles. Indeed between ourselves, Mr. Forbes, I soon began to suspect not merely this gentleman's enthusiasm but, well, his honesty also. So far eventually as our little book was concerned it might just as well, on his side, have been soap or sugar!

"The critics, on the other hand—though I was unable to follow all that they said, which was not, of course, at great *length*— were exceedingly kind. I don't mean that they were more than just—how could I? They were exceedingly kind. Some thirty copies of the book, I was given to understand, were sent to the newspapers, and about eight were sold. But apart from the bills I paid I have never had any particulars. For the time being, my son found a good deal of happiness in his venture. And then I think the merely practical side of it began to bother him a little. He fancied that we, that I, had been dreadfully cheated. I had gone off to this Mr. Crown, I should have mentioned, without my son's knowledge. But it wasn't so much the money involved —though I happened to learn afterwards he did *not* pay fees for the reviews—it was—well, I suppose, the humiliation. My son was grieved and ashamed at what such things come to. He had been kept by his father, for his own sake perhaps, too long out of the world to realize its sense of proportion. Nevertheless, he went on writing. But with more and more difficulty. A dreadful despair seemed to have come over him. He shunned everyone. He had been—mortally—wounded. But I, even then, was powerless to help him. We know so little of what is passing in any other mind—even those nearest to us. And then—at last . . . Well, there is no need to go into that."

She had paused again, and the pair of them, so far as their eyes were concerned, seemed to be like two funeral birds hovering over some morsel which neither of them had much appetite for—though it was part of God's plenty—and which it was hardly in the nature of things that they should be able to *share*. Nevertheless, Ronnie was conscious rather of a void than of any very definite dainty, and he could only blink.

But the pause had come at an opportune moment. So hot and airless was the low-pitched room in which they sat, so heavy the odour of the flowers around them, that but a few instants before, though his gaze had remained fixed on Mrs. Cotton's face, his glazing orbs from sheer sleepiness had actually rocked in his head. Now he was wide awake again; and he had need to be, for Mrs. Cotton was hastening on.

"To our second venture, as you may be aware, Mr. Forbes, the critics were less kind. They, too, couldn't fully understand what my son was after, though better than I could. Could you?"

At this her visitor's round and somewhat fresh-coloured face perceptibly paled. Yet again the trumpet had sounded. For a breath he hesitated, and then bolted the lump that had come into his throat. "I don't know the poems well enough to say," he said.

Mrs. Cotton turned away. "Well, I am grateful to you for *that*," was her unexpected retort. But her voice had trailed off a little as if from some inward rather than from any mere physical fatigue.

"That being so, you will the more readily realize, then," she continued, "that when, after the publication of my son's second book—which was, as a matter of fact, destined to be his last— it became clear to me that even those who are supposed to understand such things were unable to follow him, to grasp his meaning, to share even his *intention*—when I saw that *so far* he had absolutely failed, it was a very bitter grief to me. Not for my

own sake, though what mother is not *practically* ambitious for
her children?—but for his. I had realized you see—and it is
here that I hope you will be most patient with me and will
forgive me if I repeat myself—I had realized that to some minds
and to some spirits poetry is what religion is to others—the
most precious, the most certain, the most wanted thing life has
to give. And now that he had fallen silent I could at least
realize too if only in part the affliction it meant to him. Not
that, because he was silent, the beauty and meaning—the divination—of life were gone *too*. Not that; surely not that! That
would be such a lie as no Cyril Charlton even is capable of.
It was still there—within him; between himself and his Maker.

"I once came across somewhere a passage in a book—I can't
remember its title or even its author, but being eager and
interested as I was then, it stamped itself on my memory: 'He
that has never seen this beauty must hunger for it as for all his
welfare, he that has known it must love and reverence it as the
very beauty; he will be flooded with awe and gladness.' Well,
surely, even if it be averred that these early hopes and desires
were nothing but a fool's paradise—and *that* I refuse to believe;
and even though you may regret the folly, still you cannot deny
that to my son they *were* a paradise? No more then would I deny
the hope of its continuance, though the gates should be shut for
ever that gave others a glimpse of it." She paused, her small
square hands clenched in her lap.

"I have finished, Mr. Forbes. As you see, I live here a quiet
and retired life. I believe that no good thing in this world—since
it is a world founded on divine reason—can be eventually wasted.
I believe therefore that whatever there is of this infinite grace
in my son's poems will find in time its own haven, even though
they may be completely forgotten here on earth. Meanwhile I
keep my lesson. Cyril Charlton, and much else that I won't
burden you with, taught me at any rate once and for all that
there is a danger worse than death to this 'very beauty,' and
that it comes, not from the enemies, but from these so-called
'*lovers*' of poetry—these parasites—their jealousies, their quarrels,
their pretences, their petty curiosity, their suffocating silliness.
I will have none of it. I am determined—determined that this

precious 'world-at-large'—your own words—shall leave my son
and all he loved and the dreams from which there is now no
waking, at *peace*. His memory, himself, safe here with me; to
the end."

She had risen from her chair as she finished speaking. With
hands clutched on her bodice, her small pupils glinting like semi-
precious stones, she stood over poor Ronnie, and dared him to
do his worst. There were tears in the eyes now challenging him,
tears, he realized, not of weakness but of strength, and squeezed
out of a spirit, stable as adamant, which would not swerve by
an inch if the need came to stride off exulting to the stake.

And as, not apparently in any desire for air, and certainly
not for retreat, but merely to conceal her feelings—and maybe
from herself—Mrs. Cotton turned her back on her visitor and
marched over to the French windows, Ronnie stirred awkwardly in his chair. The attitude in which he had been listening
to this prolonged declamation had become a little strained. He
stirred—as if he were "coming to." And, "What the devil," he
was thinking ruefully, if a little vacantly, what the devil had
he or his young American friend to do with any *"stake"*!

The windows had been flung open to their fullest gape. The
tepid April air of the garden thinned in on the boxed-up atmosphere. It pierced with its sweet earthly freshness the pent-in
odours of the forced flowers. Ronnie breathed and breathed
again. The drowsy cadences of a blackbird from some shrubbery
out of view fell on his ear like waterdrops into the basin of a
fountain. And then suddenly from quite near at hand resounded
the sudden shrill battle-cry—incredibly defiant, even formidable,
for a creature so minute—of a wren.

Mrs. Cotton had paused, her hand on the window-frame, only,
it seemed, to regain her self-possession. She turned at last, and
with a gesture waved as it were all these last few confidences
between them aside.

"So you see, Mr. Forbes," she said, "now that I have said
what I have said, and it has not been an easy task, I must resign
the rest to you. You will forget any resentment I may have
shown. But as I look back on Mr. Charlton I find it difficult
to be fair to him. I believed at the time that he at least meant

well, that he had my son's reputation at heart only and solely because he himself really *cared* for poetry, whereas I . . . What else can I do then but commit myself entirely into your hands? You have come this long distance. You are bound to consider your friend's interests. I feel then I must leave you absolutely at liberty to use your own judgment as to what shall be proclaimed on the housetops and what not. You have not supposed, at least, that I want what my son has done to be forgotten. Though its innermost secrets may be hidden from me, I can at least be aware that to other minds they *may* be very precious." Her arms fell loosely to her sides. Even in youth her short, rather dumpy figure could never have been of any particular feminine grace; yet Ronnie was fated to remember that gesture. It had reminded him, absurdly enough, not of Velasquez's "Surrender," but of a ballet dancer by Degas.

"And now"—she was almost timidly inviting him—"I hope you will stay and take tea with us—my daughter-in-law will join us presently."

Ronnie dutifully murmured a word or two about trains, but she tossed them aside. "You must let it be part of our compact," she said, eyeing him almost archly but with an ironic intentness. "Meanwhile I must leave you for a moment."

She paused at the door at which Ronnie had entered. "The picture immediately behind you," she said, "is a portrait of James when he was a child of seven. It was painted by an artist —an R.A.—who is now, I believe, out of fashion. But he was not so then. The old gentleman with the pug-dog in his lap next to it (a really good picture, I have been told), is my son's great-grandfather—on my husband's side. And in that album on the what-not you will find photographs and some pieces of manuscript. Please look at anything that may interest you."

A moment afterwards the door had been firmly shut behind her, the sound of her footsteps had died away, and Ronnie was alone. He sat for a few moments perfectly still, his brown eyes fixed almost gloatingly on the garden. Then a sudden shuddering yawn overtook him. He knew how sleepy, but had not noticed how physically exhausted, he was. Heavens, what a labyrinth of a trap he had walked into! . . . But how amusing!

His glance strayed at last to the three-tiered galaxy of flowers on their white-painted shelves in the alcove—early geraniums, wax-like hyacinths, modest flowering musk, and, above all, the peach-like exotic freesia. Then he got up from his chair, yawned again as he turned about, took a pace or so backwards, and fixed his eyes on the portrait of the poet as a boy of seven.

The heavy gilt frame had woefully tarnished. But the brick red of the tartan kilt and plaid and the mustard yellow of the flaxen corkscrew curls that dangled from under a glengarry about the apple-cheeked, china-blue-eyed face had kept all their "pristine bloom." If the artist had ever really had his eye on his subject he had assuredly detected no symptom of genius there. The stolid little boy that stood in the canvas *looked* about as intelligent as a bullfinch or a Dutch cheese. None the less— as though symbols will out—he stood armed, as if for mental fight, the point of his cross-hilted wooden toy sword poised straight out of the picture and full in the direction of Ronnie's stomach.

Ronnie was nothing if not critical—but less so of pictures than of elegant literature. He could easily manage to swallow "Cherry Ripe" and even "Bubbles," but there was something in the technique of this particular painter that raised his gorge. Indeed the portrait was damnably unfair—on the part of the painter. For, after all, if there *was* a remarkable feature in the verse that little James had lived to make obscure, it was its technical mastery. "Mental fight," then, there must have been. "You can't," Ronnie adjured the child in the picture a little wearily—"you can't build any sort of Jerusalem anywhere without it, and certainly not in that rather less green and, in places, positively unpleasant land that England had rapidly been becoming since you, my poor innocent, were seven!"

Of James's particular Jerusalem, none the less, he had only the vaguest intimations. He would look it up again perhaps when he got back to London. He might even attempt to worm his way into its secret citadel. But now, anyhow, there was no need to worry about it. He was tired. Poetry of that kind is all very well while you are young and active, and the trailing clouds haven't completely shredded off. "But, heavens!" Ronnie inwardly ejaculated again, as he continued to gaze at this infant Samuel in tartan, "give *me* his mamma every time." Typically English too, almost British, in her own queer way, and overwhelmingly worth writing even to America about. How his young friend would lap her up! And the subtlety of it all!

The female spider was, of course, notorious not only for its voracity but its astuteness. They even devoured their many husbands. Mrs. Cotton had put down, it seemed, every single card in her hand face upwards on the bright green table; and Ronnie had lost—every single trick! She had hopelessly queered his pitch. And yet, as he had sat there, transfixed by those small glittering eyes, a warm (and rather un-Ronnieish) camaraderie had sprung up in his mind. Affection at first sight!

His glance drifted down from the portrait to a full-length photograph that stood in an old leather frame on the Pembroke table immediately beneath it. He stooped and looked closer. Yes, it was without any doubt a photograph of James's mother herself and one taken at about the same date as that of the picture. Square and plump and substantial in figure even then; in a neat tight-fitting bodice and flounced flow-away skirts, she stood there, one small shapely hand on a Victorian "occasional" chair, looking as straight and decisively out at the camera as her son at his R.A. And the camera had been kinder than the painter. The wide-open face was smiling; there was an almost audacious sparkle of coquetry in the eyes; and even Ronnie's worldly-wise but still susceptible masculine heart responded to this charming feminine challenge.

Indeed, he was still intent on the photograph—the album and the excellent portrait of the smiling, skull-capped old gentleman with the pug-dog on his lap having been completely ignored—when at the same moment he heard voices from far within, and the clink of teacups near at hand. When the parlour-maid entered the room with her salver he was seated on his chair again, a green-bound Moxon Tennyson in his hand, opened at "Mariana," but upside down. . . .

In the talk during the meal that followed—and Ronnie failed even to nibble at the scone on his plate until it was stone cold— the elder Mrs. Cotton took little part. The two ladies sat opposite to him, while, with his back to the door, and on a stiff barley-sugar-legged *prie-dieu* chair, he himself faced the little warrior in the portrait. In spite, however, of the hypnotic power of that infantile blue eye, Mrs. James Cotton easily held her own. She was almost embarrassingly tall and dark and flat—a tall dark flattishness accentuated rather than enhanced by the black dress she was wearing and the necklace of jet that dangled round her neck beneath a prolonged chin. Still, black against cucumber green is not an unpleasing contrast, and though (as Ronnie was thinking) this countenance was more sombre and equine in its contours even than that of the aged William Wordsworth, she was soon prattling away as if the only marvel were that circumstances had kept them so long apart.

She was enraptured and earnest and astonished and coy all in the same breath. She assured him again and again how much she adored the country and how beautiful Nature was in the spring. One of her very favourite seasons of the year—everything so fresh, so verdant, "so full of lafe, Mr. Forbes. And yet just the same—year in, year out!" Why, if you closed your eyes and listened to the birds, or opened them and looked at the flowers, they might both be exactly the same ones as you had seen *last* spring and the one before that and the one before that!

"As if, Mr. Forbes, there had been *no* winter in between!"

But, of course, that *couldn't* be so, that was only a fancy. Besides, it was just the reverse. Absolutely. What a perfectly dreadful winter they had had, to be sure: so cold, so gloomy, so protracted. "I can't like the winter, Mr. Forbes, I can't indeed." Besides, he must remember, she cried almost with elation, "we haven't any theatres here, or concert halls, or picture galleries, not one. That's where London is so different to the country, and especially in winter, and even in the spring, too." And London seemed to have been gayer than ever these last few months. So many society *functions*. She had read of them in the newspapers. Newspapers were a great resource, of course, though not the same as taking part in the functions themselves. Oh, no! At least not quite the same. And how the world changed!

Ronnie said, "Certainly," when the opportunity offered, and "But I do indeed, really," though it wasn't in the least necessary.

"You see," she was repeating yet again, as she peeped for the fourth time into the cream-jug in case Mrs. Cotton had forgotten whether it was empty or not, "one is so *removed* from things hidden away here in the country—though the country, of course, as I say, *is* the country after all—that I sometimes positively pine to see a policeman!"

She lowered her long head, gazed out of her dark mournful eyes at him, and giggled.

And the sun was wheeling lower and lower into the west, and a thrush had followed the blackbird on to the concert platform, and the flowers in the pots were continuing to unfurl—Ronnie had seen with precisely how pertinacious yet gentle a motion on the movies. But though a machine may accelerate or slow up the appearances of life, man's consciousness is as obedient as her flowers to the pace set by Nature. A fact which Mrs. Cotton, senior, was herself demonstrating as she munched steadily on, her eyes never now meeting his own, her only share in this sprightly conversation an occasional nod, or a "Thank you, Emma," or a prompt hand outheld (and again and again, for Ronnie's thirst was extreme), for his empty cup, or an impatient flick of her fingers at the crumbs in her lap.

"I was so de*l*ated to hear," said Emma at last, "that you are an admirer of my husband's poetry."

"Indeed I *am,*" cried Ronnie, in a voice that even in his own ear sounded as hollow as a tub.

"And yet, do you know, Mr. Forbes, I am sure it must be *ages* since I have seen any mention of him in the newspapers. But then you don't even see Lord Tennyson's name mentioned very much now. Do you?"

She glanced a little uneasily at her mother-in-law, but only for a moment; her dark uncertain gaze had immediately settled on their visitor again.

"He hasn't been dead long enough," broke in. Mrs. Cotton abruptly.

"No," Ronnie retorted with spirit, in the forlorn hope of wooing her into the talk, "that's just the very point. I was only saying . . ."

But at this moment, though he had been conscious of no

interruption, the door behind him seemed to have opened, for the two ladies had simultaneously raised and fixed their eyes on something or somebody behind him and out of his view. It must have been the parlour-maid, for though for the moment a curious transfixedness had spread over Mrs. Cotton's features, and her daughter-in-law looked positively alarmed; as soon as the door had been as softly shut again, Emma, after yet another glance at Mrs. Cotton, had instantly begun talking away again at Ronnie with an almost galvanic zest, and apparently with less intention than ever of waiting for his replies.

"I do so *hope*," she said, when Ronnie rose at last to make his adieux, "I do so hope that if you *should* compose anything in print about my husband, you will let me see it, Mr. Forbes. Just *Willows*, near *Ashenham*, would always find me; the post-man knows us; and I should be so very interested to hear what is being thought now about books, and things like that. For being, as I say, in the country as we are, we . . ."

Her voice trailed away. The long pale lids of her aggrieved eyes had flickeringly descended, and Mrs. Cotton had at last and finally hastened into the breach. She, too, had risen, and had given a decisive tug at the flowered china bell-handle beside the fireplace.

"Good-bye, Mr. Forbes," she said, as abandoning "Emma," black as a rook on the green of the velvet sofa, she firmly grasped his hand. "Good-bye. It has been an absorbing afternoon. And yet I'm afraid . . ." They had reached the door; parting was imminent; and she sighed out her regret in so low a voice it seemed it must have been intended for Ronnie's ear alone, and his inward ear, too—"I'm afraid I must have seemed very remiss. If only I had been a little more accustomed to being interviewed! No pencil, no note-book! And now it is too late. Still," she smiled at him, "not only am I convinced you have a far better memory for such things than Mr. Charlton—whom I must say the two of us have treated *very* harshly—but there is nothing which I feel I could not have securely—securely confided to your keeping. Or in the future either—if the need should ever come."

The memorable voice had broken a little at these last few words, and Ronnie gazed back with all his soul into the small

grey-green eyes that seemed to have darkened now that her face
was no longer in the light of the window.

"Thank you very much indeed for that, Mrs. Cotton," he
cried gallantly. "You may rely on me. I assure you. I will be
discretion itself!"

The stiff maidservant was already awaiting him. He seized
his hat, his cane, his light overcoat, and turned; for, as he expected, Mrs. Cotton's steady regard was still fixed on him from
the drawing-room door. They exchanged what seemed to Ronnie
a last swift full glance of understanding, an intent, almost intimate glance that went even a little deeper into his mind than
he could follow it. The next moment the door had been firmly
closed behind him, and he was out in the open once more.

Huge billowy clouds, like enormous bolsters, had ranged
themselves on the horizon beneath the infantile blue of the sky.
Though the sun-bright dandelions that had greeted him were
now raggedly shut for the night, the bladed grass, the leafy
willows by the water's brim stood as if enchanted in an ocean of
light and colour, and the air resounded with a mellay of song
so wild and vehement that the birds that uttered it seemed to
have been seized with an anguish of fear lest the dark to come
should deprive them of every hope of ever singing again.

And Ronnie, too, was conscious of springtime in his blood.
He stepped out buoyantly and in uncommonly high spirits.
What a hotchpotch of an afternoon, and yet on the whole how
novel, how odd, and how very amusing!

In less than no time he had come almost to the turn in the
weedy drive that would take him clean out of sight even of the
upper windows of the house he had left behind him. But there
his self-congratulations were suddenly interrupted. A low, clear,
but mysterious hail had sounded in his rear. He wheeled about.
These were not Mrs. Cotton's now familiar tones.

No, there could be no mistaking whence the summons had
come. The straw-hatted, neatly clad figure of a tubby little man
had emerged from under the trees to his left, and was now—so
extreme was his haste—almost trotting over the grass to intercept
him. And Ronnie waited. Psychologists may maintain that it is

humanly impossible to think of more than one thing at a time.
But Ronnie knew better. Two perfectly distinct "reactions" had
at this moment flashed through his mind. One, the vivid recollection of Tenniel's Tweedledum and Tweedledee; the other
the lightning conviction that he knew—that he seemed to have
known for centuries, who precisely this little man *was*.

Ought he to fly? Surely, in spite of those last few words in the
house, no such encounter as this had been included in the
compact he had but just now signed and sealed with the poet's
mother? But it was too late. Breathless, triumphant, the little
man had caught him up. Bright blue eyes of an extraordinary
intensity were surveying him from beneath arched brows under
the brim of the antiquated black straw hat.

"I am speaking," the little man inquired with a charming
courtesy, "to . . . ?"

"My name is Forbes," said Ronnie.

"Ah, yes, Forbes. I was not aware of that, Mr. Forbes. Forgive
me. I am kept a little in the dark. And better so, perhaps," he
smiled, "for even in a place as remote as this and with very few
visitors, you never know, do you . . . ?" He faltered. "At least,
so I am told. But that said, or not said, as the case may be, I
couldn't let this opportunity go by without—without, as a matter
of fact, asking you to accept this. At times I find them crumpled
up in the grass. But what can be expected of errand-boys? It is,
and I hope"—he cast a furtive glance over his shoulder as he
thrust a folded piece of paper that had apparently been torn
from a tradesman's paper bag, into Ronnie's hand—"I hope you
will let it be a little *private* matter between us—it's in the nature
of an epigram. My last."

The candid blue eyes in the countenance on which it seemed
age had decided to leave not one disfiguring mark became a
little troubled as they searched Ronnie's smiling and aware face.

"You will agree, Mr. Forbes," he pressed on earnestly, raising,
like a bishop, his small white hand a little into the summer air,
"there are things—evidences, messages, that may be *shared,*
though even the very meaning of the words may have become
corrupted—decayed—*all rotted away?*"

It isn't always that any inmate is looking out of a human eye.

But at this particular moment an exceedingly alert inmate, as keenly and austerely challenging as the gaze of an angel, was confronting Ronnie from the tranquil deeps of this little man's stare. His fingers fluttered an instant, as if inclined to snatch back what he had given.

"I must not distrust . . . I must leave it at that, Mr. Forbes," he said hurriedly, raised his straw hat, and was gone.

Ronnie remained for a moment where he was, the paper in his hand. He, too, glanced over his shoulder. The house was still just in sight, nestling, with its willows, low in the gold of the western sun. But there was too much of a glare in the sky to be sure if any of its occupants were looking out after him from the upper windows.

He went on until he had come again to the narrow stone bridge over the stream. There he unfolded the poet's scrap of paper and scanned the four lines of tiny and almost illegible script it contained. He picked his way through them again and again and again; and there could be no doubt whatever at last of their intrinsic obscurity. Worse, Ronnie had grave misgivings even of the soundness of their metrical technique. Not so the writer of them, apparently, for at the foot of the four lines which had been placed with extreme care in the very middle of the paper, there sprawled a long-looped, an almost Napoleonic *J. C.*

Baa, baa, sang out the woolly sheep on the other side of the green-springing hedge. But Ronnie paid no heed. He had instantly realized what a treasure for transatlantic academicism, or English either for that matter, he held in his hand. It was a fragment of holograph—of an unpublished poem—very late—in mint condition—recently signed with this said-to-be-deceased and unique minor poet's own initials!

He refolded this odd manuscript and placed it carefully in his pocket-book. Nor did he spend any more idle moments on the minnows in the brook beneath the bridge, but continued rapidly on his way to the railway station. Having there inquired for a later—and as it proved to be, its last—train back to London, the next being due in a few minutes, he set off for Ashenham itself.

The old woman in the little smelly village post office to whom he handed in his message to his young American friend had never heard of Wellspring, Ohio. By the deep look she gave Ronnie over her spectacles she seemed, indeed, for a moment to have supposed it was a piece of untimely jocularity. But she managed to produce at last an official *Guide*; and Ronnie, horn-rimmed spectacles on *his* fastidious but rather stubby nose, helped her all he could with the infinitesimal print. And to such effect that he all but charged himself twice the official rate *per* word. But lavish telegraphing was one of his many little weaknesses.

"*Have visited Willows,*" ran his ultimatum. "*Immensely sorry. Nothing doing. All gone. Am emphatically convinced only course to keep exclusively to text. Strongly advise complete abandonment of the ineffable Cyril. Heaven be with you. Writing. Ronnie Forbes.*"

He then withdrew J. C.'s scrap of paper from his pocket-book and slipped it without any accompaniment into a stamped envelope—a little fly-blown—which the old lady supplied from a wooden drawer on the other side of the counter. On this he scribbled Mrs. Cotton's address, and having stuck it down, himself dropped it—with a sigh just nicely enough tinged with regret—into the little red box outside.

On the Edge (1931)

MISSING

It was the last day of a torrid week in London—the flaming crest of what the newspapers called a *heat wave*. The exhausted inmates of the dazzling, airless streets—plate glass, white stone, burnished asphalt, incessant roar din, fume and odours—have the appearance at such times of insects trapped in an oven of a myriad labyrinthine windings and chambers: a glowing brazen maze to torture Christians in. To have a *mind* even remotely resembling it must be Satan's sole privilege!

I had been shopping; or rather, I had been loafing about from one department on to another in one of the huge "stores" in search of bathing-drawers, a preventative of insect bites, and a holiday "shocker," and had retired at last incapable of buying anything—even in a world where pretty well everything except peace of mind can be bought, and sold. The experience had been oppressive and trying to the temper.

Too hot, too irritable even to lunch, I had drifted into a side street, and then into a second-hand bookshop that happened still to be open this idle Saturday afternoon; and having for nine-pence acquired a copy of a book on psychoanalysis which I didn't want and should never read, I took refuge in a tea-shop.

In spite of the hot-water fountain on the counter it was a degree or two cooler in here, though even the marble-top tables were tepid to the touch. Quiet and drowsy, too. A block of ice sur-mounted the dinner wagon by the counter. The white clock face said a quarter to three. Few chairs were now occupied; the midday mellay was over. A heavy slumbrousness muffled the place—the flies were as idle as the waitresses, and the waitresses were as idle as the flies.

I gave my order, and sat back exhausted in a listless vacancy of mind and body. And my dazed eyes, having like the flies little of particular interest to settle on, settled on the only fellow reveller that happened to be sitting within easy reach. At first glimpse there could hardly be a human being you would suppose less likely to attract attention. He was so scrupulously respectable, so entirely innocent of "atmosphere." Even a Chelsea psychic would have been compelled to acknowledge that this particular human being had either disposed of his aura or had left it at home. And yet my first glimpses of him had drawn me out of the vacuum into which I had sunk as easily as a cork is drawn out of an empty bottle.

He was sitting at a table to the left, and a little in front of me. The glare from the open door and the gentler light from the

.cream-blinded shop window picked out his every hair and
button. It flooded in on him from the sparkling glittering street,
focused him, "placed" him, arranged him—as if for a portrait
in the finest of oils for next year's "Academy." Limelight on the
actor manager traversing the blasted heath is mere child's play by
comparison.

Obviously he was not "the complete Londoner"—though that
can hardly be said to be a misfortune. On the other hand, there
was nothing rural, and only a touch or so of the provincial in his
appearance. He wore a neat—an excessively neat—pepper-and-salt
tweed suit, the waistcoat cut high and exhibiting the points of a
butterfly collar and a triangle of black silk cravat slipped through
a gold mourning-ring. His ears maybe were a little out of the
mode. They had been attached rather high and flat on either side
of his conical head with its dark, glossy, silver-speckled hair.

The nose was straight, the nostrils full. They suggested courage
of a kind; possibly, even, on occasion, bravado. He looked the
kind of man, I mean, it is well to keep out of a corner. But the
eyes that were now peering vacantly down that longish nose over
a trim but unendearing moustache at the crumbs on his empty
plate were too close together. So, at least, it seemed to me. But
then I am an admirer of the wide expressive brow—such as our
politicians and financiers display. Those eyes at any rate gave this
spruce and respectable person just a hint, a soupçon of the fox. I
have never heard though that the fox is a dangerous animal even
in a corner; only that he has his wits about him and preys on
geese—whereas my stranger in the tea-shop had been refreshing
himself with Osborne biscuits.

It was hot. The air had grown more stagnant. And heat—unless
in Oriental regions—is not conducive to exquisite manners; far
otherwise. I continued to watch this person, indolently speculating
whether his little particularities of appearance did not match, or
matched too precisely. Those ears and that cravat, for example; or
those spruce-moustached nostrils and the glitter of the close-neigh-
bouring eyes. And why had he brought to mind a tightly-packed
box with no address on it? He began to be a burden, yet I could
not keep my eyes away from him—nor from his hands. They were
powerful and hairy, with large knuckles; and now that they were

not in use he had placed them on his knees under the dark polished slab of his marble table. Beneath those knees rested his feet
(the toes turned in a little) in highly-polished boots, with thickish
soles and white socks.

There is, I agree, something peculiarly vulgar in thus picking
a fellow creature to pieces. But then Keats so dissected Miss
Brawne even when he was in love with her, and it was certainly
not love at first sight between myself and this stranger.

Whether he knew it or not, he was attaching himself to me; he
was making his influence felt. It was odd, then, that he could remain so long unconscious of so detached a scrutiny. Maybe that
particular nerve in him had become atrophied. He looked as if
a few other rather important nerves might be atrophied. When
he did glance up at me—the waitress having appeared with my
tea at the same moment—there was a far-away startled look in his
bleak blue-black eyes—as if he had been called back.

Nothing more; and even at that it was much such a look as had
been for some little time fixed on the dry biscuit crumbs in his
empty plate. He seemed indeed to be a man accustomed to being
startled or surprised into vigilance without reason. But having
seen me looking at him, he did not hesitate. He carefully took
up his hat, his horn-handled and gold-mounted umbrella, and a
large rusty scaling leather bag that lay on a chair beside him;
rose; and stepping gently over with an almost catlike precision,
seated himself in the chair opposite to mine. I continued to pour
out my tea.

"You will excuse me troubling you," he began in a voice that
suggested he could sing tenor though he spoke bass, "but would
you kindly tell me the number of the omnibus that goes from here
to King's Cross? I am a stranger to this part of London."

I called after the waitress: "What is the number of the 'bus," I
said, "that goes from here to King's Cross?"

"The number of the 'bus, you si, that goes from here to King's
Cross?"

"Yes," I said, "to King's Cross."

"I'm sure I don't know," she said. "I'll ask the counter." And
she tripped off in her silk stockings and patent-leather shoes.

"The counter will know," I assured him. He looked at me,

moving his lips over his teeth as if either or both for some reason had cause to be uneasy.

"I am something of a stranger to London altogether," he said, "and I don't usually come these ways: it's a novelty to me. The omnibuses are very convenient."

"Don't you? Is it?" I replied. "Why not?" They were rather point-blank questions (and a gentleman, said Dr. Johnson, does not ask questions) but somehow they had slipped out as if at his pressing invitation.

He looked at me, his eyes seeming to draw together into an intenser focus. He was not exactly squinting, but I have noticed a similar effect in the eyes of a dog when its master is about to cry "Fetch it!"

"You see," he said, "I live in the country, and only come to London when I seem to need company—badly, I mean. There's a great contrast between the country and this. All these houses. So many strange faces. It takes one out of oneself."

I glanced round at the sparsely occupied tables. A cloud apparently had overlaid the sun, for a faint coppery glow was now reflected from the drowsy street. I could even hear the white-faced clock ticking. To congratulate him on his last remark would hardly have been courteous after so harmless an advance. I merely looked at him. What kind of self, I was vaguely speculating, would return into his hospitality when he regained his usual haunts.

"I have a nice little place down there," he went on, "but there's not much company. Lonely: especially now. Even a few hours makes all the difference. You would be surprised how friendly a place London can be; the people, I mean: helpful."

What can only be described as a faint whinny had sounded in his voice as he uttered that "helpful." Was he merely to prove yet another of those unfortunate travellers who have lost the return halves of their railway tickets? Had he marked me down for his prey?

"It is not so much what they say," he continued, laying his hand on the marble table; "but just, well, their company, you know." I glanced at the heavy ring on its third finger and then at his watch-chain—woven apparently of silk or hair—with little gold rings at intervals along it to secure the plait. His own gaze continued to rest on me with so penetrating, so corkscrew-like an intensity, that I found myself glancing over my shoulder in search of the waitress. She however was now engaged in animated argument with the young lady at the pay-desk.

"Do you live *far* from London?" I ventured.

"About seventy miles," he replied with an obvious gulp of relief at this impetus to further conversation. "A nice old house too considering the rent, roomy enough but not too large. Its only drawback in some respects is there's nothing near it—not within call, I mean; and we—I—suffer from the want of a plentiful supply of water. Especially now."

Why so tactless a remark on this broiling afternoon should have evoked so vivid a picture of a gaunt yellow-brick building perched amid sloping fields parched lint-white with a tropical drought, its garden little more than a display of vegetable anatomies, I cannot say. It was a house of a hideous aspect; but I confess it stirred my interest. Whereupon my stranger, apparently, thought he could safely glance aside; and I could examine him more at leisure. It was not, I have to confess, a taking face. There was a curious hollowness in its appearance. He looked like the shell of a man, or rather, like a hermit crab—that neat pepper-and-salt tweed suit and so on being a kind of second-hand accumulation on his back.

"And of course," he began again, "now that I am alone I become"—he turned sharply back on me—"I become more conscious of it."

"Of the loneliness?" I suggested.

Vacancy appeared on his face, as if he had for the instant stopped thinking. "Yes," he replied, once more transfixing me with those clear close eyes of his, "the loneliness. It seems to increase more and more as the other slips away into the past. But I suppose we most of us have much the same experience; just of that, I mean. And even in London . . ."

I busied myself with my tea things, having no particular wish at the moment to continue the conversation. But he hadn't any intention of losing his fish as easily as all that.

"There's a case now here in the newspaper this morning," he went on, his glance wandering off to a copy of the *Daily Mail* that lay on the chair next the one he had just vacated. "A man not very much older than I am—found dead. Dead. The only occupant of quite a good-sized house, I should judge, at Stoke Newington— though I don't know the place personally. Living there for years on end without even a charwoman to do for him—to—to work for him. Still even there there was some kind of company, I suppose. He could look out of the window; he could hear people moving about next door. Where I am, there isn't another house in sight, not even a barn, and so far as I can see, what they call Nature doesn't become any the more friendly however long you stay in a place—the birds and that kind of thing. It may get better in time; but it's only a few months ago since I was left quite like this —when my sister died."

Obviously I was hooked beyond hope of winning free again until this corkscrew persistent creature had had his way with me. The only course seemed to be to get the experience over as quickly as possible. It is not easy, however, to feign an active sympathy, and mention of his dead sister had produced in my mind only a faint reflex image of a dowdy lady no longer young in dingy black. Still, it was an image that proved to be not very far from the actuality.

"Any close companionship like that," I murmured, "when it is broken is a tragic thing."

He appeared to have seen no significance in my remark. "And you see, once there were three of us. Once. It never got into the papers—at least not into the London papers, except just by mention, I mean." He moistened his lips. "Did you ever happen to come across a report about a lady, a Miss Dutton, who was 'missing'?"

It was a pretty stupid question, for after all, few human beings are so gifted as to be able to recall the names even of the protagonists in genuine *causes célèbres*. To bear in mind every sort of Miss Dutton whose disappearance would be referred to only in news-snippets borrowed by the Metropolitan press from the provincial, would be rather too much of a tax even for those interested in such matters. I sipped my tea and surveyed him as sagaciously as possible; "Not that I can actually recall," I said. "Miss— Dutton? It isn't a very uncommon name. You knew her?"

"Knew her!" he repeated, placing his hands on his knees and sitting stiffly back in his chair, his eyes unflinchingly fixed on mine. "She lived with us a matter of two years or more. It was us she left. It was my house she was missing from. It caused quite a stir in the neighbourhood. It was the talk of the countryside. There was an Inquiry; and all that."

"How long ago?"

"Pretty near a year ago. Yes; a year yesterday."

"Do you mean the inquiry, or when Miss Dutton disappeared?"

"The inquiry," he replied in a muffled fashion, as if a little annoyed at my want of perspicacity. "The other was—oh, a month or more before that."

The interview was becoming rather a laborious way of extracting a story, but somehow its rudiments had begun to interest me. I had nothing to do. Judging from the look of the street, the quicksilver in the thermometer was still edging exquisitely upwards. I detested the thought of emerging into that oven. So apparently did my companion, unless the mere sound of his voice seemed to him better entertainment than, say, the nearest "picture palace"—where at least one would be out of sight and it would be dark.

"I should have thought," I began again in a voice as matter-of-fact as I could manage, "that living as you do, a stir in the neighbourhood would not much matter, though I agree that the mystery itself must have mattered a good deal more. It must have been a great shock to you both."

"Ay," he said, with a gleam in his eye, "but that's just what you Londoners don't seem to understand. You have your newspapers and all that. But in most ways you don't get talked about much. It's not so in the country. I guarantee you might be living right in the middle of the Yorkshire Fells and yet, if it came to there being anything to keep their tongues wagging, you'd know that your neighbours were talking of you, and what about, for miles around. It gets across—like those black men's drums one hears about in West Africa. As if the mere shock of the thing wasn't enough! What I feel about it is that nowadays people don't seem to show any sympathy, any ordinary feeling with—with those in such circumstances; at least, not country people. Wouldn't you say yourself," he added, with feline rapidity, "that if you were reported as missing it would be rough luck if nobody cared?"

"I don't quite see what you mean," I replied. "I thought you said that the disappearance of your friend made a stir in the neighbourhood."

"Yes; but they were not thinking so much of her as of the cause of it."

We exchanged a long glance, but without much addition to my own small fund of information. "But surely," I ventured, "that must depend upon where she was supposed to have disappeared *to*?"

"That," he replied, "they never knew. We couldn't find out not one iota about it. You've no idea"—he drew his hand down over his face as if to clear away a shadow from his eyes—"you've no idea. Since she has gone I feel almost sometimes as if she can never have been real. *There,* but not real; if you understand me. I see her; and then the real thing goes again. It never occurred to me, that."

"The psychologists would tell us something about that."

"The what?" he asked sharply.

"People interested in the working of the mind, you know. After all, we can't definitely say whether that teapot there is real—what it is in itself, I mean. And merely to judge from its looks," I added, "one might hope it was a pure illusion."

He looked hard at the teapot. "Miss Dutton was a very well-preserved woman for her age," he said. "And when I say 'not real,' it's only in a manner of speaking, I mean. I've got her portrait in the newspaper in my pocket-book. That ought to prove her real enough. I never knew any one who was more 'all there,' as they say. She was a good friend to me—I have every reason to remember her. She came along of her own free will—just a chance meeting, in Scarborough, as a matter of fact. And she liked the comforts of a home after all those hotels and boarding-houses."

In the course of these ruminating and mournful remarks—and there was unmistakable "feeling" in his tones—he was rather privily turning over the contents of an old leather pocket-book with an inelastic black band. He drew out a frayed newspaper cutting, and put it down on the table beside the teapot.

"Looking at that, you wouldn't be in much doubt what Miss Dutton was in herself, now, would you? You'd recognize her," he raised his eyes, "if she were—if you met her, I mean, in these awful streets? I would myself."

It was impossible to decide whether this last remark was ironical, triumphant, embittered, or matter-of-fact; so I looked at Miss Dutton. She was evidently a blonde and a well-preserved woman, as my friend had intimated; stoutish, with a plump face, a plump nose, infantile blue eyes, frizzy hair, and she wore (what a few years ago were old-fashioned and are now new-fashioned) long ear-rings.

It was curious what a stabilizing effect the ear-rings produced. They resembled the pole Blondin used to carry as he tripped across his rope over the Niagara Falls. Miss Dutton was looking out of her blurred image with a sort of insouciance, gaiety, "charm," the charm that photographers aim at but rather seldom convey. Destiny, apparently, casts no retrospective shadow. I defy anybody to have found the faintest hint in that aware, vain, commonplace, good-natured face which would suggest Miss Dutton was ever going to be "missed"—missed, I mean, in the sense of becoming indiscoverable. In the other sense her friends would no doubt miss her a good deal. But then boarding-houses and hotels are the resorts rather of vagrant acquaintances than of friends.

The owner of the newspaper snippet was scrutinizing the gay, blurred photograph with as much interest as I was; though to him it was upside down. There was a queer fond look on his face, a little feline, perhaps, in its sentimentality.

I pushed back the cutting across the marble table and he carefully reinterred it in his pocket-book. "I was wondering," he rambled on as he did so, "what you might have thought of it—without prejudice, so to speak, if you had come across it—casually-like; in the newspaper, I mean?"

The question was not quite so simple as it sounded. It appeared as if my new acquaintance were in wait for a comment which he himself was eager to supply. And I had nothing much to say.

"It's difficult, you know, to judge from prints in newspapers," I ventured at last. "They are usually execrable even as caricatures. But she looks, if I may say so, an uncommonly genial woman:

feminine—and a practical one, too. Not one, I mean, who would
be likely to be missing, except on purpose—of her own choice,
that is." Our eyes met an instant. "The whole business must have
been a dreadful shock and anxiety to you. And, of course, to Miss
. . . to your sister, I mean."

"My name," he retorted abruptly, shutting his eyes while a be-
wildering series of expressions netted themselves on his face, "my
name is Bleet."

"Miss Bleet," I added, glancing at the pocket into which the
book had by now disappeared, and speculating, too, why so preposterous an *alias* should have occurred to apparently so ready a
tongue.

"You were saying 'genial,'" he added rapidly. "And that is
what they all agreed. Even her only male relative—an uncle, as
he called himself, though I can swear she never mentioned him in
that or in any other capacity. She hadn't always been what you
might call a happy woman, mind you. But they were bound to
agree that those two years under my care—in our house—were the
happiest in Miss Dutton's life. We made it a real home to her.
She had her own rooms and her few bits of furniture—photographs and boxes and so on, quite private. It's a pretty large house
considering the rent—country, you know; and there was a sort
of a new wing added to it fifty years or more ago. Old-fashioned,
of course—open fireplace, no bath, enormous kitchen range—
swallows coal by the bushel—and so on—very inconvenient, but
cheap. And though my sister was not in a position to supervise the
housekeeping, there couldn't be a more harmless and affectionate
creature. To those, that is, who were kind to her. She'd run away
from those who weren't—just run away and hide. I must explain
that my poor sister was not quite—was a little weak in her in-
tellects—from her childhood. It was always a great responsibility.
But as time went on," he drew his hand wearily over his face,
"Miss Dutton herself very kindly relieved me of a good deal of
that. You said she looked a practical woman; so she was."

The narrative was becoming steadily more personal, and disconcerting. And yet—such is humanity—it was as steadily intensi-
fying in interest. A low grumble of thunder at that moment
sounded over the street, and a horse clattered down with its van

beyond the open door. My country friend did not appear to have noticed it.

"You never know quite where you are with the ladies," he suddenly ejaculated, and glanced piercingly up—for at that moment our waitress had drawn near.

"It's a 'Ighteen," she said, pencil on lip, and looking vacantly from one to the other of us.

"'Ighteen,'" echoed her customer sharply; "what's that? Oh, the omnibus. You didn't say what you meant. Thank you." She hovered on, check-book in hand. "And please bring me another cup of coffee." He looked at me as if with the intention of duplicating his order. I shook my head. "One cup, then, miss; no hurry."

The waitress withdrew.

"It looks as if rain was coming," he went on, and as if he were thirsting for it as much as I was. "As I was saying, you can never be quite sure where you are with women; and, mind you, Miss Dutton was a woman of the world. She had seen a good deal of life—been abroad—Gay Paree, Monte Carlo, and all that. Germany before the war, too. She could read French as free and easy as you could that mennoo there. Paper-bound books with pictures on them, and that kind of thing." He was looking at me, I realized, as if there were no other way of intimating the particular kind of literature he had in mind.

"I used to wonder sometimes what she could find in us: such a lonely place; no company. Though, of course, she was free to ask any friends if she wanted to, and talked of them too when in the mood. Good class, to judge from what she said. What I mean is, she was quite her own mistress. And I must say there could not be more good-humour and so on than what she showed my poor sister. At least, until later. She'd talk to her as if conversing; and my sister would sit there by the window, looking back at her and smiling and nodding just as if she were taking it all in. And who knows, perhaps she was. What I mean is, it's possible to have things in your head which you can't quite put into so many words. It's one of the things I look for when I come up to London: the faces that could tell a story though what's behind them can't."

I nodded.

"I can assure you that before a few weeks were over she had got to be as much at home with us as if we had known her all our lives. Chatty and domesticated, and all that. And using the whole house just as if it belonged to her. All the other arrangements were easy, too. I can say now, and I said it then, that we never once up to then demeaned ourselves to a single word of disagreement about money matters or anything else. A woman like that, who has been all over the continent, isn't likely to go far wrong in that. I agree the terms were on the generous side; but then, you take me, so were the arrangements.

"She asked herself to raise them when she had been with us upwards of twelve months. But I said 'No.' I said, 'A bargain's a bargain, Edna'—we were 'Edna' and 'William' to one another, by then, and my sister too. She was very kind to my poor sister; got a specialist up all the way from Bath—though for all his prying questions he did nothing, as I knew he wouldn't. You can't take those things so late. Mind you, as I say, the business arrangements were all on one side. Miss Dutton liked things select and comfortable. She liked things to go smoothly, as we all do, I reckon. She had been accustomed to smart boarding-houses and hotels—that kind of thing. And I did my level best to keep things nice."

My stranger's face dropped into a rather gloomy expression, as if poor humanity had sometimes to resign itself to things a little less agreeable than the merely smooth and nice. He laid down his spoon, which he had been using with some vigour, and sipped his coffee.

"What I was going to explain," he went on, rubbing at his moustache, "is that everything was going perfectly easy—just like clockwork, when the servant question came up. My house, you see, is on what you may call the large side. It's old in parts, too. Up to then we had had a very satisfactory woman—roughish but willing. She was the wife, or what you might just as well call the widow, of a sailor. I mean he was one of the kind that has a ditto in every port, you know. She was glad of the place, glad to be where her husband couldn't find her, even though the stipulation was that her wages should be permanent. That system of raising by driblets always leads to discontent. And I must say she was a fair tyrant for work.

"Besides her, there was a help from the village—precious little good *she* was. Slummocky—and *stupid!* Still, we had got on pretty well up to then, up to Miss Dutton's time, and for some months after. But cooking for three mouths is a different thing to two. Besides, Miss Dutton liked her meals dainty-like: a bit of fish, or soup occasionally, toast-rack, tantalus, serviettes on the table—that kind of thing. But all that came on gradual-like—the thin edge of the wedge; until at last, well, 'exacting' wasn't in it.

"And I must say," he turned his wandering eye once more on mine, "I must say, she had a way of addressing menials which sometimes set even my teeth on edge. She was a lady, mind you— though what *that* is when the breath is out of your body it's not so easy to say. And she had the lady's way with them—those continental hotels, I suppose. All very well in a large establishment where one works up against another and you can call them names behind their backs. But our house wasn't an establishment. It wouldn't do there: not in the long run, even if you had an angel for a general and a cook to match.

"Mind you, as I say, Miss Dutton was always niceness itself to my poor sister: never a hard word or a contemptuous look—not to her face nor behind her back, not up to then. I wouldn't have tolerated it either. And you know what talking to a party that can only just sit, hands in lap, and smile back at you means, or maybe a word now and then that doesn't seem to have anything to do with what you've been saying. It's a great affliction. But servants were another matter. Miss Dutton couldn't demean herself to them. She lived in another world. It was, 'Do this'; and 'Why isn't it done?'—all in a breath. I smoothed things over, though they got steadily worse and worse, for weeks and weeks, ay, months. It wore me to a shadow.

"And one day the woman—Bridget was her name—Irish, you know—she flared up in earnest and gave her, as they say, as good as she got. I wasn't there at the time. But I heard afterwards all that passed, and three times over—on the one side at least. I had been into the town in the runabout. And when I came home, Mrs. Tantrums had packed up her box, got a gig from the farm, and was gone for good. It did me a world of harm, that did.

"Pretty well upset, I was too, as you can imagine. I said to Miss

Dutton, 'Edna,' I said, 'all I am saying is, was it necessary to go to such extremes? Not,' I said, 'mind you, Edna that she was all sugar and honey even to me. I knew the wrong side of her mouth years before *you* appeared on the scene. What you've got to do with such people is—to manage—be firm, keep 'em low, but manage. It isn't common sense to cut off your tongue to spite your teeth. She's a woman, and Irish at that,' I said, 'and you know what to expect of them.'

"I was vexed, that's a fact, and perhaps I spoke rather more sharply than need have been. But we were good friends by that time: and if honest give-and-take isn't possible between friends, where are you? I ask you. There was by that time, too, nothing left over-private between us, either. I advised her about her investments and so on, though I took precious good care not to be personally involved. Not a finger stirring unless she volunteered it first. That all came out too. But it was nothing to do with me, now, was it, as man to man, if the good lady took a fancy into her head to see that my poor sister was not left to what's called the tender mercies of this world after my death?

"And yet, believe me, they fixed on that, like leeches. My hell, they did! At the Inquiry, I mean. And I don't see how much further their decency could have gone if they had called it an Inquest; and . . ."

Yet another low (almost gruff) volley of thunder interrupted his discourse. He left the sentence in the air; his mouth ajar. I have never met any one that made such active use of his chin in conversation, by the way, as Mr. Bleet did. It must have been exceedingly fatiguing. I fancy he mistook just then the expression on my face for one of inquiry. He leant forward, pushing down towards me that long hairy finger on the marble table-top.

"When I say 'tender mercies,'" he explained, "I don't mean that my sister would have been left penniless, even if Miss Dutton or nobody like her had come into the house. There was money of my own too, though, owing to what I need not explain"—he half swallowed the words—"not much." He broke off. "It seems as if we are in for a bit of a thunderstorm. But I'd sooner it was here than down my way. When you're alone in the house you seem to notice the noise more."

"I fancy it won't be much," I assured him. "It will clear the air."

His eyes opened as if in astonishment that any mere act of nature could bring such consolation.

"You were saying," I exclaimed, "that you lost your maid?" He glanced up sharply. "Though of course," I added hastily, "you mustn't let me intrude on your private affairs."

"Not at all; oh, not at all," he interrupted with relief. "I thought you said, 'lost my head.' Not at all. It makes all the difference to me—I can assure you, to be able to go over it like this. Friendly-like. To get a listener who has not been fed up on all that gossip and slander. It takes some living down, too. Nothing satisfies them: nothing. From one week's end to another you can't tell where they'll unearth themselves next."

It was becoming difficult to prevent a steadily growing distaste for my companion from showing itself in my face. But then self-pity is seldom ingratiating. Fortunately the light where we sat was by now little better than dusk. Indeed, to judge from the growing gloom in our tea-shop, the heavens at this moment were far from gracious. I determined to wait till the rain was over. Besides, though my stranger himself was scarcely winning company, and his matter was not much above the sensational newspaper order, the mere zigzagging of his narrative was interesting. Its technique, I mean, reminded me of the definition of a crab: "The crab is a little red animal that walks backwards."

"The fact is," he went on, "on that occasion—I mean about the servant—Miss Dutton and I had words. I own it. Not that she resented my taking the thing up in a perfectly open and friendly way. She knew she had put me in a fair quandary. But my own private opinion is that when you are talking to a woman it's best not to bring in remarks about the sex in general. A woman is herself or nothing, if you follow me. What she thinks is no more than another skin. Keep her sex out of it, and she'll be reasonable. But no further. As a matter of fact, I never argue with ladies. And I soon smoothed that over. It was only a passing cloud. And I must say, considering what a lady she *was,* she took the discomforts of having nothing but a good-for-nothing slattern in the house very generously, all things considered.

"Mind you, I worked *myself,* fit for any couple of female serv-

ants: washed up dishes, laid the table, kept the little knick-knacks
going. Ay, and I'd go into the town to fetch her out little delica-
cies: tinned soups and peaches, and suchlike: anything she might
have a taste to. And I taught her to use the runabout for herself,
though to hear her changing gear was like staring ruin in the face.
A gallon of petrol to a hank of crimson silk—that kind of thing.
Believe me, she'd go all those miles for a shampoo-powder, or to
have tea at a tea-shop—though you can't beat raw new-laid eggs
and them on the premises. They got to know her there. She was
a rare one for the fashions: scarves and motor-veils, and that kind
of thing. But I never demurred. It wasn't for me to make objec-
tions, particularly as she'd do a little shopping on the housekeeping side as well, now and then. Though, mind you, she knew sixpence from a shilling, and particularly towards the last.

"What was the worst hindrance was that my poor sister seemed
to have somehow come to know there were difficulties in the
house. I mean that there had begun to be. You don't know how
they do it; but they do. And it doesn't add to your patience, I
grant, when what you have done at one moment is done wrong
over again the next. But she meant well, poor creature: and scolding at her only made things worse. Still, we got along happily
enough for a time, until"—he paused once more with mouth ajar
—"until Miss Dutton took it into her head to let matters come to
a crisis. Now judging from that newspaper cutting I showed you,
what would you take the lady's age to be? Allowing, as you might
say, for all that golden hair?"

It was an indelicate question. Though why the mere fact that
Miss Dutton was now missing should intensify its indelicacy, it
is not easy to say.

"Happiness makes one look younger than one really is," I suggested.

He gaped at me, as if in wonderment that in a world of woe he
himself was not possessed of a white beard as long as your arm.

" 'Happiness?' " he echoed.

"Yes, happiness."

"Well, what I mean is, you wouldn't say she was in the filly
class; now, would you? High-spirited, easy-going, and all that;

silly, too, at times: but no longer young. Not in her heyday, I mean."

I pushed my empty cup aside and looked at him. But he looked back at me without flinching, as if indeed it was a pleasant experience to be sharing with a stranger sentiments so naïve regarding "the fair sex."

"Mind you, I don't profess to be a young man either. But I can assure you on my word of honour, that what she said to me that evening—I was doing chores in the kitchen at the time, and she was there too, arranging flowers in a vause for supper; she had a dainty taste in flowers—well, she asked me why I was so unkind to her, so unresponsive, and—it came on me like a thunderbolt."

As if positively for exemplification, a sudden clap of thunder at that moment resounded overhead. The glasses and crockery around us softly tinkled in sympathy. We listened in silence to its reverberations dying away across the chimney-tops; though my companion seemed to be taking them in through his mouth rather than through his ears. His cheek paled a little.

"That's what she asked me, I say. And I can tell you it took me on the raw. It was my turn to flare up. We had words again; nothing much, only a storm in a teacup." Instead of smiling at this metaphor in the circumstances, he seemed astonished, almost shocked, at its aptitude. But he pushed on boldly.

"And then after I had smoothed things over again, she put her cards on the table. Leap Year, and all that tomfoolery, not a bit of it! She was in dead earnest. She told me what I had guessed already, that she had scarcely a friend in the world. Never a word, mind you, of the Colonel—interloping old Pepper-face! She assured me, as I say, she hadn't not only a single relative, but hardly a friend; that she was, as you might say, alone in life, and—well, that her sentiments had become engaged. In honour bound I wouldn't have breathed this to a living soul who knew the parties; but to a stranger, if I may say so, it isn't quite the same thing. What she said was—in the kitchen there, and me in an apron, mind you, tied round me—doing chores—she said—well, in short, that she wanted to make a match of it. She had taken a fancy to me, and was I agreeable." There was no vanity in his face; only a stark unphilosophical astonishment. He seemed to think that to explain all is to forgive all; and was awaiting my concurrence.

"You mean she proposed marriage," I interposed with needless pedantry, and at once, but too late, wished the word back. For vestiges of our conversation had evidently reached the counter. Our waitress, still nibbling her pencil, was gazing steadily in our direction. And for some obscure reason this heat that we were sharing with the world at large, combined with this preposterous farrago, was now irritating me almost beyond endurance. The fellow's complacency was incredible.

I beckoned to the young woman. "You said this gentleman's 'bus to King's Cross was No. Eighteen, didn't you?"

"Yes, 'Ighteen," she repeated.

"Then would you please bring him an ice."

Mr. Bleet gazed at me in stupefaction; a thick colour had mounted into his face. "You don't mean to say," he spluttered, "that *I* made any such mention of such a thing. I'm sure I never noticed it."

My impulse had been nothing more than a protest against my own boredom and fatigue; but the way he had taken it filled me with shame. What could the creature's state of mind be like if his memory was as untrustworthy as that? The waitress retired.

"It's so devilishly hot in here," I explained. "And even talking is fatiguing in this weather."

"Ay," he said in a low voice. "It is. But you aren't having one yourself?"

"No, thank you," I said, "I daren't. I can't take ices. Indigestion —it's a miserable handicap. . . . You were in the kitchen."

There was a pause. He sat looking foolishly at the little glass dishful of ice-cream: as surprising a phenomenon apparently as to an explorer from the torrid zone earth's northern snows must first appear. There was a look upon his face as if he had been "hurt," as if, like a child, at another harsh word he might burst out crying.

"I hardly know that it's worth repeating," he said at last lamely. His fine resonant voice had lost its tone. "I suppose she intended it kindly enough. And I wouldn't say I hadn't suspected which way the wind was blowing: Willie this, and Willie that. I've always been William to them that know me, except Bill at school. But it was always Willie with her; and a languishing look to match. Still, I never expected what came after that. It took me aback.

"There she was, hanging on my every word, looking volumes, and me not knowing what to say. In a way too, I was attached to her. There were two sides to her, I allow that." He turned away but not, it seemed, in order to see the less conspicuous side more clearly. "I asked her to let me think things over, and I said it as any gentleman would. 'Let me think it over, Edna,' I said. 'You do me honour,' I said. Her hand was on my arm. She was looking at me. God being my witness, I tried to spare her feelings. I eased it over, meaning it all for the best. You see the prospect of it had no more than occurred to me. Married life wasn't what I was after. I shouldn't be as old as I am now—and unmarried, I mean —if that had been so. It was uncomfortable to see her carrying on like that: too early. But things having come to such a pass, well, as you might say, we glided into an understanding at last. And with what result? Why she made it an occasion for putting her foot down all the way round. And hadn't I known it of old?"

He looked at me searchingly, with those dog-bright eyes, those high-set ears, as if to discover where precisely I now was in relation to his confidences.

"She took the reins, as they say. All in good temper for the most part; but there was no mistaking it. Mistress first and Mrs. after, in a manner of speaking. But when it came to speaking sharply to my poor sister on a matter which you wouldn't expect even a full-witted person to be necessarily very quick about at the uptake —I began to suspect I had made a mistake. I knew it then: but forewarned isn't always forearmed. And mistakes are easier to make than to put right. It had gone too far. . . ."

"If you really don't want that ice, I can easily ask the waitress to take it away," I assured him, if only to bring back that wandering empty eye from the reverie into which he seemed to have fallen. Or was it that he was merely absorbed in the picture of the rain-drenched street that was reflected in the looking-glass behind my chair?

"Thank you," he said, taking up the spoon.

"And Miss Dutton left you at last. Did she tell you she had any intention of going?"

"Never," he asseverated. "Not a word. No, not a single word. And if you *can't* explain it, well then, why go on trying? I say. Not at this late day. But you might as well argue with a stone wall. The heat had come by then. Last summer, you know: the drought. Not the great drought, I mean—but round our parts in particular. The whole place was dried up to a tinder; cracks in the clay; weeds dying; birds gone. Even the trees flagging: and the oaks half eaten up by caterpillars already. Meantime, I don't know how it was—unless, perhaps, the heat—but there had been another quarrel. They never got *that* out of me at the Inquiry, though; I can tell you. And that was patched up, too. I apologized because she insisted. But she had hurt me; she had hurt my feelings. And I couldn't see that marriage was going to be a very practical experiment on those lines. But she came round; and considering what a genial woman of the world she looks like in that photograph, you wouldn't have guessed, would you, that crying, weeping, I mean, was much in her way? I found that out, too. And it didn't suit her, either. But she was what they call a woman made for affection. And I mean by *that*," he broke in emphatically, "she liked to monopolize. She wasn't a sharer. We were badly in want of a servant ourselves by that time, as you may imagine. Going from bad to worse, and me with a poisoned thumb, opening tins. But *she* was in want of a servant still more. She wanted me. Husbands often are nothing much better. What's more, I don't wish to say anything against the—against her now; but for the life of me I can't see any reason why she should have gone so far as to insult me. And not a week since we were like birds on one roost. To insult me, mind you, with my poor sister there, listening by!

"But I had learned a bit by then. I held my tongue, though there was a plenty of things to say in reply if I could have demeaned myself to utter them. Plenty. I just went on looking out of the window, easing myself with my foot—we were in the drawing-room at the time—and the very sight of the dried-up grass, and the dead vegetables, and the sun pouring down out of the sky like lava from a volcano would have been enough in themselves to finish off most people's self-restraint. But as I say, I just stood there thinking of what I might have said, but saying nothing— just let her rant on.

"Why, for instance, do you suppose she had made out weeks before that her investments were bringing in twice as much as they really did? Why all that stuff about Monte Carlo and the lady from America when it was only Boulogne and what they call a *pension,* which in plain English is nothing more than lodgings? Mind you," he said, as if to intercept the remark I had no intention of making, "mind you, I agree there *was* a competence, and I agree that, apart from a silly legacy to the Home for Cats and Dogs and that Belgian knacker trade, she had left all there was to leave to my sister—and long before what I told you about just now. I saw that in black and white. It was my duty. That was all settled. On the other hand, how was I to know that she wouldn't change her mind; that she hadn't been paving the way, as you may call it? And why had she deliberately deceived me? I thought it then, and I think it now, more than ever—considering what I have been through. It wasn't treating me fairly, and particularly before she was in a position when things couldn't be altered, so to speak, as between husband and wife."

Owing to the noise of the rain—and possibly in part to his grammar—it was only with difficulty that I could now follow what the creature was mumbling. I found my attention wandering. A miniature Niagara at least eighteen inches wide was at this moment foaming along the street gutter while the rain in the middle of the street as it rebounded above the smoking asphalt was lifting into the air an exquisite mist of spray. I watched it enthralled; it was sweet as the sight of palm trees to my tired hot eyes, and its roar and motion lulled me for a moment or two into a kind of hypnotic trance. When I came back to myself and my trivial surroundings, I found my companion eyeing me as if he had eagerly taken advantage of these moments of oblivion.

"That's the real thing," he said, as if to humour me, beckoning with his thumb over his shoulder. "That rain. But it's waste on only stones." He eyed it pensively, turning his head completely round on his narrow shoulders to do so. But only for a moment. He returned to the business in hand as promptly as if we gossipers had been called to order by the Chairman of a Committee.

"Now it says in that report there which you have just been reading, that Miss Dutton had not been seen after she left Crow-stairs that afternoon of the 3rd of July. That's what it says—in so much print. And I say that's a lie. As it came out later on. And it doesn't make it any truer being in print. It's inaccurate—proved so. But perhaps I ought to tell you first exactly how the whole thing came about. Things get so confused in memory." Once more he wearily drew his hand over his face as if to obliterate even the memory itself. "But—quite apart from the others—it's a relief to get things clearer even in one's own mind. The fact is, the whole thing was over between us a day or two before. As I say, after the last little upset which I told you about, things were smoothed out again, as usual. At least on her side, though there was precious little in which I was really myself at fault. But my own belief is that she was an hysterical woman. What I mean is, she didn't need anything to make a fuss about; to fire up over. No foundation except just her own mood and feelings. I never was what they call a demonstrative person; it isn't in our family. My father himself was a schoolmasterish kind of man. 'It hurts me more than it hurts you'; that kind of man. And up to the age of ten I can honestly say that I never once heard my mother an-swer him back. She felt it, mind you. He thrashed me little short of savage at times. She'd look on, crying; but she kept herself in. She knew it only made matters worse; and she died when I was twelve.

"Well, what I think is this—that Miss Dutton made a mistake about me. She liked comfort. Breakfast in bed; slippers at night; hot water to wash in; that kind of thing. I'll go further: she was meant for luxury. You could see it in her habits. If she had been twice as well off, she'd have wanted three times as many luxuries: lady's maid, evening dress, tea-gowns, music in the drawing-room —that sort of thing. And maybe it only irritated her when she found that I could keep myself in and just look calm, whatever she did or said. Hesitate to say whatever came into her mind?— not she!—true or untrue. Nor actual physical violence, either.

Why, months before, she threw a vause full of flowers at me:
snowdrops."

The expression on his face suddenly became fixed, as if at an
unexpected recollection.

"I am not suggesting," he testified earnestly, "considering—
considering what came after, that I bear her any grudge or malice
on account of all that. All I mean is that I was pressed and pushed
on to a point that some would say was beyond human endurance.
Maybe it was. But what I say is, let," his voice trembled, "bygones
be bygones. I will say no more of that. My point is that Miss Dutton, after all, was to be, as they say, a bird of passage. There had
been a final flare-up and all was over between us. Insult on insult
she heaped on me. And my poor sister there, in her shabby old
black dress, out peering at us, from between her fingers, trembling
in the corner like a dumb animal. She had called her in.

"And me at my wits' end, what with the servant trouble and
the most cantankerous and unreasonable lot of tradespeople you
could lay hands on, north or south. I can tell you, I was pretty
hard pressed. They dragged all that up at the Inquiry. Oh, yes,
bless you. Trust 'em for that. Once it's men against man, then
look to it. Not a *public* Inquiry, mind you. No call for that. And
I *will* say the police, though pressing, and leaving no stone un-
turned, in a manner of speaking, were gentlemen by comparison.
But such things leak out. You can't keep a penny-a-liner from
gabbing, and even if there had been nothing worse to it they'd
have made my life a hell upon earth."

"Nothing worse to it? How do you mean?"

His glance for the instant was entirely vacant of thought. "I
mean," he said stubbornly, after a moment's hesitation, "the hurt
to my private feelings. That's what I mean. I can hear her now.
And the first thing I felt after it was all over was nothing but relief. We couldn't have hit it off together, not for long: not after
the first few weeks, anyhow. Better, I say, wash your hands of
the whole thing. I grant you her decision had left me in a nasty
pickle. As a matter of fact, she was to go in a week, and me to
clear up the mess. Bills all over the place—fresh butter, mind you,
olives, wine, tinned mock turtle—that kind of thing; and all down
to my account. What I feel is, she oughtn't to have kept on at me

like that right up to the last. Wouldn't you have thought, considering all things, any woman with an ounce of common sense—not to speak of common caution—would have let sleeping dogs lie?"

He was waiting for an answer.

"What did her uncle, the Colonel, say to that?"

"Oh, him," he intimated with an incredible sneer. "In the Volunteers! I was speaking as man to man."

"And she didn't even wait the two or three days, then?"

"It was the 3rd of July," he repeated. "After tidying things up for the day—and by that time, mind you, every drop of water had to be brought in buckets across the burnt-up fields from a drying-up pond half a mile away. But it was done. I did it. After finishing, I say, all the rest of the morning chores, I was sitting there thinking of getting a snack of lunch and then what to do next, when I heard a cough—her door had opened; and then her footstep on the stairs—slippers." He held up his forefinger as if for caution, and he was speaking with extreme deliberation as if, with eyes and senses fixed on the scene, he were intent to give me the exactest of records in the clearest of terms. "And I said to myself, 'She's coming! and it's all to begin again!' I said it; I knew it. 'And face it out? . . . then—me?'" He shook his head a little like a cat tasting water, but the eyes he showed me were like the glazed windows of an empty shop. "No, I made myself scarce. I said to myself: 'Better keep your distance. Make yourself scarce; keep out of it.' And heaven help me I had been doing my best to forget what had passed the night before and to face what was to come. And so—I went out.

"It was early afternoon: sultry, like now. And I wandered about the fields. I must have gone miles and never met a soul. But if you ask me to say where, then all I can say is, isn't one field the living image of another? And what do you see when your mind isn't there? All round Winstock way—lanes, hedges, cornfields, turnips—tramp and tramp and tramp. And it was not until about seven o'clock that evening that I got back again. Time for supper. I got out the crockery and—and raked out the fire. No sign of nobody, nor of my sister either—though there was nothing in that: she had a habit of sitting up at her bedroom window, and looking out, just with her hands in her lap. And the house as still as a—as still as a church.

"I loafed about a bit in the kitchen. Call *her*? Well, hardly! There was plenty to do. As usual. The supper, and all that. The village woman had left about eleven that morning—toothache. She owned to it. Not that that put me about. I can cook a boiled egg and a potato well enough for most Christians. But hot meals —meals for—well, anyhow, there was nothing hot that evening. It was about seven-thirty by then, I suppose; and I was beginning to wonder. Then I thought I'd go out in the yard and have a look at the runabout—an old Ford, you know—I hadn't had time then for weeks to keep it decent. When I got to the shed, there was a strange cat eating up some fish-bones; and when I looked in, it was gone."

"You mean the Ford?"

"Yes, the Ford. There wasn't a sign of it. That froze me up, I can tell you, for there had been gipsies about a day or two before. I rushed into the house and called out, 'Miss Dutton, are you there? The Ford's gone.' No answer. I can tell you I was just like a frenzied man. I looked in the drawing-room—teapot and cup on a tray but empty: just sunshine streaming in as if nothing had happened. Then I looked into her little parlour: boudoir, she called it. Nothing doing. Then I went upstairs and tapped on her bedroom door. 'Miss Dutton,' I said, 'have you seen anything of the Ford? It's gone.' And then I looked in. That was the queer thing about it. They all said that. That it never occurred to me, I mean, that she was not in the car herself. But what I say is— how can you think of everything before you say it, and wasn't it I myself that *said* I had said it?

"Anyhow, I looked in: I suppose a man can do *that* in his own house and his car gone from under his very eyes! And believe me, the sight inside was shocking. I'm a great stickler myself for law and order, for neatness, I mean. I had noticed it before: it irritated me; in spite of all her finery, she was never what you would call a tidy woman. But that room beat everything. Drawers flung open, dresses hugger-mugger, slippers, bags, beadwork, boxes, gimcracks all over the place. But not a sign of her. I looked—everywhere. She wasn't there, right enough. Not—not a sign of her. She was gone. And—and I have never seen her since."

The rain was over, and the long sigh he uttered seemed to fill the whole tea-shop as if it were a faint echo of the storm, which had ceased as suddenly as it had begun. The sun was wanly shining again, gilding the street.

"You at once guessed, I suppose, the house had been broken into, while you were out?"

He kept his eyes firmly on mine. "Yes," he said. "That's what I thought—at first."

"But then, I think you said a minute or two ago that Miss Dutton *was* actually seen again?"

He nodded. "That's just it," he said, as if with incredulous lucidity. "So you see, the other couldn't have been. The facts were against it. She was seen that very evening," he said, "and driving my Ford. By more than one, too. Our butcher happened to be outside his shop door, no friend of mine either. It was a Saturday; cutting up pieces for the 4d. and 6d. trays, and he saw her going by: saw the number, too. It was all but broad daylight, though it's a narrow street. It was about seven then, he said, because he had only just wound his clock. There she was; and a good pace too. And who could be surprised if she looked a bit unusual in appearance? It's exactly what you'd expect. You don't bolt out of a house you have lived in comfortable for two or three years as neat as a new pin."

"What was wrong with her?"

"Oh, the man was nothing better than a fool, though promptitude itself when it came to asking a good customer to settle up. He said he'd have hardly recognized her. There, in my car, mind you, and all but broad daylight."

"But surely," I said as naturally as possible, "even if it is difficult sometimes to trace a human being, it is not so easy to dispose of a car. Wasn't that ever found?"

He smiled at me, and in a more friendly way than I should have deemed possible in a face so naturally inexpressive.

"You've hit the very nail on the head," he assented. "They did find the car—on the Monday morning. In fact it was found on the

Sunday by a young fellow out with his sweetheart, but they thought it was just waiting—picking flowers, or something. It had been left inside a fir-copse about a couple of hundred yards from a railway station, a mile or so out of the town."

"Just a countryfied little railway station, I suppose? Had the porter or anybody noticed a lady?"

"Countryfied—ay, maybe: but the platform crowded with people going to and fro for their week's marketing, besides a garden party from the rectory."

"The platform going into the town?"

"Yes, that's it," said my friend. "Covering her tracks."

At that moment I noticed one of our waitress's bright-red "Eighteens" whirling past the tea-shop door. It vanished.

"She had had a letter that morning—postmark Chicago," the now far-too-familiar voice pushed on industriously. "The postman noticed it, being foreign. It's my belief *that* caused it. But mind you, apart from that, though I'm not, and never was, complaining, she'd treated me, well—" But he left the sentence unfinished while he clumsily pushed about with his spoon in the attempt to rescue a fly that had strayed in too far in pursuit of his sweet cold coffee. He was breathing gently on the hapless insect.

"And I suppose, by that time, you had given the alarm?"

"Given the alarm?" he repeated. "Why?"

The sudden frigidity of his tone confused me a little. "Why," I said, "not finding Miss Dutton in the house, didn't you let anybody know?"

"Now, my dear sir," he said, "I ask you. How was *I* to know what Miss Dutton was after? I wasn't Miss Dutton's keeper; she was perfectly at liberty to do what she pleased, to come and go. How was I to know what she had taken into her head? Why, I thought for a bit it was a friendly action considering all things, that she should have borrowed the car. Mind you, I don't say I wasn't disturbed as well, her not leaving a word of explanation, as she had done once before—pinned a bit of paper to the kitchen table—'Yours with love, Edna'—that sort of thing. Though that was when everything was going smooth and pleasant. What I did first was to go off to a cottage down the lane and inquire there. All out, except the daughter in the wash-house. Not a sight or sound of car or Miss Dutton, though she did recollect the honk of a horn sounding. 'Was it my horn?' I asked. But they're not very observant, that kind of young woman. Silly-like. Besides, she wasn't much more than a child."

"And your sister: where actually was she, after all?"

He looked at me as if once more in compliment of my sagacity.

"That, I take it—to find and question *her,* I mean, was a matter of course. I went up to her room, opened the door, and I can hear myself actually saying it now: 'Have you seen anything of Edna, Maria?'

"It was very quiet in her room—stuffy, too, and for the moment I thought she wasn't there; and then I saw her—I detected her there—sitting in the farthest corner out of the light. I saw her white face turn round, it must have been covered up. 'Where's Edna, Maria?' I repeated. She shook her head at me, sitting there beyond the window. I could scarcely see her. And you don't seem to have realized that any kind of direct or sudden question always confused her. It didn't seem she understood what I was saying. In my belief it was nothing short of brutal the way they put her through it. I mean that Colonel, as he calls himself. Over and over and over again.

"Well, we weren't in any mood for food, as you may guess, when eight, nine, went by—and no sign of her. At last it was no use waiting any longer; but just to make sure, I went over to the farm two miles or so away—a little off the road, too, she must have taken to the town. We were still pretty friendly there. It was about half past nine, I suppose, and they had all gone to bed. The dog yelled at me as if it was full moon and he had never seen me before. I threw a handful of gravel up at the old man's window, and I must say, considering all things, he kept his temper pretty well. Specially as he had seen nothing. Nothing whatever, he said.

" 'Well,' I said, speaking up at him, and they were my very words, 'I should like to know what's become of her.' He didn't seem to be as anxious as I was—thought she'd turn up next morning. 'That kind of woman knows best what she's about,' he said. So I went home and went to bed, feeling very uneasy. I didn't like the feel of it, you understand. And I suppose it must have

been about three or four in the morning when I heard a noise in
the house."

"You thought she had come back?"

"What?" he said.

"I say, you thought she had come back?"

"Yes, of course. Oh yes. And I looked out of my bedroom door
over the banisters. By that time there was a bit of moonlight showing, striking down on the plaster and oilcloth. It was my sister,
with an old skirt thrown over her nightgown. She was as white
as a sheet, and shivering.

" 'Where have you been, Maria?' I asked her in as gentle a
voice as I could make it. The curious thing is, she understood me
perfectly well. I mean she answered at once, because often I think
really and truly she did understand, only that she couldn't as
quickly as most people collect her wits as they say.

"She said, mumbling her words, she had been looking for her.

" 'Looking for who?' I said, just to see if she had taken me
right.

" 'For her,' she said.

" 'For Edna?' I asked. 'And why should you be looking for
Edna this time of night?' I spoke a little more sternly.

"She looked at me, and the tears began to roll down her face.

" 'For God's sake, Maria, why are you crying?' I said.

" 'Oh,' she said, 'she's gone. And she won't come back now.'

"I put my arm round her and drew her down on to the stairs.
'Compose yourself,' I said to her, 'don't shiver and shake like that.'
I forgot she had been standing barefoot on the cold oilcloth.
'What do you mean, gone? Don't take on so. Who's to know
she won't come back safe and sound?' I am giving you the words
just as they came out of our mouths.

" 'Oh,' she said, 'William, you know better than me—I won't
say anything more. Gone. And never knowing that I hadn't forgotten how kind she was to me!'

" 'Kind, my girl!' I said. 'Kind! In good part, maybe,' I said,
'but not surely after what she said to you that day?'

"But I could get nothing more out of her. She shrank up
moaning and sobbing. She had lost herself again, her hair all
draggled over her eyes, and she kept her face averted from me,

and her shoulders were all humped, shaking under my hands—you know what women are. So I led her off to her room and made her as comfortable as I could. But all through the night I could hear her afterwards when I went to listen, and talking too.

"You can tell I was by now in a pretty state myself. That was a long night for me. And what do you think: when I repeated that conversation to the Colonel, and the Inspector himself standing by, he as good as told me he didn't believe me. 'Friendly questions'! I could have wrung his nose. But then by that time my poor sister couldn't put two words together, he bawled at her so; until even the Inspector said it was not fair on her, and that she wouldn't be any use, anyhow, whatever happened."

Once again there fell a pause in my stranger's disjointed story. He took two or three spoonfuls in rapid succession of his half-melted ice-cream. Even though the rain and the storm had come and gone, the air was not appreciably cooler, or rather it was no less heavy and stagnant. Our waitress had apparently given us up as lost souls, and I glanced a little deprecatingly at the notice: "No gratuities," on the wall.

"How long did the drought last after that?" I inquired at last.

"The drought?" said my friend. "The questions you ask! Why, it broke that very night. Over an inch of rain we had in less than eight hours."

"Well, that, at any rate, I suppose, was something of a comfort."

"I don't see quite why," he retorted.

"And then you informed the police?"

"On the Sunday." He took out a coloured silk handkerchief from the pocket of his neat pepper-and-salt jacket, and blew his nose. It is strange how one can actually anticipate merely from the general look of a man such minute particulars as the trumpeting of a nose. Strange, I mean, that all the parts and properties of human beings seem to hang so closely together, as if in positive confusion. Anyhow, the noise resounded through the glass-walled marbled room as sharp as cockcrow.

"Well," he said, "that's where I stand. Looking at me, you wouldn't suppose perhaps that everything that a man wants most in this world has been destroyed and poisoned away. I had no call perhaps to be confiding in a mere stranger. But you couldn't credit the relief. I have nothing left now. I came up here to lose myself in the noise—so shocking quiet it is, there, now. But I have to go back—can't sleep much, though: wake up shouting. But what's worst is the emptiness: it's all perished. I don't want anything now. I'd as lief die and have done with it, if I could do it undriven. I've never seen a desert, but I reckon I know what the inside of one's like now. I stop thinking sometimes, and get dressed without knowing it. You wouldn't guess that from my appearance, I dare say. But once begin living as you feel underneath living *is,* where would most of us be? They have hounded me on and they've hounded me down, and presently they'll be sealing me up, and me never knowing from one day to another what news may come of—of our friend. And my sister gone and all."

"She isn't 'missing' too, I hope?" As I reflect on it, it was a vile question to have put to the man. I don't see how anything could have justified it. His face was like a burnt-out boat. The effect on him was atrocious to witness. His swarthy cheek went grey as ashes. The hand on the marble table began to tremble violently.

"Missing?" he cried. "She's dead. Isn't *that* good enough for you?"

At this, no doubt because I was hopelessly in the wrong, I all but lost control of myself.

"What do you mean?" I exclaimed in a low voice. "What do you mean by speaking to me like that? Haven't I wasted the better part of a Saturday afternoon listening to a story which I could have picked up better in your own county newspaper? What's it all to me, may I ask? I want to have nothing more to do with it—or you either."

"You didn't say that at the beginning," he replied furiously, struggling to his feet. "You led me on."

"Led you on, by God? What do you mean by such a piece of impudence? I say I want nothing more to do with you. And if that's how you accept a kindness, take my advice and keep your troubles to yourself in future. Let your bygones *be* bygones. And may the Lord have mercy on my soul."

It was a foul outburst, due in part, I hope, to the heat; in part to the suffocating dehumanizing fœtor which spreads over London when the sun has been pouring down on its bricks and mortar as fiercely as on the bones and sands of some Eastern mud village.

My stranger had sat down again abruptly, had pushed his ice away from him and covered his face with his hands. His shoulders were jumping as if with hiccups. It was fortunate perhaps that at the moment there was no other eater in the café. But the waitresses were clustered together at the counter. They must have been watching us for some little time. And the manageress was there, too, looking at us like a scandalized hen over her collar through her pince-nez. We were evidently causing a disturbance —on the brink of a "scene." A visionary placard flaunted across my inward eye: *Fracas in a Restaurant.*

I too sat down, and beckoned peremptorily to the young lady who had been so attentive about the 'bus.

"My bill, please," I said—"this gentleman's and mine."

And then, foolishly, I added, "It's hot, isn't it?"

She made no reply until, after damping her lead pencil, she had added up her figures and had handed me between her fingertips the mean scrap of paper. Then she informed me crisply, in fastidious Cockney, that some people seemed to find it hotter than most, and that it was nearly closing-time, and would I please pay at the desk.

My accomplice had regained a little of his self-restraint by now. He put out a wavering hand and took up his hard felt hat. It was almost incredible that so marked a change should have come over so insensitive a face in that brief space of time. Its touch of bravado, its cold clear stare as of a watchful dog, even the neatness of it, had disappeared. He looked ten years older—lost and abandoned. He put out his other hand for the check. It was a curious action for a man with an intense closeness—if not meanness—clearly visible on his features: "I should prefer, if you don't mind, to pay my bill myself," he said.

"Not at all," I replied brusquely. "It was my ice-cream. I must apologize for having been so abrupt."

He tried to smile; and it was like the gleam of a sickly evening sunshine after heavy winter rain.

"It's broken me: that's all I can say," he said. "What I say is, you read such things in the newspapers, but you don't know what they mean to them as are most concerned. I don't see how you can."

I hesitated. A furious contest—dim spread-eagled figures silhouetted, as it were, against a background of utter black—seemed to be proceeding in some dream in my mind, a little beyond actual consciousness. "Well," I blurted, "I hope time will make things better. I can guess what I should feel like myself in similar circumstances. If I were you, I should . . ." But at sight of him, the words, I am thankful to say, faded out before I could utter them. 'If I were you'—how easy! But how is that metamorphosis possible?

He looked at his hat; he looked at his ice-cream, now an insipid mush; he looked anxiously and searchingly at the table—marked over with the hieroglyphics of dark ugly marble. And at last he raised his eyes—those inexpressive balls of glass—and looked at me. He changed his hat from his right to his left hand, and still looking at me, hesitated, holding the empty hand out a little above the table. Then turning away, he drew it back.

I pretended not to have noticed the action. "There should be another Eighteen in a few minutes," I volunteered. "And I think I noticed a stopping-place a few yards down."

Nevertheless I couldn't for the moment leave him there—to the tender mercies of those censorious young waitresses in their exquisitely starched caps. "I am going that way," I said. "Shall I see you into it?"

"It's the heat," he said. "No, thank you. You have been a . . ."

With a gasp I repelled as well as I could the distaste for him that was once more curdling as if with a few drops of vinegar my very blood. What monsters of hatred and uncharitableness we humans can be! And what will *my* little record look like, I wonder, when the secrets of all hearts are opened.

It seemed for the time being as though the whole of my right arm had become partially paralysed. But with an effort I put out my hand at last; and then he, too, his—a large green solitaire cuff-link showing itself against his wristband as he did so. We shook hands—though I doubt if a mere fleshly contact can express much while the self behind it is dumb with instinctive distaste.

Besides, the effect on him even of a friendly action as frigid as this was horribly disconcerting. It reminded me of ice pitted and crumbling in a sudden thaw. He seemed to have been reduced to a state of physical and spiritual helplessness, as if by an extremity of emotion, or by a drug. It was nauseating. It confused me and made me ashamed and miserable. I turned away abruptly; paid our bill at the desk, and went out.

The Connoisseur and Other Stories (1926)

THE CONNOISSEUR

Park Street

It was a narrow discreet street, and, in this late evening twilight, all but deserted. There had been rain, bringing with it an earthy fragrance from the not far-distant park, and small clear puddles of water filled the hollows of the paving-stones. Clumsily picking his way between them, St. Dusman came shuffling along between the houses to keep a rather belated tryst. He paused now and again to examine the numbers on the fanlights, and at last halted, at No. 13, where he stood for a few moments peering in over the spear-headed palisade that guarded its area. As yet the curtains of the shallowly curved window abutting on the street had not been drawn nor its shutters closed.

From a candelabrum on a lacquer Chinese table in the midst of the room electric tapers cast their beams upon the exquisite objects that stood around them. This sharp metallic light bathed ivory and porcelain, the wax-like flowers in their slim vase, the few pictures, as if they were the sacred relics of a shrine.

The old creature's eyes gazed vaguely through their magnifying spectacles at this scene of still life, then groped onward towards the figure of a man, as yet apparently in his early thirties, who now stood in the doorway, slim, sleek, dark—as if for foil to the very vase on the table with its pale green leaves and flowers. His neat head was stooping forward and inclined a little towards his left shoulder, for at that moment with intense interest and vigilance he was vainly endeavouring to see the old man out there in the darkening street as clearly as St. Dusman could see him.

The old man hesitated no longer. With the aid of its wrought-steel handrail he mounted the three shallow steps of the outer door, under its narrow shell-shaped porch, and rapped softly with his knuckles on the panel. The stranger himself hastened to open it, though for an instant or two he seemed to have paused with fingers on its catch, and after the briefest scrutiny of the face of his visitor from penetrating green-grey eyes, led him, almost as though surreptitiously, into the very room which the saint had surveyed from without. And he himself drew their curtains over the windows.

"You may not have been expecting me, Mr. Blumen?" said the old man courteously, still a little breathless. "Although, indeed, I am a little late. My friends detain me at times. And this is my last errand for the day."

Mr. Blumen's eyes were now steadily fixed on his visitor's face. "I must confess," he replied, "that I was *not* expecting you. Not, I mean, to-night."

"But you had not entirely forgotten me?" the old man pressed him whimsically. "You have now and then given a passing thought to me? I leave footprints outside."

Mr. Blumen smiled, at least with his lips. "You bring back at least one old memory—an experience often repeated when I was

a small boy in Bath, you know. The experience, I mean, of being
'called-for.' Now and then, for there are many kinds of parties,
it was a relief, a positive godsend."

There was just a hint of the formal in this rapid and not unfriendly speech. It had been uttered too in a lowish voice, though,
even at that, the characteristic slight lisp and blurred r's had been
detectable.

The old saint peered up at the young man over his thick-glassed
spectacles. "I can well understand it," he said at last. "It meant
returning home. Ours is a longer journey, Mr. Blumen."

The dark eyes had sharpened. "It *has* a goal, then?"

"Surely!" replied the old man. "Were you uncertain even of
that? Not," he added candidly, "not that the metaphor carries us
quite all the way. Lassitude follows after most races; and what
are called goals and prizes may be disappointing. But what—if I
may venture—suggested to you that any journey in this world, in
any precise meaning of the word, has an *end*?"

"Well," replied Mr. Blumen, "there are many philosophies, and
one may listen to all without being persuaded to accept any."

"But hardly without divining any—just on one's own account?"
returned the old man, almost as if he were smilingly bent on
coaxing a secret out of a child. "Wouldn't that be a little unfair
to the mere facts of the case? Now I'll be bound, Mr. Blumen,
when you were a small boy you must have dreamed now and
then? So far at least you were conscious of circles within circles
—and without—so to say?"

There was remarkably little of the childish in the keen, ashen
face confronting him. The dark, large-pupilled eyes had wandered
almost stealthily from point to point of the objects around them,
every one of which seemed now to be flashing secret signals one
to the other in this motionless creek of air.

"Well, possibly," replied Mr. Blumen. "But even a pessimist
would agree that it is as well to make the best one can of the one
'circle'—without vexing oneself too much with shallow and futile
speculations concerning any other. And optimists; well—" a slight
shrug of the narrow shoulders completed the sentence. "I must be
quite candid, though. I am unconscious of the least wish in the
world to bid adieu to what they call 'things as they are'—to

things, that is, as they appear to me to be. I realize, none the less, that you have obligations. And—thank you for fulfilling them so considerately."

At this, the old man folded one hand over the other under his loose sleeves, sighed, and quietly seated himself on the edge of a chair that stood near by. "Thank *you*, Mr. Blumen," he said; "I will enjoy a moment's needed rest."

"Forgive me," cried the other hastily, turning as he spoke towards the tiny sideboard—riding there in the offing, as it were, of this bright inward pool of silence, with its delicate cargo of Venetian glass and wine.

But his visitor pleasantly waved this little courtesy aside. "To tell you the truth, Mr. Blumen," he explained, "and you are exceedingly tolerant, I haven't the head for it. And though I am familiar with our route—almost excessively familiar—we shall still need our combined cold wits to face it out. You were saying 'things as they are'—a stimulating phrase enough in itself. Still, I have no very close knowledge of what you call the world; apart, I mean, from my daily duties. May I assume that 'things as they are' now surround us?" The aged eyes peered carefully and cautiously once more through their thick glasses. "That is so? Please, then, tell me why you are disinclined to leave them. You have seen a good deal of them?"

Mr. Blumen drew in his underlip as if to moisten it with his tongue. He paused; in search of words. "Well," he ventured at last, "partly, I suppose, because of those weeds of superstitious fear planted in one's mind when one is young; partly because life *can* be uncommonly entertaining; and partly because I dislike leaving what I have spent a good many years making my own."

"Making your own!" echoed the gentle old voice a little dryly; though there was a twinkle in its owner's eye. "But you will not be ceasing to *think* when we make a start. And surely it is only thoughts, hopes, desires, dreams, and so on that you can really claim as having been made your own.

"In a sense," agreed his quarry. "But then I'm no Platonist, either. One's friends, one's pursuits, one's possessions"—he made a little gesture with his right hand that till that moment had been reposing in his pocket—"surely they are the very proofs of one's *self* that one hungers for. Not of course that they can be permanent; or need be."

"Friends are friends," said the old man. "I can understand that. But possessions? I take it, Mr. Blumen, that you would include in that category what I see around me. Perhaps you would tell me why you value them so highly. Were there not things less perishable to possess; things that of their own nature would be less inclined to bid *you* good-bye? That old image of Kuan Yin over there, for example, is she any the more or less a symbol than the very ferocious onion-green dragon displaying his tail on that pot yonder? Better both in the imagination, don't you think, Mr. Blumen, than—well, round one's neck? Besides, earth-time is fleeting. Was it ever, do you feel, worth while to do more than merely borrow its energies, apart from much else; and be grateful?"

"To whom?" Mr. Blumen blurted.

"That is a question," retorted the old man serenely, hugging his hands a little closer under their wide sleeves—"that is a question which would take rather more earth-time than you and I have at our disposal just now to answer."

The shoulders beneath the neat dinner-jacket slightly lifted themselves. "We don't always expect answers to our questions," he said.

"Well now, see here," said the old man, and he vigorously readjusted his spectacles on the bridge of his broad and rather stumpy nose. "There are many similar things to these in every house in every neighbouring street, are there not? Is it just the sense of possession that is the charm? Or of being possessed?"

"Things *similar,* perhaps," smiled Mr. Blumen indulgently. "But I need hardly suggest to an adept like yourself that many of the specimens around us at this moment are practically unique. And do you mean to imply, sir, that the beauty and rarity of a thing amount to nothing in what perhaps—whether expressed in earth-time or otherwise—you would agree to call the long run?"

"Come, come," said the old man, "surely rarity is the reward of a mere acquisitiveness? While as for beauty; indeed, Mr. Blumen, in my humble office—a little arduous, too, at times, if I may confess it—there is not much leisure for beauty. Still, I think you will agree that what you and I mean by the word, and so far as we are personally concerned, it depends solely upon the eyes in our heads. And we have a good many, you know. With the exception, too, of the rare flowers on your table—specimens, I suspect, which would hardly be recognized even by their less remote ancestors—everything here, I notice, is—what shall we call it—of human workmanship."

"They are works of art," agreed Mr. Blumen. "They represent years of human skill, human delight, and human devotion and desire. What have you against them? For that matter what has *he* against them who has so punctually provided me with your company this evening?" A very sober countenance now scrutinized Mr. Blumen—and the old man, as if to suit posture to face, seemed to have composed himself even more heavily in his chair. He gazed hard, but made no answer; then turned his head and almost cautiously surveyed the objects around him as one by one they met his eye.

All the *familles* were there: *noire, verte,* and *rose;* each of them signally represented by elegant ambassadors, only the more amiable and acceptable for their extreme age. On half a dozen varieties of gods, on fabulous heroes and monsters renowned in old tales, and on exquisite Tanagra figures, and shapes of beast, bird, and fable, made small in priceless images of stone, earthenware, porcelain, enamel, ivory, metal, alighted his gentle glance. The faintly greenish glass on table and sideboard, like colourless and heatless crystal flame, lifted its burden of gimcracks, sweetmeats, and liqueurs, a few inches aloft.

The rugs beneath the old man's mud-stained feet by far excelled in blended colour and design the minute French masterpieces in paint, and the worn dimmed tapestry that here and there relieved the delicate gilt of the walls and of the few chairs. A smiling cherub disguised as Father Time stood on tiptoe with uplifted scythe above the minute gilt clock ticking out Mr. Blumen's envious moments upon the carved chimney-piece. The fragile peace around him and his visitor indeed was so tenuous it seemed that at any moment it might explode, and shatter itself into its component atoms. When the old man's voice again broke the silence, it was positively as if he himself had shattered in sheer actuality some crystal image lifting itself into the still, elastic air.

"You would, I believe, Mr. Blumen, be surprised," that voice was murmuring gently, "you would be surprised at the range of humanity that lies reflected around us. Here and there our company—and, as you well know, whatever a man does is to some extent a mirror of what he is: here and there (and forgive me for confessing it) that company, I say, is detestable to the last degree. You will be well rid of it. There are poisons that enter by the eye as well as in the blood. What is even worse— except for that moth searching the shadows over there, whose presence no doubt is explained by my poor company—I perceive here no faintest sign of life. Of life, I mean, here and now."

A thin dark cloud had mounted into Mr. Blumen's pallid face. "If you had consented to delay your visit even by half an hour," he retorted, with a contemptuous gesture towards the two chairs drawn up to the table, "your last remark would hardly have been to the point."

"Do not misdoubt me," replied his visitor courteously. "I have no very acute intelligence. But I have heard the rumours of busy domestic sounds from below; and I detect preparations for a visitor. But I meant by life a happy freedom of the spirit rather than mere amusement of the body. A life *delighted* in."

"A pet canary, perhaps?" But the voice was almost too tired to be insolent.

"Why not indeed?" replied the old man, "if you took a lively pleasure in it. Still, cages remain cages; and you yourself would agree with me that heart and soul you yourself are something of a recluse. And this I gather is your hermitage. And I have seldom in a pretty wide experience of such things seen a cage more elaborate. You are content with it?"

Mr. Blumen stared a little heavily into the face of his visitor. "If you know anything of the society in this neighbourhood, and if you mean that I enjoy solitude, then I am in complete agreement with you."

"So would any chrysalis be," said his visitor almost gaily. "I grieve with all my heart that you are compelled to resign things you have grown to care for—hoarded, Mr. Blumen; that it is now too late, I mean, to have *given* them away."

Mr. Blumen laid a gentle hand upon the corner of the chimney-piece. For an instant their ashen wax-like lids descended over his green-grey eyes.

"And now," went on his visitor gently, rising to his feet, "that last taxicab has passed out of hearing. There is more than half a moon to-night over Whinnimoor. It is time for us to be off."

Sasurat

The soft white glare of snow fringed the crests of the mountains that surrounded the tortuous valley beneath them. Blossoming trees and coloured drifts of flowers mounted up almost to their frozen margin. The sun ascending into the dark-blue vault of the sky, though it was but an hour or two after break of day, cast beams so fierce upon their flanks that the lawn-like mists were already swirling in the heat, showering their dew on leaf and flower and rock.

St. Dusman had made his way into the valley in the small hours, and now sat drowsing on a stone beside which roared a torrent of green water. He had removed his sandals in order to lave his feet in the coldness, and now it would appear as if every flame-plumed bird in the thickets around him, and every puffing breath of wind that came wandering across the precipitous gorges, were inviting the spirit of the old man to return to the world, to slip out of sleep and waken again. With mouth agape, however, he nodded on. Flies and butterflies of innumerable dyes flashed and fluttered in the empty air around him. Fish of hardly less brave a livery sported with fin and tail over the coloured stones that tessellated the bed of the stream that flowed beside him.

Two or three hundred feet above, at the foot of one of the lower peaks glittering in the sun-rays with rainbow flashes from its exposed face of rock and quartz, a mountain leopard now stole into view, lifting its gentle head into the sunshine. With twitching brows and whiskers, it snuffed the morning air, while its amber eyes rested for a moment upon the stooping figure of the old man crouched up and motionless in sleep far beneath him. With a faint uneasy mew, it then lifted its gaze upwards towards a pair of eagles circling in the enormous cavity of the now starless heavens. Then curling its narrow beautiful body upon the sward under the rocky wall of the mountain, it couched with head on paws, and composed itself to sleep.

It was the scream of a parrakeet that pierced through the old man's dreams at last. His eyes opened, he raised his head and looked around him. Where all had been dark with the gloom of night was now radiant with day. He rose to his feet and shuffled towards a huge spreading tree from amid whose swaying branches of foliage, almost brushing the ground beneath them with their blooms, he could wait and watch unseen. Resting his hand upon a smooth bough of the tree a little above his head, he contemplated the scene around him.

A smile spread over his seamed, weather-worn old face as his eyes roved to and fro. For twenty or thirty paces distant from him on a smooth drift of sward stood, as it were, a low small arbour woven of dried grass and rushes, and roofed with patches of moss and coloured feathers even. No bigger than a beehive though it was, it showed as conspicuous on the turf as a green oasis in the wilderness, or an isle of coral rising gently with its palms and tamarisks from out of the sea.

Some small creature, it was evident, had diligently collected together for its pleasure a few of the more sparkling and garish objects that lay within reach—muscous growths, for example, that flourished only in the denser and darker thickets of the surrounding forest, the bark of a silvery shrub that ventured nearest of all on the hill-tops to the never-melting snows, a fossil shell or two. While scattered about the rounded entrance to the arbour lay bright pebbles, bright "everlasting" flowers, scraps of quartz, and what appeared to be flakes of a shining metal.

The old man sighed, though he did not stop smiling, as he feasted himself on these simple artifices and awaited the appearance of the hidden designer. The hours of eternity are no longer than those of time. Contrariwise, a century of earth's seasons may be in thought but as transitory as the colours of a rainbow. But, whatever his ruminations might be, St. Dusman made no attempt to suppress the look of humorous compassion that now wrinkled

his face at this showing of yet another renewed attempt to make
a haven in the wilderness.

He had not very long to wait. For sunbeams had but just
gilded the fringe of the water in its cold rocky channel, when
there came a sudden scurry of wings from above his sheltering
tree, and there alit on the very stone that had been his nocturnal
stool, a bird.

From claw to crest it reared itself about eighteen inches from
its resting-place, and in plumage was of a uniform saddish green,
though tinged at the extremities of its primaries and of its tail
feathers with a dull cinnamon, its breast deepening to a faint
shot purple towards the belly.

With dipping and sidling head it surveyed the minute surrounding plateau, showing in its quick movements a faint unease
as if its senses were dimly aware of strange and dangerous
company.

So translucent was the surrounding air that even at this distance
the old man could mark the silvery rim to the iris of its eye, and
could count the horned, outspread claws that clutched the stone.
He had long since descried too, even to the delicate markings of
its rosettes, the leopard apparently sleeping away its vigil on the
height above.

The bird that had thus alighted on the stone near by, appeared
to be in quest of company. It bowed and becked now a little this
way, now a little that; it stretched and sleeked a wing until every
speck on its neutral-patterned feathers displayed itself in the sun.
Then crouching lower and amorously into its soft plumage, with
stealthy movements it twisted its neck upon its shoulders until
its beak, as if in maternal joy and quietude, lay gently upon its
bosom. The old man smiled at the realization that while this
last gesture had come straight from nature's teaching, what had
preceded it seemed to have been learned by mimicry and to have
been practised with reluctance.

A slight stir within the arbour now caught his attention. Instantly the visitor on the stone drew herself down and sped
swiftly into cover behind and beneath the boulders that lay along
the margin of the stream. Many minutes passed. The sun swept

upward into the heavens, rejoicing in his strength. By infinite degrees the shadows cast by mountain peak and crest moved in a vast curve like the hands of an enormous timepiece. At faintest touch of their chill in its lair the leopard had stirred, lifted and stretched itself, and after one swift glance over the scene spread out beneath it, had vanished from sight, as if in obedience to a secret cue.

And now from out the pitch-black arch of its nesting-place, issued into the blazing glare of the morning a creature compared with whom the visitor to its domains was but as a handmaid in the train of the Queen of Sheba compared with King Solomon in all his glory. Its crested head was of molten gold—a gold which swam and rippled down towards its folded wings into a lively green seen only in rare mosses and in the shallows of the oceans. Green, blue, and purple then mingled their beauty. The wing tips were black as soot; the tail coverts, interrupted with snow, resembled them; while above them, arched over its back, flowed upwards two paler shafts terminating in a lyre-shaped pattern of hues almost indistinguishable the one from the other, as they glinted, flashed, and melted in the sun.

This lordly creature, having surveyed a moment the surrounding day, trod delicately onwards to its bathing-place; and after a while returned once more to preen itself amid the odd riches which it had collected and strown in devices recognizable only by itself, around its arbour. And not until now stole out again its humble infatuated visitor.

The old man almost laughed outright to see the disdain with which his lordship refused to recognize his visitor's presence there. Indolently, methodically he continued his exquisite toilet. While she, poor creature, as if now utterly ashamed of her former wiles, cowered half in shadow, half in sun, gently observing him. "O Lucifer, Son of the Morning," muttered the old man—beads of sweat, in spite of the sheltering branches above him, glistening on his bald pate, "O Lucifer, Son of the Morning, by pride fell the angels."

Sheer curiosity seemed at last to overcome her as she drew a little nearer to watch the adored one rearrange his treasury. Now one shell, then another, a fragment of quartz or of glint-

ing metal, he lifted with his beak and disposed in place. There
appeared to be singularly little method in his peculiar hobby,
for as often as not he returned to its former place in the pattern
what but a moment or two before he had with extreme deliberation deposited elsewhere. Possibly some outlying province of
his birdlike mind and attention was concerned with his faithful
visitor. But not the faintest ripple of neck or plume betrayed
it. His complete heed seemed to be solely for his pretty collection.

"How strange it is," thought the old man, "that even in the
simplest of her creatures nature consistently endeavours to reach
the least bit farther than she can stretch." There was something
almost human in the queer devices these creatures of the same
kin and kind were exhibiting, though neglect and contempt
were steadily reducing the unwanted one to her own sovran
and instinctive self. She rose out of the shadow, displayed once
more an indolent wing, and emitted from her throat a curious,
bubbling, guttural note.

And apparently, as if at last in heed of her entreaties, her
disdainful idol had suddenly thrust forward his golden head;
every feather on his body seeming to bristle and roughen itself
as he stared. Yet even this could be but small comfort to her
meekness and vanity, for his silver-lined eyes were now fixed
not upon herself but a few paces beyond her.

There was a deathly pause. For an instant or two the small
lovely universe around them, snow-masked mountain-top to
brawling stream, seemed to have been swept up in a soundless
swoon. Then, as if at a signal, three sentient objects flashed into
movement, so rapid as to be individually indistinguishable.

With a mighty whirr of wing, scattering with its talons as
it rose the shells and pebbles strown around it, the Bird of the
Arbour flashed into the air; and the crouching leopard leapt
towards its prey.

Distracted an instant by the foe swooping to attack it, the
beast swerved in its leap, missing by a few inches its assured
victim, succeeding merely in tearing out a few dull feathers
from her wing. She screamed piteously as she fled, then turned
too late to observe what had befallen. Plunging with beak and
claw, the master of the arbour had cowed for a moment her

assailant. The leopard crouched snarling, with lashing tail, defending its eyes against plunging beak and claw. Then suddenly, and with one lightning buffet of its paws, it leapt into the air, and smote its aggressor down.

St. Dusman drew his roughened hand over his forehead; and seizing his staff issued out from his retreat towards the fray. If he had intended to intervene to any purpose in what was passing, he had come too late. After one glimpse of this advancing Strangeness, the leopard with cringing body turned swiftly and fled.

The old man approached the wounded and dying bird, which feebly endeavoured to beat off his advances. He raised it gently in his arms, and carrying it back into the shadow of its arbour, laid it down among its treasures. The creature's dimming eye gazed vacantly on these vanishing possessions.

"Poor soul, poor soul," the old man whispered. Then hastening down to the stream, he dipped the hem of his outer garment into the water and returning, squeezed out a few drops into its yawning bill.

Strange changes of hue seemed to be chasing, like wind over wheat, across its miraculous plumage. Its glazing eye was fixed, hardly in terror now, but in mute hopeless entreaty, upon the old man's face.

"There, there, my dear," he said, as if an old bachelor of a hundred generations had somehow learned to croon to a hurt child. "There, there, my dear; it's only time to be whispering adieu again. The longer the journey the more numerous the inns. And perhaps a moment or two's rest in each."

But as he watched its quickening pangs the old man suddenly rebuked himself for his stupidity in not reminding himself that other comfort—tenderer than any human heart could offer— was near at hand. He lifted his eyes and searched the surrounding thickets. It was not yet too late. The carcass of the creature beneath his hands was not yet wholly insensitive. And having moistened once again the pointed tongue within its beak, the old man rose to his feet and shuffled off as quick as his old bones would allow, down into the ravine where brawled the mountain river.

Nor while the morning hours lasted did he attempt to look behind him. He merely sat there lost in reverie.

And since the tongues of the water kept up an incessant roar and babblement, no faintest murmur of the plaintive farewells behind him told whether, like the fabulous swan, the Bird of the Arbour sings only at the approach of death.

Kootoora

Even the keenest eye slowly and circumspectly directing its gaze in as remote an ambience as it could command from any one of the blackened crests that lifted themselves fifteen to twenty feet, like the billows of a frozen sea on this Plain of Kootoora, would have discerned no sign of life. Minute slender steel-coloured midges, it is true, their burnished wings like infinitesimal flakes of mica beating the arid air, their horn-shaped snouts curved beneath their many-prismed eyes, drifted in multitudinous clusters in every hollow. They might be animate ashes.

Specks even more minute circling at ethereal altitudes above the vast crater of distant Ajubajao betokened the haunt of some species of vulture, though what meat nourished them more substantial than the air in which they circuited there was nothing to show.

Their towering vans commanded, however, an immense range of scene, and they long since must have descried from so dizzying a coign a tiny erect shape scrambling toilsomely from out of the east towards the centre of this wild and hideous plateau. From crest to crest of the parched savanna of lava, now pausing to recover his breath and to survey what lay before him, now sliding and swaying into the yawning hollow beneath him; clambering to his feet when some unnoticed obstacle or more dangerous glissade had sent him sprawling; he pushed steadily on.

In his pertinacity, in the serene indomitableness of his age-raddled countenance he resembled no less a personage than the first Chinese patriarch, Bodhidharma, as—muffled in his mantle —he is depicted crossing the Yangtze River, his broad soles poised upon a reed.

For this very reason, maybe, the vultures of Ajubajao wheeled no nearer. Or it may be that a pilgrim or traveller who of his own free will, or at the promptings of a bizarre romance, or in service of some incalculable behest, dares the confines of a region as barren as this, quickly dissipates whatever pleasant juices his body may contain. Or it may be some inscrutable intuition in those carrion-fed brains had revealed that destiny had him in keeping beneath her brazen wing. Abject and futile creature though he appeared to be, he came undeviatingly on.

Its last filmy wreaths of sulphurous smoke had centuries before ceased to wreathe themselves from Ajubajao's enormous womb. Leagues distant though its cone must be, its jagged outlines were sharply discernible, cut clean against that southern horizon. The skies shallowly arching the plain of lava that flowed out annularly from its base in enormous undulations, league on league until its margin lay etched and fretted against the eastern heavens—this low-hung firmament was now of a greenish pallor. In its midst the noonday's sun burned raylessly like a sullen topaz set in jade.

But utterly lifeless though the plain appeared to be, minute susurrations were occasionally audible, caused apparently by scatterings of lava dust lifted from their hollows on heated draughts of air. These gathering in volume, raised at last their multitudinous voices into a prolonged hiss, a sustained shrill sibilation as if the silken fringes of an enormous robe were being dragged gently across this ink-black Sahara.

As they subsided once more, drifting softly to rest, a faint musical murmur followed their gigantic sigh, like that of far-distant drums and dulcimers from a secret and hidden borderland. Then this also ceased, and only the plaintive horns of the midges and the scurry of beetles scuttling beneath their shards to and fro in their haunts in the crevices of the lava broke the hush.

In a deep angular hollow of the nearest of these lava dunes lay basking a serpent, flat of head and dull of eye, its slightly rufous skin mottled and barred in faintest patternings of slate and chocolate. So still she lay, her markings might appear to be but the vein of an alien stone or metal embedded in the lava.

But now and again, at the dictate of some inward whim, her blunted tail arched itself an inch or two above the floor of its black chamber, emitting a hollow and sinister rattling—as if in admonishment or endearment of the brood of her young that lay drowsing in an apparently inextricable knot of paler colouring near by.

The hours of Kootoora's morning glided on, revealing little change except an ever-increasing torridity, until the thin air fairly danced in ecstasy—like an exquisitely tenuous gas boiling in a pot—above every heat-laved arch and hollow. The skies assumed a yet paler green, resembling that of verdigris, and deepening towards the north to a dull mulberry. Strange tremors now shook the air, and thicker-crusted though its skin might be than any leviathan, a sinister insecurity haunted the plain. Here took its walks that spectre, danger, but more appallingly bedizened than in any other region of the earth.

Sluggish stirrings, the warning of some obscure instinct, in the serpent's blood now quickened her restlessness, though the lidless eyes set in that flat and obtuse head betrayed no glimmerings of intelligence or fear. She drew in closer to her brood, and again and yet again her rattle drummed sullenly in the heat. A sound alien from any experience that had ever been hers in these familiar haunts had broken the silence. It was the footstep of approaching fear.

Writhing swiftly beneath and towards the face of the lava incline, wherein a black splash marked the crannied entrance of her secret chamber, she swept aside the fragments of dried skin which she had sloughed in bygone years. An increasing movement in the lively tangle behind her showed that her last insistent summons had been heeded. One by one her restless younglings disentangled their coils from the general knot, and slid noiselessly into cover. But a few yet remained, semi-torpid, and, as her inscrutable wits warned her, in imminent danger beneath the glare of the sun, when suddenly the presence and influence of a human shape struck down across the lava wall; and the diffused purple shadow cast by the rayless sun lay over its hollow.

The body that caused it was invisible to the serpent. But her rattle sounded unceasingly, as with groping coils she turned now this way, now that, in endeavour to repel this menace to her solitude and her young's safety. Rearing herself at last in a blind fury of terror and anguish, with blunt head and flickering tongue she struck again and again not at the dreadful human gently surveying her out of his smiling yet anguished face, as draggled, parched, and half-fainting he watched her every movement, but merely at the insensitive shadow that overhung her lair.

The hollow desperate thumping of her slenderly boned head knocking its own knell grew fainter. But the last of her brood had made its way into safety before, bruised and bleeding, it drooped motionless in the dust. At this the old man scrambled down into the hollow. It had been an arduous journey for what might seem so trivial an errand, but there was no symptom of impatience in his gestures as, having moistened with spittle the ball of his thumb, he gently smeared the muzzle of his victim.

Then he too bent his head, heedless of the still feebly flickering tongue, and seemed to be whispering into the creature's sense some far-brought message of his own.

And, yet again, from across the parched precipitous flanks of Ajubajao, moved, as it were, a vast suspiration of wind, sulphurously hot, of a dense suffocating odour, bestirring in its course the hovering multitudes of the midges, and driving before it a thin cloud of lava dust, as the wind drives shadow across the flats of a sea. Yet again that insidious whispering filled the quiet; and the remote dulcimers tattooed their decoy.

The saint crouched low, hooding as best he could beneath his mantle his eyes, mouth, and nostrils against the smothering skirring particles. A minute whirlpool of air came dancing like a host of dervishes into the she-serpent's hollow. Lifting the dried scaly fragments of her discarded skin, it dispersed them here, there, everywhere, in its minute headlong rout. . . .

The Seven Valleys

The Rest House at the mouth of the Seventh Valley was made of a supple withy woven together layer above layer, with a

shell-shaped thatch roofing it in. Seen from a distance this
smiling morning, perched among the green undulations surrounding it, it had the appearance of a beehive. For these
withies or osiers, as they dry in that temperate air, fade from
their first willow grey-green into a gleaming bronze. Sprouting
out of the thatch, too, bloomed and flourished whole families
of minute plants, their round-budded clusters showing like the
heads of some congregation of insects engaged in prayer.

It was the only dwelling completely within view, rising
above the sward on which it stood some thirty yards within
the mouth of the valley, the sides of which yawned smoothly
wider and wider until they narrowed again towards the entry
of the Sixth. Beyond that, yet again—farther away than it
looked in this translucent atmosphere—tapered into the stillness the summit of yet another Rest House. And so on and on,
as it would seem, valley by valley, to the very gates themselves.

The shelving hollow of the nearer expanse was of a tranquil
yet lively green. The close turf moulded itself over these verdant
contours as delicately as the bloom on the cheek of a sleeping
baby or a plum. Clumps, here and there, of a low blossoming
tree, its fragrance rilling and wreathing into shallows of sweetness upon the still air, alone interrupted its surface. While in
drifts of sapphire blue, over which now hovered and fluttered
hosts of a narrow-winged silver butterfly, shimmered like a
diapered carpet the myriads of yet another tiny-statured flower.

Winding their way between them, skirting always as near
as possible each grove in turn, green paths, faintly patterning
the darker green around them, converged like the outspread
claws of a gigantic bird, towards the Rest House, the two
westernmost of them dipping suddenly out of sight into azure
space, as if here they plunged into an abyss of air.

Little traffic, it would appear, could occasion tracks so faint.
Up and inward, beyond the Rest House indeed, the broader
track was fainter yet; while, bordering it closely in a clean
straight line, descended yet another, shallowly printed over with
the gallopings of innumerable hoofs.

At a few paces distant from the Rest House, on a rough
wooden seat sat the young man Cuspidor. "A humble office,"

had smiled his old friend, "merits a humble name. Not all the saints, you will find, have endearing manners. The eager hunter has only his quarry in mind. He does not pause to examine every small chit-chat bird that scolds at him from a bush. Others of the saints, my son, discern only too keenly. The modest syllables of the name you now possess may therefore bring a trace of indulgence into their scrutiny. That of shoe-cleaner of the Seventh Valley may appear to be a humble occupation. It is an unworthy one, however, only if one pay regard not to the wearer but merely to the worn."

Cuspidor, though little else than a mere mortal, had been fairly content with his new office. But he sometimes pined for more company and even for rather more work. Saints only of the First Hierarchy, he had been told, had occasion to traverse in turn each of the Seven Valleys. Of these by far the greater number made no stay in the Seventh, and had no need of his ministrations. And even of the First Hierarchy there were many Orders.

"So, too, of the stars, my son," St. Dusman had explained. "Those which to our groping eyes appear the dimmest, may so appear not because they are of inferior splendour but because they are the more remote."

Cuspidor indeed had little need to complain of undue courtesies. Wayfarers who were bound only for the nearer valleys, to await such biddings as might reach them there, frequently passed on their way with downcast head as if lost in reverie, and without so much as lifting their eyes to glance at the shoe-cleaner and his hostel, or even at the galloping messengers that, like drifts of sunbeams in a forest, swept past them across the turf, bound on errands the goal and purpose of which even the farthest-travelling of the saints themselves seemed content to be ignorant.

Cuspidor had no clock. But he possessed a little wit, and had set up on end a switch of wood, and had cut out on the turf a circle round it, marked at intervals with a XII, a III, a VI, and a IX. And though he had no clear notion of what exact quantity of time consisted his day, he had some clumsy notion of the

number of the days themselves, as they glided like flowing
water through the weeds of his consciousness.

Much else, apart from realization of, those days, so glided.
Even irrevocable dreams may leave behind them in the mind
of the dreamer the empty shell of their being; and Cuspidor
was as vaguely aware of events and experiences beyond his
comprehension as a fish in the shallows of the ocean may be
aware of the outskirts of the continents that fringe it in. His
duties though menial were light. He kept watch upon the paths
from dawn till twilight: and then no more. After nightfall—
though in this region only a deep emerald dusk, thinning to a
crystalline radiance above the remoter valleys, succeeded the
placid glory of the day—after nightfall any belated traveller
must knock, and Cuspidor must rise from his bed to bid him
welcome, and to prepare the guest room. No visitor made a
prolonged stay, and few, any.

Having come to where the shoe-cleaner stood awaiting him
with downcast eyes beside his bench, the pilgrim would rest first
one foot, then another, on the wooden block prepared for the
purpose. And the young man, having unlatched them, would
remove shoes or sandals, scrape off into the hollow beneath
whatever foreign matter, dust or mud, still adhered to their
under-surface, set them out of the sun, and have them ready
when their owner next appeared, bent on his outward journey.

Some little practice had resulted in what was by now almost
conspicuous evidence of Cuspidor's labours. A few paces behind
the hostel, where stood his beehives and grew his grain and
fruit, lay a heap of refuse. It was his little private record of
the saints' wayfarings—as well as of his own industry. Even
a casual eye might have fastened in amazement on the medley
of elements represented there: minute stones of a lustre that
must surely have once been precious to *some* discerning eye;
fine-coloured sands unlike any earth or her sister planets can
afford; scraps of what resembled ivory, infinitesimals of an
endless variety, objects far past their present owner's sagacity
to give a name to, or even to recognize, lay scattered and buried
in this heap.

While still unaccustomed to his duties and by means of a
rough sieve which he had plaited out of fibre from the bark
of his fruit trees, Cuspidor had spent his leisure hours in
separating the coarser objects in this heap into kinds. The
brighter these were in mere light and colour the more they
charmed his eye, though of their origin and value he was entirely ignorant. Next, what was rare and strange delighted him.
But here, too, he fumbled in ignorance. And he had at last
wearied of the pursuit altogether, confining his attention solely
to an ivory-coloured dust which, he discovered, if scraped together without any other admixture and kneaded with a little
water or spittle, could be converted into a smooth, plastic clay.
And this he had taught himself to model rudely into whatever
shape chanced to take his fancy. If but a word or a smile were
bestowed on his workmanship, it was ample reward. And as he
made more progress he was as content with none.

With a lump of this far-fetched clay on his knee, a pointed
twig between his fingers, and his body bent almost double, he now
sat this fresh morning, completely engrossed in yet another such
attempt. It was proving one, however, of infinitely greater
difficulty than any that had preceded it. That very daybreak,
as he had first stirred in sleep, there had risen in dream into his
imagination a phantasmal face of a beauty beyond any that he
remembered to have seen in actuality. And yet how strangely
familiar it seemed. It had outlasted the dream that gave it
birth, haunting his mind, and it now hung before his very
eyes, gazing intently out of its fairness as if at the same time
happy in his company and grieved at the faintness of his recognition.

Lest it should at any instant vanish as swiftly into the nothing
out of which it had appeared, Cuspidor, intent on his clay,
had forgotten his shoe-cleaning, the saints, the very place wherein
he sat. He kneaded and moulded and graved and smoothed—
his tongue showing its tip the while between his lips; a frown
between his wide young brows as if his destiny itself, his very
peace and being hinged upon his success. So woefully absorbed
had he become in this particular occupation that it was not the
old man's footstep on the sward, but St. Dusman's voice, as he

stood peering over his shoulder, that suddenly brought him back to himself.

The old saint must for some little while past have been drawing near the shoe-cleaner in full view—as soon indeed as he had emerged out of the abyss on the path by which he usually approached the Rest House. Nor was he the only living creature now in sight. A sudden heat coursed through Cuspidor's body when, having lifted his eyes at his greeting, he discovered already midway up the Sixth Valley, and proceeding on his journey, the figure of one whose raiment showed by its markings that he was no less sacred a personage than a saint of the Third Order.

"Your flesh may well creep, my son," said the old man gently, "but by good fortune he needed nothing of you. We made our greetings as he passed me, and I see that he has returned from regions innocent altogether of the metamorphoses of what we may call the tangible and the superfluous. But be wary. There are saints of his hierarchy who strike as swiftly as a thunderbolt."

The shoe-cleaner with trembling hands—due in part to the strain of his work and in part to recognition of the peril he had escaped—gazed after the bent and tottering shape now steadily receding from sight. His mouth was shut now; and the phantasmal face had vanished like clouded moonlight from a pool.

"And what are you after this morning, my son? Tired of your pretty baubles?"

The voice was as kindly as ever, and as ever seemed to evoke from hidden chambers in the shoe-cleaner's mind the ghosts of memories, rather than memories themselves. He rose to his feet and bowed to the old man; still grasping in his hand the orb of kneaded clay, which had stubbornly refused to become more than a clumsy and distasteful symbol of what had haunted his mind.

"If it please you, Master, a wondrous dream visited me this morning."

"Then be sure you were sleeping fitfully and in some longing, and you were not alone," replied the old man.

The intent narrow eyes in the clean-cut mobile face beneath

his own slid round in survey of the verdurous slopes beneath and above them. For Cuspidor only the phantoms of serenity now had their dwelling here. The saint of the Third Order had by this time entered the immense bottle-shaped approach to the Sixth Valley. And the continual ventriloquial silver twittering in the skies above his own of a company of small hovering birds that tenanted this tranquil wilderness was the only sound and sight of life. A shadow spread over his features as he groaned rather than sighed.

"Weary already?" insisted the old man.

"It seemed it was a dream," was the answer, "that would last on into the day. And now it is gone."

"And you were endeavouring, I see," the saint retorted, "to fashion it out of mud."

"It is a marvellously easy clay to the fingers, at any rate," said the young man. "And if only I had the skill I could prove it."

"Let me see," said St. Dusman.

The young shoe-cleaner thrust out his hand over an up-bent elbow, poising his earthen lump in his right palm. And by some secret device of the light that gently flooded the green meadow which stretched in tranquil amplitude around them, there appeared in his crude model a trace of something a little closer to his hope in its markings than the young man had first detected. After a moment or two the old man pushed his spectacles (whose rims even in this rare air showed symptoms of rust) above his eyes, and scrutinized the lump a second time.

"This then was in the image of your dream?" he inquired. "Why immure in what so soon perishes that which in imagination might remain as fresh as its original?"

The shoe-cleaner frowned and flung his lump of clay to the ground. "Why, Master, there is more than one way even of cleaning shoes. It is the best that gives the most pleasure: even though it takes the most pains."

The old man's eyes were of the dimmest blue—far paler than any flower dropped from Dis's wagon, or even than those which sprinkled their spices like dew in this celestial air. The attention in them now fined itself to a needle-point, on which, say the sages, thousands upon thousands and many thousands of angels may find an easy footing.

"You have happiness in your work then, Mr. Shoe-cleaner?" he inquired pleasantly.

A queer crisscross expression mapped its way into the young man's face. The keenness as of a bird, the guile as of a serpent, the alert fixedness as of some long-experienced adept of a craft showed in it; and all of them in the service, so to speak, of an almost childlike smile. "What amuses me," he said, "is that a wayfarer that came yesterday, after watching me awhile stooping over my work here—bending his look on me, as you will understand, just round the rim of his sandal, gave me this."

He held up for St. Dusman's inspection a slender stem of ivory expanding into a narrow spoon-like groove. "He must have noticed my miserable 'lumps of mud,'" he explained. "And there was nothing on *his* feet but a scraping of gold-dust."

"I know him," said St. Dusman. "It was St. Antioch. Can you describe your dream in words, my son?"

The narrow eyelids fell, the hands fumbled. "If I could see it in actuality in the air before me," muttered a low voice, "I should be happy for ever."

"Well, well, well," nodded the old man solemnly. "Once again, and yet again. . . . You are choosing, I fear, a very long circuit before you will have the opportunity of sharing the experience of standing, as did St. Antioch yesterday, amused at the shoe-cleaner with a pretty knack in his craft. Nevertheless, time is made of eternity, and happiness, my son, is but of a moment; and that moment lost in an oblivion of loving kindness."

Prince Ahmat Naigul

The gloom of night lay over the dense forests that spread themselves like a pall over the face of the earth on either side of the high-road—that immeasurable causeway from north of the Great River for countless leagues to the sea. The skies above their motionless crests were fiery with stars. Immediately in front of

the horsemen indeed, who were now rapidly approaching along
the dim white benighted track on their many-days' journey from
the northern mountains to the Winter Palace that reared its
walls and cupolas upon the precipitous banks of the river, stood
(rivalling each the other) above the distant fret of trees, and
but a few degrees apart, silver Venus and the flaming Dog-Star.

The horsemen—the scarlet of their headdresses and their
cloaks scarcely discernible in this dense dusk—rode so far in
advance of the cavalcade which was following after them that
the dust they raised in passing had already floated to rest again
before its leaders came into sight.

Under a milk-cupped, leaf-tressed, umbrella-like tree at the
edge of the curved dip which the gigantic highway made at
this point in its course, owing to the waters of a brackish lake
which stretched itself out like a silver dragon in the uttermost
glooms of the forest, sat a leper. Forbidden by law to show his
shape in village or city, keeping his slender hold on life as best
he could, he was a wanderer and a vagrant, dependent on the
charity of chance wayfarers. Yet his marred face, glimmering
faintly beneath this black canopy of boughs as if with a phosphorescence of its own, was in spite of its hideousness benign
with magnanimity and peace. His empty dish—formed out of
the shell of an immense nut whose kind hung in huge clusters,
like slumbering groups of monkeys, amid one of the forest
trees near by—lay empty beside him. He had composed his
emaciated limbs in an attitude of contemplation. But his bleared
eyes were now fixed on the torches and lanthorns of the approaching cavalcade, as its horsemen and broad-wheeled coaches came
sweeping towards his screened retreat along the road.

The skies were still and windless, sharing as it seemed awhile
the quiet of boundless space. Even above the swelling tumult
raised by the travellers in their journey, the leper marked the
melancholy chantings of the nightbirds in the branches above
his head and in the thickets around him. Scared by scent and
rumour of these human invaders as they approached, the cower-
ing beasts of the forest had long since retired into their further
fastnesses, though the bolder of them paused to gaze stealthily
out at the leashed hounds, the hooded hawks, the intent or

sleeping faces of the convoy, and its living lovely treasure as it swept on its way.

The crackling torch-flames and coloured lanthorns now flung meanwhile a brilliant and moving cloud of luminosity above the causeway; bridle, harness, lance, scabbard, and spur glittered amid the brilliant colourings of the throng.

It was the prince Ahmat Naigul, returning with his bride after the feasting and festivities of their marriage-rites. Coach after coach, burdened with the grandees of his court and retinue, some gently slumbering as they reclined on the low, shallow, cushioned seats within; others chattering and making merry, their eyes gleaming restlessly in the light flung into the dim recesses within their small wheeled houses from the torches of the horsemen that flanked each vehicle in turn; lumbered heavily by, grinding the powdered flint of the highway into dust yet finer. It seemed this living stream between these darkened walls would never cease.

None the less, there came an interval at last in its garish onset. Then yet another squadron followed after, their milk-white cloaks drawn back over the crimson and silver of their silken under-vests to the cruppers of long-maned horses of the colour of old ivory, their headdresses surmounted with bejewelled plumes of stiff-spined feathers. They rode in silence, spear in hand, the personal bodyguard of Prince Ahmat Naigul himself, whose coach, lightly swaying on its heavy springs and fashioned of dark wood, ivory, and silver, now drew near, drawn by its eight ink-black Tartary draught-horses, their outlandish outriders muffled to the eyes this summer evening in tippets of sable.

The leper rose shivering to his feet, and muffling with his hand the deep-cut copper bell that swung suspended by a hempen cord about his middle, he advanced to the edge of the highway.

And within the royal coach, her head at a gentle angle against its swan-white cushions, Ahmat Naigul's Princess lay asleep. About her brow was a green circlet of leaves of the everlasting Ooneetha tree. Her hair hung down on either side her quiet head in braided plaits, dangling upon her slender shoulders and thence upon the smooth inlaid feathers of the hooded cloak that enwrapped her, itself patterned in a linked soft loveliness after the fashion of the same tree. Her face resembled in its quietude and fairness the twilight of an evening in May, and she reclined in profound slumber, the orange doublet or cuirass of the dark Prince beside her shining like still sheaves of flame against her snow.

His eyes were fixed intently upon the gently moving darkness of the forest that skirted the high-road, but ever and again his gaze returned to rest upon the dreaming one beside him. And with bare hand holding his jewelled glove, he would, as it were, make to stroke the feathered folds of her cloak, and then, gently drawing it back, refrain, once more resuming his scrutiny of the vast silence that compassed them in.

At that instant, the gently rocking coach in which he sat lurched slightly on its leathern springs as if the mettlesome horses that drew it had swerved at some unexpected sight or sound. A challenging voice broke into the hush. The wheels slowly ceased to revolve; then came to rest in the dust. With a sharp turn of his head, the Prince stooped forward in the warm gloom of the carriage, and peered out of the window. Delicate shafts of light from the moon that every moment was riding higher into the vacancy of the sky, struck diagonally across, silvering the motionless wall of trees that bordered this bend of the high-road.

Full in this flooding radiance, shell in hand, his once white rags dingy and blotched, stood the leper, his matted hair falling lank on either side his half-disfeatured face. The glass-clear pupils beneath the half-closed and fretted lids were steady in their regard, and were fixed not on the Prince, not apparently on any single object within the shadow of the coach, but as if in contemplation far beyond it. Nevertheless, the first clear glimpse of this whited wayside figure seemed to turn Ahmat Naigul's body to stone. He desisted even from breathing, nor dared to glance behind him into the shadow, lest the eyes that had been so gently slumbering were now wide agape. And yet the terror that had suddenly assailed a heart at least as courageous as that of any beast that prowled the forests around him had sprung solely from instinct. Such dreadful shows of God's providence as this mendicant were none too rare, even in a country magnanimously governed.

A profound foreboding darkened his mind as in the twilight reflection of the dust and foliage of the wayside Prince Ahmat Naigul now turned to scrutinize his bride. Their lids lay gently on her rounded eyes, though above them the pencilled brows were lifted as if in a faint and delicious astonishment. A rose-like flush had risen into her cheek; her lips were a moth's wing apart. The feathered cloak—needled together of down from the plumage of the swans that haunt the still green creeks of the Great River—almost imperceptibly rose and fell above the quiet breast. No dream even, unless a dream of peace, haunted the spirit within.

Stealthily as a serpent the Prince lifted himself to his feet and stepped down out of the carriage. A tense silence now lay over this loop of the great highway. All tongues had fallen still, and though curiosity had turned not one head by a hair's breadth in his direction, the complete cavalcade was arrested as if at a secret word of command. It might have been the assemblage of a dream.

With a word to the horseman that now stood dismounted in the dust a little behind the royal coach, Prince Ahmat Naigul passed on, preceded by the leper, and at a few paces distant came to a pause and confronted him.

The wolf of disease had all but gnawed away the nose. The cheek was sunken, the coarse hair hung limp and matted over the eroded ears. The hand that held the bowl to his breast shimmered as if it were inlaid with the scales of a fish, while the other grasped tight its copper bell as if with the talons of a bird. None the less, the glass-like eyes beneath their withering lids continued to gaze out as if in reverie. And not only humility, but an inward gentleness and peace, like that burthening the sails of an incoming ship in a squalid haven, shed their influences from this appalling shape. As in a lamp fashioned out of the coarsest horn, a gentle flame seemed to be burning from within the emaciated physiognomy.

Amid the folds of Ahmat Naigul's dimmed orange and scarlet, the jewels glowed softly in the moonlit atmosphere. His narrow head was flung back a little as if his nostrils were in doubt of the air they breathed. Poverty, it has been recorded, is a gift of the Infinite. And the Prince made a slight obeisance as he drew a ring from his finger and advancing a pace nearer dropped it into the leper's bowl.

"A voice within," he muttered, "tells me that life is brief. I am prepared, Sorrowful One, and of your mercy would be thankful to follow at once."

The leper inclined his head a little towards the Prince, but his eyes remained unstirring.

"How knowest thou," the parched lips gasped, "how knowest thou the message has come for *thee*? Brief though the hour may be, it has its meed of minutes. Empty your mind of all but its most secret memories; have you peace at last?"

"Is rest possible where happiness dwells?" returned Ahmat Naigul.

"Only where rest is is happiness. Your journeyings have brought you here. Nor is it my bidding to call you yet away."

"Who then?" answered the thread-like voice, as the hand beneath the cloak groped upwards towards the dagger concealed beneath it.

"I have your alms," said the leper; "and now, if, as it seems, Your Highness's will is to lead while others follow, our one and only need is that we exchange the kiss of peace."

And it seemed to the Prince as he stooped forward, resting his trembling hands upon the leper's shrivelled shoulders, that the infinitely aged face beneath his eyes might be that of Death, so utterly serene it was. But no dreadful horror of mortal malady now showed itself. Even the holes, where nostrils as sweet with health as his should be, were now dark casements commanding a secret country; and the narrowed eyes above them were as windows lit with such sunlight as springs reflected from untrodden snows. And as if Ahmat Naigul had sipped of some potent syrup, consciousness lost count for one instant of eternity of time and space. Memories as of a myriad lifetimes swept pleasantly before his eyes.

He drew back at last, and there broke upon his ear, loud as the clang of a temple gong, the clink of a horseman's silver bridle. And even yet the leper had not bent his eyes in his direction. Releasing his bell from his grasp and letting it swing soundlessly above the dust, the leper stooped, and having groped, hoarsely breathing, with his fingers in the dust, raised himself up once more and thrust out from his body his dried-up palm, at angles with his wrist, and almost as narrow as a monkey's.

Ahmat Naigul in turn outstretched his ungloved hand, from beneath his cloak, and the leper deposited in it an object so minute that the Prince had to press it firmly into the skin with his third finger lest he should lose it.

"The seven ways remain," said the leper. "And the easternmost is the way of life. My gift, Highness, is but for remembrance's sake." And without more ado this saint of poverty swathed his miserable rags around his body, and turned back towards the blossoming tree where he had been resting his bones beside the waters of the lake.

Ahmat Naigul remounted into his coach, and the horsemen swept on. Time passed unheeded while he sat bolt upright, finger still fixed to palm, his lips like ice above his gums, and his eyes dark with the fear that had clouded them.

And with daybreak, the forest by the roadside now withdrew itself a little. Dark herbage scattered with flowers nodded its dews in the first rays of the sun, as the eyes of the gentle unstirring one beside him opened, to gaze once more at the companion of her journey; and her beauty was like a looking-glass to the beauty of the morning.

"You have been gathering flowers," she said; "and the narrow air herewithin is sweeter far than that of the country in which I have been wandering."

"And what country was that?" whispered the Prince.

"I dreamed," she said, "that you were once a man, and a bird, and a serpent. And I dreamed, Ahmat Naigul, that you were once a scullion to the Sages of the Most High. And that sometimes—forgive me, beloved—you sipped of their winecups when the veil of the entering-in had hidden you from their sight."

She drew a warm hand from beneath her feathers. "Why," she said, touching his, "your lips are stained with it yet. They are like crimson threads upon a honey ground. And what have you there beneath your fingertip?"

She paused awhile. But Ahmat Naigul made no movement.

"And what have you there beneath your fingertip?" she questioned him again, a remote accent of disappointment lurking in her voice.

"If, Princess, I had tasted the wine of that other sage whose glance none can resist, what would you say then?"

"Silence is golden, beloved. I would do just like this."

And heedless of sunbeams, of strange eyes amid the thickets, of birds wandering on their pathless ways from tree to tree, she bent upwards her fair face, and kissed Ahmat Naigul.

But not until the Prince's chief magician had toiled laboriously and for days together over his hoard of polished crystal was the Princess enabled at last to detect with clearness the speck that had lain so closely imprisoned beneath the finger of his hand; and this even though the magician had succeeded in so adjusting his workmanship that it enlarged it almost to the magnitude of a grain of mustard-seed.

So it was still by faith rather than by direct evidence of her gentle senses that she believed the frettings and mouldings on its infinitesimal surface resembled the features and hollows and fairnesses of a human face. And that, her own. . . .

En Route

The mud houses at the western end of the vast city, crammed hugger-mugger together within its enormous sun-baked walls, showed no signs of life, even though the first frigid grey of dawn already showed in the eastern skies; even though from point to point in the distance the cocks crowed acknowledgment one to another of this mysterious though often repeated fragment of news. A peculiar odour lay heavy on the air, compounded of the sweet and the offensive. The beaten road wound out between the outlying huddle of houses, but was soon lost in the gloom that still overlay the desert.

The watchman at the slit of window in his turret, which looked inwards towards the city, muffled up in his sheepskin coat, his grey beard spread spadewise upon his chest, sat with so fixed and motionless an attention on the long vista of narrow street which stretched out beneath his eyes, that he was probably asleep. But one accustomed to sleep with caution, can also wake with it. Not a hair of him stirred, except his eyelashes, at sound of a shuffling footstep approaching his eyrie.

A bent old man in the attire and with the symbols of a pilgrim dangling round his neck and affixed with a slender iron chain to his brow, was approaching the watch-tower. In spite of his feebleness and the cobwebs of age that seemed to hang about him even more visibly than the folds of his pilgrim's garb, a serenity, a gravity haunted his appearance which roused the watchman clean out of the last lingering fumes of sleep that yet hung over his senses, and brought him hastily down to the thick-barred door below. Thence his eyes—their whites just touched with the light that was rilling on and on into this country's dark—peered out at this untimely intruder.

News that a princeling, more gracious than springtime in the wilderness, and yet of tender age, was now seated upon the throne of his father, had become the common property of the marketplace the whole long day before. He had himself heard the High Officer of the Court, his retinue attired in silver and purple, read out for all to hear, a proclamation announcing that father's abdication. Universal sorrow had been its effect, and universal gladness also that Fate had sweetened her medicine with a successor of such high promise.

The watchman continued to glare out of his window at the pilgrim in the street—who at length approached and was accosted. Pilgrims of any faith which the experience of life in this world may instil or fail to shatter, had long since been free to come and go without other question than could be answered by the symbols and relics which they bore.

Still, the watchman was human, and this particular pilgrim one of uncommon interest. None the less, the colloquy that followed in the murk of the deserted street and gatehouse, was brief. The watchman was given to understand (though he had difficulty in distinguishing the quavering muffled words) that the pilgrim had here expected to meet an acquaintance, a fellow wayfarer, a friend. One of renowned punctuality, even though his assignations might be one-sided.

According to his own showing, the watchman could have slumbered never so much as a wink during the hours of his vigil, for he assured the old man that no human figure had entered or passed through under the gatehouse during the whole of the preceding night. Feastings and junketings, he explained, even at this less ornate end of the great city, were over betimes. There was little need to enforce order where laws were so beneficent, and the people who obeyed them so content.

None the less, the old man persisted in assuring the watchman that this particular tryst was one impossible of failure. Could perchance the friend he looked for have concealed himself in the watch-tower? Was he, maybe, at this very moment surveying the street from the ancient battlements above—too far overhead for the discernment of his own faded sight? Could he have crept in under the shadows, secret and unseen?

The watchman's chin sunk deeper into his straggling beard. By the intensity of his scrutiny it might be guessed that he both desired and feared the increasing light which would enable him to pierce a little further under the peak of the pilgrim's hood. His next natural question concerned the appearance of the expected stranger. And at sound of the reply, the pupils of his eyes showed even a little more stonily in their sockets. With a hasty and furtive glance over his shoulder he perceived that the great door was securely barred. "That being so, I can show you—" he muttered in the face of the old man pressing close against his barred window, "I can show you the very likeness of him you seek."

At this the pilgrim paused and looked gently and gravely around him. Nothing living, however, except a stray cur which had stretched itself up out of its dusty corner and now stood shaking the dried dung from its mangy slate-grey hide, appeared in view. He turned once more to the watchman, and explained that he would be able to recognize that likeness even at a glance.

The watchman withdrew and (his lamp having been extinguished) groped his way unsteadily up the narrow staircase, muttering what might be prayers or maledictions beneath his breath. There he paused awhile, consulting anxiously his hazy old wits whether or not he dare venture to betray his instant recognition of this august visitor. The lean black cat that shared his small earthen chamber in the turret stretched itself and yawned.

It was an omen, and he returned at last, carrying in his hand a platter of burnished metal, by means of which he was accustomed to trim his beard and hair when they were in urgent need of it. Between finger and thumb of both hands he held this mirror up to the window so that his own eyes over the rounded rim were only just able to watch its effect upon the pilgrim.

To free himself from any possible offence or discourtesy he explained rapidly that the features now reflected in the mirror answered as precisely as he could remember to the description which the old man had given of his friend.

The pilgrim gazed long and earnestly. "Ah, my friend," he said at last, "you have a discerning eye, and an unflattering tongue. You have not only freed my mind of any mistrust of one whom I was prepared to find awaiting me here—lest, I mean, that he had perchance forgotten me; but you fill me with a happiness beyond even the voice of youth itself to express. I understand, as if he himself uttered it, that he and I are at one; and that I must forthwith continue my pilgrimage towards the Seventh Valley. Meanwhile, I pray you to accept of me for his remembrance this most precious keepsake and relic. Guard it safely; and present it to him —press it into the very palm of his hand—when he shall himself come your way."

The watchman drew down his blurred old mirror and thrust a horny hand close to the lattice. Into its palm the pilgrim pressed an object that appeared to have been carved out of ivory, but which in magnitude was whole worlds smaller than a pea. It was strange, too, that in these few moments the light of dawn seemed to have intensified to such a degree that it surrounded the bent old hooded head at the window with a vague radiance like that of a lunar rainbow. Having bowed a blessing, he was gone.

The watchman, being, as it has already been related, of an unusually cautious and sluggish brain, refrained from stirring for some minutes afterwards. Having then for safety deposited beneath his tongue the relic he had received for keepsake, he stealthily ascended the deep worn stone steps of his staircase, and from well within the chamber peeped out across the flat roofs towards the desert.

By this time, slow though his progress had been, the figure of the pilgrim was almost out of sight; even though the first shoots of the gigantic sun had by now struck his garments, transmuting them to their own colour—that of red and gold. And when the watchman sat down to examine his infinitesimal gift, he gave thanks to his lucky stars that he had not broken into his visitor's confidence with any of the urbanities appropriate to converse between a subject and a king.

For though his faded sight was utterly unable to discern what similitude it bore, or his wits to skip from its fretted surface to the Queen Mother who now had no one but her son for inmost company, he realised that here was a jewel of great price. And he vowed within himself, too, that when the moment came for its presentation, he would do his utmost to secure that Bugghul Dur, his fellow watchman, should then be on duty.

The Connoisseur and Other Stories (1926)

THE NAP

THE AUTUMNAL afternoon was creeping steadily on towards night; the sun after the morning's rain was now—from behind thinning clouds—glinting down on the chimney-pots and slate roofs of Mr. Thripp's suburb. And the day being a Saturday, across Europe, across England, an immense multitudinous stirring of humanity was in progress. It had begun in remote Australia and would presently sweep across the Atlantic into vast America, resembling the rustling of an ant-heap in a pine wood in sunny June. The Christian world, that is, was preparing for its weekly half-holiday; and Mr. Thripp was taking his share.

As if time were of unusual importance to him, two clocks stood on his kitchen mantelpiece: one, gay as a peepshow in the middle, in a stained wood case with red and blue flowers on the glass front; the other an "alarum"—which though it was made of tin had a voice and an appearance little short of the brazen. Above them, as if entirely oblivious to their ranting, a glazed King Edward VII stared stolidly out of a Christmas lithograph, with his Orders on his royal breast.

Mr. Thripp's kitchen table was at this moment disordered with the remains of a meal, straggling over a tablecloth that had now gallantly completed its full week's service. Like all Saturday dinners in his household, this had been a hugger-mugger dinner—one of vehement relays. Mr. Thripp himself had returned home from his office at a quarter to two—five minutes after his daughter Millie and Mrs. Thripp had already begun. Charlie Thripp had made his appearance a little before the hour; and James—who somehow had never become Jim or Jimmie—arrived soon afterwards. To each his due, kept warm.

But the hasty feeding was now over. Mr. Thripp in his shirt-sleeves, and with his silver watch-chain disposed upon his front, had returned once more from the scullery with his empty tray. He was breathing heavily, for he inclined nowadays, as he would sometimes confess, to the *ongbongpong*. He had remarkably muscular arms for a man of his sedentary profession, that of ledger-clerk in Messrs. Bailey, Bailey and Company's counting-house. His small eyes, usually half-hidden by their plump lids, were of a bright, clear blue. His round head was covered with close-cut hair; he had fullish lips, and his ample jowl always appeared as if it had been freshly shaved—even on Saturday afternoons.

Mr. Thripp delighted in Saturday afternoons. He delighted in housework. Though he never confessed it to a living soul (and even though it annoyed Tilda to hear him) he delighted too in imitating the waitresses in the tea-shops, and rattled the plates and dishes together as if they were made of a material unshatterable and everlasting. When alone at the sink he would hiss like a

groom currying a full-grown mare. He packed the tray full of
dirty dishes once more, and returned into the steam of the scullery.

"You get along now, Tilda," he said to his wife, who was drying up. "We shall have that Mrs. Brown knocking every minute,
and that only flusters you."

Mrs. Thripp looked more ill-tempered than she really was—
with her angular face and chin, pitch-dark eyes, and dark straight
hair. With long damp fingers she drew back a limp strand of hair
that had straggled over her forehead.

"What beats me is, you never take a bit of enjoyment yourself,"
she replied. "It isn't fair to *us*. I slave away, morning, noon, and
night; but that's just as things are. But other husbands get out
and about; why not you? *Let* her knock! She's got too much
money to waste; that's what's the matter with *her*. I don't know
what you wouldn't take her for in that new get-up she's got."

Then what the devil do you go about with her for? were the
words that entered Mr. Thripp's mind; and as for slaving, haven't
I just *asked* you to give over? Have reason, woman! But he didn't
utter them. "That'll be all right," he said instead, in his absurd
genial way. "You get on along off, Tilda; I'll see to all this. I
enjoy myself my own way, don't you fear. Did you never hear
of the selfish sex? Well, that's me!"

"Oh yes, I know all about that," said his wife sententiously: "a
pinch of salt on a bird's tail! But there's no need for sarcasms.
Now do be careful with that dish, there. It don't belong to us, but
to next door. She gave me one of her pancakes on it—and nothing
better than a shapeless bit of leather, either. Just to show she was
once in service as a cook-general, I suppose; though she never
owns to it."

A spiteful old mischief-maker, if you asked me, was Mr.
Thripp's inward comment. But "Oh well, Tilda, she means all
right," he said soothingly. "Don't you worry. Now get along off
with you; it's a hard day, Saturday, but you won't know yourself
when you come down again." As if forced into a line of conduct
she deprecated and despised, Tilda flung her wet tea-cloth over
a chair, and, with heart beating gaily beneath her shrunken breast,
hastened away.

Mr. Thripp began to whistle under his breath as he turned on the hot-water tap again. It was the one thing he insisted on—a lavish supply of hot water. He was no musician and only himself knew the tune he was in search of; but it kept him going as vigorously as a company of grenadiers on the march, and he invariably did his household jobs against time. It indulged a sort of gambling instinct in him; and the more he hated his job the louder he whistled. So as a small boy he had met the challenge of the terrors of the dark. "Keep going," he would say. "Don't let things mess over. That's waste!"

At that moment, his elder son, James, appeared in the scullery doorway. James took after his mother's side of the family. In his navy-blue serge suit, light-brown shoes, mauve socks, and spotted tie, he showed what careful dressing can do for a man. A cigarette sagged from his lower lip. His head was oblong, and flat-sided, and his eyes had a damp and vacant look. He thrust his face an inch or two into the succulent steam beyond the doorway.

"Well, dad, I'm off," he said.

Oh, my God! thought his father; if only you'd drop those infernal fags. Smoke, smoke, smoke, morning to night; and you that pasty-looking I can't imagine what the girl sees in you, with your nice superior ways. "Right you are, my son," he said aloud, "I won't ask you to take a hand! Enjoy yourself while you're young, I say. But slow and steady does it. Where might *you* be bound for this afternoon?"

"Oh, tea with Ivy's people," said James magnanimously. "Pretty dull going, I can tell you."

"But it won't be tea all the evening, I suppose?" said his father, pushing a steaming plate into the plate-rack.

"Oh, I dare say we shall loaf off to a Revoo or something," said James. He tossed his cigarette end into the sink, but missed the refuse strainer. Mr. Thripp picked it up with a fork and put it into the receptacle it was intended for, while James "lit up" again.

"Well, so long," said his father, "don't spoil that Sunday-go-to-Meeting suit of yours with all this steam. And by the way, James, I owe you five shillings for that little carpentering job you did for me. It's on the sitting-room shelf."

"Right ho. Thanks, dad," said James. "I thought it was six. But never mind."

His father flashed a glance at his son—a glance like the smouldering of a coal. "That so? Well, make it six, then," he said. "And
I'm much obliged."

"Oh, that's nothing," replied James graciously. "Cheerio; don't
overdo it, dad."

Mr. Thripp returned to his washing-up. He was thinking
rapidly with an extraordinary medley of feeling—as if he were
not one Mr. Thripp, but many. None the less, his whistling broke
out anew, as though, like a canary, in rivalry with the gushing
of the tap. After loading up his tray with crockery for the last
time, he put its contents away in the cupboard, and on the kitchen
dresser; cleansed the drain, swabbed up the sink, swabbed up the
cracked cement floor, hung up his dish-clout, rinsed his hands,
and returned into the kitchen.

Millie in a neat, tailor-made costume which had that week
marvellously survived dyeing, was now posed before the little
cracked square of kitchen looking-glass. She was a pale, slim
thing. Her smooth hair, of a lightish brown streaked with gold
and parted in the middle, resembled a gilded frame surrounding
her mild angelic face—a face such as the mediæval sculptors in
France delighted to carve on their altar-pieces. Whatever she wore
became her—even her skimpy old pale-blue flannel dressing-gown.

She turned her narrow pretty face sidelong under her hat and
looked at her father. She looked at every human being like that—
even at her own reflection in a shop window, even at a flower in a
glass. She spent her whole life subtly, instinctively, wordlessly
courting. She had as many young men as the White Queen has
pawns: though not all of them remained long in her service.

It's all very well to be preening yourself in that mirror, my girl,
her father was thinking, but you'd be far better off in the long run
if you did a bit more to help your mother, even though you do
earn a fraction of your living. More thinking and less face, *I* say.
And all that—! But "Why, I never see such a girl as you, Millie,"
he greeted her incredulously, "for looking your best! And such a
best, too, my dear. Which young spark is it to be *this* afternoon?
Eh?"

"Sparks! dad; how you do talk. Why, I don't hardly know,
dad. Sparks!" Millie's voice almost invariably ran down the scale

like the notes of a dulcimer muted with velvet. "I wasn't thinking of anybody in particular," she went on, continuing to watch her moving mouth in the glass, "but I promised Nellie Gibbs I . . . One thing, I am not going to stay out long on a day like this!"

"What's the matter with the day?" Mr. Thripp inquired.

"The matter! Why, look at it! It's a fair filthy mug of a day." The words slipped off her pretty curved lips like pearls over satin. A delicious anguish seemed to have arched the corners of her eyelids.

"Well, ain't there such a thing as a mackingtosh in the house, then?" inquired her father briskly.

"Mackingtosh! Over this! Oh, isn't that just like a man! I should look a perfect guy." She stood gazing at him, like a gazelle startled by the flurry of a breeze across the placid surface of its drinking-pool.

Now see you here, my girl, that see-saw voice inside her father was expostulating once more, what's the good of them fine silly airs? I take you for an honest man's daughter with not a ha'penny to spare on fal-lals and monkey-traps. *That* won't get you a husband. But Mr. Thripp once more ignored its interruption. He smiled almost roguishly out of his bright blue eyes at his daughter. "Ask *me* what I take you for, my dear? Why, I take you for a nice, well-meaning, though remarkably plain young woman. Eh? But there, there, don't worry. What I say is, make sure of the best (and the best that's *inside*) and let the other young fellows go."

He swept the last clean fork on the table into the drawer and folded up the tablecloth.

"Oh, dad, how you do go on!" breathed Millie. "It's always fellows you're thinking of. As if fellows made any difference." Her glance roamed a little startledly round the room. "What *I* can't understand," she added quickly, "is why we never have a clean tablecloth. How can anybody ask a friend home to their own place if that's the kind of thing they are going to eat off of?" The faint nuance of discontent in her voice only made it the more enchanting and seductive. She might be Sleeping Beauty babbling out of her dreams.

A cataract of invective coursed through the channels of Mr.

Thripp's mind. He paused an instant to give the soiled tablecloth
another twist and the table another prolonged sweep of that
formidable right arm which for twenty-three years had never
once been lifted in chastisement of a single one of his three offspring. Then he turned and glanced at the fire.

"I wouldn't," he said, seizing the shovel, "I wouldn't let mother
hear that, my dear. We all have a good many things to put up
with. And what I say is, all in good time. *You* bring that Mr.
Right along! and I can promise him not only a clean tablecloth
but something appetizing to eat off of it. A bit of a fire in the
sitting-room too, for that matter."

"You're a good sort, dad," said Millie, putting up her face to be
kissed—in complete confidence that the tiny powder-puff in her
vanity-bag would soon adjust any possible mishap to the tip of her
small nose. "But I don't believe you ever think *I* think of anything."

"Good-bye, my dear," said Mr. Thripp; "don't kiss me. I am all
of a smother with the washing-up."

"Toodle-loo, ma," Millie shrilled, as her father followed her out
into the passage. He drew open the front door, secreting his shirt-
sleeves well behind it in case of curious passers-by.

"Take care of yourself, my dear," he called after her, "and
don't be too late."

"Late!" tossed Millie, "any one would think I had been coddled
up in a hothouse."

Out of a seething expense of spirit in Mr. Thripp's mind only a
few words made themselves distinct. "Well, never mind, my
precious dear. I'm *with* you for ever, whether you know it or not."

He returned into the house, and at once confronted his younger
son, Charlie, who was at that moment descending the stairs. As
a matter of fact he was descending the stairs like fifteen Charlies,
and nothing so much exasperated his father as to feel the whole
house rock on its foundations at each fresh impact.

"Off to your match, my boy?" he cried. "Some day I expect
you will be taking a hand in the game yourself. Better share than
watch!"

Every single Saturday afternoon during the football season Mr.

Thripp ventured to express some such optimistic sentiment as this. But Charlie had no objection; not at all.

"Not me, dad," he assured him good-humouredly. "I'd sooner pay a bob to see other fellows crocked up. You couldn't lend me one, I suppose?"

"Lend you what?"

"Two tanners; four frippenies; a twelfth of a gross of coppers."

Good God! yelled Mr. Thripp's inward monitor, am I *never* to have a minute's rest or relief? But it yelled in vain.

"Right you are, my son," he said instead, and thrusting his fleshy hand into his tight-fitting trouser pocket he brought out a fistful of silver and pence. "And there," he added, "there's an extra sixpence free, *gratis,* and for nothing, for the *table d'hôte*. All I say is, Charlie, better say 'give' when there isn't much chance of keeping to the 'lend.' I don't want to preach; but that's always been *my* rule; and kept it too, as well as I could."

Charles counted the coins in his hand, and looked at his father. He grinned companionably. He invariably found his father a little funny to look at. He seemed somehow to be so remote from anything you could mean by things as they are, and things as they are now. He wasn't so much old-fashioned, as just a Gone-by. He was his father, of course, just as a jug is a jug, and now and then Charlie was uncommonly fond of him, longed for his company, and remembered being a little boy walking with him in the Recreation Ground. But he wished he wouldn't be always giving advice, and especially the kind of advice which he had himself assiduously practised.

"Ta, dad," he said; "that's doing me proud. I'll buy you a box of Havanas with what's over from the *table d'hôte*. And now we're square. Good-bye, dad." He paused as he turned to go. "Honour bright," he added, "I hope I shall be earning a bit more soon, and then I shan't have to ask you for anything."

A curious shine came into Mr. Thripp's small lively eyes; it seemed almost to spill over on to his plump cheeks. It looked as if those cheeks had even paled a little.

"Why, that's all right, Charlie, me boy," he mumbled, "I'd give you the skin off me body if it would be of any use. That's all right. Don't stand about too long but just keep going. What I can't abide is these young fellows that swallow down their enjoyments like so much black draught. But we are not that kind of a family, I'm thankful to say."

"Not me!" said Charles, with a grimace like a good-humoured marmoset, and off he went to his soccer match.

Hardly had the sound of his footsteps ceased—and Mr. Thripp stayed there in the passage, as if to listen till they were for ever out of hearing—when there came a muffled secretive tap on the panel of the door. At sound of it the genial podgy face blurred and blackened.

Oh, it's you, you cringing Jezebel, is it?—the thought scurried through his mind like a mangy animal. Mr. Thripp indeed was no lover of the ultra-feminine. He either feared it, or hated it, or both feared *and* hated it. It disturbed his even tenour. It was a thorn in the side of the Mr. Thripp that not only believed second thoughts were best, but systematically refused to give utterance to first. Any sensible person, he would say, ought to know when he's a bit overtaxed, and act according.

The gloved fingers, Delilah-like, had tapped again. Mr. Thripp tiptoed back into the kitchen, put on his coat, and opened the door.

"Oh, it's you, Mrs. Brown," he said. "Tilda won't be a moment. She's upstairs titivating. Come in and take a seat."

His eyes meanwhile were informing that inward censor of his precisely how many inches thick the mauvish face-powder lay on Mrs. Brown's cheek, the liver-coloured lip-stick on her mouth, and the dye on her loaded eyelashes. Those naturally delicate lashes swept down in a gentle fringe upon her cheek as she smiled in reply. She was a graceful thing, too, but practised; and far more feline, far far more body-conscious than Millie. No longer in the blush of youth either; though still mistress of the gift that never leaves its predestined owner—the impulse and power to fascinate mere man. Still, there were limitations even to Mrs. Brown's orbit of attraction, and Mr. Thripp might have been Neptune itself he kept himself so far out in the cold.

He paused a moment at the entrance to the sitting-room, until his visitor had seated herself. He was eyeing her Frenchified silk scarf, her demure new hat, her smart high-heeled patent-leather shoes, but his eyes dropped like stones when he discovered her own dark languishing ones surveying him from under that hat's beguiling brim.

"Nice afternoon after the rain," he remarked instantly. "Going to the pictures, I suppose? As for meself, these days make me want to be out and in at the same time. It's the musty, fusty, smoky dark of them places I can't stand."

Mrs. Brown rarely raised her voice much above a whisper. Indeed it appeared to be a physical effort to her to speak at all. She turned her face a little sidelong, her glance on the carpet. "Why, it's the dark I enjoy, Mr. Thripp," she said. "It"—and she raised her own—"it rests the eyes so."

For an instant Mr. Thripp's memory returned to Millie, but he made no comment.

"Here's Mrs. Brown, Tilda," he called up the staircase. Good heavens, the woman might as well be the real thing, the voice within was declaring. But the words that immediately followed up this piece of news were merely, "You'll be mighty surprised to hear, Tilda, Mrs. Brown's got a new hat." A faint catcall of merriment descended the stairs.

"Oh, now, Mr. Thripp, listen to that!" whispered the peculiar voice from out of the little airless sitting-room, "you always did make fun of me, Mr. Thripp. Do I deserve it, now?"

A gentle wave of heat coursed over Mr. Thripp as he covertly listened to these accents, but he was out of sight.

"Fun, Mrs. Brown? Never," he retorted gallantly; "it's only my little way." And then to his immense relief on lifting his eyes, discovered Tilda already descending the stairs.

He saw the pair of them off. Being restored to his coat, he could watch them clean down the drying street from his gatepost. Astonishing, he thought, what a difference there can be in two women's backs! Tilda's, straight, angular, and respectable, as you might say; and that other—sinuous, seductive, as if it were as crafty a means of expression as the very smile and long-lashed languishments upon its owner's face. "What can the old woman see in her!" he muttered to himself; "damned if I know!" On this problem Mr. Thripp firmly shut his front door. Having shut it he stooped to pick up a tiny white feather on the linoleum; and stooping, sighed.

At last his longed-for hour had come—the hour for which his very soul pined throughout each workaday week. Not that it was always his happy fate to be left completely alone like this. At times, indeed, he had for company far too much housework to leave him any leisure. But to-day the dinner things were cleared away, the washing-up was over, the tables fair as a baker's board, the kitchen spick and span, the house empty. He would just have a look round his own and Tilda's bedroom (and, maybe, the boys' and Millie's). And then the chair by the fire; the simmering kettle on the hearth; and the soft tardy autumnal dusk fading quietly into night beyond the window.

It was a curious thing that a man who loved his family so much, who was as desperately loyal to every member of it as a she-wolf is to her cubs, should yet find this few minutes' weekly solitude a luxury such as only paradise, one would suppose, would ever be able to provide.

Mr. Thripp went upstairs and not only tidied up his own and Tilda's bedroom, and went on to Millie's and the boys', but even gave a sloosh to the bath, slid the soap out of the basin where Charles had abandoned it, and hung up the draggled towels again in the tiny bathroom. What a place looks like when you come back to it from your little enjoyments—it's *that* makes all the difference to your feelings about a home. These small chores done, Mr. Thripp put on an old tweed coat with frayed sleeves, and returned to the kitchen. In a quarter of an hour that too more than ever resembled a new pin.

Then he glanced up at the clocks; between them the time was a quarter to four. He was amazed. He laid the tea, took out of his little old leather bag a pot of jam which he had bought for a surprise on his way home, and arranged a bunch of violets in a small jar beside Tilda's plate. But apart from these family preparations, Mr. Thripp was now depositing a demure little glossy brown teapot all by itself on the kitchen range. This was his Eureka. This was practically the only sensual *secret* luxury Mr. Thripp had ever allowed himself since he became a family man. Tilda's cooking was good enough for him provided that the others had their little dainties now and then. He enjoyed his beer, and could do a bit of supper occasionally with a friend. But the ritual of these solitary Saturday afternoons reached its climax in this small pot of tea. First the nap sweet as nirvana in his easy chair, then the tea, and then the still, profound quarter of an hour's musing before the door-knocker began again.

Having pulled down the blind a little in order to prevent any chance of draught, Mr. Thripp eased his boot-laces, sat himself in his chair, his cheek turned a little away from the window, his feet on the box that usually lay under the table, and with fingers clasped over his stomach composed himself to sleep. The eyelids closed; the lips set; the thumbs twitched now and again. He breathed deep, and the kettle began a whispered anthem—as if a myriad voices were singing on and on without need of pause or rest, a thousand thousand leagues away.

But now there was none to listen; and beyond quiet hung thick in the little house. Only the scarce-perceptible hum of the traffic at the end of the narrow side street was audible on the air. Within, the two clocks on the chimney-piece quarrelled furiously over the fleeting moments, attaining unanimity only in one of many ticks. Ever and again a tiny scutter of dying ashes rejoined those that had gone before in the pan beneath the fire. Soon even these faint stirrings became inaudible and in a few moments Mr. Thripp's spirit would have wafted itself completely free awhile from its earthly tenement, if, suddenly, the image of Millie—more vivid than even the actual sight of her a few minutes before—had not floated up into the narrow darkness of her father's tight-shut eyes.

But this was not the image of Millie as her father usually saw her. A pathetic earthly melancholy lay over the fair angelic features. The young cheek was sunken in; the eye was faded, dejected, downcast; and her cheek was stubbornly turned away from her father, as if she resented or was afraid of his scrutiny.

At this vision a headlong anxiety darted across Mr. Thripp's half-slumbering mind. His heart began heavily beating: and then a pulse in his forehead. Where was she now? What forecast, what warning was this? Millie was no fool. Millie knew her way about. And her mother if anything was perhaps a little too censorious of the ways of this wicked world. If you keep on talking at a girl, hinting of things that might otherwise not enter her head—that in itself is dangerous. Love itself even must edge in warily. The tight-shut lids blinked anxiously. But where was Millie now? Somewhere indoors, but where? Who with?

Mr. Thripp saw her first in a tea-shop, sitting opposite a horrid young man with his hair greased back over his low round head, and a sham pin in his tie. His elbows were on the marble-top table, and he was looking at Millie very much as a young but experienced pig looks at his wash-trough. Perhaps she was at the pictures? Dulcet accents echoed into the half-dreaming mind—"But I enjoy the dark, Mr. Thripp. . . . It rests the eyes." Why did the woman talk as if she had never more than half a breath to spare? Rest her eyes! She never at any rate wanted to rest the eyes of any fool in trousers who happened to be within glimpse of her own. It was almost unnaturally dark in the cinema of Mr. Thripp's fancy at this moment; yet he could now see his Millie with her pale, harmless, youthful face, as plainly as if she were the "close-up" of some star from Los Angeles on the screen. And now the young man in her company was almost as fair as herself, with a long-chinned sheepish face and bolting eyes; and the two of them were amorously hand in hand.

For a moment Mr. Thripp sat immovable, as if a bugle had sounded in his ear. Then he deliberately opened his eyes and glanced about him. The November daylight was already beginning to fade. Yes, he would have a word with Millie—but not when she came home that evening. It is always wiser to let the actual coming-home be pleasant and welcoming. To-morrow morning, perhaps; that is, if her mother was not goading at her for being late down and lackadaisical when there was so much to be done. Nevertheless, all in good time he would have a little quiet word with her. He would say only what he would not afterwards regret having said. He had meant to do that ages ago; but you mustn't flood a house with water when it's not on fire. She was but a mere slip of a thing—like a flower, not a wild flower, but one of those sweet waxen flowers you see blooming in a florist's window—which you must be careful with and not just expose anywhere.

And yet how his own little place here could be compared with

anything in the nature of a hothouse he could not for the life of
him understand. Delicate-looking! Everybody said that. God bless
me, perhaps her very lackadaisicalness was a symptom of some as
yet hidden malady. Good God, supposing! . . . He would take
her round to see the doctor as soon as he could. But the worst of
it was you had to do these things on your own responsibility. And
though Mr. Thripp was now a man close on fifty, sometimes he
felt as if he could no longer bear the burden of all these re-
sponsibilities. Sometimes he felt as if he couldn't endure to brood
over them as he was sometimes wont to do. If he did, he would
snap. People *looked* old; but nobody was really old inside; not old
at least in the sense that troubles were any the lighter, or forebodings any the more easily puffed away; or tongues easier to keep
still; or tempers to control.

And talking of tempers reminded him of Charlie. What on
earth was going to be done with Charlie? There was no difficulty
in conjuring up, in seeing Charlie—that is if he really did go
every Saturday to a football match. But Charlie was now of an
age when he might think it a fine manly thing to be loafing about
the counter of a pub talking to some flaxen barmaid with a
tuppeny cigar between his teeth. Still, Mr. Thripp refused to entertain more than a glimpse of this possibility. He saw him at this
moment as clearly as if in a peepshow, packed in with hundreds
of other male creatures close as sardines in a tin, with their check
caps and their "fags," and their staring eyes revolving in consort
as if they were all attached to one wire, while that idiotic ball in
the middle of the arena coursed on its helpless way from muddy
boot to muddy boot.

Heaven knows, Mr. Thripp himself was nothing much better
than a football! You had precious small chance in this life of
choosing which boot should give you the next kick. And what
about that smug new creeping accountant at the office with his
upstart airs and new-fangled book-keeping methods!

Mr. Thripp's mouth opened in a yawn, but managed only to
achieve a fraction of it. He rubbed his face; his eyes now shut
again. It was not as if any of your children were of much practical
help. Why should they be when they could never understand that
what you pined for, what you really needed was not only practical

help but some inward grace and clearness of mind wherewith they could slip in under your own thoughts and so share your point of view without all that endless terrifying argumentation. He didn't *always* give advice to suit his own ends; and yet whenever he uttered a word to James, tactfully suggesting that in a world like this—however competent a man may be and however sure of himself—you *had* to push your way, you had to make your weight felt, James always looked at him as if he were a superannuated orang-outang in a cage—an orang-outang with queer and not particularly engaging habits.

He wouldn't mind even that so much if only James would take his cigarette out of his mouth when he talked. To see that bit of stained paper attached to his son's lower lip wagging up and down, beneath that complacent smile and those dark helpless-looking eyes, all but sent Mr. Thripp stark staring mad at times. Once, indeed, he had actually given vent to the appalling mass of emotion hoarded up like water in a reservoir in his mind. The remembrance of the scene that followed made him even at this moment tremble in his chair. Thank God, thank God, he hadn't often lost control like that.

Well, James would be married by this time next year, he supposed. And what a nice dainty pickle he was concocting for himself! Mr. Thripp knew that type of young woman, with the compressed lips, and the thin dry hair, and the narrow hips. She'd be a "good manager," right enough, but that's a point in married life where good managing is little short of being in a lunatic asylum between two iron-faced nurses and yourself in a strait waistcoat. The truth of it was, with all his fine airs and neat finish, James hadn't much common sense. He had a fair share of brains; but brains are no good if you are merely self-opinionated and contemptuous on principle. James was not like anybody in Mr. Thripp's own family. He was a Simpkins.

And then suddenly it was as if some forgotten creature in Mr. Thripp's mind or heart had burst out crying; and the loving look he thereupon cast on his elder son's face in his mind was almost maudlin in its sentimentality. He would do anything for James within reason: anything. But then it would have to be within James's reason—not his own. He knew that. Why he would himself marry the young woman and exult in being a bigamist if only he could keep his son out of her way. And yet, and yet; maybe there were worse women in the world than your stubborn, petulant, niggardly, half-sexed nagger. Mr. Thripp knew a nagger of old. His brother's wife, Fanny, had been a nagger. She was dead now, and George was a free man—but drinking far too much.

Well, as soon as he could get a chance, Mr. Thripp sitting there in his chair decided, he would have another good think; but that probably wouldn't be until next Saturday, if then. You can't think to much purpose—except in a worried disjointed fashion—when you are in the noise of an office or keeping yourself from saying things you have no wish to say. The worst of it was it was not much good discussing these matters with Tilda. Like most women, she always went off at a tangent. And when you came down to it, and wanted to be reasonable, there was so little left to discuss. Besides, Tilda had worries enough of her own.

At this moment Mr. Thripp once more opened his eyes wide. The small kitchen loomed beatifically rosy and still in the glow of the fire. Evening had so far edged on its way now that he could hardly see the hands of his two clocks. He could but just detect the brass pendulum—imperturbably chopping up eternity into fragments of time. He craned forward; in five minutes he ought to be brewing his little private pot of tea. Even if he nodded off now, he would be able to wake in time, but five minutes doesn't leave *much* margin for dropping off. He shifted a little on his chair, and once more shut his eyes. And in a moment or two his mind went completely blank.

He seemed to have been suddenly hauled up helpless with horror into an enormous vacancy—to be dangling unconfined and motionless in space. A scene of wild sandy hills and spiky trees— an illimitable desert, came riding towards him out of nothingness. He hung motionless, and was yet sweeping rapidly forward, but for what purpose and to what goal there was not the smallest inkling. The wilderness before him grew ever more desolate and menacing. He began to be deadly afraid; groaned; stirred—and found himself with fingers clenched on its arms sitting bolt upright in his chair. And the hands of the clock looked to be by a hair's breadth precisely in the same position as when he had

started on that ghastly nightmare journey. His face blanched. He
sat appalled, listening to an outrageous wauling of voices. It was
as though a thousand demons lay in wait for him beneath his
window and were summoning him to his doom.

And all this nightmare horror of mind was due solely to a
wailing of cats! And yet even as with flesh still creeping he
listened on to this clamour, it was so human in effect that it might
be multitudinous shades of the unborn that were thronging about
the glass of his window. Mr. Thripp rose from his chair, his face
transfigured with rage and desire for revenge. He went out into
the scullery, opened the back door, and at sound of him the cater-
wauling instantly ceased.

And almost as instantly his fury died out in him. The cold
evening air fanned his forehead. He smiled quixotically, and
looked about him. There came a furtive rustle in the bushes. "Ah,
there you are!" he sang out gently into the dark. "Have your play
while you can, my fine gentlemen! Take it like your betters, for
it's—a sight too soon over."

Above the one cramped leafless elder tree in his yard a star was
pricking the sky. A ground mist, too, was rising, already smelling
a little stale. Great London and its suburbs appeared to be in for
one of its autumnal fogs. A few of the upper windows opposite
loomed dim with light. Mr. Thripp's neighbours, it seemed, were
also preparing to be off to the pictures or the music-halls. It was
very still, and the air was damp and clammy.

As he stood silent there in the obscurity a deepening melancholy
crept over his mind, though he was unaware into what gloomy
folds and sags his face had fallen. He suddenly remembered that
his rates would have to be paid next week. He remembered that
Christmas would soon be coming, and that he was getting too
old to enter into the fun of the thing as he used to do. His eyes
rolled a little in their sockets. What the . . . ! his old friend
within began to suggest. But Mr. Thripp himself did not even
enunciate the missing "hell." Instead, he vigorously rubbed his
face with his stout capable hand. "Well, fog anyhow don't bring
rain," he muttered to himself.

And as if at a signal his own cat and his next-door neighbour's
cat and Mrs. Brown's cat and the cat of the painter and decorator

whose back garden abutted his own, together with the ginger-and-white cat from a news-vendor's beyond, with one consent broke out once more into their Sabbath-eve quintette. The many-stranded strains of it mounted up into the heavens like the yells of demented worshippers of Baal.

"And, as I say, I don't blame ye neether," Mr. Thripp retorted, with a grim smile. "If you knew, my friends, how narrowly you some of you escaped a bucket of cold water when you couldn't even see out of your young eyes, you'd sing twice as loud."

He shut the door and returned to his fireside. No more hope of sleep that afternoon. He laughed to himself for sheer amusement at his disappointment. What kids men were! He stirred the fire; it leapt brightly as if intent to please him. He pushed the kettle on; lit the lamp; warmed his little privy glossy-brown teapot, and fetched out a small private supply of the richest Ceylon from behind some pots in the saucepan cupboard.

Puffs of steam were now vapouring out of the spout of the kettle with majestic pomposity. Mr. Thripp lifted it off the coals and balanced it over his teapot. And at that very instant the electric bell—which a year or two ago in a moment of the strangest caprice Charles had fixed up in the corner—began jangling like a fire-alarm. Mr. Thripp hesitated. If this was one of the family, he was caught. Caught, that is, unless he was mighty quick in concealing these secret preparations. If it was Tilda—well, valour was the better part of discretion. He poured the water into the pot, replaced the lid, and put it on to the oven-top to stew. With a glance of satisfaction at the spinster-like tidiness of the room, he went out, and opened the door.

"Why, it's Millie!" he said, looking out at the slim-shouldered creature standing alone there under the porch; "you don't mean to say it's you, my dear?"

Millie made no reply. Her father couldn't see her face, partly because the lamp-post stationed in front of the house three doors away gave at best a feeble light, and partly because her features were more or less concealed by her hat. She pushed furtively past him without a word, her head still stooping out of the light.

Oh, my God, what's wrong now? yelled her father's inward monstrous monitor, frenziedly clanging the fetters on wrist and ankle. "Come right in, my pretty dear," said Mr. Thripp seductively, "this *is* a pleasant surprise. And what's more, between you and me and the gatepost, I have just been making myself a cup of tea. Not a word to mother; it's *our* little secret. We'll have it together before the others come in."

He followed his daughter into the kitchen.

"Lor', what a glare you are in, pa!" she said in a small muffled voice. She turned the wick of the lamp down so low that in an instant or two the flame flickered and expired, and she seated herself in her father's chair by the fire. But the flame-light showed her face now. It was paler even than usual. A strand of her gilded pale-brown hair had streaked itself over her blue-veined temple. She looked as if she had been crying. Her father, his hands hanging down beside him as uselessly as the front paws of a performing bear, watched her in an appalling trepidation of spirit. This then was the secret of his nightmare; for this the Cats of Fate had chorused!

"What's wrong, Millie love? Are you overtired, my girl? There! Don't say nothing for a minute or two. See, here's my little pot just meant for you and me!"

Millie began to cry again, pushing her ridiculous little handkerchief close to her eyes. Mr. Thripp's hand hovered awkwardly above her dainty hat and then gently fumbled as if to stroke her hair beneath. He knelt down beside her chair.

For heaven's sake! for heaven's sake! for heaven's sake! a secret voice was gabbling frenziedly in his ear. "Tell your old dad, lovey," he murmured out loud, softly as the crooning of a woodpigeon.

Millie tilted back her pretty hat and dropped her fair head on his shoulder. "It's nothing, dad," she said. "It's only that they are all the same."

"What are all the same?"

"Oh, fellows, dad."

"Which one, precious?" Mr. Thripp lulled wooingly. God strike him dead! muttered his monster.

"Oh, only young Arthur. Like a fool I waited half an hour for him and then saw him with—with that Westcliff girl."

A sigh as voluminous as the suspiration of Niagara swept over

Mr. Thripp; but it made no sound. Half a dozen miraculous words of reassurance were storming his mind in a frenzy of relief. He paused an instant, and accepted the seventh.

"What's all that, my precious?" he was murmuring. "Why, when I was courting your mother, I saw just the same thing happen. She was a mighty pretty young thing, too, as a girl, though not quite so trim and neat in the figure as you. I felt I could throttle him where he stood. But no, I just took no notice, trusting in my own charms!"

"That's all very well," sobbed Millie, "but you were a man, and *we* have to fight without seeming to. Not that I care a fig for him: he can go. But—"

"Lord, Millie!" Mr. Thripp interrupted, smoothing her cheek with his squat forefinger, "you'd beat twenty of them Westcliffs, with a cast in both eyes and your hands behind your back. Don't you grieve no more, my dear; he'll come back safe and sound, or he's less of a—of a nice young feller than I take him for."

For a moment Mr. Thripp caught a glimpse of the detestable creature with the goggling eyes and the suède shoes, but he dismissed him sternly from view.

"There now," he said, "give your poor old dad a kiss. What's disappointments, Millie; they soon pass away. And now, just take a sip or two of this extra-strong Bohay! I was hoping I shouldn't have to put up with a lonely cup and not a soul to keep me company. But mind, my precious, not a word to your ma."

So there they sat, father and daughter, comforter and comforted, while Mr. Thripp worked miracles for two out of a teapot for one. And while Millie, with heart comforted, was musing on that other young fellow she had noticed boldly watching her while she was waiting for her Arthur, Mr. Thripp was wondering when it would be safe and discreet to disturb her solacing daydream so that he might be busying himself over the supper.

It's one dam neck-and-neck worry and trouble after another, his voice was assuring him. But meanwhile, his plain square face was serene and gentle as a nestful of halcyons, as he sat sipping his hot water and patting his pensive Millie's hand.

The Connoisseur and Other Stories (1926)

ALL HALLOWS

"And because time in itself . . . can receive no alteration, the
hallowing . . . must consist in the shape or countenance which we
put upon the affaires that are incident in these days."

RICHARD HOOKER

IT WAS about half past three on an August afternoon when I
found myself for the first time looking down upon All Hallows.
And at first glimpse of it, every vestige of fatigue and vexation
passed away. I stood "at gaze," as the old phrase goes—like the
two children of Israel sent in to spy out the Promised Land. How
often the imagined transcends the real. Not so All Hallows. Having at last reached the end of my journey—flies, dust, heat, wind
—having at last come limping out upon the green sea-bluff beneath which lay its walls—I confess the actuality excelled my
feeble dreams of it.

What most astonished me, perhaps, was the sense not so much
of its age, its austerity, or even its solitude, but its air of abandonment. It lay couched there as if in its narrow sea-bay. Not a sound
was in the air; not a jackdaw clapped its wings among its turrets.
No other roof, not even a chimney, was in sight; only the dark-
blue arch of the sky; the narrow snowline of the ebbing tide; and
that gaunt coast fading away into the haze of a west over which
were already gathering the veils of sunset.

We had met then, at an appropriate hour and season. And yet
—I wonder. For it was certainly not the "beauty" of All Hallows,
lulled as if into a dream in this serenity of air and heavens, which
was to leave the sharpest impression upon me. And what kind of
first showing would it have made, I speculated, if an autumnal

gale had been shrilling and trumpeting across its narrow bay—
clots of wind-borne spume floating among its dusky pinnacles—
and the roar of the sea echoing against its walls! Imagine it
frozen stark in winter, icy hoar-frost edging its every boss, moulding, finial, crocket, cusp!

Indeed, are there not works of man, legacies of a half-forgotten
past, scattered across this human world of ours from China to
Peru which seem to daunt the imagination with their incompre-
hensibility? Incomprehensible, I mean, in the sense that the passion that inspired and conceived them is incomprehensible.
Viewed in the light of the passing day, they might be the monu-
ments of a race of demi-gods. And yet, if we could but free ourselves from our timidities, realise that even we ourselves have an
obligation to leave behind us similar memorials—testaments to
the creative and faithful genius not so much of the individual as
of Humanity itself.

However that may be, it was my own personal fortune to see
All Hallows for the first time in the heat of the Dog Days, after
a journey which could hardly be justified except by its end. At
this moment of the afternoon the great church almost cheated
one into the belief that it was possessed of a life of its own. It lay,
as I say, couched in its natural hollow, basking under the dark
dome of the heavens like some half-fossilized monster that might
at any moment stir and awaken out of the swoon to which the
wand of the enchanter had committed it. And with every inch of
the sun's descending journey it changed its appearance.

That is the charm of such things. Man himself, says the philosopher, is the sport of change. His life and the life around him are
but the flotsam of a perpetual flux. Yet, haunted by ideals, egged
on by impossibilities, he builds his vision of the changeless; and
time diversifies it with its colours and its "effects" at leisure. It
was drawing near to harvest now; the summer was nearly over;
the corn would soon be in stook; the season of silence had come,
not even the robins had yet begun to practise their autumnal la-
ment. I should have come earlier.

The distance was of little account. But nine flinty hills in seven
miles is certainly hard commons. To plod (the occupant of a
cloud of dust) up one steep incline and so see another; to plod

up that and so see a third; to surmount that and, half-choked,
half-roasted, to see (as if in unbelievable mirage) a fourth—and
always stone walls, discoloured grass, no flower but ragged rag-
wort, whited fleabane, moody nettle, and the exquisite stubborn
bindweed with its almond-burdened censers, and always the
glitter and dazzle of the sun—well, the experience grows irksome.
And then that endless flint erection with which some jealous
Lord of the Manor had barricaded his verdurous estate! A fly-
infested mile of the company of that wall was tantamount to
making one's way into the infernal regions—with Tantalus for
fellow pilgrim. And when a solitary and empty dung-wagon had
lumbered by, lifting the dumb dust out of the road in swirling
clouds into the heat-quivering air, I had all but wept aloud.

No, I shall not easily forget that walk—or the conclusion of it
—when footsore, all but dead beat—dust all over me, cheeks, lips,
eyelids, in my hair, dust in drifts even between my naked body
and my clothes—I stretched my aching limbs on the turf under
the straggle of trees which crowned the bluff of that last hill, still
blessedly green and verdant, and feasted my eyes on the cathedral
beneath me. How odd Memory is—in her sorting arrangements.
How perverse her pigeon-holes.

It had reminded me of a drizzling evening many years ago.
I had stayed a moment to listen to an old Salvation Army officer
preaching at a street corner. The sopped and squalid houses
echoed with his harangue. His penitents' drum resembled the
block of an executioner. His goatish beard wagged at every word
he uttered. "My brothers and sisters," he was saying, "the very
instant our fleshly bodies are born they begin to perish; the moment the Lord has put them together, time begins to take them
to pieces again. *Now* at this very instant if you listen close, you
can hear the nibblings and frettings of the moth and rust within
—the worm that never dies. It's the same with human causes and
creeds and institutions—just the same. Oh, then for that Strand of
Beauty where all that is mortal shall be shed away and we shall
appear in the likeness and verisimilitude of what in sober and
awful truth we are."

The light striking out of an oil and colourman's shop at the
street corner lay across his cheek and beard and glassed his eye.

The soaked circle of humanity in which he was gesticulating stood staring and motionless—the lassies, the probationers, the melancholy idlers. I had had enough. I went away. But it is odd that so utterly inappropriate a recollection should have edged back into my mind at this moment. There was, as I have said, not a living soul in sight. Only a few sea-birds—oyster-catchers maybe —were jangling on the distant beach.

It was now a quarter to four by my watch, and the usual pensive "lin-lan-lone" from the belfry beneath me would soon no doubt be ringing to evensong. But if at that moment a triple bob-major had suddenly clanged its alarm over sea and shore, I couldn't have stirred a finger's breadth. Scanty though the shade afforded by the wind-shorn tuft of trees under which I lay might be—I was ineffably at peace.

No bell, as a matter of fact, loosed its tongue that stagnant half-hour. Unless then the walls beneath me already concealed a few such chance visitors as myself, All Hallows would be empty. A cathedral not only without a close but without a congregation— yet another romantic charm. The Deanery and the residences of its clergy, my old guide-book had long since informed me, were a full mile or more away. I determined in due time, first to make sure of an entry, and then having quenched my thirst, to bathe.

How inhuman any extremity—hunger, fatigue, pain, desire— makes us poor humans. Thirst and drought so haunted my mind that again and again as I glanced towards it I supped up at one long draught that complete blue sea. But meanwhile, too, my eyes had been steadily exploring and searching out this monument of the bygone centuries beneath me.

The headland faced approximately due west. The windows of the Lady Chapel therefore lay immediately beneath me, their fourteenth-century glass showing flatly dark amid their traceries. Above it, the shallow V-shaped, leaden-ribbed roof of the chancel converged towards the unfinished tower, then broke away at right angles—for the cathedral was cruciform. Walls so ancient and so sparsely adorned and decorated could not but be inhospitable in effect. Their stone was of a bleached bone-grey; a grey that none the less seemed to be as immaterial as flame—or incandescent ash. They were substantial enough, however, to cast a marvellously lucent shadow, of a blue no less vivid but paler than that of the sea, on the shelving sward beneath them. And that shadow was steadily shifting as I watched. But even if the complete edifice had vanished into the void, the scene would still have been of an incredible loveliness. The colours in air and sky on this dangerous coast seemed to shed a peculiar unreality even on the rocks of its own outworks.

So, from my vantage place on the hill that dominates it, I continued for a while to watch All Hallows; to spy upon it; and no less intently than a sentry who, not quite trusting his own eyes, has seen a dubious shape approaching him in the dusk. It may sound absurd, but I felt that at any moment I too might surprise All Hallows in the act of revealing what in very truth it looked like—and *was,* when no human witness was there to share its solitude.

Those gigantic statues, for example, which flanked the base of the unfinished tower—an intense bluish-white in the sunlight and a bluish-purple in shadow—images of angels and of saints, as I had learned of old from my guide-book. Only six of them at most could be visible, of course, from where I sat. And yet I found myself counting them again and yet again, as if doubting my own arithmetic. For my first impression had been that seven were in view—though the figure furthest from me at the western angle showed little more than a jutting fragment of stone which might perhaps be only part and parcel of the fabric itself.

But then the lights even of day may be deceitful, and fantasy plays strange tricks with one's eyes. With exercise, none the less, the mind is enabled to detect minute details which the unaided eye is incapable of particularizing. Given the imagination, man himself indeed may some day be able to distinguish what shapes are walking during our own terrestrial midnight amid the black shadows of the craters in the noonday of the moon. At any rate, I could trace at last frets of carving, minute weather marks, crookednesses, incrustations, repairings, that had before passed unnoticed. These walls, indeed, like human faces, were maps and charts of their own long past.

In the midst of this prolonged scrutiny, the hypnotic air, the heat, must suddenly have overcome me. I fell asleep up there in my grove's scanty shade; and remained asleep, too, long enough (as time is measured by the clocks of sleep), to dream an immense panoramic dream. On waking, I could recall only the faintest vestiges of it, and found that the hand of my watch had crept on but a few minutes in the interval. It was eight minutes past four.

I scrambled up—numbed and inert—with that peculiar sense of panic which sometimes follows an uneasy sleep. What folly to have been frittering time away within sight of my goal at an hour when no doubt the cathedral would soon be closed to visitors, and abandoned for the night to its own secret ruminations. I hastened down the steep rounded incline of the hill, and having skirted under the sunlit expanse of the walls, came presently to the south door, only to discover that my forebodings had been justified, and that it was already barred and bolted. The discovery seemed to increase my fatigue fourfold. How foolish it is to obey mere caprices. What a straw is a man!

I glanced up into the beautiful shell of masonry above my head. Shapes and figures in stone it showed in plenty—symbols of an imagination that had flamed and faded, leaving this signature for sole witness—but not a living bird or butterfly. There was but one faint chance left of making an entry. Hunted now, rather than the hunter, I hastened out again into the full blazing flood of sunshine—and once more came within sight of the sea; a sea so near at last that I could hear its enormous sallies and murmurings. Indeed I had not realized until that moment how closely the great western doors of the cathedral abutted on the beach.

It was as if its hospitality had been deliberately designed, not for a people to whom the faith of which it was the shrine had become a weariness and a commonplace, but for the solace of pilgrims from over the ocean. I could see them tumbling into their cockle-boats out of their great hollow ships—sails idle, anchors down; see them leaping ashore and straggling up across the sands to these all-welcoming portals—"Parthians and Medes and Elamites; dwellers in Mesopotamia and in the parts of Egypt about Cyrene; strangers of Rome, Jews and Proselytes—we do hear them speak in our own tongue the wonderful works of God."

And so at last I found my way into All Hallows—entering by a rounded dwarfish side-door with zigzag mouldings. There hung for corbel to its dripstone a curious leering face, with its forked tongue out, to give me welcome. And an appropriate one, too, for the figure I made!

But once beneath that prodigious roof-tree, I forgot myself and everything that was mine. The hush, the coolness, the unfathomable twilight drifted in on my small human consciousness. Not even the ocean itself is able so completely to receive one into its solacing bosom. Except for the windows over my head, filtering with their stained glass the last western radiance of the sun, there was but little visible colour in those great spaces, and a severe economy of decoration. The stone piers carried their round arches with an almost intimidating impassivity.

By deliberate design, too, or by some illusion of perspective, the whole floor of the building appeared steadily to ascend towards the east, where a dark wooden multitudinously-figured rood-screen shut off the choir and the high altar from the nave. I seemed to have exchanged one universal actuality for another: the burning world of nature, for this oasis of quiet. Here, the wings of the imagination need never rest in their flight out of the wilderness into the unknown.

Thus resting, I must again have fallen asleep. And so swiftly can even the merest freshet of sleep affect the mind, that when my eyes opened, I was completely at a loss.

Where was I? What demon of what romantic chasm had swept my poor drowsy body into this immense haunt? The din and clamour of an horrific dream whose fainting rumour was still in my ear, became suddenly stilled. Then at one and the same moment, a sense of utter dismay at earthly surroundings no longer serene and peaceful, but grim and forbidding, flooded my mind, and I became aware that I was no longer alone. Twenty or thirty paces away, and a little this side of the rood-screen, an old man was standing.

To judge from the black and purple velvet and tassel-tagged gown he wore, he was a verger. He had not yet realized, it seemed, that a visitor shared his solitude. And yet he was listening. His head was craned forward and leaned sideways on his rusty shoulders. As I steadily watched him, he raised his eyes, and with a peculiar stealthy deliberation scanned the complete upper regions of the northern transept. Not the faintest rumour of any sound that may have attracted his attention reached me where I sat. Maybe a wild bird had made its entry through a broken pane of glass and with its cry had at the same moment awakened me and caught his attention. Or maybe the old man was waiting for some fellow occupant to join him from above.

I continued to watch him. Even at this distance, the silvery twilight cast by the clerestory windows was sufficient to show me, though vaguely, his face: the high sloping nose, the lean cheekbones and protruding chin. He continued so long in the same position that I at last determined to break in on his reverie.

At sound of my footsteps his head sunk cautiously back upon his shoulders; and he turned; and then motionlessly surveyed me as I drew near. He resembled one of those old men whom Rembrandt delighted in drawing: the knotted hands, the blank drooping eyebrows, the wide thin-lipped ecclesiastical mouth, the intent cavernous dark eyes beneath the heavy folds of their lids. White as a miller with dust, hot and draggled, I was hardly the kind of visitor that any self-respecting custodian would warmly welcome, but he greeted me none the less with every mark of courtesy.

I apologized for the lateness of my arrival, and explained it as best I could. "Until I caught sight of you," I concluded lamely, "I hadn't ventured very far in: otherwise I might have found myself a prisoner for the night. It must be dark in here when there is no moon."

The old man smiled—but wryly. "As a matter of fact, sir," he replied, "the cathedral is closed to visitors at four—at such times, that is, when there is no afternoon service. Services are not as frequent as they were. But visitors are rare too. In winter, in particular, you notice the gloom—as you say, sir. Not that I ever spend the night here: though I am usually last to leave. There's the risk of fire to be thought of and . . . I think I should have detected your presence here, sir. One becomes accustomed after many years."

There was the usual trace of official pedantry in his voice, but it was more pleasing than otherwise. Nor did he show any wish to be rid of me. He continued his survey, although his eye was a little absent and his attention seemed to be divided.

"I thought perhaps I might be able to find a room for the night and really explore the cathedral to-morrow morning. It has been a tiring journey; I come from B—"

"Ah, from B—; it *is* a fatiguing journey, sir, taken on foot. I used to walk in there to see a sick daughter of mine. Carriage parties occasionally make their way here, but not so much as once. We are too far out of the hurly-burly to be much intruded on. Not that them who come to make their worship here are intruders. Far from it. But most that come are mere sightseers. And the fewer of them, I say, in the circumstances, the better."

Something in what I had said or in my appearance seemed to have reassured him. "Well, I cannot claim to be a regular church-goer," I said. "I am myself a mere sightseer. And yet—even to sit here for a few minutes is to be reconciled."

"Ah, reconciled, sir," the old man repeated, turning away. "I can well imagine it after that journey on such a day as this. But to live here is another matter."

"I was thinking of that," I replied in a foolish attempt to re-trieve the position. "It must, as you say, be desolate enough in the winter—for two thirds of the year, indeed."

"We have our storms, sir—the bad with the good," he agreed, "and our position is specially prolific of what they call sea-fog. It comes driving in from the sea for days and nights together—gale and mist, so that you can scarcely see your open hand in front of your eyes even in broad daylight. And the noise of it, sir, sweep-ing across overhead in that woolliness of mist, if you take me, is most peculiar. It's shocking to a stranger. No, sir, we are left pretty much to ourselves when the fine-weather birds are flown. . . . You'd be astonished at the power of the winds here. There was a mason—a local man too—not above two or three years ago was blown clean off the roof from under the tower—tossed up in the air like an empty sack. But"—and the old man at last allowed his eyes to stray upwards to the roof again—"but there's not much doing now." He seemed to be pondering. "Nothing open."

"I mustn't detain you," I said, "but you were saying that serv-

ices are infrequent now. Why is that? When one thinks of—"
But tact restrained me.

"Pray don't think of keeping me, sir. It's a part of my duties.
But from a remark you let fall I was supposing you may have
seen something that appeared, I understand, not many months
ago in the newspapers. We lost our Dean—Dean Pomfrey—last
November. To all intents and purposes, I mean; and his office has
not yet been filled. Between you and me, sir, there's a hitch—
though I should wish it to go no further. They are greedy monsters—those newspapers: no respect, no discretion, no decency,
in my view. And they copy each other like cats in a chorus.

"We have never wanted to be a notoriety here, sir: and not of
late things of all times. We must face our own troubles. You'd
be astonished how callous the mere sightseer can be. And not
only them from over the water whom our particular troubles cannot concern—but far worse—parties as English as you or me.
They ask you questions you wouldn't believe possible in a civi-
lized country. Not that they care what becomes of us—not one
iota, sir. We talk of them masked-up Inquisitors in olden times,
but there's many a human being in our own would enjoy seeing
a fellow creature on the rack if he could get the opportunity. It's
a heartless age, sir."

This was queerish talk in the circumstances: and after all I myself was of the glorious company of the sightseers. I held my
peace. And the old man, as if to make amends, asked me if I
would care to see any particular part of the building. "The light
is smalling," he explained, "but still if we keep to the ground level
there'll be a few minutes to spare; and we shall not be interrupted
if we go quietly on our way."

For the moment the reference eluded me: I could only thank
him for the suggestion and once more beg him not to put himself
to any inconvenience. I explained, too, that though I had no personal acquaintance with Dr. Pomfrey, I had read of his illness in
the newspapers. "Isn't he," I added a little dubiously, "the author
of *The Church and the Folk*? If so, he must be an exceedingly
learned and delightful man."

"Ay, sir." The old verger put up a hand towards me; "you may well say it: a saint, if ever there was one. But it's worse than illness, sir—it's oblivion. And, thank God, the newspapers didn't get hold of more than a bare outline."

He dropped his voice. "This way, if you please"; and he led me off gently down the aisle, once more coming to a standstill beneath the roof of the tower. "What I mean, sir, is that there's very few left in this world who have any place in their minds for a sacred confidence—no reverence, sir. They would as lief All Hallows and all it stands for were swept away to-morrow, demolished to the dust. And that gives me the greatest caution with whom I speak. But sharing one's troubles is sometimes a relief. If it weren't so, why do those Cartholics have their wooden boxes all built for the purpose? What else, I ask you, is the meaning of their fasts and penances?

"You see, sir, I am myself, and have been for upwards of twelve years now, the Dean's verger. In the sight of no respecter of persons—of offices and dignities, that is, I take it—I might claim to be even an elder brother. And our Dean, sir, was a man who was all things to all men. No pride of place, no vauntingness, none of your apron-and-gaiter high-and-mightiness whatsoever, sir. And then that! And to come on us without warning; or at least without warning as could be taken as *such*." I followed his eyes into the darkening stony spaces above us; a light like tarnished silver lay over the soundless vaultings. But so, of course, dusk, either of evening or daybreak, would affect the ancient stones. Nothing moved there.

"You must understand, sir," the old man was continuing, "the procession for divine service proceeds from the vestry over yonder out through those wrought-iron gates and so under the roodscreen and into the chancel there. Visitors are admitted on showing a card or a word to the verger in charge: but not otherwise. If you stand a pace or two to the right, you will catch a glimpse of the altar-screen—fourteenth-century work, Bishop Robert de Beaufort—and a unique example of the age. But what I was saying is that when we proceed for the services *out* of here *into* there, it has always been our custom to keep pretty close together; more seemly and decent, sir, than straggling in like so many sheep.

"Besides, sir, aren't we at such times in the manner of an *array;* 'marching as to war,' if you take me: it's a lesson in objects. The third verger leading: then the choristers, boys and men, though sadly depleted; then the minor canons; then any other dignitaries who may happen to be present, with the canon in residence; then myself, sir, followed by the Dean.

"There hadn't been much amiss up to then, and on that afternoon, I can vouch—and I've repeated it *ad naushum*—there was not a single stranger out in this beyond here, sir—nave or transepts. Not within view, that is: one can't be expected to see through four feet of Norman stone. Well, sir, we had gone on our way, and I had actually turned about as usual to bow Dr. Pomfrey into his stall, when I found to my consternation, to my consternation, I say, he wasn't there! It alarmed me, sir, and as you might well believe if you knew the full circumstances.

"Not that I lost my presence of mind. My first duty was to see all things to be in order and nothing unseemly to occur. My feelings were another matter. The old gentleman had left the vestry with us: that I knew: I had myself robed 'im as usual, and he in his own manner, smiling with his 'Well, Jones, another day gone; another day gone.' He was always an anxious gentleman for *time,* sir. How we spend it and all.

"As I say, then, he was behind me when we swept out of the gates. I saw him coming on out of the tail of my eye—we grow accustomed to it, to see with the whole of the eye, I mean. And then—not a vestige; and me—well, sir, nonplussed, as you may imagine. I gave a look and sign at Canon Ockham, and the service proceeded as usual, while I hurried back to the vestry thinking the poor gentleman must have been taken suddenly ill. And yet, sir, I was not surprised to find the vestry vacant, and him not there. I had been expecting matters to come to what you might call a head.

"As best I could I held my tongue, and a fortunate thing it was that Canon Ockham was then in residence, and not Canon Leigh Shougar, though perhaps I am not the one to say it. No, sir, our beloved Dean—as pious and harmless a gentleman as ever graced the Church—was gone for ever. He was not to appear in our midst again. He had been"—and the old man with elevated eyebrows and long lean mouth nearly whispered the words into my ear—"he had been absconded—abducted, sir."

"Abducted!" I murmured.

The old man closed his eyes, and with trembling lids added, "He was found, sir, late that night up there in what they call the Trophy Room—sitting in a corner there, weeping. A child. Not a word of what had persuaded him to go or misled him there, not a word of sorrow or sadness, thank God. He didn't know us, sir—didn't know *me*. Just simple; harmless; memory all gone. Simple, sir."

It was foolish to be whispering together like this beneath these enormous spaces with not so much as a clothes-moth for sign of life within view. But I even lowered my voice still further: "Were there no premonitory symptoms? Had he been failing for long?"

The spectacle of grief in any human face is afflicting, but in a face as aged and resigned as this old man's—I turned away in remorse the moment the question was out of my lips; emotion of any kind is a human solvent and a sort of friendliness had sprung up between us.

"If you will just follow me," he whispered, "there's a little place where I make my ablutions that might be of service, sir. We could converse there in better comfort. I am sometimes reminded of those words in Ecclesiastes: 'And a bird of the air shall tell of the matter.' There is not much in our poor human affairs, sir, that was not known to the writer of that book."

He turned and led the way with surprising celerity, gliding along in his thin-soled, square-toed, clerical springside boots, and came to a pause outside a nail-studded door. He opened it with a huge key, and admitted me into a recess under the central tower. We mounted a spiral stone staircase and passed along a corridor hardly more than two feet wide and so dark that now and again I thrust out my fingertips in search of his black velveted gown to make sure of my guide.

This corridor at length conducted us into a little room whose only illumination I gathered was that of the ebbing dusk from within the cathedral. The old man with trembling rheumatic fingers lit a candle, and thrusting its stick into the middle of an old oak table, pushed open yet another thick oaken door. "You will find a basin and a towel in there, sir, if you will be so kind."

I entered. A print of the Crucifixion was tin-tacked to the panelled wall, and beneath it stood a tin basin and jug on a stand. Never was water sweeter. I laved my face and hands, and drank deep; my throat like a parched river-course after a drought. What appeared to be a tarnished censer lay in one corner of the room; a pair of seven-branched candlesticks shared a recess with a mousetrap and a book. My eyes passed wearily yet gratefully from one to another of these mute discarded objects while I stood drying my hands.

When I returned, the old man was standing motionless before the spike-barred grill of the window, peering out and down.

"You asked me, sir," he said, turning his lank waxen face into the feeble rays of the candle, "you asked me, sir, a question which, if I understood you aright, was this: Was there anything that had occurred *previous* that would explain what I have been telling you? Well, sir, it's a long story, and one best restricted to them perhaps that have the goodwill of things at heart. All Hallows, I might say, sir, is my second home. I have been here, boy and man, for close on fifty-five years—have seen four bishops pass away and have served under no less than five several deans, Dr. Pomfrey, poor gentleman, being the last of the five.

"If such a word could be excused, sir, it's no exaggeration to say that Canon Leigh Shougar is a greenhorn by comparison: which may in part be why he has never quite hit it off, as they say, with Canon Ockham. Or even with Archdeacon Trafford, though he's another kind of gentleman altogether. And *he* is at present abroad. He had what they call a breakdown in health, sir.

"Now in my humble opinion, what was required was not only wisdom and knowledge but simple common sense. In the circumstances I am about to mention, it serves no purpose for any of us to be talking too much; to be for ever sitting at a table with shut doors and finger on lip, and discussing what to most intents and purposes would hardly be called evidence at all, sir. What is the use of argufying, splitting hairs, objurgating about trifles, when matters are sweeping rapidly on from bad to worse. I say it with all due respect and not, I hope, thrusting myself into what doesn't concern me: Dr. Pomfrey might be with us now in his own self and reason if only common caution had been observed.

"But now that the poor gentleman is gone beyond all that, there is no hope of action or agreement left, none whatsoever. They meet and they meet, and they have now one expert now another down from London, and even from the continent. And I don't say they are not knowledgeable gentlemen either, nor a pride to their profession. But why not tell *all*? Why keep back the very secret of what we know? That's what I am asking. And what's the answer? Why, simply that what they don't want to believe, what runs counter to their hopes and wishes and credibilities— and comfort—in this world, that's what they keep out of sight as long as decency permits.

"Canon Leigh Shougar *knows,* sir, what *I* know. And how, I ask, is he going to get to grips with it at this late day if he refuses to acknowledge that such things are what every fragment of evidence goes to prove that they are. It's *we,* sir, and not the rest of the heedless world outside, who in the long and the short of it are responsible. And what I say is: no power or principality here or hereunder can take possession of a place while those inside have faith enough to keep them out. But once let that falter—the seas are in. And when I say no power, sir, I mean—with all deference —even Satan himself." The lean lank face had set at the word like a wax mask. The black eyes beneath the heavy lids were fixed on mine with an acute intensity and—though more inscrutable things haunted them—with an unfaltering courage. So dense a hush hung about us that the very stones of the walls seemed to be of silence solidified. It is curious what a refreshment of spirit a mere tin basinful of water may be. I stood leaning against the edge of the table so that the candlelight still rested on my companion.

"What is *wrong* here?" I asked him baldly.

He seemed not to have expected so direct an inquiry. "Wrong, sir? Why, if I might make so bold," he replied with a wan, far-away smile and gently drawing his hand down one of the velvet lapels of his gown, "if I might make so bold, sir, I take it that you have come as a direct answer to prayer."

His voice faltered. "I am an old man now, and nearly at the

end of my tether. You must realize, if you please, that I can't get
any help that I can understand. I am not doubting that the gentlemen I have mentioned have only the salvation of the cathedral at
heart—the cause, sir; and a graver responsibility yet. But they refuse to see how close to the edge of things we are: and how we are
drifting.

"Take mere situation. So far as my knowledge tells me, there is
no sacred edifice in the whole kingdom—of a piece, that is, with
All Hallows not only in mere size and age but in what I might
call sanctity and tradition—that is so open—open, I mean, sir, to
attack of this peculiar and terrifying nature."

"Terrifying?"

"*Terrifying,* sir; though I hold fast to what wits my Maker has
bestowed on me. Where else, may I ask, would you expect the
powers of darkness to congregate in open besiegement than in
this narrow valley? First, the sea out there. Are you aware, sir,
that ever since living remembrance flood-tide has been gnawing
and mumbling its way into this bay to the extent of three or four
feet *per annum?* Forty inches, and forty inches, and forty inches
corroding on and on. Watch it, sir, man and boy as I have these
sixty years past and then make a century of it.

"And now, think a moment of the floods and gales that fall
upon us autumn and winter through and even in spring, when
this valley is liker paradise to young eyes than any place on earth.
They make the roads from the nearest towns well-nigh impassable; which means that for seven months of the year we are to all
intents and purposes clean cut off from the rest of the world—as
the Schindels out there are from the mainland. Are you aware,
sir, I continue, that as we stand now we are above a mile from
traces of the nearest human habitation, and them merely the relics
of a burnt-out old farmstead? I warrant that if (and which God
forbid) you had been shut up here during the coming night,
and it was a near thing but what you weren't—I warrant you
might have shouted yourself dumb out of the nearest window
if window you could reach—and not a human soul to heed or
help you."

I shifted my hands on the table. It was tedious to be asking
questions that received only such vague and evasive replies: and

it is always a little disconcerting in the presence of a stranger to be spoken to so close, and with such positiveness.

"Well," I smiled, "I hope I should not have disgraced my nerves to such an extreme as that. As a small boy, one of my particular fancies was to spend a night in a pulpit. There's a cushion, you know!"

The old man's solemn glance never swerved from my eyes. "But I take it, sir," he said, "if you had ventured to give out a text up there in the dark hours, your innocent young mind would not have been prepared for any kind of a congregation?"

"You mean," I said a little sharply, "that the place is haunted?" The absurd notion had flitted across my mind of some wandering tribe of gipsies chancing on a refuge so ample and isolated as this, and taking up its quarters in its secret parts. The old church must be honeycombed with corridors and passages and chambers pretty much like the one in which we were now concealed: and what does "cartholic" imply but an infinite hospitality within pre-scribed limits? But the old man had taken me at my word.

"I mean, sir," he said firmly, shutting his eyes, "that there are devilish agencies at work here." He raised his hand. "Don't, I entreat you, dismiss what I am saying as the wanderings of a fool-ish old man." He drew a little nearer. "I have heard them with these ears; I have seen them with these eyes; though whether they have any positive substance, sir, is beyond my small knowledge to declare. But what indeed might we expect their substance to *be*? First: I 'take it,' says the Book, 'to be such as no man can by learning define, nor by wisdom search out.' Is that so? Then I go by the Book. And next: what does the same Word or very near it (I speak of the Apocrypha) say of their *purpose*? It says—and correct me if I go astray—'Devils are creatures made by God, and *that for vengeance.*'

"So far, so good, sir. We stop when we can go no further. Vengeance. But of their power, of what they can *do*, I can give you definite evidences. It would be a byword if once the rumour was spread abroad. And if it is *not* so, why, I ask, does every ex-pert that comes here leave us in haste and in dismay? They go off with their tails between their legs. They see, they grope in, but they don't believe. They *invent* reasons. And they *hasten* to leave us!" His face shook with the emphasis he laid upon the word. "Why? Why, because the experience is beyond their knowledge, sir." He drew back breathless and, as I could see, profoundly moved.

"But surely," I said, "every old building is bound in time to show symptoms of decay. Half the cathedrals in England, half its churches, even, of any age, have been 'restored'—and in many cases with ghastly results. This new grouting and so on. Why, only the other day . . . All I mean is, why should you suppose mere wear and tear should be caused by any other agency than—"

The old man turned away. "I must apologize," he interrupted me with his inimitable admixture of modesty and dignity, "I am a poor mouth at explanations, sir. Decay—stress—strain—settling —dissolution: I have heard those words bandied from lip to lip like a game at cup and ball. They fill me with nausea. Why, I am speaking not of dissolution, sir, but of *repairs, restorations*. Not decay, *strengthening*. Not a corroding loss, an awful *progress*. I could show you places—and chiefly obscured from direct view and difficult of a close examination, sir, where stones lately as rotten as pumice and as fretted as a sponge have been replaced by others fresh-quarried—and nothing of their kind within twenty miles.

"There are spots where massive blocks a yard or more square have been *pushed* into place by sheer force. All Hallows is safer at this moment than it has been for three hundred years. They meant well—them who came to see, full of talk and fine language, and went dumb away. I grant you they meant well. I allow that. They hummed and they hawed. They smirked this and they shrugged that. But at heart, sir, they were cowed—horrified: all at a loss. Their very faces showed it. But if you ask me for what purpose such doings are afoot—I have no answer; none.

"But now, supposing you yourself, sir, were one of them, with *your* repute at stake, and you were called in to look at a house which the owners of it and them who had it in trust were disturbed by its being re-edificated and restored by some agency unknown to them. Supposing that! *Why,*" and he rapped with his knuckles on the table, "being human *and not one of us* mightn't you be going away too with mouth shut, because you didn't want to get talked about to your disadvantage? And wouldn't you at last dismiss the whole thing as a foolish delusion, in the belief that living in out-of-the-way parts like these cuts a man off from the world, breeds maggots in the mind?

"I assure you, sir, they don't—not even Canon Ockham himself to the full—they don't believe even me. And yet, when they have their meetings of the Chapter, they talk and wrangle round and round about nothing else. I can bear the other without a murmur. What God sends, I say, we humans deserve. We have laid ourselves open to it. But when you buttress up blindness and wickedness with downright folly, why then, sir, I sometimes fear for my own reason."

He set his shoulders as square as his aged frame would permit, and with fingers clutching the lapels beneath his chin, he stood gazing out into the darkness through that narrow inward window.

"Ah, sir," he began again, "I have not spent sixty years in this solitary place without paying heed to my own small wandering thoughts and instincts. Look at your newspapers, sir. What they call the Great War is over—and he'd be a brave man who would take an oath before heaven that *that* was only of human designing —and yet what do we see around us? Nothing but strife and juggleries and hatred and contempt and discord wherever you look. I am no scholar, sir, but so far as my knowledge and experience carry me, we human beings are living to-day what ought to have been done yesterday, and yet are at a loss to know what's to be done to-morrow.

"And the Church, sir. God forbid I should push my way into what does not concern me; and if you had told me half an hour gone by that you were a regular churchman, I shouldn't be pouring out all this to you now. It wouldn't be seemly. But being not so gives me confidence. By merely listening you can help me, sir; though you can't help *us*. Centuries ago—and in my humble judgment, rightly—we broke away from the parent stem and rooted ourselves in our own soil. But, right or wrong, doesn't that of itself, I ask you, make us all the more open to attack from him who never wearies in going to and fro in the world seeking whom he may devour?

"I am not wishing you to take sides. But a gentleman doesn't scoff; you don't find him jeering at what he doesn't rightly understand. He keeps his own counsel, sir. And that's where, as I say, Canon Leigh Shougar sets me doubting. He refuses to make allowances; though up there in London things may look different. He gets his company there; and then for him the whole kallyidoscope changes, if you take me."

The old man scanned me an instant as if inquiring within himself whether, after all, I too might not be one of the outcasts. "You see, sir," he went on dejectedly, "I can bear what may be to come. I can, if need be, live on through what few years may yet remain to me and keep going, as they say. But only if I can be assured that my own inmost senses are not cheating and misleading me. Tell me the worst, and you will have done an old man a service he can never repay. Tell me, on the other hand, that I am merely groping along in a network of devilish *delusion,* sir—well, in that case I hope to be with my master, with Dr. Pomfrey, as soon as possible. We were all children once; and now there's nothing worse in this world for him to come into, in a manner of speaking.

"Oh, sir, I sometimes wonder if what we call childhood and growing up isn't a copy of the fate of our ancient forefathers. In the beginning of time there were Fallen Angels, we are told; but even if it weren't there in Holy Writ, we might have learnt it of our own fears and misgivings. I sometimes find myself looking at a young child with little short of awe, sir, knowing that within its mind is a scene of peace and paradise of which we older folk have no notion, and which will fade away out of it, as life wears in, like the mere tabernacling of a dream."

There was no trace of unction in his speech, though the phraseology might suggest it, and he smiled at me as if in reassurance. "You see, sir—if I have any true notion of the matter—then I say, Heaven is dealing very gently with Dr. Pomfrey. He has gone back, and, I take it, his soul is elsewhere and at rest."

He had come a pace or two nearer, and the candlelight now cast grotesque shadows in the hollows of his brows and cheekbones, silvering his long scanty hair. The eyes, dimming with age, were fixed on mine as if in incommunicable entreaty. I was at a loss to answer him.

He dropped his hands to his sides. "The fact is," he looked cautiously about him, "what I am now being so bold as to suggest, though it's a familiar enough experience to me, may put you in actual physical danger. But then, duty's duty, and a deed of kindness from stranger to stranger quite another matter. You seem to have come, if I may say so, in the nick of time: that was all. On the other hand we can leave the building at once if you are so minded. In any case we must be gone well before dark sets in; even mere human beings are best not disturbed at any night work they may be after. The dark brings recklessness: conscience cannot see as clear in the dark. Besides, I once delayed too long myself. There is not much of day left even now, though I see by the almanac there should be a slip of moon to-night—unless the sky is overclouded. All that I'm meaning is that our all-in-all, so to speak, is the calm untrammelled evidence of the outer senses, sir. And there comes a time when—well, when one hesitates to trust one's own."

I have read somewhere that it is only its setting—the shape, the line, the fold, the angle of the lid and so on—that gives its finer shades of meaning and significance to the human eye. Looking into his, even in that narrow and melancholy illumination, was like pondering over a grey, salt, desolate pool—such as sometimes neighbours the sea on a flat and dangerous coast.

Perhaps if I had been a little less credulous, or less exhausted, I should by now have begun to doubt this old creature's sanity. And yet, surely, at even the faintest contact with the insane, a sentinel in the mind sends up flares and warnings; the very landscape changes; there is a sense of insecurity. If, too, the characters inscribed by age and experience on a man's face can be evidence of goodness and simplicity, then my companion was safe enough. To trust in his sagacity was another matter.

But then, there was All Hallows itself to take into account. That first glimpse from my green headland of its louring yet lovely walls had been strangely moving. There are buildings (almost as though they were once copies of originals now half-forgotten in the human mind) that have a singular influence on the imagination. Even now in this remote candlelit room, immured between its massive stones, the vast edifice seemed to be gently and furtively fretting its impression on my mind.

I glanced again at the old man: he had turned aside as if to leave me, unbiased, to my own decision. How would a lifetime spent between these sombre walls have affected *me,* I wondered. Surely it would be an act of mere decency to indulge their worn-out hermit! He had appealed to me. If I were ten times more reluctant to follow him, I could hardly refuse. Not at any rate without risking a retreat as humiliating as that of the architectural experts he had referred to—with my tail between my legs.

"I only wish I could hope to be of any real help."

He turned about; his expression changed, as if at the coming of a light. "Why, then, sir, let us be gone at once. You are with me, sir; that was all I hoped and asked. And now there's no time to waste."

He tilted his head to listen a moment—with that large, flat, shell-like ear of his which age alone seems to produce. "Matches and candle, sir," he had lowered his voice to a whisper, "but—though we mustn't lose each other; you and me, I mean—*not,* I think, a naked light. What I would suggest, if you have no objection, is your kindly grasping my gown. There is a kind of streamer here, you see—as if made for the purpose. There will be a good deal of up-and-downing, but I know the building blind-fold and as you might say inch by inch. And now that the bell-ringers have given up ringing it is more in my charge than ever."

He stood back and looked at me with folded hands, a whimsical childlike smile on his aged face. "I sometimes think to myself I'm like the sentry, sir, in that play of William Shakespeare's. I saw it, sir, years ago, on my only visit to London—when I was a boy. If ever there was a villain for all his fine talk and all, commend me to that ghost. I see him yet."

Whisper though it was, a sort of chirrup had come into his voice, like that of a cricket in a baker's shop. I took tight hold of the velveted tag of his gown. He opened the door, pressed the box of safety matches into my hand, himself grasped the candle-stick, and then blew out the light. We were instantly marooned in an impenetrable darkness. "Now, sir, if you would kindly remove your walking shoes," he muttered close in my ear, "we should proceed with less noise. I shan't hurry you. And please to tug at the streamer if you need attention. In a few minutes the blackness will be less intense."

As I stooped down to loose my shoe-laces I heard my heart thumping merrily away. It had been listening to our conversation apparently! I slung my shoes round my neck—as I had often done as a boy when going paddling—and we set out on our expedition.

I have endured too often the nightmare of being lost and abandoned in the stony bowels of some strange and prodigious building to take such an adventure lightly. I clung, I confess, desperately tight to my lifeline, and we groped steadily onward—my guide ever and again turning back to mutter warning or encouragement in my ear.

Now I found myself steadily ascending; and then in a while, feeling my way down flights of hollowly worn stone steps, and anon brushing along a gallery or corkscrewing up a newel staircase so narrow that my shoulders all but touched the walls on either side. In spite of the sepulchral cold in these bowels of the cathedral, I was soon suffocatingly hot, and the effort to see became intolerably fatiguing. Once, to recover our breath, we paused opposite a slit in the thickness of the masonry, at which to breathe the tepid sweetness of the outer air. It was faint with the scent of wild flowers and cool of the sea. And presently after, at a barred window, high overhead, I caught a glimpse of the night's first stars.

We then turned inward once more, ascending yet another spiral staircase. And now the intense darkness thinned a little, the groined roof above us becoming faintly discernible. A fresher air softly fanned my cheek; and then trembling fingers groped over my breast, and, cold and bony, clutched my own.

"Dead still here, sir, if you please." So close sounded the whispered syllables the voice might have been a messenger's within my own consciousness. "Dead still, here. There's a drop of some sixty or seventy feet a few paces on."

I peered out across the abyss, conscious, as it seemed, of the huge superincumbent weight of the noble fretted roof only a small space now immediately above our heads. As we approached the edge of this stony precipice, the gloom paled a little, and I guessed that we must be standing in some coign of the southern transept, for what light the evening skies now afforded was clearer towards the right. On the other hand, it seemed the northern windows opposite us were most of them boarded up, or obscured in some fashion. Gazing out, I could detect scaffolding poles—like knitting needles—thrust out from the walls and a balloon-like spread of canvas above them. For the moment my ear was haunted by what appeared to be the droning of an immense insect. But this presently ceased. I fancy it was internal only.

"You will understand, sir," breathed the old man close beside me—and we still stood, grotesquely enough, hand in hand—"the scaffolding over there has been in position a good many months now. It was put up when the last gentleman came down from London to inspect the fabric. And there it's been left ever since. Now, sir!—though I implore you to be cautious."

I hardly needed the warning. With one hand clutching my box of matches, the fingers of the other interlaced with my companion's, I strained every sense. And yet I could detect not the faintest stir or murmur under that wide-spreading roof. Only a hush as profound as that which must reign in the Royal Chamber of the pyramid of Cheops faintly swirled in the labyrinths of my ear.

How long we stayed in this position I cannot say; but minutes sometimes seem like hours. And then, without the slightest warning, I became aware of a peculiar and incessant vibration. It is impossible to give a name to it. It suggested the remote whirring of an enormous millstone, or that—though without definite pulsation—of revolving wings, or even the spinning of an immense top.

In spite of his age, my companion apparently had ears as acute as mine. He had clutched me tighter a full ten seconds before I myself became aware of this disturbance of the air. He pressed closer. "Do you see that, sir?"

I gazed and gazed, and saw nothing. Indeed even in what I had seemed to hear I might have been deceived. Nothing is more treacherous in certain circumstances—except possibly the eye—than the ear. It magnifies, distorts, and may even invent. As instantaneously as I had become aware of it, the murmur had

ceased. And then—though I cannot be certain—it seemed the
dingy and voluminous spread of canvas over there had perceptibly
trembled, as if a huge cautious hand had been thrust out to draw
it aside. No time was given me to make sure. The old man had
hastily withdrawn me into the opening of the wall through which
we had issued; and we made no pause in our retreat until we had
come again to the narrow slit of window which I have spoken of
and could refresh ourselves with a less stagnant air. We stood
here resting awhile.

"Well, sir?" he inquired at last, in the same flat muffled tones.

"Do you ever pass along here alone?" I whispered.

"Oh, yes, sir. I make it a habit to be the last to leave—and often
the first to come; but I am usually gone by this hour."

I looked close at the dim face in profile against that narrow
oblong of night. "It is so difficult to be sure of oneself," I said.
"Have you ever actually *encountered* anything—near at hand, I
mean?"

"I keep a sharp look-out, sir. Maybe they don't think me of
enough importance to molest—the last rat, as they say."

"But *have* you?"—I might myself have been communicating
with the phantasmal *genius loci* of All Hallows—our muffled
voices; this intense caution and secret listening; the slight breathlessness, as if at any instant one's heart were ready for flight: "But
have you?"

"Well, yes, sir," he said. "And in this very gallery. They nearly
had me, sir. But by good fortune there's a recess a little further on
—stored up with some old fragments of carving, from the original
building, sixth-century, so it's said: stone capitals, heads and
hands, and suchlike. I had had my warning, and managed to
leap in there and conceal myself. But only just in time. Indeed,
sir, I confess I was in such a condition of terror and horror I
turned my back."

"You mean you heard, but didn't look? And—something
came?"

"Yes, sir, I seemed to be reduced to no bigger than a child, huddled up there in that corner. There was a sound like clanging
metal—but I don't think it was metal. It drew near at a furious

speed, then passed me, making a filthy gust of wind. For some instants I couldn't breathe; the air was gone."

"And no other sound?"

"No other, sir, except out of the distance a noise like the sounding of a stupendous kind of gibberish. A calling; or so it seemed —no human sound. The air shook with it. You see, sir, I myself wasn't of any consequence, I take it—unless a mere obstruction in the way. But—I have heard it said somewhere that the rarity of these happenings is only because it's a pain and torment and not any sort of pleasure for such beings, such apparitions, sir, good or bad, to visit our outward world. That's what I have heard said; though I can go no further.

"The time I'm telling you of was in the early winter—November. There was a dense sea-fog over the valley, I remember. It eddied through that opening there into the candlelight like flowing milk. I never light up now: and, if I may be forgiven the boast, sir, I seem to have almost forgotten how to be afraid. After all, in any walk of life a man can only do his best, and if there weren't such opposition and hindrances in high places, I should have nothing to complain of. What is anybody's life, sir (come past the gaiety of youth), but marking time? . . . Did you hear anything *then,* sir?"

His gentle monotonous mumbling ceased and we listened together. But every ancient edifice has voices and soundings of its own: there was nothing audible that I could put a name to, only what seemed to be a faint perpetual stir or whirr of grinding such as (to one's over-stimulated senses) the stablest stones set one on top of the other with an ever slightly-varying weight and stress might be likely to make perceptible in a world of matter. A world which, after all, they say, is itself in unimaginably rapid rotation, and under the tyranny of time.

"No, I hear nothing," I answered: "but please don't think I am doubting what you say. Far from it. You must remember I am a stranger, and that therefore the influence of the place cannot but be less apparent to me. And you have no help in this now?"

"No, sir. Not now. But even at the best of times we had small

company hereabouts, and no money. Not for any substantial out-
lay, I mean. And not even the boldest suggests making what's
called a public appeal. It's a strange thing to me, sir, but whenever the newspapers get hold of anything, they turn it into a byword and a sham. Yet how can they help themselves?—with no
beliefs to guide them and nothing to stay their mouths except
about what for sheer human decency's sake they daren't talk
about. But then, who am I to complain? And now, sir," he continued with a sigh of utter weariness, "if you are sufficiently rested,
would you perhaps follow me on to the roof? It is the last visit I
make—though by rights perhaps I should take in what there is
of the tower. But I'm too old now for that—clambering and climbing over naked beams; and the ladders are not so safe as they
were."

We had not far to go. The old man drew open a squat heavily-
ironed door at the head of a flight of wooden stairs. It was latched
but not bolted, and admitted us at once to the leaden roof of the
building and to the immense amphitheatre of evening. The last
faint hues of sunset were fading in the west; and silver-bright
Spica shared with the tilted crescent of the moon the serene
lagoon-like expanse of sky above the sea. Even at this height, the
air was audibly stirred with the low lullaby of the tide.

The staircase by which we had come out was surmounted by a
flat penthouse roof about seven feet high. We edged softly along,
then paused once more; to find ourselves now all but *tête-à-tête*
with the gigantic figures that stood sentinel at the base of the but-
tresses to the unfinished tower.

The tower was so far unfinished, indeed, as to wear the appearance of the ruinous; besides which, what appeared to be scars and
stains as if of fire were detectable on some of its stones, reminding me of the legend which years before I had chanced upon,
that this stretch of coast had more than once been visited centuries
ago by pillaging Norsemen.

The night was unfathomably clear and still. On our left rose
the conical bluff of the headland crowned with the solitary grove
of trees beneath which I had taken refuge from the blinding sunshine that very afternoon. Its grasses were now hoary with faintest
moonlight. Far to the right stretched the flat cold plain of the

Atlantic—that enormous darkened looking-glass of space; only a distant lightship ever and again stealthily signalling to us with a lean phosphoric finger from its outermost reaches.

The mere sense of that abysm of space—its waste powdered with the stars of the Milky Way; the mere presence of the stony leviathan on whose back we two humans now stood, dwarfed into insignificance beside these gesturing images of stone, were enough of themselves to excite the imagination. And—whether matter-of-fact or pure delusion—this old verger's insinuations that the cathedral was now menaced by some inconceivable danger and assault had set my nerves on edge. My feet were numb as the lead they stood upon; while the tips of my fingers tingled as if a powerful electric discharge were coursing through my body.

We moved gently on—the spare shape of the old man a few steps ahead, peering cautiously to right and left of him as we advanced. Once with a hasty gesture he drew me back and fixed his eyes for a full minute on a figure—at two removes—which was silhouetted at that moment against the starry emptiness: a forbidding thing enough, viewed in this vague luminosity, which seemed in spite of the unmoving stare that I fixed on it to be perceptibly stirring on its wind-worn pedestal.

But no; "All's well!" the old man had mutely signalled to me, and we pushed on. Slowly and cautiously; indeed, I had time to notice in passing that this particular figure held stretched in its right hand a bent bow, and was crowned with a high weather-worn stone coronet. One and all were frigid company. At last we completed our circuit of the tower, had come back to the place we had set out from, and stood eyeing one another like two conspirators in the clear dusk. Maybe there was a tinge of incredulity on my face.

"No, sir," murmured the old man, "I expected no other. The night is uncommonly quiet. I've noticed that before. They seem to leave us at peace on nights of quiet. We must turn in again and be getting home."

Until that moment I had thought no more of where I was to sleep or to get food, nor had even realized how famished with hunger I was. Nevertheless, the notion of fumbling down again out of the open air into the narrow inward blackness of the

walls from which we had just issued was singularly uninviting.
Across these wide flat stretches of roof there was at least space for
flight, and there were recesses for concealment. To gain a moment's respite, I inquired if I should have much difficulty in
getting a bed in the village. And as I had hoped, the old man
himself offered me hospitality.

I thanked him; but still hesitated to follow, for at that moment
I was trying to discover what peculiar effect of dusk and darkness
a moment before had deceived me into the belief that some small
animal—a dog, a spaniel, I should have guessed—had suddenly
and surreptitiously taken cover behind the stone buttress near by.
But that apparently had been a mere illusion. The creature, whatever it might be, was no barker at any rate. Nothing stirred now;
and my companion seemed to have noticed nothing amiss.

"You were saying," I pressed him, "that when repairs—restorations—of the building were in contemplation, even the experts
were perplexed by what they discovered? What did they actually
say?"

"Say, sir!" Our voices sounded as small and meaningless up
here as those of grasshoppers in a noonday meadow. "Examine
that balustrade which you are leaning against at this minute.
Look at that gnawing and fretting—that furrowing above the
lead. All that is honest wear and tear—constant weathering of the
mere elements, sir—rain and wind and snow and frost. That's
honest *nature*-work, sir. But now compare it, if you please, with
this St. Mark here; and remember, sir, these images were intended to be part and parcel of the fabric as you might say,
sentries on a castle—symbols, you understand."

I stooped close under the huge grey creature of stone until my
eyes were scarcely more than six inches from its pedestal. And,
unless the moon deceived me, I confess I could find not the
slightest trace of fret or friction. Far from it. The stone had been
grotesquely decorated in low relief with a gaping crocodile—a
two-headed crocodile; and the angles, knubs, and undulations of
the creature were cut as sharp as with a knife in cheese. I drew
back.

"Now cast your glance upwards, sir. Is that what you would
call a saintly shape and gesture?"

What I took to represent an eagle was perched on the image's lifted wrist—but louring and vulture-like. The head of the figure was poised at an angle of defiance—the ears unnaturally high up on the skull; the lean right forearm extended with pointing forefinger as if in derision. Its stony gaze was fixed upon the stars; its whole aspect was undeniably sinister and intimidating. The faintest puff of milk-warm air from over the sea stirred on my cheek. I drew aside.

"Ay, sir, and so with one or two of the rest of them," the old man commented, as he watched me, "there are other wills than the Almighty's."

At this, the pent-up excitement within me broke bounds. This nebulous insinuatory talk!—I all but lost my temper. "I can't, for the life of me, understand what you are saying," I exclaimed in a voice that astonished me with its shrill volume of sound in that intense lofty quiet. "One doesn't *repair* in order to destroy."

The old man met me without flinching. "No, sir? Say you so? And why not? Are there not two kinds of change in this world? —a building-up and a breaking-down? To give strength and endurance for evil or misguided purposes, would that be time wasted, if such was your aim? Why, sir, isn't that true even of the human mind and heart? We here are on the outskirts, I grant, but where would you expect the activity to show itself unless in the outer defences? An institution may be beyond dying, sir: it may be being restored for a worse destruction. And a hundred trumpeting voices would make no difference when the faith and life within is tottering to its fall."

Somehow, this muddle of metaphors reassured me. Obviously the old man's wits had worn a little thin: he was the victim of an intelligible but monstrous hallucination.

"And yet you are taking it for granted," I expostulated, "that, if what you say is true, a stranger could be of the slightest help. A visitor—mind you—who hasn't been inside the doors of a church, except in search of what is old and gone, for years."

The old man laid a trembling hand upon my sleeve. The folly of it—with my shoes hanging like ludicrous millstones round my neck!

"If you please, sir," he pleaded, "have a little patience with me.

I'm preaching at nobody. I'm not even hinting that them outside the fold circumstantially speaking aren't of the flock. All in good time, sir; the Almighty's time. Maybe—with all due respect—it's from them within we have most to fear. And indeed, sir, believe an old man: I could never express the gratitude I feel. You have given me the occasion to unbosom myself, to make a clean breast, as they say. All Hallows is my earthly home, and—well, there, let us say no more. You couldn't *help me*—except only by your presence here. God alone knows who can!"

At that instant, a dull enormous rumble reverberated from within the building—as if a huge boulder or block of stone had been shifted or dislodged in the fabric; a peculiar grinding nerve-racking sound. And for the fraction of a second the flags on which we stood seemed to tremble beneath our feet.

The fingers tightened on my arm. "Come, sir; keep close; we must be gone at once," the quavering old voice whispered; "we have stayed too long."

But we emerged into the night at last without mishap. The little western door, above which the grinning head had welcomed me on my arrival, admitted us to *terra firma* again, and we made our way up a deep sandy track, bordered by clumps of herb agrimony and fennel and hemlock, with viper's bugloss and sea-poppy blooming in the gentle dusk of night at our feet. We turned when we reached the summit of this sandy incline and looked back. All Hallows, vague and enormous, lay beneath us in its hollow, resembling some natural prehistoric outcrop of that sea-worn rock-bound coast; but strangely human and saturnine.

The air was mild as milk—a pool of faintest sweetnesses—gorse, bracken, heather; and not a rumour disturbed its calm, except only the furtive and stertorous sighings of the tide. But far out to sea and beneath the horizon summer lightnings were now in idle play—flickering into the sky like the unfolding of a signal, planet to planet—then gone. That alone, and perhaps too this feeble moonlight glinting on the ancient glass, may have accounted for the faint vitreous glare that seemed ever and again to glitter across the windows of the northern transept far beneath. And yet how easily deceived is the imagination. This old man's talk still echoing in my ear, I could have vowed this was no reflection but the glow of some light shining fitfully from within outwards.

The old man paused beside a flowering bush of fuchsia at the wicket gate leading into his small square of country garden. "You'll forgive me, sir, for mentioning it; but I make it a rule as far as possible to leave all my troubles and misgivings outside when I come home. My daughter is a widow, and not long in that sad condition, so I keep as happy a face as I can on things. And yet: well, sir, I wonder at times if—if a personal sacrifice isn't incumbent on them that have their object most at heart. I'd go out myself very willingly, sir, I can assure you, if there was any certainty in my mind that it would serve the cause. It would be little to me if—" He made no attempt to complete the sentence.

On my way to bed, that night, the old man led me in on tiptoe to show me his grandson. His daughter watched me intently as I stooped over the child's cot—with that birdlike solicitude which all mothers show in the presence of a stranger.

Her small son was of that fairness which almost suggests the unreal. He had flung back his bedclothes—as if innocence in this world needed no covering or defence—and lay at ease, the dews of sleep on lip, cheek, and forehead. He was breathing so quietly that not the least movement of shoulder or narrow breast was perceptible.

"The lovely thing!" I muttered, staring at him. "Where is he now, I wonder." His mother lifted her face and smiled at me with a drowsy ecstatic happiness, then sighed.

And from out of the distance there came the first prolonged whisper of a wind from over the sea. It was eleven by my watch, the storm after the long heat of the day seemed to be drifting inland; but All Hallows, apparently, had forgotten to wind its clock.

The Connoisseur and Other Stories (1926)

THE WHARF

SHE gave a critical pat or two to the handsome cherry bow, turning her head this way then that, as she did so; pulled balloonishly out its dainty loops; then once more twisted round the small figure with its dark little face and dancing burning eyes, and scanned the home-made party frock from in front.

"What does it *look* like, mother?" the small creature cried in the voice of a mermaid: then tucked in her chin like a preening swan to see herself closer. The firelight danced from the kitchen range. There was an inch of snow on the sill of the window, and the evergreen leaves of the bushes of euonymus beyond bore each its platterful of woolly whiteness.

"Please, mother. What does it look like?" the chiming voice repeated; "my frock?"

With that wearer within it, it looked for all the world like the white petals of a flower; its flashing crimson fruit just peeping out from beneath. It looked like spindle-tree blossom and spindle berries both together. And the creature inside danced up and down with the motion of a bird on its claws, at sight, first, of the grave intentness and ardour and love in its mother's eyes; and next, in expectation of the wonderful party, which was now floating there in the offing like a ship in full sail upon the enormous ocean.

"Then I look nice, mother, nice, nice, nice?" she cried. And her mother smiled with half-closed eyes, just as if she were drinking up a tiny little glass of some strange far-fetched wine.

"You are my precious one," she said, still gazing at her. "And you will be *very* good? And eat just a little at a time, and not get over-excited?"

"Oh dear, oh dear," cried the mite, her dark face turning aside in dismay like a tiny cloud from the sunrise; "they won't never, never be done dressing."

"There, now, be still, my dear," her mother pleaded. "You mustn't excite yourself. Why, there they are, you see, coming down the stairs."

And when the three—the two elder fair ones and this—were safely off, she returned to the fire, knelt down to poke it into a blaze, and then reclining softly back upon her heels, remained there awhile, quite still—brooding on a distant day indeed.

Something had reminded her of a scene—a queer little scene when you came to think of it, but one she would never forget, though she seldom had even the time to brood over it. And now there was one whole long hour of peace and solitude before her. She was with herself. It was a scene, even in this distant retrospect entangled, drenched, in a darkness which, thank Heaven, she could only just vaguely recall. To return back even in thought into that would be like going down into a coal-mine. Worse; for "nerves" have other things to frighten one with than merely impenetrable darkness. The little scene itself, of course, quite small now because so far away, had come afterwards. It shone uncommonly like a star on a black winter night. And yet not exactly winter; for cold wakens the body before putting it to sleep. And that time was like the throes of a nightmare in a hot still huge country—a country like Africa; enormous and sinister and black.

And so, piece by piece, as it had never returned to her before, she explored the whole beginning of that strange experience. She remembered kneeling as she was now, half sitting on her heels, and looking into a fire. A kitchen fire, then, as now; though not this kitchen. And not winter, but early May. And behind her the two elder children were playing, in their blue overalls, the fair hair gently shimmering in the napes of their necks as they stooped over their toys. It was, of course, before this house, before tiny Nell had come—dark and different from her two quiet sisters. And yet—good gracious me, how strange things are!

As now at this moment, she had been alone in that kitchen, even though the children were there. And alone as she had never been before. It seemed as though she had come to the end of things—a vacant abyss. Her husband had gone on to his work after having been with her to the doctor. She remembered that doctor—a taciturn, wide-faced man, who had listened to her symptoms without the least change of countenance, just steadily fixing his grey eyes on her face. Still, however piercing their attention, and whatever the symptoms, they could only have guessed at the horror within.

And then her husband had brought her home again, and after consoling her as best he could, had gone off late and anxious to his work, leaving her in utter despair. She must go away at once into the country, the doctor had said, and go away without company: must leave everything and rest. Rest! She had hated the very thought of the country: its green fields, its living things, and the long days and evenings with nothing to do; and then the nights! Even though a farm was the very place in the world she would have wished to have been born in, to live in, and there to die, she would be more than ever at the mercy there of those horrors within. And country people can stare and pry, too. They despise Londoners.

The extraordinary thing was that though her husband had reeled off to the doctor, as if he had learned it all by heart, as if he wanted to get rid of it once and for all, the long list of her symptoms, the one worst symptom of them all he had never had the faintest glimpse of. His pale face, that queer frown between his eyebrows, and the odd uncertain way in which he had moved his mouth as he was speaking, though they showed that, though he was talking by rote, or, rather, talking just as men do, with the one idea of making himself clear and business-like, were yet proof too of what he was feeling. But not a single word he had said had touched her inmost secret. He hadn't an inkling that her awful state, body and soul, was centred on *him*.

She could smile to herself now to think what contortions the body may twist itself into when anything goes wrong in the mind. That detestation of food, those dizzying moments when you twirl helplessly on a kind of vacant devilish merry-go-round; that repetition of one thought on and on like a rat in a cage; those forebodings rising up one after the other like clouds out of the sea in an Arabian tale. Why, she had had symptoms enough for every patent medicine there was. She smiled again at thought of her portrait appearing in the advertisements in the newspapers for pills and tonics, her hand clutching the small of her back, or clamped over a knotted forehead.

Still, though she quite agreed now, and had almost agreed then, that it had been wise to see the doctor, and though she agreed now beyond all telling that she owed him what was infinitely more precious even than life itself; still she hadn't breathed to her husband one word about that dream; not a word. And never would. Not even if she lay dying, and if its living horror came to her then again—though it never would—in the hope of crushing her once for all, utterly and for ever.

It was something no one could tell anybody. There were vile things enough in the world for every one to read and share, but this was one not even a newspaper could print, simply because she supposed no one could realize except herself how abject, how unendurable it was. Perhaps this was because it was a dream, she wondered. Dreams are more terrible than anything that happens in the day, in the real world.

A gentle quietude had descended upon her face lit up by the firelight there. It was as if the very thought of a dream had endued it with the expression of sleep. Nor, of course, was there anything to harm her now. This was yet another mystery concerning the life one's spirit lives in a dream, in sleep. The worst of haunting dreams may lose not only its poison, its horror, it may even lose its meaning, just as dreams of happiness and peace, in the glare and noise of day, may lose the secret of their beauty. Not that *this* particular dream had ever lost its meaning. It had kept its meaning, though what came after had completely changed it—turned it outside in, so to speak.

And now, since she was sane and "normal" again, just the mother of her three children, with her work to do, and able to do it—the meanings did not seem really to matter very much. You must just live on, she was thinking to herself, and do all you have to do, and not push about or pierce too much into your hidden mind. Leave it alone; you will be happier so. Griefs come of themselves. They break in like thieves, destroying as they go. No need to seek *them* out, anticipate *them*!

But what a mercy her husband had been the kind of man he was—so patient over those horrible symptoms, so matter-of-fact. It was absurd of the doctor to try to hurry him on, to get testy. Clever people are all very well, but if her husband had been clever or conceited he would have noticed she was keeping something back—might have questioned her. And then she would have been beyond hope—crazy.

And that, of course, put one face to face with the unanswerable question: Was what she had seen real? *Was* there such a place? Were there such dreadful beings? After all, places you could not see had real existence—think of the vast mountainous forests of the world and the deserts and all their horrors! And perhaps after death? . . . For a while the white-faced clock on the wall overhead, hanging above the burnished row of kitchen tins, ticked out its seconds, without so much as one further thought passing in her mind. The room was deliciously warm; all the familiar things in it were friendly. This was home. And in an hour or two her husband would return to it; and a little later their three girls: the two fair ones, with the little dark creature—tired probably and a little fretful—between them. And life would begin again.

She was happy now. But thinking too much was unwise. That had really been at the root of her Uncle Willie's malady. He could not rest, and then had become hopelessly "silly"—then, his "visitors!" What a comfort to pretend for a moment to be like one of those empty jugs on the dresser; or, rather, not quite empty but with a bunch of flowers in one! And a fresh bunch every day. If you remain empty, ideas come creeping in—as sleep, too, one's mind is empty, waiting for dreams to well in. It is always dangerous—leaving doors ajar.

And so—she had merely come round to the same place once more. But now, and for the first time since that visit to the country, she could afford to face the whole experience. It was surprising how its worst had evaporated. It had begun in the March by her being just "out of sorts," overtired and fretful. But she had got better. And then, while she was going up to bed that night—seven years ago now—her candle had been blown out by a draught from the dark open landing window. Nothing of consequence had happened during the evening. Her husband had been elated by a letter from an old friend of his bachelor days, and she herself had been doing needlework. And yet, this absurd little accident to her candle had resembled the straw too many on the camel's back.

It had seemed like an enemy—that puff of wind: as if a spectre had whispered, "Try the dark!" And she had sat down there on the stairs in the gloom and had begun to cry. Without a sound the burning tears had slowly rolled down her cheeks as if from the very depths of her life. "So *this* was the meaning of everything!" they seemed to tell her. "It is high time you were told." The fit was quickly over. The cold air at the landing window had soothed her, and in a moment or two she had lit her candle again, and, as if filled with remorse, had looked in on her two sleeping children, and after kissing them, gone on to bed.

And it was in the middle of that night her dream had come. After stifling in her pillow a few last belated sobs, lest her husband should hear her, she had fallen asleep. And she had dreamed that she was standing alone on the timbers of a kind of immense Wharf, beside a wide sluggish stream. There was no moon, and there were no stars, so far as she could remember, in the sky. Yet all around her was faintly visible. The water itself as if of its own slow moving darkness, seemed to be luminous. She could see that darkness as if by its own light: or rather was conscious of it, as if all around her was taking its light from herself. How absurd!

The wharf was built on piles that plunged down into the water and into the slime beneath. There were flights of stone steps on the left, and up there, beyond, loomed what appeared to be immense unwindowed buildings, like warehouses or granaries, but these she could not see very plainly. Confronting her, further down the wharf, and moored to it by a thick rope, floated on the river a huge and empty barge. There was a wrapped figure stooping there, where the sweeps jut out, as if in profound sleep. And above the barge, on the wharf itself, lay a vague irregular mass of what apparently had come out of the barge.

It was at the spectacle of the mere shape of this foul mass, it seemed, that she had begun to be afraid. It would have horrified her even if she had been alone in the solitude of the wharf—even in the absence of the gigantic apparition-like beings who stood round about it; busy with great shovels, working silently in company. They, she realized, were unaware of her presence. They laboured on, without speech, intent only on their office. And as she watched them she could not have conceived it was possible to be so solitary and terrified and lost.

There was no Past in her dream. She stood on this dreadful wharf, beside this soundless and sluggish river under the impenetrable murk of its skies, as if in an eternal Present. And though she could scarcely move for terror, some impulse within impelled her to approach nearer to discover what these angelic yet horrifying shapes were at. And as she drew near enough to them to distinguish the faintly flaming eyes in their faces, and the straight flax-coloured hair upon their heads, even the shape of their enormous shovels, she became aware of yet another presence standing close beside her, more shadowy than they, more closely resembling her own phantom self.

But though it was beyond her power to turn and confront it, it seemed that by its influence she realized what cargo the barge had been carrying up the stream and had disgorged upon the wharf. It was a heap, sombre and terrific, of a kind of refuse. The horror of this realization shook her even now, as she knelt there, the flames of the kitchen fire lighting up her fair blond face. For, as if through a whisper in her consciousness from the companion that stood beside her—she knew that this refuse was the souls of men; the souls not of utterly vile and evil men (if such there were; and no knowledge was given to her of where *their* souls lay or where the blessed) but of ordinary nondescript men, "wayfaring men, though fools." Yet nothing but what seemed to be a sublime indifference to their laborious toil and to its object showed on the faces of the labourers on the wharf.

Perhaps if there had been any speech among them, or if any sound—no more earthly than echo in her imagination—of their movements had reached her above the flowing of that vast dark stealthy stream, and above the scrapings of the timbers of the shovels, almost as large as those used in an oast-house, she would have been less afraid.

But this unfathomable silence seemed to intensify the gloom as she watched; every object there became darker yet more sharply outlined, so that she could see more clearly, up above, the immense steep-walled warehouses. For now *their* walls too seemed to afford a gentle luminosity. And one thought only was repeating itself again and again in her mind: The souls, the souls, of men! *The souls, the souls, of men!*

And then, beyond human heart to bear, the secret messenger beside her let fall into consciousness another seed of thought. She realized that her poor husband's soul was there in that vast nondescript heap; and those of loved-ones gone, wayfarers, friends of her childhood, her girlhood, and of those nearer yet, valueless, neglected—being shovelled away by these gigantic, angelic beings. "Oh, my dear, my dear," she was weeping within. And, as with afflicted lungs and bursting temples she continued to gaze, suddenly out of the nowhere of those skies, two or three angle-winged birds swooped down and alighting in greed near by, covertly watched the toilers.

And one, bolder than the rest, scurried forward on scowering wing, and leapt back into the air burdened with its morsel out of that accumulation. The sight of it pierced her being in this eternity as if that morsel were her own. And suddenly one of the shapes, and not an instant too soon, had lifted its shovel, brandishing it on high above his head, with a shrill resounding cry—"Harpy!"

The cry shattered the silence, reverberated on and on, wharf, warehouse, starless arch, and she had awakened: had awakened to her small homely bedroom. It was bathed as if with beauty by the beams of the night-light that shone on a small table beside her bed where used to sleep her three-year-old. It was safety, assurance, peace; and yet unreal. Unreal even her husband —his simple face perfectly still and strange in sleep—lying quietly beside her. And she—lost amid the gloom of her own mind.

Tell *that* dream—never, never! But yet now in this quiet firelight, so many cares over—and, above all, that dreary entanglement of the mind a thing of the past—what alone still kept the dream a secret was not so much its horror, but its shame. The shame not only that she should have dreamed such a dream, but that she should as it were have seen only its horror and had become its slave.

To have believed in such a doom; to have supposed that God . . . But she could afford to smile indulgently now at this weakness and cowardice and infidelity. She could afford it simply because of Mr. Simmonds, the farmer. That was the solemn, the really-and-truly amusing truth. It was that rather corpulent, short, red-faced Mr. Simmonds who had been responsible for the very happiest moment in her life: who had saved her, had saved far more even than her "reason."

Her husband, of course, knew how much they owed to his kindness. But he did not know that he owed Mr. Simmonds her very heart's salvation, if that was not a conceited way of putting it. And yet it was this Mr. Simmonds—she laughed softly out loud as she gazed on into the fire—it was this Mr. Simmonds who had at first sight, in his old brown coat and mud-caked gaiters, reminded her of a potato! Of a potato and then an apple, one of those cobbled apples, their bright red faded a little and the skin drawn up. His smile was like that, as dry as it was sweet like cider.

What an interminable Sunday that had been before her husband and the two children had said good-bye to her at the railway station. How that man in spectacles had stared at her over his newspaper. Then the ride in the trap, her roped box behind, and Mrs. Simmonds, and the farm. Two or three times a day at least she had rushed out in imagination to drown everything in the looking-glass-like pond among the reeds not very far from the farm. And yet all the time, though Mrs. Simmonds knew she was "queer," she could not possibly have guessed, while she was talking to her of an evening in the parlour, the things that were flaring and fleering in her mind like the noises and sights of a fair.

The doctor had said—looking at her very steadily: "But you won't, you must remember, be really much alone, because you will have your home and your children to think of. You will have them. Think as little as possible about everything else. Just rest, and be looked after."

The consequence of which had been the suspicion that she was being not merely "looked after" but watched. And she would openly pretend to set out from the farm in another direction when she was bent on looking once more at her reflection in the pond. None the less she had remembered what the doctor had said, had held on to it almost as if it had been a bag she was carrying and must keep safe. And by-and-by in the hayfields, in the lanes by the hedges, she had begun to be a quieter companion to herself and even glad of Mrs. Simmond's company, and of talking to her plump brown-haired daughter, or to the pale skimpy dairy-maid.

It was curious though that, while passing the opening in the farm wall she had never failed to cast a glance towards that dark distant mound with its flowers beyond the yard, she had never really noticed it. She had seen it, even admired its burden, but not definitely attended to it. It had taken her fancy and yet not her eye. She had been far less conscious of it, for example, than of the pretty Jersey heifer that was sometimes there, and even of the tortoise-shell cat, and the cocks and hens, and of the geese in the green meadow.

All these she saw with an extraordinary clearness, as if she were looking at them from out of a window in a strange world. They quieted her mind without her being aware of it, and she would talk of them to Mrs. Simmonds partly because she was interested to hear about them; partly to keep her in the room; and partly so that she might think of other things while the farmer's wife was talking. Of other things indeed!—when first and foremost, like a huge louring storm-cloud on the horizon of a sea, there never left her mind for a single moment the memory and influence of her dream. It would sweep back on her, so much distorting her face and clouding her eyes that she would be compelled to turn her head away out of the glare of the parlour lamp, in case Mrs. Simmonds should notice it.

And then came that calm, sunlit afternoon. She had had quiet sleep the night before. It had been her first night at the farm untroubled by sudden galvanic leaps into consciousness and by the swarming cries and phantom faces that appeared as soon as her tired-out eyes hid themselves from the tiny radiance of the night-light.

She had been for a walk—yes, and to the reed-pond—and had there promised her absent husband and her two children never to go there again unless she could positively bear herself no longer. She had promised; and, quieted in mind, she was coming back. She remembered even thinking with pleasure of the home-made jam that Mrs. Simmonds would give her for her tea.

There was no doubt at all, then, that she had been getting better—just as before (when the dream came) she had been really, though secretly, getting worse. And as she was turning in home by the farm-gate, she saw Nellie, the heifer, there; the nimble young fawn-haired creature, with its delicate head and lustrous eyes with their long lashes; and she had advanced in her silly London fashion, with a handful of coarse grass, to make real friends with her. The animal had sidled away and then had trotted off into the farmyard, and she had followed it with an unusual effort of will.

The sun was pouring its light in abundance out of the west on the whitewashed walls and stones and living creatures in the yard; midges in the air, wagtails, chaffinches in the golden straw, a wren scolding, a cart-horse in reverie at the gate, and the deep black-shadowed holes of the byres and stables.

Still eluding her, Nellie had edged across the yard; and it was then that, lifting her eyes beyond the retreating creature, she had caught sight of that mound, now near at hand, and had realized what it was. She had realized what it was almost as if because her dream had instantly returned with it, almost as if the one thing were the "familiar" of the other. But the horror now was more distant. She could not even (more than vaguely, like reflection in water) see those shapes with the shovels simply because what she now saw in actuality was so vivid and lovely a thing. It was a heap of old stable manure; and it must have lain there where it was for a very long time, since it was strayed over in every direction, and was lit up with the tufted colours of at least a dozen varieties of wild flowers. Her glance wandered to and fro from bell to bell and cup to cup; the harsh yet sweet

odour of the yard and stables was in her nostrils: that of hay
was in the air; and into the distance stretched meadow and
field under the sky, their crops sprouting, their green deepening.

And as she stood, densely gazing at this heap, she herself
it had seemed became nothing more than that picture in her
eyes. And then Mr. Simmonds had come out and across the
yard, his flannel shirt-sleeves tucked up above his thick sunburned arms, and a pitchfork in his hand. He had touched his
hat with that almost schoolboyish little gentle grin of his; then
when he noticed that she was trying to speak to him, had stood
beside her, leaning on his pitchfork, his glance following the
direction of her eyes.

For a moment or two she had been unable to utter a syllable
for sheer breathlessness, and had turned her face aside a little
under its wide-brimmed hat, stammering on, and then almost
whispering, as if she were a mere breath of wind and he a dense
deep-rooted oak tree. But he had caught the word "flowers"
easily enough.

There must have been at least a score of varieties on that
foster-mothering heap; complete little families of them: silver,
cream, crimson, rose-pink, stars and cups and coronals, and a
most marvellous green in their leaves, all standing still together
there in the windless ruddying light of the sun. And Mr. Simmonds had told her a few of their country names, the very
sounds of them like the happy things themselves.

She had explained how exquisitely fresh they looked—not
like street-flowers—though she supposed of course that to him
they were mere waste—just "wild" flowers.

And he had replied, with his courteous "ma'ams" and those
curiously bright blue eyes of his in his plain plump face, that
it was no wonder they flourished there. And as for being "waste,"
why, they were kind of enjoying themselves, he supposed, and
welcome to it.

He had been amused, too, in an almost courtly fashion at her
disjointed curious questions about the heap. It was just "stable-
mook"; and the older that is, of course, the better. It would be
used all right some time, he assured her. The wild flowers, pretty
creatures, wouldn't harm it; not they. They'd fade by the winter

and *become* it. Some were what they called annuals, he explained, and some perennials. The birds brought the seeds in
their droppings, or the wind carried them, or the roots just
wandered about of themselves. You couldn't keep them out of
the fields! That was another matter. You see there you had other
things to mind. And with that charlock over there! . . .

And still she persisted, struggling as it were in the midst of
the dream vaguely hanging its shrouds in her mind, as if towards
a crevice of light to come out by. And Mr. Simmonds had been
patience and courtesy itself. He had told her about the various
chemical manures they used on the crops. That was one thing.
But there was, she gathered, what was called "nature" in *this*
stuff. It was not exactly the very life of the flowers, for that came
you could not tell whence, it is the "virtue" in it. It and the rain
and the dew was just as much and as little their life-blood—
their sap—as the drink and victuals of humans and animals are.
"If you starve a lad, ma'am, keep him from his victuals, he don't
exactly flourish, do he?"

Oh yes, he agreed such facts were strange, and, as you might
say almost unknowledgeable. A curious thing, too, that what to
some seems just filth and waste and nastiness should be the very
secret of all that is most precious in the living things of the
world. But then, we don't all think alike; " 't wouldn't do, d'ye
see?" Why, he had explained and she had listened to him as
quietly as a child at school, the roots of a tree will bend at right
angles after the secret waters underneath. He crooked his forefinger to show her how. And the groping hair-like filaments
of the shallowest weed would turn towards a richer food in the
soil. "We farmers couldn't do without it, ma'am." If the nature's
out of a thing, it is as good as dead and gone, for ever. Wasn't
it now the "good-nature" in a human being that made him what
he was? That and what you might call his very life. "Look at
Nellie, there! Don't her just comfort your eye in a manner of
speaking?"

And whether it was Mr. Simmond's words, or the way he
said them, as if for her comfort—and they were as much a part
and parcel of his own good-nature as were his brown hairy
arms and his pitchfork and the creases on his round face; or

whether it was just the calm copious gentle sunshine that was
streaming down on them from across the low heavens, and on
the roofs and walls of the yard, and on that rich brown-and
golden heap of stable manure with its delicate colonies of live
things shedding their beauty on every side, nodding their heads
in the lightest of airs; she could not tell. At that very moment
and as if for joy a red cock clapped his wings on the midden, and
shouted his *Qui vive*.

At this, a whelming wave of consolation and understanding
seemed to have enveloped her very soul. Mr. Simmonds may
have actually seen the tears dropping from her eyes as she
turned to smile at him, and to thank him. She didn't mind.
It was nothing in the world in her perhaps that he would ever
be able to understand. He would never know, never even guess
that he had been her predestined redemption.

For a while they had stood there in silence, like figures in a
picture. Nellie had long since wandered off, grazing her way
across the meadow. She had now joined the other cows, though
she herself was but a heifer, and had not yet calved or given
milk. How "out of it" a Londoner was in country places! Her
very love of it was a kind of barrier between herself and Mr.
Simmonds.

And yet, not an impassable one. Knowing that she was "ill,"
and being a "family man," and sympathetic, he had understood
a little. She had at last hastened away into the house; and
shutting her door on herself, had flung herself down at her
bedside, remaining there on her knees, with nothing in the
nature of a thought in her mind, not a word on her lips; conscious
of no more than an incredibly placid vacancy and the realization
that the worst was over. . . .

The kitchen fire had lapsed into a brilliant glow, unbroken by
any flame. Her lids smarted; she had stared so long without
blinking into its red. She must have been kneeling there for
hours, thus lost in memory. Her glance swept up in dismay to
the clock; and at that instant she heard the scraping of her
husband's latch-key in the lock—and his evening meal not even
so much as laid yet!

She sprang to her feet and, stumbling a little because one of them had "gone to sleep," met him in the doorway. "I am late," she breathed into his shoulder, putting her arms round his neck with an intensity of greeting that astonished even his familiar knowledge of her. "But there were the children to get off. And then I just sat down there by the fire a minute. Jim: don't think I'm never thankful. You were kind to me that time I was ill. Kinder than ever you can possibly think or imagine. But we won't say anything about that."

Her arms slipped down to her sides; a sort of absentness spread itself over her faintly-lit features, her cheeks flushed by the fire. "I've been daydreaming—just thinking: *you* know. How queer things are! Can you really believe that that Mr. Simmonds is at the farm *now,* this very moment?" Her voice sank lower. "It's all snow; and soon it will be getting dark; and the cows have been milked; and the fields are fading away out of the light; and the pond with the reeds. . . . It's still; like a dream and now . . ."

And her husband, being tireder than usual that afternoon, cast a rather dejected look at the empty table. But he spoke up bravely: "And how did the youngsters get off? They must have been a handful!"

He smoothed her smooth hair with his hand. But she seemed still too deeply immerged and far-lost in her memory of the farm to answer for a moment, and then her words came as if by rote.

"'A handful'? They *were*—and that tiny thing!—I am sometimes, you know, Jim, almost afraid of those wild spirits—as if she might—just burst into tiny pieces—into bits some day—like glass. It's such a world to have to be careful in!"

The Connoisseur and Other Stories (1926)

THE ORGY: AN IDYLL

IT WAS a Wednesday morning, and May-day, and London, its West End too, crisp, brisk, scintillating. Even the horses had come out in their Sunday best. With their nosegays and ribbons and rosettes they might have been on their way to a wedding—the nuptials of Labour and Capital, perhaps. As for people, the wide pavements of the great street were packed with them. Not so many busy idlers of the one sex as of the other, of course, at this early hour—a top-hat here, a pearl-grey Homburg there; but of the feminine a host as eager and variegated as the butterflies in an Alpine valley in midsummer; some stepping daintily down from their landaulettes like "Painted Ladies" out of the chrysalis, and thousands of others, blues and browns and speckleds and sables and tawnies and high-fliers and maiden's blushes, from all parts of the world and from most of the suburbs, edging and eddying along, this way, that way, their eyes goggling, their tongues clacking, but most of them, their backs to the highway, gazing, as though mesmerized, in and in through the beautiful plate-glass windows at the motley merchandise on the other side. And much of that on the limbs and trunks of beatific images almost as lifelike but a good deal less active than themselves.

The very heavens, so far as they could manage to peep under the blinds, seemed to be smiling at this plenty. Nor had they any need for care concerning the future, for nursemaids pushing their baby-carriages before them also paraded the pavements, their infant charges laid in dimpled sleep beneath silken awning

and coverlet, while here and there a tiny tot chattered up into
the air like a starling.

A clock, probably a church clock, and only just audible,
struck ten. The sun from its heights far up above the roof-tops
blazed down upon the polished asphalt and walls with such an
explosion of splendour that it looked as if everything had been
repainted overnight with a thin coat of crystalline varnish and
then sprinkled with frozen sea-water. And every human creature
within sight seemed to be as heart-free and gay as this beautiful
weather promised to be brief. With one exception only—poor
Philip Pim.

And why not? He was young—so young in looks, indeed,
that if Adonis had been stepping along at his side they might
have been taken for cousins. He was charmingly attired, too,
from his little, round, hard felt hat—not unlike Mercury's usual
wear, but without the wings—to his neat brogue shoes; and he
was so blond, with his pink cheeks and flaxen hair, that at first
you could scarcely distinguish his silken eyebrows and eyelashes,
though thay made up for it on a second glance. Care seemed to
never have sat on those young temples. Philip looked as harmless as he was unharmed.

Alas! this without of his had no resemblance whatever to his
within. He eyed vacantly a buzzing hive-like abandonment he
could not share; first, because though he had the whole long day
to himself he had no notion of what to do with it; and next,
because only the previous afternoon the manager of the bank
in which until then he had had a stool specially reserved for him
every morning, had shaken him by the hand and had wished him
well—for ever. He had said how deeply he regretted Philip's
services could not be indulged in by the bank any longer. He
would miss him. Oh yes, very much indeed—but missed Philip
must be.

The fact was that Philip had never been able to add up pounds,
shillings, and pence so that he could be certain the total was
correct. His 9's, too, often looked like 7's, his 5's like 3's. And
as "simple addition" was all but his sole duty in the bank, he
would not have adorned its premises for a week if his uncle,
Colonel Crompton Pim, had not been acquainted with one of

its most stylish directors, and was not in the habit of keeping a large part of his ample fortune in its charge. He had asked Mr. Bumbleton to give Philip a chance. But chances—some as rapidly as Manx cats—come to an end. And Philip's had.

Now, if Colonel Pim had sent his nephew when he was a small boy to a nice public school, he might have been able by this time to do simple sums very well indeed. Philip might have become an accurate adder-up. It is well to look on the bright side of things. Unfortunately when Philip was an infant, his health had not been very satisfactory—at least to his widowed mother—and he had been sent instead to a private academy. There a Mr. Browne was the mathematical master—a Mr. Browne so much attached to algebra and to reading *The Times* in school hours that he hadn't much patience with the rudiments of arithmetic. "Just add it up," he would say, "and look up the answer. And if it isn't right, do it again."

It was imprudent of him, but in these early years poor Philip had never so much as dreamed that some day he was going to be a clerk on a stool. If he had, he might not perhaps have been so eager to look up the answers. But then, his uncle was fabulously rich and yet apparently unmarriageable, and Philip was his only nephew. Why, then, should he ever have paid any attention to banks, apart from the variety on which the wild thyme grows?

Term succeeded term, and still, though "a promising boy," he remained backward—particularly in the last of the three R's. And his holidays, so called, would be peppered with such problems as (*a*) if a herring and a half cost three halfpence, how many would you get for a shilling? (*b*) If a brick weighs a pound and a half a brick, how much does it weigh? (*c*) If Moses was the son of Pharaoh's daughter, etc.; and (*d*) Uncles and brothers have I none, and so on. And since, after successive mornings with a sheet of foolscap and a stub of pencil, Philip's answers would almost invariably reappear as (*a*) 18; (*b*) 1½lb.; (*c*) his sister, and (*d*) himself, Colonel Pim grew more and more impatient, and Nature had long ago given him a good start.

He had a way, too, when carpeting poor Philip, of flicking his shepherd-plaid trouser-leg with his handkerchief, which seemed useless to everyone concerned. And at least, instead of transferring his nephew from Mr. Browne to Christ Church, Oxford, or to Trinity College, Cambridge, or to some less delectable resort at an outlying university, he first (before setting out in pursuit of big game all around the world) consigned him to a tutor, who thanked his lucky stars the expedition would take the Colonel a long time; and, on his return, gave them both a prolonged vacation.

And *then* had fallen the bolt from the blue. On the morning of his twenty-first birthday, which had promised to be so cool, so calm, so bright, Philip received a letter from his uncle. He opened it with joy; he read it with consternation. It was in terms as curt as they looked illegible, and it was merely to tell him that what the Colonel called a post (but which was, in fact, a high stool) had been secured for his nephew, and that unless Philip managed to keep his seat on it for twelve consecutive months he would be cut off with a shilling.

Of these drear months about two and a half had somehow managed to melt away, and now not only was the stool rapidly following them into the limbo of the past, but at this very moment the Colonel was doubtless engaged, and with his usual zest, in keeping his promise. What wonder, then, Philip was not exactly a happy young man as he wandered this sunny populous May morning aimlessly on his way. There was nothing— apart from Everything around him—to make him so, except only one minute stroke of luck that had befallen him before breakfast.

When he had risen from his tumbled bed in his London lodgings, the sight of his striped bank trousers and his black bank coat and waistcoat had filled him with disgust. Opening the grained cupboard which did duty for a wardrobe—and in the indulgence of his tailor it was pretty full—he took down from a peg the festive suit he was now wearing, but which otherwise he had left unheeded since Easter. He found himself faintly whistling as he buttoned it on; but his delight can be imagined when, putting his finger and thumb into an upper waistcoat pocket, he discovered —a sovereign. And an excellent specimen of one, with St. George in his mantle and the dragon on the one side of it, and King Edward VII's head—cut off at the neck as if he had sat to its designer in his bath—on the other. This, with four others very much like it, had been bestowed on Philip many months ago by his Uncle Charles—a maternal uncle, who had since perished in Paris. As the rest of Philip's pockets contained only 7½d. in all, this coin—how forgotten, he simply could not conjecture—was treasure trove indeed.

Now, poor Philip had never really cared for money. Perhaps he had always associated it with herrings and half-bricks. Perhaps he had never needed it quite enough. Since, moreover, immediately opposite his perch at the bank there hung a framed antique picture of this commodity in process of being shovelled out of receptacles closely resembling coal-scuttles into great vulgar heaps upon a polished counter, and there weighed in brass scales like so much lard or glucose, he had come to like it less and less. On the other hand, he dearly enjoyed spending it. As with Adam and the happy birds in the Garden of Eden—linnet and kestrel and wren —he enjoyed seeing it fly. In this he was the precise antithesis of his uncle.

Colonel Crompton Pim loved money. He exulted in it (not vocally, of course) *en masse,* as the Pharaohs exulted in pyramids. And he abhorred spending it. For this (and for many another) reason he had little affection for mere objects—apart, that is, from *such* objects as golf clubs, shooting boots, or hippopotamus-hoof inkstands—and he had not the smallest pleasure in buying anything for mere buying's sake.

His immense dormitory near Cheltenham, it is true, was full of furniture, but it was furniture, acquired in the 'sixties or thereabouts, for use and not for joy. Prodigious chairs with pigskin seats; tables of a solidity that defied time and of a wood that laughed at the worm; bedsteads of the Gog order; wardrobes resembling Assyrian sarcophagi; and ottomans which would seat with comfort and dignity a complete royal family. As for its "ornaments," they came chiefly from Benares.

And simply because poor Philip delighted in spending money and hated impedimenta such as these with the contempt a humming-bird feels for the corpse of a rhinoceros, he had never been able to take to his uncle—not even for the sake of what he owned. And it was impossible—as he fondly supposed—for any human being to take to him for any other reason. No, there was nothing in common between them, except a few branches of the family tree. And these the Colonel might already have converted into firewood.

Now, as poor Philip meandered listlessly along the street, fingering his Uncle Charles's golden sovereign in his pocket, he came on one of those gigantic edifices wherein you can purchase anything in the world—from a white elephant to a performing flea, from a cargo of coconuts to a tin-tack. This was the "store" at which his uncle "dealt." And by sheer force of habit, Philip mounted the welcoming flight of steps, crossed a large flat rubber mat, and went inside.

Having thus got safely in, he at once began to ponder how he was to get safely out—with any fraction, that is, of his golden sovereign still in his pocket. And he had realized in the recent small hours that with so little on earth now left to spend, except an indefinite amount of leisure, he must strive to spend that little with extreme deliberation.

So first, having breakfasted on a mere glance at the charred remnant of a kipper which his landlady had served up with his chicory, he entered a large gilded lift, or elevator, as the directors preferred to call it, *en route* to the restaurant. There he seated himself at a vacant table and asked the waitress to be so kind as to bring him a glass of milk and a bun. He nibbled, he sipped, and he watched the people—if people they really were, and not, as seemed more probable, automata intended to advertise the Ecclesiastical, the Sports, the Provincial, the Curio, the Export, and the Cast-Iron Departments.

With his first sip of milk he all but made up his mind to buy a little parting present for his uncle. It would be at least a gentle gesture. With his second he decided that the Colonel would be even less pleased to receive a letter, *and,* say, a velvet smoking-cap, or a pair of mother-of-pearl cuff-links, than just a letter. By the time he had finished his bun he had decided to buy a little something for himself. But try as he might he could think of nothing (for less than a guinea) that would be worthy of the shade of his beloved Uncle Charles. So having pushed seven fifteenths of all he else possessed under his plate for his freckled waitress, with the remaining fourpence he settled his bill and went steadily downstairs. Nineteen minutes past ten—he would have a good look about him before he came to a decision.

Hunger, it has been said, sharpens the senses, but it is apt also to have an edgy effect upon the nerves. If, then, Philip's breakfast had been less exacting, or his lunch had made up for it, he might have spent the next few hours of this pleasant May morning as a young man should—in the open air. Or he might have visited the British Museum, the National Gallery, and Westminster Abbey. He might never, at any rate, in one brief morning of his mortal existence have all but died again and again of terror, abandon, shame, rapture, and incredulity. He might never—but all in good time.

He was at a loose end, and it is then that habits are apt to prevail. And of all his habits, Philip's favourite was that of ordering "goods" on behalf of his uncle. The Colonel in his fantastic handwriting would post him two weekly lists—one consisting of the "wanted," the other of complaints about the previous week's "supplied." Armed with these, Philip would set out for the building he was now actually in. The first list, though not a thing of beauty, was a joy as long as it lasted. The second, for he had always flatly refused to repeat his uncle's sulphurous comments to any underling, he reserved for his old enemy, the secretary of the establishment, Sir Leopold Bull. And though in these weekly interviews Sir Leopold might boil with rage and chagrin, he never boiled over. For the name of Pim was a name of power in the secretary's office. The name of Pim was that of a heavy shareholder; and what the Colonel wanted he invariably in the long run got. A chest, say, of Ceylon tea, "rich, fruity, bright infusion"; a shooting-stick (extra heavy, Brugglesdon tube pattern); a quart size tantalus, for a wedding present, with a double-spring sterling-silver Brahmin lock; a hundredweight of sago; a stymie, perhaps, or a click—something of that sort.

These "order days" had been the balm of Philip's late existence. His eyes fixed on his ledger and his fancy on, say, "Saddlery," or "Sports," he looked forward to his Wednesdays—thirsted for them. Indeed, his chief regret at the bank, apart from little difficulties with his 9's and 3's, had been that his uncle's stores were closed on Saturday afternoons. And on Sundays. His hobby had, therefore, frequently given him indigestion, since he could indulge it only between 1 and 2 p.m. It was a pity, of course, that Colonel Pim was a man of wants so few, and those of so narrow a range. Possibly the suns of India had burned the rest out of him. But for Philip, any kind of vicarious purchase had been better than none. And now these delights, too, were for ever over. His fountain had run dry. Sir Leopold had triumphed.

At this moment he found himself straying into the Portmanteau and Bag Department. There is nothing like leather, and here there was nothing *but* leather, and all of it made up into articles ranging in size from trunks that would hold the remains of a Daniel Lambert to card-cases that would hold practically nothing at all. And all of a sudden Philip fancied he would like to buy a cigarette-case. He would have preferred one of enamel or gold or morocco or tortoise-shell or lizard or shagreen; or even of silver or suède. But preferences are expensive. And as he sauntered on, his dreamy eye ranging the counters in search merely of a cigarette-case he could *buy,* his glance alighted on a "gent's dressing-case."

It was of pigskin, and it lay, unlike the central figure in Rembrandt's "Lesson in Anatomy," so that the whole of its interior was in full view, thus revealing a modest row of silver-topped bottles, similiar receptacles for soap, toothbrushes, hair-oil, and Eau de Cologne; a shoe-horn, a boot-hook, an ivory paper-knife, and hair brushes, "all complete." Philip mused on it for a moment or two, perplexed by a peculiar effervescence that was going on in his vitals. He then approached the counter and asked its price.

"The price, sir?" echoed the assistant, squinnying at the tiny oblong of pasteboard attached by a thread to the ring of the handle; "the price of that article is seventeen, seventeen, six."

He was a tubby little man with boot-button eyes, and his snort, Philip thought, was a trifle unctuous.

"Ah," he said, putting a bold face on the matter, "it looks a sound workaday bag. A little mediocre perhaps. Have you anything—less ordinary?"

"Something more expensive, sir? Why, yes, indeed. This is only a stock line—the 'Archdeacon' or 'Country Solicitor' model. We have prices to suit all purposes. Now if you were thinking of something which you might call resshersy, sir"—and Philip now was—"there's a dressing-case under the window over there was specially made to the order of Haitch Haitch the Maharaja of Jolhopolloluli. Unfortunately, sir, the gentleman deceased suddenly a week or two ago; climate, I understand. His funeral obliquies were in the newspaper, you may remember. The consequence being, his ladies not, as you might say, concurring, the dressing-case in a manner of speaking is on our hands—and at a considerable reduction. Only six hundred and seventy-five guineas, sir; or rupees to match."

"May I look at it?" said Philip. "Colonel Crompton Pim."

"By all means, sir," cried the little man as if until that moment he had failed to notice that Philip was a long-lost son; "Colonel Crompton Pim; of course. Here is the article, sir, a very handsome case, and quite unique, one of the finest, in fact, I have ever had the privilege of handling since I was transferred to this Department—from the Sports, sir."

He pressed a tiny knob, the hinges yawned, and Philip's mouth began to water. It was in sober sooth a handsome dressing-case, and the shaft of sunlight that slanted in on it from the dusky window seemed pleased to be exploring it. It was a dressing-case of tooled red Levant morocco, with gold locks and clasps and a lining of vermilion watered silk, gilded with a chaste design of lotus flowers, peacocks, and houris, the "fittings" being of gold and tortoise-shell, and studded with so many minute brilliants and seed pearls that its contents, even in that rather dingy sunbeam, appeared to be delicately on fire.

Philip's light-blue eyes under their silken lashes continued to dwell on its charms in so spellbound a silence that for a moment the assistant thought the young man was about to swoon.

"Thank you very much," said Philip at last, turning away with infinite reluctance and with a movement as graceful as that of a fawn, or of a *première danseuse* about to rest; "I will keep it in mind. You are sure the management can afford the reduction?"

Having made this rather airy comment, it seemed to Philip impolite, if not impossible, to ask the price of a "job line" of mock goatskin cigarette-cases that were piled up in dreary disorder on a tray near at hand. So he passed out into the next department, which happened to be that devoted to goods described as "fancy," though, so far as he could see, not very aptly.

Still he glanced around him as he hurried on, his heart bleeding for the unfortunates, old and helpless, or young and defenceless, doomed some day to welcome these exacerbating barbarous jocosities as gifts. But at sight of an obscure, puffy, maroon object demonstratively labelled "Pochette: Art Nouveau," his very skin contracted, and he was all but about to inquire of a large veiled old lady with an ebony walking stick who was manfully pushing her way through this *mélange,* possibly in search of a *prie-dieu,* how such dreadful phenomena were "begot, how nourished," and was himself preparing to join in the chorus, when a little beyond it his glance alighted on a minute writing-case, so frailly finished, so useless, so delicious to look at, handle, and smell, that even Titania herself might have paused to admire it. Philip eyed it with unconcealed gusto. His features had melted into the smile that so often used to visit them when as a little boy he had confided in his Uncle Charles that he preferred éclairs to doughnuts. Its price, he thought, was ridiculously moderate: only £67 10s.

"It's the décor, sir—Parisian, of course—that makes it a trifle costly," the assistant was explaining. "But it's practical as well as sheek and would add distinction to *any young* lady's boudoir, bedchamber, or lap. The ink, as you see, sir, cannot possibly leak from the bottle, if the case, that is, is held the right way up—so. The pencil, the 'Sans Merci,' as you observe, is of solid gold; and the pen, though we cannot guarantee the nib, is set with life-size turquoises. The flaps will hold at least six sheets of small-size notepaper, and envelopes to—or not to—match. And *here* is a little something, a sort of calendar, sir, by which you can tell the day of the week of any day of the month in any year in any century from one A.D. to nine hundred and ninety-nine thousand, nine hundred and ninety-nine. It could then be renewed."

"M'm, very ingenious," Philip murmured, "and even Leap Year, I see. Is it unique, and so on?"

"No doubt of it, sir. As a matter of fact a lady from Philadelphia—the United States of America, sir—ordered fifty facsillimies, platinum mounts, of this very article—only yesterday afternoon; they get married a good deal over there, sir; wedding presents."

"Quite, thank you, no," said Philip, firmly but pleasantly. "They say there is safety in numbers, but there seems to be precious little else. Have you anything less reproducible?"

"Reproducible, sir? Why, naturally, sir. You see this is only a counter article. While catering for the many, sir, we are bound to keep an eye upon the few. For that very reason, the management prefer to have the costlier specimens under cover."

"Again, thank you," said Philip hurriedly. "What evils are done in thy name, O Philadelphia! I may return later."

He emerged from the Fancy Goods Department, feeling at the same moment crestfallen and curiously elated. His mind, in fact, at this moment resembled a volcano the instant before its gloom is fated to burst into a blazing eruption. Though very hazily, he even recognized the danger he was in. So in hope to compose himself he sat down for a minute or two on a Madeira wicker chair intended perhaps by the management for this very purpose, and found himself gazing at a large black Chinese cat, in the glossiest of glazed earthenware, and as lifelike as Oriental artifice could make it. It was seated in a corner under a high potted palm, and it wore a grin upon its features that may have come from Cheshire, but which showed no symptom whatever of vanishing away. At sight of it—for Philip was not only partial to cats but knew the virtues of the black variety— a secret fibre seemed to have snapped in his head. "Good luck!" the creature smirked at him. And Philip smirked back. A flame of anguished defiance and desire had leapt up in his body. He would show his uncle what was what. He would learn him to cut nephews off with shillings. He would dare and do and die!

He rose, refreshed and renewed. It was as if he had tossed off a bumper of "Veuve Clicquot" of 1066. He must himself have come over with the Conqueror. A shopwalker lurking near was interrupted in the middle of an enormous gape by the spectacle of this Apollonian young figure now entering his department— Pianofortes and American Organs. There was something in the leopard-like look of him, something so princely and predatory in his tread, that this Mr. Jackson would have been almost ready to confess that he was moved. Frenchily dark and Frenchily sleek, he bowed himself almost double.

"Yes, sir?" he remarked out loud.

"I want, I think, a pianoforte," said Philip. "A Grand."

"Thank you, sir; this way, please. Grand pianofortes, Mr. Smithers."

"I want a Grand piano," repeated Philip to Mr. Smithers, an assistant with a slight cast in his left eye and an ample gingerish moustache. But in spite of these little handicaps Philip liked him much better than Mr. Jackson. A far-away glimpse of Mrs. Smithers and of all the little Smitherses seated round their Sunday leg of mutton at Hackney or at Brondesbury, maybe, had flashed into his mind.

"Grands, sir," cried Mr. Smithers, moving his moustache up and down with a curious rotary constriction of the lips; "this way, please."

The young man was conducted along serried ranks of Grands. They stood on their three legs, their jaws tight shut, as mute as troops on parade. Philip paced on and on, feeling very much like the late Duke of Cambridge reviewing a regiment of his Guards. He paused at length in front of a "Style 8; 7 ft. 9 in., square-legged, black-wood, mahogany-trimmed Bismarck."

"It *looks* spacious," he smiled amiably. "But the finish! And why overhung?"

"Overstrung, sir?" said Mr. Smithers. "That's merely a manner of speaking, sir, relating solely to its inside. But this, of course, is not what we specificate as a *grand* Grand. For tone and timber and resonance and pedal work and solidity and *wear*—there isn't a better on the market. I mean on the rest of the market. And if you were having in mind an everlasting instrument for the nursery or for a practice room—and we supply the new padded partitioning—this would be precisely the instrument, sir, you were having in mind. The young are sometimes a little hard on piano-fortes, sir. They mean well, but they are but children after all; and—"

"Now let—me—think," Philip interposed. "To be quite candid, I wasn't having anything of that sort in mind. My sentiments are English for the English; and Bismarck, you know, though in girth and so on a remarkable man, was in other respects, a little—well, miscellaneous. It is said that he mixed his champagne with stout—or was it cocoa? On the other hand, I have no wish to be insular, and I *may* order one of these constructions later—for a lady: the niece, as a matter of fact, of a governess of my uncle Colonel Crompton Pim's when he was young—as young at least as it was possible for him to be—who is, I believe, thinking of taking—of taking in—pupils. But we will see to that later. Have you anything that I could really look at?"

Mr. Smithers's moustaches twirled like a weathercock. "Why, yes, sir. Just now we are up to our eyes in pianos—flooded; and if I may venture to say so, sir, Bismarck was never no friend of *mine*. All this," and he swept his thumb in the direction of the avenue of instruments that stretched behind them, "they may be Grands, but they're most of them foreign, and if you want a little some-thing as nice to listen to as it is natty to look at, and *not* a mere menadjery fit only for an 'awl, there is a little what they call a harpsichord over yonder, sir. It's a bijou model, de Pompadour case, hand-painted throughout—Cupids and scallops and what not, all English gut, wire, metal, and jacks, and I defy any dealer in London to approximate it, sir, in what you might call pure form. No noise and all music, sir, and that *mellow* you scarcely know where to look. A lady's instrument—a titled lady's. And only seven hundred and seventy-seven guineas, sir, all told."

"Is it unique?" Philip inquired.

"Unique, Sir? There's not another like it in Europe."

Philip smiled at Mr. Smithers very kindly out of his blue eyes. "But what about America?" he said.

The assistant curved what seemed an almost unnecessarily large hand round his lips. "Between you and me, sir, if by America," he murmured, "you're meaning the United States, why, Messrs. Montferas & de Beauguyou refuse to ship in that direction. It ruins their tone. In fact, sir, they are what's called *difficult*. They make for nobody and nowhere but as a favour; and that instrument over there was built for—!"

He whispered the sesame so low that water rustling on a pebbled beach would have conveyed to Philip tidings more intelligible. But by the look in Mr. Smithers's eye Philip guessed that the lady in question moved in a lofty, though possibly a narrow, circle.

"Ah!" he said; "then that settles it. A home away from home. Charity begins there. I shall want it to-morrow. I shall want them both to-morrow. I mean the pianos. And perhaps a more democratic instrument for the servants' hall. But I will leave that to you."

Mr. Smithers pretended not to goggle. "Why, yes, sir, that can be easily arranged. In London, I *ho*—conjecture?"

"In London," said Philip, "Grosvenor Square." For at that very instant, as if at the summons of a jinnee, there had wafted itself into his memory the image of a vacant and "highly desirable residence," which his casual eye had glanced upon only the afternoon before, and which had proclaimed itself "to be let."

"Grosvenor Square, sir; oh yes, Sir?" Mr. Smithers was ejaculating, order-book in hand. "I will arrange for their removal at once. The three of them—quite a nice little set, sir."

"Pim, Crompton, Colonel," chanted Philip. "R-*O*-M; deferred account; *thank* you. 4-4-4, yes, four hundred and forty-four, Grosvenor Square. I am—that is, *we* are furnishing there."

But his gentle emphasis on the "we" was so courtly in effect that it sounded more like an afterthought than a piece of information. Nevertheless it misled Mr. Smithers. Intense fellow-feeling beamed from under his slightly overhung forehead. "And I am sure, sir, if I may make so bold, I wish you both every happiness. I am myself of a matrimonial turn. And regret it, sir? *never!* I always say if every—"

"That's very kind indeed of you," said Philip, averting his young cheek, which having flushed had now turned a little pale. "And if *I* may be so bold, I am perfectly certain Mrs. Smithers is of the same way of thinking. Which is the best way to the Best Man's Department, if I take in Portmanteaux and the Fancies on my way?"

Mr. Smithers eyed him with the sublimest admiration. "Straight through, sir, on the left beyond them Chappels. On the same floor, but right out on the farther side of the Building. As far as you can go."

"That is exactly what I was beginning to wonder—precisely how far I can go. This little venture of mine is a rather novel experience, and at the moment I am uncertain of its issue. But tell me, why is it our enterprising American friends have not yet invented a *lateral* lift?"

"Now that's passing strange, too, sir; for I've often fancied it myself," said Mr. Smithers. "But you see in a department like this there's not much time for quiet thought, sir, with so much what you might call hidden din about. As a matter of fact, when I was younger, sir—and that happens to us all—I did invent a harmonium key-stifler—rubber, and pith, and wool—*so*—and a small steel spring, quite neat and entirely unnoticeable. But the manufacturers wouldn't look at it; not they!"

"I don't believe," said Philip, folding up his bill, "they ever look at anything. Not closely, you know. But if ever I do buy a harmonium," he put his head a little on one side and again smiled at Mr. Smithers, "I shall insist on the stifler. I suppose," he added reflectively, "you haven't by any chance a nice pedigree Amati or Stradivarius in stock? I have a little weakness for fiddles."

Mr. Smithers, leaning heavily on the counter on both his thumbs, smiled, but at the same time almost imperceptibly shook his head.

"I fancied it was unlikely," said Philip. "What's that over there; in the glass case, I mean?"

"That, sir?" said Mr. Smithers, twinkling up, "in that glass case there? That's a harp, sir. And a lovely little piece *that* is. Child's size, sir. What they call minnychoore, and well over a century old, but still as sweet as a canary. It was made, so they say, for Mozart, the composer, sir, as you might be aware, in 1781, and up in the top corner is scratched the letters A. W. No doubt of it, sir—A. W. I've seen a picture of the mite myself playing like an angel in his nightcap, and not a day over seven; you'd hardly believe it, and his parents coming in at the door. Surprising. Then Schumann, *he* had it, sir—I mean the harp; and Schumann, though I don't know how he could dissuade himself to part with it, *he* passed it on to Brahms, another composer—and very much thought of even though a bit nearer *our* day. But you'll find it all neatly set out on the brass label at the foot. It's all there, sir. There's many a custo—"

"Indeed!" said Philip; "Brahms, Schumann, Mozart, what scenes we are recalling! And here it rests at last. The knacker's yard. How very, very sad. Why, of course, Mr. Smithers, we must have that sent on too—and packed very, very carefully. Is the glass case extra?"

Mr. Smithers gulped. "I am exceedingly sorry, sir," he said, "exceedingly sorry, but it's not for sale; I mean—*except* the case."

"Not for sale," retorted Philip impulsively. "But what is the use, Mr. Smithers, of a mercenary institution like this unless everything in it is for sale? You cannot mean for raw advertisement?"

Mr. Smithers was covered with confusion. "I am sure, sir," he said, "that the directors would do their utmost to consider your wishes. They would be very happy to do so. But if you will excuse my mentioning it, I should myself very much miss that harp. I have been in this department thirteen years now. . . . My little boy . . . It is the only thing . . ."

It was Philip's turn to be all in confusion. "Good gracious me, I quite understand," he said; "not another word, Mr. Smithers. I wouldn't *think* of pressing the point. None the less I can assure you that even if it *had* been for sale I should always have welcomed you whenever you cared to come to Grosvenor Square and take another look at it. And, of course, your little boy too—*all* your little boys."

Mr. Smithers appeared to be lost in gratitude. "If only," he began, a light that never was on sea or land in his eye—but words failed him.

At the other end of the "Chappels" Philip again encountered the walker, Mr. Jackson, still looking as much like a self-possessed bridegroom as it is possible for a high collar and a barber to achieve.

"I see," said Philip, "you exhibit specimens of the tuberphone (and, by the way, I would suggest *a* instead of 'er'), the tuba-phone, the clog-box, and the Bombaboo, iniquities at the same time negroid and old-fashioned, but though in a recent visit to Budapest I found even the charming little linden-shaded shops—along the Uffelgang, you know, not, of course, a fashionable part of the city—crammed with models of the 'Haba-Stein,' a microtonic instrument with five keyboards and Hindu effects, intended, of course, for the polytonal decompositions of the 'Nothing-but-Music' school—*most* interesting; I see *no* trace of it here. I am a neoteromanic, but still, we must keep abreast, we must keep abreast!"

He waved a not unfriendly glove over his head, smiled, and went on.

Mr. Smithers had also watched the slim grey young figure until it had turned the corner and was out of sight. He then had a word with his "floor chief."

"Pim, eh, Crompton," said Mr. Jackson, squinting morosely at his underling's open order-book. " 'Setting up house'? Then I suppose the old gent must have sent in his checks. Not that I'm surprised this nephew of his hasn't bought his black yet. Close-fisted, purple-nosed, peppery old—! There won't be many to cry their eyes out over *his* arums and gardenias."

Mr. Smithers, being a family man, felt obliged to seem to enjoy as much as possible his immediate chief's society.

"All I can say *is,*" he ventured, "that young feller, and he's a gentleman if ever there was one, is making it fly."

He *was.* At this moment Philip was assuring Assistant No. 6 in the Portmanteau Department that unless the Maharaja of Jolhopolloluli's dressing-case could be dispatched next day to reach No. 444 Grosvenor Square by tea-time he need not trouble. "A few other little things," he explained, "are being sent at the same time." No. 6 at once hastened to the house telephone and asked for the secretary's office. The line was engaged.

But he need not have hesitated, for when a young man with a Pim for an uncle and of so much suavity and resources makes his wishes known, this world is amiability itself. Philip was warming up. However bland in outward appearance, he was by this time at a very enlivening temperature. He had tasted blood, as the saying goes; and he was beginning to see the need of setting a good example. Customers, like the coneys, are usually a feeble folk. His little sortie was turning into a crusade.

By this time he had all but finished disporting himself in the Furniture Department. "Three large drawing-rooms, one of them extensive," had run his rather naked catalogue, "a ballroom, a dining-room, a breakfast-room, and a little pretty dumpy all-kinds-of-angles morning-room with a Cherubini ceiling and a Venetian chimney-piece, eighteenth-century, in lapis lazuli and glass. Bedrooms, let me see, say, twenty-two—just to go on with (but not in), eleven of them for personal use, and the rest, staff. That, I think, will do for the present. We face east or west as the case may be; and nothing, please, of the 'decorative,' the quaint, or the latest thing out. Nothing shoddy, shapeless, or sham. I dislike the stuffy and the fussy and mere trimmings; and let the beds be *beds*. Moreover, I confess to being sadly disappointed in the old, the 'antique,' furniture you have shown me. The choice is restricted, naïve, and incongruous, and I have looked in vain for anything that could not be easily rivalled in the richer museums. However, let there be as many so-called antique pieces as possible, and those as antique as you can manage. Period, origin, design, harmony—please bear these in mind."

The assistants, clustering round him, bowed.

"If I have time I will look through the Department again on my way down. Eight hundred guineas for the cheaper of the Chippendale four-posters seems a little exorbitant; and three hundred and fifty for the William and Mary wall-glass—I fear it's been resilvered and patched. Still, I agree you can but do your best—I say you can all of you but do your best—and I must put up with that. What I *must* insist on, however, is that everything I have mentioned—everything—must be in its place to-morrow afternoon—carpets and so on will, of course, precede them—by four o'clock. And let there be no trace left of that indescribable odour of straw and wrappings—from Delhi, I should think —which accompanies removals. 444 Grosvenor Square. Pim—Crompton—Colonel: R-*O*-M. Thank you. To the left? *Thank* you."

This "floor-chief" hastened on in front of his visitor as if he were a Gehazi in attendance on a Naaman, and the young man presently found himself in a scene overwhelmingly rich with the colours, if not the perfumes, of the Orient. Here a complete quarter of an hour slid blissfully by. Mere wooden furniture, even when adorned with gilt, lacquer, ivory, or alabaster, can be disposed of with moderate ease; and especially if the stock of the tolerable is quickly exhausted. But Persian, Chinese, if not Turkey, carpets are another matter.

Philip sat erect on a gimcrack gilded chair, his cane and hat in his left hand, his gloves in his right, while no less than three sturdy attendants in baize aprons at one and the same moment strewed their matchless offerings at his feet, and an infuriated and rapidly multiplying group of would-be customers in search of floorcloth, lino, and coconut matting stood fuming beyond. But first come, first served is a good old maxim, and even apart from it Philip was unaware of their company. He lifted not so much as an eyebrow in their direction.

In the meantime, however, the cash balance in his uncle's bank, and much else besides, had long since as rapidly vanished as the vapour from a locomotive on a hot summer's day. From the Carpet Department, vexed that time allowed him only one of London's chief treasuries to ransack—such are the glories of Bokhara and Ispahan—he hastened down to the wine counters. Here, childishly confident in the cellarage of No. 444, Philip indulged a pretty palate *not* inherited from his uncle: claret, Burgundy, hock, sherry, cherry brandy, green Chartreuse, and similar delicate aids to good talk and reflection. He was ingenuous but enthusiastic. Port he ignored.

From "Wines" he made his way through the galleries exhibiting curtains and "hangings" (he shuddered), and china and glass —"most discouraging." His spirits revived a little when yet another defunct and barbaric prince, this time from Abyssinia, supplied him in the Car Department with a vehicle whose only adequate use, to judge from the modesty of its dashboard, the simplicity of its engine, and its price, would be a journey from this world into the next. Nevertheless His Highness had left it behind.

Fleeting visits to counters bristling with ironmongery, turnery, kitchen utensils, and provisions—and from motives of principle he omitted all mention of mulligatawny paste, chutney, West India pickles, and similar fierce and barbarous comestibles—vanished out of memory like the patterns of a kaleidoscope. The rather noisy annexe reserved for live stock Philip left unvisited. After deserts of dead stock it sounded inviting, but Philip's was a dainty nose and he was sorry for orang-outangs:

So too with books. He had clear convictions of what a gentleman's library should be without, but decided that it would take more leisure than he could spare this morning to expound them. Even the sight of a Work of Reference, however, is an excellent sedative; he ordered the choicest of who's-whos, dictionaries, atlases, encyclopædias, bird, flower, and cookery books—with a copy of "Bradshaw"—and retired.

As for pictures and statuary, one anguished glance into the dreadful chambers devoted to the fine arts had sent him scurrying on like a March hare. Nor, as he rather sadly realized, had he any cause to linger at the portals of the Monumental Masonry Department, and he now suddenly found himself in the midst of a coruscating blaze of the precious metals and the still more precious stones. He had strayed into "Jewellery"—a feast for Aladdin. Gold in particular—goblets and bowls and tankards, plates, platters, and dishes of it; clocks, chronometers, watches—from massive turnips, memorial of the Georges, to midgets like a threepenny piece in crystal and enamel, many of them buzzing like bees, and all of them intent on the kind of time which is *not* wild or always nectarous, but of which Philip had always supposed there was an inexhaustible supply. But not, alas, for all purposes. Indeed, these officious reminders of the actual hour had for the first time a little scared him.

In the peculiar atmosphere that hangs over any abundant array of sago, cooked meats, candles, biscuits, coffee, tea, ginger, and similar wares, he had been merely a young bachelor on the brink of an establishment. But at sight of this otiose display of gewgaws in the lamplit mansion in which he now found himself, his fancy had suddenly provided him with a bride. She was of a fairness incomparably fair. The first faint hint of this eventuality had almost unnerved him. He lost his head and—his heart being uncon-cerned—his taste also. In tones as languid as the breezes of Arabia he had at once ordered her rings, bracelets, necklaces, pendants, brooches, ear-rings, not to speak of bediamonded plumes and tiaras, that would daunt the dreams even of the complete bevy of musical-comedy young ladies on the British stage—not to men-tion that of Buenos Aires. And then, oddly enough, he had come to himself, and paused.

At the very moment of opening his mouth in repetition of a solo with which he was now entirely familiar—"R-*O*-M," and so on—he sat instead, gaping at the tall, calm, bald, venerable old gentleman on the other side of the counter. He had flushed.

"Have you," he inquired almost timidly at last, his eyes fixed on a chastely printed list of cutlery and silverware that lay on the glass case at his elbow, "have you just one really simple, lovely, rare, precious, and, well, unique little trinket suitable for a lady? Young, you know? An *un*-birthday present?"

The old gentleman looked up, looked at, looked *in,* smiled fondly, reminiscently, and, selecting a minute key on a ring which he had drawn out of his pocket, opened a safe not half a dozen yards away. "We have this," he said.

"This," at first, was a little fat morocco-leather case. He pressed the spring. Its lid flew open. And for an instant Philip's eyesight failed him. But it was not so much the suppressed lustre of the jewels within that had dazed his imagination as the delicate mar-vel of their setting. They lay like lambent dewdrops on the petals of a flower. The old gentleman gazed too.

"The meaning of the word 'simple,'" he suggested rumina-tively, "is one of many degrees. This, sir, is a Benvenuto Cellini piece." He had almost whispered the last few syllables as if what in workmanship were past all rivalry was also beyond any mortal pocket; as if, in fact, he were telling secrets of the unattainable. The tone piqued Philip a little.

"It is charming," he said. "But have you nothing then of Jacques de la Tocqueville's, or of Rudolph von Himmeldommer's, noth-ing of—dear me, the name escapes me. The earlier Florentine, you will remember, no doubt referred to in *Sordello,* who designed the chryselephantine bowl for the Botticelli wedding-feast. But never mind. Nothing Greek? Nothing Etruscan—*poudre d'or*? Are you suggesting that the Winter Palace was thrice looted in vain?"

The old gentleman was accustomed to the airs and graces of fastidious clients and merely smiled. He had not been listening very intently. "You will appreciate the difficulty, sir, of keeping anything but our more trifling pieces actually within reach of the nearest burglar with a stick of gun-cotton or an acetylene lamp. This"—he stirred the little leather case with his finger as lightly as a cat the relics of a mouse, and its contents seemed softly to sizzle in subdued flames of rose and amber and blue—"this," he said, "happens not to be our property. It is merely in our keeping. And though to an article of such a nature it is absurd to put a price, we have been asked to dispose of it; and by—well, a client for whom we have the profoundest respect."

"I see"; Philip pondered coldly on the bauble, though his heart was a whirlpool of desire and admiration. He swallowed. The remote tiny piping of a bird that was neither nightingale nor sky-lark, and yet might be either or both, had called to him as if from the shores of some paradisal isle hidden in the mists of the future. He glanced up at the old gentleman, but his bald, long, grey countenance was as impassive as ever.

"I'll take it," Philip said, and for a while could say no more. When speech was restored to him, he asked that it should be de-livered not "with the other things," and not to any butler or major-domo or other crustacean that might appear in answer to a knock at No. 444, but by special messenger into his own per-sonal private hands.

"Precisely, at half past four, if you please." The old gentleman bowed. As there was not enough room in the money column of his order-book for the noughts, he had written in the price in longhand, and was engaged in printing the figures 444 in the place reserved for the customer's address, when a small but clearly actual little voice at Philip's elbow suddenly shrilled up into his ear—"Mr. Philip Pim, sir?" At echo of this summons Philip stood stock-still and stiff, his heart in his ears. "The sekkertary, sir," the piping voice piped on, "asks me to say he'd be much obliged if you would be so kind as to step along into his office on your way *hout,* sir."

The tone of this invitation, though a little Cockney in effect, was innocence and courtesy itself; yet at sound of it every drop of blood in Philip's body—though he was by no means a bloated creature—had instantly congealed. This was the end, then. His orgy was over. His morning of mornings was done. The afflatus that had wafted him on from floor to floor had wisped out of his mind like the smoke of a snuffed-out candle. Yet *still* the bright thought shook him: he had had a Run for his money. No—better than that: he had had a Run *gratis.*

He must collect his wits: they had gone wool-gathering. At last he managed to turn his head and look down at the small, apple-cheeked, maroon-tunicked page-boy at his side—apple-cheeked, alas, only because he had but that week entered the sekkertary's service and his parents were of country stock.

"Tell Sir Leopold Bull"—Philip smiled at the infant—"that I will endeavour to be with him in the course of the afternoon. Thank you. That," he added for the ear of his friend on the other side of the counter, "that will be all."

But Philip was reluctant to leave him. These four syllables, as he had heard himself uttering them, sounded on in his ear with the finality of a knell. He was extremely dubious of what would happen if he let go of the counter. His knees shook under him. A dizzy vacancy enveloped him in. With a faint wan smile at the old gentleman, who was too busily engaged in returning his treasures to the safe to notice it, he managed to edge away at last.

Every mortal thing around him, gilded ceiling to grandfather clock, was at this moment swaying and rotating, as will the ocean in the eyes of a seasick traveller gloating down upon it from an upper deck. He felt ill with foreboding.

But breeding tells. And courage is a mistress that has never been known to jilt a faithful heart. Philip was reminded of this as he suddenly caught sight of a sort of enormous purple beef-eater, resembling in stature a Prussian dragoon, and in appearance a Javanese Jimjam. This figure stood on duty in the doorway, and appeared to be examining him as closely as if he were the heir to the English throne (or the most nefarious crook from

Chicago). As Philip drew near he looked this monster full in his
fishlike eye, since he was unable to do anything else. But try as he
might he couldn't pass him in silence.

"Ask Sir Leopold Bull, please," he said, "to send an official to
show me the way to his office. He will find me somewhere in the
building."

"I can take you there meself," replied the giant hoarsely. He
could indeed—bodily.

"Thank you," replied Philip. "I have no doubt of it. But I shall
be much obliged if you would at once deliver my message."

He then groped his way to yet another wicker chair not many
yards along a corridor festooned with knick-knacks from Japan
and the Near East, and clearly intended for speedy disposal. He
eyed them with immense distaste and sat down.

"Nothing whatever, thank you," he murmured to a waitress
who had approached him with a card containing a list of soft
drinks. Never in his life had he so signally realized the joys of
self-restraint. And though at the same moment he thrust finger
and thumb into his waistcoat pocket in search of his Uncle
Charles's last sovereign, it was with a view not to material but
to moral support. Years before he had often tried the same device
when as a small boy deadly afraid of the dark he had managed
at last to thrust his fevered head up and out from under his bedclothes, and to emit a dreadful simulacrum of a croupy cough.
He had never known it to fail of effect, and it was always nice
to know his mother was *there*.

So, too, with his Uncle Charles's sovereign. It was nice to know
it was there, though it was not the dark Philip was now afraid
of but the light. Resting the ivory handle of his walking-stick on
his lower lip, he began to think. What would his sentence be? A
first offender, but not exactly a novice. Not, at any rate, he hoped,
in taste and judgment. Months or years? Hard labour or penal
servitude? So swift is the imagination that in a few seconds Philip
found himself not only—his sentence served, the smiling governor
bidden farewell—*out* and a free man again, but fuming with rage
that he had not managed to retain a single specimen of his spoils.
The Jobbli dressing-bag, for instance, or that tiny, that utterly and
inimitably "unique" little Sheraton Sheridan writing-desk.

He came back a little stronger from this expedition into the future. For reassurance, like hope, springs eternal in the human breast. His one regret was not so much that he had been found out (that might come later), but that he had been found out so soon. How much bolder, less humiliating, nobler, to have actually bearded that old curmudgeon of an uncle of his, swapp or bogey in hand, in his den!

That in any event he would have been "found out" on the morrow, as soon, that is, as the first van arrived at No. 444, he had realized long ago. He certainly would not have been found "in"! But even one brief night in May seems, in prospect, a long interval between being a Crœsus and a felon in Pentonville.

He was recalled from these reflections by a young man whose sleek black hair was parted as neatly in front and in the middle as his morning coat was parted behind. A few paces distant, like a mass of gilded pudding-stone, stood the giant from the Jewellery Department. Were they in collusion? Philip could not decide.

"If you would step this way, sir, to the secretary's office," said the young man, "Sir Leopold Bull would be very much obliged."

Philip mounted to his feet and, though he flatly refused to step *that* way, followed him—to his doom. That, however, was not to be instantaneous, for on his arrival Sir Leopold Bull, rising from his roll-top desk with a brief but thrilling smile, first proffered a plump white hand to his visitor and then a chair. It seemed to be a needlessly polite preamble to the interview that was to follow. Philip ignored the hand but took the chair.

"Thank you," he said. "I do hope you will some day take my advice, Sir Leopold, to *sim*plify the arrangement of this building. It is a perfect labyrinth, and I always miss my way." With a sigh he sank down into the cushions. He was tired.

"My uncle, Colonel Crompton Pim," he continued, "is unable to spare a moment to see you this morning. I regret to say he strongly disapproved of the Bombay ducks, or was it the Clam Chowder, you sent him on Friday. They were beneath contempt."

Sir Leopold smiled once more, but even more placatingly. "I had the privilege of seeing Colonel Crompton Pim only yesterday afternoon," he replied. "He then expressed his satisfaction, for the time being, at the golf balls—the new *Excelsior* brand—with one of which we had the pleasure of supplying him *gratis* a week or two ago. The Bombay ducks shall be withdrawn immediately. I must apologize for not seeking you out in person, Mr. Pim, but what I have to say is somewhat of a private nature, and—"

"Yes," said Philip, realizing how thin was the end of the wedge which Sir Leopold was at this moment insinuating into the matter in hand. "Yes, quite." And he opened his innocent blue eyes as wide as he could, to prevent them from blinking. He kept them fixed, too, on the close-shaven face, its octopus-like mouth and prominent eyes, with ill-suppressed repulsion. To be a fly that had fallen a victim to such a spider as this!

"It would please me better," he went on, "if you would arrive as rapidly as possible at the matter you wish to discuss with me. I am free for five minutes, but I must beg you not to waste our time. And please tell your porter over there to go away. Scenes are distasteful to me."

The face of the porter, who seemed to have been created solely for his bulk, turned as crimson as a specimen of *sang-du-bœuf*. He appeared to be hurt at having been described as a "scene." But wages are of more importance than feelings, and he withdrew.

"You have had a busy morning, Mr. Pim," said the secretary. "No less than seven of my assistants who have had the privilege of waiting upon you have been monopolizing me for some time with telephone messages. I hope I am not being too intrusive if I venture to congratulate you, sir, on what I suppose to be Colonel Crompton Pim's approaching—"

"Candidly, Sir Leopold," said Philip firmly, "that *would* be venturing too far. Much too far. Let us say no more about it. What precise charge are you intending to bring against me?"

There was a pause while the world continued to rotate.

"For which article?" breathed Sir Leopold.

Philip gazed steadily at the full, bland, secretive countenance. It was as if once again he had heard that seraphic birdlike voice sounding in the remote blue sky above the storm-clouds that now hung so heavily over his beating heart.

"Oh, I mean for delivery," he said. "Mine was—was a large order."

"But, my dear sir, we shouldn't dream of making *any* such

charge. *Any* service to Colonel Pim . . ." The faint sob in the
voice would have done credit to Caruso.

Philip stooped to hide the cataract of relief that had swept over
his face, then raised his head again. How could he be sure that
this was anything more than play-acting—the torture of suspense?
"Ah, well," he said, "that is no matter now. I gather there was
some other point you had in mind—in *view,* I should say."

"Oh, only," said Sir Leopold, "to ask if Colonel Pim would be
so kind as to subscribe as usual to our Fund for the Amelioration
of the Conditions of the Offspring of Superannuated Shop Assistants. Mainly orphans, Mr. Pim. We must all die, Mr. Pim, and
some of us have to die earlier in life than others. Still, our average
here is little worse than that of any other large London establishment. In Petrograd—or was it Los Angeles?—I am given to understand, a shop assistant at two-and-thirty is a shop assistant with
at least one foot in the grave. It is the little orphans, the fatherless
ones, who from no apparent fault of their own have to be left to
the tender mercies of a busy world! It would grieve you, sir,
which Heaven forbid, if I told you how many of these wee small
things there are now on our hands. Chubby, joysome, rosebud
little creatures, as happy as the day is long. Nevertheless it is a
little thoughtless to marry, Mr. Pim, when it is only orphans one
can leave behind one. On the other hand, there is a silver lining
to *every* cloud. Without these infants we should be deprived of a
good cause. An excellent cause. And it's causes that keep us going.
Last year I think Colonel Pim very kindly contributed half a
guinea."

"In cash?" Philip inquired sharply.

"We debited his account," said Sir Leopold.

"Well, then," said Philip, "please understand that my uncle
regrets that little laxity. He has hardened. He now entirely dis-
approves of orphans and of orphanages. The shop assistant, he
was saying to me only the other day, is a person who should be
grateful to Providence that he has *no* justification for dabbling
in matrimony. The more celibate they are, in his opinion, the better. But recollect, Sir Leopold, that until we arrive at the higher
and fewer salaried officials in your establishment, I feel myself in
no way bound to *share* my uncle's views. Your staff is as courteous

and considerate as it appears to be unappreciated. A man's a man for a' that. And *a'* that. Let us talk of brighter things."

Sir Leopold did his utmost to conceal the wound to his vanity. "I am sorry to seem to be persistent," he assured his client, "but Colonel Pim only yesterday was so kind as to say he would *consider* my appeal. I take it, then, that he has changed his mind?"

"My uncle," retorted Philip tartly, "has a mind that is the better for being changed." For an instant he saw the face before him as it would appear in due course in the witness-box; and his very soul revolted. That pitiless Machine called Society might have its merits, but not *this* cog in its wheel! "I myself implored my uncle," he added bitterly, "to give the orphans the cold shoulder. What in the chronic sirocco of his next world would be the use to him of a mere half-guinea's worth of cooling breezes? Scarcely a sop in the pan. Indeed, only a passion for the conventional prevented him from asking for his previous donations to be returned."

Sir Leopold appeared to be engaged in rapidly bolting something—possibly his pride. It was at any rate no part of his secretarial duties to detect insanity in the family of any solvent shareholder.

"There is only one other little point," he went on rather hollowly. "Colonel Pim asked me to send him a detailed account of his purchases during the last month. We met by happy chance as he was yesterday alighting from a taxicab at the entrance to his bank. After to-day's purchases that will perhaps take an hour or two. But it shall reach him to-morrow morning—without fail."

Philip had risen. It is better to stand when one is at bay. While with a gentle absent smile he stood drawing on his gloves he was faced with the wildest effort of his life—to make sure of what lay in hiding behind these last remarks. Anything *might*.

"Oh, he did—did he?" he remarked very softly. "I fancy"— and at last he lifted his gentle eyes to meet his adversary's—"I *believe* there's an empty whisky jar that has not yet been credited to him. Perhaps that was on his mind."

"Well, Mr. Pim," said Sir Leopold, "turning" at last, "if *that's* his only jar it's soon adjusted."

Philip took a deep breath. He playfully wagged a finger.

"Now *that,* Sir Leopold," he said, "was blank verse. I hope you don't intend to put my little purchases of this morning into *rhyme!* The effort, I assure you, would be wasted on my uncle."

He wheeled lightly, and turned towards the door. Sir Leopold, his face now at liberty to resume its office of expressing his feelings, accompanied him. Indeed he continued to accompany him to the very entrance of his gigantic abode. And there Philip almost fainted. A deluge, compared with which that of Noah and his family was nothing but an April shower, was descending on the street.

"A taxi," roared Sir Leopold at a group of his satellites in the porch, caparisoned in shiny waterproofs, and armed with gigantic *parapluies.*

But though at least nineteen of these vehicles were instantly battling their way towards this goal, Philip with incredible agility had eluded their attention. Before Sir Leopold had had time even to arrange his face to smile a farewell, our young friend had gone leaping up the staircase behind him, and had without a moment's pause vanished into the Tropical Department. One fugitive glance at its pith and pucka contents, and at the dusky assistants in attendance, had only accelerated his retreat. In less than half a minute he found himself confronting a young woman seated in midst of a stockade of umbrellas.

The coincidence was too extreme to be ignored. He would at least carry off *some* little souvenir of his morning's outing. What better value could he get for hard cash than an implement that would be at the same time a refuge from the elements—for other he would soon presently have none—and a really formidable weapon at hand for his next interview with Sir Leopold?

He had but just enough breath left to express himself. He pointed.

"I *want* one, please," he cried at the young woman. "Cash."

"One, two, three, four, *five* guineas?" she murmured, looking as if she were less in need of her stock than of her lunch. "Partridge, malacca, horn, ivory, rhinoceros, natural, *gold?* Union, gloria, glacé, taffeta, cotton, mixture, or *twill?*"

"Not a toy; an umbrella," Philip expostulated. "To keep off rain. A nephew returning to school—ten years' wear. Gingham, alpaca, calico, cast-iron—*anything;* so long as it is hefty, solid, endurable, awful, and *cheap.*"

"We have here what is *called* an umbrella," replied the assistant a trifle coldly. "The 'Miss and Master Brand.' Lignum-vitæ stick, whalebone ribs, blunted ferrule, non-poisonous handle, guaranteed not to break, fray, fade, or scale. Nine and elevenpence complete."

"Bill; in haste; cash; just as it is; thanks," cried Philip, and seized the dreadful object. With a groan he laid his Uncle Charles's sovereign in the narrow brass trough of the pay-desk. The obese young person in the wooden box seemed about to lift it to her lips, glanced at him again, put it aside, smiled, and gave him his change.

"The way to the back exit, I think, is over here?" Philip murmured, waving his gloves due west.

The young person smiled again, and he withdrew. He withdrew down the back steps and into the deluge: there to face a watery world, the possessor of ten shillings and a penny (in his pocket), a wardrobe of old suits, about a hundred and fifty books, three of them unmerited prizes for good conduct, a juvenile collection of postage stamps, a hypothetical legacy of a shilling, and an uncle who, if he faced his liabilities as an English gentleman should, had to all intents and purposes overdrawn his bank account that afternoon by, say roughly, a couple of hundred thousand pounds.

On the Edge (1931)

CAPE RACE

IT WAS still early—marvellously sharp and clear and early; and the tang of the open sea simply swept over Lettie from head to foot as she stepped over the brass-bound coaming of the doorway on to the water-darkened deck. Cooped up in her cabin, it seemed that she had been listening to the sailors swabbing down that deck for hours. "All through the night," in fact. The muffled swish and thump of their mops had sounded faintly on even in her dreams as she lay, rocked in her narrow berth, between sleeping and waking. But now the deck was not only swept and garnished, it was deserted. It just dipped with its slow gentle lurch and then swam back again. And along the whole length of it there was nothing but empty chairs to be seen—chairs in a long gaping wooden row, naked and vacant, that had themselves watched out life together the whole dark through.

Just now, however, chairs as empty as possible were all the company Lettie needed, and she pushed off into the full glare of the bright windy morning. Like a guinea embedded in black sealing-wax her gold-sleeked head stood out sharply against the diamond-clear deep darkness of the sea—which, having recovered from its childish fit of rage and petulance overnight, was now with its scattering crystal foam-beads rocking itself to sleep. Even if the brine-laden breezes were not actually bragging about it, it was plain how early the morning was, for the globe of the burning sun was still low in the east, immense and refulgent, and Lettie was alone.

George shut up in his stateroom, and George's mamma in hers, were still blind leagues away from this vast welcoming scene that

had now burst in with all its radiance upon her senses. Poor
George, you couldn't blame *him* for clinging to his blankets. It
was indeed bad luck not only to have been so forlornly and stubbornly seasick, but for such a humiliatingly long spell. And to
be worried to death with forebodings, too—such unnecessary,
shapeless, vaporous forebodings. And all these horrors all at the
same time! No, indeed; as much as possible of that dreamless
slumber which knits up the ravelled sleeve of care for George,
poor dear!

As for George's mamma, since like a drowsy mouse-wearied
pussy-cat she was always miles and miles away from the Here and
Now, it was a joy to think of her not bothered with it at all. You
can't lose *real* things in your sleep, that's one blessing. And after
all she had in some degree lost even her beloved George. So Lettie
was positively exulting in having the North Atlantic entirely to
herself. Her own little secret bout of *mal de mer* had lasted only a
few hours. She felt as fresh as a linnet in an April copse. She
gloried in the fatuous but lovely motions of the great ship—its
faint murk of smoke thinning up from its yawning funnels—as it
wallowed like some vast imperturbable monster along its watery
pathway to New York.

They that go down to the sea in ships and have their business
in great waters—Lettie pushed and dipped and danced her way
along the slippery deck, and lo and behold, as she came forging
on towards the bows of the ship, *there,* as sharp as a tiny picture
across the tumbling sea, lay land. Land! As astonishing, as unexpected and welcome as it was lovely: a flattish land mounding
beyond into low bluish hills. And on its coast a huddle of coloured
shingle-roofed houses, a red and a red and a green, and what she
was morally certain must be a wireless station—its exquisite an-
tennæ tapering up into the crystalline blue.

A man in an old blue jersey, and with bits of the sky for eyes
—a seaman too, and not one of these mere urban and obsequious
deck stewards—was coming along.

"What's that?" said Lettie, pointing her finger.

"That?" said the seaman. "That's Cape Race. Newfoundland,
miss. We don't sight this coast like that once in a blue moon. Not
usually. Fog."

"So that's Cape Race—Newfoundland!" echoed Lettie, her small head poised on her shoulders like a young she-kestrel's as she gazed across at it. "Cape Race. How far to go now, then?"

"A bit over a thousand miles, miss, I should reckon."

How romantic and how amazing! Newfoundland indeed! And that it should have been there for centuries upon centuries continually in sound of its perpetual breakers beneath its low moulded hill, and that she had never seen it before! What completely commonplace things could sometimes almost suffocate you, not of course with any *novelty,* but with some hidden meaning. And if she herself could count those mute dark windows beneath those smokeless chimneys—obviously there might be eyes behind them even at this moment steadfastly scanning this great painted stranger on the deep, as it forged its stealthy course from east to west—eyes of people half-asleep, in their night-clothes, peering at the ship from beneath those low roofs.

"And what," asked Lettie, exceedingly loth to let the sailor go, "what is the name of that bit of land jutting out to the left there?"

"That, miss? That's Mistaken Point," he said.

"Why was it mistaken?"

He shook his head, and smiled out of his sea-clear eyes at her. "That's got me, miss," he replied.

"Anyhow," cried Lettie with decision, "we are not mistaking it now." At which little witticism the young sailor laughed and went on his way.

So this was land! and the journey which was to end in two wonderful beginnings, George's new career, and, if everything went well, her own marriage, would soon be over. Another day or two and the vast bronze face of Liberty, with her spiked headdress and uplifted torch, would heave into view and stand sightlessly gazing at her from the harbour mouth. And beyond Liberty the serried austerities of poor George's abhorred and inexorable skyscrapers. But sufficient unto the morrow are the perils thereof. Why is it that what may seem absolutely unendurable to think of before it comes, can swim up so easily and predestinedly on the day?

Anyhow, she wasn't going to bother about the future. Not now; and no; never more. Indeed she couldn't possibly have told any-

body how every electric particle of her was exulting in the buffet-
ing wind, in the flecked light-bright beads of spray, in the glitter
and the splendour and motion of it all, and not least in that queer
huddled little nest of humans over there, tucked away beyond its
surf on this remote coast line. And all as natural and like a picture
as a village in the Cotswolds!

Should she, or should she *not,* tap on George's little round thick
glass port? No daisy of the sea, no marine heartsease flowed in
those smooth dark hollows of water, else Ophelia-wise she might
have put the question to the test. So doubtful she herself remained
that she had actually stepped in from off the open deck on her
way below long before she had decided that she would. But here
she was; and the long wide glass-walled saloon—that too was
perfectly empty.

But no, yet another marvel. It was not empty. For even as she
came stooping in on its light and solitude some winged thing
flashed before her eyes, and had dashed with a sullen tiny thump
against the plate-glass window. It was only a bird, a very slender
bird with coloured feathers, as small as one of her own English
warblers; but now it was fluttering in frenzy against the crystal
walls of its strange prison-house in vain exhausting efforts to
escape this human stranger and to reach the sun.

"You poor *poor* little creature," Lettie was whispering to herself
as she watched it. "It's silly to do that. Just stay still awhile and
wait!" Why, it must have come dipping in overnight or possibly
at daybreak from the very hills she had just been contemplating
across the few severing miles of the sea. And alas, how could she
hope to free the mite unharmed? If she ran out for help, it might
beat itself to death while she was gone. What an omen!

She would have to remain completely still, then seize her opportunity. In this inner hush she could hear the fluttering of its wings
and the tapping of its small horny beak against the glass even
above the vast wash and soughings of the ocean. Grief and dismay
filled her heart; she stood tautly stooping, utterly at a loss how
to save it from its own wild fears. And perhaps because she had
meanwhile never stirred by so much as an inch, head or foot, perhaps, also, because compassion may make itself felt even between
things so alien to one another as wild bird and Man, it had now,

wearied out for the while, pushed its small bony framework into a corner and crevice of the window, its head crooked on its ruffled neck, its sun-diamonded round eye fixed, it seemed, on herself, its primrose-tinted wing forlornly drooping.

With infinite caution Lettie pushed a chair the least bit nearer. Then poising herself, as stealthily as a weasel, on feet and ankles almost as slender in proportion as the bird's own legs and claws, she gradually raised herself towards its lair. And still this panting little atom of life in its damp-darkened feathers just eyed her glassily back.

"There now," she whispered seductively with pursed-up lips, "it's only me, *I'll* take care of you. Just—yes, there!—just trust yourself for one—sigh of—an instant—and . . ."

It was almost as if she had hypnotized the wild and tiny creature. It had neither struggled any longer, nor pecked at her fingers; it had scarcely stirred; and Lettie with extreme caution had climbed inch by inch down from her rocking perch again, and now held her throbbing, warm-downed, living prey clasped safely in her hand. Its flat and pointed head lay gently couched on the knuckle of one of her forefingers, while with the tip of the other she smoothed its exquisite feathers from crown to tail. She smiled, whistling softly, but the bright black-ringed fierce grey unspeculating eyes paid no heed.

Lettie's heart was beating under her young ribs as violently as its own. It *was* an omen; she was desperately reluctant to let it go, and yet confident that, given its liberty, it would find its way back to safety and home. So bidding it be of good courage and fear nothing—as if she were talking to a child—she hooded it softly over with her scrap of a handkerchief and went out again on to the deck. There she gingerly picked her way foot by foot and yard by yard—though she had long since found her sea-legs—sternwards.

A rather pallid and heavy young man wearing shell-rimmed spectacles, whom she had more than once noticed during the voyage, had also decided to savour the morning breezes. Perhaps he was anxious to take the taste of something overnight from out of his mouth. He had come lurching round the corner like a bear after honey. And as he cocked a discreetly interrogative eye in

her direction, Lettie openly smiled at him. She would have
smiled at Beelzebub. It was as if she had seen him thousands and
thousands of times before, and she said "Good morning," as if she
really did desperately hope it would be a *very* good morning for
him. Then, still with her weightless burden in her hand, she
hastened on, and down the narrow steps of the companion ladder
to the deck below.

At the further end of this, past the tight-wedged hatches and
the bollards and the cook-house, was a niche now familiar to her.
She and George had spent many a dark stolen moment there,
gazing—he mournfully, she comfortingly—away back out over
the yeasty wake of the great vessel towards home. There with the
fumes of bacon and coffee in her nostrils she now stayed awhile,
completely screened from sight, to give her prize as long a respite
as it might need before she committed it to its fate.

The sky was as blue as a hedge-sparrow's egg—bluer. Its vast
empty vault, where still the stars in their invisible constellations
must be shining, though not even the Ancient Mariner's eye could
now have picked them out, arched itself over her head. And the
unfathomable and inexplorable sea, which she and the ship were
abandoning to its own eyeless solitude again, stretched out in its
measureless leagues beyond and beyond and beyond her. None
the less even Lettie realized—had not George himself pointed it
out to her?—how narrow a circle of its waters was actually scan-
nable from where she stood; a small horizon which was, too, continually changing as the ship plunged on.

And now, on her left hand, the silent shores, the squat vigilant
lighthouse, the smokeless shack roofs, the uplands of Cape Race
were wheeling more clearly into view. Soon they would have
drifted by, be gone, have vanished—and, so far as she was concerned, probably for ever. There was not a moment to lose. She
raised her hand to her lips, and imprinted a kiss light as thistledown on the snakelike feathery head, showering on it a host of
blessings as multitudinous as the morning dew. Her very life for
the moment seemed to be bound up with its destiny. She had
saved it from ship's cat or ship's boy, perhaps, or from one of those
odious little tallow-faced gentilities she had seen scuttling in and
out of the most expensive "suite" of staterooms on the upper deck.

How dreadful then if, in spite of it all, it should come to grief!
Why, during the last voyage of this very ship, in the latening
dusk, had not a mad miserable and heartbroken woman attempted to fling herself overboard from this very rail on which
Lettie was now leaning? "Not the ghost of a chance for her
there," George had declared, almost as if with satisfaction at *something* definite in a universe of flux. "Not a ghost!" and he had
gone on staring down into the pale-green seething pit of water
under the keel.

Lettie sighed. And at length she lifted her hand high above her
head, and with breath held tight in her bosom, relaxed the four
fingers and the thumb. The bird fell a few inches like a stone,
and dipped, fluttering a moment, helplessly. But with the next,
its wings had gained the mastery they needed over the quiet air
in the shelter of the ship. It soared up into the wind, was drifted
a few yards in its great sweeping sightless flood like weed on the
sea, and then, the gay colours of its plumage still discernible in
the sunbeams, it had sped off away towards the shore.

Lettie watched it till it had become a drifting speck—until her
eyes were overflowing from the dark dazzle of the sea. She turned
away. "Safe!" She had actually uttered the word aloud, and was
so elated at her morning's act of mercy that she very nearly repeated the prayers which she had hurried through only a few
minutes before.

How absurd, how silly people were! What ridiculous little webs
of mere coincidences they kept on spinning round themselves!
Talk about horizons! Good heavens, it was lucky she hadn't
shared her little burst of fireworks with her future mother-in-law.

Not that George's "mumsie" wouldn't have sympathized with
"the darling little bird." She would have sent one of the stewards
for some canary seed, or would have had a special bowl of bread
and milk brought up, and would probably have suffocated her
little protégé. She might even have asked the captain—"so very
approachable a man, my dear"—to back in and land the tiny creature on the nearest beach.

For you can kill, as well as save, all sorts of things by kindness.
For this very reason Lettie had made up her mind long ago that
she would scrutinize at once all kindnesses to herself when they

came her way. So many were showered on her that she was apt to shower them back, without really thinking much about them. And it was absolutely essential not to be merely sympathetic but to be reasonable with George. Not to give way too much to his absurd fits of depression. Not to pamper him. Pampered husbands become perfectly horrible: indolent, cumbrous, oily and otiose, yes and cynical. Creases appear and deepen beneath their several chins, and they always go bald early—lose every scrap of hair!

A sudden revulsion of feeling had settled over Lettie's mind. How very queer: the sea, the sky, the morning were only a few moments older and couldn't by any possibility have faded since she had bent her steps this way. And the light sparkling breezes from the twelve corners of the heavens still sang briskly about her ears, as she turned away towards breakfast. And yet, merely because she had caught a glimpse in her mind's eye of being stout and forty-four and as used to your excellent domesticated job as a cat is to cream, everything seemed to have darkened and tarnished a little. Why, only death itself can free that kind of "bird"!

It was the same old story: she was always being silly and wrought-up and impulsive like this. And by no means always with success. And invariably the reaction came; then life went flat and spiritless, and the future loomed as ghostly and ghastly before her as a London wrapt in a pea-soup November fog. And now there wasn't any captive aboard at all that could be given its freedom—a sudden headlong gust of sea-sprayed wind had slapped her blue skirts tight against her legs as she pushed on towards its bows—except, possibly, herself.

Wasn't she engaged to be married, good heavens, and wasn't there a most beautiful sapphire ring welded two joints under the third claw of her left hand? Why, even her hair was as yellow as the bird's wing. They shared the very same badge. She'd a jolly good mind to throw *herself* overboard and trust to Providence to give his angels charge over her, to fan her up and waft her away towards that cosy little cluster of houses over there, which was so very like England—never, never, perhaps, to be seen again. And then, when the fogs had drifted down once more, perhaps George could come too. She could see them both in sea-sodden clothes and rubber boots, hunting for their morning cockles along the beach. Why all these forebodings, this confusion and anxiety merely about salary and *prospects*? Who ever recognized the very handsomest of prospects—when it came? Why *not* the simple life, with mamma-in-law in an early-Victorian rocking-chair of colonial manufacture beside the kettled hob!

"Good *morn*ing," she cried suddenly, and this time entirely by mistake, to the sleek heavy young man in the tortoise-shell spectacles, and this time he cocked an inquiring eye indeed. How absurd! *That* belarded hee-haw! And yet just *this* silly little mistake had almost restored her good spirits again. If George wasn't up by now, she would make the devil of a fuss about it. It was all very well to be ranging round like a roaring young lioness in the wild bright jungle of the morning, but, after all, you did sometimes want a glimpse of your solemn shag-necked lord and master too.

Wonder of wonders, there he was! Balancing himself gingerly along the deck exactly like a reanimated flounder in a fish shop. She had never noticed before what a charmingly genteel and pacifying effect gold-rimmed spectacles have on a quiet, round, and even slightly owlish face—compared, that is, with those goggling tortoise-shell things.

"George," she said, "I found a bird just now in the concert room, a bird from the land, a land-bird—Cape Race, over *there,* never seen before—a tiny thing, as light as a postage stamp and almost dead with exhaustion and terror. Oh, such a lovely helpless little thing, and it never stirred a hair's breadth when it saw I was coming. Fancy *daring* to start off at evening or dawn just because you saw something like a faint lighted palace far out to sea. What *kind* do you suppose it was: dark head, very slim, a crest, golden yellow on its wings, and a sharp narrow bill?"

She led him in, without the least intention of waiting for an answer, and down the stairs and into the dining-saloon. Dining-saloon! They were the very first passengers to come and eat. How frigid and insecure, how select and horribly discreet it all looked. It would have been far, far better fun to have gone steerage. And they sat down at the table, the little silver vase of iced flowers right in the middle of it, and the crisp rolls and the enormous breakfast menu in front of them—steak and sturgeon and kedgeree, fifteen kinds of meats and five-and-twenty jams, not to mention "Vigorbrits," "Drenergy," and exploded rice! . . .

And there was George, just because they had sighted land, looking glummer even than twenty flounders, his cheeks no longer sea-green, but positively putty-like with anxiety, and even his silly freckled and sunburned hand trembling a little as it lay with its thumb sticking out on the damask tablecloth.

"You really are," whispered Lettie, with a swift glance round in quest of trespassing stewards, "you really *are* rather a dear, you poor thing, and I believe I love you best when you are most like a fat little boy that couldn't say Bo to a cockroach. George dear, *look* at me. Do try and be a little confident. You know—and wouldn't you just rap it out at anybody who denied it!—you know perfectly well that you could take on even that old President's job to-morrow morning without a moment's hesitation—as soon, that is, as you had recovered from dying of fright overnight. And yet! . . ."

She slid her slender cold hand under the tablecloth and clasped his right one that lay flaccid and inert upon his knee.

"Besides, haven't you *me,* you old silly? Would I have said, Go, or rather Come, all this marvellous long way across the sea, if I hadn't been absolutely certain it was Set Fair? Would I? Would I be unendurably pining to kiss you *now*—if only we weren't *here* —*would* I?"

George—his fingers still trembling a little, for three solid days of queasy seasickness does take it out of a man even with the stubbornest of constitutions—removed his gold glasses, and turned his placid anxious faithful affectionate hazel eyes on Lettie's, as she sat there, their hands clasped under the tablecloth. But out of the corner of one of them he had at that very moment spotted a steward, nimbly stepping on his way in their direction, and what he huskily *said* was, "Any cereal, Lettie?"

The Wind Blows Over (1936)

PHYSIC

EMILIA and William had been keeping one another company in the kitchen. Mary, her trusty substantial cook-general, was "out," and would not be knocking at the door until half past ten. After that there might be another hour to wait. But then Emilia would be alone. Meanwhile, just like man and wife, William and she would soon be having supper together at two corners of the kitchen table, and William would have an egg—with nine bread-and-butter fingers.

This, once fortnightly, now weekly, Wednesday-night feast had become a kind of ritual, a little secret institution. They called it their covey night. Not even Daddie ever shared it with them; and it was astonishing what mature grown-up company William became on these occasions. It was as if, entirely unknown to himself, he had swallowed one of Jack's bean-seeds and had turned inside into a sort of sagacious second husband. All that Emilia had to do, then, was merely to become again the child she used to be. And that of course needs only a happy heart.

He was a little dark-skinned boy, William—small for his age. A fringe of gilt-edged fair hair thatched a narrow forehead over his small, restless eyes. His sister Sallie—poor gaunt Aunt Sarah, whom she had been called after, having departed this life when less than a month had passed since the gay little christening party —after a restless and peevish afternoon and a wailful bath, was asleep now, upstairs, in her crib. You could tell that almost without having to creep out every now and again to listen at the foot of the stairs.

William had been even more lively and hoppity than usual.

He and Emilia had been playing Beggar-my-Neighbour, and he had become steadily more excited, when, with something very like sheer magic, every sly knave in the pack had rapidly abandoned poor Emilia and managed to sidle into his hand. And when—after an excited argument as to where the Queen of Hearts had best be hidden—they changed the game, he laughed and laughed till the tears came into his eyes to see her utter confusion at finding herself for the third time an abject Old Maid! And when supper-time came—plates, spoons, forks—he had all but danced from dresser to table, from table to dresser again. They had borrowed Mary's best blue-check kitchen tablecloth; he had said it looked cooler. "Don't you *think* so, Mummie?" And every now and again he had ejaculated crisp shrill remarks and directions at Emilia, who was looking after the cooking in the outer room, a room she had steadfastly refused to call the "scullery." Merely because she disliked the word! Though one day in a sudden moment of inspiration she had defended this priggishness by exclaiming, "Well, spell it with a *k* and then see what you think of it!"

It was a little way Emilia had. As tenaciously as she could she always put off until to-morrow even what it was merely difficult to put up with to-day. Never trouble trouble till trouble troubles you, was her motto when driven into a corner. She hated problems, crises, the least shadow of any horror, though they would sometimes peer up at her out of her mind—and from elsewhere—when she wasn't looking, like animals at evening in the darkening hills. But when they actually neared, and had to be faced; well, that was quite another matter.

For some minutes now, busied over her sizzling pan at the gas stove, she hadn't noticed that William's galvanic sprightly conversation piped up from the kitchen had been steadily dwindling, had almost ceased. He had decided to have his supper egg fried, though "lightly boiled" was the institution. And Emilia had laughed when, after long debate, he had declared that he had chosen it fried because then it was more indigestible. She was dishing it up from the smoke and splutter—a setting sun on a field of snow, and with a most delicate edging of scorch.

When she came back into the kitchen William was standing

by the table, gazing across it at the window. He couldn't be look-ing *out* of the window, for although there was a crevice a few inches wide between the flowered chintz curtains that had been drawn over it and where the blue linen blind had not been pulled down to the very bottom, it was already pitch-dark outside. Yet even at this distance she saw that he couldn't also be staring solely at his own reflection.

He stood motionless, his eyes fixed on this dark glassy patch of window, his head well above the table now. He had not even turned at sound of her footstep. So far as Emilia's birdlike heart was concerned, it was as if a jay had screeched in a spinney. But best not notice too much. Don't put things into people's heads. "There!" she exclaimed. "Well now, you *have* cut the bread and butter thick, Mr. Stoic! *I'm* going to have that scrap of cold fish. Eat this while it's hot, my precious!"

But William had continued to wait.

"I don't think, Mummie," he said slowly, as if he were reciting something he had been learning by heart, "I don't *think* I'll have my egg after all. I don't think I feel very hungry just now."

All his eagerness and excitement seemed to have died down into this solemn and stagnant reverie; and for a child to have the air and appearance of a sorrowful old dwarf is unutterably far away from its deliciously pretending to be a sedate grown-up.

"Not have it!" said Emilia. "Why, look, blessing, it's cooked! Look! Lovely. You wouldn't know it wasn't a tiny half of a peach in cream. Let's pretend."

"I couldn't like even that, Mummie," he said, glancing at it, a slight shudder ending in a decisive shake of the head as he hastily looked away again. "I don't think, you know, I want *any* supper."

Emilia's eyes widened. She stood perfectly still a moment, the hot plate in her hand, staring at him. Then she hurriedly put it down on the table, knelt with incredible quickness beside him, and seized his hand.

"That's what it is," she said. "You don't feel very well, William. You don't feel very well? Your hands are hot. Not sick? Not sore throat? Tell Mummie."

"I'm *not* ill," wailed William obstinately. "Just because I don't want the egg! You *can't* like that horrid cold fish, and if I did feel sick, wouldn't I say so? That's only what *you* say." He paused as if the utmost caution and precision were imperative, then added, nodding his head mournfully and sympathetically in time to the whispered words, "I *have* got a teeny tiny headache, but I didn't notice it until just now." His mouth opened in a prodigious yawn, leaving tears in his eyes. "Isn't it funny, Mummie —you can't really see anything out of the window when it's black like that, yet you needn't look at your*self* in the glass. It's just as if . . ."

His eyes came round from examining the window, and fixed themselves on her face.

"That's what it is," said Emilia, raising herself abruptly from the floor. "That's what it is." She kept squeezing the thin, unresponsive fingers of his hand between her own. "You're feverish. And I knew it. *All* the time. Yes—*how* stupid of me." And instantly her voice had changed, all vain self-recriminations gone. "I'll tell you what we'll *do,* William. First, I'll fill a hot-water bottle. Then I'll run up and get the thermometer. And *you* shall be the doctor. That's much the best thing." And she did not even pause for his consent.

"I expect you know, Dr. Wilson," she had begun at once, "it's something that's disagreed with my little boy. I expect so. Oh, yes, I expect so."

William, pale and attentive, was faltering. "Well, yes, Mrs. Hadleigh, p'r'aps," he said at last, as if his mouth were cram-full of plums. "You *may* be right. And that depends, you know, on what he has been *eating."*

"Yes, yes, I quite understand, Doctor. Then would you perhaps wait here just for one moment, while I see if my little boy is ready for you. I think, you know, he might like to wash his hands first and brush his hair. And *pray* keep on your overcoat in case you should feel cold." She took a large dry Turkish towel that was airing on a horse near by, and draped it over William's shoulders. "I won't be a moment," she assured him. "Not a moment."

Yet she paused to glance again at his shawled-in pale face and fever-bright eyes, as if by mere looking she could bore clean through his body; and stooping once more, she pressed her cheek against his, and then his hand to her lips.

"You said," half tearfully chanted the little boy, "that I was the doctor; and now you are kissing me, Mummie!"

"Well, I could often and often kiss lots of doctors," said his mother, and in a flash she was gone, leaving him alone. She raced up the dark staircase as if she were pursued by twenty demons, not even waiting to switch on the light. And when she came to her bedroom it was as if everything in it were doing its utmost to reassure her. The shining of the street lamp was quietly dappling its walls with shadow. The whole room lay oceans deep in silence; the duskily mounded bed, the glass over the chimney-piece, the glass on the dressing-table. They may until that very moment have been conferring together, but now had, as usual, instantly fallen mute, their profound confabulations for the time being over. But she did not pause even so much as to sip of this refreshing stillness. Her finger touched the electric switch, and in an instant the harmless velvety shadows—frail quivering leaf-shadows—the peace, the serenity, had clean evaporated. It was as if the silence had been stricken with leprosy, so instantaneous was the unnatural glare—even in spite of the rose-pink lamp-shades. For now Emilia was staring indeed.

How, she was asking herself, how by any possibility could that striped school tie of her husband's have escaped from its upper drawer on to the bedspread? How by an utter miracle had she failed to see it when she had carried Sallie into the room only an hour or two ago? Ties don't wriggle out of top drawers across carpets and climb up valances like serpents in the tropics. Husbands miles away cannot charm such things into antics like *these*!

Mary had been out all the afternoon. She herself had been out for most of it with the children, and she could have vowed, taken her oath, *knew,* that *that* couldn't have been there when she had come up to put on her hat. In the instant that followed, before even she could insist on raising her eyes from this queer scrap of "evidence," her mind suddenly discovered that it was dazed and in the utmost confusion. It was as if, like visitors to a gaudy Soho restaurant, a jostling crowd of thoughts and images, recollections, doubts, memories, clues, forebodings, apprehensions, and reiterated stubborn reassurances had thronged noisy and jostling into consciousness—and then were gone again. And at that, at once, as if by instinct and as unforeseeably as a night moth alights on one out of a multitude of flowers, her stricken glance had encountered her husband's note.

At sight of it her heart had lept in her body, and then cowered down like a thing smitten with palsy. Novels told you of things like these, but surely not just ordinary life! The note had been scribbled on a half-sheet of her own note-paper, and hastily folded into a cocked hat—perhaps the only old-fashioned device she had ever known that husband to be capable of. It seemed that she had learned by heart the message it contained before even she had unfolded the paper and read it. Indeed, it did not matter what it had to say. It hardly even mattered *how* it had said it. So considerately, yet so clumsily, so blastingly. "She"—that alone was enough. When shells explode why be concerned with fuse or packing? Edward was gone. That was all that mattered. She had been abandoned—she and the children.

So far, so inevitably. You can in vile moments of suspicion, incredulity, and terror foresee things like that. Just that he was gone —and for good. But to have come stealing back in the afternoon into a vacant house, merely for a few clothes or a little money, and she out, and Mary out, and the children out—and everything else out; well, that seemed a funny, an unnecessary thing to do!

"I wouldn't have so much minded . . ." she began to mutter to herself, and then realized that her body was minding far too much. A thin acid water had come into her mouth. Unlike William, she felt sick and dizzy. She had gone stiff and cold and goose-flesh all over. It was as if some fiendish hand were clutching her back hair and dragging the scalp from her forehead taut as the parchment of a drum over her eyes. It was as if she had swallowed unwittingly a dose of some filthy physic. Her knees trembled. Her hands hung down from her arms as though they were useless. And the only thing she could see at this instant was the other woman's face. But it wasn't looking at her—on purpose. It was turned three-quarters away—at a very becoming angle to the long, fair cheekbone, the drooping eyelashes, the feline line of the jaw. Clara. And then, suddenly, she saw them both together, stooping a little, at a railway station, it seemed; talking close. Or was it that they had just got out of a cab?

Emilia might as well have been dreaming all this, since although these picturings, this misery, this revulsion of jealousy, and the horror of what was to come persisted in a hideous activity somewhere in her mind, she herself had refused for the time being to have anything to do with it. There was something infinitely more important that must be done at once, without a moment's delay. Husbands may go, love *turn,* the future slip into ruin as silently and irretrievably as a house of cards. But children must not be kept waiting; not sick children. She was already clumsily tugging at the tiny middle drawer of the old mirror, one of their first bargains, on the dressing-table, and she caught at the same instant a glimpse of the face reflected in its glass; but so instantaneously that the eyes of the image appeared to be darkened and shut, and therefore blind.

What a boon a little methodicalness may be. What a mercy that in this world *things* stay where they are put; do not hide, deceive, play false, forsake and abandon us. Where she always kept it, *there* lay the slim, metal, sharp-edged case of the thermometer. It was as if it had been faithfully awaiting this very reunion—ever since she had seen it last. In the old days, before she was married and had children, even if she had possessed such a thing, she might have looked for it for hours before discovering it. She had despised thermometers. Now, such a search would have resembled insanity.

She hesitated for scarcely the breadth of a sigh at the door, and then with decision switched off the light. Stuffing her husband's scribbled note into her apron pocket, she flew into the next room, put a match to the fire laid in the grate, pushed the hot-water bottle between the sheets of the bed, and hastened downstairs. Her legs, her body, her hand flitting over the banisters, were as light and sure again as if she had never experienced so much as an hour even of mere disappointment in her life. Besides, for some little time now, that body had been habitually told what it had to do. And so long as her orders came promptly and concisely, it could be trusted to continue to act in the same fashion, to be instantly obedient. That was what being a mother taught you to become, and even taught you to try within limits to teach a young child to become—an animated automaton.

Dr. Wilson stood where she had left him beside the table and in precisely the same attitude. He had not even troubled to sit down. He had, apparently, not even so much as moved his eyes.

"Now, Doctor," said Emilia.

At this, those eyes first settled on her fingers, then quietly shifted to her face.

"You were a long time gone, Mrs. Hadleigh," he remonstrated in a drawling voice, as if his tongue were sticking to the roof of his mouth. "A very long time." He took the thermometer and pushed it gingerly between his lips, shutting them firmly over the thin glass stem. Then his blue and solemn eyes became fixed again, and, without the faintest stir, he continued to watch his mother, while she in turn watched him. When half a minute had gone by, he lifted his eyebrows. She shook her head. In another half-minute he himself took the thermometer out of his mouth, and, holding it between finger and thumb, gravely scrutinized it under the light. "A hundred and forty-seven," he announced solemnly. "H'm." Then he smiled, a half-secret, half-deprecatory smile. *"That's* nothing to worry about, Mrs. Hadleigh. Nothing at all. It looks to me as if all you did was to worry. Put him to bed; I will send him round a bottle of very nice medicine—*very* nice medicine. And . . ." his voice fell a little fainter, "I'll look in again in the morning."

His eyes had become fixed once more, focused, it seemed, on the far-away. "Mummie, I do wish when Mary pulls down the blinds she would do it to the very bottom. I *hate* seeing—seeing myself in the glass."

But Emilia had not really attended to this fretful and unreasonable complaint. She herself was now examining the thermometer. She was frowning, adjusting it, frowning again. Then she had said something—half-muttered, half-whispered—which Dr. Wilson had failed to catch.

"I'd give him," he again began wearily, "some rice pudding and lemonade, and—" But before the rest of his counsel could be uttered she had wrapped him tighter in his bath towel, had stooped down to him back to front so that he could clasp his hands round her neck, pick-a-back; and next moment he was being whisked up the dark staircase to the blue and white nursery.

There she slid him gently down beside the fender, took off his shoes, smoothed his fringe, and tenderly kissed him.

"You have very bright eyes, Dr. Wilson. You mustn't let them get too bright—just for my sake."

"Not at all, Mrs. Hadleigh," he parroted, and then suddenly his whole body began to shiver.

"There," she said, "now just begin to take off your clothes, my own precious, while I see to the fire—though *that,* Dr. Wilson, should have been done *first.* Look, the silly paper has just flared up and gone out. But it won't be a minute. The sticks are as dry as Guy Fawkes' Day. Soon cosy in bed now."

William with unusually stupid fingers was endeavouring to undo his buttons. He was already tired of being the doctor. "Why," he said, "do your teeth chatter, Mummie, when you are very hot? That seems funny. And why do faces come in the window, horrid faces? Is *that* blind right down to the very bottom? Because I would like it to be. Oh dear, my head does ache, Mummie."

It was extraordinary with what cleverness and dexterity Emilia's hands, unlike her son's, were now doing as they were bidden. The fire, coaxed by a little puffing in lieu of bellows, in a wondrous sheet of yellow, like crocuses, was now sweeping up the chimney as if to devour the universe. A loose under-blanket had been thrust into the bed, the hot bottle wrapped up in a fleecy old shawl, the coal-scuttle had been filled, a second pair of small pyjamas had been hung over the fender to air, a saucepan of milk had been stood on the stove with its gas turned low—like a circlet of little blue wavering beads; and William himself, half-naked for less than the fraction of a second, had been tucked up in his bed, one of her own tiny embroidered handkerchiefs sprinkled with lavender water for company. There, he had instantly fallen asleep, though spasmodic jerks of foot and hand, and flickering eyelids showed that his small troubles had not wholly been left behind him.

So swiftly and mechanically had her activities followed one upon the other that Emilia had only just realized that she was still unable to make up her mind whether to telephone at once to the doctor or to venture—to dare—to look in on Sallie.

Blind fool! *Blind* fool!—foreseeing plainly open or half-hidden hint and threat of to-night's event, smelling it, tasting it, hearing it again and again knocking at the door of her mind, she had yet continually deferred the dreadful moment when she must meet it face to face, challenge and be done with it, and accept its consequences. The mere image in her mind of her husband's school tie left abandoned on the bed had made the foreboding of looking at Sallie a last and all but insupportable straw. The futility, the cowardice! What needs most daring must be done instantly. There had not been the least need to debate such a question. You can't do twenty-*one* things at once!

Having stolen another prolonged scrutiny of William's pale dream-distorted face and dilating nostrils, she hastened into her own bedroom again, groped for the tiny switch-pull that dangled by the bed-rail, stooped over the cot beside it, and, screening its inmate's face as much as possible from the glare, looked down and in. The small blonde creature, lovelier and even more delicate to the eye than any flower, had kicked off all its bedclothes, the bright lips were ajar, the cheeks flushed—an exquisite coral red. And the body was breathing almost as fast and shallowly as a cat's. That children under three years old should talk in their sleep, yes; but with so minute a vocabulary! Still, all vocabularies are minute for what they are sometimes needed to express—or to keep silent about.

No sickness, no sore throat; but headache, lassitude, pains all over the body, shivering attacks and fever—you just added up the yeses and substracted the nots; and influenza, or worse, was the obvious answer. Should she or should she not wheel the cot into William's room? Sallie might wake, and wake William. Whereas if she remained here and she herself lay down in the night even for so much as an hour—and began to think, she wouldn't be alone, not hopelessly alone. It was the fear of waking either patient that decided the question. She very gently drew blanket and counterpane over Sallie's nakedness, draped a silk handkerchief over the rose-coloured shade, switched on the electric stove in the fireplace, and ran downstairs. There for a few moments, eyes restlessly glancing, she faced the stark dumbness and blindness of the mouthpiece of the telephone.

Dr. Wilson *was* in. Thank Heaven for that. Incredible, that was his voice! There might have been a maternity case—hours and hours. He might have had a horde of dispensary patients. But no, he would be round in a few minutes. Thank Heaven for that. She put back the receiver with a shuddering sigh of gratitude. All that was now needed—superhuman ordeal—was just to wait.

But this Emilia was to be spared. For midway up the staircase, whose treads now seemed at least twice their usual height, she had suddenly paused. Fingers clutching the banister rail, she stood arrested, stock still, icy, constricted. The garden gate had faintly clicked. There could be only one explanation of that—at least on a Wednesday. Edward's few friends and cronies, every one of them, must have discovered long ago that Wednesdays were now *his* "evenings out." And she—she hadn't much fancied friends or company recently. It was he himself, then. He had come back. What to do now? A ghastly revulsion took possession of her, a knawing ache in the pit of her stomach, another kind of nausea, another *kind,* even, of palpitation.

If only she could snatch a few minutes to regain her balance, to prepare herself, to be alone. Consciousness was like the scene of a fair—a dream-fair, all distortion, glare, noise, diablerie, and confusion. And before she was even aware of her decision—to make use of a deceit, a blind, a mere best-thing-for-the-time-being —she had found herself in her bedroom again, had somehow with cold and fumbling fingers folded the note into its pretty cocked-hat shape again, and replaced it where she had first set eyes on it, beside the charming little travelling clock, the gift of Aunt Sarah, in the middle of the mantelpiece.

What light remained in the room behind the blinded and cur-tained windows could not possibly have been detectible outside. That was certain. In an instant she was in William's room once more—listening, her heart beating against her ribs like the menac-ing thumping of a drum. She had not long to wait. The latch of the front door had faintly squeaked, the lower edge of the door itself had scraped very gently across the coarse mat within, had as softly and furtively shut.

"Is that you, Edward?" she heard herself very gently and in-sidiously calling over the banisters from the landing. "How lovely! You *are* home early. I didn't expect you for—for hours and hours!"

And now she had met and kissed him, full in the light of the hall lamp. "Why, what's the matter, darling . . . ? You are ill!" She was peering as if out of an enormous fog at the narrow, beloved, pallid countenance, the pale lips, the hunted, haunted, misery-stricken light-brown eyes in those pits of dark entreaty and despair.

"Is it *that's* brought you home?"

He continued to stare at her as if, spectacles lost, he were endeavouring to read a little book in very small print and in an unfamiliar language. His mouth opened, as if to yawn; he began to tremble a little, and said, "Oh, no; nothing much. A headache; I'm tired. Where *were* you?"

"Me?" But her lips remained faintly, mournfully, sympathetically smiling; her dark eyes were as clear and guileless and empty of reflections as pools of water under the windless blue of the sky. "I was in William's room. It's hateful to say it now, Edward— now that you are so tired yourself—but—but I'm rather afraid, poor mite, he's in for another cold—a little chill—and I shouldn't be surprised if Sallie . . . But don't worry about that—because, because there's nothing of course at all yet to worry about. It's you I'm thinking of. You look so dreadfully fagged and—what a welcome! . . . There's nothing . . . ?"

Her vocabulary had at last begun to get a little obstinate and inadequate. "You don't mean, Edward, there's anything *seriously* wrong? I fancy, you know"—she deliberately laid her hand for an instant on his—"I fancy *you* may be the least little bit feverish yourself—you too. Well . . ." She turned away, flung up a hand as if to flag off a railway train. "I'll get you something hot at once.

"And Edward"—she turned her head over her shoulder, to find him as motionless as she had left him, in almost as stolid and meaningless an attitude as "Dr. Wilson's" had been in the kitchen, as he stood brooding on the nightmare faces in the darkness of the glass. "There is just one thing, if you could manage it. Just in *case*, would you in a moment or two first wheel Sallie's cot into William's room. I've lit the fire—and I *had* to ask Dr. Wilson to come. I'm so dreadfully stupid and anxious, when—even when there's no reason to be."

The two faces had starkly confronted one another again, but neither could decipher with any absolute certainty the hitherto unrevealed characters now inscribed on them. Each of them was investigating the map of a familiar country, but the cartographer must now have sketched it from an unprecedentedly eccentric angle. The next moment she had turned away, had whisked upstairs and down again, leaving him free, at liberty, to dispose of himself—and of anything else he might be inclined to. In every family life there are surely potential keepsakes that would be far better destroyed; and perhaps a moment *some* time might come. But now . . .

When she returned with her tray and its contents—a steaming tumbler of milk, a few biscuits, and a decanter containing a little whisky—she found him standing beside William's bedroom fire. He watched her, as with the utmost care she put down her burden on the little wicker table.

"Millie," he said. "I'm not sure. . . . But, well—it was, I suppose, because of William's being ill that you haven't yet been into —into the other room, our bedroom. And so"—he had gulped, as if there was some little danger of producing his very heart for her inspection—"you have not seen *this?*" He was holding towards her the unfolded note, and with trembling fingers she found herself actually pretending to read its scribbled lines again.

Her face had whitened; she had begun to despair of herself, conscious beyond everything else—the tumult in her mind, the ravaging of her heart—that she could hardly endure the mingled miseries, remorse, humiliation in his eyes, in the very tones of his voice, yet listening at the same time to a message of ineffable reassurance. He has not then deceived me again! At last she had contrived to nod, her chin shaking so stupidly for a while that she could scarcely utter a word. "Yes. I *have* read it. I put it back . . . couldn't face it when I heard you. The children—I had to have time. I'm *sorry,* Edward."

" '*Sorry!*' " he echoed.

"I mean—it *was* an awful, well, revelation; but I was stupid; I

ought to have seen . . . I did see. But we won't—I *can't* go into
that now. You are tired, ill; but you are back . . . for the present."

Her eyes had managed at last to glance at him, and then to
break away, and to keep from weeping. And, as if even in his
sleep his usual small tact and wisdom had not deserted him,
William had suddenly flung back his scorching sheet and in a
gasping voice was muttering to an unseen listener in some broken,
unintelligible lingo that yet ended with a sound resembling the
word "faces." "There, darling," she answered him, smoothing
back his fair fringe from his forehead, "*I* know. They are gone;
all gone now; and the blind *is* down—to its very last inch."

She stayed watching him, couldn't look back just yet.

"You see, Millie . . . She"—her husband was trying to explain
—"that is, *we* had arranged to meet. It's hopeless to attempt to
say anything more just now. . . . I waited. She sent. . . . She
didn't come."

"I see. And so?"

"Millie, Millie. It wasn't, it wasn't *you*. Oh, I can't bear it
any longer. If I had dreamed—the children!" He had flung himself into a pretty round basket chair and sat shuddering, his face
hidden in his lean, bloodless hands.

The few minute sounds in the room, the peevish creakings of
the chair, William's rapid, snoring breathing, the fluttering of
the fire, were interrupted by the noise of brakes and wheels
rasping to a standstill in the street below. A brisk yet cautious
knocking had followed, awakening an echo, it seemed, in the
very hollow of her breast bone.

"Look," she said, "that's where *that* goes. There's no *time* now."
The scrap of paper, more swiftly than a vanishing card in a
conjuring trick, had been instantly devoured by the voracious
flames, had thinned to an exquisitely delicate fluttering ash, and
then, as if with a sudden impulse, wafted itself out of sight like
a tiny toy balloon into the sooty vacany of the chimney.

"Listen. Must *you* see the doctor, to-night? Unless it's not—
you know—well, *bad* 'flu? Wouldn't it be better not? I'll tell
him; I could find out; I could say you had gone to bed. Quick,
I must go." Every nerve in her body was clamouring for motion,
action, something to face, something to do.

He nodded. "And you'll come back?"

"Yes. . . . I'll try. Oh, Edward, I'm sorry, sorry. If only there were words to say it. It must have been awful—awful!" She hesitated, gazing at his bent head, the familiar hands. . . .

And now the doctor, having deftly packed up Sallie again, burning hot but seemingly resigned to whatever fate might bring, and having carefully wiped his thermometer on the clean huckaback towel Emilia had handed him, was stuffing his stethoscope back into his little brown case. An almost passionate admiration filled her breast at his assured, unhurried movements, and with it a sort of mute, all-reconciling amusement to see how closely, deep within, behind these gestures, and the careful choice of words, he resembled his small and solemn understudy, William.

She was returning earnestly glance for glance, intently observant of every least change of expression in his dark decisive face, of timbre in his voice. Practically every one of the hungered-for, familiar, foreseen, all-satisfying assurances—like a tiny flock of innocent sheep pattering through a gateway—had been uttered and sagaciously nodded to: "It may be just a feverish attack; it might, it *might* be 'flu." "Don't forget, Mrs. Hadleigh, they are down one moment and up the next!" "I'll send round a bottle of medicine to-night, almost at once, and some powders." "I'll look in again first thing in the morning." Then he had paused, little leather case in hand, his eyes fixed on the fire.

Some day, she told herself, she *must* retaliate in kind: "You must understand, Dr. Wilson, that at this hour of the night it would be utterly stupid of you to breathe the word 'pneumonia,' which takes weeks and weeks and weeks; may easily be fatal; and one has just to wait for the crisis!" Or, "Don't be mistaken, Dr. Wilson, even if you were at death's door yourself I shouldn't hesitate to ring you up if their temperatures go over 103"—that kind of thing.

"You know, Mrs. Hadleigh," he was beginning again, "it just beats me why you mothers—quite rational, sensible, almost cynically practical creatures some of you, simply wear yourselves out with worry and anxiety when there's scarcely a shred of justification for it. Quite uselessly. Getting thin and haggard, wasting away, losing all that precious youth and beauty. I say I often *think* these things—wish I could express them. You simply refuse to heed *the* lesson in life: that really great Englishman's, Mr. Asquith's—'Wait and See.' *Condensing,* don't you see, and not squandering all energy, impulse and reserves. 'Never trouble trouble until trouble troubles you.' Isn't *that* good sense? It's what's called an old wives' saying, of course—not a mother's. But I could have saved dozens of precious lives and bodies and all but souls, if only . . . well, literally saved them, I mean, a deuce of a lot of wear and tear."

She was drinking in his words, this delicious lecture, these scoldings; devouring them, as if they were manna dipped in honey, the waters of life. They were a rest and peace beyond expression. A ready help in time of trouble. He shall lead his flock like a shepherd. Yea, though I walk . . . Why all this Bible? Dr. Wilson was not a parson; he was just a doctor. And then another Dr. Wilson had piped up in memory again, " 'You *said* that I was the doctor; and now you are kissing me, Mummie!' . . . 'I could often kiss lots of doctors!' "

"I know, I know," she heard herself meekly assuring him. "I'm utterly stupid about these things. And of course if we were all sensible savages or gipsies there wouldn't be . . . Even—oh, but you can't think what a comfort it is to—to be reassured."

He was eyeing her now more closely, totting up and subtracting yeses and nots, it seemed, on his own account, and on hers. It was with difficulty she met the straight clear scrutiny. "Well, there we are," he decided. "Just look what lovely babies you have. Everything a woman could wish for! Gipsies be dashed. There are, I assure you, my dear Mrs. Hadleigh, spinsters galore in this parish who . . . How's your husband?"

Her dark shining eyes had now at last quivered in their sockets, if only for the fraction of a second.

"It sounds very silly," the words were squeezing out like cooing turtle doves through too narrow an exit, "but *he's* not very well either! It's, it's almost funny, ridiculous—all three at once. Isn't it? He came home rather late from—from the office, and he's gone to bed." It seemed a pity that one's cheeks should flatly refuse not to flame up, when one's eyes were hard as brass. "The fact is, Dr. Wilson, he refused to see you. You know what men are. But could it be, do you think," a little nod towards William's bed had helped her out, "that too?"

"I think," Dr. Wilson had replied dryly, a scarcely perceptible forking frown between his eyebrows, "it might very well be that too. But listen, Mrs. Hadleigh. Husbands, of course, are not really of much importance in life—not really. Necessities perhaps; but here to-day and gone to-morrow. *Children* are what the kernel is to the nut; the innermost part of it. And so must be taken great care of. *Therefore*—and this is not advice; this is *orders*: I forbid you to worry; forbid it. I shall throw up the case! If you *must* stay up—you have a maid, a good solid, stolid one too. Wake her up and chance it; she'll love you all the better. And you can share the night between you. Otherwise—unless of course you need me again, and you won't, though I should be *easily* handy —you are not only not to worry (more than you can help) but you are on no account to get up more than twice until the morning to look at your patients—at *our* patients, mind you. It's bad for them, worse for you. When they've had their dose, they'll soon quieten down—unless I'm *wrong*. And—imagine it!—I sometimes am." He was holding out his hand, a look of unadulterated, generous, wholly masculine admiration on his vigilant, assured features.

"By gad!" he said. "All three! But then *you* know *I* know what you can manage when hard pressed. So that's all right." He was plunging downstairs into the night, and Emilia was trying in vain to keep up with him.

"And after the first dose and the powders, Dr. Wilson, I shouldn't, I suppose, wake either of them up to give them any *more* medicine—not until the morning?"

"As a general rule, Mrs. Hadleigh," replied the doctor, carefully putting on his hat and glancing as he did so into the strip of looking-glass on the wall, "it's wiser never to wake *anybody* up, merely to give them physic—even mere doctor's physic."

The Wind Blows Over (1936)

THE TRUMPET

"For Brutus, as you know, was Caesar's angel. . . ."

"And he said . . . Am I my brother's keeper?"

THE MINUTE church, obscurely lit by a full moon that had not yet found window-glass through which her direct beams could pierce into its gloaming, was deserted and silent. Not a sound, within or without, disturbed its stony quiet—except only the insect-like rapid ticking of a clock in the vestry, and the low pulsating thump of a revolving cogwheel in the tower above the roof. Here and there a polished stone gleamed coldly in the vague luminous haze—a marble head, a wing tip, a pointing finger, the claws and beak of the eagle on the brazen lectern, the two silvergilt candlesticks flanking the colourless waxen flowers upon the altar. So secret and secluded seemed the church within its nocturnal walls that living creature might never have been here at all—or creatures only so insignificant and transitory as to have left no perceptible trace behind them.

Like a cataleptic's countenance it hinted moreover at no inward activity of its own. And yet, if—fantastic notion—some unseen watcher through the bygone centuries had kept it perpetually within gaze, he might at last have concluded that it possessed a *sort* of stagnant life or animation, at least in its passive obedience to the influences of time, change, decay, and the laws of gravitation. Now it revealed not the faintest symptom of it. If, on the other hand, any immaterial sentinel were still, as ever, on guard within it, he made no sign of his presence here.

Unhasteningly, like water dripping from the fateful urn, the thump-recorded moments ebbed away; and it was approaching midnight and first cockcrow when from beyond the thick stone chancel walls there came the sound of a stealthy footfall, crunching the rain-soaked gravel. An owl squawked, the footsteps ceased; and after a brief pause, began again. The groping rattle of a key in the wards of a lock followed, and presently—with a motion so slow that it was barely perceptible—the heavy curtain that hung over the entrance to the vestry began as if with an infinite caution to be drawn aside; and the slender cone-shaped rays from the thick glass of a small bull's-eye lantern—its radiance thinning into the dusk of the moonlight as it expanded in area—to funnel inquisitively to and fro.

The lantern-bearer himself now appeared—a small boy. His thick fair hair was tousled over a pale forehead, his mouth was ajar and his lips were drawn back a little above his teeth, his eyes gleamed as they moved. The collar of his dark greatcoat had been turned up about his ears, but nevertheless disclosed in the crevice between its lapels the stripes of a pyjama jacket which had been tucked into a pair of old flannel breeches. Stockinged ankles and damp mud-stained rubber shoes showed beneath the greatcoat. His cheeks at this moment were so pale as scarcely to be tinged with red, and since the pupils of his blue eyes were dilated to their full extent they appeared to be all but jet-black. He was shivering, in part by reason of the cold, in part because of certain inward qualms and forebodings. Only by an effort was he preventing his teeth from beginning to chatter. Still acutely cautious and intent, his head thrust forward, his eyes searching the darker recesses of the building around him as they followed the direction of his tiny searchlight, he stole a pace or two forward, the border of the heavy curtain furtively swinging to behind him. In spite of the door-key safe in his pocket, he appeared to be divided in mind between hope and dread that he might prove to be not the sole occupant of the church.

Where there is space enough for the human cranium to pass, the shoulders, it is said, can follow; and particularly if they all three belong to a child. One small diamond-paned window in the vestry he had already observed was open. Images, too, less substantial in appearance than those of human beings were occupying his mind's eye. When then a little owl in the dark of the yew tree over the south gate in the moonlit churchyard again suddenly screeched, he started as if at an electric shock. And twice his mouth opened before he managed to call low and hoarsely, "Are you there, Dick? . . . Dick, are you there?"

Not a stony eyelid in the heads around him had so much as flickered at this timid challenge. The stooping eagle—a large shut Bible on its outstretched wings—had stirred not a feather; the pulpit remained cavernously empty. But a few high-panelled pews, relics of the past, were within view, and even moonlight and lantern-light combined were powerless to reveal anything or anybody that might be hiding behind them. The trespasser appeared to be on the point of retiring as secretly as he had come, when a jangling gurgle, as of some monster muttering in its sleep, began to sound above his head, and the clock chimes rang out the second quarter of the hour. The vibrant metal ceased to hum; and, as if reassured by this interruption, he drew out of his pocket a large stone—a flint such as his remote ancestors would have coveted—roughly dumb-bell in shape, and now waisted with a thick and knotted length of old blind-cord. This primitive weapon, long treasured for any emergency, he gently deposited on the shelf behind him, and then followed it into the pew.

Lantern still in hand, he seated himself on the flat faded red cushion that lay along the seat. It was that of one of the mighty, the rector's warden. Even in this half-light, as easily as a cat in the dark, he could spy out all about him now, organ-recess to gallery; but he opened his brand-new lantern none the less and trimmed as best he could with his fingernail its charred and oily wick. The fume and stench of the hot metal made him sneeze, whereupon he clicked-to the glass, covered it with his hand, and began listening again. "Sneak," he muttered, then suddenly plumped down on the hassock at his feet, rapidly repeated a prayer, with a glance over his shoulder half-covertly crossed himself, then as promptly sat up again; glancing as he did so at the pulpit over his head, which he was accustomed to find comfortably brimmed with his father's portly presence.

Fortified by his prayer and by his wrath with the friend who it seemed at the last moment had abandoned their enterprise, he was now comparatively at ease. Tortoise-fashion he snuggled down in his greatcoat in the corner of the pew, having discovered that by craning his neck a little he could fix his vacant eyes on the brilliant disc of the still-ascending moon.

She was the Hunter's moon, and her beams had now begun to silver a clear-glassed square-headed window high up in the south wall of the chancel. He watched her intently, lost in astonishment that at this very moment she should be keeping tryst with him here. But before she had edged far enough above the sill to greet the gilded figure of an angel that surmounted an ornate tomb opposite her peephole, a faint thief-like shuffle from the direction of the vestry door caught his ear. He instantly dropped out of sight into the shelter of his pew. The shuffling ceased, the door creaked. He crouched low; a smile at once apprehensive and malicious creasing his still-childish face. He would give his friend Dick a taste of his own physic.

In the hush, a lamentable *Oh, oh, oh, oh!*—like the cry of a captured mermaid wailed up from his lips into the dusk of the roof. *Oh, oh, oh!* Then silence—and silence. And still there came no response. The smile faded out of his face; he had begun to shiver again. He was positively certain that this must be the friend whom he was expecting. And yet—suppose it was not! He leapt up, flashing at the same instant his toy lantern full into the glittering eyes of a dwarfish and motionless shape which were fixed on him through the sockets of a pitch-black battered mask—a relic of the last Fifth of November.

He had realized what trick was being played on him almost before he had had time to be afraid. Nevertheless, for a few moments, his mouth wide open, he had failed to breathe; and stood shuddering with rage as well as terror. His friend Dick, however, having emerged from his lair in the folds of the curtain, was now plunging about half doubled-up and almost helpless with laughter.

"You silly fool!" he fumed at him in a whisper, "what did you want to do that for? Shut up! Shut *up*, I tell you! You think

it's funny, I suppose. Well, I don't. You're hours late already, and
I'm going home. Stop it, do you hear? Can't you remember
you're in a *church*?"

From beneath its mask a small sharp-nosed and utterly sober
face now showed itself—all laughter gone. "Who began it, then?"
Dick expostulated, dejectedly squeezing his pasteboard mask into
his pocket. "You tried it first on me, with your Oh-oh-oh-ing.
And now just because . . . You didn't think of 'church' then."

"Well, I do now. Besides, it's near the time, and I might have
broken my neck for all you cared, getting out of the window.
What made you so late?"

Dick had been eyeing his friend as might a sorrowful mouse a
slice of plum cake a few inches out of its reach. "I'm sorry, Philip,"
he said. "I didn't mean any harm; honest, I didn't. It was only
a lark." He turned penitently away, and the next instant, as if
all troubles were over and all discord pacified, began peeping
about him with the movements and anglings of some little night-
creature on unexpectedly finding itself in an utterly strange place.

"I say, Philip," he whispered, "doesn't it look creepy just, the
moon shining in? I had a dream, and then I woke. But I couldn't
have come before. My father was downstairs with a lamp, reading. Besides I was waiting for you *out*side, under the trees. Why
did you come *in*? It's by the gate you see them. That's what my
mother heard *your* mother say. Oh, I'm glad I came; aren't you?"

The sentences were sprayed out in minute beads of words like
the hasty cadenzas of a bird. The neat black head, the small
bright eyes, the shallow wall of close-cropped hair, the sloping
shoulders—every line, movement, and quick darting variation
of posture gave him a resemblance to a bird—including the alert,
quick, shy yet fearless spirit within that neat skull's brittle walls.

Philip, who had been intently watching him meanwhile, had
now recovered his equanimity, his pulse had sobered down, but
he was still only partially placated, and querulous.

"Of course I came in. What was the good of loafing out there
where *any*body might see us? It's cold and mouldy enough in
here. You don't seem to remember I mustn't go out at night,
because of my chest. I've been waiting until my feet are like
stones. Did you hear that owl just now—or something?"

Dick having at last ventured in from the other end of the pew, had now seated himself beside his friend on the flat crimson cushion.

"Golly!" he exclaimed, his sharp eyes now fixed on the flint, "what's that for? I shouldn't care to have a crump over the head with that!" He peered up winningly into his companion's fair face. "I didn't really expect you would come, Philip. But," he sighed, "I'm glad."

"Didn't I *say* I would come?" retorted Philip in a small condescending voice. "That's nothing." He nodded at his stone. "I always carry that at night. How was I to know . . . ? *Didn't* I?"

The neat small head nodded violently. "M'm."

"Then why didn't you expect me to?"

"Oh, well, I didn't." A thin ingratiating little smile passed over Dick's face and as quickly vanished. "It wasn't so easy for you as it was for me. That's why."

"That stone," said Philip incisively, "keeps any harm from happening to me. It's got magic in it."

"Has it, Philip? . . . What did *that*?" He was eyeing the patch of dried blood on the hand that clutched the bent wire handle of the lantern.

"Oh, that?" was the lofty reply. "That's nothing; that was only the rope. It burned like billy-oh, and I fell halfway from my bedroom window-sill on to the lawn. An awful crack. But nobody heard me, even though the other windows were wide open round the corner. You could see them against the sky. My mother always sleeps with her windows open—all the year round. A doctor in London told her it would be good for her. I don't believe that about your father reading, though. When everybody is in bed and asleep! I didn't even know your father *could* read."

"Well, he was, or I wouldn't have said so. He was reading the Bible. How could I tell that if he wasn't reading at all?"

"Anyhow, I bet it wasn't the Bible. Even my father wouldn't do that—not after evening prayers. Would he whack you much if he caught you?"

Dick shook his head. "No fear. My mother won't have *him* punishing me, whatever happens. He preaches at me no end;

and says I'll never be good for anything. Once," he added pensively, as if scarcely able to believe his own ears, "once he said I was a little imp of hell. Then my mother flared up. But he wouldn't beat me; oh no, he wouldn't beat me. Yesterday my mother came back with a big bundle of old clothes. There was a black silk jacket, and some stockings and hats and feathers and things, an *enormous* bundle. And this—look!"

He undid a button of his jacket and pulled out from underneath it a pinch of an old green silk dressing-gown.

"Why, that's mine!" said Philip. "I've had it for ages." He stared at it censoriously, as if dubious whether or not to ask for it back. "But I don't think I want it now, because it's miles too small for me. My grandmother gave it me for a Christmas present donkey's years ago. She's so rich she doesn't mind *what* things cost—when she gives me anything. That's real Spitalfields silk, that is; you can't get it anywhere now. You'll crumple it up and spoil it if you wear it stuffed in like that." He peered closer. "What have you got on underneath it? You're all puffed out like a turkey-cock."

Dick promptly edged back from the investigating finger, a sly look of confusion passing swiftly over his face. "That's my other clothes," he explained.

"What *I* say," said Philip, still eyeing his companion as if only a constant vigilance could hope to detect what he might not be up to next, "what *I* say is, your mother's jolly lucky to get expensive things given to her—good things, even if they *are* left-offs. Most of our old stuff goes to the Jumble Sales. I bet," he suddenly broke off, "I bet if your *real* father found you skulking here, he'd whack you hot and strong."

The alert and supple body beside his own had suddenly stiffened, and the dangling spindle legs beneath the pew ceased to swing.

"No, he wouldn't," Dick hardly more than whispered.

"Why not?"

"For one thing he just wouldn't. He knows he's nothing to do with me; not now; and leaves me alone. For all that, I went out rabbiting with him one night last summer. And nobody knew. It was warm and still and pitch-dark—not like this; and when

the moon began to come up over the woods, he sent me home.
I know *he* wouldn't either. Besides," he drew in his chin a little
as if the words were refusing to come out of his throat, "he's
dead."

"Dead! Oh, I say! I like that! Oh no, he isn't; *that's* not true.
He isn't dead. Why, I heard them reading out about in the newspaper only a few weeks ago. That's what you *say*. I know what
has become of him; and I bet your tongue is burning. What's
more, if your other father hadn't been Chapel you would never
have had *any* father—not to show, I mean. Your mother would
have been just like any other woman, though I don't suppose she
could have gone on living in the village. But as he *is* Chapel,
and, according to what you say, sits up as late as this reading the
Bible, I can't understand why he lets you sing in our choir. I call
that being a hypocrite. I'd like to see my father letting *me* go to
chapel. He must be just a hypocrite, Bible or not."

Dick made no attempt whatever to examine this delicate moral
question. "Oh no, he isn't," he retorted hotly. "He's as good as
yours any day. He goes by what my mother says: if you are
Chapel, keep Chapel. *She's* not a hypocrite. And you'd better
not say so, either."

"I didn't say it. I didn't say that your mother was a hypocrite;
not a *hypocrite*. I like your mother. And nobody's going to prevent me from going with you either, if I want to. Not if I want
to. Your mother's been jolly decent to me—often. Mrs. Fuller
sneaks: *she* doesn't."

"So is your mother to me—when you aren't there. At least
she talks to me sometimes then. And I'm glad you're my friend,
Philip. The other day she gave me a hunch of cake, and she
made me share a sip of wine from my mother's glass. Because
it was her birthday. Some day I'm going to be a sailor, and
going to sea. She had been crying, because her eyes were red;
and *your* mother said that crying was no use at all—because I'm
growing up more and more like her every day, and shall be a
comfort to her when I'm a man. And so I will; you see!"

" 'Wine'! Did she just? But that was only because she's always
kind to people—to everybody. She doesn't mind *who* it is. That's
why she likes being liked by everybody. But after what my father

read out in the newspaper, he said he entreated her to be more careful. She must think of *him,* my father said. He didn't want to have the village people talking. He tapped his eyeglasses on the paper and said it was a standing scandal. That's what he said. He was purple in the face." His voice rather suddenly fell silent, as if, like a dog, he had scented indiscretions. "But I say: *if* your real father is just dead, he would be the very person according to you to be coming here to-night. *Then* you'd look mighty funny, I should think."

Dick's legs, like opposed pendulums, had begun very sluggishly to swing again. "Oh no, I wouldn't, because that's just what doesn't happen; and I told you so. It's the people who are going to die soon—next year—who come: *their* ghosts. Wouldn't they look white and awful, Philip, coming in under the yew tree? . . . I expect its roots go down all among the coffins. Shall we go out now and watch? It's as bright as day; you could see a bird hopping about."

" 'Ghosts'!" was the derisive reply. "I like that! *You* can. I'm not. How can they be ghosts, silly, if they're still alive? Besides, even if there are such things, and even if what your mother told you is really true, you said yourself that they would come *into* the church. So if any *should* come and we keep here and hide and peep over the edge, they can't possibly see us—if ghosts do see. And then we shall be near the door in there. They would be surprised to find that one open, I should think. But even if they were, and ghosts don't mind doors, they wouldn't come in at a potty little door like that."

He paused as if to listen, and continued more boldly. "Not, mind you, that I believe a single word of anything you've said— all that stuff. Not really. I came . . ." he faltered, turning his head away, "only just for a game, and because you dared me to. Why you asked me to come *really* is because you were frightened of being here alone. You wait and see, I'll dare *you* in a minute. Besides, how do you know anybody *is* going to die in the village next year—except old Mrs. Harrison? And she's been dying ever since I can remember. She takes snuff, but she can't stir a foot out of her bed. I bet she hasn't any ghost left. *She* wouldn't come." The sentence suddenly concluded in a prodigious shudering yawn. It reminded him that he was cold and that the fatal moment was rapidly nearing. "Did they say, before, or after, the clock strikes?"

Dick paused a moment before replying, and then piped up confidently: "It's the very second while the last clump of the bell is sounding. That's when they get to the church. Because it's midnight. And all the ghosts begin to walk then. Some come up out of their graves. But"—he sighed, as if saddened at the poverty of his expectations—"only very seldom. The people who go to heaven wouldn't want to, and the Devil wouldn't let the others out. At least that's what I think."

"What *you* think! And yet," retorted Philip indignantly, "you talk all that stuff about ghosts; and believe it too. I'd just like to see your ghost. That'd be a skinny one if you like—like a starved bird. Would *you* come back?"

Dick leant his body forward; he was sitting on his hands; and at this his black, close-cropped head nodded far more vigorously than a china Mandarin's. "I don't *know*," he said; "but I like being out at night. I like—oh, everything. . . . If ghosts can smell," he began again in small matter-of-fact tones, "they'd soon snuff *us* out. Look at it smoking."

The two boys sat mute for a while, watching the tiny slender thread of sooty smoke from the lantern wreathing up in the luminous air; and in the silence—which, after their tongues had ceased chattering, immediately flooded the church fathoms deep —they stayed, listening; their senses avid for the faintest whisper. But the night was windless, and the earth coldly still in the glassy radiance of the moon. And if the saints in their splendour were already assembling in the heavens to celebrate their earthly festival, no sound of their rejoicings reached these small pricked-up human ears.

"If," at last Dick exploded, gazing up into the vaporour glooms of the roof above his head, "if any more light comes in, the walls will burst. I love the moon; I love the light. . . . *I'*m going to have a peep."

With a galvanic wriggle he had snatched his arm free from Philip's grasp, had nimbly whipped out of the pew, and vanished behind the curtain that concealed the vestry door.

Philip shuffled uneasily in his seat, hesitating whether or not to follow him. But from a native indolence and for other motives, and in spite of his incredulity, he decided to stay where he was. It seemed safer than the churchyard. From a few loose jujubes in his greatcoat pocket he chose the cleanest, and sat quietly sucking, his eyes fixed on the monument that not only dominated but dwarfed the small but lovely chancel. The figure of its angel was now bathed with the silver of the moon. With long-toed feet at once clasping and spurning the orb beneath them, it stood erect, on high. Chin outthrust, its steadfast sightless eyes were fixed upon the faded blue and geranium-red of the panelled roof. Its braided locks drawn back from a serene and impassive visage, its left hand lay flat upon its breast, and with the right it clasped a tapering, uplifted, bell-mouthed, gilded trumpet, held firmly not against but at a little distance from its lips.

Unlike Dick, Philip was not a chorister. He was none the less his father's son, and as soon as he had learned to behave himself, to put his penny in the plate, and to refrain from babbling aloud, he had been taken to church every Sunday morning. This had been as natural an accompaniment of the Sabbath as clean underclothes, Etons, and hot sausages for breakfast. Thus he had heard hundreds of his father's sermons—sermons usually as simple as they were short. If only he had listened to them he might by now have become well-founded in dogma, a plain but four-square theologian. Instead of listening, however, he would usually sit "thinking." Side by side with his mother, his cheek all but brushing her silks, with their delicate odours, his fingers—rather clammy fingers when the weather was hot—lightly clasping hers while he counted over and over the sharp-stoned rings on her dainty fingers, he had been wont to follow his fancies.

Morning service had been the general rule. During the last few years however his mother had become the victim of periodical sick headaches, of lassitude and palpitations, and had been given strict injunctions not to overdo things, to rest. Occasionally too she had worldly-minded visitors, including a highly unorthodox sister, whom it would be tactless even to attempt to persuade to spend her Sundays as, usually, she felt dutifully impelled to spend her own. All this she would confide to Philip. She must on no account, she repeatedly admonished him, be alarmed or worried, distressed or disturbed. As for his stout and rubicund father, who was at least ten years her senior, he adored every bone in her body. But though by nature placable and easy-going, he was also subject to outbursts of temper and fits of moroseness as periodical as her attacks of migraine. It was therefore prudent, if only for her sake, to avoid anything in the nature of a scene. "So, Philip," she would cajole him, "you will *promise* me to be a good boy, and you'll go to church this evening, won't you—instead of now? And you won't make any fuss about it? You know your father wishes it."

Philip might demur, and, if it was practicable, bargain with her; but at heart he much preferred this arrangement. It meant that on these particular Sundays he was safe from interference, and could spend the whole morning as he pleased. It was too the darkening evenings about the time of the equinox, when it was not yet necessary to light the brass oil-lamps that hung in the nave, and two solitary candlesticks alone gleamed spangling in the pulpit—it was these he loved best. Only the village and farm people came to evening service, and not many even of them. Philip would sit in his pew, and, absorbed in his secret cogitations, enjoy the whole hour. The church changed then its very being. It welled over with mystery. Even in the joy of a Harvest Festival, when he could admire the flowers and vegetables and the gigantic loaf of bread under the lectern, the bloom of grapes and apples, the minute sheaves of wheat and barley gently nodding their heads to the more impulsive strains of the organ, there was still a faint tinge of sadness. And the unheeded sermon drowsed his senses like an incantation. His father's honeyed pulpit voice rose and fell like that of some dulcet Old Man of the Sea; and he himself, though not, like Dick, sporting and whispering noiselessly with his surpliced choir-mates out of sight of the preacher, was at any rate beyond any direct scrutiny. Meanwhile the bulky family cook, his mother's usual proxy on these occasions, would settle down beside him into a state of apathy so complete, her cotton-gloved hands convulsively clasped over her diaphragm, that it was only by an occasional sniff he could tell that she was perhaps lead-ing as active an internal life as he was, and was neither asleep nor dead.

Now and then he had himself been wafted away in sleep into regions of the most exorbitant scenery, events, and vagaries; to be aroused suddenly by, "And now to God, the Father . . . ," blear-eyed, lost, and with so violent a start that it had all but dis-located his neck. The most beguiling and habitual of these rev-eries had been concerned with the angel. How and when his spec-ulations on it had originated, what random bird had dropped this extravagant seed of a hundred daydreams into his mind, was be-yond discovery now. But it was to the cook that he had confided his first direct questions concerning it.

One low thundery evening, during their brief solitary journey through the churchyard into the hedged-in narrow lane by the coach-house and stables, and so through the garden and back to the rectory, he had managed to blurt out, "Mrs. Sullivan, why did they make the angel so as she can't *blow* the trumpet?" And this although his mind had been busied over the wholly different and more advanced problems— What exactly would happen if for any reason she ever did?

Until this moment Mrs. Sullivan had been unaware of the an-gel's perpetual predicament, and her attitude was cautious and tentative.

"I *expect*," she said, "it was because they couldn't help them-selves. Besides, Master Philip, what you are talking about isn't a real angel, no more than what her trumpet is a real trumpet. And who's to say if even a real angel could blow a trumpet that isn't real. I wouldn't care to go so far as that myself. Besides, who's to know as it is a she?"

Here, in this darker quiet, under the thick-leaved ilexes, Philip always drew a little nearer to his stout and panting companion; and sometimes for reassurance slipped a hand under her elbow. Free again, and the stars visible in the autumn sky, he had ven-tured to protest.

"But *why* couldn't they? And of course it's a she. Besides it was *I* who said she can't. *I* told *you*. It's three inches at least from her mouth. Like this. I've measured it heaps and heaps of times."

" '*Measured* it,' Master Philip! Well, that's a nice thing to be getting up to! All I can say is if that's the kind of mischief you are after I don't know what your father wouldn't say."

"I didn't mean *really*," was the impatient reply. "How could I? I meant by looking, of course. How *could* I mean 'really'?" There was scorn in his voice, even though his question had fallen like a hint from heaven into the quiet of his mind.

"If it's just guessing," Mrs. Sullivan had complacently decided, "I wouldn't suppose it could be *three*. And, though *your* young eyes may be better than mine, it might be no more than just a shadow. . . . It looks as if it had been raining, according to all these puddles."

Philip had paid no attention to the puddles, except that he had continued to enjoy quietly walking through them. "But you said just now," he persisted, "that you'd never even seen the angel. So how can you possibly tell? Anyhow, it *is* three, it's more than three, it's more likely four or five. You don't seem to remember how far she is up under the roof. Why, the end of her trumpet nearly touches the ceiling. *I* think that was silly. *Why* didn't they?"

They were drifting back to his original riddle again. But Mrs. Sullivan, reminded of another kind of trumpet, was meditating vaguely at this moment on a deaf bedridden sister who lived in the Midlands. "I never knew a boy with so many questions," she answered him ruminatively, almost as if she were explaining the situation to a third party. "I suppose it's because the Last Day hasn't risen on us as yet. That at least is what it was meant to mean for the gentleman that's laid in the tomb beneath it—and for any of us for that matter. God send it never may!"

"You mean *you* think *she* is waiting for the Last Day? I don't know what you mean by 'never.' There must be *a* Last Day, and that would be *the* Last Day. And if she's waiting for that, what will happen then—*after* the last?"

"Well, Master Philip, if you are the son of your own father, which I take you to be, you should best be able to answer that question for yourself. I don't hold with such pryings. It's far from ready *I'm* likely to be."

"Why not?"

"Because," said Mrs. Sullivan, "I'm getting old, and time is not what it was. When I was a young girl I nearly brooded all the blood out of my body thinking of things like that; though you might not suppose so now. Not that the young should or need be doing so, though I'm not saying there's no need even for *them* not to mind their p's and q's. There is."

"What are p's and q's?"

But this tepid and lifeless inquiry might have been borne on the winds of Arabia, it seemed so far away.

"Goodness gracious, you've got a tongue like an empty money-box. I see your mamma has gone to bed. Let's hope her sick head-ache is no worse. And here comes the rector."

Philip had accepted Mrs. Sullivan's complex solution of his difficulty with reservations, and had pondered continually on parts of it. After that, apart perhaps from a stray dog or bird, or a strange human face, nothing in church, or in the Scriptures, not even Jezebel or the Scarlet Woman, or Gideon, or Og, or Samson's foxes in the wheat, or golden Absalom hanging in the oak tree, or hairy Esau with his mess of pottage, or Elisha and the widow's cruse—nothing had so instantly galvanized him into a rapt attention as the least word he heard uttered about an angel or a trumpet. He had even taken to searching the Bible on his own account to satisfy his craving.

To-night, none the less, was the first time he had ever been alone with his angel—wholly alone. And he had risked a good deal for her sake—a caning from his father; a break-neck fall from his bedroom window if the clothesline had proved as rotten as it looked; a scurry, heart in mouth, through the fusty dark of the shrubbery; and the possibility, far more affrighting than he had confessed, of strange meetings at the lych-gate. Besides there was the humiliation of having been beguiled into this crazy expedition by a friend who was frowned at if not forbidden, and who was not only one of the "village boys," but clouded and compromised at that.

It was a companionship that fretted Philip at times almost beyond bearing, but from which he could not contrive to break free. Scrubbed and polished Dick might be, but he never *looked* clean.

He could be stupider than an owl, and yet was as sharp and quick as a pygmy sparrowhawk, and feared nothing and nobody. Sometimes even the mere sight of his intent, small-nosed face, and its dark eyes, now darting with life and eagerness, now laden with an inscrutable melancholy; of his very hands, even—small and quick, and his tiny pointed ears, filled Philip with an acute distaste. Yet there was a curious and continual fascination in his company.

He was like a mysterious and unintelligible little animal, past caging or taming, and possessed of a spirit of whose secret presence he himself was completely unaware. Contrariwise, he could be as demure, submissive, and affectionate as a little girl, and it was past all hope to find out where his small mind was ranging. Philip admired, despised, was jealous of, and sometimes bitterly hated him.

Why, he wondered, did his father always become so flustered and unreasonable at the mere mention of his name; or why, his mother either, for that matter? If an unexpected tradesman's bill from London or the county town accompanied his *Morning Post,* why was the heated discussion of this particular topic almost bound sooner or later to follow? First a few "words"—and of a steadily densening drift; a desultory wrangle; but at last his mother, flaming with anger, in tears, would flare up like a loose heap of gunpowder, and his father would subside into a sulky and cowed acquiescence.

Even if Dick was *not* the son of the sober and crusted old wheelwright at the other end of the village, what did that matter? And if Dick's mother *was* so close a confidante of his own mother, what did that? Wasn't there every reason why she should be? Only a few years before this, she had been parlour-maid at the rectory, a quiet, fair, meditative creature. And then all of a sudden she had left and got married. But she was still the best "help" in the house imaginable. No one could wait at table so deftly and sedately as she could; and not even Philip's indolent and elegant mother was such a marvel with her needle. And yet she was so quiet and so far away that when suddenly spoken to she would start and flush as if she had but just come out of some secret hiding-place.

It was only the spiteful new cook, Mrs. Sullivan's successor, who had steadily refused to be won over; and Philip hated *her* anyhow. His father, on the other hand, took no more notice of Dick when he passed him by in the rectory garden than if he had been a toadstool.

It was a mystery. If ever on any rare feast or festival, there was a solo to be sung in the minute village choir, it was Dick who sang it—"As pants the hart," "With verdure clad"—and as roundly and sweetly and passionlessly as the strains of some small woodland flute. His voice at any rate would need no angelic tuition—even in a better world. Nevertheless, although the rector had been known to boast of the prowess of his choir, Philip could not recall a single word of commendation from his father after the service was over, not even so much as a pompous little pat on the head. So far as *he* was concerned, Dick might have been a deaf-mute.

Yet if nuts, or peppermints, or marbles, or a grasshopper, or a glow-worm in a matchbox was brought into church for furtive display, and Dick was discovered to be the culprit, very little happened. Other boys when they were caught were given a good lecture in the rector's study, and one runagate far less enterprising than Dick had been expelled from the choir.

However closely he listened, Philip could never unravel the secret of this mystery. Even when he most enjoyed Dick's company, he could never for a moment conceal his own sense of superiority. At one moment he might be green with envy of Dick's silly, dare-devil, scatter-brained ways; at the next utterly despise him. There was a perpetual conflict in his mind between affection, jealousy, and contempt. And Dick would detect these secret feelings, as they were expressed solely in his face and actions, as neatly and quickly as a robin pecks up crumbs. Yet he never referred to them, or for more than a minute or two together seemed to resent a single one.

Just now, however, his protective stone and the increasing stench of his lantern unheeded, Philip had all but forgotten what had brought him into his present extraordinary situation. Like the restless imp he always was, Dick had taken himself off. Let him stay away, then! Meanwhile he had himself sat stolidly on, lost in contemplation, the prey of the most fantastic and ridiculous hopes and forebodings.

The church was brimmed so full of limpid moonlight that at any moment, it seemed, the stone walls, the pulpit, the roof itself might vanish away like the fabric of a dream. Its contents appeared to have no more reality than the reflections in a glass. Every crevice in the mouldings of the arches, every sunken flower and leaf in the mullions of the windows, even the knot in the wood of the pew beneath his nose stood out as if it had been blacked in with Indian ink. Every jut and angle, corbel and finial, marble nose and toe and finger seemed to have been dipped in quicksilver. And Philip, his eyes fixed on the faintly-golden, winged, ecstatic figure—mutely "shaking her gilded tresses in the air"—whose gaze he pined and yet feared even in imagination to meet, was lost for the time being to the world of the actual. He failed even to notice urgent reminders that one of his legs from knee to foot had gone numb, and that he was stone cold.

The premonitory whirring rumble of the clock over his head and the chimes of midnight roused him at last from his lethargy. He "came to," and listened starkly to the muffled, sullen booming of the bell, as if he had suddenly escaped from the mazes of a dream. ". . . Eleven . . . Twelve." The sonorous vibrations ebbed into inaudibility, and a dead and empty silence again prevailed. He had steadily assured himself, from the moment the project had been decided on, that nothing would happen. Nothing *had* happened. He felt spiritless and vacant, and now realized miserably that in spite of this radiance and beauty, he was further away from his angel than he had ever been before. It was she who had withdrawn herself from him, and with that withdrawal a faltering speechless faith and belief in her powers had faded out of his heart.

And as he crouched there, chilled and sick, there rose suddenly into the night beyond the chancel windows a restrained yet fiendish screech, compared with which his own *Oh, oh, oh,* had been sweet as the lamentations of a mermaid. Even though he had instantly guessed its origin, he sat appalled. His eyes fixed on the heavy folds of the curtain that had softly swayed forward as if in a waft of the wind through the open door, he had in his horror almost ceased to breathe. What if he were mistaken? What ghoulish wraith might *not* be skulking there! All but indetectibly the curtain was edging apart to disclose at length a lean faceless shape draped as if with a shroud from its flat-topped shapeless and featureless head downwards. Even in his consternation he marvelled at the delicate play of the moonlight in the folds of the cambric. With pointing sooty finger, this ridiculous scarecrow had now begun noiselessly edging towards his pew. The effort to prevent a yell of terror from escaping his throat had brought the taste of blood to Philip's lip; and he at once fell into a violent passion.

"You're nothing but a damn silly little fathead," he bawled, as it were, under his breath, "and it would serve you jolly well right if I gave you a good licking. Stop that rot! Stop it! Come *out*, I say!"

The spectre, notwithstanding, had fallen into a solemn yet nimble Negro shuffle and a voice out of its middle began to intone:

> "Dearly beloved brethren, is it not a sin
> To eat raw potatoes and throw away the skin?
> The skin feeds the pigs and the pigs feed you;
> Dearly beloved brethren, is—it—not—TRUE?"

Pat with the last word, and having flung off the rector's surplice and discarded the semi-hairless broom of the old church charwoman, Dick skipped out from his disguise, looking smaller and skinnier than ever. It was as if his high spirits, having learned that the same jest is seldom successful twice, had been crushed out of him for good by this rebuke. He stood dumbly staring at Philip, like a stricken and downcast little monkey that has been chastised by its master.

"Keep your silly wig on," he expostulated at last. "That's what you always do. You can't take any joke unless you've made it yourself. I'm tired of being here. There's nothing coming—and there never was. Perhaps if you had been alone . . ." Unstable as water, his mood began to revive again. "*I* know! Let's go down to the mill-pond, Philip, and look at the fish. The moon's like glass. You could catch 'em with your hands with that lantern. Let's try. Come on."

"Oh no, you don't," retorted Philip morosely. "You needn't suppose you're going to wriggle out like that. You dared me to come, and I dare *you* to stay. Anyhow, you shan't put your nose ever into our house again or into the garden, either, I can promise you, if you're nothing but a sneak—and afraid. I know something that will soon put a stop to that."

Dick stood irresolute, eyeing him sharply, his high cheekbones a bright red, his eyes shining, his mouth ajar.

"I'm not a sneak. And who"—a doleful quaver jarred his thin clear treble voice—"who *wants* to come into your silly old garden. If my mother . . . Besides, you *know* I'm not afraid!"

"Oh, do I!" A crafty stealthy designing look had crept into Philip's fair face, and a slight haze into his blue eyes. A faint ambiguous smile faded out of his angel features. He glanced covertly about him. "What's more likely is you only want to show off," he sneered. "Wheedle." He half yawned. "You know perfectly well that I shouldn't be here now except for some silly story you told me and couldn't have understood. Dare for yourself! Why, you haven't even the pluck to climb up into belfry and give the least tiny ding on one of the bells. Not all alone."

"Oh, wouldn't I! Yes, I would. Where's the key? There's an old owl's nest in the belfry. . . . *'One!'*—why, even if anybody in the village woke and heard it, they'd think it was nothing but the wind."

"Well, *three* dings, then. Anybody can make excuses. And you knew I hadn't the key! What's more, you wouldn't take a single flower, not even a scrap of a green leaf, from one of those vases up there."

Dick's gaze angled swiftly over the silver candlesticks upon the altar, the snow-white linen, the rich silk embroidered frontal, with its design in gold thread—I.H.S., the flat hueless shields of hot-house flowers. "Yes, I would, if I can reach them."

"Oh, would you! And there you are again—*'if!'* But you shan't —not while *I'm* here. That would be worse than stealing even, because this is a church, and that's the altar. And that's holy. This is not one of your mouldy old chapels." Once again he glanced about him. "I bet this, then. You wouldn't go up into the gallery and scratch out the eye in *that*—not even if I lent you my knife to do it with. Why, you'd be scared even of falling off the chair!"

The "that" he was referring to was an ancient painted lozenge-shaped hatchment, fastened by tenpenny nails in its clumsy black frame to the lime-washed western wall. It was blazoned with a coat of arms, and above the coat was a crest—the turbaned head of a Saracen in profile; and beneath the coat, in bold Gothic lettering, the one word, *Resurgam*.

Dick gazed motionlessly at its darkened green and vermilion and at the sinister head. "Yes, I would," he muttered. "What does *Resurgam* mean?"

"It's Latin," replied Philip, as if he were a little mollified by the modesty of the inquiry. "And it means, *I shall rise up again*. But it *might* be the subjunctive. It's what's called a motto, and the head's the crest, and the body's down in the vault. I expect he was a crusader. Anyhow, *any*body could do that; because you know very well it mightn't be noticed for ages. Never, p'r'aps. Besides, what's the use? . . . I'll give you a last chance. I'll tell you what you *wouldn't* do, not if you stayed here for a month of Sundays, and not a single soul came into the church to see you!"

His cheek had crimsoned. He nodded his head violently. "You wouldn't climb up that, and—and blow that trumpet."

Dick wheeled about, lifting his dark squirrel-bright eyes as he did so towards the angel, and looked. He continued to look: the angel at this moment of its nightly vigil, though already the hand that clasped the trumpet had lost its silver, seemed with an ineffable yearning as if about to leap into a cataract of moonlight, like a siren erecting her green-haired head and shoulders out of a rippleless sea to scan the shore.

"You *said*, what would be the use?" he protested at last in a small, scarcely audible voice, and without turning his head. "Even if I did, no one would hear. . . . Why do you *want* me to?"

"*Who* wants you to!" came the mocking challenge. "You asked me to give you a dare. And now—what did I say! Shouldn't *I* hear? I don't believe you've ever even looked at it, not even *seen* it before!"

"Oh, haven't I!" Dick faltered. "You say that only because on Sundays I don't sit on your side. And what's the use? Staring up gives you a crick in the neck. But it's not because I am afraid. . . .

Besides, she's only made of stone." In spite of this disparagement he continued to gaze at the angel.

"*Is* she then! Stone! That's all you know about it. She's made of wood, silly. How could she be that colour if it were marble or even *any* stone? Anybody could see that! And even if she *is* only wood, there are people all over the world who worship idols and —and images. I don't mean just savages either. If she"—for an instant his eyes shut and revolved beneath their pale rounded lids —"if she or anybody else was to blow through that trumpet, it would be the Last Day. I say it, and I *know*. Even if your father has ever heard of angels, I bet he doesn't believe in them. I'm *sure* he doesn't. My father does believe in them, though. And if you had ever really listened to what he reads out about them in the Lessons you'd know too. *I—have.*"

He sat for a moment, torpid as a spider engaged in digesting or contemplating a visitor to its nets. Dick's small, alert, yet guileless face was still turned away from him, upwards and sidelong. As one may put one's ear to a minute device in clockwork and listen to the wheels within going round, the very thoughts in his cropped, compact head seemed audible. And then, as if after a sudden decision to dismiss the subject from his mind, Philip casually picked up his bull's-eye lantern, idly twisted its penthouse top, and directed first a greenish, then a thin red beam of light towards the lustrous monument. But the moon made mock of this trivial rivalry.

"What," was Dick's husky inquiry at last, "what *does* the Bible say about angels? It must be a lovely place where they are, Philip."

Philip ignored the sentimental comment. "Oh, heaps of things. I couldn't tell you; not half of them, not a quarter." A mild, absent-minded, almost hypnotic expression now veiled his pale cold features. He began again as though he were repeating a lesson, in tones low yet so confident that the whole church could easily play eavesdropper to his every word. Nevertheless the sentences followed one another tardily and piecemeal, as if, like a writer of books, he could not wholly trust his memory, as though words and ideas were stubborn things to set in order and be made even so much as to hint at what was pent up in his mind.

"Well, first there was St. Paul; he went to a man's house who had *seen* an angel. Then there was the angel who came to tell his mother about Samuel, when she was sitting alone sewing in her bedroom. . . . And there was the angel that spoke to a man called Lot before he came out of a place called Sodom that was burned in the desert and his wife was turned into a pillar of salt. Because she turned back. Oh, heaps! *You* seem to suppose that because people can't see them now, there never were any angels. What about the sea-serpent, then; and what about witches? And what about the stars millions and billions of miles out in space, and mites and germs and all that, so teeny-tiny *no*body ever saw them until microscopes and telescopes were invented? I've looked through a microscope, so I know."

Dick nodded vacantly. "If people can *see* them," he admitted, "there must be sea-serpents. And I *have* seen a witch. There's one lives in Colney Bottom, and everybody says she's a witch. She's humpty-backed, with straggly grey hair all over her shoulders. I crept in through the trees once and she was in her garden digging potatoes. At least I *think* it was potatoes. She was talking; but there was nobody there and it wasn't to *me*. But you were telling me about the angels, Philip. Won't you go on?"

" 'Go on'!" echoed Philip in derision, and began again fumbling with his lantern. "Good heavens, you don't expect me to tell you half the Bible, do you? Why don't you listen? I don't believe you've any more brains than a parrot. 'Go on'! Why *everybody* has heard of the angel that when Moses was with his sheep called to him out of the middle of the burning bramble bush on the mountains. Its leaves and branches were all crackling with flames. That's another. And when Elijah was once lying asleep in the desert under a juniper tree an angel came in the morning and touched him to wake him because he had brought him some cake, and some fresh water to drink. That," he pondered a moment or two, "that was before the ravens. And I suppose you've never even heard of Joshua either? He was a captain of Israel. And when he was standing dressed in his armour on the sand, with his naked sword in his hand, and looking at the enormous walls of Jericho, he saw an angel there beside him, in ar-

mour too, just as you might see a man in a wood at night. They
stood there together looking at the *enormous* walls of Jericho.
But you couldn't see them very plainly because it was getting
dark, and there weren't any lamps or lights in the houses. So nobody inside knew that they were there, not even the woman who
had talked to the two spies who had stolen the bunches of grapes."

Philip, unperceived, had quickly and suddenly glanced at his
friend, who, his face wholly at peace, had meanwhile been emptily watching the coloured lights succeeding one another in the
round, glass, owl-like eye of the toy lantern.

"I should like to see an angel," he said.

"Oh, would you? Then that's all you know about it. There are
thousands upon thousands of them, most of them miles taller than
any giant there ever was and others no bigger than—than ordinary. Not all of them have only two wings either; some of them
have six—here, and here, and here; with two they fly and with
two they cover their faces when they are asleep. And they have
names too; else God wouldn't be able to call them. But don't you
go and think they are like *us;* because they aren't. They are more
like demons or ghosts—real ghosts, I mean, not the kind *you* were
talking about. And I don't believe either that just because anything is made of wood or stone, it hasn't any life at all—not at *all*.
Even savages couldn't be as stupid as all that. You only *think* you
could touch angels. But you couldn't. And some angels, though I
don't know even myself if they are most like women or men"—
his voice ebbed away almost into a whisper, like that of a child
murmuring in its sleep, as if he were not only nearing the end of
his resources, but was losing himself in the rapture of some ineffable vision in his mind—"some angels are far far more beautiful
to look at than any woman, even the most beautiful woman there
ever was. And even than—*that!*"

Yet again Dick lifted his intense small eyes towards the image.
It had, it seemed, as if in an instant, returned to an appearance of
mute immobility; but only in the nick of time to elude his silent
questioning.

"I shouldn't mind any angel," he said, "if it were only like that.
Not *mind* I mean. If she *looked* at me, perhaps I might. She's like

Rebecca, the girl that lives up at the farm. My mother taught me
a hymn once to say when I am in bed. I can't remember the beginning now, but some of it I can:

> Four corners to my bed;
> Four angels round my head:
> One to bless, and one to pray,
> And one to bear my soul away. . . .

If you are not afraid, she says, not anywhere, ever, nothing can
do anything against you."

"Oh, they can't, can't they! That just shows all *you* know about
it. Besides, what you've been saying is only a rhyme for children.
It's only a rhyme. My nurse told me that ages ago. Those angels
are only one kind. Why, there are angels so enormously strong
that if one of them no more than touched even the roof of this
church with the tip of his finger it would crumble away into dust.
Like that"—he firmly placed his own small forefinger on the
dried-up corpse of a tiny monkey-spider that had long since expired in the corner of the pew—"absolutely into dust. And their
voices are as loud as thunder, so that when one speaks to another,
the sound of their shouting sweeps clean across the sky. And some
fly up out of the sea, out of the east, when the sun rises; and some
come up out of a huge frightful pit. And some come up out of
the water, deep dangerous lakes and great rivers, and they stand
on the water, and can *fly*—straight across, as if it was lightning,
from one edge of the world to the other—like huge tremendous
birds. I should jolly well like to see what a pilot of an aeroplane
would do at the edge of the night if he met one. They can"—he
bent forward a little, his pale face now faintly greened with his
own lantern—"they can see without looking; and they stay still,
like great carved stones, in a light—why, this moon wouldn't be
even a candle to it!

"And some day they will pour awful things out of vials down
on the earth and reap with gigantic sickles not just ordinary corn,
but men and women. Men and women. And besides the sea," his
rather colourless eyes had brightened, his cheeks had taken on a
gentle flush, his nervous fingers were clasping and unclasping
themselves over the warm metal of his lantern, "and besides the

sea, they can stand and live exulting in the sun. But on the earth here they are invisible, at least *now,* except when they come in dreams. Besides, everybody has two angels; though they never get married, and so there are never any children angels. They are called cherubs. And I know this too—you can tell they are there even when you cannot see them. You can hear them listening. If *they* have charge of you, nothing can hurt you, not the rocks— nor the ice—not even of the highest mountains. And that was why the angel spoke to Balaam's donkey when they were on the mountain pass, because he wished not to frighten him; and the donkey answered. But if you were cursed by one for wickedness, then you would wither up and die like a gnat, or have awful pains, and everything inside of you would melt away like water. And don't forget either that the Devil has crowds of angels under his command who were thrown out of heaven millions of years ago, long before Adam and Eve. They are as proud as he is, and they live in hell. . . . They are awful."

It was doubtful if Dick had been really attending to this pro- longed, halting, almost monotoned harangue; his face at any rate suggested that his thoughts had journeyed off on a remote and marvelling errand of their own.

"Well," he ventured at last, with a profound half-stifled sigh, "I *would* climb it anyway. And not because you dared me to, either. Even *you* couldn't say what I might not see up there."

He tiptoed a pace or two nearer the shallow altar steps and again fixed his eyes on his quarry. "What about the trumpet?" he suddenly inquired, with a ring of triumph in his voice, as if he had at last managed to corner his learned friend. "The trum- pet? You didn't say a single word about the trumpet."

"Well, what if I didn't?" was the flat acrimonious answer. "I can't say two things at once, can I? You don't know *any*thing. And that is simply because you never pay any attention. You're just like a fly buzzing about among the plates seeing what you can pick up. I don't suppose, if I asked you even now, you could tell me a single word of *all* that I've been saying!"

Dick turned, glancing a little sadly and wistfully at his friend. "I could, Philip. At least, I think I could. Besides flies do settle sometimes; I suppose then they are asleep."

"Oh, well, anyhow," replied Philip coldly, "I don't think I want to. But I could if I had the time." He sighed. "You don't even seem to understand there are so many *kinds* of trumpets. You don't seem ever to have heard even of Gideon's trumpets. Some are made of brass and some are silver and some are great shells and some are made out of sheep's horns, rams'. And in the old days, ages ago, war-horses loved the sound of trumpets—I don't mean just men going hunting. It made them laugh and prance, with all their teeth showing. *'Ha, ha!'*—like that. Simply maddened to go into battle. And besides, clergymen, priests they were called in those days, used to have trumpets, but that was ages before Henry VIII. And they used to blow them, like that one, up there, when there was a new moon; and when," he glanced sidelong, his eyelids drooping a little furtively over his full eyes, and his voice fell to a mumble, "and when there was a *full* moon too. And at the end there will be incense, and dreadful hail, and fire, and scorpions with claws like huge poisonous spiders. And there's a Star called Wormwood; and there will be thousands and thousands of men riding on horses with heads like lions. . . ." He fell silent and sat fumbling for a few moments. "But I wasn't really going to talk about all that. It's only because *I* have listened. And it's just what I've said already, and I know the very words too." He nodded slowly as if he were bent on imparting a deathless and invaluable secret: " 'The trumpet shall sound and the dead shall be raised.' Those are the very words. And *I* see what they mean."

Dick had meanwhile become perfectly still, as if some inward self were lost in a strange land. He appeared to be profoundly pondering these matters. "And supposing," he muttered at length, as though like the prophet he had swallowed Philip's little book and it were sweet as honey, "supposing *nothing* happens, Philip? If I do? Perhaps *that* trumpet is only solid wood all through. Then it wouldn't make *any* sound. Then you would only burst your cheeks, trying. Wouldn't it be funny—if I burst my cheeks, trying!"

"That," replied Philip, disdaining the suggestion, "that would only mean that it isn't really a trumpet. But you wouldn't even be *thinking* of that if you weren't too frightened to try. You're only talking."

"*You* wouldn't."

"I like that!" cried Philip, as if in a brief ecstasy. "Oh, I like that! Who *thought* of the angel, may I ask? Who *asked* to be dared? Besides, as I have said again and again, this is my father's church; and chapel people don't believe in angels. They don't believe in anything that really matters."

"You can say what you like about chapel people," said Dick stubbornly, his eyes shining like some dangerous little animal's that has been caught in a snare. "But I'm *not* afeard, even if you won't go yourself."

"Oh, well"—a cold and unforeseen fit of anxiety had stolen into Philip's mind as he sat staring at his friend. "I don't care. Come on, let's clear out of this, I say. You can *try* if you want to, but I'm not going to *watch*. So don't get blaming anything on to me. It's nothing to do with me. That's just what you always do. You're a silly little weathercock. First, yes; then, no."

Cramped and spiritless, he had got down from his pew and, as if absent-mindedly, had pushed his magic dumb-bell flint into his greatcoat pocket and shut off the light of his lantern. The moonlight, which a few moments before, from pavement to arching roof, had suffused the small church through and through, had begun to thin away into a delicate dusk again; and at the withdrawal even of the tiny coloured lights of the lantern, its pallor on the zigzag-fretted walls and squat thick stone shafts of the piers had become colder. Moreover the quietude around them had at once immeasurably deepened again now that the two boys' idle chirruping voices were stilled.

Philip took up the lantern, and looked at his friend. A curious, crooked, scornful alarm showed on his own delicate features. But it was the scorn in it that his ardent, undersized, and peeping devotee had detected most clearly. His intensely dark eyes were searching Philip's face with an astonishing rapidity.

"You said, 'blaming,'" he half entreated. "And did I ever? I—I . . . Haven't I always shown that we—I . . . ! It's only because

I didn't think anything might happen. But I'm not afeard, what-ever you may think. Besides, you asked me, Philip. And anything —*any*thing you asked me. . . . So it couldn't be *only* a dare."

Like a cork on a shallow stream that has come momentarily to rest in the midst of rippling and conflicting currents, Philip stood motionless, his pondering eyes intent on the young adventurer whom he had at last decoyed into action. A faintly apprehensive, faintly melancholy expression had now crept into his features. The cold detaining fingers he had thrust out of his coat-sleeve fell slackly to his side again. For Dick had already straddled over the thick red plaited cord that dangled between nave and chancel, disclosing as he did so a frayed gaping hole in the canvas of one of his shoes. Their rubber soles made not the faintest sound as he trod lightly over the thick Persian rug and the stone slabs towards the great monument in the further corner, only a few paces from the altar.

It was a monument constructed of many ornate marbles, and these supplied cold couch and canopy for the effigy in alabaster of a worthy knight who, as its inscription declared, had long ago surrendered the joys and sorrows of this world. He reposed, rather uneasily, on his left elbow; his attire, ruff and hose, not less dec-orative and rococo than the wreathings and carvings, the cherubs and pilasters of his tomb. But like an Oriental bed in a small English bedroom, the tomb was a size or two too large for the church.

Until this moment Philip had not fully realized its loftiness, and how angularly its pinnacles soared up under the roof. Dark and dwarfed against the whiteness of its marble, Dick had now begun to climb. But he had mounted only a few feet from the ground when Philip noticed that the moon had now abandoned the carved ringlets, the rounded cheeks, the upturned sightless face of his angel. Though her pinions and feet were still chequered with its silvering beams, her trumpet now lifted its mouth into a cold and sullen gloom. An unendurable misgiving had begun to stir in him.

"The moon's gone, Dick," he whispered across. "What's the good? Come down!"

"I say," came the muffled but elated answer, "the ledges are simply thick with dust, and don't they just cut into the soles of your feet. I can't hear what you're saying."

"I said," repeated Philip, still patiently, "come down!" But he might as well have been pleading with the angel itself. There came no response. "Dick, Dick," he reiterated, "I said, come down! Oh, I'm going." In a sudden fever he pushed his way under the curtain into the vestry and vanished. But it was only a ruse. He came flying back in a few moments as if in utter consternation.

"Quick, Dick; quick, I say!" he all but shouted. "Come down! There's someone, something *coming*. It isn't a man and it isn't a woman. Quick! It won't be a minute before it's in the church. Oh you silly, silly fool! I tell you there's someone coming!" His voice broke away into a sob of bewilderment, rage, apprehension, and despair. "By God," he called, "I'll tell my father of this! You see if I don't."

But the snail-slow groping figure, still radiantly lit with the moon's downcast beams as it continued to scale the monument, was far too much engrossed in its mission to pay any attention to him now, and hardly paused until with a small, black broken-nailed hand it had securely clasped the angel's foot. "I'm nearly up, Philip," he called down at last. "Look! *Look* where I am! I'm even with the gallery now, and can hardly see because of the dazzle. It's cold and still and awful, but oh, *peace*ful; and I can see into the moon. The angel's lovely too, close to, but much, much bigger. Supposing I blow with all my might and the trumpet doesn't sound? It won't be my fault, will it? And we will still keep friends, always, won't we, Philip?"

"Oh, you fool, you idiot crock fool," called Philip hoarsely. "Didn't I *tell* you, didn't I tell you, what might come to *every*body? . . . And you believed it! Oh, it was all a story, a lie, a story. Dick, I will give you anything in the world if you will only come down."

"I don't want anything in the world," was the dull, stubborn retort. Even as he spoke, the lower dust-dried hand had crept cautiously up to join its fellow, and in a few moments, himself half in and half out of the moonlight, his fingers were clutching the acorn tassels of the cord that bound its convoluted hood to the angel's head. Philip was now all but past motion or speech. He was shivering from head to foot, and praying inarticulately in his terror, "O God, make him come down! O God, make him come down!"

"I believe," a calm but rapturous voice was declaring, "it *is* hollow, and I *think* she knows I'm here. You won't say I was afraid now! Philip, I'd do anything in the world for you."

But at this moment, it seemed, the ancient guardians of the sanctity of the edifice had deemed it discreet to intervene. A cock crowed from its perch in the hen-roost at the farm where Rebecca now lay fast asleep. A vast solemn gust of wind evoked from no-where out of space had swept across the churchyard and in at the open vestry door, powerful enough in its gust to belly out the dark green felt curtain and to add its edge of terror to Philip's appalled state of mind. "Look! Quick! It's coming. Didn't I *say* it was all . . ."

And this time the small human creature clinging to its goal, a lean skinny arm outstretched above his head, had heard the warn-ing cry. "Who? What's coming?" he called, faint and far. "Oh, it's lovely up here. I'm alone. I can't stop now. I'm nearly there."

"I say, you are *not* to, you are *not* to." Philip was all but dancing in helpless fear and fury. "It's wicked! It's *my* angel, it's *my* trum-pet! I hate you! Listen!—I tell you! I *command* you to come down!"

But his adjurations had become as meaningless as is now the song the Sirens sang.

A rending snap, abrupt as that of a pistol shot, had echoed through the church. The tapering wooden trumpet, never since its first fashioning visited by any other living creature than capri-cious fly and prowling spider, had splintered off clean from the angel's grasp. And without a cry, a syllable, either of triumph or despair, Dick had fallen vertically on to the flagstones beneath, the thud of his small body, and the minute crack as of some ex-quisitely delicate and brittle vessel exposed to too extreme a ten-sion being followed by a silence soft, and thick, and deep as deep and heavy snow.

The stolid pendulum had resumed its imperturbable thumping again, the fussy vestry clock its protest against such indifference. By any miracle of mercy, *could* this be only yet another of this intrepid restless little Yorick's infinite jests? The sharp-nosed crusader continued alabaster-wise to stare into his future. The disgraced angel, breast to lock-crowned head, stood now in shadow as if to hide her shame. Her mute wooden trumpet remained clutched in a lifeless hand. . . . No.

"Dick! Dick!" an anguished stuttering voice at last contrived to whisper. "I didn't mean it. On my oath I didn't mean it. Don't let me down. . . . Dick, are you dead?"

But since no answer was volunteered, and all courage and enterprise had ebbed into nausea and vertigo, the speaker found himself incapable of venturing nearer, and presently, as thievishly as he had entered it, crept away out into the openness of the churchyard, and so home.

The Wind Blows Over (1936)

THE CREATURES

It was the ebbing light of evening that recalled me out of my story to a consciousness of my whereabouts. I dropped the squat little red book to my knee and glanced out of the narrow and begrimed oblong window. We were skirting the eastern coast of cliffs, to the very edge of which a ploughman, stumbling along behind his two great horses, was driving the last of his dark furrows. In a cleft far down between the rocks a cold and idle sea was soundlessly laying its frigid garlands of foam. I stared over the flat stretch of waters, then turned my head, and looked with a kind of suddenness into the face of my one fellow traveller.

He had entered the carriage, all but unheeded, yet not altogether unresented, at the last country station. His features were a little obscure in the fading daylight that hung between our four narrow walls, but apparently his eyes had been fixed on my face for some little time.

He narrowed his lids at this unexpected confrontation, jerked back his head, and cast a glance out of his mirky glass at the slip of greenish-bright moon that was struggling into its full brilliance above the dun, swelling uplands.

"It's a queer experience, railway-travelling," he began abruptly, in a low, almost deprecating voice, drawing his hand across his eyes. "One is cast into a passing privacy with a fellow stranger and then is gone." It was as if he had been patiently awaiting the attention of a chosen listener.

I nodded, looking at him. *"That* privacy, too," he ejaculated, "all that!" My eyes turned towards the window again: bare, thorned, black, January hedge, inhospitable salt coast, flat waste of northern water. Our engine-driver promptly shut off his steam, and we slid almost noiselessly out of sight of sky and sea into a cutting.

"It's a desolate country," I ventured to remark.

"Oh, yes, 'desolate,' " he echoed a little wearily. "But what frets me is the way we have of arrogating to ourselves the offices of judge, jury, and counsel all in one. As if this earth . . . I never forget it—the futility, the presumption. It *leads* nowhere. We drive in—into all this silence, this—this 'forsakenness,' this dream of a world between her lights of day and night time. We desecrate. Consciousness! What restless monkeys men are." He recovered himself, swallowed his indignation with an obvious gulp. "As if," he continued, in more chastened tones—"as if that other gate were not for ever ajar, into God knows what of peace and mystery." He stooped forward, lean, darkened, objurgatory. "Don't we *make* our world? Isn't that our blessed, our betrayed responsibility?"

I nodded, and ensconced myself, like a dog in straw, in the

basest of all responses to a rare, even if eccentric, candour—caution.

"Well," he continued, a little weariedly, "that's the indictment. Small wonder if it will need a trumpet to blare us into that last 'Family Prayers.' Then perhaps a few solitaries—just a few—will creep out of their holes and fastnesses, and draw mercy from the merciful on the cities of the plain. The buried talent will shine none the worse for the long, long looming of its napery spun from dream and desire.

"Years ago—ten, fifteen, perhaps—I chanced on the queerest specimen of this order of the 'talented.' Much the same country, too. This"—he swept his glance out towards the now invisible sea—"this is a kind of dwarf replica of it. More naked, smoother, more sudden and precipitous, more 'forsaken,' moody. Alone! The trees are shorn there, as if with monstrous shears, by the winter gales. The air's salt. It is a country of stones and emerald meadows, of green, meandering, aimless lanes, of farms set in their clifts and valleys like rough time-bedimmed jewels, as if by some angel of humanity, wandering between dark and daybreak.

"I was younger then—in body: the youth of the mind is for men of a certain age; yours, maybe, and mine. Even then, even at that, I was sickened of crowds, of that unimaginable London—swarming wilderness of mankind in which a poor lost thirsty dog from Otherwhere tastes first the full meaning of that idle word 'forsaken.' 'Forsaken by whom?' is the question I ask myself now. Visitors to my particular paradise were few then—as if, my dear sir, we are not all of us visitors, visitants, revenants, on earth, panting for time in which to tell and share our secrets, roving in search of the marks that shall prove our quest not vain, not unprecedented, not a treachery. But let that be.

"I would start off morning after morning, bread and cheese in pocket, from the bare old house I lodged in, bound for that unforeseen nowhere for which the heart, the fantasy aches. Lingering hot noondays would find me stretched in a state half-comatose, yet vigilant, on the close-flowered turf of the fields or cliffs, on the sun-baked sands and rocks, soaking in the scene and life around me like some pilgrim chameleon. It was in hope to lose

my way that I would set out. How shall a man find his way unless
he lose it? Now and then I succeeded. That country is large, and
its land and sea marks easily cheat the stranger. I was still of an
age, you see, when my 'small door' was ajar, and I planted a solid
foot to keep it from shutting. But how could I know what I was
after? One just shakes the tree of life, and the rare fruits come
tumbling down, to rot for the most part in the lush grasses.

"What was most haunting and provocative in that far-away
country was its fleeting resemblance to the country of dream. You
stand, you sit, or lie prone on its bud-starred heights, and look
down; the green, dispersed, treeless landscape spreads beneath
you, with its hollows and mounded slopes, clustering farmstead,
and scatter of village, all motionless under the vast wash of sun
and blue, like the drop-scene of some enchanted playhouse centuries old. So, too, the visionary bird-haunted headlands, veiled
faintly in a mist of unreality above their broken stones and the
enormous saucer of the sea.

"You cannot guess there what you may not chance upon, or
whom. Bells clash, boom, and quarrel hollowly on the edge of
darkness in those breakers. Voices waver across the fainter winds.
The birds cry in a tongue unknown yet not unfamiliar. The sky
is the hawks' and the stars'. *There* one is on the edge of life, of
the unforeseen, whereas our cities—are not our desiccated jaded
minds ever continually pressing and edging further and further
away from freedom, the vast unknown, the infinite presence, picking a fool's journey from sensual fact to fact at the tail of that
he-ass called Reason? I suggest that in that solitude the spirit
within us realizes that it treads the outskirts of a region long
since called the Imagination. I assert we have strayed, and in our
blindness abandoned—"

My stranger paused in his frenzy, glanced out at me from his
obscure corner as if he had intended to stun, to astonish me with
some violent heresy. We puffed out slowly, laboriously, from a
"Halt" at which in the gathering dark and moonshine we had for
some while been at a standstill. Never was wedding-guest more
desperately at the mercy of ancient mariner.

"Well, one day," he went on, lifting his voice a little to master

the resounding heart-beats of our steam-engine—"one late afternoon, in my goal-less wanderings, I had climbed to the summit of
a steep grass-grown cart-track, winding up dustily between dense,
untended hedges. Even then I might have missed the house to
which it led, for, hairpin fashion, the track here abruptly turned
back on itself, and only a far fainter footpath led on over the hill-
crest. I might, I say, have missed the house and—and its inmates,
if I had not heard the musical sound of what seemed like the
twangling of a harp. This thin-drawn, sweet, tuneless warbling
welled over the close green grass of the height as if out of space.
Truth cannot say whether it was of that air or of my own fantasy.
Nor did I ever discover what instrument, whether of man or
Ariel, had released a strain so pure and yet so bodiless.

"I pushed on and found myself in command of a gorse-strewn
height, a stretch of country that lay a few hundred paces across
the steep and sudden valley in between. In a V-shaped entry to
the left, and sunwards, lay an azure and lazy tongue of the sea.
And as my eye slid softly thence and upwards and along the
sharp, green horizon line against the glass-clear turquoise of space,
it caught the flinty glitter of a square chimney. I pushed on, and
presently found myself at the gate of a farmyard.

"There was but one straw-mow upon its staddles. A few fowls
were sunning themselves in their dust-baths. White and pied doves
preened and cooed on the roof of an outbuilding as golden with
its lichens as if the western sun had scattered its dust for centuries
upon the large slate slabs. Just that life and the whispering of the
wind: nothing more. Yet even at one swift glimpse I seemed to
have trespassed upon a peace that had endured for ages; to have
crossed the viewless border that divides time from eternity. I
leaned, resting, over the gate, and could have remained there for
hours, lapsing ever more profoundly into the blessed quietude
that had stolen over my thoughts.

"A bent-up woman appeared at the dark entry of a stone shed
opposite to me, and, shading her eyes, paused in prolonged scrutiny of the stranger. At that I entered the gate and, explaining
that I had lost my way and was tired and thirsty, asked for some
milk. She made no reply, but after peering up at me, with something between suspicion and apprehension on her weather-beaten

old face, led me towards the house which lay to the left on the slope of the valley, hidden from me till then by plumy bushes of tamarisk.

"It was a low grave house, grey-chimneyed, its stone walls traversed by a deep shadow cast by the declining sun, its dark windows rounded and uncurtained, its door wide open to the porch. She entered the house, and I paused upon the threshold. A deep unmoving quiet lay within, like that of water in a cave renewed by the tide. Above a table hung a wreath of wild flowers. To the right was a heavy oak settle upon the flags. A beam of sunlight pierced the air of the staircase from an upper window.

"Presently a dark long-faced gaunt man appeared from within, contemplating me, as he advanced, out of eyes that seemed not so much to fix the intruder as to encircle his image, as the sea contains the distant speck of a ship on its wide blue bosom of water. They might have been the eyes of the blind; the windows of a house in dream to which the inmate must make something of a pilgrimage to look out upon actuality. Then he smiled, and the long, dark features, melancholy yet serene, took light upon them, as might a bluff of rock beneath a thin passing wash of sunshine. With a gesture he welcomed me into the large dark-flagged kitchen, cool as a cellar, airy as a belfry, its sweet air traversed by a long oblong of light out of the west.

"The wide shelves of the painted dresser were laden with crockery. A wreath of freshly-gathered flowers hung over the chimney-piece. As we entered, a twittering cloud of small birds, robins, hedge-sparrows, chaffinches fluttered up a few inches from floor and sill and window-seat, and once more, with tiny starry-dark eyes observing me, soundlessly alighted. I could hear the infinitesimal *tic-tac* of their tiny claws upon the slate. My gaze drifted out of the window into the garden beyond, a cavern of clearer crystal and colour than that which astounded the eyes of young Aladdin.

"Apart from the twisted garland of wild flowers, the shining metal of range and copper candlestick, and the bright-scoured crockery, there was no adornment in the room except a rough frame, hanging from a nail in the wall, and enclosing what appeared to be a faint patterned fragment of blue silk or fine linen.

The chairs and table were old and heavy. A low light warbling, an occasional *skirr* of wing, a haze-like drone of bee and fly—these were the only sounds that edged a quiet intensified in its profundity by the remote stirrings of the sea.

"The house was stilled as by a charm, yet thought within me asked no questions; speculation was asleep in its kennel. I sat down to the milk and bread, the honey and fruit which the old woman laid out upon the table, and her master seated himself opposite to me, now in a low sibilant whisper—a tongue which they seemed to understand—addressing himself to the birds, and now, as if with an effort, raising those strange grey-green eyes of his to bestow a quiet remark upon me. He asked, rather in courtesy than with any active interest, a few questions, referring to the world, its business and transports—*our* beautiful world—as an astronomer in the small hours might murmur a few words to the chance-sent guest of his solitude concerning the secrets of Uranus or Saturn. There is another, an inexplorable side to the moon. Yet he said enough for me to gather that he, too, was of that small tribe of the aloof and wild to which our cracked old word 'forsaken' might be applied, hermits, lamas, clay-matted fakirs, and suchlike; the snowy birds that play and cry amid mid-oceanic surges; the living of an oasis of the wilderness; which share a reality only distantly dreamed of by the time-driven thought-corroded congregations of man.

"Yet so narrow and hazardous I somehow realized was the brink of fellow-being (shall I call it?) which we shared, he and I, that again and again fantasy within me seemed to hover over that precipice Night knows as fear. It was he, it seemed, with that still embracive contemplation of his, with that far-away yet reassuring smile, that kept my poise, my balance. 'No,' some voice within him seemed to utter, 'you are safe; the bounds are fixed; though hallucination chaunt its decoy, you shall not irretrievably pass over. Eat and drink, and presently return to 'life.' And I listened, and, like that of a drowsy child in its cradle, my consciousness sank deeper and deeper, stilled, pacified, into the dream amid which, as it seemed, this soundless house of stone now reared its walls.

"I had all but finished my meal when I heard footsteps approaching on the flags without. The murmur of other voices, distinguishably shrill yet guttural even at a distance, and in spite of the dense stones and beams of the house which had blunted their timbre, had already reached me. Now the feet halted. I turned my head—cautiously, even perhaps apprehensively—and confronted two figures in the doorway.

"I cannot now guess the age of my entertainer. These children —for children they were in face and gesture and effect, though as to form and stature apparently in their last teens—these children were far more problematical. I say 'form and stature,' yet obviously they were dwarfish. Their heads were sunken between their shoulders, their hair thick, their eyes disconcertingly deep-set. They were ungainly, their features peculiarly irregular, as if two races from the ends of the earth had in them intermingled their blood and strangeness; as if, rather, animal and angel had connived in their creation.

"But if some inward light lay on the still eyes, on the gaunt, sorrowful, quixotic countenance that now was fully and intensely bent on mine, emphatically that light was theirs also. He spoke to them; they answered—in English, my own language, without a doubt: but an English slurred, broken, and unintelligible to me, yet clear as bell, haunting, penetrating, pining as voice of nix or siren. My ears drank in the sound as an Arab parched with desert sand falls on his dried belly and gulps in mouthfuls of crystal water. The birds hopped nearer as if beneath the rod of an enchanter. A sweet continuous clamour arose from their small throats. The exquisite colours of plume and bosom burned, greened, melted in the level sun-ray, in the darker air beyond.

"A kind of mournful gaiety, a lamentable felicity, such as rings in the cadences of an old folk-song, welled into my heart. I was come back to the borders of Eden, bowed and outwearied, gazing from out of dream into dream, homesick, 'forsaken.'

"Well, years have gone by," muttered my fellow traveller deprecatingly, "but I have not forgotten that Eden's primeval trees and shade.

"They led me out, these bizarre companions, a he and a she, if I may put it as crudely as my apprehension of them put it to me then. Through a broad door they conducted me—if one who

leads may be said to be conducted—into their garden. Garden!
A full mile long, between undiscerned walls, it sloped and narrowed towards a sea at whose dark unfoamed blue, even at this
distance, my eyes dazzled. Yet how can one call that a garden
which reveals no ghost of a sign of human arrangement, of human slavery, of spade or hoe?

"Great boulders shouldered up, tessellated, embossed, powdered
with a thousand various mosses and lichens, between a flowering
greenery of weeds. Wind-stunted, clear-emerald, lichen-tufted
trees smoothed and crisped the inflowing airs of the ocean with
their leaves and spines, sibilating a thin scarce-audible music.
Scanty, rank, and uncultivated fruits hung close their vivid-
coloured cheeks to the gnarled branches. It was the harbourage of
birds, the small embowering parlour of their house of life, under
an evening sky, pure and lustrous as a waterdrop. It cried 'Hospital' to the wanderers of the universe.

"As I look back in ever-thinning nebulous remembrance on my
two companions, hear their voices gutturally sweet and shrill,
catch again their being, so to speak, I realize that there was a kind
of Orientalism in their effect. Their instant courtesy was not
Western, the smiles that greeted me, whenever I turned my head
to look back at them, were infinitely friendly, yet infinitely remote. So ungainly, so far from our notions of beauty and symmetry were their bodies and faces, those heads thrust heavily between their shoulders, their disproportioned yet graceful arms and
hands, that the children in some of our English villages might be
moved to stone them, while their elders looked on and laughed.

"Dusk was drawing near; soon night would come. The colours
of the sunset, sucking its extremest dye from every leaf and blade
and petal, touched my consciousness even then with a vague
fleeting alarm.

"I remember I asked these strange and happy beings, repeating
my question twice or thrice, as we neared the surfy entry of the
valley upon whose sands a tiny stream emptied its fresh waters—
I asked them if it was they who had planted this multitude of
flowers, many of a kind utterly unknown to me and alien to a
country inexhaustibly rich. 'We wait; we wait!' I think they cried.
And it was as if their cry woke echo from the green-walled valleys

of the mind into which I had strayed. Shall I confess that tears came into my eyes as I gazed hungrily around me on the harvest of their patience?

"Never was actuality so close to dream. It was not only an unknown country, slipped in between these placid hills, on which I had chanced in my ramblings. I had entered for a few brief moments a strange region of consciousness. I was treading, thus accompanied, amid a world of welcoming and fearless life—oh, friendly to me!—the paths of man's imagination, the kingdom from which thought and curiosity, vexed scrutiny and lust—a lust it may be for nothing more impious than the actual—had prehistorically proved the insensate means of his banishment. 'Reality,' 'Consciousness': had he for 'the time being' unwittingly, unhappily missed his way? Would he be led back at length to that garden wherein cockatrice and basilisk bask, harmlessly, at peace?

"I speculate now. In that queer, yes, and possibly sinister, company, sinister only because it was alien to me, I did not speculate. In their garden, the familiar was become the strange—'the strange' that lurks in the inmost heart, unburdens its riches in trance, flings its light and gilding upon love, gives heavenly savour to the intemperate bowl of passion, and is the secret of our incommunicable pity. What is yet queerer, these beings were evidently glad of my company. They stumped after me (as might yellow men after some Occidental quadruped never before seen) in merry collusion of nods and wreathed smiles at this perhaps unprecedented intrusion.

"I stood for a moment looking out over the placid surface of the sea. A ship in sail hung phantom-like on the horizon. I pined to call my discovery to its seamen. The tide gushed, broke, spent itself on the bare boulders, I was suddenly cold and alone, and gladly turned back into the garden, my companions instinctively separating to let me pass between them. I breathed in the rare, almost exotic heat, the tenuous, honeyed, almond-laden air of its flowers and birds—gull, sheldrake, plover, wagtail, finch, robin, which as I half-angrily, half-sadly realized fluttered up in momentary dismay only at *my* presence—the embodied spectre of their enemy, man. Man? Then who were these? . . .

"I lost again a way lost early that morning, as I trudged inland at night. The dark came, warm and starry. I was dejected and exhausted beyond words. That night I slept in a barn and was awakened soon after daybreak by the crowing of cocks. I went out, dazed and blinking into the sunlight, bathed face and hands in a brook near by, and came to a village before a soul was stirring. So I sat under a thrift-cushioned, thorn-crowned wall in a meadow, and once more drowsed off and fell asleep. When again I awoke, it was ten o'clock. The church clock in its tower knelled out the strokes, and I went into an inn for food.

"A corpulent, blonde woman, kindly and hospitable, with a face comfortably resembling her own sow's, that yuffed and nosed in at the open door as I sat on my stool, served me with what I called for. I described—not without some vanishing shame, as if it were a treachery—my farm, its whereabouts.

"Her small blue eyes 'pigged' at me with a fleeting expression which I failed to translate. The name of the farm, it appeared, was Trevarras. 'And did you see any of the Creatures?' she asked me in a voice not entirely her own. 'The Creatures'? I sat back for an instant and stared at her; then realized that Creature was the name of my host, and Maria and Christus (though here her dialect may have deceived me) the names of my two gardeners. She spun an absurd story, so far as I could tack it together and make it coherent. Superstitious stuff about this man who had wandered in upon the shocked and curious inhabitants of the district and made his home at Trevarras—a stranger and pilgrim, a 'foreigner,' it seemed, of few words, dubious manners, and both uninformative.

"Then there was something (she placed her two fat hands, one of them wedding-ringed, on the zinc of the bar-counter, and peered over at me, as if I were a delectable 'wash'), then there was something about a woman 'from the sea.' In a 'blue gown,' and either dumb, inarticulate, or mistress of only a foreign tongue. She must have lived in sin, moreover, those pig's eyes seemed to yearn, since the children were 'simple,' 'naturals'—as God intends in such matters. It was useless. One's stomach may sometimes reject the cold sanative aerated water of 'the next morning,' and my ridiculous intoxication had left me dry but not yet quite sober.

"Anyhow, this she told me, that my blue woman, as fair as flax, had died and was buried in the neighbouring churchyard (the nearest to, though miles distant from, Trevarras). She repeatedly assured me, as if I might otherwise doubt so sophisticated a fact, that I should find her grave there, her 'stone.'

"So indeed I did—far away from the elect, and in a shade-ridden north-west corner of the sleepy, cropless acre: a slab, scarcely rounded, of granite, with but a name bitten out of the dark rough surface, *'Femina Creature.'*"

The Riddle and Other Stories (1923)

THE VATS

MANY years ago now—in that once upon a time which is the memory of the imagination rather than of the workaday mind, I went walking with a friend. Of what passed before we set out I have nothing but the vaguest recollection. All I remember is that it was early morning, that we were happy to be in one another's company, that there were bright green boughs overhead amongst which the birds floated and sang, and that the early dews still burned in their crystal in the sun.

We were taking our way almost at haphazard across country, there was now grass, now the faintly sparkling flinty dust of an English road, underfoot. With remarkably few humans to be seen, we trudged on, turning our eyes ever and again to glance laughingly, questioningly, or perplexedly at one another's, then slanting them once more on the blue-canopied countryside. It was spring, in the month of May, I think, and we were talking of Time.

We speculated on what it was, and where it went to, touched in furtive tones on the Fourth Dimension and exchanged "the Magic Formula." We wondered if pigs could see time as they see the wind, and wished we could recline awhile upon those bewitching banks where it grows wild. We confessed to each other how of late we had been pining in our secret hearts for just a brief spell of an *eternity* of it. Time wherein we could be and think and dream all that each busy, hugger-mugger, feverish, precipitate twenty-four hours would not allow us to be or to think or dream. Impracticable, infatuate desire! We desired to muse, to brood, to meditate, to embark (with a buoyant cargo) upon that quiet stream men call reverie. We had all but forgotten how even to sleep. We lay like Argus of nights with all our hundred eyes ajar. There were books we should never now be able to read; speculations we should never be able to explore; riddles we should never so much as hear put, much less expounded. There were, above all, waking visions now past hoping for; long since shut away from us by the stream of the hasty moments—as they tick and silt and slide irrecoverably away. In the gay folly of that bright morning we could almost have vowed there were even other "selves" awaiting us with whom no kind of precarious tryst we had ever made we had ever been faithful to. Perhaps they and we would be ready if only the world's mechanical clocks would cease their trivial moralizings.

And memories—surely they would come arrowing home in the first of the evening to haunts serene and unmolested, if only the weather and mood and season and housing we could offer were decently propitious. We had frittered away, squandered so many days, weeks, years—and had saved so little. Spendthrifts of the unborrowable, we had been living on our capital—a capital bringing in how meagre an "interest"—and were continually growing poorer. Once, when we were children, and in our own world, an hour had been as capacious as the blue bowl of the sky, and of as refreshing a milk. Now its successors haggardly snatched their way past our sluggard senses like thieves pursued.

Like an hour glass that cannot tell the difference between its head and its heels; like a dial on a sunless day; like a timepiece wound-up—wound-up and bereft of its pendulum; so were we.

Age, we had hideously learned, devours life as a river consumes flakes of the falling snow. Soon we should be beggars, with scarcely a month to our name; and none to give us alms.

I confess that at this crisis in our talk I caught an uncomfortable glimpse of the visionary stallions of my hearse—ink-black streaming manes and tails—positively galloping me off—wreaths, glass, corpse, and all, to keep their dismal appointment with the grave: and even at that, abominably late.

Indeed, our minds had at length become so profoundly engaged in these pictures and forebodings as we paced on, that a complete æon might have meanwhile swept over our heads. We had talked ourselves into a kind of oblivion. Nor had either of us given the least thought to our direction or destination. We had been following not even so much as our noses. And then suddenly, we "came to." Maybe it was the unwonted silence—a silence unbroken even by the harplike drone of noonday—that recalled us to ourselves. Maybe the air in these unfamiliar parts was of a crisper quality, or the mere effect of the strangeness around us had muttered in secret to our inward spirits. Whether or not, we both of us discovered at the same instant and as if at a signal, that without being aware of it, and while still our tongues were wagging on together on our old-fashioned theme, we had come into sight of the Vats. We looked up, and lo!—they lay there in the middle distance, in cluster enormous under the cloudless sky: and here were we!

Imagine two age-scarred wolf-skinned humans of prehistoric days paddling along at shut of evening on some barbarous errand, and suddenly from a sweeping crest on Salisbury Plain descrying on the nearer horizon the awful monoliths of Stonehenge. An experience resembling that was ours this summer day.

We came at once to a standstill amid the far-flung stretches of the unknown plateau on which we had re-found ourselves, and with eyes fixed upon these astonishing objects, stood and stared. I have called them Vats. Vats they were not; but rather sunken Reservoirs; vast semi-spherical primeval Cisterns, of an area many times that of the bloated and swollen gasometers which float like huge flattened bubbles between earth and heaven under the sunlit clouds of the Thames. But no sunbeams dispread themselves here.

They lay slumbering in a grave, crystal light, which lapped, deep as the Tuscarora Trough, above and around their prodigious stone plates, or slats, or slabs, or laminæ; their steep slopes washed by the rarefied atmosphere of their site, and in hue of a hoary green.

As we gazed at them like this from afar they seemed to be in number, as I remember, about nine, but they were by no means all of a size. For one or two of the rotundas were smaller in compass than the others, just as there may be big snails or mushrooms in a family, and little ones.

But any object on earth of a majesty or magnitude that recalls the Pyramids is a formidable spectacle. And not a word passed between us, scarcely a glance, as with extreme caution and circumspection we approached—creeping human pace by pace—to view them nearer.

A fit of shivering came over me, I recollect, as thus advantaged I scanned their enormous sides, shaggy with tufts of a monstrous moss and scarred with yard-wide circumambulations of lichen. Gigantic grasses stooped their fatted seedpods from the least rough ledge. They might be walls of ice, so cold their aspect; or of a matter discoverable only in an alien planet.

Not—though they were horrific to the *eye*—not that they were in themselves appalling to the soul. Far rather they seemed to be emblems of an ineffable peace; harmless as, centuries before Noah, were the playing leviathans in a then privy Pacific. And when one looked close on them it was to see myriads of animated infinitesimals in crevice and cranny, of a beauty, hue, and symmetry past eye to seize. Indeed, there was a hint remotely human in the looks of these Vats. The likeness between them resembled that between generations of mankind, countless generations old. Contemplating them with the unparalleled equanimity their presence at last bestowed, one might almost have ventured to guess their names. And never have I seen sward or turf so smooth and virginally emerald as that which heaved itself against their brobdingnagian flanks.

My friend and I, naturally enough, were acutely conscious of our minuteness of stature as we stood side by side in this unrecorded solitude, and, out of our little round heads, peered up at them with our eyes. Obviously their muscous incrustations and the families of weeds flourishing in their interstices were of an age to daunt the imagination. Their ancestry must have rooted itself here when the dinosaur and the tribes of the megatherium roamed earth's crust and the pterodactyl clashed through its twilight—thousands of centuries before the green acorn sprouted that was to afford little Cain in a fallen world his first leafy petticoats. I realized as if at a sigh why smiles the Sphinx; why the primary stars have blazed on in undiminishing midnight lustre during Man's brief history, and his childish constellations have scarcely by a single inch of heaven changed in their apparent stations.

They wore that air of lovely timelessness which decks the thorn, and haunts for the half-woken sense the odour of sweet-brier; yet they were grey with the everlasting, as are the beards of the patriarchs and the cindery craters of the Moon. Theirs was the semblance of having been lost, forgotten, abandoned, like some foundered Nereid-haunted derelict of the first sailors, rotting in dream upon an undiscovered shore. They hunched their vast shapes out of the green beneath the sunless blue of space, and for untrodden leagues around them stretched like a paradisal savanna what we poor thronging clock-vexed men call Silence. Solitude.

In telling of these Vats it is difficult to convey in mere words even a fraction of their effect upon our minds. And not merely our minds. They called to some hidden being within us that, if not their coeval, was at least aware of their exquisite antiquity. Whether of archangelic or dæmonic construction, clearly they had remained unvisited by mortal man for as many centuries at least as there are cherries in Damascus or beads in Tierra del Fuego. Sharers of this thought, we two dwarf visitors had whispered an instant or so together, face to face; and then were again mute.

Yes, we were of one mind about that. In the utmost depths of our imaginations it was clear to us that these supremely solitary objects, if not positively cast out of thought, had been abandoned.

But by whom? My friend and I had sometimes talked of the divine Abandoner; and also (if one can, and may, distinguish between mood and person, between the dream and the dreamer) of It. Here was the vacancy of His presence; just as one may be aware of a filament of His miracle in the smiling beauty that hovers above the swaying grasses of an indecipherable grave-stone.

Looking back on the heatless and rayless noonday of those Vats, I see, as I have said, the mere bodies of my friend and me, the upright bones of us, indescribably dwarfed by their antediluvian monstrosity. Yet within the lightless bellies of these sarcophagi were heaped up, we were utterly assured (though *how*, I know not), floods, beyond measure, of the waters for which our souls had pined. Waters, imaginably so clear as to be dense, as if of melted metal more translucent even than crystal; of such a tenuous purity that not even the moonlit branches of a dream would spell their reflex in them; so costly, so far beyond price, that this whole stony world's rubies and sapphires and amethysts of Mandalay and Guadalajara and Solikamsk, all the treasure-houses of Cambalech and the booty of King Tamburlane would suffice to purchase not one drop.

It is indeed the unseen, the imagined, the untold-of, the fabulous, the forgotten that alone lies safe from mortal moth and rust; and these Vats—their very silence held us spellbound, as were the Isles before the Sirens sang.

But how, it may be asked; No sound? No spectral tread? No faintest summons? And not the minutest iota of a superscription? None. I sunk my very being into nothingness, so that I seemed to become but a shell receptive of the least of whispers. But the multitudinous life that was here was utterly silent. No sigh, no ripple, no pining chime of rilling drop within. Waters of life; but infinitely still.

I may seem to have used extravagant terms. My friend and I used none. We merely stood in dumb survey of these crusted, butt-like domes of stone, wherein slept *Elixir Vitæ,* whose last echo had been the Choragium of the morning stars.

God knows there are potent explosives in these latter days. My friend and I had merely the nails upon our fingers, a pen-knife, and a broken pair of scissors in our pockets. We might have scraped seven and seventy score growths of a Nebuchadnezzar's talons down to the quick, and yet have left all but unmarked and unscarred those mossed and monstrous laminæ. But we had tasted the untastable, and were refreshed in spirit at least a little more endurably than are the camel-riders of the Sahara dream-ridden by mirage.

We knew now and for ever that Time-pure *is;* that here—somewhere awaiting us and all forlorn mankind—lay hid the solace of our mortal longing; that doubtless the Seraph whose charge is the living waters will in the divine hour fetch down his iron key in his arms, and—well, Dives, rich man and crumb-waster that he was, pleaded out of the flames for but one drop of them. Neither my friend nor I was a Dives then, nor was ever likely to be. And now only I remain.

We were Children of Lazarus, ageing, footsore, dusty and athirst. We smiled openly and with an extraordinary gentle felicity at one another—his eyes and mine—as we turned away from the Vats.

The Riddle and Other Stories (1923)

STRANGERS AND PILGRIMS

To me, who find,
Reviewing my past way, much to condemn,
Little to praise, and nothing to regret,
(Save some remembrances of dream-like joys
That scarcely seem to have belonged to me)
If I must take my choice between the pair
That rule alternately the weary hours,
Night is than day more acceptable; sleep
Doth, in my estimate of good, appear
A better state than waking; death than sleep:

Feelingly sweet is stillness after storm,
Though under covert of the wormy ground!
                                        William Wordsworth

IT WAS later even than Mr. Phelps had supposed. But now his day
was nearly over. Not an arduous, and perhaps a rather vacant day,
spent as it had been like thousands of its forerunners between his
three-roomed cottage—resembling at this season a mound of
flowers more than a house—and the great church. Lank and as-
cetic, in his old many-buttoned cassock, ponderous key in hand
and the heavy door yawning behind him, he had paused as was
his habit in the southern porch to lift his eyes towards the smooth,
low, bright-green hills that rose beyond it. Dotted with dwarfed
and scattered thorn trees and bushes of juniper in their mounded
hollows, they lay there—mantled with light and colour. They
were his constant companions, unchanging and serene.

Shadows in the oblique sunshine were now encroaching upon
them. High in the vault of the blue air a few gulls were circling;
the plaintive sweet call of a peewit fell faintly on his ear. And
behold, one solitary human figure was descending the rough cart-
track towards the church. Mr. Phelps had at once fixed his eyes
on this unlikely fellow creature.

Head bowed down, he came slowly, steadily, ploddingly on;
now treading the grass between the wheel-ruts, and now stumbling into the ruts themselves, though he raised no dust into the
gilding evening light. Like all ancient buildings, the old church
attracted an odd assortment of visitors; but few—at least so late
in the day—came from this direction: that of the sea. Mr. Phelps
kept his quarry closely in view. For a moment, but only for a
moment, his cautious but discerning soul had uncharitably de-
bated whether or not he could be perfectly sober.

It was as yet no more than on the fringe of the holiday season,
and little opportunity had recently been offered him for descant-
ing on the glories of the edifice in his charge—a privilege of which
he never wearied. This individual, however, had no trace of
the holiday-maker in his aspect. From head to foot he was in
black. And yet, the verger, long practised in these little matters,
had at once decided that he was not in holy orders. He was the

better pleased to think so. Layman make the more docile listeners. And you might be excessively odd, yet orthodox. At this moment there could be no question of the odd. "In the name of God," the old man heard himself muttering, "and who can this be?"

Unwilling to be caught resembling a spider in wait for a fly, he withdrew a few paces into the church, and in this seclusion kept an ear cocked beyond it. At length the iron latch of the lych-gate had clicked. Peering out, he still kept watch. The stranger had paused before a vast palisaded vault, but rather as if to make certain that he was alone than to read what was inscribed on its panels. Indeed, as he came on, his face had oddly contracted at the discovery that the heavily-hinged door within the porch was a few inches ajar. He hesitated again—like an animal wary of a trap. It was Mr. Phelp's opportunity.

"Good evening, sir," he said, sallying out pleasantly. "And a very beautiful evening it is!"

The stranger became completely motionless, as motionless as some animal or insect "shamming dead." The deep-set inward eyes under his black hat-brim seemed to be slightly asquint, so fixed was his scrutiny. A prolonged murmuration had ebbed away into silence in the sunlit calm of the evening—the placid breaking of a seventh wave along the low beach beyond the hill—a sigh as of time itself in the quiet.

"Is this St. Stephen's, Langridge?" came at length the inquiry—but in tones so mumbled and muffled that Mr. Phelps had detected no motion in the questioner's mouth.

He smiled urbanely; but, he *knows* it is Langridge, was the conviction that had swiftly flitted through his mind. "Indeed, yes, sir; this is Langridge. The village you'll find is only a few minutes' distance beyond the trees round the bend of the road; and *this* is St. Edmund's, King and Martyr." With but a lift of a forefinger he had indicated the great beautiful stone church behind him.

"You may perhaps, sir, have already noticed in the niche above our heads the crossed arrows and the crowned head—with open mouth—between the fore-paws of the wolf. And as you may be aware, the body of the saintly King was not discovered and reattached to the head until some fifty years afterwards—after he was martyred, sir. A pitiless affair. There is a scrap of old glass too in the vestry showing him one among a happy group of the halt and the lame—and all of them *carrying* their crutches!"

The loose creaseless trousers were powdered with dust; the dark hands hung squat and swollen from their cuffs. Owing in part to his having spent so many years within walls and in part to a bilious constitution, the verger's lean ecclesiastical countenance was somewhat tallowy in hue. His visitor's might have been modelled out of wax. The lips had lost their red, his eyes resembled little flat agates beneath their heavy lids—the eyelids, one might conjecture, of one so wearied out with this world's travailings that they could never be surfeited enough with sleep. It was a face burdened with a profound secretiveness. Only an extreme solitude surely could have produced the appearance of so dark a lethargy. And yet, no countryman, Mr. Phelps had concluded; possibly a lay reader, though he hardly thought so.

"I was just about to lock up, sir. The key, as you see, is in my hand. But if you had anything in particular in view . . . ?"

The stranger withdrew his glance from the time-pocked dismembered stone head that graced the porch and slowly eyed him. He drew in his lips. "As a matter of fact," he said, and as if he were repeating a lesson, "I am—and have been for some time—in search of . . . of an inscription. But I agree; yes, it is growing late. And you must be gone?" He raised his head as though to measure the advance of darkness with his eyes, but stealthily, one by one, surveyed instead the grinning row of gargoyles that jutted out above the weathered groining of the windows, then glanced back at the track he had recently descended.

"Why, yes, sir, but that's of no account," Mr. Phelps assured him. " 'At length it ringeth to evensong,' as the old rhyme says, but I should be very glad to give you any assistance in my power. We are not, as you can see, *short* of inscriptions—inside or out! In fact our population here must now far exceed what is left in the village yonder. In these days, sir, we cannot even make good our losses. All sheep, and few lambs. There will presently, I sometimes say, be nobody and nothing left but me and the church! If you would give me the name, or even as much as the year and place, there might be no difficulty. In late summer we have visitors from all parts of the world, most merely from hearsay, but a good sprinkling of them hunting up ancestors, coats of arms, pedigrees, and so forth. Anything for deep-laid English roots, sir; and no wonder. There was a party from the United States of America, a very talkative lady, sir, who I myself tracked down only a few weeks ago to 1616—the year of the lamented death, you will remember, of the poet William Shakespeare. And highly gratified she was."

The stranger appeared to have listened, but made no comment. You would hardly associate him just now, mused the verger, with the heraldic. There are individuals who in spite of copious hints at a private history suggest neither roots nor pedigree. This one, indeed, to judge from his appearance, might himself be one of his more recent ancestors—the slack ill-fitting black clothes, the elastic-sided boots, the shield-shaped cravat decked with a garnet pin, the shapeless black-banded hat. They reminded Mr. Phelps of an enlarged and tinted photograph of his own father which graced the chimney-piece of his crowded little sitting-room. He had been posed by the genial photographer of the county town standing in his Sunday best beside a canvas depicting a large urn—a rather funereal effect.

In this case the funereal seemed to have been carried to an extreme. The verger—dust in hand—had helped to officiate at many "interments" in his day, but never before had he encountered a human being so eloquent of mourning. His black was almost dazzling in its intensity—as dazzling as the dark outer blue of the Atlantic. On glancing away for an instant a faintly green after-image was left within the eye. Only guilty sorrow has a blackness as much bereft of light; and despair one as dense. And the more repeatedly Mr. Phelps examined the stranger before him the less he could make of him, except that he resembled a receptacle which however much you might pour into it in the way of information, you could never hope to brim. Still, any listener was better than none; he must craftily play his catch, and hope for the best.

With a mild sacerdotal gesture he invited his visitor to follow him in. "Perhaps," he explained ingenuously, "we might first take a glance at the interior. As you see, sir, we have some uncommonly fine Norman work—early Norman, some of it, too. Before the Conqueror, they say; though there seems to be no end to their disputings. And that, sir, is a unique angel roof in the chapel yonder. There are only three, I am told, to match it in these islands. The rood-screen has been carefully restored but not re-coloured; and we are proud of our pews; the poppyheads are very little damaged. Them old high pews may have had their abuses, sir—sleeping, snoring, and children monkeying—but rush chairs with Norman I never could away with. Our brasses, too. Mostly in Latin of course; but you will find the English in the pamphlet. If, that is," he added gallantly, "you should require it. In fact, as I often repeat, we are packed from crypt to belfry with the Past. Yes, sir; and with all due respect, I might say that this church has become a second home to me. Indeed, believe it or not, I can detect the presence of a stranger in it even before I've either seen or heard him."

This particular stranger's eyes had meanwhile settled vacantly on a slab of grey marble which had been inset in the stone of the wall opposite to him. It was surmounted by the flat square head of a cherub, but the words beneath it must at this distance have been competely indecipherable.

"The 'Past,' " he repeated dully, as if the meaning of the word were no longer worth even the effort of speech. "Yes. And yet . . . The truth is, there *is* no past. There is only what is here now. For all that," he added, his flat husky tones sinking almost into inaudibility, "I must, even recently, have read over hundreds—I say, hundreds of inscriptions."

"Indeed, sir?" said the verger tactfully. "And I see you have already detected one which attracts practically every visitor that comes along; especially our female visitors."

He rapidly sidled his way between the pews, and in a tenoring voice, a little throaty but not unpleasing, intoned aloud:

> "Here lies—how sad that he is no more seen—
>   A child so sweet of mien
> Earth must with Heaven have conspired to make him.
>   As wise a manhood, 'tis said,

Promised his lovely head;
As gentle as nature
His every youthful feature.
But now no sound, no word, no night-long bird—
Not even the daybreak lark can hope to awake him.

"Not even the daybreak lark," he repeated, and paused to look back. "Why, sir, in the spring, as you might well guess, there's scarcely a minute of the day without its circling skylark over these quiet hills; and no doubt it has always been so." His visitor was continuing to listen. "But 'youthful' notwithstanding, sir, if this little lad had lived up to now, he would be *one hundred and twenty-four* years of age! And that is a fact, seeing him so young in the mind's eye, that never fails to strike me as pathetic. I agree it's nothing to the point," he added, after yet another glance at his listener, "since it is the age that we die at we remain—at least in memory. Tidings sad enough, sir, for the old and infirm. Still, you cannot put an old man back into his youth again, however much he may covet it."

"It's the human way," Mr. Phelp's visitor had huskily interposed, as if he were unaccustomed to the sound of his own voice. "But what is age? No more than a mask; even if what is done is done for ever. The cocoon may perish, but not the deathless worm. You said 'the Past'; but it's the same thing. Its all is all *we* have."

The verger had discovered little coherency in these remarks; he was intent, however, not on receiving but on giving. "Certainly, sir," he agreed. "And here, though six and thirty years divide them, another child lies buried; and he was only seven. Not that at such an age he can have known what he would be missing." Again he spared his visitor's eyesight.

"Here lies a strangely serious child,
Called on earth Emmanuel.
Never to laughter reconciled,
This day-long peace must please him well;
He must, forsooth, in secret keep
Smiling—that he is so sound asleep.

"Yet you'll notice, sir, solemn-soever a child as he may have been, the stone-cutter has notwithstanding put in here—and here—and here—the usual and common toys of children—a rattle, a nursery trumpet, a top and so forth; pretty no doubt in intention, sir, but still wide of the mark. And *there,* close adjacent," he rapidly continued, as if to stifle an incipient interruption, "a weeping willow, as you see, spreading its stony leaves and branches from summit to base of the complete memorial stone. That's where"—he pointed—"*that* one's mother lays, and the child beside her. Not, as I take it, the father, sir. Though why, I cannot tell you. There may have been good reasons; or bad.

> "Art thou a widow? Then, my Friend,
> By this my tomb a moment spend,
> To breathe a prayer o'er these cold stones
> Which house-room give to weary bones.
> And may God grant, when thou so lie,
> Dust of they loved one rest near by!

"Widow or not, I always say, *that* is a supplication it's hard to pass entirely unheeded, sir. They lie so near, what remains of them, and yet so seldom in memory's sight." With no more than a fleeting glance out of his watery grey eye, the verger had led the way on; like a dog on a familiar scent. "Now this," he was explaining, his lean forefinger laid on a tablet flush with the wall, and no more than half the size of a pocket handkerchief, "this is our smallest and shortest—a tailor's; though he'd have small trade here now, I fancy, if he came back! Of the name of Hackle, William Hackle. They say he was a one-eyed old man—like his implement, sir.

> Here's an old Taylour, rest his eye:
> Needle and thredde put by.

And it couldn't have been put shorter. Next we have Silas Dwight—the memorial only; the remains themselves having been interred outside. Not that that need have been intended for any slight on them, sir. There are many no doubt who would prefer the open. According to our records he was choirmaster here for seventeen years, so the horn spoken of is mainly what they call a figure of speech." His voice rose a little to do justice to his theme:

> "Though hautboy and bassoon may break
> This ancient peace with, Christians, Wake!
> We should not stir, nor have, since when
> God rest you, merry Gentlemen!
> He of the icy hand us bid,
> And laid us 'neath earth's coverlid.
> Yet oft did Silas Dwight, who lies
> Under this stone, in cheerful wise
> Make Chancel wall and roof to ring
> With Christmas Joys and Wassailing;
> And still, maybe, may wind his horn
> And stop out shrill, This Happy Morn.

"The days here spoken of, as you may recollect, sir, were those before the church organs, at least in village churches, fine as ours may be. And speaking for myself, though the instrument you see yonder, three manuals, cost us a thumping sum of money, I like the old single fiddles and clarinets better than the yowling and bumbling of the stops and pedals. All depends, of course," he had lowered his voice into the confidential, "on who's handling them; but, no matter who, I never did care much for the clatter —nor the notion of the lad, neither, cracking his nuts behind her and blowing her up."

The stranger had rather belatedly met his glance. It was encouragement enough. "Now here, sir," the verger, eager as a schoolboy, had shuffled across to the south aisle again, "here, talking of age, we have our Parr. Not, I must warn you, the famous Thomas, who outlived ten kings of England and begot a child, sir, so the story goes, when he was twenty years over his century. Which, I may add, is nothing much to boast of by comparison with some of these old patriarchs mentioned in the Scriptures. No, *our* Parr—William—departed this life three days *short* of his century; a sad vexation, I have no doubt, to his relatives, sir, wishful to be bruiting him abroad. I've heard tell of some old Greek who did the same, but his name escapes me. Well, sir, so much for William Parr. And his lettering's so cut, you'll notice,

on his "decent and fair Marble" as I've seen it described, that it's
easiest to read sideways, though for my part I could manage it
upside down! This is how it goes:

> He that lies here was mortal olde,
> All but a hundred, if truth be told.
> His pinpricke eyes, his hairless pate,
> Crutch in hand, his shambling gaite—
> All spake of Time: and Time's slow stroke,
> That fells at length the stoutest Oke.
> Of yeares so many now he is gone
> There's nought to tell except this stone.
> His name was Parr: decease did he
> In Seventeen Hundred Sixty Three."

The old verger had once more intoned the lines loud, since the
stranger had remained where he had left him. "Outside," he
added, "a yard or so beyond this wall, in fact, there is a similar
inscription, and one that strikes nearer home, at least to me, sir.
I'll show you the stone itself in a few minutes; but this is how that
runs:

> Three score years I lived; and then
> Looked for to live another ten.
> But he who from the Hale and Quick
> Robs the pure Oile that feeds the Wick
> Chanced my enfeebled frame to mark—
> Hence, this unutterable Darke.

"Which is only to declare, sir, that there is more than one way
of looking at the same occurrences in life—a point by your leave
to which we will return later. In the meantime, sir, if you please,
would you step this way?"

Even Mr. Phelps had paused a moment to give dramatic effect
to his next exhibit. "The tomb now before us," he announced,
"is reputed, sir, to be the finest specimen of sepulchral art we
have. Not only in St. Edmund's, but in these parts. And not
merely that, neither. The medicos tell me—gentlemen, I mean,
learned in such things—that there is not a single bone in the
human anatomy missing in this skeleton here—of the finest ala-

baster. It represents, as you see, the figure of Death, scythe over
shoulder, lantern in hand; though, as I've heard say, he can as
often manage his private business in the dark. Sir Willoughby
Branksome was quondam owner, sir, of the old Manor House
beyond the village—a family going back into mediæval times—
and the house was built much about the same period as the roof
over our heads."

The stranger had drawn nearer, and was emptily surveying the
ornate details of the tomb.

> Alas! Alack!
> We come not back.
> Adieu! and Welladay!
> Yet, if we could,
> No wise man would;
> What more is left to say?

"Considering the cost and the sculpture work, I must confess,"
remarked the verger, "that *that* has a disappointing ring; at least
to my ear, sir. Words and effigy don't rightly match. Besides, as
you can see for yourself, counting the two rows of them there, he
left nine ungrown children behind him, not including the smallest
already gone, and holding a skull in her infant hands. Ten, sir,
must be a burden to any mother. Quality, or otherwise. And she
did well by some of them, too; as you can see by the marbles to
either hand—a countess there, and a Lord Admiral here. The
truth is, times change. What is common human nature in one age
is unbefitting levity in another." He turned for a word of ap-
proval, and so met for an instant the direct leaden lustreless gaze
of his companion in the church. "Here, for example," he hastened
on, "is such doggerel as no chisel would be allowed to cut on
sacred walls in these days—a Henry the Eighth in private life.
And yet, are we any more conscionable of the *facts*?

> Here rests in peace, Rebecca Anne,
> Spouse of Job Hodson, Gentleman.

> Here also Henrietta Grace,
> Destined to lie in this same place.

And Jane, who three brief years of life
Did bear the honoured name of wife.

Here also Caroline (once Dove).
And him, the husband of the above.

"And that, sir, is a standing example, as I have heard our good
Bishop himself declare, of God's plenty!"

Daylight had been steadily draining out of the church, and
dusk seeping in. The last hues of the sunset had long since vanished from the stone walls beyond the dog-toothed arcade of the
clerestory windows. A small indistinct shape had begun soundlessly flitting to and fro beneath the timbers of the roof overhead.
The great church, cold, serene, motionless as if frozen, was preparing itself for the night.

Visitors to it—ignorant, frivolous, inquiring, learned, indifferent, were all in Mr. Phelps's daily round. Never had he encountered one so frigid and irresponsive. There hung too about him a
vague hint of the earthy; as if he might have slept overnight in
a cellar. Was he intelligent enough—that tallow-flat face—to
have followed what had been said? Or was perhaps the gentleman a little hard of hearing? Or was he merely humouring his
cicerone, passing the time away, until he could get about his own
private business? A word or two of inquiry, Mr. Phelps was well
aware, might at once set him on the right track. Nevertheless he
refrained from uttering it. Patience no doubt would at last be its
own reward, even if the sands of day were ebbing low.

"If only, sir," he remonstrated, with a disarming smile, "you
had happed in on me a few minutes earlier, I could have shown
you our crypt. There's many who visit us solely for that purpose.
But it's beyond hours already now, and down there it must be
long ago pitch-dark. What's more, the rector has a mortal dread
of fire." He held his head sidelong a little, and a childishly naïve
and deprecating smile descended into the furrows of his long
jaw as he added—"both here, and hereafter. Besides, we should
have no light left for the churchyard."

With the faintest indication of a gesture the other seemed to
intimate that there was no necessity for haste, that time was of

no concern to him, and a church as pleasant a lodging for the night as any. He had sluggishly followed the verger into the bell-chamber under the west tower, glancing up narrowly, as he did so, at the slack ropes looped dangling through the holes in its ceiling.

"Now here, sir," said Mr. Phelps, coming to a standstill again, "is what was in my mind to speak of a moment or two ago. Some four or five summers since, not to put too fine a point on it, there came here a grey-faced, stunted little old brat of a man —and I had my misgivings the moment I set eyes on him—who first listened me out, and then, quite deliberately, sir, told me to my face that all I had been repeating was nothing but *holy hocum*: his very words. 'I don't give that for your old stones and bones,' he said, and spat on the floor. Now in my humble estimation, sir, that man's was the soul of nothing short of a maniac's. He had gone bad, and the Devil had entered into him. I gave him a look, sir: and I shook the dust of him from off my feet.

"That's one side, one extreme of the story. On the other; that we mortals should dread the tomb—that's only natural. And it's when we are nearing the end that what may be called the real takes on another colour, sir. You look at those about you and can't any more so surely rely on what they *are,* if you take me. As once you could. There is so thin a crust, sir, in a manner of speaking, between being awake and asleep—very fast asleep indeed. A sip of a doctor's drug, and not only the lantern goes out but everything it shone on. I had that experience myself not more than a month or two since—only a decayed tooth, sir: outer darkness, and then the awakening. If that *comes.* It is like as if we were treading a flat fall of untrodden snow and suddenly it is thin ice—cat ice, as we used to call it when we were boys—and we are gone. Not, mind you, that the waters of death, however cold they may be, are not—well, the waters of life. Faith is faith. What then do you conjecture must the infidel think of finding statements in stone in a Christian church which are sheer contrary to its own beliefs? Not that I should be repeating this to *every* visitor. That would be neither meet nor proper; besides, few would care. But even in this small parcel of ground around us here we have no fewer than five diametrically different views on

the subject—diametrically different. Here, for one, is the grave
of a child named Blackstone, Timothy Blackstone, who, as we
read for ourselves, 'was borne a Weakling and lived but to be
three years old.' But what is said of him?—

> O Death, have care
> Only a Childe lies here.
> A fear-full mite was he,
> My last-born, *Timothy*.
> Shroud then thy grewsome face,
> When thou dost pass this place;
> Lest his small ghoste should see,
> And weep for me!

"The ghost of a *child*, sir, mark you, and a very young child.
And no doubt it is his mother who is speaking, or one who is
speaking *for* his mother. And yet, poor lamb, he is considered as
being still frightened and still forsaken—at evils that were long,
long ago all safely over!"

The stranger had raised his hand again, had turned with mouth
ajar, as if to expostulate. "One moment, sir, if you please," cried
Mr. Phelps. "Cheek by jowl with it, as you see, we have 'O. A.'—
no more than the initials, and the years, 1710–1762—and this!

> Who: and How: and Where: and When—
> Tell their stones of these poore men.
> Grudge not then if one be bare
> Of Who, and How, and When, and Where.
> Such is nought to them who sigh
> Still with their last breath, Why?

"That's *another* way of looking at the riddle, and, I grant you,
in our low moments there's a good deal to be said for the 'Why.'
But what I am bearing towards, if you follow me, is whether we
are not already edging into the neighborhood of the heathen,
sir? And yet, mark you—light itself by comparison—here's another, clean contrary to both:

> Son of man, tell me,
> Hast thou at any time lain in thick darkness,
> Gazing up into a lightless silence,

A dark void vacancy,
Like the woe of the sea
In the unvisited places of the ocean?
And nothing but thine own frail sentience
To prove thee living?
Lost in this affliction of the spirit,
Did'st thou then call upon God
Of his infinite mercy to reveal to thee
Proof of his presence—
His presence and love for thee, exquisite creature of his creation?
To show thee but some small devisal
Of his infinite compassion and pity, even though it were as
    fleeting
As the light of a falling star in a dewdrop?
Hast thou? O, if thou hast not,
Do it now; do it now; do it now!
Lest that night come which is sans sense, thought, tongue, stir,
    time, being,
And the moment is for ever denied thee,
Since thou art thyself as I am.

"While here again, sir, beneath the very soles of our feet," he tapped the stone with the capless toe of his shoe, "here we have Richard Halladay, and a very fine piece of lettering, I allow—though a few words, as you see, have been worn flat by the bell-ringers' treadings, sir." He glossed the inscription as he read:

"Each in place as God did 'gree
    Here lie all ye Bones of me.
But what made them walke up right,
And, cladde in Flesh, a goodly Sight,
One of the hostes of Living Men—
    Ask again—ask again!

"And last this, which, being human, we all can share. It was, sir, my poor dear mother's favourite of them all:

O onlie one, Fare-well!
Love hath not words to tell
How dear thou wert, and art,
To an emptie heart."

He had paused before attempting the last line. "But now, sir," he went rapidly on, "to continue my argument. We all feel and realize *that* when the grief is on us. But what I am asking myself is what one of these Mohometans or suchlike, heretics as we call them, would think of so much of the contradictory, sir, in so little space! The fact is, when it comes to a question of truth— and, 'What *is* Truth?' said Pontius Pilate—it's as if each and every one of us had his own private compass. From birth, sir. The needle pointing not due north, mark you, never that, but a few hairs' breadths or more short of it. As life goes on, now this way it veers, now that; and the most we can do as it seems to me, is to see that it doesn't jam."

A little breathless, a fresh apprehension transfixing his pale face, he paused a moment—his own needle hovering rather more widely than usual—as if to let this reflection sink in. Mr. Phelps's stranger had at last found voice again.

"You forget," he was saying, "that every syllable inscribed on these walls was put there by the living. None *by*, but only *of* the dead. Better, a thousand times, I agree, a single word of pity and forgiveness than—nothing at all. As for any attempt to return, a mere child could have little occasion for it. But these others—do *they*, do you suppose, never come back?" The last few hollow, challenging, half-stifled words had rung out oddly in the silence of the church—and far more exclamatorily than Mr. Phelps's pleasant tenoring.

Back, back, back, had quietly fainted away the echo—as if in-deed the masons of the ancient building when fitting stone to stone had childishly so adapted its acoustics as to ensure a device of which the Elizabethan dramatists and the old poets never wearied. A long pause followed. But the set black eyes in the expressionless face were still apparently expecting an answer. The verger thrust his hand into his cassock pocket, drew out an immense handkerchief, and replaced it. He temporized.

"I agree, sir," he smiled inquiringly, "that the dead cannot compose their own epitaphs! They might make queer, ay, and moving reading if they did. The riddle to *me* is what sort of question you could put to such a one as Lazarus as you'd most wish to have answered, as would *assure* the point. But taking *your* question merely as it is put, I would not deny the possibility of such occurrences. God forbid. One may become aware of what is unusual, yet not know. You would be astonished, sir, how even the hopping of a bird, or the skirring of a withered leaf in the draught over the stones, will sound out in these walls when I'm alone here. And it's seldom so late. Nor would I deny that now and again I have fancied that other occupants . . ." His glance fixed on his visitor, a temporary confusion had spread over his mind, and he failed to complete his sentence. "But there; the human eye, sir, can be a great deceiver!"

"That indeed is so," the low insistent voice rejoined, "but there may be those who prefer *not* to be seen?"

The verger disliked being cornered, but he had sat under many preachers.

"The points as I take it, sir, are these. First," he laid forefinger on forefinger, "the number of those gone as compared with ourselves who are still waiting. Next, there being no warrant that what is seen—if seen at all—is wraiths of the departed, and not from elsewhere. The very waterspouts outside are said to be demonstrations of that belief. Third and last, another question: What purpose could call so small a sprinkling of them back—a few grains of sand out of the wilderness, unless, it may be, some festering grievance; or hunger for the living, sir, or duty left undone? In which case, mark you, which of any of us is safe?"

His visitor lifted a heavy head and looked at him. "But the living themselves," he said, "have instincts, hidden impulses, are driven, beaten, incited on to what may at last appear the unevadable. Then why not *they*? What proof is there . . . only 'duty'? They might, no more than the living, be aware of any purpose, yet be compelled to pursue it. And assuredly," he hesitated, "if, at the end, there had been extreme trouble and—horror."

The harsh screaming of the swifts coursing in the twilight beyond the leaded windows before they retired into the heavens to sleep out the night upon the wing, was for the moment the only comment on these remarks.

"Well, sir," said Mr. Phelps uneasily at last, "I confess you press me close. But we are still no nearer what you had in mind, and I must be locking up. Perhaps you would care to take a glance at a few of the stones in the churchyard, if there is light enough left? But, first," he added, with a little bow of old-fashioned courtesy, "and I trust I haven't been detaining you, sir; would you very kindly put your name in our Visitor's Book?"

The well-worn volume stood on a table by itself. He set it open at the current page, and himself dipped the pen into the inkpot. His visitor accepted the pen, paused, and, without again raising his heavy eyes, stooped over the book.

Mr. Phelps politely retired, drew open the great door, and his visitor, rather reluctantly, it seemed, and still as far as space permitted keeping his distance, presently edged out and preceded him into the churchyard. From their haunts in the green hills came yet again the sweet and sorrowful cry of the peewits. The air in the porch, after the stony chill within, struck warm on the cheek, and mild as new milk, laden faintly with the earth-sweet fragrance of the hills and the remote freshness of the sea. The evening star in the tarnished gold of the west shone liquid and solitary. The verger feasted his eyes a moment on this quiet scene.

It was as if he had half-forgotten but had now retrieved it, after some dark passage of the mind. An unusual sense of fatigue, mind and body, had stolen over him, and he was relieved that his catechism was over. Few visitors volunteered many questions. If they did, they were questions expected, easy to answer—concerning dates, styles, uses, rituals, and so forth. He regretted now, but only because he was unwontedly tired, that he had not a moment ago seized his opportunity to bid this stranger Godspeed. He was none the less astonished to discover on issuing from the porch that he had already vanished. Since he was nowhere within sight, he cannot but have made his way around the east side of the church. Had this, he mused a little forlornly, been merely with the notion of evading the customary tip?

He could recall many such hints of human nature—pious and prosperous pilgrims absent-mindedly debating if perhaps sixpence would be enough. To describe as sardonic any smile on so mild, horse-resembling, and pensive a face as the verger's would be absurd. In his own small way he was an artist. Tips were not his sole incentive. Besides, his comfortable little balance in the Savings Bank needed no refreshing, not at this late day. He could, then, easily afford this faint grin of amusement. "The horseleach hath two daughters, crying Give, give!"

No, it was the *gaucherie,* the unfriendliness that piqued the old man. And not merely that, something else, less easy to describe. Should he let him go, or be after him? This was not his first visit to the church—of that he was convinced. Then why pretend it? Had the stranger hoped to find himself alone there? For what purpose? Now that Mr. Phelps was no longer listening to his own voice—perhaps his favourite occupation—hitherto unheeded impressions had begun to coagulate in his mind.

Clothes, manner, gait, speech—never in his long experience had any specimen of a human being embodied so many peculiarities. And there was yet another, pervading all the rest, but more elusive. The verger was a confirmed dreamer. His office, perhaps, and his daily surroundings accounted for a more active night-life. In this he was apt to have strange experiences—to find himself surveying vast shelves of sloping rocks, the sea, enormous buildings, their bells ringing, but not to summon humanity within their walls. At this very moment—wide-awake though he had supposed himself to be—he might have issued from such a dream. The body sometimes seems as precarious as if it had but just been put on. And now, quite another suspicion had struck across his mind. Was this man—was he—quite *sane?* That taciturnity, the vigilance, the dark, fixed, lightless eye, the galvanic gestures, the evasiveness. No; to put it crudely, it would be as well to see him safely off the premises.

He hastened away, the hem of his iron-black cassock rustling over the grass as, in spite of his sixty-odd years, he stepped nimbly across the intervening mounds. And though he was half prepared to find no trace of his visitor, there was nothing unexpected in that visitor's appearance when, on skirting the outer walls of the Lady Chapel, he set eyes on him again. He was standing in engrossed contemplation of yet another tomb-stone, and evidently unaware that he was observed.

Solitary thus in this dusky green on the colder north side of the high old ecclesiastical mansion, and motionless as an image in a waxwork show, he looked, if not exactly more real, at least more conspicuously actual than anything around him. It was almost as though he had dressed up to simulate a certain part on the stage of life, and had overdone it. But perhaps Mr. Phelps himself was now overdoing it a little. He was at any rate taking liberties, and had no intention of playing the spy. He coughed discreetly. But his visitor had either not heard this announcement, or had taken no notice of it. He had remained unmoved, peering, as if short-sightedly, at the defaced inscription at his feet, one which Mr. Phelps could easily have repeated to him, word-perfect:

> He who hath walked in darkest night,
> Stars and bright moon shut out from sight,
> And Fiends around him cruel as sin,
> Finds welcome even the coldest Inn.

With no more than a slow unsteady movement of his head, he presently turned aside to the stone of Susanna Harbert, "Spinster of this Parish":

> Let upon my bosom be
> Only a bush of Rosemary;
> Even though love forget, its breath
> Will sweeten this ancient haunt of Death.

But if any bush had ever been planted there, it was gone. Instead, a delicate forest of summer grasses and a few wild flowers concealed the flattened mound.

"You will pardon me breaking in, sir," interposed the verger, but drawing no nearer, "there are very few inscriptions in this part of the churchyard; it is seldom visited. If you would give me even so much as a name to go by, it *might* be, sir, within my recollection. I have been here for many years. But the stone itself will almost certainly be on the south side."

The stranger, looking, as Mr. Phelps afterwards put it himself, more like a copy of a human being than ever, continued for some moments merely to gaze at him; but not as if there were any activity of speculation behind his fixed eyes. "The name?" he repeated at last, as if he had drawn the word cold and dripping out of some unfathomable well of memory. "The name was Ambrose Manning. . . . It was said he had made away with himself. It was said . . ." But nothing further came.

"Ah!" ejaculated the verger in unfeigned dismay. . . . "And the date, sir, perhaps?"

"1882."

"Well, in that case," was the hesitant reply, "we *are* on the right side." The syllables he had heard, though they had been uttered in so low and lifeless a voice, were now being called, whispered, echoed in every chamber of the old man's memory. Where, where, had he seen, heard, that name before? "You see," he was explaining, "at that time, and perhaps even now, his remains would not so much as have entered the church; not *felo de se,* sir. The whole service, a special one, would be at the grave's side. There was one, I recollect, many years ago, the rain pouring in torrents, and a heavy sea running. But," he added, as if in apology, "not *fifty* years ago!"

By this time he was thoroughly wearied of his task. He had been ill-advised to linger so long—this craving for *any* listener. His one desire was to get back to his cottage and to the cold supper that was awaiting him. Nevertheless he was still reluctant to leave such a visitor at large and to his own devices in the precincts of the church. Only two grave-stones, however, now remained between him and freedom; he would at any rate wait them out. They leaned slightly askew under a much-lopped but still hardy old yew tree, one of them encrusted from summit to base with a thin, pale mantling of grey and green.

> Traveller, forbear
> To brood too secretly on what is here!
> Death hath us in his care.
> *There is no Fear.*
> But thou, in life—Oh, but I thee implore,
> Stray thou amidst these dangerous shades no more!

Mr. Phelps was observing his visitor with some anxiety. He looked like a man upon the verge of a trance, a cataleptic, a somnambulist. "I have never *myself*," he told him, "been aware of any 'danger' here. And, as you yourself pointed out but a few minutes since, though I confess the thought had never occurred to me, not in that shape, sir—it is the *living* who are speaking to us from these stones—not the dead. Or at least, those who were living at that time. And last," he went on, since no response had been vouchsafed to him, "there's this." He emphasized the word, in a tone of finality, pointing with his finger. "But it's 'N. F.'—as you see, sir; and so the initials don't suit with the names you mentioned. A very tragic case, too—for more than one; as I remember hearing when a boy:"

Here lies the Self-Dishonoured Body of N. F. who perished miserably by his own Hand on October 31 in the year of our Lord 1875.

> See now, if thou have any heed
> For thine own soul, now hence make speed!
> Here in this waste of briar and thorn
> Sojourns one hungry and forlorn,
> Self-murdered, unassoiled, unshriven,
> Haunting these shades twixt Earth and Heaven.
> O get thee gone; no biding make;
> Lest the Unsleeping find the Wake!

The stranger (having as it appeared digested these words also), with a peculiar motion of the head, again glanced gently around him, then lifted his colourless face towards the dimly gilded hands of the clock in the church tower. Whereupon, the bells within, as if in response to a silent invitation, chimed out the hour—that of compline. Perplexed, even vexed at this taciturnity and poor fellowship, Mr. Phelps remarked a little coldly that "this" was "the nearest way out." But again to unlistening ears, for his visitor with no more than a last furtive and empty yet concentrated glance at him, had turned aside, and was already making his way under the dark trees towards a stile which gave egress to a plank bridge over a brook, and so to the hills beyond.

Mr. Phelps watched him until he had vanished—not merely from sight, but as if the dense motionless foliage had swallowed him up. There was not a sigh of wind to stir the flowering grasses. The waters of the brook in their narrow ravine were singing a quiet tune; a corncrake was calling in the meadows beyond the low stone wall. All was as it had ever been. The verger turned about at length and paced slowly back to the south porch. Should he or should he not re-enter the church? Should he postpone what he had in mind until the morning? He was aware of a distaste to linger any more. And yet . . .

He adjusted the key, stepped across the threshold into the darkened building, paused, drew-to the heavy door behind him, paused again, then deliberately locked it. Having lit a stub of candle, which in its brass dish-shaped holder he took from a cupboard in the vestry, he unlocked a small iron safe and laid the burial book on the table. The gilt of its title—*Register of Burials; Church of St. Edmund; Langridge*—had nearly faded from out of its covers. Having adjusted his eyeglasses on the extremity of his long stooping nose, he stood there in the stony silence, the radiance of the candle striking up into his long face, etching in with black shadow the lines upon it, chiefly the kindliness, long service, and curiosity. Then with a wetted finger he slowly turned over the leaves until he came to January 1, 1882.

After that he drew his finger steadily down each of the following few pages in turn until he came to November 4. Memory had not deluded him; at least not wholly. *"November 4. Ambrose Manning,"* he read. Nothing more than that, and even this had proved to be erroneous. A thin line in red ink had been drawn through both names, and in another hand there followed a scrawled—"Nothing known. Not buried here."

Mr. Phelps—his eyebrows mounted high on his conical bare forehead—continued for a few moments to scrutinize the entry: he could recall no other example of the kind. How many years had it been since he had chanced on it? "H'm, not buried here," he muttered to himself. "Strange. . . . Why not, then . . . ? And where?"

"Where?" an excessively faint voice from nowhere had muttered as if in reply. Scrupulous servant of habit that he was, though a little jarred, he put back the book into the iron chest, locked it, and, cupping the lighted candle with his bony fingers, made his way out of the vestry. The Visitors' Book lay open, as he had left it, on its narrow table, the pen beside it, now dry. Mr. Phelps glanced down at the scribbled page. The latest entry on it was the signature of Helen Jane Wilkinson (Mrs.) of 1a Portsea Terrace, High Wycombe. His last visitor then, taking advantage of his own courtesy, had merely pretended to write his name.

There was no reason to suppose that he could have forgotten it!

The verger's grey eyes wandered vacantly over the scribbled page. He felt a trifle cold, empty, anxious and oppressed. And as he stood pondering, momentarily severed and estranged as it seemed for the first time in all these years from the beloved, familiar building in his charge, a faint sound arrested his attention. A sound that was no more than a whisper, as of a minute clot of plaster falling from the roof on to the flags beneath. He jerked his head sidelong towards the door that he had but a few minutes before locked behind him.

He held his breath to listen again; then, puffing out his candle-end, crept to the cranny of the door, remaining there as motionless for a while as a cat at a mouse's hole. Slowly and stealthily at length he pushed the key into the lock, turned it in the oiled wards, and drew open the door. But no. The sound he had heard can have been no more than a mere fancy. The ancient porch stood empty; the southern sky now framed beyond it was studded with a few brightening stars. He was unutterably relieved; and yet not wholly so. A hitherto unheeded misgiving was gnawing in his mind. Poor creature—he was debating within himself; this man had come to him hungry, famished, it seemed, for help, and had gone away unsatisfied. He realized now that he had swallowed an extreme distaste for his visitor only in order to indulge his own love of talking. Yet, even at the worst there had been nothing of active evil in that mask of a human face, only an animal-like patience and obstinacy, clay-cold, impassive. No signal of hope either, or of comradeship; only the sediment of an unspeakable obsession. He might have been searching for years. But why?

Nor had it occurred to the verger, he ruminated mutely, to offer his belated visitor even so much as a glass of cold water. A few words of comfort, of reassurance—*they* would not necessarily have been cold. And—least commendable perhaps of all motives —you can never tell when you may not be needing them yourself.

The Wind Blows Over (1936)

Walter de la Mare

A PARTIAL CHECK-LIST

POEMS

> Poems (1906)
> The Listeners, and Other Poems (1912)
> Motley, and Other Poems (1918)
> The Veil, and Other Poems (1921)
> The Fleeting, and Other Poems (1933)
> Memory, and Other Poems (1938)
> Collected Poems (1941)
> The Burning Glass (1945)
> The Traveller (1946)

NOVELS AND TALES

> Henry Brocken (1904)
> The Return (1910, 1922)
> Memoirs of a Midget (1921)
> The Riddle and Other Tales (1923)
> Ding Dong Bell (1924)
> The Connoisseur and Other Stories (1926)
> On the Edge (1930)
> The Wind Blows Over (1936)

465

BOOKS FOR CHILDREN

A) Poems

> *Songs of Childhood*   (*1902*)
> *A Child's Day*   (*1912*)
> *Peacock Pie*   (*1913*)
> *Flora* (with Pamela Bianco)   (*1919*)
> *Down-a-down-Derry: A Book of Fairy Poems*   (*1922*)
> *Stuff and Nonsense*   (*1927*)
> *This Year, Next Year* (with Harold Jones)   (*1937*)
> *Bells and Grass*   (*1942*)
> *Rhymes and Verses*   (*1947*)

B) Stories

> *The Three Mulla-Mulgars*   (*1910*) *
> *Broomsticks, and Other Tales*   (*1925*)
> *Told Again*   (*1927*)
> *Stories from the Bible*   (*1929*)
> *The Dutch Cheese*   (*1931*)
> *The Lord Fish, and Other Stories*   (*1933*)
> *Animal Stories*   (*1939*)
> *Mr. Bumps and His Monkey*   (*1942*)

C) Drama

> *Crossings: A Fairy Play*   (*1921*)

D) Anthologies

> *Come Hither*   (*1923*)
> *Readings* (with Thomas Quayle)   (*1927*)
> *Tom Tiddler's Ground*   (*1931*)

---

* Republished as *The Three Royal Monkeys*.

CRITICISM AND BELLES-LETTRES

M. E. Coleridge, An Appreciation (*1907*)
Rupert Brooke and the Intellectual Imagination (*1919*)
Some Thoughts on Reading (*1923*)
Desert Islands and Robinson Crusoe (*1930*)
Nonsense and Lewis Carroll (*1932*)
Early One Morning in the Spring (*1935*)
Pleasures and Speculations (*1940*)

ANTHOLOGIES, EDITED BY MR. DE LA MARE

Behold, This Dreamer! (*1939*)
Love (*1943*)

SELECTIONS FROM MR. DE LA MARE'S WORK

Story and Rhyme (*1921*)
Seven Short Stories (*1931*)
Stories, Essays and Poems (Everyman's Library) (*1938*)
Best Stories of Walter de la Mare (*1943*)

A NOTE ON THE TYPE

This book is set in GRANJON *a type named in compliment to Robert Granjon, type-cutter and printer—Antwerp, Lyons, Rome, Paris—active from 1523 to 1590. The boldest and most original designer of his time, he was one of the first to practise the trade of type-founder apart from that of printer.*

This type face was designed by George W. Jones, who based his drawings upon a type used by Claude Garamond (1510–61) in his beautiful French books, and more closely resembles Garamond's own than do any of the various modern types that bear his name.

The book was composed, printed, and bound by Kingsport Press, Inc., Kingsport, Tennessee. The binding was designed by Warren Chappell.